FATHER AND SON

FATHER AND SON

James T. Farrell

with an Introduction by

Charles Fanning

University of Illinois Press
Urbana and Chicago

Manufactured in the United States of America
1 2 3 4 5 C P 5 4 3 2 1
♾ This book is printed on acid-free paper.

Library of Congress Cataloging-in-Publication Data
Farrell, James T. (James Thomas), 1904–1979.
Father and son / James Farrell ; with an introduction
by Charles Fanning. — [Cloth & Paper ed.].
p. cm.
ISBN 978-0-252-03264-6 (cloth : alk. paper)
ISBN 0-252-03264-0 (cloth : alk. paper)
ISBN 978-0-252-07495-0 (pbk. : alk. paper)
ISBN 0-252-07495-5 (pbk. : alk. paper)
I. Title.
PS3511.A738F38 2008
813'.52—dc22 2007044104

James T. Farrell's O'Neill-O'Flaherty Novels: An Introduction

Charles Fanning

Background

James T. Farrell's 1935 story, "The Oratory Contest," presents George O'Dell, a middle-aged Chicago streetcar driver, and his sixteen-year-old son Gerry, who is about to compete in the senior oratorical contest at Mary Our Mother School on the city's South Side. This story opens with Gerry practicing before the bathroom mirror, "imagining the thunder of applause that would greet him at the conclusion of his oration." The scene recalls the opening of Farrell's first novel, *Young Lonigan*, published three years earlier, where Studs Lonigan strikes hard-boiled poses before his mirror on the night of graduation from eighth grade at St. Patrick's School. I believe that this is a deliberate echo, and that Farrell is making the point that two boys from the same neighborhood and Catholic school system can go in very different directions. That point would have been sharp in 1935, for the third Lonigan novel, *Judgment Day*, in which the hapless Studs dies at twenty-nine, had appeared in April, and the trilogy was published in one volume in November. The contrast is pronounced, for Gerry O'Dell is a successful student, encouraged by his teachers and considering college, although he can't afford to go unless, as his father suggests, he can "get a job and study law in the evenings downtown at St. Vincent's."

As he and his other son Michael approach the high school, George feels "increasingly timid," and realizes "that Gerry, instead of waiting for him and Michael, had gone ahead. Gerry, he suddenly felt, was ashamed of him. He argued with himself that the boy had had to get there early, and that, anyway, he had been nervous about the contest and restless, like a colt before the start of a race. But still, no, he could not rid his mind of that thought." In the ensuing competition, Gerry speaks eloquently and wins the gold medal. George

O'Dell is moved to tears and "a simple and childlike joy" by his son's victory. After rushing out to a drugstore to telephone the news to his wife, he returns to congratulate his son, only to find the stage empty: "Gerry must have gone. He told himself that Gerry had known that his father would wait to see him, congratulate him, buy him a treat, and that then they would go home together. And Gerry had not waited." George O'Dell searches the few remaining faces, asks a crowd of boys if anyone has seen his son, and then the story ends: "He stood with Michael. Only a few scattered groups remained in front of the hall. Feeling blank, he told himself, yes, Gerry had gone. He solemnly led Michael away, both of them silent. He asked himself why Gerry hadn't waited, and he knew the answer to his question."[1]

When I first read this story in the late 1970s, I felt the shock of recognition, because it's my story too. My father was a school custodian, and on the night when I competed in the local high school essay contest, he was not seated in the audience, but on duty in the building, standing at the back of the auditorium. When I emerged from the hall clutching the first-prize check for $25, he was in the foyer leaning on a push broom. I remember always having been proud of how hard he worked, especially in winter when he'd have to get up at four in the morning to shovel snow. And my memory of that evening is that I went right over and shook his hand. But I could so easily have been Gerry O'Dell, and I'm sure that sometimes I was. There is no more effective rendering in American fiction of the gulf that can develop between working-class parents and their better-educated children than "The Oratory Contest." The story exemplifies the great strengths of James T. Farrell's fiction: plain-style austerity in the telling, realistic presentation of pain that can be understood but not alleviated, and a mutually reinforcing combination of clarity and compassion—the whole rendered without a scrap of condescension toward the characters and situations.

"The Oratory Contest" points straight toward the second phase of Farrell's achievement, his five O'Neill-O'Flaherty novels: *A World I Never Made* (1936), *No Star Is Lost* (1938), *Father and Son* (1940), *My Days of Anger* (1943), and *The Face of Time* (1953). His first two major cycles, the *Studs Lonigan* trilogy (published in 1932, 1934, and 1935) and the O'Neill-O'Flaherty pentalogy, share a setting (the South Side neighborhood around Washington Park where Farrell himself grew up), a time frame (roughly 1890 to 1930), and many characters. Farrell's own childhood around Fifty-eighth Street had much more in common with the experience of young Danny O'Neill in the second series than with that of Studs Lonigan. However, with a wisdom unusual in young writers, Farrell knew that in order to deal in a balanced way with his own emotionally laden personal experience, he ought to tell Studs's story first. But Farrell's eight Washington Park novels actually comprise one coherent grand design with two contrasting movements: the downward, negative alternative embodied in the passive, doomed

Studs, and the upward, positive possibility embodied in Danny, who grows up to become a writer.

In June 1929 Farrell had written a publisher that he was "working on two novels. One is a realistic story of a corner gang at Fifty Eighth and Prairie Avenue of this city. . . . The other novel is a tale of a boy in a Catholic high school of this city during the early part of the jazz age." After finishing *The Young Manhood of Studs Lonigan* in 1934, Farrell reported to Ezra Pound: "one more Lonigan book to come, and I'm writing it, . . . and also am working on a long story of a family, Irish American, with a lot of autobiography, that extends from 1911 to 1933, and intends to shoot the works, and include a number of things I've held back in my other books. It may be anywhere from one to five volumes." Farrell published the first O'Neill novel, *A World I Never Made*, in October 1936. Shortly thereafter, he explained to a friend that the new series "is conceived as a complementary study to 'Studs Lonigan.' One [of] the main characters, Danny O'Neill, is planned as a character whose life experience is to be precisely the opposite of Studs." Farrell held to this conception through the writing of the remaining volumes. While finishing up the final draft of *My Days of Anger*, he wrote his publisher that "I think now, it'll come out right, and be a fitting end to the series—and a fitting companion series to *Studs Lonigan*—and that Danny and Studs will stand as I conceived them—dialectical opposites in their destinies—one goes up, the other goes down."[2] The two sequences and the many short stories that share the same South Side setting (there are at least fifty stories about Danny O'Neill) constitute a full-scale fictional chronicle of three generations of urban Americans, from nineteenth-century immigrant laborers to Depression-era intellectuals, grounded in a specific place with clear reference points like the markings on a compass. Farrell's sense of the scope and the integrity of his Chicago fiction was already clear by August 1934 when he wrote to a friend: "I hope to run to at least twenty volumes of novels and short stories attempting to describe, represent, analyze and portray connected social areas of Chicago that I have lived in, and that I have more or less assimilated. In these terms, then, the various books and stories are all panels of one work."[3]

The grandson of Irish immigrants and the son of a teamster and a former domestic servant, Farrell was born on February 27, 1904, raised in South Side Chicago neighborhoods near Washington Park, and educated at Corpus Christi and St. Anselm's Catholic grammar schools and St. Cyril's Carmelite High School, graduating in 1923. Because his parents had many children and little money, he lived from age two with his maternal grandparents and his unmarried uncles and aunts who were better off, and this double perspective of belonging to two families both enriched and complicated his youth. Farrell was first encouraged to write by his eighth-grade teacher at St. Anselm's, Sister Magdalen. He recalls sitting at the parlor window of his grandmother's apartment on South Park Avenue overlooking Washington Park on a rainy Saturday in autumn. Planning out an essay on Andrew Jackson and the United States Bank, "for the first time in my life I experienced that absorption, that exhilaration, and that compulsion which drives you to sit alone and write with the immediate world about you walled out of your consciousness and with your impulses to have fun in the present put to sleep." At St. Cyril's, which is still open at the same location at Sixty-fourth Street and Dante Avenue as Mount Carmel High School, he was further encouraged by two of the Carmelite fathers who were his English teachers, Father Leo J. Walter and Father Albert Dolan. He remembers that in his first year he wrote "an essay of two pages about two boys who didn't want to fight and who talked toughly to one another. Here was a dim forecast of my future writing." This piece became "Helen, I Love You," the first Farrell story to appear in a national publication—H. L. Mencken's *American Mercury* in July 1932. He wrote "out of passion and interest," often about baseball and the White Sox, including a long piece about the Black Sox scandal, which broke during his second year of high school, and the school magazine published his first piece of fiction, "Danny's Uncle," a vignette of the street encounter of young "Danny O'Neil" with his wealthy uncle. "We boys were naive," Farrell remembered. "We did not come from cultivated households. We did not live in a cultural milieu." And yet, under the tutelage of the Carmelites, he took his first "slow step" toward "self-expression and self-consciousness."[4]

Over the next five years, Farrell worked for an express company and as a gas station attendant, took a semester of prelaw courses at De Paul University night school, and enrolled for several quarters at the University of Chicago. In March 1927 he had resolved to be a writer, and embarked on a fierce regimen of reading and writing, in and out of schools, from which he never subsequently deviated. On February 27, 1929, he turned twenty-five. Soon after, he enrolled for what would turn out to be his last quarter at the University of Chicago, taking one course, Advanced Composition, from a favorite professor, James Weber Linn. This year also saw the first commercial publication of a Farrell story, the writing of a second and crucially important story, and the conception of the Lonigan and O'Neill fictional cycles. In June 1929, in the first number of a local little magazine, appeared the story "Slob," which describes an unnamed young man struggling with his drunken aunt in an apartment on Chicago's South Side. And a month or so previously, Farrell had written for Professor Linn's course another South Side Irish story, in which a thoughtful young man attends the wake of a former acquaintance who has died of dissolute living. Its title was "Studs." The narrating consciousness in these two stories is the precursor of Danny O'Neill.[5]

Farrell took the chance of a creative life by quitting the University of Chicago after the spring quarter of 1929. He later wrote of this "drastic step" that "there was a cost to success, and I would not pay that cost. I could not pay it, because, if I did, then I could not write." Over the next two years, unfazed by the stock-market crash (except as it would provide a certain dénouement for his novel in progress), he traveled to New York City twice, did odd jobs while living at home or flopping on couches in his friends' Hyde Park apartments, and read and wrote feverishly, day in and day out. He recalled of these years that in order to give "as much of my time as I could to study and writing, . . . in a sense, the Depression caught up with me. By early 1928, I had brought on my own Depression. I got myself jobless, not through inability to hold a job, but because I did not want one."[6] The result was, as Edgar Branch has said, that the young Farrell had, like the young Herman Melville, "swum through libraries." Among the writers he had read in depth by 1930 were "William James, Dewey, and George H. Mead, Nietzsche, Max Stirner, Bertrand Russell, Thorstein Veblen, R. H. Tawney, Sigmund Freud, Walter Pater, Ibsen, Chekhov, H. L. Mencken, Theodore Dreiser, Sherwood Anderson, Carl Sandburg, Sinclair Lewis, Ernest Hemingway, and James Joyce."[7] "There were ways," recalls Murray Kempton in his memoir of the thirties, "in which [Farrell] was the best-educated young writer of his time. He had read philosophers well outside the realm of discourse of conventional critics; he was a deep, though perhaps narrow, student of history; he had great resources in the European tradition. He was a perceptive enough critic to argue for William Faulkner in the early thirties, when Faulkner was at his peak of creation and his nadir of reputation. He was certainly better educated than Hemingway and Fitzgerald, who in many areas were not educated at all."[8]

By early 1931, Farrell had written thousands of manuscript pages of fiction, including much that would be incorporated into the *Studs Lonigan* trilogy and the O'Neill-O'Flaherty series. He got almost none of it published. In April 1931, dead broke and still without a publisher except for the smallest of the Midwest's little magazines, Farrell did the next logical thing—he got married, to Dorothy Butler, and the newlyweds sailed off to Paris for a year. There he expanded his reading by absorbing great amounts of Balzac, Proust, Henry James, Spinoza, and Trotsky. Then came his breakthrough. Shortly after arriving in Paris, Farrell learned that his first novel, *Young Lonigan: A Boyhood in Chicago Streets*, had been accepted by the Vanguard Press in New York. In April 1932, the novel was published and James T. Farrell was off and running.

What followed was one of the most extraordinary creative flowerings in the history of American letters. One thinks of Herman Melville's eight novels and several stories between 1846 and 1857, his entire fictional corpus but for *Billy Budd*, and William Faulkner's eleven books, including his masterworks, between 1929 and 1942. When he finished writing *My Days of Anger*, the fourth O'Neill-O'Flaherty novel, in February 1943, Farrell wrote a friend that "I have accomplished what I set out to. Shortly after I will have reached thirty nine, I will have accomplished my two major literary objectives—not of course that I haven't more that I want to write. But this much I have done. I have now written the books I said I would write a little over ten years ago when this seemed like a wild prediction."[9] In eleven years he had published eleven novels, four collections of short fiction, one book of literary criticism, and over 300 essays and reviews. The *New York Times* had hailed the *Studs Lonigan* trilogy as "one of the most powerful pieces of American fiction," and its inclusion in the Random House Modern Library in 1938 ensured a continuing audience of intelligent readers. As both an artist and an intellectual, James T. Farrell was a force to be reckoned with in American letters.

Farrell was far from alone in having made this sort of journey at this time in American cultural life. Although his output was uniquely prodigious, he was but one of many children and grandchildren of immigrants and the working class who made up a chorus of new voices starting out in the 1930s to expand the boundaries of American literature. Indeed, Michael Denning has argued that the extraordinary artistic and intellectual energies unleashed in that decade constituted "a birthing of a new American culture, a second American Renaissance," when "for the first time in the history of the United States, a working-class culture had made a significant imprint on the dominant cultural institutions."[10] Among the new "proletarian" writers bent on bringing their experiences and those of their parents' generation to fiction were (with some of their books): Mike Gold (*Jews without Money*, 1930); Edward Dahlberg (*Bottom Dogs*, 1930); Langston Hughes (*Not without Laughter*, 1930); Catherine Brody (*Nobody Starves*, 1932); Grace Lumpkin (*To Make My Bread*, 1932); Jack Conroy (*The Disinherited*, 1933); Marita Bonner (*The Black Map*, 1933); Daniel Fuchs (*Summer in Williamsburg*, 1934); Albert Halper (*On the Shore*, 1934); Henry Roth (*Call It Sleep*, 1934); Tillie Olsen, "The Iron Throat" (1934); Nelson Algren (*Somebody in Boots*, 1935); Clara Weatherwax (*Marching, Marching*, 1935); Thomas Bell (*All Brides Are Beautiful*, 1936); Meyer Levin (*The Old Bunch*, 1937); John Fante (*Wait until Spring, Bandini*, 1938); Pietro Di Donato (*Christ in Concrete*, 1939); and Richard Wright (*Uncle Tom's Children*, 1938, and *Native Son*, 1940). These were writers who shared a faith in literature as an uncondescending chronicle of working-class and underclass lives and, at its best, a potential vehicle for social change.[11]

Farrell marked his own consciousness of this community in his April 1935 speech before the First American Writers' Congress in New York, a widely publicized, Communist-led event. He took as his ambitious subject "the development of literary traditions" in "a succession of patterns," using as his main illustration an inclusive look at the new African American literature and an insightful analogy with the Irish tradition. The first pattern of "Negro literature" that he sees is "the Uncle Remus story of the dark-skinned Southern Handy Andy." The reference is to the stereotyped Irish peasantry in books such as Samuel Lover's *Handy Andy* of 1842, in which there is also implied "a condition of master and slave, oppressor and oppressed." The "Uncle Remus" pattern "presents a vaudevilized conception of the Negro, portray[ing] him as obsequious, shiftless, childishly humorous and simple, . . . the subject of comedy which, as we know, slurs and distorts the story of the tragic history of the Negro in capitalist America." Farrell sees this conception as still very much abroad in the land in 1935. He cites the *Saturday Evening Post*, the movies, and the Amos and Andy radio show, and he analyzes this pattern as "a combination of the conventions forced upon the Negro to permit, on one hand, some harmonious interaction between the Negro and the privileged class of whites living on his back, and, on the other, a wish fulfillment of what that privileged class desires the Negro to be."

Farrell goes on to connect the "literature of realism and social protest which has come to be the dominant literary tradition in twentieth-century American writing" with "an increasingly apparent contradiction between the hopes of the American dream and the manner in which human destinies unraveled in actual life." In this movement, contemporary American writers have "been introducing us to a new kind of American life, to the life of poor farmers and sharecroppers in backward rural areas, to the scenes, sights, and dialects of the urban streets, to the feelings of Slavic immigrants, the problems and discontents of sweat-shop workers, the resentments and oppressions of the factory proletariat. . . . In brief, it has been dipping us down toward the bottom of the so-called American melting pot." Farrell goes on to criticize the lack of "internal conviction" in "many of the new revolutionary short stories." Authors "seek[ing] to express a revolutionary point of view, . . . instead of making their aim functional within the story so that the aim impresses the reader as a natural and integral aspect of the story, it seems to be glued on," in the worst cases, "as a slogan or revolutionary direction sign that possesses no coherent and vital or necessary relation to the body of the story."[12]

One conference participant who paid close attention to Farrell's speech was Richard Wright, who had come east from Chicago, where his family was living on the South Side at 3743 Indiana Avenue, ten blocks north of Farrell's childhood home on the same street and twenty blocks north of the Studs Lonigan/Danny O'Neill neighborhood. A few years earlier, Wright had lived even closer, at 4831 Vincennes. In fact, the Chicago South Side neighborhoods around Washington Park constitute an outstanding example of the resilience of urban communities as genius loci for artistic expression in the earlier twentieth century. Much has been made of the disruption to patterns of living in the wake of the great migration of African Americans from the rural South to northern cities between the two world wars. And yet, where the arts were concerned, there was significant continuity as well. It was just that the dominant art form changed from literature to music. Among the jazz greats who came of age in the 1930s on the same streets where Farrell and Wright had matured in the 1920s were Dorothy Donegan, Joe Williams, Johnny Board, Viola Jefferson, Milt Hinton, John Young, Johnny Hartman, and Nat "King" Cole. Most attended DuSable High School at Forty-ninth and Wabash, where they were trained by the legendary bandmaster, Captain Walter Dyett.[13]

When he arrived in New York for the American Writers' Congress, Richard Wright was twenty-six, four years younger than Farrell, and had published a few poems and stories in little magazines. He also spoke at the conference—on "The Isolation of the Negro Writer." Michel Fabre has said that Wright "was enthralled to hear James T. Farrell speak on the revolutionary story," particularly Farrell's "true defense of art against propaganda and political tyranny." As Wright was just then becoming interested in short fiction, "Farrell's vigorous observations could not help but influence him, especially because he had his own reservations about the political demands of the Party. This was the beginning of a literary friendship that benefitted Wright enormously."[14]

Farrell spent impressive critical energies in the 1930s warning artists against the contaminating influence of politics on literature and distancing himself from those who would judge books ideologically. In 1936 he published *A Note on Literary Criticism*, his book-length analysis of the relationship between literature and Marxist cultural criticism. There, with detailed discussion of sources as varied as the Japanese *Tale of Genji*, Spinoza, Thomas Aquinas, Dickens, Proust, Dostoyevsky, and Joyce, he defended the integrity of art against the corruption of political propaganda, which he saw as an urgent threat from the intellectual left.[15] In this campaign, Farrell's was an early and very strong voice. Similarly, in his preface to the 1937 single-volume edition of his first three story collections, Farrell discussed the most conspicuous example of his era's blind faith in content: the demand in left-wing magazines such as *The Anvil* for didactic, so-called proletarian fiction featuring "a purely conceptualized, hypothetical, and non-existent worker [as] the hero. The stories produced in this movement were bad, lifeless, wooden. In place of the happy ending of *The Saturday Evening Post* variety, they had an 'uplifting' conclusion based on a sudden conversion to the sole correct faith in progress and the future of humanity." Thus, Farrell attacked distortions of content in the name of form in the mechanical "plot story" of popular magazines and college writing courses, and distortions of form in the name of content in "local color" and "proletarian" stories about minorities and the working class. There is little to choose, he declared, between fiction produced and endorsed by political standards or by short-fiction handbooks: "The former hypostasizes, narrows, and freezes content; the latter achieves a similar effect with form."[16]

Farrell's candid critique made him several enemies, and, as luck would have it, some of these people (among them Malcolm Cowley, Granville Hicks, and Alfred Kazin) went on to become influential shapers of literary reputation in the 1940s and 1950s. These New York–based critics utilized an embrace of high modernism and a "new critical" aesthetic to try to blackball Farrell from consideration as a serious writer. This vindictive crusade began with the publication of the first O'Neill-O'Flaherty novels, *A World I Never Made* in 1936 and *No Star Is Lost* in 1938. A good example of the level of much of this was the dismissal of the third novel in the series, *Father and Son*, by Edmund Wilson in *The New Republic* in October 1940. After confessing that he hadn't read Farrell's "last two or three novels," Wilson had the gall to declare that Farrell was "writing book after book about Irish boys growing up in Chicago," and "continuing to tell the same story." Instead of reviewing this new one, Wilson says, "I should like to ask you to state yourself why you expect people to go on reading your books. . . . Why do you keep on with this interminable record?" The magazine did allow Farrell to respond: "As for Studs Lonigan and Danny O'Neill," he says, "they can be pronounced alike only by a critic who could confuse Becky Sharp and Mrs. Wiggs of the Cabbage Patch." And as for Wilson's disingenuous questions: "I answer, because I have an unshakeable conviction that I have a true and representative story to tell of how people have lived, suffered and enjoyed, striven and forged ideals, loved and hated, died in my time. . . . When I began writing, I determined not to compromise with passing fads that come and go. I have rigidly tried to adhere to this intention. I have always been prepared to breast every hostile current that my books required and I am still prepared to do this. I make these statements not with any arrogance, but rather out of a full realization that each writer must find his own way in accordance with his temperament and his talents."[17]

Actually, the O'Neill-O'Flaherty novels were greeted in many of the most respected journals and newspapers as major literary events. For example, in his review of the first volume for the *Nation*, Carl Van Doren pointed out that the characters' "consciences make up nearly as much of the story as their acts. This helps to give to *A World I Never Made* that habitual tenderness which is quite as characteristic of Mr. Farrell's novels as their toughness." Further, Van Doren's sense of the overall effect of the style is fully congruent with Farrell's own aims: "He has an extraordinarily capacious mind which holds the persons and events of a novel as if they were, somehow, in solution, to be poured out in a full stream in which his own share as narrator may be lost sight of. You forget that you are seeing this life through the eyes of a selecting novelist. It seems merely to be there before you." As to subject matter, he went on to praise Farrell as the American city's "truest historian." Indeed, "Mr. Farrell seems to me to go beyond any other American novelist in his knowledge of the common life of an American city and his understanding of the city culture."[18] The novel sold over 5,000 copies in its first year, making it Farrell's most successful book up to that point.

When the fourth volume, *My Days of Anger*, appeared in 1943, Carlos Baker said in the *New York Times Book Review* that it "reveals in the author a heartening accession of philosophical gentleness and narrative power. It is in many ways a better book than Farrell has done before," and "if there is an accession of tenderness and even a kind of optimism in the present novel, there is also a gain in narrative power and incisiveness." The critics who praised the books of the O'Neill-O'Flaherty series as they appeared also included Bernard De Voto, Harold Strauss, Lewis Corey, Weldon Kees, Diana Trilling, and H. L. Mencken. In February 1937, Van Doren, De Voto, and Heywood Broun also testified in the successful court action against the New York Society for the Suppression of Vice, which had petitioned that *A World I Never Made* be banned as "obscene, lewd, and lascivious."[19]

What was missing from the criticism, however, was a developed sense of the projected scope and ultimate achievement of the O'Neill-O'Flaherty series as a whole. Had this been registered strongly in either 1943 with *My Days of Anger* or 1953, when the fifth volume, *The Face of Time*, appeared, then all of these books would be much better known. Militating against the articulation of full perspective on the series was everything that constituted the uniqueness of Farrell's accomplishment—the setting, characters, and style of his portrait of the artist in Washington Park on the South Side of Chicago. These all ran counter to the ultimately elitist hegemony of the "New Criticism" in the late 1940s and 1950s, which favored and praised high style, the veins of irony and allusion that cry out for exegesis, and an erudite controlling narrative consciousness, as in iconic works such as *Ulysses*, *The Waste Land*, and *To the Lighthouse*.

A clarifying visual analogy to both Farrell's achievement in the O'Neill-O'Flaherty series and the lack of critical recognition thereof is Peter Brooks's discussion of Gustave Courbet's revolutionary "Burial at Ornans" of 1849, a huge painting (ten by twenty-two feet) of a "humble" subject (an ordinary funeral in his own home village). This was the first volley in the campaign for *réalisme* in which Courbet was the salient standard-bearer. Brooks asserts that Parisian critics were scandalized both by the "heroic scale usually reserved for the grandeur of history painting" and the spectacle of a straggling parade of "low, vulgar" villagers, "in fact, portraits done by Courbet from his fellow townspeople," ranged around the "gaping hole" of a grave.[20] Similarly, Farrell chose to work on the largest literary canvas, a sequence of related novels that would reach 2,500 pages, and to take as his subject the works and days, lives and deaths of the ordinary people among whom he had grown up.

Contexts: Joyce, Proust, Chekhov, the Pragmatists

The O'Neill-O'Flaherty series is, among other things, a portrait of the growth of an artist, and in the design and ambition of his own project, Farrell's great tutelary spirits were James Joyce and Marcel Proust. With his own Irish American

Catholic background, he could hardly have failed to be affected by Joyce. After reading the galleys of *Young Lonigan* in February 1932, Ezra Pound had jibed to Farrell, "Effect a bit too much Joyce of the Portrait," to which Farrell replied, "As to the Irishness of it. I generally feel that I'm an Irishman rather than an American, and [*Young Lonigan*] was recommended at the nrf [Nouvelle Review Française, its French publishing house] as being practically an Irish novel. I had read Joyce [meaning *Ulysses*] and pretty well forgotten him in all details at least a year, and the Portrait a year and a half before even starting the book, and any similarity was all unconscious." However, upon rereading "most of the Portrait a month or so ago," Farrell continued, "I did feel that, with differences of time, climate, and country, there were certain similarities to the exterior conditions and experiences and even the personal ones portrayed there and the ones I bumped into in the course of growing up as a Catholic young man, attending a Catholic high school taught by Carmelites rather than Jesuits etc."[21]

In *My Days of Anger*, in which Danny O'Neill reaches maturity, he discusses *A Portrait* and *Ulysses* with friends at the University of Chicago. Shortly after completing that novel, Farrell wrote two essays on Joyce for the *New York Times Book Review* that were later expanded and published separately, in which he located the *Portrait* firmly in its innovative contexts. First, he insists that nineteenth-century Irish political history is necessary to understanding the book, for "Joyce was a kind of inverted nationalist," for whom "the nationalism he rejects runs . . . like a central thread." Second, he asserts that "it was Joyce who introduced the city realistically into modern Irish writing. The city—Dublin—is the focus of Ireland in his work, and in his life. We see that this is the case with Stephen [Dedalus], the genius son of a declassed family. Stephen lives, grows up in a Dublin that is a center of paralysis. Is he to have a future in such a center? Is he to prevent himself from suffering paralysis, spiritual paralysis? Stephen's painful burden of reality can be interpreted as a reality that derives from the history of Ireland's defeats and that is focused, concretized, in the very quality of the men of Dublin." Third, Farrell emphasizes Stephen's Catholicism as crucially formative: "From his considerable reading in the literature of the church the boy gained not only a sense of the past but also a sense of an ordered inner world and of a systematized *other* world. Eternity has filled his imagination." Furthermore, "his greatest sufferings are not imposed by the Dublin reality which disturbs him so much but by images of inferno as terrifying as that of Dante. He quivers and cowers before the vision of an other world which must make that of the Irish legends seem the most pale of mists. His spiritual struggle is one involving acceptance or rejection of this ordered other world."

Farrell goes on to place Joyce in the context of the European tradition of the bildungsroman, which he charts as a three-part progression through the nineteenth century. "Early in the century we see the young man—for instance Julien

Sorel of *The Red and the Black*, or Balzac's Lucien and Rastignac—seeking glory and fame. Their aim is success, and the plane of action is the objective one of society." At mid-century, "in the Russian novel—Pierre of *War and Peace*, Levin of *Anna Karenina*, Bazarov of *Fathers and Sons*, and Dostoyevsky's Raskolnikov and Ivan Karamazov—there is a shift of emphasis. These young men probe for the meaning of life; they seek to harmonize their words and their deeds." Toward the century's end, "we see the young man seeking freedom in the realm of feeling. This is the object of Frederic Moreau in *A Sentimental Education*—and of Des Esseintes (in a purely decadent fashion) in Huysmans's *Against the Grain*. Marius [Pater's Epicurean] and Stephen are both of this line; they, too, seek freedom in the realm of feeling and of culture." Farrell sees this substitution of artistic for worldly or ontological goals by fiction's protagonists as a reflection of "the evolving conditions of life in the nineteenth century. The character of public life changes and decreases the opportunities to be free. The idea of culture (as the realm of freedom) begins to grow. Thus, the logic of art for art's sake. The artist, crushed by the weight of contemporary culture, adopts the attitude that art is its own end, becomes the rebel artist." Stephen Dedalus fits here. He is "the artist as rebel, questioning the whole moral sensibility of his age."

Having recently finished his fourth and, at that point, the final O'Neill-O'Flaherty novel, Farrell must also have been locating his own bildungsroman as an advance into twentieth-century America of this venerable Old World tradition. Moreover, it is clear from Farrell's description that Stephen Dedalus and Danny O'Neill are as different as their differing places, times, gifts, and limitations dictate. Farrell notes that "almost from childhood, Stephen is an exceptional character. He is separated from others. He is aloof, lonely, different. His childhood is not a normal one in which he shares the common experiences of give-and-take between boys. He seldom participates in games; he is bookish, introspective. By the time he becomes a university student his mind is monkish, cloistered, and he regards it as such." Danny O'Neill hasn't the precocity, arrogance, or self-confidence of Stephen Dedalus. Though they are about the same age at the conclusions of *My Days of Anger* and *Ulysses*, Stephen is much further along on the road toward conviction and self-sufficiency in his vocation of artist.[22]

This distinction between the two protagonists relates to Farrell's lifelong ambivalence about Joyce, which had mostly to do with aspects of literary style. In his Joyce essay, Farrell explains Joyce's brilliant melding of style and theme in *A Portrait* by observing that "Joyce's realism is a realism of the mind, of the consciousness. Stephen's life is described in a highly concentrated and selective manner, deriving from this point of view. His own mind serves as the frame of reference for the story." Thus, "in many parts of the narrative the very style in which it is written has direct bearing on the theme." Because "the inner life of the artist is what is significant in [Stephen's] life, . . . the style, the perspective, the organization of the novel all seem to harmonize beautifully with its content." That is, Joyce makes his protagonist's exceptionalism clear by making the dominant style in the last chapter of *A Portrait* and in *Ulysses* a reflection of Stephen's brilliance, isolation, and self-absorption. In Farrell's view, this was a double-edged sword. As early as 1934, he had written that "parts of *Ulysses* seem like stunt performances to permit the author the luxury of showing off. I feel that the question and answer chapter is of such a nature. But such performances remain the privilege of genius." Farrell went even further a few years later in writing a friend that *Finnegans Wake* was "a signal of a man of genius with colossal egotism," which ultimately failed to meet John Dewey's "only demand" of an artist: "that his product be communicable in some sense to someone."[23]

Dennis Flynn has pointed out that a measure of Farrell's fluctuating opinion about Joyce is his "repeated comparison of Joyce and Proust. Early in his career, he favored Joyce's 'rigorousness, restraint, and stern dignity' as opposed to Proust's 'narrowness of range' and 'repetitive succession of agonies of heart.' Later he wrote that, though Joyce was a great genius, his work no longer seemed as stimulating. He came to reconsider his earlier estimate: 'Among writers of the twentieth century, the one whom I love the most is Marcel Proust.'"[24] Farrell had read Proust's first volume, *Swann's Way*, in Chicago in about 1927, and he went on to read all seven volumes of *In Search of Lost Time* while in Paris in 1931. The many references to Proust in *A Note on Literary Criticism*, Farrell's 1936 defense of literature against propaganda, demonstrate the strong connection between them at this early stage of Farrell's career. Farrell first mentions Proust in his summary dismissal of the extraliterary critique of literature coming from the cultural left, citing the "usual Marxmanship" of Mike Gold, Granville Hicks, and others. Class and politics be damned, is Farrell's message, for a "proletarian writer" (whatever that may mean) will be influenced by all sorts of art, by the fiction of James Joyce, bizarrely condemned by D. S. Mirsky as "inseparably connected with the specifically decadent phase of the bourgeois culture," and "by literature that is unqualifiedly non-proletarian, like Proust's works, or unqualifiedly non-revolutionary, in the political sense, like T. S. Eliot's."[25]

Overall, there are at least four areas of fruitful connection between Proust and Farrell. First is their shared focus on consciousness, especially in their shared sense of the pernicious effects on consciousness of habit. Here Proust's fiction reinforced Farrell's own philosophic roots in American pragmatism, which will also be discussed a bit later in this essay. Second, there is a clarifying similarity between Proust's concept of involuntary memory and the use of daydream and reverie in Farrell's fiction. Third is the primacy of place for both writers as the object of cathexis (the objective locus for concentration of emotional energy) through which the artist realizes his overarching aim of defeating time. Fourth is the way that Proust's narrator serves as a model for Farrell's portrait of the artist.

In *A Note on Literary Criticism,* Farrell emphasizes the centrality of Proust's view of habit in an extended analysis of a passage from Proust's second volume, *Within a Budding Grove.* Farrell cites "a most excitingly exact description of certain impressions of a railroad journey taken by the 'I' of the novels," which is followed by a passage where the narrator stresses the uniqueness of the impressions of the outside world registered by each individual consciousness and the aesthetic (and moral) falseness of generalization. Here Farrell quotes Proust at length:

> We invariably forget that these [qualities that we perceive through the senses] are individual qualities, and, substituting for them in our mind a conventional type at which we arrive by striking a sort of mean amongst the different faces that have taken our fancy, the pleasures we have known, we are left with mere abstract images which are lifeless and dull because they are lacking in precisely that element of novelty, different from anything we have known, that element which is proper to beauty and happiness. And we deliver on life a pessimistic judgment which we suppose to be fair, for we believed that we were taking into account when we formed it happiness and beauty, whereas in fact we left them out and replaced them by syntheses in which there is not a single atom of either.

By extension, Farrell asserts, "so it is with a character in a novel, no matter what class he belongs to. He is not just a copy of all the other members of his class. He is a person with resemblances to all the other members of his class, and with a difference from all the other members of that class." To explain further, Farrell again quotes Proust: "As a rule it is with our being reduced to a minimum that we live, most of our faculties lie dormant because they can rely upon Habit, which knows what there is to be done and has no need of their services." And yet, the railroad journey stimulated the narrator to use more of his faculties because, Proust explains, the sights and sounds presented "a project which would have the further advantage of providing with subject matter the selfish, active, practical, mechanical, indolent, centrifugal tendency which is that of the human mind."[26]

Here Proust supports Farrell's argument in *A Note on Literary Criticism* that politics is irrelevant or worse as motivation or measuring stick for art. I also believe that this is the heart of Farrell's own design for fiction, toward which Proust's masterpiece is a model of belief in the validity for extended artistic rendering of individual consciousness. The result is the O'Neill-O'Flaherty series—*In Search of Lost Time* in Washington Park. Farrell had no illusions, by the way, as to the potential receptiveness of an American literary audience to his emphasis on the interior life. He pointed out in a lecture that "perhaps the greatest literary tradition in modern times is that of France. . . . When the novel developed in France, there was already a very highly developed culture." He cites *La Princess de Cleves* (1678), *Adolphe* (1815), and *Les Liaisons Dangereuses* (1880s) as examples of novels in which "the characters understand a great deal about their own emotions. There is a high level of sophistication, of sophistication in a good sense, and there was an audience that could understand it." In contrast, America has been "a crude and primitive" place ("except in New England"), where "it was impossible for us to have a developed awareness, a developed consciousness of self, such as the French had, because we didn't have stabilized classes, a stabilized culture or even a stabilized language."[27]

The second link between Proust and Farrell is their shared understanding of how the mind can find release from the enslaving ballast of habit. For Proust, liberation comes only in the fresh, unbidden visitations of "involuntary memory," the most famous of which is the first—when a tea-soaked biscuit brings the narrator's entire childhood world vividly into his adult mind.[28] In Farrell's fiction, the unbidden epiphanies of involuntary memory come in experiences of daydream and reverie, and these contribute to his pioneering expansion of the possibilities for literature of the consciousness of so-called ordinary people. In his first two fictional cycles, the *Studs Lonigan* trilogy and the O'Neill-O'Flaherty pentalogy, examples include Studs Lonigan's recurrent dream of perching in a tree with Lucy Scanlan, Mrs. Mary O'Flaherty at her husband's grave, Old Tom O'Flaherty on his deathbed, Jim O'Neill dozing over Shakespeare after having suffered three strokes, and the boy Danny O'Neill drifting aimlessly through Washington Park at all seasons of the year.

The third element, place, is pervasive for both writers. When he first read *Swann's Way* in 1927, Farrell was surely struck by renderings of and attitudes toward important locations that echoed his own experience. One such is the depiction of Proust's narrator's sickly Aunt Léonie, whose "bed lay by the window, she had the street there before her eyes and on it from morning to night, to divert her melancholy, like the Persian princes, would read the daily but immemorial chronicle of Combray, which she would afterward comment upon with [her maid] Françoise." Another is the narrator's remembered perception that the steeple of the Catholic church organized the entire country town of Combray: "It was the steeple of Saint-Hilaire that gave all the occupations, all the hours, all the viewpoints of the town their shape, their crown, their consecration." Reading these passages, Farrell would have seen his own grandmother, Julia Daly, sitting at her window "reading the daily but immemorial chronicle" of Washington Park, and he would have felt the echo of his own childhood neighborhood, in which Corpus Christi and St. Anselm's churches focused everyone's works and days.

Swann's Way ends with the section titled "Place-Names: The Name," and more than half of *Within a Budding Grove* is the section called "Place-Names: The Place." In both books and throughout Proust's entire sequence of seven novels, evocations abound of place as catalyst for remembered experience. As it happens, two more of the earliest and most important also involve church steeples. Early in the "Combray" section of *Swann* comes the lovely passage in which the narrator confesses: "And even today," if someone answers his question for directions in a strange town by pointing to a steeple, he finds himself "forgetting the walk I had begun or the necessary errand," and "remain[ing] there in front of the steeple for hours, motionless, trying to remember, feeling deep in myself lands recovered from oblivion draining and rebuilding themselves. . . . I am still seeking my path, I am turning a corner . . . but . . . I am doing so in my heart." And at the climax of "Combray," the narrator recalls one of his earliest experiences of the mystery and the power of place. While out walking, "suddenly a roof, a glimmer of sun on a stone, the smell of the road would stop me because of a particular pleasure they gave me, and also because they seemed to be concealing, beyond what I could see, something which they were inviting me to come take and which despite my efforts I could not manage to discover." And then, one day,

> At the bend of a road I suddenly experienced that special pleasure which was unlike any other, when I saw the two steeples of Martinville, shining in the setting sun and appearing to change position with the motion of our carriage and the windings of the road. As I noted the shape of their spires, the shifting of their lines, the sunlight on their surfaces, I felt that I was not reaching the full depth of my impression, that something was behind that motion, that brightness, something which they seemed at once to contain and conceal.

This time he asks the family friend who is driving the carriage for a pencil and paper, and he writes out his impressions of the steeples. The result is the narrator's first attempt to make art, and although the result is clumsy and tentative, he nonetheless recognizes immediately that the act of writing will be his weapon against time.[29]

From the outset of his writing life, place was equally important in Farrell's fiction. "Helen, I Love You," the first story, dated 1930, in his first collection of short fiction opens with "two boys . . . in front of one of the small gray-stone houses in the 5700 block of Indiana Avenue, glaring at each other." And he begins his first novel, *Young Lonigan: A Boyhood in Chicago Streets*, published in 1932, with an abundance of detailed place lore. About to graduate from eighth grade, the young protagonist Studs Lonigan defines himself in terms of "St. Patrick's" church and parochial school at Michigan Avenue and Sixty-first Street, Indiana Avenue where he walked his first girlfriend home, the "corner of Sixtieth" where he broke some basement windows, the Carter Playground where he had his first fight, and the elevated railroad structure at Fifty-ninth Street, the site of his brave acceptance of a challenge to climb a girder. This boy's reverie is followed by the stock-taking daydream of Studs's father, Paddy Lonigan, who recalls his own childhood as the son of a "pauperized greenhorn," with a wider-ranging litany of place names: Blue Island, St. Ignatius church, dances at Hull-House, "back of the yards," Canaryville, "Luke O'Toole's place on Halsted." Place is similarly paramount from the opening pages of the first O'Neill-O'Flaherty novel, *A World I Never Made*, as six-year-old Danny O'Neill stands looking "wistfully out the parlor window. He saw the vacant lot at the corner of Fiftieth and Calumet Avenue with the elevated tracks in the alley behind the lot and the advertising signboards running all around the front of the lot." He notes "an elevated train" going north, and thinks that "he rode on that train when Uncle Al took him to see the White Sox play." And when "an electric" passes, "headed for Fifty-first Street," he looks down "at the moving black roof" and "wished that he was riding in it," instead of having to get ready to go to Sunday Mass.

Indeed, the connectedness of mind and milieu infuses every page of Farrell's fiction. "No ideas but in things," as William Carlos Williams puts it, and Farrell once wrote (in an unpublished essay) that the world of Washington Park "was tremendously and vividly real to me. It was as real to me as I was to myself," and that "Santa Claus and God were real to me as a child—'There's nothing either good or bad but thinking makes it so'—as real, as true as the building off of the alley between Calumet Avenue and Grand Boulevard and set back from a gravelly, rectangular-shaped little school yard: the building was Corpus Christi School." Here, Farrell continues, "I played, and grew, and dreamed."

Thoughts such as these do not appear as often in Farrell's art as in Proust's because of the radically different narrative positions of each novelist. Proust's aim is recovery of the past from the doubled, reflexive perspective of the consciousness of one highly sophisticated narrator in full adulthood. Farrell's aim is the recovery of the past from the single perspective of the consciousness of a character living a life moment by moment—that is, recovery of the past by imagining it as the present. As Farrell put it in that same unpublished piece, "a novelist, of course, must have knowledge of many details." This is especially true of his fiction, because story, happenings, characters "are all presented from the standpoint of immediate experience."[30] In addition, even when the character is Danny O'Neill, the future artist, the insights day by day are less startling, incisive, lyrical—whatever can be said about Proust—because Danny is not looking back, but registering the moments as he lives them. Furthermore, Danny and his family are not French aristocrats and aesthetes, but working-class and lower-middle-class Irish immigrants and second-generation Americans.

And yet, despite the obvious distances between them, Proust's narrator and Danny O'Neill have much more in common with each other as portraits of the artist than either has, for example, with Stephen Dedalus. Here is the fourth way in which Proust served as a crucial, directing model for Farrell. To be sure,

Proust's, Joyce's, and Farrell's large fictional projects all conclude in similar anticlimax. At the end of the seventh volume of *In Search of Lost Time*, of *Ulysses*, and of Farrell's *My Days of Anger*, none of the three protagonists has written anything of consequence. All artistic achievement lies beyond the pages with which these sequences end. This makes practical sense because the novelists would have realized that, after the artist has committed to his vocation, he's not so interesting to the prospective reader. Better grist for fiction's mill is the fits and false starts, the hard slog through the tangle of unmediated experience through which Proust's narrator, Stephen Dedalus, and Danny O'Neill fight their way toward enlightenment. The end of this inward journey marks the outer limit of the portrait in each case. But young Stephen Hero is much farther along the road than either of the other two. He knows, and thus we know, that he's definitely going to get there. In contrast, Proust's narrator is a dismayingly unprecocious seeker, stumbling, vulnerable, and maddeningly tentative in his development. So is Danny O'Neill, and Farrell got from Proust the courage of his conviction to give extended narrative treatment to so slow and painful a pilgrim's progress toward a life in art.

Thus, encouraged in so many ways by the example of Marcel Proust, James T. Farrell began fashioning a body of fiction in which the relentless, deadening force of habit faces off against the fitful, countervailing blessings of daydream and reverie. The great enemy is time, but in these novels, the characters in whose minds this war plays out are fixed in the writer's amber of fully realized place. Much in Walter Benjamin's succinct elucidation of Proust also illuminates Farrell. Benjamin declares that Proust's "true interest is in the passage of time in its most real—that is, space-bound—form." Although "there has never been anyone else with Proust's ability to show us things," he uses experience "not to drink from it, but to dream to its heartbeat," and his bass note is a "hopeless sadness" that springs from acknowledgment of "the incurable imperfection in . . . the present moment." Add to this Benjamin's assertion that "Proust approaches experience without the slightest metaphysical interest, . . . without the slightest tendency to console," and you have much of the truth about Farrell as well.[31]

Farrell's investigation of consciousness in the O'Neill-O'Flaherty novels is especially inclusive and challenging. In addition to the development of the artist's mind, he also sets out to render the inner lives of some half-dozen members of the two families from which Danny O'Neill springs, most of whom have not had the luxury of advanced education and circumstances that allow for or encourage reflection. Even in *My Days of Anger*, which focuses on the young artist's coming of age, Farrell does not abandon Danny's parents, grandmother, brothers, and sisters. All continue to contribute their individual thoughts to the interwoven pattern. It is here that the example of a third writer was crucially reinforcing for Farrell's project, an artist without either the stylistic egotism of Joyce or the focus on characters from the cultured elite of Proust. This was Anton Chekhov, whom Farrell had first read seriously in 1927 while beginning work on his own fiction. Farrell's 1942 essay on Chekhov elucidates the connection between them. He describes Chekhov's characters as "idle dreamers who live sunk in the commonplace; men and women who cannot react to cruelty, who cannot be free, who cannot lift themselves above the terrible plain of stagnation—people in whom human dignity is dissolving." Farrell emphasizes two characteristics of Chekhov's work, both noted by Maxim Gorky, which were central to Farrell's own aims. The first was Gorky's assessment that "banality always found in him a discerning and merciless judge," to which Farrell adds, "Chekhov raised the portrayal of banality to the level of world literature." The second was Gorky's statement of Chekhov's essential message: "You live badly, my friends. It is shameful to live like that." Farrell goes on to indicate the motive behind that portrayal by quoting a Chekhov letter that articulates the faith of the literary realist: "The best of [writers] are realists and paint life as it is, but, through every line's being soaked in the consciousness of an object, you feel, besides life as it is, the life that ought to be, and that captivates you. . . . Man will only become better when you make him see what he is like." Farrell underscores his sense of this passage, which also expresses his own goal for fiction: "great and good writers saturate us with a consciousness of life, and, by achieving this effect, endow us with a sense not only of what life is but also of what it ought to be."[32]

Elsewhere, in a piece on "Nonsense and the Short Story," Farrell cites a number of spurious opinions about the genre, then asks, "Which of these definitions is best suited to the stories of Chekhov?—in my opinion the greatest short-story writer who ever lived. Or which one is most applicable to the stories in Joyce's *Dubliners*? To *Winesburg, Ohio*?" Rejecting the formulaic criterion that a story should create a "*single* or a *unified* impression," he described Chekhov's "A Woman's Kingdom," as "literally, a cross section of many phases of life [in czarist Russia]. One gets from it impressions of class relationships, of characters, of moods. What, then, of the singleness of impression? In fact, Chekhov's stories are an excellent refutation of all these definitions. His stories are, in my opinion, like doors of understanding and awareness opening outward into an entire world."[33]

The idea of grafting Chekhovian concern for inclusion of the mundane on Joycean and Proustian attention to consciousness involved a dramatic change of narrative orientation for Farrell. He recalled later that his first stories came easily—too easily, and when he had first tried to write an autobiographical novel about "my boyhood and high school days" in April 1927, he had failed utterly: "I went back to my short-pants days, and attempted to create a character who had been much like myself, and who would reveal himself, and tell a story of others around him and of himself; this would be done in a stream-of-consciousness flow. In a Standard Oil filling station at Thirty-fifth and Morgan, the last of the stations in which I worked, I stood at the desk and wrote in pencil. It was a sunny afternoon in April and I thought that I had found a way of writing, one that I could do easily, rolling it off, in a swift succession of pages. But it was not that easy; it wasn't that way. I came to a dead halt."[34] Two years later, shortly after conceiving the character of Studs Lonigan, he recognized the major flaw in his early fiction to be lack of objectivity: "I analyzed my character as I considered him in his relations to his own world, his own background. I set as my aim that of unfolding the destiny of Studs Lonigan in his own words, his own actions, his own patterns of thought and feeling. I decided that my task was not to state formally what life meant to me, but to try and re-create a sense of what life meant to Studs Lonigan. I worked on with this project, setting up as an ideal the strictest possible objectivity."[35]

The result of Farrell's thinking was the reinvention of his style. Most of the proletarian realists of the 1930s had as one of their aims speaking for people for whom self-expression comes hard. This theme of tragic inarticulateness suggests a stylistic challenge, a problem of narrative voice: how to speak for people who cannot easily speak for themselves. Farrell's solution was to create a third-person-limited point of view that shifts from character to character. The result is a kind of omniscience—but with a difference. It is an omniscience of which one key aim is exclusion of the consciousness of the author. Except, of course, for the selection and organization of incidents, events, and the consciousness on which these register, this is the meaning of Farrell's often quoted goal of writing "so that life may speak for itself." This is Flaubert's "free indirect discourse," but without the irony that signals authorial control and judgment. The medium that Farrell fashioned is an austere style of scrupulous plainness that effectively renders the thoughts and speech of ordinary people. For this prodigiously gifted intellectual, encyclopedically well read and fiercely committed to the life of the mind, the forging of this style was likely a heroic effort of will. Taken in 1929, Farrell's hard decision to displace the central narrative consciousness from the sophisticated, autobiographical self to the limited other resulted in the creation of an urban plain style that is one of his great gifts to American literature. Analogues for this achievement include Mark Twain's decision to let Huck Finn tell his own story, Robert Frost's incorporation of New England idiom and rhythms into lyric poetry, and William Carlos Williams's determination to use East Coast city colloquialism in verse, including the epic.

The Farrell style can be understood in a larger literary context. Farrell has said that "I was decidedly formed and ready before the Thirties started. And I had read and been influenced by many, Ben Hecht, Maxwell Bodenheim, George Moore, James Joyce, Hemingway, Sherwood Anderson, Nietzsche, Red Lewis, etc., and not solely and simply by Teddy Dreiser." Farrell's position as a stylistic innovator with modernist roots in the twenties has been established by Donald Pizer, who credits Farrell's use of epiphany and development of stream-of-consciousness writing and links him particularly with Joyce and Anderson. Pizer identifies Farrell's stream-of-consciousness technique as a form of "indirect discourse," a third-person voice wherein "the narrator is present as reporter, structurer, and summarizer of the character's frame of mind but . . . [in which] he presents this material in the language and grammatical form habitually used by the character." And he sees *Studs Lonigan* as "a novel of the 1920s in Farrell's exploration of the inarticulate felt life of a character by means of indirect discourse."[36] Farrell's technique is notably effective in the many examples of daydream and reverie in his fiction, and his rendering of the dream life of ordinary people is part of his expansion of the literary possibilities of the consciousness of Americans. The climax of this effect in the *Studs Lonigan* trilogy is Studs's fevered death fantasy, a distorted montage of the people who have influenced his life that flickers through his failing consciousness near the end of the trilogy's 1935 final volume, *Judgment Day*. Surreal dream materials are even more prominent in *Gas-House McGinty*, his novel of 1933 set in the bustling "Wagon Call Department" of an express company, an unlikely place, before Farrell, for such literary experimentation. By the inception of the O'Neill-O'Flaherty series, these techniques were fully at his command. The result is several examples over the five novels of a hard-won, minimal eloquence that embodies Farrell's faith in the ability of relatively unreflective and uneducated people to clarify and bless their own lives, even if only in their own minds.

A final overarching influence for Farrell's fiction was the philosophy of pragmatism. In several essays and lectures in the mid-1960s, he asserted that the writings of the pragmatists William James, George Herbert Mead, and, especially, John Dewey had been the most important influence on the development of his own art. He recalls that beginning in 1929, he filled notebook after notebook with quotations and comments based on his first, excited engagement with these philosophers: "When I read book after book of John Dewey in the fall of 1929 and in 1930, I was permanently influenced. . . . John Dewey and Mead had a tremendous influence on me in the writing of *Studs Lonigan*. . . . I was concerned with how to conceive character, and I was concerned with certain general problems, both for themselves and in relationship to the writing. I was just two years a writer by then, and James on habit and John Dewey on habit in *Human Nature and Conduct* influenced me, and Mead and Dewey and the social conception of self and the personality—the social conception of individuality—and Dewey in his approach to a problem in terms of the situation rather than in an individualized way or in an abstracted generalized way."

At that time, Farrell continues, "The whole cast of my thought was really fixed and this has never changed." He recalls how much clicked into place when he read the passage from Dewey that became an epigraph for his first novel, *Young*

Lonigan: A Boyhood in Chicago Streets: "While I was working on the book about a character called Studs Lonigan, I came across the following, which I quote from *Human Nature and Conduct*, which crystallized much of my thinking in reference to the book, and thinking of mine in general. 'The poignancy of situations that evoke reflection lies in the fact that we really do not know the meaning of the tendencies that are pressing for action.' And I had begun *Studs Lonigan* from the end—that is, he was going to die as a young man in his young manhood. There was actually a situation that called for reflection, I felt." He explains that Dewey, James, and Mead "saved and short-circuited" him into "a clearer conception of naturalism," a "philosophical" naturalism that differs fundamentally from that of Emile Zola, who "took two very generalized railroad-train conceptions of heredity and environment, and counterposed them to each other and said that heredity was stronger. That was the generalization of what he thought was science, and he dismissed individual opinions and impressions as lies."[37] Harry Smith has succinctly summarized the crucial distinction that Farrell makes here and at many other places in his critical writing: "Farrell was not the last great exponent of American Naturalism. Rather, he achieved the first great synthesis of realist tradition and the newer subjectivist fiction, bringing psychological exploration to social forces and the facts of ordinary life. Farrell was more concerned with consciousness, attitudes, personality, subjective time, dream and the irrational than was any 'realist' or 'Naturalist.'"[38]

In a 1966 essay, Farrell highlights what was for him Dewey's key idea of growth as a social phenomenon, which became the grounding for Farrell's own passionate commitment to fiction that locates character in its deepest social context:

> The pragmatists in philosophy are concerned with process and particularly with growth. The living organism must function in society. A child, for example, has inner impulses and a child has to grow, intellectually as well as physically. Growth springs from those inner impulses. Because the mind is an organ, developed in society—not set apart—knowledge is essentially cooperative in character. How an individual functions is to be tested by consequences, but, in Dewey's view, this is not the same as simple success. The fulfillments of functioning are in "shared experiences." He believed that certainties do not exist. Man, in a universe of peril, can reduce uncertainties that threaten him by the cooperative acquisition of knowledge and by cooperative action. In this world void of certainty, categorical imperatives are arbitrary. The only imperative, if there be one, Dewey held, was that of growth.[39]

Robert Butler has explained most usefully how the pragmatists' conceptions of time and habit also guided Farrell's fiction from the start:

> [The pragmatists] developed an idea that is crucial to Farrell's vision, that time is an organic continuum centered in human consciousness. The mind reconstructs a past to stabilize action in the present and it simultaneously imagines a future to

> serve as a directive for such action. This is what Mead understands as "temporal perspective" and what James describes as temporal "equilibrium." For current action to be useful in the growth of individuals and the progress of society, it must be harmonized with the other two levels of time. Otherwise, time becomes fragmented and a fundamental loss of control over experience results. . . . Such a fragmentary experience of moments is what the pragmatists referred to as a 'specious' present—an assortment of isolated events which either drift into nothingness or eventually form a chain of repetition. But, as Dewey points out, the self can be whole and effective only if the consciousness which directs action is artfully balanced in all three levels of time.[40]

Here are the psychosocial models for Studs Lonigan and Danny O'Neill, the one caught in centrifugal drift and deadening habit, the other struggling to develop a secular, "temporal perspective" on which to ground a significant life.

Butler further explains that "both Farrell and the pragmatists saw entrenched habit as a serious human problem. Allowing the past to dominate the present rather than inviting the present to 'organize' the past for its own needs, habit makes time a rigid circle of necessity, stripping the here and now of novelty and making the future a dreary set of mindless repetitions." As Butler summarizes, "These theories of time helped Farrell to imagine human experience in coherently structured terms and were, therefore, immensely useful in the formal shaping of his fiction. . . . Seen in this light, . . . his fictive world is remarkable not only for its often acknowledged power but also for its little-recognized depth of vision and formal control."[41]

In a 1965 lecture, Farrell paid homage to Mead on aesthetics, and then described how his own thinking went beyond Mead in a more positive, humanistic direction. The result is one of his most moving defenses of the artist's endeavor: "[Mead] treated aesthetics as serial processes leading to an end or a culmination. He made a distinction between the functional and the aesthetic. The functional was what you wanted in order to get on to the next step. . . . But when you pause and contemplate the pleasure and the joy and the satisfaction you will get or gain at the end of this serial process, that is aesthetic experience." And yet, while appreciating Mead's systematic approach, Farrell disagrees, especially for the artist: "I would say that all experience is both aesthetic *and* functional—or should be. . . . It is not for [the artist] to work only for himself; rather it is for him to render multiple experience as best he can—to render it with the hope that he will leave some of it to the memory of mankind, because in the first, in the last and in every analysis the memory of mankind is what sustains us. In it is the source of all belief and of all faith."[42]

I agree with Dennis Flynn, who declares that "I can think of no American novelist who begins to approach Farrell in the degree to which his work is rooted in a philosophical world view. Farrell's roots in the philosophy of pragmatism help account not only for his being realistic and dispassionate about the Catholic Church, but also for the generally experimental and innovative nature of his writing. He was able to put into fiction . . . thoughts and feelings many people have had but which had never been held worthy of inclusion in serious literature."[43] Farrell began with a solid, philosophical basis for both style and subject matter of what he wanted to write. From the outset, he committed to fiction that emphasizes consciousness as active, seeing the mind as in process, buffeted by experience, searching for "Truth" or "truths," often unaware of that distinction, often blocked by habit—the result of laziness among the comfortable or exhaustion among the underprivileged. In my view, this is most important in the O'Neill-O'Flaherty series, where the novelist's challenge is rendering the variously damaging or fruitful applications of consciousness to the placement of the self in time by a large number of characters. This philosophical justification also explains the conviction and energy with which Farrell attempted so detailed a scrutiny of the interior lives of his characters. In this deep and thoughtful context, no mind is more or less "ordinary" than any other. Novelist Thomas F. Curley put it well when he praised Farrell's "steady attempt to make art of an experience that is at once common and significant."[44]

Neighborhood, Catholicism, Childhood

Farrell's fiction is also important to American literature from the 1930s onward in its delivery of fresh and corrective perspectives in three thematic areas: city life as actually lived, the religion of ethnic Americans as actually practiced, and the nature of experience as perceived by children. Farrell recalled that the first profound catalyst for his decision to become a writer was Sherwood Anderson—in particular, *Tar, A Midwestern Childhood*, which he read early in 1927. His excited reaction mirrors that of many subsequent writers to his own work: "If the inner life of a boy in an Ohio country town of the nineteenth century was meaningful enough to be the material for a book like *Tar*, then perhaps my own feelings and emotions and the feelings and emotions of those with whom I had grown up were important. . . . I thought of writing a novel about my own boyhood, about the neighborhood in which I had grown up. Here was one of the seeds that led to *Studs Lonigan*." He goes on to explain that "the neighborhoods of Chicago in which I grew up possessed something of the character of a small town. They were little worlds of their own. Many of the people living in them knew one another. There was a certain amount of gossip of the character that one finds in small towns. One of the largest nationality and religious groups in these neighborhoods was Irish American and Catholic. I attended a parochial school. Through the school and Sunday mass, the life of these neighborhoods was rendered somewhat more cohesive. My grandmother was always a neighborhood character, well known. I became known, too, the way a boy would be in a small town."[45]

Before Farrell wrote, few American writers had presented city neighborhoods in this way. Finley Peter Dunne's "Mr. Dooley" columns about Chicago and Abraham Cahan's stories of Jewish New York in the 1890s were among the few notable exceptions. Farrell's perspective, pioneering in its balance as well as in its accurate detail, revises a number of distorted views: Stephen Crane's vision of the city as a threatening, impressionist theater set, Theodore Dreiser's view of the city as an exciting but alien destination for immigrant and rural seekers, and the local-color journalists' (Richard Harding Davis, Brander Mathews, and others) portraits of the city as a tourist stop wherein to find the quaint and picturesque. Unlike these others, the city in Farrell's fiction is a real place where daily life is presented with fullness and fairness. Crucial to that presentation is the creation of urban neighborhoods that are as richly realized as any in fiction. Farrell knew instinctively what Eudora Welty has put so memorably: "The truth is, fiction depends for its life on place. Location is the crossroads of circumstance, the proving ground of 'What happened? Who's here? Who's coming?'—and that is the heart's field."[46]

The O'Neill-O'Flaherty novels show us what it looked, sounded, smelled, tasted, and felt like to live in South Side Chicago neighborhoods, what areas such as Washington Park provided and lacked for working- and middle-class urban Americans, and how these places changed over time, specifically from the 1890s through the 1920s. Like many immigrant couples, Tom and Mary O'Flaherty begin their Chicago life in one of the city's oldest places, Blue Island Avenue, where many generations of settlers have already come and gone. In their story of internal migration to better neighborhoods, the O'Flahertys exemplify the process by which many marginally middle-class, ethnic families got ahead—young adults lived at home until they married and contributed their earnings to the family. Thus, by the time Old Tom retires from his teamster's job, his children Al, Ned, Margaret, and Louise earn enough to allow the family to move from a crowded flat on Twelfth Street to larger apartments further south. The culminating change of location in the O'Neill-O'Flaherty series puts the family in a spacious apartment overlooking Washington Park. Similarly, Farrell documents Jim and Lizz O'Neill's laborious movement toward a better life for their large family in terms of their three homes over the course of the five novels: a cold-water tenement flat, a ramshackle cottage with outhouse behind, and, finally, a comfortable apartment with indoor plumbing, gas, and electricity. The map accompanying this introduction demonstrates the congruence between these places and the homes of Farrell's parents, James Francis and Mary Daly Farrell, and maternal grandparents, John and Julia Brown Daly.[47]

The depth of neighborhood place lore in the O'Neill-O'Flaherty novels is partly because they were very much a family affair. On February 2, 1934, begins the remarkable group of letters in which, like Joyce writing back to his relatives in Dublin, Farrell asks his brothers and sisters for help. The first is to his sister Mary: "I've started the family saga, and maybe you could help me, by, without making it apparent that you're doing it, picking up whatever you can about LaSalle Street, and Mrs. Butcher, Mrs. Meyers, etc. I'd appreciate anything you can send me, and as you can get it, and so on." These letters go back and forth for the entire writing life of the series, and include questions and answers about street addresses and neighborhood characters, racing forms and "linguistic habits," and the mechanics of various jobs. "No details will be negligible, I'm sure," Farrell writes early on, "so don't hesitate any time you feel so inclined to write more."[48] It is possible that Farrell's powerful evocation of the few square blocks that make up a city neighborhood is a vestigial link with his family's Irish heritage. After all, the literature of Ireland is remarkable in this same way, and its origins are in the ancient Irish poetic tradition of *dindshenchas*, which means a poetry explanatory of place and place lore. Whatever its roots, the South Side Chicago world that emerges in Farrell's fiction is as complete and coherent as Proust's Combray, Joyce's Dublin, and Faulkner's Yoknapatawpha County.

Farrell's rendering of Catholicism is another of his pioneering contributions to American fiction. For his Irish characters, a second familiar charted boundary, at least as vital and defining as the neighborhood, is the immigrant/ethnic Catholic parish, which provided both continuity with Ireland and help toward adjustment in America, as well as religion's traditional gifts of meaning and solace. In nineteenth-century urban America, the Irish found more negative echoes of the old country than one might have assumed. Here again, they were renters—apartment dwellers to be sure, but renters nonetheless. Here again, they were living in the worst available housing—flimsy, fire-prone, overcrowded, disease-ridden tenements. (Mr. Dooley tells us that "th' Hogan flats on Halsted Sthreet" was "wan iv thim big, fine-lookin' buildings that pious men built out iv celluloid an' plasther iv Paris.") Here again, they were at the bottom of the economic ladder in terms of remuneration for labor, with destitution and beggary looming just below the surface of daily life. Here again, as Catholics, they faced prejudice and discrimination from a Protestant governing class—with the difference being that this time the Protestants were in the majority, constituting a true demographic establishment. And here again, their religion provided both spiritual comfort and social adhesive. However, in the New World, there were formidable counterweights to second-class citizenship. The Irish in America were able to practice their religion freely, they could earn wages that increased over time, and they had the opportunity to rise in the world. As a result, they soon had the economic wherewithal—albeit often by accretion of nickels and dimes—to progress from frame and basement churches to that wonder of the late-nineteenth-century American religious world, the urban Catholic parish—a strong and vibrant complex of church, school, public meeting hall, rectory, and convent, with significant outlying institutions—Catholic hospitals, orphanages, and social settlement facilities.

Farrell's Washington Park novels describe this sophisticated cultural milieu in full swing, and they also illustrate the various attitudes toward the Church among three generations of Irish Americans. Like no other American writing when he was starting out, Farrell's fiction is bursting with descriptions of what went on in Catholic schoolrooms and schoolyards, at populous Sunday masses and quotidian visits to the peaceful, empty church, at the administration of the sacraments of penance and extreme unction, and at all sizes and manners of wakes. Notable in this vivid rendering is Farrell's balanced presentation of opposing aspects of American Catholic culture. True to his realist aesthetic, these contrasts are also a significant part of the dialectical opposition in the two fictional cycles. In the *Studs Lonigan* trilogy, St. Patrick's church and its pompous and hypocritical pastor, Father Gilhooley, fail everyone. Despite his flirtations with street life, Studs remains a conventional Catholic, never questioning the teachings of the Church, and reacting typically right up to his last illness. Although he tries to save his sinking life by joining parish groups and making countless acts of contrition, nothing avails. As a child, Danny O'Neill is terrorized by the fear of everlasting perdition instilled by the nuns at Crucifixion School, and yet, Catholic education also provides him with models of spiritual, educated, and ideologically dedicated men and women who eventually inspire the boy to translate his imaginative life into words. In addition, the Church exposes Danny to positive attributes unavailable elsewhere on the South Side of Chicago: a sense of order and ritual, historical continuity, and mystery. Although far from being the only writer in the thirties raised as a Catholic, Farrell was unique in the fullness of his exploration of Catholicism as a shaping institutional force in American life, from the graduation ceremony at St. Patrick's grammar school at the beginning of *Young Lonigan* to Danny's grandmother Mary O'Flaherty's black rosary beads at the end of her life in *My Days of Anger*. In the next decade, many would follow his lead, but it is important to understand just how innovative Farrell's fiction was in this regard. He brought Catholicism into the mainstream of American literature.[49]

The consciousness observing Washington Park and its Catholic parishes in Farrell's novels is often that of a child, for whom perceptions of urban life are fresh and formative. Here Farrell is also innovative. In his critique of the sorry state of American fiction at the First American Writers' Congress in 1935, he declared that much of "the writing about children by adults" was "of the same nature" as Harris's Uncle Remus stories and Lover's Handy Andy stage Irish stereotype: "Booth Tarkington's *Penrod*, for instance, is put into the same kind of mold, and it is a combination of certain conventions necessary for the intercourse between children and certain types of parents, on one hand, and, on the other hand, of a wish fulfillment or an adult fantasy about childhood." With his deep grounding in the works of John Dewey, Farrell saw education as the central issue. He wrote of his first novels that "the story of Studs Lonigan was conceived as the story of the education of a normal American boy in this period. The important institutions in the education of Studs Lonigan were the home and the family, the church, the school, and the playground. These institutions broke down and did not serve their desired function." In their place, "the streets became a potent educative factor in the boy's life."[50] Conversely, the path of Danny O'Neill makes it clear that education broadly defined in the Deweyan sense can have opposite, positive results for a city boy from a background much less stable than Studs's. This is another contribution to the dialectical force field that connects the two series of novels.

The Five Novels

The O'Neill-O'Flaherty series is sweeping and symphonic in structure. *A World I Never Made* is the prelude in which major themes are introduced. *No Star Is Lost* is a dark movement in a shattering, minor key. *Father and Son* consists of contrapuntal variations between the two title figures. *My Days of Anger* contains a large, focused statement of the major theme of the entire series. *The Face of Time* is a lyrical coda recapitulating the opening themes. Two streams of experience mingle in these pages: the outer stream of social life, a chronicle of the works and days of three generations of Chicagoans, and the inner stream of consciousness, the perceptions of that chronicle and of themselves in the minds of several individuals living it. Throughout the series, the same two watershed experiences recur—death and illuminating reverie. Deaths in the family constitute the central events of the outer stream and emphasize the social themes of alienation and failed community in urban America in the 1910s and 1920s. Solitary reveries are the central events of the inner streams of consciousness, and these emphasize the psychological theme of individual isolation. Clarifications of life and honest self-assessment come only in dreams and daydreams, and they are almost never shared. This theme gathers force in the last three volumes of the series, in which major characters die without having spoken their minds to anyone else. Against this choking tide, the young protagonist Danny O'Neill moves toward understanding of the social and psychological tragedies of his family's thwarted lives. His growth toward the resolution to use art as his weapon against these dual tragedies is the binding theme of the whole project. Through the first four books, Danny experiences the start of formal schooling, early adolescence, high school, and college. In the fifth novel, he comes around again to early childhood when home is the whole world. The slow and painful nature of his intellectual journey enforces another continuing motif—how hard we must work for enlightenment in this tough world. Here Farrell's love of the poetry of W. B. Yeats, from "Adam's Curse" to "The Circus Animals' Desertion," stood him in good stead. In the series overall, Farrell achieves a balance between the bump and flow of experience, both inner and outer, and a structural ordering into large thematic blocks and recurrent motifs. The mixture that results comes as close as fiction can to the rag and bone of reality. Most of the characters in these novels are caught in the flow and catch only brief glimpses of larger meanings. The Deweyan "poignancy of situations that evoke reflection" comes only to the reader, who is the one abiding witness to both confusing detail and clarifying pattern. The reader's perspective generates the sole, yet great and governing, irony that Farrell the author allows between his epigraphs and the last page of fictive text. And this whole consort makes for a powerful, compelling, and memorable reading experience.

The O'Neill-O'Flaherty series is autobiographical in obvious ways. Places and times often correlate with James T. Farrell's own facts of life. These include the ages and abodes of Danny O'Neill's grandparents and parents in the years covered in the novels, the number of his siblings and their approximate dates of birth (and death, in one case), and Danny's own formal markers of development: the start of elementary school (1911), graduation from high school (1923), and attendance at the University of Chicago (from 1925). But this is really neither here nor there for the novels. Here, once again, the example of Proust is useful. In the introduction to her translation of *Swann's Way*, Lydia Davis describes Proust's narrative in terms that also apply to Farrell's series: "The book is filled with events and characters closely resembling those of Proust's own life, yet this novel is not autobiography wearing a thin disguise of fiction but, rather, something more complex—fiction created out of real life, based on the experiences and beliefs of its author, and presented in the guise of autobiography."[51]

A World I Never Made takes place over five months, opening in August 1911 when Danny O'Neill is seven years old, and closing at Christmastime. *No Star Is Lost* covers two years, late 1914 (World War I is on in Europe) and 1915, when Danny is ten and eleven. *Father and Son* begins in 1918 with Danny fourteen and in eighth grade, and ends after his high school graduation in June 1923. *My Days of Anger* spans four years, 1924 through 1927, which include Danny's unfulfilling and abortive experiences of higher education at St. Vincent's night law school and the University of Chicago. The novel ends in the summer of 1927 when he is twenty-three. The fifth O'Neill-O'Flaherty book, *The Face of Time*, brings the series full circle, opening in the summer of 1909, when Danny O'Neill is five years old, and ending in December 1910.

In 1947, the World Publishing Company (Cleveland and New York) reprinted the four volumes of the O'Neill-O'Flaherty series that had appeared so far. The occasion prompted Farrell to write short introductions to the novels in which he outlines his aims with clarity and conciseness. He begins the first of these with a crucial distinction. Unlike *Studs Lonigan*, "which is mainly concerned with one central character," in this second series, "there are a number of major protagonists. . . . Each of them exists in his or her own right. Attention shifts from one to another of these characters. With this shift of attention the novel is unfolded in terms of a complicated series of contrasts. This story deals with two branches of one family, the O'Neills and the O'Flahertys. The former is a working class family; the latter is lower middle class. Three generations of this family appear in the work. There are contrasts in age, contrasts which have a class character and which are mirrored in different social attitudes, and, further, contrasts among the individual characters." And yet, Farrell continued, the lines from Housman that provide the first novel's epigraph and title—"I, a stranger and afraid, / In a world I never made"—indicate that "the central aim of this whole series has been that of portraying the emergence of Danny O'Neill." "An anxious little boy who has many fears," Danny "seen here first at the age of seven, is being prepared, educated in the day by day patterns of urban life." Thus, this bildungsroman begins.

In the World reprint introduction, Farrell stresses seven-year-old Danny's anxieties and alienation: "living with his grandmother, he is something of a stranger. . . . He is not in his own home." Furthermore, "it can equally be said that all of the characters here live in a world they never really made. All of them carry in their very consciousness the values of their past, of their *milieu.*" Indeed, the "feeling of homelessness" experienced by Danny O'Neill and his two families is "noticeable in our whole modern period." Here, Farrell's deep reading of Dewey, Mead, and the pragmatists comes to bear. This vexed pervasive condition provoked Farrell's consideration of "one of the problems with which I was concerned in this novel. . . . What is the precise content of life of people in environments such as the environments described in this work? What does poverty mean in the intimate daily lives of those who must live in deprivation? Needless to say," he continues, "the novel does not seek to answer such questions in any formal and sociological manner. It seeks to describe, to recreate, to present in terms of immediate characterization." Not that these questions have no ramifications off the page. In the World reprint introduction, thirty-five years and one great international depression after 1911, the year in which *A World I Never Made* has its setting, Farrell declares that the "conditions of life under which the characters of this story live" and remain "strangers and afraid," still persist. Hence, the cultural relevance of the 1947 editions of the O'Neill-O'Flaherty series: "Before a world can be changed, it is necessary to know what the *nature of experience* [italics in text] is like in that world. This novel is one of the efforts I have made to go as deeply as possible into the nature of experience during the period of my own lifetime."[52] In my view, the stunning accomplishment in the O'Neill-O'Flaherty series of Farrell's dual purposes, aesthetic and cultural, justifies the present new editions from the University of Illinois Press. We are another sixty years down the road, and the value of such books is no less urgently evident. As William Carlos Williams so memorably said:

> It is difficult
> to get the news from poems
> yet men die miserably every day
> for lack
> of what is found there.

A World I Never Made begins in August 1911 with emphasis on the central characterization of seven-year-old Danny O'Neill as defined by his anxious, conflicted interactions with the other members of the two families between which he feels himself torn. In the first fifty pages Farrell introduces the essential dramatis personae of the entire series. First come the lower-middle-class O'Flahertys. Danny's grandmother, Mary O'Flaherty, is an aging immigrant matriarch. Recently widowed, she is devoted to her grandson but combative and cantankerous toward everyone else. Danny's Aunt Margaret O'Flaherty ("Peg") is twenty-four, a cashier in a Loop hotel, attractive but unstable. Resentful of the demands of her family and unhappy as the mistress of a married businessman whose promise of marriage she distrusts, Peg is drifting toward alcoholism. Danny's Uncle Al O'Flaherty, thirty-eight, is a fairly successful traveling shoe salesman and the main family breadwinner. Poignantly earnest, he reads Emerson and Lord Chesterfield for "self-improvement," and works hard to sustain a positive outlook in the face of the increased responsibilities and expenses of "two deaths in the family this year"—his father, Old Tom O'Flaherty, of stomach cancer, and his twenty-one-year-old sister Louise, of consumption. This is a household reeling from recently inflicted, deep dynastic wounds. In it, to young Danny's great confusion (and sometimes dread), brief periods of calm, often elicited by soothing music on the gramophone, alternate with fights that can escalate into vicious verbal and even physical pummeling, as when Mrs. O'Flaherty excoriates Peg for being an adulterous "chippy," who "goes out with the Devil," and Peg responds by accusing her mother ("you Irish whoremonger!") of nagging Old Tom into his grave.

Danny's "real" family, the impoverished O'Neills, live twenty-five blocks north in a much worse neighborhood. Lizz is an O'Flaherty, the hard-luck sister of Peg and Al. Now in her mid-thirties, she has already borne eight children. Three have died at birth, and the five surviving are Bill, eleven; Danny, seven; "Little Margaret," five; Dennis, four; and Bob, eighteen months. Small wonder, given what she has already endured, that Lizz is old-country superstitious, fiercely pious, and sometimes hysterical. She is, when the novel opens, suffering the throes of yet another pregnancy approaching term. This new baby will be born healthy and named Catherine. Lizz's husband, Jim O'Neill, is forty years old. An overworked teamster, he is trapped in a physically punishing job, ashamed of how poorly he provides for his family, and apprehensive about the future with another child on the way. It especially bothers him that he has been forced to send his second son away to be raised by his wife's parents, and that the boy is happy with the O'Flahertys: Danny calls his grandmother "Mother." Prone to violence when drinking, Jim is nonetheless a decent, thoughtful man who still loves his wife and kids and hopes against hope for better days. The O'Neills also fight, mostly when Jim's practicality clashes with his wife's escapist otherworldliness. For example, when they come into some money, he urges Lizz to get her teeth fixed, rather than buying "high masses for all your dead relations."

Farrell begins *A World I Never Made* by placing Danny O'Neill in the four milieus from which his character will emerge: at home (chapter 1, in his grandmother O'Flaherty's apartment), at play (chapter 3, at a White Sox game), and at school (in chapter 4, his first day at Corpus Christi school). Chapter 2 introduces the contrasting world from which Danny has been removed, that of his parents, Jim and Lizz O'Neill. Throughout this novel, Danny's mind swings between fear (of the consequences of missing Mass on Sunday morning, of the recent deaths of his grandfather and Aunt Louise, of the violent fights among the adults in his two households, of the strange new world of school) and escape into daydreams of mastery. Constant throughout this novel and those that follow, Danny's reveries also point, however tentatively, toward an artist's vocation. At the beginning of *A World I Never Made*, he sees himself as Buffalo Bill saving his Aunt Louise from the Indians, "Danny Dreamer in the funny papers," and the White Sox catcher, Billy Sullivan, warming up for a big game. Later, he pretends to be a laundryman, a butcher, and an artist selling his drawings. At the end of the novel, the boy has two related imaginative experiences at Christmas of 1911—a daydream of art and a nightmare of death. The first occurs on his way to the Loop with his Aunt Margaret to see Santa Claus: "He saw himself as two Danny O'Neills. One of him was sitting in the elevated train that was going along, swish, zish. The other of him was outside, running, going just as fast as the train was, jumping from roof to roof." Here is the artist's dream of doubleness and control—to step outside the self and walk easily through a recognizable world. The second experience occurs on Christmas Eve, when Danny dreams of hissing snakes and "a boy as big as Mother, with a beard like a dwarf and a black suit like the Devil," come to carry him off and kill him. These two daydreams connect in the fourth volume of the series, *My Days of Anger*, when the use of art to answer the finality of death becomes an article of faith at the start of Danny's life as a writer.

For the second O'Neill-O'Flaherty novel, *No Star Is Lost*, once again Farrell takes both title and epigraph from Housman. Here the second reverses the charge of the first. The title could be mistakenly read as supporting divine intentionality—until the epigraph provides the bleak context of philosophical naturalism (any man's death does *not* diminish the universe) combined with the irremediable human stain:

> Stars, I have seen them fall,
>   But when they drop and die
> No star is lost at all
>   From all the star-sown sky,
> The toil of all that be
>   Helps not the primal fault;
> It rains into the sea
>   And still the sea is salt.

In his introduction to the World reprint edition, Farrell indicates that "the note of Christmas quiet" at the end of *A World I Never Made* "carried, also, a note of foreboding," for "nothing truly tragic had happened to any of the characters." In this new novel, "the treatment of poverty" represented by the O'Neill family "is extended, further developed. The tragic consequences of poverty on the lives of the children are shown in what happens to the child, Little Arty, at the end of this novel." Overall, *No Star Is Lost* "deals more with the life of the children than did its predecessor. This is especially the case with the treatment of the boy, Danny O'Neill. Here we see Danny living more completely in the public world of a boy as well as in the private world of the home, the family." The clash and contrast thus evidenced, "creat[es] in Danny a tension and bewilderment which, I trust, suggests what will be the character of the problems and the resolution of these problems that he will face in the future, when he is seen at an older age."[53]

No Star Is Lost is a lacerating novel to read, especially in its advancement of two of Farrell's strongest themes with harrowing verisimilitude: the rendering of alcoholism and the use of children as witnesses to disaster. In its tracing of the O'Neill family's painful and failing struggle toward a decent life, the book focuses Farrell's central theme of social injustice. In 1914 and 1915, the O'Neills are living in a small, cramped cottage at Forty-fifth and Wells, and on cold days the children "take turns sticking their feet in the oven." Jim O'Neill is working a backbreaking six-day week as a poorly paid teamster for Continental Express. Again, Danny is spared the physical discomfort because he continues to live at the O'Flahertys. And yet, he experiences humiliation on the streets and playgrounds, where kids make fun of his grandmother's clay pipe and other Irish ways and his Aunt Margaret's drinking. Because he is more and more interested in baseball, Danny, now ten, is outside a lot, but he wishes he could move to a new neighborhood to escape the embarrassment of his family's worsening reputation. Farrell establishes the child's perspective by presenting the first seventy-five pages from Danny's point of view, the longest such stretch in the series. His dreams of guilt and dominance continue. In one, black and white angels vie for the boy's soul and he hears the latter ordered to "Go back and be a guardian angel to the White Sox." In another, he is grown up, "a man so big he could almost touch the ceiling," walking fearlessly through the neighborhood, past the convent of the Little Sisters of the Good Shepherd on Prairie Avenue and the Willard Theater on Fifty-first and Calumet.

Jilted by her married lover and frightened by the erosion of her good looks, Peg O'Flaherty goes on a terrifying, extended self-destructive binge of several weeks that nearly tears her family apart. All through this period, she and her mother engage in verbal and sometimes physical battles of epic ferocity, many of them observed by Danny. Night after night, Peg reels home comatose, incontinent, and hounded with delirium tremens so horrifying that she attempts suicide by turning on the gas. Her Hieronymus Bosch hallucinations feature snakes and devils, waiters pouring gin from bottles shaped like phalluses, hideous animals, mud, slime, and excrement. These nightmare visions stand in stark contrast to Danny's recurrent creative daydreaming.

There is a third type of vision here as well. An effective technique of Farrell's for revealing his characters, so many of whom have trouble expressing their deepest affections and motives aloud, is a kind of daydream-soliloquy, the first of which appears in *No Star Is Lost* when Mary O'Flaherty goes out to Calvary Cemetery and has a fine long chat with her husband Tom, who has been dead for five years. Recalling Ireland, the Mullingar Fair where they met, their first hard years in America, and the death of their first son, Mary realizes that this grave site is "the only plot of ground that they had ever owned in America." Suddenly, Tom O'Flaherty is standing there beside her, "a small old man in a white nightgown, with a slightly drooping gray mustache." Not fazed in the least, Mary reverts to her everyday self by administering a typical scolding to poor Tom, for whom even the grave is no protection. Having been annoyed several times by Lizz O'Neill's reports that her dead father has been speaking to her, Mary tells her husband to stop visiting Lizz: "If you have messages, you give them to me. It's me that should get them, and not her. . . . I'm a hard woman when I'm crossed, Tom, a hard woman, and I'll make you toe the mark, dead or alive."

The death of the youngest O'Neill child, two-year-old Arty, of diphtheria in 1915 is the climactic event of *No Star Is Lost.* All the O'Neill children come down with the disease, and Lizz is about to deliver another child as well. With his brothers and sisters falling down around him, Arty dies unattended by either the doctor or the priest. Neither will risk contagion by entering the O'Neill cottage. As the delirious Lizz attempts to feed her own mother's milk to Arty, it is five-year-old Bob who realizes that his brother is dead. "There's only one crime in this world, Lizz," says the heartsick Jim: "to be a poor man." Returning on a streetcar from his son's burial in Calvary Cemetery, Jim sees middle-class homes and says to himself: "In these homes the kids were happy and well-fed and had the care of a doctor when they were sick. And in these homes, the kids were alive." That same day, the rest of the O'Neill children are packed off to a public hospital in the police wagon and Lizz bears a stillborn son. This is not melodrama, but one of the places in the O'Neill-O'Flaherty series where Farrell's own family life matches that of his characters most closely. His baby brother Frankie had died of diphtheria, similarly unattended, in the Farrell cottage at Forty-fifth and Wells on June 21, 1918. That same afternoon, Mary Daly Farrell was delivered of a stillborn son. She was to have in all fifteen pregnancies, including eight stillbirths. So much, in this far from uncommon situation, for the "wages of whiteness," the heavily theorized and poorly evidenced idea that great numbers of Irish ethnics opted for the benefits of an improved quality of life by "becoming white" at the expense of people of color.

No Star Is Lost ends with a detailed example of neighborhood placement that is also a reminder that Danny O'Neill has been spared all this suffering. The boy gets his wish of a fresh start as the O'Flahertys move further south to a new apartment at Fifty-seventh and Indiana. This also means that Danny will attend a new school, St. Patrick's, at Sixty-first and Michigan. On his first day in the new neighborhood, he meets two older kids—Johnny O'Brien and Studs Lonigan.

Father and Son, the third novel, has a span of six years, the longest in the series. The two families have moved again, but most characters continue in established patterns. The marriage of Jim and Lizz O'Neill bumps along with fights, reconciliations, thwarted resolutions for change, and increasing anxieties related to Jim's health. Promoted to night dispatcher at the express company, Jim is able proudly to move his family south to Fifty-eighth and Calumet in Washington Park into an apartment with "a bathroom inside, running hot and cold water, steam heat, gas and electricity." The O'Flahertys have also moved further south—to 5816–1/2 South Park Avenue overlooking the park. Their home life is still a buzzing hive of contentious personalities: Peg drinks to excess, though less often; Al becomes more frustrated with his job and his autodidactic optimism takes on a willed, cast-iron aspect; and their mother continues to stir the pot of controversy. If anything, the tensions in this family are greater now, because second son Ned O'Flaherty has moved back home from Madison after the death of his wife. A preening narcissist and sometime soap-box speaker at the Washington Park "Bug Club," Ned has embraced the cockeyed spirituality of "New Thought," whose main tenet is the "power of the wish." He's no help to anyone.

The great theme of *Father and Son* is the struggle of Jim and Danny O'Neill to understand one another in the context of Jim's downward spiral to unemployment and helplessness because of three crippling strokes and Danny's painful stumbling through high school toward emotional and intellectual maturity. Theirs is the story of George and Gerry O'Dell writ large, and few readers will not recognize and be moved by the fully elaborated drama of this largely failed attempt at communication. In the World reprint introduction, Farrell explains that "the effect of the years of separation from [Danny's] father begin to tell. The misunderstanding between the father and the callow boy deepens. In difficult moments, Jim can only become angry with his son. Danny can only feel guilty towards his father, and, at the same time, sorry for him."

There is epiphany for both father and son, but, in keeping with Farrell's realist aesthetic, it is muted, inconclusive, and far from clearly revealed to the characters themselves. Heartbreakingly, Jim O'Neill in his last illness sees himself as having failed his family. And yet, in this novel he faces progressive debilitation and boredom with courage, dignity, and deepening compassion. Sitting alone by the apartment window, Jim meditates on the mystery of having children, the unreflective profligacy of youth, the solace of Catholicism (and its limits, for he rejects the view that contraception is sinful), the lack of justice in the world. Shakespeare is Jim's companion and consolation, as he often sits up at night reading *Julius Caesar* and *Hamlet.* His insights include a doubleness that, unbeknownst to either, echoes his son's artistic perspective: "Lying alone in bed, as he began coming back to himself, lying there so much alone, he had felt half in this world and half not in it, watching it. Yes, men tried and fought and raised hell and wanted all kinds of things, and yes, yes, *vanity, all is vanity.*" In his finest hour, Jim hears that the doctor who refused to attend his dying child Arty has himself died suddenly, and Jim forgives him his trespass. Farrell's depiction of Jim O'Neill's lonely struggle to understand his life and approaching death is one of the great achievements of modern fiction.

Jim's final weeks are filled with petty indignities. Another of his children is farmed out to the O'Flahertys, and Lizz suggests that he check into a public hospital. He is shamed by having to accept a Christmas basket from a Protestant charity. He has to make an X to get money at the bank, and he loses a five-dollar bill in the street. People on the El think he's drunk, kids mock and mimic his limp, and an apartment-house janitor accuses him of loitering. On Jim's last day, it is once again the children who register the tragic. Twelve-year-old Catherine sees that her father has wet his pants, and it is Bob, a year older, who discovers that his father has died. The social and economic dimension of this novel published in 1940 is also clear. Farrell declares in the World introduction that "the tragedy of the worker is the central social tragedy of our times. Jim's life is but one illustration of this tragedy." Furthermore, "it could well pose for the reader the question—is this a fair and open fight?"

As for Danny, "Now, on the threshold of manhood, he must find a place and a career in that world. He is still afraid, and he remains something of a stranger. But he has, among the other lessons he has learned, the example of his father's life. He gains the conviction that his father never had a chance. His father's death meant something, but he doesn't know exactly what."[54] Farrell describes Danny's abortive diary keeping and other failed writing projects, his clumsy attempts at male and female friendships, the superficial compensation of success in high school athletics, the persistent angst of his situation vis-à-vis his two families. And yet, despite the blunders and embarrassments of what Yeats called "the ignominy of boyhood; the distress / Of boyhood changing into man," *Father and Son* also contains an artistic breakthrough for Danny O'Neill. With a family fight raging around him, he is able to finish a story that he knows is good enough for the St. Stanislaus literary magazine. Here, life and art intersect again, because this turns out to be the same story, a romantic tale of a priest's martyrdom in Elizabethan Ireland, that Farrell wrote in 1922 for his high school magazine, the St. Cyril *Oriflamme*. In one sense, appropriating here his own adolescent version of sentimental Catholic fiction is Farrell's way of saying that, as a mature writer, he will not contribute to this genre of literature as propaganda. But in another sense, the story documents the milieu of the Catholic high school in the 1920s as an environment somewhat encouraging to the imagination.

Here again, Farrell's epigraphs speak volumes. For Jim O'Neill, he quotes Tolstoy: "Ivan Ilych's life had been most simple and most ordinary and therefore most terrible." For Danny, there is the Baudelaire of *Les Fleurs du Mal:* "—Ah! Seigneur! Donnez moi la force et le courage / De contempler mon coeur et mon corps sans dégoût!" And for himself, Farrell provides a credo of Bertrand Russell, who counters man's brief, powerless, suffering condition with an admonition "to cherish, ere yet the blow falls, the lofty thoughts that ennoble his little day; disdaining the coward terrors of the slave of Fate, to worship at the shrine that his own hands have built; undismayed by the empire of chance, to preserve a mind free from the wanton tyranny that rules his outward life."

As Farrell points out in his World introduction, *My Days of Anger* "differs in method of presentation from its three predecessors. . . . Here, the story is told with auctorial concentration on one central character, Danny O'Neill." Farrell will do this by limiting twenty-eight of the twenty-nine arabic-numbered chapters of the book to the consciousness of this protagonist. The thoughts of everyone else are relegated to brief, italicized interchapters. His aim is "to present the way in which the disposition of an American artist is forged." This word naturally echoes Joyce's *Portrait of the Artist*, where Stephen Dedalus sets out for Paris "to forge the uncreated conscience of my race." Because of the challenges of his background and upbringing, Farrell explains, Danny's "disposition as an artist is forged in bewilderment and anxiety, in confusion and insecurity." However, along his difficult way, he makes "small decisions and resolutions [that] suggest a tension within him, a tension which is symptomatic of his need for change, for escape from the circumstances of his life." And when he prepares to leave for New York at the novel's end, "his mood is one of determination. He asks no quarter. He looks forward to struggle. In this sense, *My Days of Anger* is an optimistic book." Further, Danny "rejects the values of his past, but he does not completely destroy his sense of identification with his own people. He feels that he is going forth to fight not only war but their war. His conception of art, of writing, is a militant one." Again, as a realist, Farrell knows that anger is a limited and, ultimately, a distorting tool for the artist, and so this novel will end with Danny not quite launched into the concerted action of a life committed to writing. The novel's first epigraph, from Baudelaire's *Intimate Journals*, makes this proviso clear: "Nevertheless, I will let these pages stand—since I wish to record my days of anger."

In the World introduction, Farrell refutes the idea that his book is in any way a pastiche of Joyce by pointing out that his aspiring artist/protagonist "emerges from a background which is common rather than special; it is the background known to millions of Americans. Here, in short, I feel, is a detailed story of the American Way of Life."[55] At the same time, that *My Days of Anger* is Farrell's "common," "American" *Portrait* is clear from its second epigraph, an homage that takes the form of a poetic fragment by Joyce:

> Ah star of evil! star of pain!
> Highhearted youth comes not again
>
> Nor old heart's wisdom yet to know
> The signs that mock me as I go.

The poem is dated "*Bahnhofstrasse*, Zurich, 1918," when Joyce was thirty-six. Farrell had turned thirty-nine in February 1943, the year he completed and published *My Days of Anger*.

This novel's great emphasis on Danny is the capstone of Farrell's pioneering presentation of the growth of an American artist from working-class, urban, ethnic, and Catholic backgrounds. Again, scrupulous detail is all. In the outside world, Farrell continues to describe Danny's home life among the O'Flahertys and O'Neills, who appear in the counterpointing interchapters as stuck in familiar troubles. Peg steals at work, is fired, and gets drunk for a week. Al's shoe company fails and he has to go back out on the road in a lesser position. The aging Mary O'Flaherty becomes ill. Danny's brothers and sisters are growing up aware of their social and economic limits and restless for change. When *My Days of Anger* opens, Danny is a year out of high school and still working at the Continental Express Company. He goes on to a South Side gas station, where he has more time to read and also learns about American capitalism firsthand. Farrell also breaks new ground for American fictional milieus by detailing Danny's "pre-legal" night-school classes at "St. Vincent's" in the Loop, and then taking us into his economics, history, and writing classes at the University of Chicago and the lunchroom dialectic among his fellow students. Emotionally, although he is now out of high school, Danny still suffers the tortures of the damned in his relationships with the opposite sex. He cannot find a steady girlfriend, he loses his virginity in a casual encounter on his twenty-first birthday in February 1925, and he picks up the habit of going to whorehouses with friends from the neighborhood. Intellectually, Danny's continuing fascination with words evolves at last into his first honest "Thought Diary" entries, and then into a torrent of fiction produced for his creative-writing teacher at the university, Professor Saxon. He loses his faith, at first in a dream, and wakes up a nonbeliever, "free of lies." (Studs Lonigan brings the news of Danny's atheism to the pool hall, diagnosing the cause as "too many books.") Other liberating rejections follow: of his pseudo-Nietzschean friend Ed Lanson, of the University of Chicago, and of Chicago as a place to live. At the same time, Danny's days of anger and confusion slowly give way to understanding of and sympathy for his family, friends, and other exploited Chicagoans, especially African Americans. In this process, the crucial experience is his grandmother's death in the spring of 1927.

A classic immigrant matriarch who has held her family together by sheer force of often vituperative will, Mary O'Flaherty, a self-described "hard woman from a hard country," has never been able to express love or compassion for her family—with the single exception of her grandson. As she nears death at eighty-six, a last extended daydream-soliloquy—the only full chapter in this novel from inside a mind other than Danny O'Neill's—provides a summary of her character and concerns. Farrell had been planning Mrs. O'Flaherty's reverie at least since 1938, when he traveled to Ireland for the first time to verify the immigrants' background. Upon completing *My Days of Anger* in 1943, he wrote a friend announcing the conclusion of this phase of his writing life, the "years of driving work, years of eight to fourteen hour days concentrating on these connected books." He was especially proud of the "long chapter, in Anglo-Irish, when Grandmother O'Flaherty sits by the window in a wheel chair, hip broken, slowly fading out of this life; it is a long reverie, more or less Joycean, in which past and present jumble, time loses significance, she dreams and she awakes." The writing here "is something fresh—the fading consciousness of an old woman, further, an old Irish immigrant woman, illiterate, who came out to America, raised her family here, [has] seen them grow up, and sits doing this while her grandson sits preparing to write, even about her own life."[56] As with Jim O'Neill's lonely meditations, Farrell here solves the problem of speaking for those for whom self-expression comes hard with a restrained eloquence that is a hallmark of his achievement as a novelist.

When his grandmother dies, Danny finds his rejection of Catholicism tempered by understanding that "the sorrows of death remained, remained in the hearts of the living. . . . He understood now why people did what he could not do, what he could never do—pray." In an earlier conversation with friends at the university, Danny had agreed with Stephen Dedalus's refusing to pray at his dying mother's bedside in *Ulysses:* "What has kindness got to do with conviction? I won't bend my knees." And yet, on the morning of his grandmother's death, Danny kneels down, blesses himself, and pretends to pray with his family. A month later, as he prepares to leave Chicago for New York and a new life as a writer, Danny walks home down Fifty-eighth Street from the El, and feels the weight of the Washington Park neighborhood as "a world in itself . . . a world in which another Danny O'Neill had lived." Realizing that he has "finally taken off a way of life . . . as if it were a worn-out suit of clothes," he now has confidence in the "weapons" of his writer's trade: "now he was leaving and he was fully armed." In this, he echoes Stephen Dedalus leaving Dublin for Paris in 1902 with his own weapons of "silence, exile, and cunning." Danny also has a mature understanding of his position as an artist in relation to his family: "His people had not been fulfilled. He had not understood them all these years. He would do no penance now for these; he would do something surpassing penance. There was a loyalty to the dead, a loyalty beyond penance and regret. He would do battle so that others did not remain unfulfilled as he and his family had been." Rather than ending the novel here, Farrell goes on to create one final contrast between honest and false consciousness in the form of an overheard conversation back at the Continental Express Company, where the bosses who used to ridicule Danny look back with distorting nostalgia at his time with them, declaring that he was "a crackerjack clerk" and "one of the best kids I ever had."

Ten years after finishing *My Days of Anger*, Farrell published the fifth and final O'Neill-O'Flaherty novel. Although not part of his original plan, *The Face of Time* is an appropriate coda for the series. Opening in the summer of 1909, this book brings the design full circle to the final illnesses of Old Tom O'Flaherty and his youngest daughter Louise, the memory of which hangs over the first volume, *A World I Never Made.* Farrell also renders the elder O'Flahertys' memories of Ireland, the journey to America, and their early years in Brooklyn, Green Bay, and Chicago, thus returning his narrative to the beginning of this family's story. The result is one of the finest American fictional treatments of the felt experience of immigration.

For most of this novel, the focus alternates between the minds of the aging

Irish immigrant, Old Tom O'Flaherty, and his five-year-old American grandson, Danny O'Neill. Again, the child is witness to pain and conflict. The family fights among Mary O'Flaherty and her children are well under way, and Danny is also precociously aware that living with his grandparents has wounded his parents, especially his father. In addition, he is the terrified observer of his favorite aunt's worsening health and his beloved grandfather's decline and death. Old Tom lives out a restless retirement, bored or harassed within the family, and dies of a painful stomach cancer. In his characterization, Farrell's theme of thwarted communication of the heart's urgent concerns has a last statement here as well. Only in the unshared daydream-soliloquies of his final illness does Tom reveal his sad secrets: the "greenhorn" humiliations of his first displacements in the New World still disturb the old man; he has never felt at home in America; he is puzzled and embittered by having worked so hard and ended up with so little; and he wishes he could go back to die in Ireland. Tom's closest bond is not with his wife Mary, who tends to ignore him, but with his son-in-law, Jim O'Neill, representative of a new generation of hardworking, ill-rewarded laborers, people for whom the American dream remains unfulfilled. In turning over the insults and injustices to which the working man is prone and the compensating mysteries of marriage and children, these two share the closest moments in this novel.

The Face of Time is most moving in the variations—sometimes harsh, sometimes lyrical—that Farrell plays on the theme of elemental loneliness. In his fiction, immigration is but the prototype and metaphor for what he sees as an inevitable condition of humanity. The other most important voice here is the consciousness of Louise O'Flaherty, dying of consumption at twenty-one and holding terror at bay with dreams of the arrival of "Prince Charming," marriage, and children of her own. It is she who asks the big question, though only to herself: "And was this the end of love, one going, dying, the way her father was dying? Must you, in the end, always be alone?" Farrell's answer pervades this novel's conclusion. On his way to the hospital, Old Tom's voice breaks and he is unable to say good-bye to Danny. During the family's last visit to his bedside, Tom can hear his wife and daughter discussing his imminent death, but he cannot speak to them. When the hospital calls with the news of Tom's passing, Mary O'Flaherty shuts the bedroom door to grieve alone. Standing in front of his grandfather's casket, six-year-old Danny thinks, "There was Father. He couldn't talk. He was Father all right, and he wasn't Father." Underscored by the deaths of Old Tom and Louise, the inability of the O'Neill and O'Flaherty families to articulate the heart's speech of love and compassion brings *The Face of Time* around again to the initial provocations for Danny O'Neill's hard journey through the course of the other four novels of the series out of this stalemate and toward the solution of art.

In Farrell's materialist/pragmatist universe, time is the archenemy of all such solutions, a point underscored by this novel's title and epigraph from Yeats's "Lamentation of the Old Pensioner." Relegated to "shelter from the rain / Under a broken tree," the speaker in the poem recalls his youthful participation in talk of love, politics, and revolution. Now, "My contemplations are of Time / That has transfigured me." And yet, he continues to affirm the storyteller's power of memory and to defy the changes rung by Time:

There's not a woman turns her face
Upon a broken tree,
And yet the beauties that I loved
Are in my memory;
I spit into the face of Time
That has transfigured me.

This is also the novel in which Farrell provides his most positive rendering of place. Grandfather and grandson walk abroad in their neighborhood world thoroughly at ease. Because they are absolved by age and youth from the crises and challenges faced by the other family members who are in the responsible middle way of their lives, Old Tom and Danny encounter fewer obstacles. Through them, Farrell presents Washington Park as home on a human scale. The two companions take great pleasure in the daily round: feeding the ducks on the pond in Washington Park, talking to the cop on the beat and the clerk at the corner grocery, checking in with a sympathetic priest who knows their story, watching Ty Cobb in town against the White Sox at Comiskey, and "rushing the can" for beer at the saloon. Given the fullness and fairness of his presentation throughout the series, Farrell is entitled to the lyrical backward glance at his native city in *The Face of Time*. In fact, it's part of the novel's overall elegiac tone. But he nonetheless avoids distorting nostalgia by keeping illness and isolation as the grounding bass notes.

Shortly after publishing the last O'Neill-O'Flaherty novel, Farrell wrote an essay, "How *The Face of Time* Was Written," that speaks tellingly of his method, themes, aims, and a crucial influence. He recalls the origin of this unplanned fifth volume on "a raw and sunless September afternoon in 1951" in the Chelsea Hotel in New York, just eight days after he had completed *Yet Other Waters*, the final volume of his Bernard Carr trilogy of novels: "Then suddenly . . . I had an impulse to write a short story which would tell of the death of Old Tom. I sat down and began it in longhand. Immediately, I thought of the old man and his grandson Danny. I began by putting them together on Forty-ninth Street in Chicago." Again, the imagination's catalyst is place. As he worked on, day by day, the conception blossomed into "a long story or novelette," and then into a novel. "When a story or book evolves in this manner," Farrell continues, "I know that I have a clear path from my unconscious. I have always believed that one must trust the unconscious and write out of it."

While completing the first draft in Paris in August 1952, "I thought of Proust, to me the greatest writer of the twentieth century. *Remembrance of Things Past* ended in that deeply tragic death mask scene and in Proust's mystical sense of time and existence in two times at once. I was living in two times at once. I had no mystical sense of time, but I felt, too, the dual sense of time." His working title, "to me very exact," was *A Legacy of Fear*, but to avoid mislabeling ("It could seem like a detective story"), he searched for another and found it in Yeats's poem. Farrell concludes this essay by generalizing from the completion of *The Face of Time* to the central goal that drove his working life: "In that novel I tried to achieve what is my constant and major aim as a writer—to write so that life may speak for itself. And life, speaking for itself, tells us again and again of the transfiguration of time. Joy and sadness, growth and decay, life and death are all part of the transfiguration of time. To look into the Face of Time, and to master its threat to us—this is one of the basic themes and purposes of art and literature."[57]

An appropriate gloss for James T. Farrell's commitment and career is the last poem, "Epilogue," in Robert Lowell's last book, *Day by Day*. What Lowell comes around to after his circus animals have deserted is what Farrell's life of unremitting literary labor represents and accomplishes:

> Yet why not say what happened?
> Pray for the grace of accuracy
> Vermeer gave to the sun's illumination
> stealing like the tide across a map
> to his girl solid with yearning.
> We are poor passing facts,
> warned by that to give
> each figure in the photograph
> his living name.

Notes

1. James T. Farrell, *Chicago Stories*, ed. Charles Fanning (Urbana and Chicago: University of Illinois Press, 1998), 106–15.

2. Letters to Clifton Fadiman, 24 June 1929; Ezra Pound, 14 February 1934; Ernest W. Burgess, 9 January 1937; James Henle, 12 February 1943; James T. Farrell Archives, University of Pennsylvania (hereafter, Farrell Archives).

3. Letter to Jack Kunitz, 7 August 1934, Farrell Archives.

4. "My Beginnings as a Writer," in *Reflections at Fifty and Other Essays* (New York: Vanguard Press, 1954), 157–63.

5. Farrell recalled that he made "the decision to write" on "a March morning in 1927." It was spring, and he was looking for a metaphor "to make new the miraculous unity of life. . . . I know that my sentimentalities were just that, and no more." Unpublished manuscript, Box 495, Farrell Archives. See also "Beginnings," unpublished manuscript, 1961, Box 494, Farrell Archives.

6. "Beginnings," Box 494, Farrell Archives; "The World Is Today," *Park East* (New York), 8 May 1975.

7. Edgar M. Branch, *James T. Farrell* (New York: Twayne Publishers, 1971), 23. See also Branch's elegant short book, *A Paris Year, Dorothy and James T. Farrell, 1931–1932* (Athens: Ohio University Press, 1998), and Robert K. Landers, *An Honest Writer, the Life and Times of James T. Farrell* (San Francisco: Encounter Books, 2004). Wholly inadequate as criticism, Landers's biography is useful for details of Farrell's life.

8. Murray Kempton, *Part of Our Time: Some Ruins and Monuments of the Thirties* (New York: Simon and Schuster, 1955), 128–29.

9. Letter to James J. Geller, 16 February 1943, Farrell Archives.

10. Michael Denning, *The Cultural Front: The Laboring of American Culture in the Twentieth Century* (New York: Verso, 1997), xvii, xx.

11. Farrell preferred the term "bottom-dog literature," which he borrowed from the title of Edward Dahlberg's novel: "If we use 'proletarian' in the strictly Marxist sense, many of these works cannot be said to deal with the proletariat but rather with the lower middle class, the urban lumpen proletariat, the poor farmer." "Social Themes in American Realism," in *Literature and Morality* (New York: Vanguard Press, 1947), 21. See also Douglas Wixson, *Worker-Writer in America* (Urbana: University of Illinois Press, 1999), passim.

12. "The Short Story" [Speech before the First American Writers' Congress], in *The League of Frightened Philistines and Other Papers* (New York: Vanguard Press, 1945), 136–48.

13. Dempsey J. Travis, *An Autobiography of Black Jazz* (Chicago: Urban Research Institute, 1983), passim.

14. Michel Fabre, *The Unfinished Quest of Richard Wright*, 2nd ed. (Urbana: University of Illinois Press, 1993), 118–19.

15. *A Note on Literary Criticism* (1936; repr., New York: Columbia University Press, 1992).

16. Preface to *The Short Stories of James T. Farrell* (New York: Vanguard Press, 1937), l–li.

17. "James Farrell on James Farrell," *The New Republic*, 28 October 1940, 595–96. Murray Kempton recognized the class divide between Farrell and some, like Wilson, who opposed him: "Farrell once said that a writer's style is his childhood; in middle age, he chose to put on the title page of his *Bernard Carr* a terrible reflection of Anton Chekhov's: 'What writers belonging to the upper class have received from nature for nothing, plebeians acquire at the cost of their youth.' . . . Farrell's world, like Dreiser's, was one whose inhabitants understood the price the artist pays. They looked at the New York literary world and thought it commercial, supercilious, log-rolling, and absolutely alien." *Part of Our Time*, 128–29.

18. Carl Van Doren, "The City Culture," *Nation* 143 (24 October 1936): 483.

19. Carlos Baker, "Another Milestone in the Long Saga of Danny O'Neill," *New York Times Book Review*, 24 October 1943, BR 3; *New York Times*, 4 February 1937, 19; 12 February 1937, 21.

20. Peter Brooks, *Realist Vision* (New Haven and London: Yale University Press, 2005), 71–75.

21. Letters, Ezra Pound to James T. Farrell, 3 February 1932; James T. Farrell to Ezra Pound, 17 February 1932; Farrell Archives.

22. "Joyce's *A Portrait of the Artist as a Young Man*," in *League of Frightened Philistines*, 45–59.

23. "A Note on Ulysses" (1934); letter to Meyer Schapiro, 6 August 1938, both quoted in Dennis Flynn, ed., James T. Farrell, *On Irish Themes* (Philadelphia: University of Pennsylvania Press, 1982), 86, 169. Flynn's book is the invaluable guide to Farrell's engagement with all things Irish.

24. Flynn, introduction to Farrell, *On Irish Themes*, 4.

25. *Note on Literary Criticism*, 78, 83, 88.

26. *Note on Literary Criticism*, 118–23. Another writer who grasped fully and early on the importance of this concept in Proust was Samuel Beckett, whose brilliant little book, *Proust* (New York: New Directions), appeared in 1931. Here is Beckett:

> Memory and Habit are attributes of the Time cancer. They control the most simple Proustian episode, and an understanding of their mechanism must precede any particular analysis of their application. . . .
>
> The laws of memory are subject to the more general laws of habit. Habit is a compromise effected between the individual and his environment, or between the individual and his own organic eccentricities, the guarantee of a dull inviolability, the lightning-conductor of his existence. Habit is the ballast that chains the dog to his vomit. (7–8)

27. "The Writer and His Audience," Indiana, Pennsylvania, 12 June 1958, in Donald Phelps, ed., *Hearing Out James T. Farrell, Selected Lectures* (New York: The Smith, 1985), 108–10.

28. Here again, Beckett understood this fully in 1931: "Involuntary memory is explosive, 'an immediate, total and delicious deflagration.' It restores . . . the past object. . . . Because in its flame it has consumed Habit and all its works, and in its brightness revealed what the mock reality of experience never can and never will reveal—the real. But involuntary memory is an unruly magician and will not be importuned. It chooses its own time and place for the performance of its miracle." In all of Proust, Beckett counts "twelve or thirteen" of these miracle moments, "but the first—the famous episode of the madeleine steeped in tea—would justify the assertion that his entire book is a monument to involuntary memory and the epic of its action. The whole of Proust's world comes out of a teacup, and not merely Combray and his childhood. For Combray brings us to the two 'ways' and to Swann, and to Swann may be related every element of the Proustian experience and consequently its climax in revelation" (19–23).

29. Marcel Proust, *Swann's Way*, trans. and ed. Lydia Davis (New York: Viking Press, 2003), 53, 68, 182, 184–85.

30. "Beginnings," unpublished manuscript, Box 494, Farrell Archives.

31. Walter Benjamin, *Illuminations* (New York: Knopf, 1969): 203–13.

32. "On the Letters of Anton Chekhov," in *League of Frightened Philistines*, 60–71. Farrell returned to this idea in judging John O'Hara to be a gifted short-story writer but a failure as a novelist, except for *Appointment in Samarra:* "In this novel, O'Hara attained what Henry James called 'saturation.' I interpret this word to mean that the characters and their environment, including their cultural, social, and moral background, became a world, or a segment of a world, with a past and a present, and an assumable future, and with a play of meanings." "The Eternal Question of John O'Hara," in Jack Alan Robbins, ed., *Literary Essays 1954–1974* (Port Washington, N.Y.: Kennikat Press, 1976), 90–92.

33. "Nonsense and the Short Story," in *League of Frightened Philistines*, 81.

34. Unpublished manuscript, Box 495, Farrell Archives.

35. "How *Studs Lonigan* Was Written," in *League of Frightened Philistines*, 86.

36. Farrell, quoted in the introduction to Ralph F. Bogardus and Fred Hobson, eds., *Literature at the Barricades: The American Writer in the 1930s* (Tuscaloosa: University of Alabama Press, 1982), 3–4; Donald Pizer, "James T. Farrell and the 1930s," in *Literature at the Barricades*, 75, 81.

37. Unpublished manuscript, "Memories of John Dewey by James T. Farrell," 5 November 1965, Newberry Library, Gift of Cleo Paturis. Farrell registered the excitement of first absorbing the pragmatists in a June 1930 essay published in *Earth*, a little magazine out of Wheaton, Illinois. The piece, "Half Way from the Cradle," is a concise anatomy of the serial engagement with and rejection of belief systems among adolescents and young adults in Jazz Age America: from athletics, sex, and rote education to the ideals of success, family life, and organized religion (for the less adventurous), and to Bohemianism, "art for art's sake," and engagement with "the twin [philosophical] problems of duality and certainty" (for the more thoughtful). His own resolution, a young man's bold declaration, is straight out of William James, Mead, and Dewey: "Only by eliminating certainties that are not referable to human experience can we be men—human beings—rather than parasites on an extra-experiential source of immutable Being." *Earth* (Wheaton, Illinois) 1, no. 3 (June 1930): 1–3, 14.

38. Harry Smith, "Defictionalizing Farrell," *The Smith* 22: 8.

39. "Topics: The Democratic Faith of John Dewey," *New York Times*, 22 October 1966, 25. See also James T. Farrell, "Reflections on John Dewey," *Thought* (New Delhi, India) 19 (27 May 1967): 14–16.

40. Robert James Butler, "Parks, Parties, and Pragmatism: Time and Setting in James T. Farrell's Major Novels," *Essays in Literature* 10, no. 2 (Fall 1983): 242.

41. Robert James Butler, "Christian and Pragmatic Visions of Time in the Lonigan Trilogy," *Thought* 55, no. 219 (December 1980): 465, 475. Butler points out that Farrell cogently reviewed G. H. Mead's *The Philosophy of the Present* in 1930 while he was working on the Lonigan material. The review demonstrates the importance for the beginning novelist's plan for fiction of the pragmatists' ideas on the consciousness of time as a three-part exercise in integration. Farrell explains that in Mead's thought, "the locus of both consciousness and value is the present, and it is in terms of this present that the past and the future are organized"; "Christian and Pragmatic Visions," 464.

42. "Continuity and Change" (2 July 1965, Austin, Tex.), in Phelps, *Hearing Out James T. Farrell*, 136–37.

43. Dennis Flynn, "James T. Farrell and His Catholics," *America*, 15 September 1975, 111–13.

44. Thomas F. Curley, "Catholic Novels and American Culture," *Commentary* 36 (July 1963): 34–42. Curley's essay remains one of the most insightful analyses of Catholic literary culture in the middle of the twentieth century.

45. "A Note on Sherwood Anderson," in *Reflections at Fifty*, 164–68.

46. Eudora Welty, "Place in Fiction," *South Atlantic Quarterly* 55 (January 1956): 57–72.

47. See also Charles Fanning and Ellen Skerrett, "James T. Farrell and Washington Park: The Novel as Social History," *Chicago History* 8, no. 2 (Summer 1979): 80–91.

48. Letters to Mary Farrell, 2 February 1934; 6 March 1934; 21 March 1935; 12 April 1935; 26 August 1935; 12 July 1937; Farrell Archives.

49. Farrell's example was followed by many Irish American writers of the 1940s, among them Thomas Sugrue, Leo R. Ward, Jack Dunphy, Harry Sylvester, Mary Deasy, Mary Doyle Curran, Betty Smith, Edward McSorley, and J. F. Powers. See Charles Fanning, *The Irish Voice in America, 250 Years of Irish-American Fiction*, 2nd ed. (Lexington: University Press of Kentucky, 2000), 292–312.

In an unpublished manuscript, "The Church in My Fiction," Farrell rejected the term "Catholic novelist" as inappropriate (given his unbelief) and limiting (given his wider aims). He continues: "However, my fiction is saturated with Catholicism. Many of my characters are Catholics. They are from cradle to the grave Catholics, and I bury a number of them in Calvary Cemetery, in Evanston, Illinois. The fundamental point to be made concerning my fiction is that being a Catholic in the world of my expressed imagination is a normal experience that need not be explained and defended. The Church is in their lives. It is part of their lives. Their reactions are those of persons who have lived in relationship with and to the Church. Their thoughts, emotions, actions are wound through the body of belief, ritual and practice of the Catholic Church"; Box 640, Farrell Archives.

50. "The Short Story," in *League of Frightened Philistines*, 137–38; "How *Studs Lonigan* Was Written," in *League of Frightened Philistines*, 87–88.

51. Lydia Davis, introduction to *Swann's Way* by Marcel Proust (New York: Viking Press, 2003), ix. Davis goes on to assert Proust's great theme—"how time will be transcended through art"—in terms that also describe Farrell's artistic faith: "For only in recollection does an experience become fully significant, as we arrange it in a meaningful pattern, and thus the crucial role of our intellect, our imagination, in our perception of the world and our re-creation of it to suit our desires; thus the importance of the role of the artist in transforming reality according to a particular inner vision: the artist escapes the tyranny of time through art"; *Swann's Way*, xi.

Interestingly, the French publisher of *Young Lonigan*, Nouvelle Revue Française, was the second of three houses to reject *Swann's Way*. André Gide was in charge at the time, and he later said this decision was one of the greatest mistakes of his life. With its name changed to Gallimard, the house did publish later editions of Proust. Gallimard has continued to publish Farrell as well.

52. Introduction to *A World I Never Made* (Cleveland and New York: World Publishing, 1947), ix–xii.

53. Introduction to *No Star Is Lost* (Cleveland and New York: World Publishing, 1947), ix–x.

54. Introduction to *Father and Son* (Cleveland and New York: World Publishing, 1947), xi–xii.

55. Introduction to *My Days of Anger* (Cleveland and New York: World Publishing, 1947), xi–xii.

56. Letter to Jim Putnam, 18 February 1943, Farrell Archives.

57. "How *The Face of Time* Was Written," in *Reflections at Fifty*, 35–41.

Selected Bibliography

Works by James T. Farrell

Novels and Novellas

Studs Lonigan: A Trilogy. New York: Vanguard Press, 1935. Comprised of *Young Lonigan: A Boyhood in Chicago Streets* (New York: Vanguard Press, 1932); *The Young Manhood of Studs Lonigan* (New York: Vanguard Press, 1934); and *Judgment Day* (New York: Vanguard Press, 1935). There have been many reprints since, including in the Library of America in 2004.

Gas-House McGinty. New York: Vanguard Press, 1933; London: United Anglo-American Book Company, 1948; revised edition, New York: Avon, 1950.

Tommy Gallagher's Crusade. New York: Vanguard Press, 1939.

Ellen Rogers. New York: Vanguard Press, 1941; London: Routledge, 1942.

O'NEILL-O'FLAHERTY PENTALOGY:

A World I Never Made. New York: Vanguard Press, 1936; London: Constable, 1938.

No Star Is Lost. New York: Vanguard Press, 1938; London: Constable, 1939.

Father and Son. New York: Vanguard Press, 1940; [as *A Father and His Son* (London: Routledge, 1943)].

My Days of Anger. New York: Vanguard Press, 1943; London: Routledge, 1945.

The Face of Time. New York: Vanguard Press, 1953; London: Spearman and Calder, 1954.

BERNARD CARR TRILOGY:

Bernard Clare. New York: Vanguard Press, 1946 [as *Bernard Clayre* (London: Routledge, 1948); as *Bernard Carr* (New York: New American Library, 1952)].

The Road Between. New York: Vanguard Press, and London: Routledge, 1949.

Yet Other Waters. New York: Vanguard Press, 1952; London: Panther, 1960.

This Man and This Woman. New York: Vanguard Press, 1951.
Boarding House Blues. New York: Paperback Library, 1961; London: Panther, 1962.

UNIVERSE OF TIME SEQUENCE:

The Silence of History. New York: Doubleday, 1963; London: W. H. Allen, 1964.
What Time Collects. New York: Doubleday, 1964; London: W. H. Allen, 1965.
When Time Was Born. New York: The Smith-Horizon Press, 1966.
Lonely for the Future. New York: Doubleday, 1966; London: W. H. Allen, 1966.
New Year's Eve/1929. New York: Smith-Horizon Press, 1967.
A Brand New Life. New York: Doubleday, 1968.
Judith. Athens, Ohio: Duane Schneider Press, 1969.
Invisible Swords. New York: Doubleday, 1971.
The Dunne Family. New York: Doubleday, 1976.
The Death of Nora Ryan. New York: Doubleday, 1978.
Sam Holman. Buffalo, N.Y.: Prometheus Books, 1983.

Short Fiction Collections

Calico Shoes and Other Stories. New York: Vanguard Press, 1934 [as *Seventeen and Other Stories* (London: Panther, 1959)].
Guillotine Party and Other Stories. New York: Vanguard Press, 1935.
Can All This Grandeur Perish? and Other Stories. New York: Vanguard Press, 1937.
The Short Stories of James T. Farrell. New York: Vanguard Press, 1937 [as *Fellow Countrymen: Collected Stories* (London: Constable, 1937)]. Reprints the preceding three volumes.
$1,000 a Week and Other Stories. New York: Vanguard Press, 1942.
Fifteen Selected Stories. Avon Modern Short Story Monthly, No. 10. New York: Avon Book, 1943. Reprints stories from several volumes.
To Whom It May Concern and Other Stories. New York: Vanguard Press, 1944.
Twelve Great Stories. Avon Modern Short Story Monthly, No. 21. New York: Avon Book, 1945. Reprints stories from several volumes.
When Boyhood Dreams Come True. New York: Vanguard Press, 1946.
More Fellow Countrymen. London: Routledge, 1946. Reprints stories from several volumes.
The Life Adventurous and Other Stories. New York: Vanguard Press, 1947.
Yesterday's Love and Eleven Other Stories. New York: Avon Book, 1948. Reprints stories from several volumes.
A Misunderstanding. New York: House of Books, 1949. Small-press printing of a single story.
An American Dream Girl. New York: Vanguard Press, 1950.
French Girls Are Vicious and Other Stories. New York: Vanguard Press, 1955; London: Panther, 1958.
An Omnibus of Short Stories. New York: Vanguard Press, 1957. Reprints *$1,000 a Week and Other Stories*, *To Whom It May Concern and Other Stories*, and *The Life Adventurous and Other Stories*.

A Dangerous Woman and Other Stories. New York: New American Library, 1957; London: Panther, 1959.

Saturday Night and Other Stories. London: Panther, 1958. Reprints stories from several volumes.

The Girls at the Sphinx. London: Panther, 1959. Reprints stories from several volumes.

Looking 'Em Over. London: Panther, 1960. Reprints stories from several volumes.

Side Street and Other Stories. New York: Paperback Library, 1961.

Sound of a City. New York: Paperback Library, 1962.

Childhood Is Not Forever and Other Stories. New York: Doubleday, 1969.

Judith and Other Stories. New York: Doubleday, 1973.

Olive and Mary Anne. New York: Stonehill, 1977.

Eight Short Short Stories and Sketches. Ed. Marshall Brooks. Newton, Mass.: Arts End Books, 1981.

Chicago Stories of James T. Farrell. Ed. Charles Fanning. Urbana: University of Illinois Press, 1998.

Literary Criticism and Other Publications

A Note on Literary Criticism. New York: Vanguard Press, 1936; London: Constable, 1937.

The League of Frightened Philistines and Other Papers. New York: Vanguard Press, 1945; London: Routledge, 1947.

The Fate of Writing in America. New York: New Directions, 1946; London: Grey Walls Press, 1947.

Literature and Morality. New York: Vanguard Press, 1947.

[Jonathan Titulescu Fogarty, Esq., pseud.] *The Name Is Fogarty: Private Papers on Public Matters*. New York: Vanguard Press, 1950.

[with Jeannette Covert Nolan and Horace Gregory] *Poet of the People: An Evaluation of James Whitcomb Riley*. Bloomington: Indiana University Press, 1951.

Reflections at Fifty and Other Essays. New York: Vanguard Press, 1954; London: Spearman, 1956.

My Baseball Diary: A Famed Author Recalls the Wonderful World of Baseball, Yesterday and Today. New York: A. S. Barnes, 1957.

It Has Come to Pass. New York: Herzl Press, 1958.

[edited] *Prejudices*, by H. L. Mencken. New York: Knopf, 1958.

[edited] *A Dreiser Reader*. New York: Dell, 1962.

Selected Essays. New York: McGraw-Hill, 1964.

The Collected Poems of James T. Farrell. New York: Fleet, 1965.

Literary Essays 1954–74. Port Washington, N.Y.: Kennikat Press, 1976.

On Irish Themes. Ed. Dennis Flynn. Philadelphia: University of Pennsylvania Press, 1982.

Hearing Out James T. Farrell: Selected Lectures. New York: The Smith, 1985.

Secondary Sources

Our understanding of the writings of James T. Farrell springs from the work of Edgar M. Branch, whose essays, books, and bibliographies have created Farrell criticism and made further work possible. See his *James T. Farrell* (New York: Twayne Publishers, 1971), and *A Bibliography of James T. Farrell's Writings 1921–1957* (Philadelphia: University of Pennsylvania Press, 1959). Branch has published bibliographical supplements as follows: "A Supplement to the Bibliography of James T. Farrell's Writings," *American Book Collector* 11 (Summer 1961): 42–48; "Bibliography of James T. Farrell: A Supplement," *American Book Collector* 17 (May 1967): 9–19; "Bibliography of James T. Farrell: January 1967–August 1970," *American Book Collector* 21 (March–April 1971): 13–18; "Bibliography of James T. Farrell, September 1970–February 1975," *American Book Collector* 26, no 3: 17–22; and "Bibliography of James T. Farrell's Writings: Supplement Five, 1975–1981," *Bulletin of Bibliography* 39, no. 4 (December 1982): 201–6. Branch has also published the beautifully illustrated *Studs Lonigan's Neighborhood and the Making of James T. Farrell* (Newton, Mass.: Arts End Books, 1996), and an elegant short study of *A Paris Year: Dorothy and James T. Farrell, 1931–1932* (Athens: Ohio University Press, 1998).

Corroborating Branch, other critics have placed Farrell firmly in the context of American realism. See Horace Gregory, "James T. Farrell: Beyond the Provinces of Art," *New World Writing: Fifth Mentor Selection* (New York: New American Library, 1954), 52–64; Blanche Gelfant, *The American City Novel* (Norman: University of Oklahoma Press, 1954), 175–227; Charles C. Walcutt, *American Literary Naturalism, A Divided Stream* (Minneapolis: University of Minnesota Press, 1956), 240–57; Charles C. Walcutt, *Seven Novelists in the American Naturalist Tradition* (Minneapolis: University of Minnesota Press, 1974), 245–89; Nelson M. Blake, *Novelists' America, Fiction as History, 1910–1940* (Syracuse, N.Y.: Syracuse University Press, 1969), 195–225; Richard Mitchell, "*Studs Lonigan:* Research in Morality," *Centennial Review* 6 (Spring 1962): 202–14; Barbara Foley, *Telling the Truth: The Theory and Practice of Documentary Fiction* (Ithaca, N.Y.: Cornell University Press, 1986); and Barbara Foley, *Radical Representations: Politics and Form in U.S. Proletarian Fiction, 1929–1941* (Durham, N.C.: Duke University Press, 1993).

William V. Shannon began the consideration of Farrell's ethnic dimension with a section in *The American Irish: A Political and Social Portrait* (New York: Macmillan, 1966), 249–58. On Farrell and Irish America, see also Charles Fanning, *The Irish Voice in America: 250 Years of Irish-American Fiction,* 2nd ed. (Lexington: University Press of Kentucky, 2000), 257–91; Fanning, "Death and Revery in Farrell's O'Neill-O'Flaherty Novels," *MELUS* 13, nos. 1 and 2 (Spring–Summer 1986): 97–114; and Fanning and Ellen Skerrett, "James T. Farrell and Washington Park," *Chicago History* 7 (Summer 1979): 80–91; Ron Ebest, "The Irish Catholic Schooling of James T. Ferrell, 1914–23," *Eire-Ireland* 30, no. 4 (Winter 1996): 18–32; Patricia J. Fanning, "'Maybe They'd Call the Doctor': Illness Behavior in the Novels of James T. Farrell," *New Hibernia Review* I, no. 4 (Winter 1997): 81–92. A breakthrough book for placement of Farrell in the larger context of American ethnicity is Ron Ebest, *Private Histories: The Writings of Irish Americans, 1900–1935* (Notre Dame: University of Notre Dame Press, 2005).

Other useful criticism of many aspects of Farrell's work includes: Jack Salzman and

Dennis Flynn, eds., Special Issue: "Essays on James T. Farrell," *Twentieth Century Literature* 22, no. 1 (February 1976); Leonard Kriegel, "Homage to Mr. Farrell," *Nation* 223 (16 October 1976): 373–75; Celeste Loughman, "'Old Now, and Good to Her': J. T. Farrell's Last Novels," *Eire-Ireland* 20, no. 3 (Fall 1985): 43–55; Shaun O'Connell, "His Kind: James T. Farrell's Last Word on the Irish," *Recorder* 1, no. 1 (Winter 1985): 41–50; Bette Howland, "James T. Farrell's Studs Lonigan," *Literary Review* 27 (Fall 1983): 22–5; Blanche Gelfant, "*Studs Lonigan* and Popular Art," *Raritan* 8 (Spring 1989): 111–20; Donald Pizer, "James T. Farrell and the 1930s," in Ralph F. Bogardus and Fred Hobson, ed., *Literature at the Barricades: The American Writer in the 1930s* (Tuscaloosa: University of Alabama Press, 1982), 69–81; Marcus Klein, *Foreigners: The Making of American Literature 1900–1940* (Chicago: University of Chicago Press, 1981), 206–15; Lewis F. Fried, *Makers of the City* (Amherst: University of Massachusetts Press, 1990), 119–58; Arnold L. Goldsmith, *The Modern American Urban Novel* (Detroit: Wayne State University Press, 1991), 39–58; Charles Fanning, ed., Special Issue: "Irish-American Literature," *MELUS* 18, no. 1 (Spring 1993), which contains essays on "Farrell and Richard Wright" by Robert Butler (pp. 103–11) and "Farrell and Dostoevsky" by Dennis Flynn (pp. 113–25), as well as a recently discovered 1931 essay by Farrell on "The Dance Marathons," edited by Ellen Skerrett (pp. 127–43).

Explorations of Farrell's relevance as a social critic include: Ann Douglas, "Studs Lonigan and the Failure of History in Mass Society: A Study in Claustrophobia," *American Quarterly* 26 (Winter 1977): 487–505; Alan M. Wald, *James T. Farrell: The Revolutionary Socialist Years* (New York: New York University Press, 1978); Alan M. Wald, *The New York Intellectuals* (Chapel Hill: University of North Carolina Press, 1987): 83–5, 249–63; Douglas Wixson, *Worker-Writer in America: Jack Conroy and the Tradition of Midwestern Literary Radicalism, 1898–1990* (Urbana and Chicago: University of Illinois Press, 1994); Daniel Shiffman, "Ethnic Competitors in *Studs Lonigan*," *MELUS* 24, no. 3 (Fall 1999): 67–79; Kathleen Farrell, *Literary Integrity and Political Action: The Public Argument of James T. Farrell* (Boulder, Colo.: Westview Press, 2000); and Lauren Onkey, "James Farrell's *Studs Lonigan* Trilogy and the Anxieties of Race," *Eire-Ireland* 40, nos. 3 and 4 (Fall/Winter 2005): 104–18.

Robert James Butler has established both the philosophical underpinnings and the subtle architectonics of Farrell's fiction in these essays: "Christian and Pragmatic Visions of Time in the Lonigan Trilogy," *Thought* 55 (December 1980): 461–75; "The Christian Roots of Farrell's O'Neill and Carr Novels," *Renascence* 34 (1982): 81–97; "Parks, Parties, and Pragmatism: Time and Setting in James T. Farrell's Major Novels," *Essays in Literature* 10 (Fall 1983): 241–54; and "Scenic Structure in Farrell's *Studs Lonigan*," *Essays in Literature* 14 (Spring 1987): 93–103.

Dennis Flynn was the first to open the rich Farrell Archive at the University of Pennsylvania, a voluminous collection of letters, diaries, and manuscripts that constitutes one of the great personal records available to us of the social and intellectual history of America in the earlier twentieth century. See James T. Farrell, *On Irish Themes* (Philadelphia: University of Pennsylvania Press, 1982), edited by Dennis Flynn. Flynn's work in progress is an edition of Farrell's selected letters and diary notes, which will open up the possibilities of the collection for other scholars to follow. Much remains to be done to elucidate the full range and accomplishment of James T. Farrell as a writer. His work and influence in short fiction needs to be further explored. His last, unfinished sequence, *A Universe of Time*, has only just begun to be considered critically. In his later fiction he often left Chicago and the Irish to continue his explorations of time, death, and the possibilities in modern life for self-knowledge, growth, and creativity. Recent evidence of renewed interest in Farrell studies includes the completion since 1978 of at least twenty-five doctoral dissertations in which Farrell is a major figure.

Farrell's first posthumously published work, *Sam Holman* (Buffalo, N.Y.: Prometheus Books, 1983), is a novel of New York intellectual life in the 1930s, and there are other valuable works in manuscript form that have yet to be made generally available. One story published since Farrell's death is "Cigarette Card Baseball Pictures," in *Crab Orchard Review* 1, no. 2 (Spring/Summer 1996): 3–12. His novel of the 1919 Chicago "Black Sox" scandal, *Dreaming Baseball*, appears in 2007 in the Kent State University Press Writing Sports Series.

In Farrell's centennial year of 2004, a new hardbound edition of *Studs Lonigan: A Trilogy* was published by the Library of America. This was followed by several new paperback editions of *Studs*. The publication of the five O'Neill-O'Flaherty novels by the University of Illinois Press guarantees that Farrell's grand design of the eight Washington Park novels will again be accessible to the American audience. Also in 2004, Robert K. Landers's biography of Farrell appeared. *An Honest Writer: The Life and Times of James T. Farrell* (San Francisco: Encounter Books) is useful for its collection and organization of the facts of Farrell's life, especially the early years. It is, however, inadequate as literary criticism. The integrated critical biography that Farrell deserves remains to be written.

From Rand McNally Atlas of Chicago for 1913

1. 4816 S. Indiana, Daly ("O'Flaherty") home, 1906-1910
2. 4953 S. Calumet, Daly ("O'Flaherty") home, 1910-1911
3. 5131 S. Prairie, Daly ("O'Flaherty") home, 1911-1915
4. 5704 S. Indiana, Daly ("O'Flaherty") home, 1915-1916
5. 5816 S. Park, Daly ("O'Flaherty") home, 1917-1928
6. 5939 S. Calumet, Farrell ("O'Neill") home, 1918-1923
7. 4831 S. Vincennes, Richard Wright home, 1929
8. 5730 S. Michigan, "Studs Lonigan" home
9. Corpus Christi ("Crucifixion") church and school, 49th and Grand
10. St. Anselm ("St.Patrick") church and school, 61st and Michigan
11. St. Cyril College ("St. Stanislaus High School"), 6410 S. Dante: one block south and five blocks east of this marker
12. University of Chicago

FATHER AND SON

James T. Farrell

To

the memory of

my father

"Iván Ilých's life had been most simple and most ordinary and therefore most terrible."

—Leo Tolstoy, *The Death of Iván Ilých*

"—Ah! Seigneur! donnez moi la force et le courage
De contempler mon coeur et mon corps sans dégoût!"

—Charles Baudelaire, *Les Fleurs du Mal*

"Brief and powerless is Man's life; on him and all his race the slow, sure doom falls pitiless and dark. Blind to good and evil, reckless of destruction, omnipotent matter rolls on its relentless way; for Man, condemned today to lose his dearest, tomorrow himself to pass through the gate of darkness, it remains only to cherish, ere yet the blow falls, the lofty thoughts that ennoble his little day; disdaining the coward terrors of the slave of Fate, to worship at the shrine that his own hands have built; undismayed by the empire of chance, to preserve a mind free from the wanton tyranny that rules his outward life; proudly defiant of the irresistible forces that tolerate, for a moment, his knowledge and his condemnation, to sustain alone, a weary but unyielding Atlas, the world that his own ideals have fashioned despite the trampling march of unconscious power."

—Bertrand Russell, *Mysticism and Logic*

SECTION ONE

1918–1919

1

I

Jim O'Neill sat up in bed and yawned. The bedroom was dark and needed air. Lizz must have closed the window while he was asleep. From the vacant lot outside he could hear children playing. Perhaps his own kids were out there.

"Oh, Lizz!" he called, sitting up in bed.

"What do you want, Jim?"

"What time is it?"

"What do you want?"

"What time is it?"

"Three o'clock."

Still sitting in bed, Jim stretched. He got up and put on his socks, shoes, and pants. He went to the dining room.

"I'm going to shave, Lizz, and then can you fix me something to eat?"

He went to the bathroom. He lathered his stiff and heavy beard. He'd been living six months in this new place, with a bathroom inside, running hot and cold water, steam heat, gas and electricity. He was used to these conveniences, and now it seemed as if they had never been without them. He sharpened his razor on the strap and began to shave carefully.

Yes, no more winters in the cottage where the kids used to gather around the stove and take turns sticking their feet in the oven to get warm. And the new furniture they'd bought when he'd been promoted and they'd moved in here was almost paid for. At least it should be. Lizz handled all that, but he figured she had it about paid for by now. He'd had a good time the day he and Lizz had gone downtown and picked out his new Morris chair.

He wiped his razor and ran it over the strap a few times.

What made him most happy was Bill. Bill was working now at the express company. He'd always had faith in Bill. What settled Bill was when he and that fellow, Kahler, had been caught after snatching a woman's pocketbook in Washington Park. When he'd come home, Bill was there, white and scared. But he hadn't hit him. He'd talked to Bill like a father. Lizz had gone to see McCarthy, the police sergeant whose boys played with Bill and Danny, and McCarthy had quashed it all. He'd paid for the pocketbook, and it was all forgotten. After that, Bill had settled down. Now, you couldn't want for a decenter boy.

He looked at his leathery face in the mirror. He washed it, dried himself, cleaned out the wash bowl, and left the bathroom. He put on his khaki shirt, passed through the small hallway to the dining room, and was ready to eat.

The dining-room table was covered with dishes and papers. In the center of it there was a large glass cake-dish, which contained crumbs and a stale chunk of cake. Lizz pushed dishes aside and set coffee, sugar buns, and a plate of ham and eggs before him. She wore an old apron and had a rag tied under her chin. She looked sloppy.

Jim pitched into the ham and eggs.

"I was over to see my mother yesterday," Lizz remarked, sitting down to talk with him.

He nodded, but said nothing. He bit into a sugar bun. He was waiting to see whether or not she'd had another scrap with her people.

"Mother said that Al isn't well," she said.

"You wouldn't think he would be, having a doctor like Mike Geraghty," Jim said, suddenly bitter.

His face clouded. He remembered his Little Arty, now three years dead. All their good luck had to come after Arty was long since dead. He wiped up the yolk from the plate with a bun and ate it, and then he shoved his plate aside and handed Lizz his cup for more coffee. She returned with a filled cup and sat down.

"Lizz, it's a long time since the little fellow left us. You really ought to take off your mourning. If you do that you won't be sad so often. You have to let time heal old wounds," he said, his voice kindly.

"Oh, Jim, I see the children playing on Calumet Avenue, and it breaks my heart. Not one of them is as beautiful as our Arty was."

"Come on now, Lizz, we've got to brace up. We've got lots to be thankful for, even with the tough breaks we had in the past," he said, but the image of little Arty stood in his mind, a lovely, light-haired boy in a dirty dress, staring with those wonderful sad eyes and saying "Fither."

Lizz wiped her eyes with her apron.

"Jim, I can't help it. I look at our new house and I think of him. Oh, how he would have loved it. He'd be going to school this year or next. Everywhere I see, Jim, makes me think of him. I can't help it. I can't take off my mourning," she said in tears.

Jim watched her, realizing that a mother's loss was something that only a mother could understand. But still, wasn't three years more than enough for her to wear mourning? He watched her. Tears rolled unrestrained down her fat cheeks.

"Lizz, I know how you feel. But the living must go on living."

He had no sooner said this than he was overcome with a sense of the futility of his words.

"If he was alive, he could be playing out in the prairie, and I could keep my eyes on him while I did the housework," she sobbed.

There was no comfort, no solace he could give her. And it all might have been averted, too. How could he ever forget what they had gone through? He remembered how he had been called home from work and had buried the child. And how, after that, he and Lizz had been alone in the cottage. All the kids had been taken to the hospital, and they had sat down alone to supper, realizing how silent the house was with no children in it.

"Jim, I still say it was Mike Geraghty's fault. Oh, why didn't he come after we kept calling him up?"

Jim could not hide his bitterness. It showed in his face.

"Well, thank God, we didn't lose more," he finally said.

"I thought it was going to take my little Margaret, too, but the Lord spared her. My dead father and sister in Heaven saved the rest of my children with their prayers of intercession."

Lizz dried her eyes. She went out to the kitchen and came back with a cup of tea.

"She's going to be a brave girl now," Jim coaxed, smiling at Lizz.

"Jim, I went to church today and I lit a candle for Patsy McLaughlin. It was so good of him, first promoting you and then finding a good job for my Bill," she said.

"They tell me that Bill is getting along damned fine in the Call Department," Jim said, proud.

"I'm never done thanking God and praying because of it. But, Jim, I do wish you could get on day work."

"I can't ask for the moon all at once."

"Jim, maybe if I went down to see Patsy and told him that you have to work days to be with your family more, he'd fix it."

"Don't you dare try that!"

"You needn't talk to me in that tone of voice."

"I didn't mean to, Lizz. But what would I look like with my wife going down to Patsy about me gettin' on days? There are other men working nights in the supervision who have wives and children besides myself. If you did that, I'd be the laughingstock of the company."

"I didn't mean no harm, Jim."

"Forget it, Lizz."

Jim got up.

"Lizz, get me those shoes of Bob and Dennis. I got an hour or so to spare before I go to work, and I can half-sole them now."

"They can wait," she said.

"No, go ahead, get them, and I'll fix them."

He went to the kitchen and got out his tools and leather, and then he sat by the dining-room window and slowly and carefully worked, half-soling his boys' shoes. Damn it, he could have been a good shoemaker if he hadn't been an expressman.

Well, he hadn't done bad as an expressman. Here he was, paying fifty dollars a month rent, earning his one seventy-five a month now. No, it was good he'd stuck in the express company all these years. In the end he'd gotten somewhere.

II

It was almost dark and the street lights were going on when Jim left home for work, carrying his lunch under his arm, wrapped up in a newspaper. Kids were playing on either side of the street, but he couldn't see his own. Catherine usually met him and walked to the elevated with him, but she was playing elsewhere, he guessed, and hadn't shown up. He walked with a loose, shambling gait. He was chewing on a gob of tobacco and occasionally he spat out the juice. As he came near Fifty-ninth Street, he saw a parlor first-floor window light up. A man passed him. Now men were beginning to come home from work to have supper and spend the night with their families. He wished he were coming home from work now. But then, he had no complaints. He was used to night work by now.

Continuing along Calumet Avenue, past a solid row of apartment buildings, he saw Liberty Bond signs in many windows. There was none in his. He had more important places for his money. Let the rich pay for the war. And he didn't like this war. Maybe we had to get into it, and maybe we didn't. Of course, it was good for the workingman who didn't have to go, but not for the one who did. And if it hadn't been for the war and the wartime business, and the amalgamation of all the express companies, he wouldn't have been promoted. But he felt that it was about time for the human race to be able to find some other way to settle its rows besides war and wholesale killing.

He and Bill had already had to register for the draft. If he didn't have a family, he'd be willing to go and fight for the flag. But he didn't want to see his son drafted, transported to France, and killed. If the war kept on, Bill would be called. The idea of Bill having to go to war terrified him. Suddenly he stood dead still on the sidewalk. Yes, they might draft Bill and take him away. He walked on.

He spat tobacco juice angrily. Goddamn it, what the hell kind of a business was it when a man had the time he'd had raising a family, and then, when the oldest boy gets his first job and is helping out, he is taken away, maybe killed across an ocean. The prospect made him sore. God, hadn't he and Lizz had enough to go through already without having to lose Bill in a war. Bill was just a boy, too young to be a soldier.

But then, maybe he was counting his chickens before they were hatched. The papers said the Germans were being licked. He hoped so, and that it would end the war. He wanted the Kaiser licked, and he wanted to see it happen before they took Bill away.

As he approached Fifty-eighth and Calumet, Jim saw Danny, his fourteen-year-old son, race by. Jim hurried to the corner.

"Hey!" he called.

Danny turned around, surprised, and then came back toward his father. Danny wore glasses, and he was skinny, a little undersized. He had long arms, and Jim could see that when he developed he'd have big shoulders.

"Oh, hello, Pa."

"How are you, boy?"

"I'm all right, Pa. I was playing touch football over on Indiana Avenue."

"You don't come over to see us very often, and we only live a block away from you and your grandmother."

"I was over last night, but you were at work."

"Your mother must have forgotten to mention it to me."

There was an awkward pause in the conversation, as if neither Jim nor Danny knew what to say.

"How you gettin' along in school?"

"Oh, pretty good, Pa. I got an average of ninety on my report card for last month."

"That's fine. I'm proud of you. But why don't you bring it over and let me see it? You know, Dan, your father is always interested to know how you're gettin' on in school."

"I will next month," Danny said.

"Be sure to."

"I will, Pa," Danny repeated with boyish sincerity and with a slight exaggeration of tone that was intended to assure his father that he meant to keep his promise.

"Tomorrow is Sunday. Why don't you come over after mass and say hello to us?"

"I will, Papa."

Danny stood before his father, awkward, continually shifting his weight from one foot to the other.

"Well, Dan, I got to be getting on to work, but I'll see you tomorrow," Jim said.

"Yes, Pa."

"So long."

"Goodbye, Papa."

Jim took a couple of steps away.

"Dan!" he called in a stern voice.

Danny came back, timid, unsure of himself.

"Here," Jim said, his voice changing; he handed Danny a nickel.

"Oh, thanks," Danny said, accepting the coin.

"Now, be a good kid and don't forget about tomorrow morning."

Jim watched Danny run toward the alley between Calumet and South Park. Danny was a good kid. He turned and walked on to the Fifty-eighth Street elevated station.

III

Jim hurried along a street lined with factories and warehouses, and men and girls swarmed past him. The street was crowded with express vehicles, motor trucks, and horse-drawn wagons. Jim waved to drivers he knew, remembering how he had so often waited in a lineup like this to get into the terminal to get unloaded, check out for the stable, and then call it quits for the day. Well, those days were over. Jim O'Neill wasn't a teamster any more. He was in the supervision now.

Billing Station V was a long, low, shedlike building covering a freight platform. Several ramps led into it. Jim walked through one of the entrances and nodded to the gumshoe man on duty. He climbed a short pair of steps onto the platform. He heard the noises and saw all the signs of activity that were so familiar to him. Wagons and motor trucks were lined side by side along the platform. Platform men were sweating away, unloading them, pushing, pulling, and carting the freight off to be billed and sorted. Stepping onto the platform, he smelled an odor of sawdust and wood. Through a cloud of dust, smoke, and electric light, he could see the freight handlers hustling for their fifty-five cents an hour. He heard the crash of boxes, the shouts and commands of foremen, the steady singsong of the billers who droned out the weight, value, and destination of each article of freight, and then pasted onto each piece a label giving this information. He threaded his way in and out of clusters of freight, side-stepped and dodged platform men, who scuttled past him with loaded arms or little carts, and walked by bins already jammed with freight.

"Hi Jim!"

It was a man of Jim's age, who wore the uniform cap and badge of a wagon-man.

"How's it comin', Jackie?"

"They're workin' my pants off these days."

"Yeh, it's war business. This looks like a lot of freight for a Saturday night, don't it?"

"Well, it's better than the old days. Things is different from what they used to be. More pay, time and a half for overtime, hell, Jim, it ain't so goddamned bad being a manure whaler like it was when you and I was young bucks startin' in on the wagons."

"Yeh, times have changed, Jackie."

"No gainsayin' that. That's why I say they can keep this war goin' forever."

"Well, see you in church. And don't take no counterfeit nickels, Jackie," Jim said.

Jim shambled on through the confusion to a small coop, built of light boards and glass in the center of the platform. Inside it there were two chairs, a small board desk containing papers and spindles, a bulletin board with notices, hooks for hats and coats, and next to the hooks a shelf on which there were coffee cans, tin cups, and odds and ends.

"I'm leaving you plenty tonight, Jim, old boy," said Tommy Murphy, the day Wagon Dispatcher.

"We're here to move it, Tommy," Jim said.

"What's the paper say? They still got the Dutchmen on the run?"

"Yes, it seems so."

"If I was younger, I'd like to be there. Say, it wouldn't be so bad, Jim, tastin' what the dames is like in Berlin," Tommy said.

"We're gettin' too old for that, Tommy."

"Not me, but I'm hauling ass home. Don't work too hard, my boy," Tommy said.

Jim got out a clean set of record sheets from a stack under the board desk and marked and dated them for the evening. The telephone rang, and Jim answered it.

IV

Going home on the elevated, Jim had dozed off. He woke up just in time and rushed out of the car at the Fifty-eighth Street station. The train rumbled on, and Jim paused on the platform, looking off to the west. Dawn was breaking. There was a misty gray filling the air. The weather was damp and chilly. Jim blinked. He was sleepy. He went downstairs to the street.

Coming out of the elevated station, he saw a white milk wagon. The horse pulling it jogged along. It seemed for a moment like some object appearing fantastically in a dream. Jim turned to the left, hearing the clatter of the milk wagon behind him. The lamppost at Calumet Avenue was still lighted. There were several empty liquor bottles in front of the poolroom close to the station. The wind scraped bits of paper along the sidewalk. Above the buildings he saw the fading moon disappear behind a cloud. He could make out the bushes at the edge of Washington Park ahead of him. They were faintly outlined, as if they had been drawn by a pencil. It was very quiet. Every morning when he came home at this hour, he was impressed by the quiet as if it were something new, never experienced before. The city, the streets now were so utterly different from what they were in the daytime. Fifty-eighth Street at this hour, with the gray dawn filtering over it and the sharp autumn wind cruising through it, it was like some street in a dream. There was something mysterious about the deserted street. A hidden meaning seemed to be lurking in it.

Jim turned down Calumet Avenue. He heard an elevated train, and then all was quiet again. He saw a light go on in an apartment window. Some man going to work. He wondered what the man did. Jim's thoughts seemed as vague as the dawn. He seemed to want to grasp at some idea, some impression, but it was as illusive as the meaning in the fresh day that was now marching slowly over the city. He liked it, coming home at this hour. The air was clean and fresh, such a change from the close air at the terminal. He was tired, and the prospect of sleep was sweet and comforting. He shambled on. As he entered the building where he lived, he heard another elevated train. The first colors of dawn were tentatively shifting in the sky.

V

Jim didn't look quite at ease in his Sunday clothes. He wore a well-made black overcoat with a velvet collar, and an expensive black suit, both hand-me-downs from his cousin, Joe O'Reilley. He had on a crushed black felt hat which he had worn on Sundays for years. His clothes seemed to hang unevenly on his loose, lanky frame, and although his trousers were pressed, they didn't quite look as if they had been. Lizz wore mourning, a large black hat with a veil, and an old black dress spotted in the front. One button hung loose from her plain black coat. Her face was washed, her hair was combed, and her skin was fresh and clear. She was carrying a thick, worn prayer book.

Lizz and Jim left for church.

Calumet Avenue was lazy and peaceful. Jim, walking on the outside, thought how quiet it was here, and how, in Europe, the terrible fighting, shelling, killing, destruction was going on at this very moment. Again he feared that Bill would be drawn into that bloody fighting.

A sprinkling of people were on the street, going to church. Jim thought of mass as a duty to be performed. He always found it hard to keep his mind fixed on what was going on during mass. But then, he knew he should go. He believed in God. He guessed he just wasn't like his wife. She was devout, too devout. But then, the women were generally more pious than the men.

He shambled along at Lizz's side. Lizz held her head high, and her expression was serious. She thought that all the ladies of the parish went to a late mass, and that now, Lizz O'Neill was one of the ladies of the parish going to a late mass.

"Jim, there's Mrs. Doyle. She's Mother's neighbor," Lizz said, jabbing Jim's ribs and nodding her head at a stout woman on the other side of the street. "Her husband owns his own building."

They continued on their way. Lizz told herself that other ladies of the parish might look at her. She wondered would they be saying that there goes Mr. and Mrs. O'Neill? And would they notice her mourning and wonder about it? Would they pity her?

"Oh, Jim, there goes Mrs. Cannon."

"Who's she?" Jim asked, smiling genially.

"You don't know who Mrs. Cannon is? I told you about her and her husband, he works in the stockyards."

Mrs. Cannon, a thin little woman with a wart prominent on her nose, passed them. She tightly held a prayer book in her thin, gloved hands.

"I thought you knew her?" Jim asked.

"Oh, no. But I know all about her. And, Jim, I want you to know I'm like my mother. I don't talk to everybody I see on the street."

Jim glanced at Lizz, amused. They crossed Sixtieth Street. Jim was wishing that mass were over. Father Gilhooley, the pastor, always said the late masses. He was slower than the other priests. Jim suddenly smiled. He'd bet that during the sermon Father Gilhooley would say something about the collections. Father Gilhooley was always complaining about the size of the collection.

"Good morning, Mrs. Monahan," Lizz said as a ruddy and stout woman passed with a wizened red-nosed husband creeping along at her side.

The Monahans bowed formally.

"He's got a cousin on the police force and he's a contractor, and when Mother lived on Wabash Avenue years ago, just after we got married, there was a Monahan who lived next door to us. He was a stew and his wife left him. I never knew a Monahan that was any good."

As Lizz was speaking to him, Jim's eyes wandered. He saw a gold star hanging from a first-floor window. Somebody's son killed in France.

Lizz was talking on about the Monahans. He didn't hear a word she was saying. He guessed it didn't do Lizz any harm to pick up a little gossip. Lizz had had a hard life. Now, for the first time in their lives, they could be without real worries to dog them. Yes, maybe the war wouldn't last long and Bill wouldn't be killed. No, no real worry there. He could look ahead these days.

He took Lizz's arm and guided her across Calumet Avenue, and then on along Sixty-first Street.

2

I

Al O'Flaherty stood by the low bedroom window looking out, beyond the front porch, at Washington Park across the street. It was a pleasant view. The park was alive with the colors of autumn. Through the trees and shrubbery he could see the lagoon. People were strolling about the park and they seemed to be so at ease. They seemed to be living in another world. He reflected on what he saw, telling himself it was an idyllic sight.

Ned O'Flaherty came in, but Al paid no attention to him. Ned was taller than his older brother. He was a man of thirty-four, with a soft, handsome face, gray-blue eyes, and light brown hair. He looked like a dandy. He hung up his coat, and rolling up his shirt sleeves, he faced Al.

"Al, close that door! I want to talk with you!"

"What the hell's the matter?"

Ned closed the bedroom door.

"Al, you're a damned fool."

"Say, for Christ sake!"

"Keep your temper. I'm going to talk to you for your own good."

"I'm not losing my temper. You're the one who's getting sore," Al countered.

"Me? What the hell do you mean?"

"Sure, you! Coming in like this, telling me to close the door. What the hell is this?"

"Why do you want to have this damned-fool operation? Tell me that!"

"I had another attack on the road. Suppose I'm in some jerkwater town and my appendix bursts, then where'll I be? I have a chronic appendicitis, and the best course for me to take is to have it out. Mike examined me, and he's a good doctor. And he sent me to Doctor Collins, a crackerjack, and he says the same as Mike. I'm doing what they advise me to do."

"What the hell does a doctor know?"

"They're educated to know what the layman like you and I don't know."

"Yes? Then tell me this! Why haven't I got appendicitis?" Ned asked.

"How in hell do I know?"

"I'll tell you why. It's because I have faith. And listen to me, I can save you money and cure you, if you'll let me."

"Faith is all right in its place, but I got a bum appendix, and if I don't have it out, no doctor can predict what'll happen to me," Al said.

"Answer this question! Why did Jesus walk on the water?"

"Because He was God."

"Because He had faith. And you, too, can walk on water, and you can cure yourself of appendicitis without getting yourself hacked by some butcher—you can do all that if you have faith."

"Ned, don't be a goddamned fool."

"I'm not a goddamned fool. I'm telling you! With faith, you can attune yourself properly to the universe and cure yourself. Did Jesus ever have appendicitis? No!"

"I agree with you about the efficacy of faith, but action is also necessary."

"Action is in the heart," Ned said, pointing to his breast.

"Now you listen to me! Don't be a goddamned fool all your life," Al said sharply.

"Don't you call me a goddamned fool."

"Aw, nuts!"

Ned stood in the center of the bedroom, scowling, with fine wrinkles forming on his forehead.

"Fathead!" Ned said half aloud.

II

Danny had gone over to see his father, and when he came back he flopped in a chair in the parlor and continued his re-reading of Guy Empey's *Over the Top*. It made him feel as if he were an American Sammy fighting in the trenches. He wanted to be a hero for his country, a devil dog maybe, who would go over the top and capture a German machine-gun nest singlehanded. He had gone to the library last week and read a book by a Belgian priest telling about how the Germans raped women, even old women like Mother. Of course he didn't want to be killed fighting. He wanted to be a live hero, not a dead one. And he was awfully worried. Suppose the Germans won in Europe and came over here. He set the book aside and went to the center parlor window, the one with a Liberty

Bond sign hanging in it. He looked out and imagined Washington Park as No-Man's Land. He saw himself in the trenches facing the Huns at the zero hour, going over the top, leading the charge at the beginning of a drive that wouldn't end until the dirty Germans were driven clean out of America and wiped off the map. He turned back again, dropped into a rocking chair, swung his legs awkwardly over one side, and glued his eyes on the book.

But now he couldn't read because Uncle Al and Uncle Ned were arguing in their bedroom right off the parlor. They were yelling so loudly at each other that he couldn't keep his mind on the book. He heard the steady and angry sound of their voices, but he couldn't make out the words. Whenever they quarreled like this he was always afraid, because it might lead to a real fist fight, especially since Uncle Al was so hot tempered.

Suddenly the bedroom door flew open and Uncle Al rushed out. Danny pretended to be absorbed in his reading. But Uncle Al went down the hall to the bathroom. Danny tried to read. Uncle Al came into the parlor.

"Well, Sport, how you feeling?" Uncle Al asked, and Danny looked up from the book.

"Oh, I'm all right." But he felt that Uncle Al was worried about something.

"Getting along all right in school?" Uncle Al asked, his voice kind and gentle.

"Yes, I am," Danny said.

"Fine! Fine! That's fine, and I'm proud of you."

Al sat down opposite Danny. He was very moody. He was wondering would he come through this operation, or wouldn't he? Was this perhaps the last time he'd talk with his nephew? It might be, he sadly reflected. And if it were, he ought to have a long talk with Danny. But somehow he couldn't bring himself to say the things he probably ought to say. He should give Danny advice about sex and life, and about decorum. He had determined to do this before, but he hadn't done it. He had often wondered how much Danny knew. What went on in his mind? Was he still innocent? He remembered his own boyhood, how he had picked up information on the streets when he was pretty young, false information, too, in most instances. Yes, he should tell the boy. He wanted to do it, right now, but he was embarrassed. He didn't know how to begin.

"Sport, while I'm away, you're going to study, obey your aunt and grandmother, and help around the house?" he said.

"Yes."

Danny sensed a strange mood in Uncle Al. He was embarrassed, and he wished Uncle Al would leave the room. Maybe Uncle Al was going to talk about the Sixth Commandment. So many times of late he'd had a feeling that Uncle Al was going to do that. He'd be ashamed of himself if he talked with Uncle Al about this subject. He was ashamed of himself sometimes, ashamed of the little bit of hair he was beginning to get. He didn't know why he had the feeling Uncle Al wanted to talk about such a subject, and yet he had it. He sat with his feet twisted up in the chair, squirming, wishing very much that Uncle Al would go out of the room.

"You're going to write me regularly, too, Sport?"

Al looked tenderly at Danny. He determined to have the talk with the boy now. It was his duty to instruct him in this matter. He would lead up to it by first going into other matters.

"And you'll forward my mail to me regularly, won't you?"

"Uh huh," Danny exclaimed, retreating into a shell of shyness.

"Your aunt has been behaving and is in a good mood. Now don't do anything that will make her go off the handle."

"I'll try not to, Uncle Al."

There was a pause. Al racked his brain for a way to begin.

"I've had a book around here a long time, *The Letters of Lord Chesterfield*. I want you to promise me you'll read it," he said.

"I will."

"It contains letters you should read. You're a boy in the eighth grade now," Al said. It occurred to Al in a flash that here was his opening. He made a noise as if clearing his throat. "Yes, you're in the eighth grade now and you're fourteen years old. You should learn about deportment and manners. You want to be a regular fellow, don't you?"

"Of course I do."

"Well, you read those letters, and you will." Al looked at Danny fondly.

"Danny, your aunt wants you. She wants you to go to the store," Ned said at the parlor entrance.

Danny jumped to his feet and hurried out of the room, glad for once that he was being sent to the store. It relieved him of all this embarrassment he had been feeling in there with Uncle Al.

III

Al left home, looking forward to seeing Mike Geraghty. It was a chilly fall evening, the kind that always caused him to brood. He wondered whether he should walk or ride over to Mike's? There wouldn't be any danger in walking. And he would walk carefully, not in that quick, nervous stride of his. The walk would be nice. It would give him a chance to enjoy thoughts and memories, a nice time by himself.

He went on along South Park Avenue, toward Garfield Boulevard. Ned had tried to argue with him again, but he had cut Ned off. Of course you could do a lot with faith and the right attitude, and of course it helped if you sent out the right thoughts and harmonized them with the universe. But these thoughts had to harmonize with something else besides the law of the universe. They had to be harmonized with action. This rule applied to selling as it did to everything else. In selling, action meant getting up and going out, seeing people, trying to sell, keeping on your toes, co-operating with the laws of the universe that worked for your own good. And when you were sick, you had to act in a way to help the unseen forces of faith and goodness so that they could help you. And that meant going to see the doctor and having the doctor do all that he could for you. God helped those who helped themselves.

Ned only saw one side of the situation. That was Ned's trouble. In selling he was the same way. He wouldn't go out and get things. But thank old Harry, he was working again and doing good. If he kept at it and didn't fight with his boss, it would be a great help and it would lighten the burden of the family that rested on his own shoulders. Yes, that was good, and he, also, was now in better circumstances. He had fine prospects, and his sales record this fall had started off with a real bang. Fortune was smiling on him. Fortune was a friendly goddess.

But he was plunged deeply into a fit of gloom. Why did something like an appendicitis have to come upon him just when everything in life was taking a turn for the good? When everything was perking up and the world was giving himself and his family a great big bright ray of sunshine? At such a time, that this should happen to him.

He saw himself dead, laid out in a coffin. What would happen to everybody? Could Ned carry the burden? Would Ned give Danny a high-school and college education, the chance in life he wanted the boy to have? Of course, he wouldn't die and leave the family nothing. There was his thousand-dollar life insurance policy. He had a couple of Liberty Bonds, and a few others, mainly in public utilities. Public utilities were good investments. And of course there were the shares in the factory he'd bought from his salary. But that couldn't keep them forever. And he had a thousand dollars cash in the bank, but this operation would take some of that. Mother might live for many years to come. God willing, she would. She was old, but in the best of health. God willing, they would all live for many years to come and enjoy the fruits of a fine, happy, and prosperous life together.

He stopped and stood motionless on the sidewalk for a moment. It was dark, and lighted windows and the lampposts made him feel only the more alone. He could hear the wind in the bare trees across the street on the park edge. He held an image of himself in his mind, dead. He had seen others dead, gone to their wakes, paid his last respects to them. And would he be dead now and would others come to see him, a corpse, sit there and talk about him and smoke cigars, follow him to his last resting place? He walked on. Should he heed what Ned said and not go through with the operation? No, Mike knew more about it than Ned. Ned wasn't a doctor, he was a shoe salesman. Ned didn't know anything about medicine. Why, Ned was damned near being a Christian Scientist. Hell, Ned had never had so many cockeyed, half-baked ideas when he was younger. Where had he picked them up? Mildred, Ned's dead wife, had always been a fine and sensible woman. Ned never talked of her. After she died in 1916, he'd come home again to live with them.

Al again imagined himself lying dead in a coffin. He pitied himself. Here he had struggled to get along in life, and just when he had his head really above the water and was swimming fine with an easy, tireless stroke, and the waters were calm and he could see ahead of him the safe snug harbor, this danger had to come upon him.

He had to live. God would keep him alive. God was good. God wanted people to be happy when they were decent. He wouldn't want a promising boy and a widowed old mother like his to be left unprotected, unprovided for.

And there was so much in life that he wanted. Books, Danny, and Danny's future. Danny was growing up and soon would be a real companion for him. Marriage? Well, he would like that, but he'd put it out of his head. After all, he had a home and responsibilities. And Danny was like a son to him.

Al walked along Garfield Boulevard, and he decided that before he went to Mike's he'd stop in and say a few prayers for himself at Saint Rose's church. It was right on his way.

IV

Al sat with Dr. Mike Geraghty in the downstairs part of the Geraghty house.

"All I can say is don't act on Ned's cracked ideas. You know, Al, the body is something separate from the soul. If you have an abscessed tooth, you got to have it out whether it hurts or not. All this Christian Science is boloney."

"I imagine there must be something in it, some grain of truth."

"Well, maybe there is, but not as far as the body goes when you have a bug or an infection in you. Al, if I gave my patients the advice Ned gives you, I'd get myself in a hell of a lot of trouble. I'd be disgraced."

"Ned's a fine fellow, but he's cracked on some subjects."

"Al, now don't you worry. I'm sure you'll come out fine, and you're doing what you ought to under the circumstances. Your heart's in pretty good shape now. I don't think you'll have any worry from that source. You've got a good surgeon, as good as there's to be found. I know you'll come through with flying colors. Don't worry."

"Sure! Sure, Mike, I agree with you. I didn't tell the folks, except Ned, because I didn't want to worry them."

"That was wise. After all, your sister is a nervous girl. Is she behaving herself these days?"

"Perfect. Perfectly. Just like a lady. Yes, everything is tranquil on the domestic front."

"I think this is going to eliminate any source of worry for you. You'll be yourself again in a few weeks."

"What really causes appendicitis, Mike?"

"It's an infection. I suppose there must be a reason for a man having a vermiform appendix. Otherwise the Lord wouldn't have put one in us. But whatever its purpose is in the human body, I don't know. The best thing to do with 'em the minute they give you any trouble is to get 'em out. Sometimes they may clear up, but I don't like to gamble on that. You may use ice bags and your temperature may go down, and everything might look good. But you can't be sure. They can take a turn for the worse and burst on you and develop into peritonitis. So I say, get 'em out if they cause any trouble."

"That makes sense."

The two friends sat there. Al had wanted to have a long and confidential talk with Mike. And yet suddenly there seemed to be little to say.

"Mike, if anything happens, I want to ask you a favor. Keep your eye on my nephew, Danny."

"Of course, Al. But now, don't you worry and cross bridges you probably won't have to go over."

"It's not that I'm worrying, Mike. I say it only in case something does go wrong. No matter what the chances are in anything, something can go wrong about the best-laid plans of mice and men, that's all I mean."

Mike nodded.

"You know, Mike, I was just thinking. It seems like it was only yesterday that I was a young shoe clerk in a store. Ned worked in a shoe store then, too. It was because of me, you know, that he entered the shoe game."

"He's getting along in that line, isn't he, Al?"

"Yes, he's a good shoe man."

Al puffed at his cigar and watched the smoke rise to the ceiling.

"You know, it'll be kind of nice to rest in the hospital after it's over. I'll get a lot of reading done, too. I bought some good books."

"Good, Al."

Again a pause.

"Business good?" Mike asked.

"No complaints. Fine and dandy. Fine. I'm having one of my best years."

"I guess the war's helped everything."

"It's put men to work, given them higher salaries, and money is pouring out all over," Al said.

"Well, we'll win it. You're not likely to be drafted, are you?"

"I won't have to go. I have a family to support, but I'm worried that they might take Ned."

"Well, I'm married, that'll let me out," Mike said.

Al continued puffing on his cigar. The friendship he felt for Mike was deep. Friendship was one of the finest things in a man's life. There was a feeling of warmth and security sitting here. He was with a friend and away from the troubles of the world.

3

I

The classroom was large. Its seven rows of seats were sufficient for sixty-three pupils. The seventh-grade boys were over by the windows, while the eighth-grade class sat in the rows near the blackboard and hall door. Sister's desk was on a dais in the corner near a window. Up front, a picture of the Sacred Heart of Jesus hung on the wall, and there were doors on either side leading into the dressing room which was also used by the seventh- and eighth-grade girls in the room next door.

Sister Magdalen was a tall, swarthy, middle-aged, bespectacled nun with down on her upper lip. Her black eyes were piercing. After leading both classes in prayer, she sat at her desk. While she heard one class recite, the other class studied. Now the seventh-grade boys were peering into opened catechisms.

"Instead of hearing the catechism lesson today, I'm going to talk to all of you boys," she said in a modulated voice.

The seventh-grade boys closed their books. Danny, in the first row, glanced around the room. Mickey Feehan, over near the window, wriggled his ears and grinned at him.

"Yesterday I had a little talk with Father Gilhooley about this school. He is very proud of his parish school and he thinks that there is none better in the city. But he told me that he was disappointed because this school has not sent one boy to study for the priesthood in the last ten years. That is a very poor record. I told him that it would be a shame if the class of 1919 doesn't give a few priests to God. And I said that this morning I would talk to my classes about vocations."

Danny chewed on a pencil and watched Sister. He put the pencil down and sat listening, immobile.

"A vocation is a call from God to a human soul, telling a person that he or she has been specially chosen to be a priest or a nun. Some of you may ask, 'How will I know if I have the call?' First of all, to have the call, a boy must have the makings in him. He must be good and pure in his heart. He must be an intelligent boy."

"That lets Roman Dombrowski out," Fat Malloy yelled from the seventh-grade side of the room.

There was laughter.

Sister Magdalen raised her heavy dark brows. She snapped her knob-shaped clapper, and everyone instantly stopped laughing.

"Thomas Malloy, come up here!"

"Sister, I didn't mean anything. I'm sorry I said that," Fat Malloy said, standing up; he was a plump, genial, round-faced boy.

"Come up here, Thomas!"

He obeyed, slowly. She stepped off her dais and met him in front of the row of seats.

"I don't want tomfoolery when I am talking about a serious subject. Put out your hand! No, not that way—with the knuckles up!"

She grabbed his hand and smacked his knuckles with the clapper. He begged her to stop and cried out in pain.

"Now kneel down with your face to the wall. If you turn around you'll get worse."

She sat down.

"I want no more such conduct. It is a disgrace, and if Thomas Malloy's mother knew of his misbehavior, she would punish him more severely than I have. It is a disgrace to the seventh-grade class."

She glanced around the room. She had perfect attention.

"There are certain conditions under which it is not likely that God will call a boy to the priesthood. For instance, if a boy is sickly by nature it is not very probable that God will call him. But even in such a case, you can never be sure. Or if a boy's father and mother are very poor and they will need him to go to work and help to take care of younger brothers and sisters, then again the chances are that God will not plant a vocation in his heart. But even there, you can never be sure. God might just call such a boy. But if He does, of course God will find a way for that boy's family to get along.

"But now, who are the boys whom we would most expect God to call? The type of boy whom God is most likely to call to the priesthood is one of a deep religious nature who has a good head on his shoulders. A priest must be a very smart man and he must study deep problems, the deepest problems in the whole world. And the boy is likely to come from a family that can afford to put him through the priesthood. And he is a boy who has no secret sins."

Pensive, Danny asked himself if he was such a type.

"The call to the priesthood can come to a boy in many different ways. God's ways are a mystery to man. Of course, there can be a visitation from God, from His Blessed Mother, or from one of the Communion of Saints. That is how Saint Paul was called on the road to Damascus, as you boys already know. But such visitations, while they have been very numerous in the past, do not happen very often nowadays. And there is a reason why they don't. After all, if God comes to a boy and tells him he has a vocation, that boy would have to be very bad and heedless indeed to refuse to do what God has told him. Why, if God appeared to everyone who had the call, boys who are called would answer it without making any effort of will on their own part. They wouldn't pray as often or be as holy as they should. And of course, it is only to an especially holy person that God will show Himself. Some of us would become too proud if we were used to having God appear before us. And we mustn't forget that it was pride which led to the fall of Lucifer and all of his bad angels.

"Even though God does not come and tell us in so many words that we have the call, He nevertheless makes it known to us in a way that we cannot mistake. There is no person on earth who ever received the call and did not know of it. So if you are going to be called, you need have no fear that you will not know it. *You will know!*

"In my own case, there was no mistake. When I was a girl, I had many dreams. Now these were not visitations. But in my dreams I would say to myself that I had the call to be a nun. It must have been the voice of my guardian angel speaking to me. And when I would go to parties with other boys and girls—yes, I went to parties and played and liked fun when I was a girl—I would sometimes find that I was telling myself in the middle of a game that I had the call. I knew it because it grew in me; it grew in my heart and my soul. That is usually the way you know you have the call. It grows in you. Your guardian angel knows if you have a vocation or not, and if you have he will find ways of keeping you reminded of it.

"But you must prepare yourself to find this out. You must pray. Prayer is most important to any boy who thinks he might have the call. All of the great saints and holy men and women of God dedicated themselves to prayer; they prayed much more than any of us ever will. They prayed not only for themselves, but for others. There were many saints who devoted themselves to almost nothing except prayer, and the stories of their beautiful lives are wonderful stories. For instance, there was a great Italian mystic saint, Saint Mary Magdalen of Pazzi, whose vocation it was to pray and to do penance. With her prayers and her penance she wanted to reform everyone in the church, even the heretics and the pagans. She said: 'I desire to offer Thee, O my God, all creatures class by class. Would that I had the strength to gather all infidels to lead them into the bosom of Thy Church.' I just mention her as one example. The history of the church is full of saints who prayed as their main vocation. You must pray. It is by prayers, by keeping the Ten Commandments, by daily keeping yourself among the pure in heart, by receiving the Sacraments regularly, that you must prepare yourself so that your soul, your mind, your heart will be in the right condition of piety and purity for you to receive the call.

"Nothing disappoints God more than for one called to the priesthood to ignore the call."

Danny, his face intent, raised his hand.

"Yes, Daniel," Sister Magdalen said, nodding.

"Sister, if someone has the call and doesn't answer it and become a priest, can that person still save his soul?"

"That's a very intelligent question, Daniel, and I'm glad you asked it," she answered; Danny was uncomfortable because a number of eyes were turned toward him.

The nun cleared her throat and paused a moment before answering.

"No one of you could have asked me a better question. The answer is that no one in this world is damned unless that person sins. We all have free will and the knowledge of good and evil. If you have the call and you do not heed it, you can still save your soul from the torments of Hell. But it will be very difficult, very hard indeed. If you fling away the special grace He has given you by endowing you with a vocation to serve Him as a priest, you must not forget that you have then used up a great store of God's grace. You cannot expect much more. God has then already helped you to save your soul, helped you more than he has the great majority of the faithful. The person who ignores the call has deeply disappointed God. Of course, it can be done, but it is not easy to save your soul under such circumstances. I can tell you boys that the unhappiest people in the world are those who have spurned the call."

She paused.

Danny rested his elbows on the desk and cupped his chin in his hands. He was dreamy-eyed. He could still go to Heaven by fighting the Devil if he *really* did have the call and didn't answer it.

"You must think of what a favor God bestows on the boy whom he calls to the priesthood. Just think of what an honor it is. A priest is the minister and the messenger of God on this earth. He is one of the successors of the Apostles. His mission is the highest and noblest a man can have—that of saving souls. God gives the priest special powers granted no other human being. A priest is given the power to change bread and wine into the body and blood of our Saviour. He is given the power to forgive sins, to take away from the poor sinner the heaviest of all burdens. The priest feeds to God's flock of faithful souls the bread of everlasting life. He is the most honored of men. Even non-Catholics look with awe and respect on a priest. He is a man whom God has set apart. And he is the happiest of men. I am a nun. I can tell you boys from my own experience and my own life that the nun's life is a very happy one. But my happiness, the happiness of any nun, is nothing compared to that of the priest. The rewards of being a priest are finer than the rewards of money and fame. They are the rewards of the soul. Why, when you think of what it means to be a priest, when you once realize that the priest is the representative of our Lord on earth, then you begin to see that any boy who turns his back on the call is a fool. It is impossible to imagine what reason there could be to lead one to refuse a vocation. Think of it a moment!"

She stopped and glanced around the room, seeing the many boyish faces, some intent, others blank.

"If your mother or father wants to give you a wonderful present, you don't say that you won't take it. But that is what you are doing if you turn down the most wonderful gift that God can give to us, His children."

She made it seem so easy to answer the call. But of course, he didn't know if he had it or not. Danny jerked about in his seat.

"Most mothers and fathers," the nun continued, "are highly pleased when a child of theirs becomes a priest or a nun. There is no joy in the heart of a Catholic mother to equal that which she has when her own son is ordained and she is blessed by his own hands. But sometimes, not very often, of course, but sometimes a mother or father objects to a boy answering the call. And I say the Lord forbid that it happen in the case of any of you. I don't think it will. I know most of your mothers and fathers, and I know that if any of you boys were to be called, they would be very happy. But if it does happen, you must remember that while you owe much to your father and mother, you owe still more to God. Our first loyalty is to God, and that is above all other loyalties."

Danny bit the eraser off his pencil. Sister Magdalen was going on. Suppose he had been sick, too sick to come to school today. Then he wouldn't have heard what she said and maybe he wouldn't be worrying and afraid that he had a vocation. What was there in him that made him worry for fear he had a vocation when it was the greatest gift God could give anyone?

"Now, I want all of you to ask yourself this question: 'Have I a vocation?' I want you to think about it very seriously. If you have any doubts, come and speak to me. And tell the priest in confession. If any of you think that you have the call, but are not sure, nothing, absolutely nothing else in the world, is as important as making up your mind. For if you disregard a call from God, you are risking your immortal soul.

"For what doth it profit a man, if he gain the whole world, and suffer the loss of his own soul?"

The ten o'clock bell rang. Danny took the pencil out of his mouth. It was dented with tooth marks. He pulled his arithmetic book out of his desk.

II

Danny waited while Sister straightened up some papers. He was alone with her in the classroom. He wondered what she wanted. He was apprehensive. He had an idea of what she might have on her mind.

"All right, Danny, we can talk now," she said.

Danny went up to her. He stood on the dais facing her, and she sat at her desk.

"You didn't get along very well last year with Sister Bertha, did you?" she asked.

"Well, Sister—" he began, but he halted, not knowing what to say.

"Such things happen, and often it is neither the fault of the pupil nor of the teacher. But I didn't ask you to stay here to talk to you about bygones. I always say, let bygones be bygones. You know, Danny, in the short time that I have been teaching you, I have grown to think a lot of you."

He smiled sheepishly.

"I'm telling you this because I don't think that it will go to your head. I don't think you can be spoiled. I have observed that you possess some fine qualities."

He grinned, ill at ease.

"Yes, you are a very loyal boy. And you have stick-to-itiveness. Without these virtues, a boy is not going to amount to anything in this world. But you have these qualities and you are a very smart boy."

"Well, Sister, I try to learn my lessons and do my homework," he began, and then he paused; he waited for her to go on.

"But also, there are other things about you. You have the germ of destruction in you. I have never seen a boy with more of the germ of destruction in him than you have. I watch you closely. You are always destroying something. You mark up your books. You chew pencils. You get in fights. Last summer when Sister Bertha learned that I was coming here in her place, she spoke to me about all you boys. She told me how you like to fight. It's because you have this germ of destruction in you. But she evidently didn't see the other qualities you have. If you didn't have them, you would be destroying something every minute of the day."

He didn't know what to say. He didn't know how true it was. Of course, he did like to break windows, and last summer he and Dick Buckford used to go around and throw rotten tomatoes at people on back porches, break windows, and throw things in houses, but he didn't know.

"Your grandmother is a wonderful woman. I can see that your home life with her has been very wholesome. Its good influence must have helped save you."

He didn't know where she got all these ideas, but it was swell to know she didn't even suspect how things had been at home, and about Aunt Margaret. She didn't know how a few years ago on Indiana Avenue some kids wouldn't play with him because their mothers said there was too much cursing in his house.

She paused a moment and then went on:

"Danny, this morning, when I talked of vocations, you were one of the boys to whom I was really talking."

That was what he had been suspecting. He had been thinking about what she had said all day. Going home at noon with the gang, he had deliberately cursed to make it look as if he wasn't one of the kids she meant.

"Danny, look me in the eye!"

She held him in a piercing but sympathetic gaze. He looked at her, struggling with himself, to make his expression as honest a one as he could. He told himself that he would tell the truth and he would be honest and answer her questions. This was too important for him to lie about.

"Danny, have you ever thought that you might have a vocation?"

He didn't want to have a vocation. All day a voice inside him kept telling him he had a vocation. He hesitated answering her.

"Yes, Sister," he blurted out.

Immediately he wished he hadn't said it. He wished he had taken time really to think it over.

"I was certain I was right about you," she said, suddenly smiling with gratification.

He had never spoken with any person who could look you in the eye as steadily and for as long a time as Sister could.

"How long have you had thoughts about it?"

"Well, Sister, today, when you talked to us in catechism," he answered haltingly.

"Before that?"

He tried to think.

"Now and then the idea came to me. It would sometimes come and go, just like sometimes I would think that the most wonderful way to die would be as a martyr. But I can't say for how long."

"Danny, I knew it. That explains why the germ of destruction is so strong in you. It's your temptation. God has given you that kind of a tendency, and He has given you the character to have loyalty and stick-to-itiveness to counteract it. The reason is because He has singled you out as a boy to receive the call."

She was sure a smart nun. She knew more about him than he knew himself.

"Have you made up your mind, Danny?"

"Well . . . No, not exactly."

He lowered his head and scraped his feet on the dais.

"Danny, I want you to know that I'm your friend. You don't want to look at me just as the teacher who makes you do homework and sometimes has to punish you. You must feel that I am a real friend of yours."

No nun had ever talked to him like this. But then no teacher had ever been as wonderful as Sister Magdalen.

"Danny, I am certain you have a vocation."

Outside, the sun had gone down. From the street, faint echoes of children at play could be heard.

"Your grandmother has money, and she can put you through the schooling to be a priest. That won't be a handicap to you as it would be to some boys."

What gave her that idea? But then he couldn't say it really wasn't so, because he'd like it thought that his folks had a lot of money.

"You have all the qualities needed for a priest. As a priest a boy like you should have a wonderful career open to him. Danny, keep this in mind. God needs boys like you. The Church needs boys like you."

He hated to think of all the dreams he'd have to give up if he became a priest.

"And you were right by instinct in not making up your mind too soon. But I do want you to think this over. We will talk about it again, and we'll talk like two friends, not merely as teacher and pupil."

It was rapidly growing dark. The light seeping through the window was getting faint. Danny glanced off. The sky seemed sad. Life suddenly seemed sad to him.

"But, goodness, it's getting late. I have to go over to the convent. I have this stack of papers to correct," she said, pointing to a large, neatly arranged pile of papers on her desk.

She picked up her papers and books and got to her feet. She towered over him. Her beads rattled as she crossed the room.

"Are you playing football these days, Danny?" she asked, walking down the back stairs with him.

"Sometimes, Sister, but not a lot."

"You like baseball better, don't you?"

"Yes, Sister."

He walked with her across a short stretch of sidewalk from the high stairs of the school building to the back door of the yellow brick convent which faced on Indiana Avenue. It stood at the end of the large schoolyard.

"Now, Danny, you think over what I said—carefully. And you better run along."

"Yes, Sister. And goodbye, Sister."

She smiled at him. The convent door closed. He suddenly felt very much alone. His feelings were so mixed up and confused that he was hardly able to have any thoughts. He walked by the side of the convent and out the gate of the iron picket fence.

4

I

Danny sat at the supper table, moody and quiet. He had a secret from Mother, Uncle Ned, and his sister, Little Margaret. He felt set off, not only from them, but from everyone he knew—except from Sister.

"Mud, I can tell you something now," Uncle Ned said; he sat in Uncle Al's place at the head of the table.

"What's that you say, Ned?" Mrs. O'Flaherty asked.

"Al's all right. He didn't go away. He had to go to the hospital and he was operated on for appendicitis today, but he's come through it all right. There's no need to worry."

Danny, Little Margaret, and Mrs. O'Flaherty all turned toward Ned, shocked and frightened. Mrs. O'Flaherty looked stunned. She kept her eyes on Ned and suddenly she blessed herself. Danny thought of how he had often read in the newspapers about people dying of appendicitis. He said a silent prayer, asking God to spare Uncle Al.

"Mother, Al's all right. Don't be upset. There's no cause for worry," Ned said.

She stared at her son, bewildered.

"Come on, eat your supper," Ned urged.

"I knew he wasn't himself, poor boy," Mrs. O'Flaherty said faintly.

"Mother!" Ned began, annoyed. "Mother, will you please not start hanging crepe. I tell you he's all right."

Mrs. O'Flaherty didn't listen. Her eyes welled up with tears.

"Merciful God, what will we all do now?" she exclaimed, folding her hands together prayerfully and raising her tear-filled eyes to the ceiling.

Ned gazed helplessly at his mother.

"Come and eat your supper, Mud. Al's all right and there's nothing to worry about," he said, leaning over and patting her on the shoulder.

“Are you sure my son is all right?”

“Yes, he is. Now please eat your supper.”

“When can I see him? Take me to him.”

“Please eat your supper before it gets cold. I’ll take you tomorrow or the day after.”

A gloomy silence pervaded the room.

“Mother, don’t cry,” Little Margaret said; she was a skinny, lanky girl.

“For God’s sake, do we have to turn our home into a funeral parlor?” Ned said, leaving the table.

He returned almost immediately. The supper proceeded mournfully. The old lady couldn’t eat. She gazed from one to the other, almost like a hurt animal.

II

“Peg! Peg! Ask Ned about Al,” Mrs. O’Flaherty cried out excitedly when Margaret came home at about nine-thirty.

“Why, what’s the matter?”

Ned immediately rushed to Margaret. He saw that she was apprehensive.

“Tell me what’s happened to Al?” Margaret asked, anxious.

“He’s in the hospital,” Mrs. O’Flaherty said.

“Oh, God!” Margaret exclaimed.

“Peg, be calm. Al’s perfectly all right. He went to the hospital today,” Ned began in a reassuring voice.

“Good God, why must this happen to me!” she bemoaned.

“He was operated on for appendicitis and he’s doing well and out of danger,” Ned said.

“Why didn’t he tell me? Why didn’t you tell me? When did it happen? Scaring the life out of me this way! I have enough on my mind without this,” Margaret said rapidly, a threatening hysteria in her voice.

“Al wouldn’t let me. I didn’t think he should have let it be done, and I tried to get him not to, but he wouldn’t listen to me. He made me promise not to tell you. Well, thank the Lord, he’s out of danger,” Ned said.

“When can we see him?” asked Margaret.

“In a day or so,” Ned said.

III

Danny sat at the table in the back parlor, studying his Cathedral’s *History of the United States.* But he couldn’t keep his mind on the book. It was a warning from God. This was the way God must have taken to warn him, and now if he didn’t answer the call, God was letting him know that He might really punish him.

Now if he didn't, he was sure God would make him be such a lousy ballplayer he couldn't ever get in the big leagues.

And suppose Uncle Al should die? No one in this house had died since his Aunt Louise had, down on Calumet in 1911 before he had started to school. But Uncle Al might. Sometimes when people were supposed to be getting better, they weren't at all, but were getting worse, and they died.

He got up and walked to the parlor window and looked out at the dark park. It made him feel more sad. He could hear the wind. He turned from the window.

Oh, God, please have Uncle Al not die, please have him live.

IV

Margaret sat in her bedroom crying. She really didn't know why. She just felt like crying. Life was sad, and she was sad, and no person on earth had to live a sadder life than she.

If Al died, everything would be thrown on her poor shoulders. Well, she would carry the cross on her poor weak back. But it wasn't fair. Ned would have to help her.

Would she never be happy? Here she was, already over thirty, getting old, and she had never been happy.

Oh, if she could only see Lorry Robinson! Her Lorry!

She'd write him another letter. He would see the heartfelt agony of her soul in her letter and answer her. In tears, she got out pen and paper and tried to write.

V

Ned was lying down in the front bedroom, tired. He hadn't realized that he'd been under such a heavy strain. He'd been more worried than he'd realized. And then the waiting in the hospital. Now that it was over and Al seemed out of danger, he was tired. And of course, this end of it had to be his. He always got the dirty end of the stick. Poor Mother didn't understand what it all meant, and Peg was so damned nervous. God, he hoped that this business wouldn't set her off again on another one of her drunks. That'd be the last straw. But he mustn't even have such thoughts. He lay there, sending good thoughts out into the universe to make everything come out harmoniously and happily, and soon he was asleep.

VI

Lizz paid the O'Flahertys a surprise visit around ten o'clock. She wore her black mourning hat and veil, a shabby coat, and a dirty apron.

"Al is in the hospital," Mrs. O'Flaherty said.

"Blessed Mother of God!" Lizz exclaimed in astonishment.

She got down on her knees, blessed herself, and prayed with eyes closed and her face shining with piety. Liberty, the Airedale dog, approached and sniffed at her. She pushed the dog away and continued praying.

"Oh, my poor brother, what's happened to him?" she asked, getting off her knees.

"What do they call it, apprendicitis?"

"Blessed Sacred Heart of the Saviour!"

Mrs. O'Flaherty sat by the kitchen table, cried, wiped her eyes with her gingham apron.

"Hello, Lizz," Margaret said, coming out to the kitchen in her kimono; her eyes were red.

The dog looked bewilderedly from one woman to the other.

"My poor baby sister," Lizz said, clutching Margaret.

"Did Mother tell you?" Margaret asked, removing herself from Lizz's embrace.

"Peg, mark my words! Don't trust those doctors and hospitals. They want you to die there so they can cut you open and let the medical students look at your insides," Lizz said.

"Peg, are you sure me son is all right?" Mrs. O'Flaherty cut in.

"Yes, Mother. I talked with Mike Geraghty on the telephone, and he assured me there was no need to worry."

"I must go to church the first thing tomorrow and say a Stations of the Cross," Lizz said.

"Pray for me, too, Lizz," Margaret said.

"I never let a visit to the Blessed Sacrament go but that I pray for my darling, lovely, baby sister."

"Liz, you're so good. Next payday I'll give you a little something for you and the children."

Ned suddenly appeared in the kitchen doorway.

"Don't you have to be going home and putting your kids to bed? Isn't it pretty late to be leaving them alone?" he said.

"My Bill is with them," Lizz said. She turned to her mother. "Mother, appendicitis put Tim Curtin under the ground, poor man. I went to the wake and I told his poor wife, Sadie, I said, 'Sadie, they butchered your Tim. Sue them!

My man's cousin, Joe O'Reilley, is a big lawyer for the breweries and he'll handle your case for nothing. Sue them!'"

"Say, who asked you over here?" Ned said, interrupting Lizz.

"The law gives me the right to see my mother. And our Lord says: *Honor thy father and thy mother.*"

"Well, honor her with more pleasant thoughts. There's enough sorrow in the world without you coming over here late at night to give us your line of gab."

"Say, you, who died and made you boss?" Lizz cried out.

Danny and Little Margaret came out to the kitchen.

"What do you want?" Ned asked them.

They looked at their uncle.

"If you touch my children, I'll call the police," Lizz yelled.

"Go on and do your homework and go to bed," Ned said, shuttling the two children out of the kitchen.

"Ned, I have to be to work at the hotel at seven in the morning. Let's not have any trouble," Margaret said.

"All I'm doing is asking her to cut out hanging crepe."

"You're not going to insult me, a decent woman, a mother," Lizz yelled.

"Nobody's insulting you. I'm only asking you not to talk the way you do. Don't you ever think of sunshine and happiness?"

"Lizz, when did you say Timmy Curtin died of the appendix?" Mrs. O'Flaherty asked.

"See, Peg, now she's got Mud going."

"Mother, who did he get his bossiness from? He didn't get it from you or my father," Lizz said.

The dog alertly watched Lizz.

"Go on home, you crepe-hanging scarecrow. You give me a pain in the ass," Ned shouted at Lizz.

"Lizz!" Margaret entreated as Lizz advanced a step toward Ned.

"Now go ahead! Dig graves in the back yard! Put headstones all over the kitchen," Ned said.

"Ah, Ned, let her talk," Mrs. O'Flaherty said.

Danny and Little Margaret stood frightened at the kitchen door.

"Get out of here!" Ned yelled, taking a step toward Lizz.

"Don't hit her, Ned," Margaret pleaded.

"Don't hit my Mama!" Little Margaret shrieked.

"If you so much as lay a hand on me, Ned O'Flaherty, I'll bring a wagonload of men from the express company out here after you. They'll turn you into hamburger."

"Go home and wash your face," Ned said, stamping out of the kitchen.

"Mother, when he was little, I used to take him out for a walk and he'd piss in his pants," Lizz said.

She put on her hat and veil crookedly. She got into her coat.

"Mother, I'm never coming here again. If you want to see me, you come to my house where we are civilized and never insult our guests," she said.

Sticking her nose in the air, she marched majestically out of the kitchen.

"Jesus, Mary and Joseph, what will me poor son do on this misfortunate night!" Mrs. O'Flaherty exclaimed.

The Airedale looked from Mrs. O'Flaherty to Margaret. Then she went and lay down by the radiator near the stove.

VII

"Good morning, Mud," Ned said, coming out to the kitchen in a purple bathrobe.

"Ned, when you go see Al this afternoon, tell him that me and Peg and the children are coming to see him tonight."

"I will, Mud."

Ned got a cup of coffee and sat down at the kitchen table. Liberty came over to him and sniffed. She sat on her haunches and looked at him with sad, begging eyes.

"Ah, Lib, you're a good dog, a good dog," he said, petting her.

"Don't be speaking to her. I'm mad at her," Mrs. O'Flaherty said.

"Why, Mother? She's only a poor dumb beast."

"She was out running with the tinkers again in the alley and she'll be having more pups again when her time comes."

"Cripes, won't anybody ever watch the dog! What the hell's the matter with Danny? Didn't he take her out today?"

"That he did. But she was after me to go out again, so I let her, and there she was with the tinkers. I ran out with the broom and shooed them off her but it was too late."

"Well, Mud, don't blame the poor dog."

"That beast is the shame of the neighborhood."

The dog went over to the old lady.

"Get away from me, you scamp!" Mrs. O'Flaherty yelled.

The dog dejectedly moved away and returned to sit before Ned. He gave her a chunk of bread and patted her head.

"Ah, Ned, the poor dumb beast knows I'm mad at her."

"Oh, say, Mud, I forgot to tell you. I saw Lizz on the street yesterday, and she wouldn't speak to me because of what happened here last week. You should have seen her. She looked like a washer woman or something."

“Ned, there goes that Mr. Hancock on the first floor. Sure he doesn’t like the dog or the boys to be playing ball in the back yard.”

“He and his wife seem very nice and quiet, decent.”

“Well they might be, and him only a guard on the elevated. Sure I don’t know how he can afford to live in as fine a building as this. Complaining about our poor dog when the poor beast wouldn’t hurt a flea, let alone that little girl of his. There he goes to work now, the long-legged Protestant drink of water.”

Mrs. O’Flaherty turned from the window in the kitchen door.

Ned finished his coffee and left the kitchen.

VIII

Ned dipped his finger in the tub to be sure that the temperature was right. Then took off his pajamas and bathrobe, lit a cigarette, and got in the tub, sinking his soft white flesh under the water and lying there in sensuous enjoyment. He soaked himself comfortably, and a dreamy, absorbed look came upon his face.

He thanked the Lord that the war would soon be over. Now there was going to be peace on earth. He didn’t want to kill. He wanted to love thy neighbor as thyself. And if the war went on, they might draft him. He was lucky to have been just over the age for the first draft. Well, if they took him now, he wouldn’t go. He would say that he believed in live and let live. If they said he had to go, he would ask them if they were Christians or barbarians, and what right had they to demand that a Christian murder somebody he never saw before and had nothing against? If they said anything more to him, he’d ask them if they knew the Fifth Commandment, *Thou shalt not kill.* He made a face of disgust. What right had they to make him murder? Hell, he didn’t like the pigheaded Germans and their Kaiser in his funny steel hat. He was glad that they weren’t winning the war. But Christ forgave every man. You even had to forgive the German for his pigheadedness.

He ought to send out good thoughts into the world to help the cause of peace. He concentrated and told himself:

I am sending out good thoughts to have peace in the world.

I am sending out good thoughts to have peace in the world.

I am sending out good thoughts to have peace in the world.

I am sending out good thoughts to have peace in the world.

I am sending out good thoughts to have peace in the world.

Amen!

He squashed his butt in an ash tray by the side of the tub.

What he couldn’t understand was why there were so few people in the world who didn’t know the simple key to Goodness and Happiness. The Power of the Wish was Almighty when it was joined with Faith. Wish, Have Faith, Send Your

Thoughts Out Into the Cosmos, and you would get what you wanted if it was Good.

Ask, and it shall be given you;

Knock, and it shall be opened unto you.

The water had gotten a trifle cool. He reached forward and turned on the hot-water faucet for a moment. When the water again was right, he sank back.

He lifted up one leg and admired his slender thigh. He set it back in the water.

Here, right now in the bathtub, he had performed an action of faith that would accomplish more than a lot of the long-winded talk of statesmen and generals and all these Napoleons and Kaisers in the world. What damned fools they had all been!

Jesus had come into the world to make men good and to make them happy. And cripes, look at the damned fools!

He was comfortable, warm. He wished he didn't have to go to the damned hospital this afternoon. Well, no use having unpleasant thoughts now. Time enough to think of the hospital when he was there.

He lay in the tub a half hour before he washed himself. Then he lay back and let the cold water run until the water was good and cold so as to close his pores. He got out of the tub and slowly rubbed himself dry. He fiddled around with the water in the sink until it was right for him to shave. Using a safety razor, he took his time shaving. Almost coddlingly, he ran his hands over his smooth cheeks. He held a hot, and then a cold, washrag to his face, and after that he rubbed a shaving lotion on his cheeks. He stood back from the mirror and studied his face.

Catherine thought he was handsome.

He rubbed talcum powder on his cheeks. He put on his bathrobe again and left the bathroom.

IX

Ned dallied getting on his underwear, socks, shoes, shirt and trousers. He studied his ties to find one that would go with his pink silk shirt. He selected a brown knit tie and tied it meticulously. He leaned forward close to the dresser mirror and observed the knot he had made. He drew back against the bed and studied the knot from that distance.

He could hear his mother talking in the kitchen with Danny and Little Margaret, who were home for their lunch.

He wiped off his shoes with a shoe cloth. He brushed his trousers with a whisk broom, and then applied it to his vest and coat. He put on his vest and coat, fiddled around with his arms and shoulders and then with his shirt cuffs.

He selected a pure white linen handkerchief and folded it attractively before placing it in his suit-coat pocket. He put on his spats, and again ran a shoe cloth over his shoes.

He looked at himself in the mirror again. He bent forward and gave a last straightening tug at his tie. He took his derby hat out of a hatbox and brushed it with a stiff brush. He put it on at an angle, and twice adjusted that angle. He got out his top coat and, holding it over his arm, went to study himself before the parlor mirror. He approached and retreated from the mirror in order to see himself at different distances. He put on his top coat, buttoned it, and again studied himself in the mirror. Now he was ready to leave.

He called goodbye and left by the front door. It was twenty minutes to one when he stepped onto the sidewalk of South Park Avenue.

X

Al was propped up in bed. He was a trifle pale, but he did not look ill. He was reading a thick book when Ned came in and he set it on the table beside him.

"Oh, hello, Ned. I'm glad you came. How's everyone at home?"

"They're all fine and dandy. Fine and Dandy, Al. How are you feeling?"

"Fine, Ned. Good. I'll be getting out of here soon. Hell, this was a very bad time to get this. The fall, with business good, but then, it's over with now, thank the Lord. Mike was around to see me. He says I'm in good shape."

"That's good. I have to be getting back on the road, too. I'm leaving next week."

"Well, here's a little wish from the fairy wishing-ring that you knock 'em dead with sales, Ned."

"Thanks, Al. But I'd sell better if that goddamn fool I'm working for, Tommy Grayson, had some horse sense and would listen to me."

"Ned, you can't tell the boss anything. You know that by now."

"I never tell. That's not good psychology. I suggest. There's a difference between telling a man and suggesting to him. You never want to tell. You always want to suggest."

He sat down by the bed and lit a cigarette. He carefully pulled his trousers up at the knees.

"You have something there, Ned. That's a very good idea."

"Sure it is. It's psychology. But say, Al, what's the book you were reading when I came in?"

"Boswell's *Life of Samuel Johnson*," Al answered proudly.

"What the hell?" Ned exclaimed, wrinkling up his brows in a frown.

"Have you ever read it?"

"Me, read a book that long! What do you take me for, one of those long-haired, absent-minded professors who has to read Greek and sputter out something in long Latin words that you can say quickly in English?"

"It's a fine book, a classic," Al said.

"Classic in a pig's eye. Al, what the hell do you want to be reading a book that long for? Cripes, you'll sprain your wrist or get muscle-bound holding it."

"It's a good book, Ned, a classic. I'm reading it because of its mellifluous style."

"What's that you said?" Ned asked, reaching over and dumping cigarette ashes in a wastebasket.

"I like reading it because of its mellifluous style."

"That's a hot sketch. What dictionary have you been chewing on for breakfast?"

"What's wrong with that? I said I like it for its mellifluous style."

They frowned at one another. Ned squashed his cigarette and dropped it in the wastebasket.

"The dog is going to get puppies again. Mother, like a damned fool, let her out after Danny went to school and she was with the dogs again."

"Christ sake!"

"Al, you be careful. Don't excite yourself."

"That's right. But goddamn it, Ned, it's such a damned nuisance."

"You should kick. You were away when she had the last batch, and where in the devil does she have them? Right under my bed. I had to sleep in a room smelling like the stockyards."

"Well, we'll have to drown them when they come."

"You can't do that."

"We can't keep them, can we?"

"We can sell them."

"Who the hell wants to buy mongrel pups?"

"Lots of people might. If we can't sell them, we'll give them away. It's cruel to kill them."

"Aw, rats on that stuff."

"What do you mean, rats on it? Wanting to kill little dogs deliberately. Don't you think they want to live as well as you? Haven't they got as much right to live as you or me?"

There was a pause.

"Peg, Mother and the kids are coming to see you tonight," Ned said.

"Good. And is Peg behaving?"

"She's all right. Only do you know, she's still telephoning the hotel about that goddamned Robinson?"

"She is?"

"Yes, I heard her a couple of times. She didn't know I heard her. It seems to me she could forget him."

"I hope she doesn't go back seeing him."

"What I can't understand, Al, is why she wants to chase after him. He doesn't want to see her. Cripes, you'd think our sister would have some dignity and decency."

Al's face clouded. He didn't know what to say.

"We'll have to do some wishing or something about that matter," he finally said.

"Wishing, hell, if I saw that guy, I'd tell him something besides wishes. You're damned right, I would."

Al said nothing. He was thoughtful.

"Well, since everything is going better now, let's hope for the best," he said moodily.

They started talking about shoes, lasts, shoe ads, and the shoe business.

XI

Ned was relieved when he was able to leave the hospital. The knowledge that so many people were in the rooms suffering, the smell of medicine and disinfectants, everything about a hospital depressed him.

Outside, he drew a deep breath. He lit a cigarette. It was getting dark, and the day was gone.

Some day, would he be in a hospital, dying, dying of cancer, t.b., of some dreadful disease? Suppose some day he had to be operated on, butchered? How would he feel when he was put under? What would his thoughts be? But no use having such unpleasant thoughts now. As long as a man was well and in good health, he had death conquered.

He walked from the hospital, through a deteriorated section inhabited by Negroes. He saw old buildings that once had been the mansions of the rich. Now it was all slums. Dirty Negro children played in the street. Negro men and women passing him or standing on corners and in doorways looked poor and shabby. Because he was well-dressed and white, he was self-conscious. He quickened his pace.

He couldn't get the thought of death out of his mind. Some day he would be dead. Some day everyone he loved would be dead. Mud would die. She was old. How many times had he not felt that this year would be her last. Now winter was coming soon. She might catch a cold, and it might turn into pneumonia. Then off she would go. There already had been a serious flu epidemic this fall. Schools and theaters had even been closed because of it, and you were no longer allowed to smoke on the front platform of the street cars. He remembered his father. The old man had lain in the same hospital he'd just visited, dying of cancer, dying in agony. God, think of it. It was sad. It was ugly. Why was he even letting himself dwell on it?

He walked on sprucely, and he remembered Mildred, his wife, as she lay dying. That was two years ago. To watch a loved one pass away as he had had to watch Mildred, trying to be cheerful, pretending that he wasn't worried and that his heart wasn't being torn out of him! The day before she had died he had sat by her bedside and talked of how they would go away on a vacation as soon as she got well. For years she had been in failing health. He had lived those years with sickness and with a half-crippled woman. And people couldn't understand why he didn't like to hear talk about death.

He turned onto Twenty-second Street, walked to the El station, bought a newspaper, and climbed the elevated steps to go home. He glanced at the headlines while he waited for his train. Peace was expected. That was something to thank God for.

XII

Ned and Danny were playing checkers, for a nickel a game.

"Well, Dan, you got me again," Ned said.

Danny smiled.

"Yes, it's your game."

Ned gave Danny another nickel, and then laid five cents by the board. They set up the checkers and Ned moved. Ned looked at Danny. Just a boy. Sometimes he had to be called to turn, but a damned good kid, young and innocent. He wasn't touched by life, by the sadness of life.

Danny moved.

"Well, you think you're going to beat me with the old army game now?" Ned said, watching the pattern of movements Danny was initiating at the start of the game.

Ned moved. He noticed Danny's grin. A happy boy! Boyhood, the happiest time of one's life. Crowning a king for Danny, he tried to remember his own boyhood. He looked at Danny. How did Danny feel? A man often thought of that. How do kids feel? He couldn't remember enough of how he himself used to feel to know how a kid felt. And the world had changed since he was a kid. How they used to sneak in to prize fights. And earlier, running and playing ball and playing tricks over on Twelfth Street when they had lived in Saint Ignatius parish.

"Move, your turn, Uncle Ned."

"Oh, I thought it was your turn," Ned said.

He studied the board.

"Well, I guess you got me again," Ned said.

Danny grinned. He had won five out of eight games from his uncle. He had a composition book in which he kept all his records, his batting and fielding averages for all the ball games in which he played, the times he boxed and wrestled, the games of checkers he played, his performances in every kind of sport in which he participated. He went to his bedroom, got out his book, and marked down the results of his checker games with Uncle Ned.

XIII

"Danny, will you help me do my arithmetic homework?" Little Margaret asked plaintively.

"I got my own to do," Danny answered peevishly.

"Oh, please, Danny? It won't take you long," she begged in a loud, whining voice.

"What the hell's the matter with you?" Uncle Ned asked, coming out of his bedroom.

"Nothing," Danny said.

"Well, why don't you help your sister?"

"Why can't she do her own?"

"It's too hard. You're good in arithmetic and you had all this, and I'm not good in arithmetic."

"You can be out fooling around with a goddamned football or something, and you can't come home, go to the store for your grandmother, and help your sister with her homework. Cripes, what kind of a guy are you?" Ned said.

"She's lazy and doesn't want to do her own work," Danny said.

"Go ahead and help her!" Ned commanded.

"I can't. I got to do my own," Danny pouted, turning to his own arithmetic lesson.

"Then don't. I'll fix you. If I was Roslyn Hayes and asked you to do it, you'd fall over your neck backward to help me," Little Margaret said.

"I wouldn't. I don't care about her, see!"

"You damned pup, I told you to help your sister!"

Danny looked down at his arithmetic.

"Now, goddamn it, don't make me tell you to do it again!" Ned said, grabbing Danny's arithmetic and throwing it on the floor.

Danny trembled. Tears came against his will.

"Go ahead!"

"These problems. They'll be easy for you," she said, pointing out the lesson.

Danny wiped his eyes. He sniffled.

"I'm gonna tell Uncle Al."

"And I'll tell him plenty more," Ned said. Ned looked down at them. "Now do it and quit this crabbing."

Sobbing, crying, but trying not to, Danny worked out the problems in his sister's homework lesson. He writhed inside of himself with a sense of the injustice he felt had been done to him.

"I didn't mean to get you in trouble, Danny. Only, gee, I couldn't do the lesson by myself. It was too hard," Little Margaret said.

"Don't talk to me."

Danny went to his bedroom. He was still filled with shame, with the sense of a lack of manliness because he had cried. When he was a man nobody would order him around. He'd get even for a lot of things when he was a man.

XIV

"Mud, I just got time to catch the last movie down the street," Ned said, coming out into the kitchen where Mrs. O'Flaherty and Margaret sat talking.

"All right, Ned."

He went to the front and fiddled around for about twenty minutes getting ready to go out to the movie. He felt sorry for the way he had talked to his nephew, but it was so little for Danny to do. Looking at himself in the mirror, he suddenly became nostalgic and wished that he were a boy again. Men got old and died. But he had to auto-suggest and psychologize himself out of dark thoughts. It was the hospital, that was what it was. But a man had to attain self-mastery over the spirit. He took a final look at himself, put on his derby and left.

XV

"Peg, do you think he's going out to see a woman?" Mrs. O'Flaherty asked when she heard Ned go out.

"It would be good for him if he did. I don't know why he doesn't get married again," Margaret answered curtly.

"If he does, I'll tan the hide off him."

"He ought to get married. He's like an old maid around here."

"Peg, I swear that he's going out to see a woman. That one is always calling him up, you know."

"I wish he would get married."

"Peg, there was a man in the old country, by the name of Podgeen McNamara. And what does he do but meet a girl one market day. He lived by the side of a road near a hill, and his mother told him he couldn't marry this girl. And he did, and when his mother told him he shouldn't, he cursed his poor old mother. And do you know what happened, Peg? The tongue fell out of his mouth and went into the fire and burned, and Podgeen never was able to utter another word as long as he lived. Let the boy that marries against his mother beware."

"Mother, don't talk that old Irish stuff to me. Let him marry and good riddance."

XVI

Ned walked over to the theater at Fifty-eighth and Prairie. It was windy. He felt it was a ghosty night. Too bad he wasn't seeing Catherine tonight, but she was with a girl friend. He was lonely. Here he was already a man of over thirty. Mildred was dead. Father was dead. This windy night, bringing back these memories. These ghosts. Yes, he was going to see a nice cheerful moving picture and get rid of such thoughts. He walked briskly. Tomorrow was going to be a day full of sunshine. Tomorrow night he would see Catherine. No, there was nothing wrong in what he and Catherine did. It was good. When he went on the road, he was going to have lots of business. Life was good, and he was going to dwell on the goodness of life.

5

I

Danny couldn't fall asleep tonight. It used to be that he would go to bed and think about Roslyn and baseball and hardly a minute would pass before he would be asleep. Lying in the darkness with the bed so comfortable and nothing to distract him, he found it easier to make himself believe that what he was thinking about as happening was really happening. Every night, too, he told himself that he wanted to dream about Roslyn and baseball when he fell asleep. But he almost never did. When he lay in bed imagining, he could pretend what he wanted to. But when he dreamed, that wasn't so. But here he was letting his mind wander instead of keeping his promise to God.

He had promised God and the Blessed Virgin that every night before he fell asleep he would try to say a decade of the Rosary, offering it to God in thanks for Uncle Al's recovery from the operation. He reeled off Hail Marys, trying to keep his mind on God as he prayed. The image of God suddenly seemed to vanish from his mind, and without realizing it he had stopped praying. He thought of how Uncle Ned had often told him that if you really wanted something, all you had to do to get it was to wish for it. You kept wishing for what you wanted again and again, and you told yourself that you were going to get it. If you had faith, your wishes came true. He'd tried this and it had worked. Earlier this year he had gotten up one morning and he'd wished that before the week was over he would talk to Roslyn and kiss her. That sounded crazy and impossible, because when she would hardly even recognize that he was alive, how could he expect to kiss her? But that very morning, her cousin, Glenn, had said he was having a party on Friday night. And on the day of the party he'd gone to Glenn's house after school and she was there, wearing the green sweater she always wore. They'd talked about the party, and he'd told her how he took his dog, Liberty, out to the park, and how Liberty ran through the bushes behind the tennis courts and always found tennis balls. He never had to buy tennis balls with his dog. And she'd said she wished he'd have his dog get her some tennis balls, and he'd said some day he would.

Hail Mary, full of Grace! the Lord is with thee; blessed art thou amongst women; and blessed is the fruit of thy womb, Jesus. Holy Mary, Mother of God, pray for us sinners, now and at the hour of our death. Amen.

He began tossing and kicking in bed. He twisted from one side to the other, and repeated Hail Marys. When they'd played post office at the party hardly any of the girls had called him. Every so often one of them had noticed that he wasn't being called, and then they'd call him. But she hadn't called him, not even once. Natalie O'Reedy, the prettiest girl in Saint Patrick's, had called him in the first time, but he'd felt that she was just taking pity on him. He'd kissed her cheek, and then stood alone, wondering what girl to call. He'd felt that what he should do was not call Roslyn until she called on him, and that way to show her that if she didn't like him, then he didn't care and ish kabbible. But he'd called her just the same. She'd come into the room, held her cheek up, let him kiss her, and said not a word.

Yes, he'd felt as if he didn't belong at the party, and he'd told himself that he belonged on the ball diamond. Well, he was right. That stuff wasn't for him. At the party, he had felt so out of place, not even knowing what to do with his hands, that he'd pretended he had a headache. That got him more attention than anything else that happened at the party. Glenn's mother had given him aspirin, and every so often someone had asked him if his headache was gone. But she hadn't even asked him that much. If anything proved that she didn't give a darn about him, didn't that?

Hail Mary, full of grace. . . .

Maybe the fact that he didn't get along with girls, and was so bashful in their presence, and didn't know what to say to them or how to act, maybe that all proved that he had the call. Other kids were so different from him. They never seemed to have any trouble talking to girls. Glenn, Dick, Billie, Ralph, all the gang could dance and think up funny things that made girls laugh, but not him. He didn't even get along with kids too well. He never had. Many times he felt that he didn't really belong with them, and that they didn't accept him as one of the gang the same way they accepted others.

He turned over on his side. He wasn't sleepy. And here he was doing everything except keep his promise to God and the Blessed Virgin.

He made an effort of will and forced himself to finish his decade of the Rosary. He tossed in bed until he fell asleep.

II

Feeling dopey, Danny came out to the kitchen. He had had terrible dreams that he couldn't remember except that they were awful.

"Did you sleep sound, Son?" his grandmother asked, already preparing his breakfast.

"Uh huh!" he exclaimed listlessly. "Isn't Little Margaret up yet?"

"Ah, let her sleep."

"She has to go to school. How is she ever going to graduate if she always stalls to get out of going to school?"

"Why in the name of God should a girl be educated? I never had any education."

"But, Mother, times are different, and girls should be educated."

"Here, have your breakfast, and be damned to the girls," she said, putting his eggs before him.

As he ate breakfast, he asked himself if his terrible dreams last night were a temptation. And if he overcame temptation, maybe he would be the first American saint. After he died, he might be Saint Daniel O'Neill of Chicago. Saint Ignatius Loyola. Saint Patrick. Saint James. Saint Peter. Saint Anselm. Saint Jude. Saint Augustine. Saint Daniel O'Neill of Chicago. That didn't sound right, thinking of becoming a saint when he had a bad confession on his conscience. That had made every confession he had ever made, and every time he had ever gone to Holy Communion, a sacrilege. But it would be wonderful to be a saint. Of course, nowadays saints didn't become martyrs for the Church as they did when the pagan Romans had them eaten by the lions in the amphitheater. Nowadays it was harder to become a saint. Why should he feel his destiny maybe was to be Saint Daniel O'Neill of Chicago instead of a greater baseball player than Eddie Collins or Ty Cobb?

But it was nerve of him to have such thoughts. He well knew that his own sins and his own weaknesses were like some terrible weight crushing his soul in mud. He could imagine his guardian angel on his right side sad and disappointed, looking at him with an accusation in each eye, while the devil, who was his bad angel on his left side, danced and laughed and grinned at the guardian angel.

He finished breakfast and dreamily washed and dressed.

He took Liberty down in the yard, and stood by the steps watching her while she gamboled about, sniffed, and did her job. It was a sharp, clear morning, and the sun was breaking through the morning mist. He breathed deeply and waited. Suppose he should take Liberty out and he should see Roslyn, and just then Liberty would have to do something? What would he do? He would be so darned ashamed. The thought of this made him ashamed of life and of his body, ashamed of the fact that he had to go to the bathroom, and that girls had to also. Maybe he should be a priest. But even priests had to.

The dog ran around. He got bored and called her. She followed him upstairs.

He set out for school, with his strapped books over his shoulder. He was deliberately not going to school by way of South Park and Sixty-first Street, as he so often did when he hoped to see Roslyn. She was his temptation. If he was going to be a priest, he had to forget all his daydreams about some day marrying her. And he was going to conquer his temptation. He was going to drive her out of his mind, forget her. If she really cared about him, it would serve her right. He walked down to Fifty-ninth and Calumet and then over toward Indiana Avenue.

If he became a priest, and then maybe a monsignor, and then maybe a bishop, and then maybe an archbishop, and then maybe a cardinal, he would be repaid and repaid a hundredfold in Heaven for having resisted and won out over his temptations in this world. And he had made a beginning this morning by going to school this way instead of her way.

He drooped along to school.

III

It was a little after ten, and Dick Buckford was at the blackboard working problems in arithmetic. The pupils heard an unusual ringing of the bell in the hallway and looked at one another, surprised.

"Why, I wonder what the matter is?" Sister Magdalen said from her dais, as surprised as were her pupils.

She hurried out of the room, her robes swishing and her beads rattling as she walked.

"The Germans are coming," Danny called out.

"Well, take your big shoes off quick and let us all get in your gunboats to fight 'em, O'Neill," Glenn called back, and there was much laughter.

Dick Buckford aimed an eraser at Fat Malloy, but missed him; Fat stuck his tongue out.

Sister Magdalen reappeared. The boys quieted down immediately.

"Boys, the war is over," she said, smiling.

"Sister, did we lick the Germans?" Fat Malloy yelled.

Her face was all smiles. She shook her head affirmatively.

"Hurrah for our side!" Fat called out.

Suddenly and spontaneously, they yelled and shouted and cheered. The nun raised her hand for silence.

"There will be no more school today. You can all go home now," she said.

They broke into cheers. They rushed pell-mell into the dressing room for their hats and coats, shouting, pounding one another on the back, and making as much noise as they pleased. Sister beamed as she watched them from her desk. They rushed out of the room, and, joining the children from other classes, they jumped and pushed one another down the stairs. Outside, Danny started going down the rear stone steps two at a time. He landed on the edge of a step, lost his balance, tripped, and sprawled down on his face. He felt a burning pain around his lips.

"Yuh goof!" Fat Malloy yelled.

"You cut your lip, Drippy," Billie Morris said.

Danny put a dirty handkerchief to his lip and examined it; there were blood stains.

He rushed upstairs, past noisy little kids, and bounded down a stairway to the boys' toilet. He saw his face in a dirty mirror. It was bleeding under the lower lip and it was smeared with dirt. He let water run on his dirty handkerchief and put it to his lip, and then he wiped off his face. He hurried outside, where the whole school was yelling its lungs out.

"The war's over!" Danny shouted, thumping Fat Malloy on the back.

Fat turned around, gasping for breath. He doubled up his fists and took a step forward. He saw that it was Danny. He unclenched his fists.

"Watch out what you're doin'!" he bellowed.

"The war's over!" Danny yelled at him.

They both rushed at Billie Morris.

"The war's over!" they yelled, slamming Billie so hard on the back that he went sprawling.

"Watch what you guys do!" Billie said, almost in tears as he got to his feet.

"Why?" Fat yelled.

"Well, watch yourself and who you're shoving!"

"What'll you do if I don't?" Fat asked.

"I know you can lick me, but I'll fight you if you shove me!"

"Can it!" Fat said.

"Danny, you gonna let him get away with that stuff on me?" Billie asked; Danny was gratified that Billie should turn to him this way.

"He's not gonna fight your battles for you, are you, O'Neill?" Fat asked, turning to Danny.

Just then Danny was catapulted from behind and fell on his face. He got up sore and rushed at Dick Buckford.

"Pardon me, I thought you was the Kaiser," Dick shouted, laughing and dodging as Danny swung at him.

They laughed. Danny touched his lip with his handkerchief.

"I'll kick the crap out of you!" he yelled at Dick.

"Try it on the Kaiser," Dick answered, standing off at a safe distance, prepared to run if Danny came at him.

"Come on, you guys!" Fat yelled.

They formed a gang and went around the schoolyard shoving other kids from behind. They laughed as they apologized to their victims, saying they were sorry but they thought they'd pushed the Kaiser on his ear.

IV

Walking northward along Indiana Avenue where he used to live, Danny was lonely. Now that the war was over, he wished it wasn't. He wished it would have gone on until he would have been old enough to go to France and defend Old Glory. He sang the chorus of *Over There*. He liked it the best of all the war songs he knew. Well, he certainly was glad that the Kaiser was licked. We had won the American Revolution, the War of 1812, the Mexican War, the Civil War, the Spanish American War, and now we'd won this war. He wished America had fought more wars and won them and licked every country in the world. We could, too, even England. We were the greatest country in the world. Maybe when he grew up he'd be a soldier and we'd fight the Japs and lick them, clean up the Mexican greasers, take Canada away from England, and chase Lenin and Trotsky out of Russia, and he'd be a hero in all these wars.

He passed the Methodist Church at Fifty-sixth Street. He had a thoughtful expression on his face and his hands were jammed in his pockets. He didn't know where the kids were. Mother and Uncle Ned had told him he couldn't go downtown because he might get hurt in the crowds. Everybody was going downtown and raising hell and he wasn't allowed to.

The other day, the rumors about the war being over had only been a false alarm, but today it had really ended. So everybody was celebrating all over again. Mama had come over and said Papa had gotten drunk celebrating, and they'd all talked about Papa in the kitchen, and when he tried to listen, Uncle Ned had chased him out, asking him why did he want to listen to something that didn't concern him? The other day when there was the false rumor about the armistice, he'd fallen down the back stairs at school and cut his lip and got a big scab on it. Mother asked him what did he do that for, and Uncle Ned had asked him what kind of a guy was he to go falling down stairs? Studs Lonigan and all the older guys were downtown raising hell, and he wished he was with them. It was just like last week. The elevated trains were jammed with people blowing horns and making all the noise they could, and men and women as well as kids were acting just like it was Halloween. This morning the men yelling extra papers had waked them all up, and he heard somebody from a back porch shooting off a pistol, and then the whistles started blowing and there was more noise than on New Year's Eve. They all got up and read the papers and had coffee and buns and talked, and Mother had said over and over again thank God and now the men wouldn't be killing one another. But Mother was an old woman and she didn't understand how you had to fight sometimes, and all men must want to be heroes for their country and cover themselves with glory, and if they didn't, what kind of men were they? And this morning Uncle Ned had said there shouldn't be any more killing and wars and now he hoped humanity would live by the Golden Rule. There were things that Uncle Ned didn't understand either.

And at school this morning, Sister wouldn't let them run out and yell their heads off as she had last week. She took them all down to church, and they prayed for peace, and Father Gilhooley talked to them, telling them to thank God their country won. And then they had gone out in the schoolyard and stood around the flag pole with their hats off while Dick Buckford and Billie Morris raised the flag and they all pledged allegiance to it, and then they'd gone home, and now here he was and he couldn't find the kids.

Well, he was going to see Mabel Normand in a good movie; he liked her and would never forget her in *Mickey.*

V

When Danny came out of the Michigan Theater on Garfield Boulevard, it was getting dark. He thought of the newsreel he'd seen with Woodrow Wilson reviewing American soldiers. Already, he was beginning to feel about the war the same as he felt about things that had happened in sixth grade that he wished could happen all over again, like the surprise party on Little Margaret and the birthday he had three days later. That had been in Lent, and they'd played kissing games, and when Sister Cyrilla heard about it, she'd bawled him out, and he'd talked back to her and then he got sick with a bad cold and she told him it was his punishment.

He wondered could he ever become as great a man as Woodrow Wilson? He stuck his hands in his pockets and asked himself why not? Woodrow Wilson had been a kid once, and then had he known he was going to become the greatest man in the world like he now was . . . well, the greatest next to the Pope? But to lots of kids he was just a goof. Wouldn't they laugh at him if they knew what he sometimes thought he might become when he was a man, or, anyway, what he wished he could become. Well, let them wait and just see what he would be. And he would really rather be a great baseball player than anything else, even than President of the United States like Woodrow Wilson. Gee, maybe some day kids in school would be having Woodrow Wilson's birthday off just as they now had George Washington's.

Anyway, he shouldn't feel sorry because he couldn't be a devil dog fighting at Château Thierry. What road of life offered him greater glory than that of the priesthood? He could be something better than a soldier of America. He could be a soldier of Christ.

He jumped over a railing and then back again onto the sidewalk. A voice inside kept telling him that he didn't want to be a soldier of Christ. That must be his bad angel. Even so, he knew the voice was telling him the truth. And he couldn't hide any of his thoughts from God. God knew what he was. And him the other day thinking he would be a saint.

Other kids didn't have the troubles and worries he had over his thoughts. At least they didn't act like they did. Of course he never let on that he had them either. Were other kids the same?

Well, anyway, there was one thing he was glad about. With the war over there was sure to be a baseball season next year, and all the White Sox stars like Joe Jackson and Eddie Collins would be back, and would they win the pennant! He wished it was next season already.

He started stepping on sidewalk squares and counting the number of steps he took.

6

I

Jim O'Neill waited on the corner across the street from the drugstore at Fifty-eighth and Calumet. Swaying drunkenly, he looked bleary-eyed at people who passed him.

"Well, I'll be double-damned two times over," he told himself, seeing Danny approach.

"Oh, hello, Papa," Danny said, surprised, realizing immediately that his father was drunk and growing fearful because he was always afraid of drunkenness.

"I'm glad to see you."

"I went to a movie. We didn't have school today on account of the war being over."

"Yes, Boy, the war's over and your old man is a happy man."

Danny started trying to think up an excuse that would help him get away from Papa as quickly as possible.

"Look! Look!" Jim said, pointing to a passing elevated train jammed with people who were yelling, blowing horns, and ringing cowbells.

Jim patted Danny's head gently.

"And now they won't be taking my boys, you and Bill, when you get old enough to go off and fight. Yeh, the war's over, Boy, and your old man is celebratin'."

"Jim! Jim!"

Jim watched Lizz, unkempt and in old clothes, cross from the drugstore.

"Hey, Lizz, look what I picked up!"

"Oh, my precious son, my lost sheep," Lizz exclaimed loudly.

Danny, seeing a small crowd gather and stare at them, started to get nervous and anxious.

"Mama, I have to hurry home."

"That's all right, tell the O'Flahertys you was with your old man, and then just let there be one bat out of them."

"Come on, Jim, I have to get home and cook supper."

"Sure, got to take care of the kids. You go home, and I'll walk Danny home and then come home myself."

"No, you come home with me. I talked to Mr. Wolfe. He said it would be all right for you to miss tonight and he says he hopes you'll be feeling better tomorrow."

"Lizz, I want to tell you, the hull company isn't moving freight tonight. It's movin' elbows, liftin' glasses from the bar to the mouth. Lizz, you should have seen Patsy McLaughlin lap them up. The hull company."

Danny started to edge away.

"Come on, Danny, walk with your old man," Jim said.

Danny asked himself why he hadn't come another way, say Garfield Boulevard to South Park and down. Then he wouldn't have bumped into Papa drunk. He hoped they would let him go home the back way by the alley, but Papa clutched his arm firmly and led him on past the alley.

"Lizz, why don't you go home and take care of the kids? I'll be home later."

"Yes, and have you go out to get stinking drunk at some damned saloon full of bums."

"I'm not drunk. And I'm not getting drunk. I'm just walking my son home to his grandmother's."

"Please, Mama!" Danny said, sensing that a fight was impending, right out on the street.

"When you take him home, what are you going to do?"

"What the hell's it to you?"

"Jim O'Neill, don't you dare talk to me like that," Lizz shouted.

His mother and father would disgrace him in public. Suppose one of the kids from school passed and saw it all and then told everyone at school?

"Jim O'Neill, I'll have you know that this is no way to treat a mother, a poor mother," Lizz said, halting and facing him.

"Lizz, don't be such a bad sport."

"Papa, I have to hurry home."

"See, the Boy has to get home, and you won't let him," Jim said, and Danny noticed a passing man stare at them.

Jim took Danny's arm and they walked on toward South Park Avenue.

"Boy, your old man thinks the world of every one of his kids."

Danny didn't answer.

They turned the corner, Lizz walking as if her feet ached. He was glad it was dark and they weren't seeing anyone he knew. It would be almost as bad to see kids from the neighborhood as it would be to see kids from school. He'd get ragged as much either way.

In front of the gray stone apartment building, Jim fumbled in his pocket, and then handed Danny a half dollar.

"Gee, Papa . . ."

"Never mind, take it. And come over and see your old man. Because there's this that I want you never to forget. Your old man thinks the world of every one of his kids, every damned one of you."

"Kiss Mama goodbye," Lizz said.

Danny kissed his mother perfunctorily.

"Goodbye, Mama! Goodbye, Papa!"

Relieved, he tore up the stone steps to go inside.

II

Jim walked with a slight stagger. He was in dutch with Lizz. My wife's gone to the country, hurray! He was in dutch with his wife.

After taking Danny home, he'd run away from Lizz. She'd run after him, yelling, but he'd ducked down the alley and come out a gangway. Now he was back on Fifty-ninth Street and he'd given her the slip. And he would just bet his boots that she was sore as all holy hell with him. His legs were buckling on him just a trifle. But he wasn't drunk. He was just happy. If anybody thought he was drunk, they had a lot more thinks coming. He could hold his liquor like a man. And a man wasn't happy every day in the week, not by a damned sight.

A dour fellow passed him. Jim glared. The man said nothing. Now, just let someone say something. Come to think of it, he hadn't had a fight in a long time, and he was just about due for one.

But why should he want to fight? He was just going to have a few more nips and then go home. He turned the corner of Fifty-ninth and State Street and found a saloon.

The saloon was crowded. This is what he wanted, a good saloon, a regular he-man's saloon with talk and lots of people. He edged up to the bar, frowning. He didn't know who these guys were, and he had to be on his guard in case some fellow thought himself tough. There were lots of fellows in the world who thought they were tough. Well, he'd handled guys like that, more than once.

"Whiskey and a chaser," Jim told the dumpy, bald-headed bartender, laying a coin on the bar.

Gulping down his liquor and drinking his chaser, Jim noticed the man on his right. He was tall and had dark brows. He wore a cap and a blue shirt and looked like a workingman.

After some drinks, he really liked the taste of liquor and wanted more. But he didn't want to get drunk. Just have a few drinks and feel on top of the world.

"They sure were going crazy downtown in the Loop today. It was like a madhouse. I took three hours gettin' my old nag out of the crowds. No use workin' today. Nobody worked, I guess," the fellow on his right said.

"I didn't go to work tonight myself. A war doesn't come to an end every day in the week," Jim said.

"If I was Pershing, I'd have kept right on goin' and not stopped until I was in Berlin," a fellow on Jim's left said.

"You drive a wagon?" Jim asked the fellow on his right.

"For the Cunard Hauling Company."

"I used to for the express company," Jim said, drinking.

"Them's good jobs, ain't they?"

Jim nodded.

"My name's Kramer."

"Mine's Jim O'Neill," Jim said, shaking hands with Kramer. "I think I'll have a bite," Jim said, and he wandered over to the free-lunch counter, opposite the bar up front. He grabbed slices of ham and ate them greedily. His eyes watered. He watched the line of men along the bar.

"Man, I'm telling you, Wilson's pro-British," a red-faced Irishman proclaimed.

"Ain't we fighting with England now on our side?"

"Man, what am I after telling you? I leave it to the gent on me right." The Irishman turned to a lean man. "Sir, and answer me, am I or am I not after saying that Woodrow Wilson is pro-British?"

"What if he is?"

"What if he is, be damned, and Ireland not free."

"Why did the Irish start all that shootin' in Dublin? I got a brother on the other side. Suppose a German submarine got him? Huh?"

"Sure, me name is O'Malley, and did you ever hear tell of Robert Emmet?"

"What's his batting average, Paddy?" someone yelled.

Jim went over to the group. His legs were unsteady. He signaled for another drink and paid for it.

"You don't think you're smarter than Wilson do you?" the lean fellow asked.

"O'Malley, if you Irish were free, you wouldn't know what to do. You'd be fighting with yourselves instead of the English," another fellow said.

"Time and time again I've stood by this very bar and stated me profound conviction that if Ireland wasn't divided, we'd lick John Bull," O'Malley said. He turned to the bartender. "Give me another."

"You don't like the English, huh?" Jim said, drinking.

"Sir, and what is your name?"

"O'Neill."

"Mine's O'Malley. Shake hands, O'Neill. Have a drink."

"You, too," Jim said.

"Just a minute and I will," O'Malley said, moving off.

"Where you goin', Paddy?"

"Sir, the victory of bladder over mind is inevitable," O'Malley said with gravity.

Jim smiled genially, watching O'Malley stagger to the lavatory.

III

Jim sat at a table, drinking with Kramer, O'Malley, and a crowd of others. The bar was jammed, and the saloon was noisy. In one corner a group of barroom tenors struggled with the chorus of *The Rose of No Man's Land.*

"When I get home, my old lady will raise the roof. But here I am, just the same. O'Neill, think I'd be here if it wasn't a swell gang?" Kramer said.

"My old lady's sore at me, too," Jim said, swigging a drink.

"How about your old lady, O'Malley?" Kramer asked.

"She's home knittin' and prayin', and be damned to her. Don't be interruptin' me with irrelevancies," O'Malley said, and they laughed.

"Boy, I'd like to be in France marching into Germany. I wouldn't at all mind sampling some High Dutch, Low Dutch, Middle Dutch, and just Plain Dutch nooky," a fellow named Hanrahan said.

"His mind's in a pig sty," O'Malley said.

They had another round of drinks.

Jim kept eyeing a fellow at the end of the table. He was about twenty-five, and had a wide, brutal face. His name was Cooney. Jim didn't like Cooney's voice or the way Cooney was looking at him all the time. Was the guy looking for trouble?

O'Malley sang *The Rose of Tralee.* They clapped, and several men from the bar drifted over to their table.

"Sing us another, O'Malley."

"I can't. I got a frog in me throat. Whiskey interferes with me voice, so I say to hell with me voice."

"Leave it to the Irish to have a sense of humor," Kramer said, laughing with many others.

"Well, I'm glad that the war's over. I got a boy, eighteen. Best kid you ever saw. Eighteen and working. Best kid you ever saw. I'm glad the war's over," Jim said to a thin fellow beside him.

"I guess everybody's glad," the thin fellow answered.

"I know I am. Partner, my name's O'Neill."

"Mine's Pete Thompson. Glad to meet you."

"Glad to meet you, Thompson. Well, I was saying, I got six kids, and the oldest is eighteen. Finest damn kid you ever saw. I'm damned glad the war's over because of him. Goddamn it, Thompson, there ain't no more war," Jim said.

"What the hell do you care, Long Legs, you wouldn't have to go!" Cooney shouted at Jim.

"What?"

"I said it."

"What do you want to be scrappin' for, Cooney?" asked a pimply-faced young lad.

"Are you talkin' to me?" Jim asked.

"I don't talk to no wall or to myself," Cooney said with an insulting laugh.

"Say that again!" Jim said.

"Forget it, he's drunk, O'Neill," Thompson said.

"This is a celebration, not a fight," Kramer said.

"I said what the hell do you care about the war? You don't have to go."

Jim stood up.

IV

Jim and Cooney squared off in the center of a circle of men in the alley in back of the saloon. They were both drunk.

Cooney plunged in, but Jim hooked him with a left to the jaw.

"Whoo, see that? The guy can swing."

"Go on and fight, you bum," yelled a fellow who wore a derby and was chewing on a cigar.

Swinging both fists, Jim lurched at Cooney.

"Break! Break! Fight fair!" someone yelled as they clinched.

They pushed, mauled, and shoved one another back and forth across the alley, raising a cloud of dust. They squared off. A ray of light from a lamplight over the back door of the saloon fell over Jim's face. There was a welt under his eye. He stood poised, left fist extended, his right cocked.

"Come on, you little yellow squirt," Jim said contemptuously.

Cooney rushed Jim and pounded him backward into a fence. The crowd cheered.

"He talks too much. Give it to the drink-of-water."

"Kill the bastard, Cooney!"

"Up the Irish, O'Neill," O'Malley yelled.

Jim was pinioned against the fence. Cooney caught him flush on the jaw. Jim shook his head. He used the heel of his hand on Cooney's chin and shoved him back. He followed up with his right and drove Cooney across the alley. He smashed Cooney into the stone wall of the saloon building.

The gang now cheered Jim instead of Cooney.

Jim knocked Cooney down. Cooney knelt on one knee, his nose bleeding.

"Get up and take your medicine," Jim yelled, standing over Cooney.

"Get back and give him a chance," someone yelled.

Jim stepped back. Cooney got up. Jim rushed at him. They slugged each other. Jim caught Cooney with a sock on the cheek bone which everyone heard.

Jim's hands and face were smeared with Cooney's blood. Cooney struggled to defend himself and turn the tide of the fight. The crowd pressed in on them, yelling and exultant.

They continued slugging, toe to toe. Cooney suddenly drove Jim back and followed up, pumping his tired fists, left, right, left, right. Jim side-stepped, regained his balance, and ripped Cooney with hooks and uppercuts. Cooney tried to rush Jim, but he was wearied and he punched lumberingly.

Kramer, who was holding Jim's coat, watched anxiously. Cooney got in close and tried to come up with his knee. Jim, tired, but sobered by the punishment he had taken, crooked up his leg and checkmated Cooney.

"You dirty sonofabitch!" Jim yelled, losing his temper.

He hit Cooney with everything he had. Cooney's knees buckled. He sagged, crumpled up, went down. He lay in the dust, glassy-eyed, semi-conscious, bleeding profusely.

Jim turned to face the crowd. His shirt was torn. His face was swollen. His hands and shirt were smeared from Cooney's blood. He did not speak, but stared at the crowd defiantly.

"Come on, O'Neill, you better get out of here," Kramer whispered.

"What for?"

"Come on," Kramer said, taking Jim's arm and leading him off.

Behind them the crowd stood over the battered young fellow.

"Some of his friends might gang up on you," Kramer said.

"I'll take 'em on."

"You're a married man and got kids. Come on."

"The wise pup. Who does he think he is?"

"I'm glad you trimmed him. He's a nasty, no-good sonofabitch. He's always around the saloon," Kramer said.

O'Malley caught up with them and patted Jim on the back.

"I got to get a drink," Jim said.

"I could stand one meself," O'Malley said.

"Let's go back," Jim said.

"Come on, I know another place," O'Malley said.

He and Kramer hurried Jim along.

V

"We were minding our business, and he gets snotty. I don't take anything from a pup like that," Jim said, sitting with Kramer and O'Malley in the dim corner of a saloon on Sixty-first Street. Jim was washed and sober, but his face was marked from the fight.

"Have another," O'Malley said, motioning for drinks.

A waiter brought the drinks. Jim dug into his pocket to pay.

"This is mine," O'Malley said, throwing a dollar on the table.

"He got me so sore I'd have fought the hull saloon," Jim said.

"You're lucky. He's got some mean friends," Kramer said.

"Listen, most of these tough guys, they're punks! Punks!" Jim said with contempt, feeling his face as he spoke.

"O'Neill, you got a wallop in your mitt that does me heart good," O'Malley said.

Jim yawned. He was getting sleepy. He had a headache, and his stomach was heavy. His arms were weary. The whiskey he'd drunk had taken its effect on the nerves and muscles of his legs. These men he was talking with were nice fellows, but they were strangers. His kids were home asleep, and Lizz was probably worried to death. He felt blue and lousy as hell.

"And when you think, O'Neill, that the guy you licked is almost young enough to be your son," O'Malley said.

Jim nodded to the waiter and got another drink. So did his companions. He told himself that he'd had enough. Did he want to go rolling home? He gulped it down. He sat slouched in his chair. Kramer and O'Malley faced him, bleary-eyed. They yawned.

"Where to, man?" asked O'Malley as Jim stood up.

"Home," Jim muttered.

"Home!" O'Malley muttered. He belched. "Home!" He stared emptily at Jim. "Home!" He looked bleary-eyed at Kramer. "Uh!"

"Have one more, O'Neill," Kramer muttered drunkenly.

Jim slid back into his chair. They had another drink.

"Why in hell is the man wanting to go home for? Home! Kramer, home!"

O'Malley's head suddenly dropped. He rested his chin on his chest and snored. Kramer sat in a stupor.

"So long," Jim said, getting up and leaving.

VI

It was late. The night was foggy. Sixty-first Street was deserted. Jim staggered along, eastward. His legs were rubbery, and he floundered all over the sidewalk.

You're drunk, he told himself.

With a kind of drunken curiosity, he watched a street car pass. He tipped his hat in front of Saint Patrick's church and lurched onward. The stores were all darkened. A young couple passed him, but he didn't notice them.

He vomited. Some of his vomit splashed on his shoes and trouser cuffs. He staggered on. The foggy night seemed to have entered his head. His mind was blurred and so was his sight.

Drunk, he told himself.

He stood at the corner of Calumet Avenue.

Calumet Avenue! he told himself.

He turned in the right direction and floundered on toward home, tiring rapidly with each step. The fog in his head seemed to thicken.

VII

Jim struggled to get his key in the lock. Lizz opened the door.

"This is a fine how-do-you-do," she said in blazing anger.

Jim's tall frame swayed in the doorway. There was a stupefied grin on his face. She pulled him in and closed the door.

"What the hell do you come home to me like this for?"

"Uh!"

"If you could only see yourself. Where were you, in the stockyards?"

"Uh," he muttered, hardly able to stand up, smelling rankly of alcohol and vomit.

"Coming home to your wife and family just like a stew bum."

"Lizz!" He leaned over. "The war's over. Had . . . had a fight. . . ."

"Where were you? Who hit you? How did you get that face? Were you robbed?" she asked excitedly.

"Sleepy, Lizz. Put me to bed."

After wiping his hands and face with a wet cloth, she dragged his weighty bulk to the bedroom and put him to bed. He filled the bedroom with the fumes of alcohol. He snored. Lizz and Catherine, who was at the foot of the bed, could not sleep because of the way he kicked and flung his arms about.

7

I

Jim sat in his Morris chair and glanced out the window. Catherine was playing hopscotch on the sidewalk with some of the neighborhood girls.

He had a headache. The balls of his eyes pained him. His tongue was coated and his stomach felt as if he had lead in it. His whole body seemed to be a heavy, ugly, uncomfortable mass, a weight which he had to carry.

He glanced toward the window again and watched Catherine hopping on one leg between chalked-off squares. Reaching the end, she bent down and picked up her marker. He heard her giggle.

He didn't even have the energy to wind the phonograph and play some records. He didn't used to get such lousy hangovers. Sometime in the saloon last night his mind had gone blank. All he could remember about getting home was a recollection of himself standing on the corner of Sixty-first and Calumet Avenue and muttering *Calumet*. After that he had only a vague memory of crowded excitement. He wished he hadn't been a damned fool and gotten so drunk. Well, he was paying for it today.

Slouching further down in his chair, he rested his chin in his hands. His headache wouldn't go away. Perhaps a bath would make him feel better. But he couldn't even get up that much ambition. Maybe when Lizz got home she'd run the tub for him.

Drinking wasn't worth it when it left you so nervous and jumpy and feeling so all-around rotten the next day. It made you feel good for a while, as if you were the lord of the world. That feeling was wonderful—while it lasted. But you went on drinking, and pretty soon you were pissy-assed and didn't know what you were saying or doing or whether you were coming or going.

At least he wasn't likely to be docked for missing these two days. If he were, he'd feel even worse. Yes, there were advantages in being more than an ordinary workingman. When he'd been on the wagons and gone off on his bats and lost time, plunk, it went right out of his pay envelope.

But then, he only had a hangover. It would pass and, after all, why shouldn't a man get drunk once in a while. What was wrong in getting drunk? When a man had worked as hard as he had worked all his life, he at least had earned the right to go on a bat now and then.

He felt his face where it had been bruised and welted from the fight. He ran his hands over his beard. He'd shave tomorrow. He rubbed and examined the sore knuckles on his right hand. There was one wise young garter-snapper named Cooney who knew that he'd been hit.

II

Jim had fallen asleep. The bell woke him up. He heard Lizz answering it. He hadn't heard her come in.

"Oh, it's you, Dolly."

"Where's Papa?"

"Don't you wake him up now. He's asleep."

"Here I am," Jim called out.

Catherine ran into the parlor. She was a pretty, dirty-faced, bobbed-hair little girl of seven.

"Are you going to work tonight, Papa?" she asked, smiling at him.

"No. And aren't you glad?"

"Of course I am."

Jim was pleased. There was a benign look on his face.

"Papa, can I sit on your lap?"

He lifted her onto his lap and held her. Her little buttocks grew warm against his thigh.

"Papa, can I feel your whiskers?"

"Of course," he answered, grinning.

She ran her hand over his beard.

"Gee!" she exclaimed.

"What's the matter?"

"They could hurt you easy if you were rubbed hard with them."

"Want me to hurt you with 'em?"

"No," she answered, laughing.

"What's the joke?"

"Oh, something."

"Tell your father what it is."

"I was thinking something. I was thinking that it would be fun to watch you hurt Bob with your whiskers."

"Just for that, I'll hurt you."

Frowning fiercely and making strange noises in his throat, Jim bent forward. She ducked her head. He rubbed his whiskers against her arm. She pretended to be more hurt than she actually was. Then she giggled.

She snuggled herself comfortably in his arms. Suddenly he noticed that she was staring at him intently and with what seemed like awe and adoration. He noticed that her dark eyes seemed larger than their normal size and that they glistened. A sense of mystery pervaded him. This warm little girl in his arms was his daughter, the daughter of himself and of Lizz. Some day she would grow up to be a woman. He was proud. There was nothing in the world to match being a father. She was his daughter, and she was like a little angel, innocent and with such lovely eyes. Yes, just think of it, he and Lizz had produced this little soul.

And though she was his daughter, she was a stranger. What was she really like? What did she really have going on in her little mind? A father didn't really know what his own little girl was like.

He kissed her tenderly.

III

Jim sat at the head of the table. Lizz was on his left, and Bill on his right. Bob, Catherine, and Dennis were ranged around the lower end. They all had greasy hamburger and fried potatoes on their plates.

Jim was still jumpy. His head felt light, and now and then he would get a weak spell.

"Eat, Jim, and you'll feel better," Lizz said.

"I'm all right. I'm just not hungry."

"Papa, tell us about the fight you had," Dennis said.

"Say, you shyster, wipe that catsup off your chin," Lizz yelled at Dennis.

Jim grinned. The three sons, so disparate in age, all looked at their father with frank admiration. Jim shoved a chunk of hamburger into his mouth and chewed it.

"Papa, did you lick the guy?" asked Bob.

"Sure I licked him."

"Pa's a good fighter, you dummy. Of course he licked him," Dennis said to Bob.

"Well, let Papa tell me about it. I don't want you to," Bob said.

"Then keep still so he can," Dennis said.

Bill waited expectantly for his father to talk. Catherine, wide-eyed, stared at Jim.

"Sure I licked him," Jim said.

"You didn't look like you did, on my word, you didn't, when you came home last night," Lizz said.

"You should have seen what the other fellow looked like," Jim said, and Bill smiled proudly.

"Papa, where was the fight?" Dennis asked.

"In an alley."

"How did you fight?" Bob asked.

"What do you mean?" Jim asked, thinking that as far as fighting went, his children would never be ashamed of their old man.

"Did you rush him or did he rush you?"

"Sometimes I rushed him and sometimes he rushed me."

"But I bet you rushed him more times," Bob said, and Jim grinned.

"Papa, who started the fight?" Dennis asked.

"I didn't like something he said. I don't believe in taking any man's sass." Jim paused. "I don't want you kids to take sass, either, but I don't want you to go around fightin' or lookin' for fights."

"Children, when your father was younger, could he fight?" Lizz jumped up from the table. "Jim, remember the time you took me to a dance at Flanagan's?"

Jim's eyes lit up.

"And a tough guy named Bugs Canavan thought he could take me away from your father. And, children, you should have seen what your father did to him!" Lizz began waving her fists.

Jim beamed. Momentarily he forgot his hangover.

"Jim, I remember what happened as clear as if it was this morning. You asked him: 'Bugs Canavan, are you a tough guy?'"

"All I remember is that I didn't like him, and he said something snotty, and so I cleaned him up."

"Mama, what did Papa do to Bugs Canavan?" Bob asked.

"He made mincemeat out of him. Mincemeat! Oh, my, was it a fight! Everybody was yelling, and the police came, and I was afraid your father would clean up the flatfoots," Lizz said, talking loudly, her enthusiasm carrying over into her gestures.

"Papa, did you give the guy last night a shiner?" Bob asked.

"He knocked two of Bugs Canavan's teeth out," Lizz said. She sat down and added, "Your father was a fighter."

"Pa, did you give him a shiner last night?" Bob asked.

"I punched him all over the alley and I knocked him cold," Jim answered, and then he bent over his plate and took some more to eat.

"Papa, the next time you're gonna have a fight, will you take me with you so I can see it?" Bob asked.

"Say, you, what do you think your father is, a brawler? He has to work and make a living."

"Well, you seen him fight, didn't you?" Bob asked.

"Don't talk back to your mother, you," Jim said.

"Well, she said she did," said Bob.

"I told you, don't talk back to your mother!" Jim said.

"Papa, when he hit you in the eye, did he hurt you?" asked Bob.

"Gee, I don't remember. I just went after him, and every time he hit me, I hit him harder."

"Papa socked him, didn't you, Jim?" Lizz said.

"You kids better eat before your supper gets cold," Jim said, grinning.

He suddenly felt he was bragging. Then, he told himself, no, he wasn't. He was telling what happened, and telling the truth, and it wasn't bragging to tell the truth, was it?

IV

The young children sat on the floor, near their father who was in his Morris chair, wearing carpet slippers. Dennis worked at his arithmetic homework, and Bob pored over his catechism, repeating the words of the lesson half aloud. Catherine watched her father.

"Well, how's everything at the Wagon Department, Bill?" Jim asked.

"Oh, everything is all right."

"I guess the only thing to do is to take things as they come; go along and do your work, and no one will bother you."

"That's what I do."

"You get along with Bryan?"

"He seems to like me. He likes you too, Pa."

"I never had any trouble with Bryan."

"We got a new kid today named Casey, from the West Side. He seems to be quite wise."

"I don't like these wise alecks. Don't have much to do with 'em. And don't be wise yourself."

"I don't. I try to do what I got to do. And we're always busy. The phones keep you going, you know, Pa."

Jim relaxed. He still was feeling lousy. Well, he'd go to bed early and get a good night's sleep and he'd be able to be back to work tomorrow. No more such drunks for him.

A pain shot through his head, and his eyeballs throbbed. Well, he could take a bath and go to bed. Just think, it wasn't so long ago when he wasn't able to afford a house in which he could take a bath in a comfortable tub.

"Well, Pa, I guess I'll go and see a movie," Bill said.

"Just a minute, Bill, I want to talk to you."

Bill blushed and turned his head aside so his father wouldn't observe this reaction.

"Bill, I been at the express company a long time. And I'm a lucky man to be where I am."

Bill waited.

"Now, Bill, you ain't ever going to get anywhere in this world unless you try to. You know that, don't you?"

"Yes, Pa."

"I think you ought to study. Take Joe O'Reilley. He went to law school and studied and look where he is. Now me, I wouldn't do it, so I ain't where Joe is today. I don't expect I'll ever go any higher than I am. But I'll be able to help you kids get an education."

He paused and waited. Bill said nothing.

"Bill, there's many fellows at the express company who never are going to get anywhere. They're decent fellows. And I'm the last man in the world to look down at the workingman. I'm one myself and I always been one. I'm not saying I want you to be a dude or anything like that. But I want to see every damned one of you kids amount to something."

Bill shook his head in agreement.

"I want you to study, take up something nights so you can get somewhere."

"I was thinking of doing something like that and I was going to talk to you about it."

"Pa! Pa!" Bob yelled.

"What do you think you'd like to take up?"

"Well, now, Pa, I ain't thought about that yet. I just thought maybe I'd take up something."

"Pa! Pa!" Bob yelled.

"I'm glad to hear you say that, Bill. Now, do you think you'd like to go in for the law? There's good night schools, and maybe Joe O'Reilley can help you."

"Well, you see, I haven't decided just exactly what I ought to take up."

"Papa, I'm going to be a fireman when I grow up," Bob yelled.

"Shut up, I'm talking," Jim said curtly.

"I was always best in school in mathematics and arithmetic, and maybe if I took up something along that line, bookkeeping and accounting now."

"That's good. I just want you to take something up so you can get ahead and not have to look forward to answering telephones all your life."

"Yes, I will. But I better go now so I can catch the show and get home early," Bill said as he left the room.

"All right, Bill."

"Papa, can I feel your muscle?" Bob asked.

Jim smiled. Bob went to him, followed by Dennis and Catherine. Jim flexed his muscles. They all felt his biceps and uttered exclamations of admiration.

"I want to have hard muscles like yours, Pa, when I grow up," Bob said.

"Goodbye, Pa," Bill called.

"So long, Bill."

Jim went out to the dining room, where Lizz was darning socks.

"Lizz, fix the tub for me. I think I'll take a warm bath and turn in."

He followed her to the bathroom and began undressing. He looked at his discolored face in the mirror and rubbed his beard. He yawned.

8

I

Father Gilhooley was celebrating five o'clock mass. The church was crowded and the altar blazed with candles. Danny knelt in a center pew at the rear of the church. He'd forgotten his prayer book and was trying to follow the parts of the mass from memory. He kept saying *Hail Marys* and *Our Fathers*, and at the same time tried to keep episodes from the life of Christ in his mind.

Behind him, and a little to his right, the small choir was filled with children from the school. He had been excluded from the choir because he had such a foghorn voice. But he liked the singing in church, particularly on Christmas and Holy Thursday. It was beautiful. He regretted that he didn't have a good voice so he could be back there and sing *Adeste Fidelis* this morning.

Uncle Al was having Mother give five dollars in the collection. That wasn't so bad, but if they were richer, they could give more. Roslyn's father always gave fifty or a hundred dollars to the Christmas and Easter collections. He wondered what Papa and Mama were giving. He was ashamed that they couldn't afford to give much, just as he'd been ashamed because there wasn't a Liberty Bond sign hanging in Papa's windows. In the church calendar next month, under the Calumet Avenue list, his father's name might be there—*James O'Neill $1.00*. All the kids would see it, too.

But this wasn't praying, and he was at mass. He had to keep his mind on God, especially because he was receiving Holy Communion. He suddenly remembered that yesterday afternoon at confession he'd again forgotten to tell Father Doneggan about how he had made a bad confession years ago. He'd determined to tell it while he was examining his conscience, and then, when he was in the confessional, it had gone right out of his mind.

He closed his eyes and bowed his head. He struggled with himself to be in as contrite a mood as was possible. He wanted to say *An Act of Contrition* that was as near to perfect as it could possibly be.

Oh my God! I am heartily sorry for having offended Thee, and I detest all my sins, because I dread the loss of heaven and the pains of hell, but most of all because they offend Thee, my God, Who art all-good and deserving of all my love. I firmly resolve, with the help of Thy grace, to confess my sins, to do penance, and to amend my life. Amen.

He kept his head lowered and he told himself he detested with all his might every sin he had ever committed. Suddenly there formed in his mind a picture of Christ, kneeling beside a bush in the dark garden of Golgotha. A ray from Heaven lit up Christ's face, and he envisioned the face of the Saviour in agony, suffering for all the sins of all the people who had ever lived or who would live on this earth. He thought of how at that moment Jesus was seeing in His agony all the sins, all the dirty thoughts and disobediences of Danny O'Neill. He asked God to help him to sin no more, to make him worthy this minute to receive Holy Communion.

The children back in the choir sang:

> *The angels were watching the whole night long,*
> *Under the starry sky . . .*

Danny lifted his head and opened his eyes. He felt as if he had just been far away. He kept his eyes on Father Gilhooley up at the altar.

II

Father Gilhooley mounted the pulpit. He blessed himself.

In the name of the Father, and of the Son, and of the Holy Ghost. Amen.

He paused. Then he read in his bland voice:

And behold an angel of the Lord stood by them, and the brightness of God shone about them, and they feared with a great fear.

"These are the words of Saint Luke, Chapter two, ninth verse.

"My friends, there is a special significance in this Christmas morning when, once again, we all find ourselves gathered together in this little church to celebrate and to commemorate the birthday of Jesus Christ, our Lord and God. This Christmas is one of peace after four years of terrible war. War, like a plague, has scourged the earth. Mankind has expiated its sins in the bloodiest and fiercest battles of all history. And we have not escaped these dread events. In the rear of this church there hangs a flag with twenty-five gold stars. Each one of these stars represents a loved one who is not with us, a loved one from this parish who has died for his country. These stars bring home to us the war which has so recently torn mankind and divided humanity by hatred.

"One year ago this morning, while we were all gathered here together, thousands and millions of men, among them our own, were crowded in the trenches in Europe, engaged in murderous war. I spoke then from this pulpit, as a man of God, a man of peace. And while I spoke, men were fighting one another in battles in the fiercest of all wars. Today the long vigil is over for mankind, and we offer our merciful thanks to Almighty God for a Christmas of peace. Today we can participate in Christmas festivities with lightness of heart. All men can and do truly rejoice. For today mankind can love his neighbor as himself.

"One thousand nine hundred and eighteen years ago this morning the Christ Child was born in a manger in Bethlehem. That morning there was joy on the earth and joy in Heaven. Like one of us, poor and weak, with only a stable to shelter Him and His Holy Mother and saintly father, the King of Kings was born. It was a cold and frosty morning. Only the breath and the warmth of the animals provided heat in that little manger. And bearing their gifts from afar, the Three Wise Men came to join with the shepherds and the angels of Heaven in heralding the birth of the Redeemer.

"Since that first Christmas morn generations and generations of men have come and gone from the face of the earth. The gospel of the child God born that morning has carried down the ages and traveled around the world as if on wings. He came to save us, and He left us a priceless treasure–the true Church. And the Church has withstood the storms of the centuries, wars and rumors of wars, heresies, the onslaughts of the infidels, the assaults of Satan himself, who has vainly used all his wiles and his cunning to corrode the solid foundations of the rock of Peter. Today that Church is jubilant throughout the length and breadth of the world. It stands in majesty and glory, teaching and ministering to all men and all nations, healing the wounds of a war that has divided mankind. Today the Church tells all men to be brothers, brothers in Christ, Our Lord.

"There have been some Christmas days in the long procession of the centuries which have been more joyous than others. There have been Christmas morns when the faithful had to hide and herd themselves underground in the catacombs of pagan Rome in order that they might celebrate the birth of their Redeemer. And there have been Christmas mornings when the Church in all its pomp and all its majestic beauty has commemorated the birth of Christ in the great and beautiful cathedrals of Europe, the most magnificent edifices that the hand and the brain and the brawn of man has ever fashioned. But always, and in all circumstances, there is a lesson in the return of Christmas day. And this lesson is one which we should especially remember this morning.

"*Christ is born!* Dwell for a moment on these three simple words. For they describe the greatest event in all human history. They mean that the King of Kings, Our God and Saviour, He Who made us after His own image, came down to us mortals to save and redeem us, to die for us. Every Christmas morning, our realization of these three simple words should renew in us our faith. We feel as if we were better men and better women on Christmas morning. We say 'Merry Christmas' to everyone, even to strangers. A great joy wells within us. We are at the end of a long year. Many things have happened to us in that year, some joyous and happy, some sad and mournful. Some of you have become richer; others poorer. Some are in excellent health; some are ill. Some of us have welcomed little newcomers into the world; others have lost loved ones. But all of us, rich and poor, young and old, healthy and infirm, all of us in the great wide world of Christendom feel a genuine and deep sense of renewal on this glorious feast day. There is a rebirth of faith in the hearts and the souls of the faithful throughout the world. Today all we Catholics share a kindredness of spirit.

"Such is the general atmosphere and spirit of any Christmas. But how much more so does it permeate this Christmas morning of peace and of good will to men. After the Holy Sacrifice of the mass is ended here this morning, we must all go forth from this church carrying with us a feeling of renewal. We must go forth feeling that just as there is a new dawn of peace in the world at large, so is there in our hearts a new dawn of faith, of hope, and of charity and forgiveness. And when you pray this morning, when so many of you march up here to the altar rail to receive the body and blood of our Lord, I know that you will have a great thanksgiving in your hearts. I want to ask all of you to pray in thanksgiving to God for the boon of peace that He has given mankind. I want to ask you to remember to pray for the repose of the souls whose heroism is commemorated by the gold stars on the banner in the rear of our church–for the repose of the souls of all who died in the terrible war now ended–for the repose of the souls of all brave men who died in battle, whether they were friend or foe. For such is the spirit of Christmas. Yes, my friends, I want to ask you to pray for the dead and for the living. Let us thank God for peace. Let us all beseech the Lord with the petition that mankind has fought its last war. Let us hope that the faith and the Gospel which Christ brought to us will now prevail triumphant among the nations. Let us pray that the word of Mars is banished forever and that the word of Christ will guide us down the years that lay before us.

"I say to you again, my friends: *Glory to God in the highest; and on earth peace to men of good will.*

"In the name of the Father, and of the Son, and of the Holy Ghost. Amen."

Father Gilhooley turned and descended from the pulpit.

The congregation stirred. Mass continued, and the faithful knelt. Danny thrilled with pride. His mind filled with pictures of the Church in the past, in Rome, in the middle ages. He imagined missionary saints saying mass for darkies in Africa, while other priests celebrated holy mass in the cathedrals of Europe. Would he some day hear mass in these churches, in Rome itself? He was proud that he was a Catholic, a member of the One, Holy, True, and Universal Church.

He must be worthy of his religion. He had to be good, do good, avoid sin and the occasion of sin. And if he really had the call, he must answer it, bravely and with the desire to serve God firm in his heart. For ages the Church has been a solid rock. Oh, God, give him the grace and the strength to stand on that rock.

He heard the pure voice of Dick Buckford singing.

Holy night, silent night . . .

III

As soon as mass was over, Danny hurried out of church and stood on the curb, watching the crowd stream forth. It was still dark out, and the wind was raw and icy. Some parishioners paused a moment to exchange greetings with one another, and the air was filled with merry voices. The crowd quickly thinned out, but Danny still waited, stamping his chilled feet. He saw Fritzie Lonigan with her mother, father, and kid brother. Then he saw Billie Morris' old man and old lady.

But she hadn't come out yet.

"Come on home. What you waitin' for? It's cold," Fat Malloy said.

"I gotta wait for my grandmother," Danny said, thinking Fat wouldn't know his grandmother hadn't come to mass and that he was waiting for an altogether different purpose.

There she was, coming down the steps with her mother and father and little brother and kid sister.

"Well, I'm not gonna hang around and get icicles on my tail. Merry Christmas," Fat said, dashing away.

Her family was talking with the O'Reedys. But she wasn't even looking at him.

"You always keep your family in church after mass to say an extra prayer, don't you, Mr. Hayes," Mrs. O'Reedy was saying.

He didn't hear what her father said in answer. He fastened his gaze on the church door, but tried to watch them from the corner of his eye. He ought to put his ear laps down, but if he did he wouldn't be as able to overhear what they said. She was talking now, but it was just his luck to have a street car pass.

He didn't want her to think he was waiting just to see her. Pretending to be anxiously waiting for someone, he nervously watched the church doors. The Hayes family walked by him. She didn't even give him a glance. He was shivering, his ears were burning, and his feet were getting cold. He could have been almost halfway home by now, and instead he was still here waiting, and what for? He saw her family get into their automobile and drive away. He took off his cap, and the cold struck his head. He hastily pulled down the ear laps and put his cap back on. The moon was still out, and its rays turned the snow in the schoolyard into a glistening, bluish-white field. He had seen her, and she hadn't even wished him a Merry Christmas. And he wouldn't see her again today! He ran along Sixty-first Street, toward home.

IV

"We all went to mass early, and received," Mrs. O'Flaherty self-righteously and almost belligerently announced as Ned came leisurely into the kitchen, wearing his purple bathrobe.

Al was eating breakfast, and Danny sat with him, sipping a cup of coffee.

"Good for you, Mud. Merry Christmas, everybody," Ned said.

"Yes, we received and attended holy mass."

"Are you starting off on Christmas Day with a chip on your shoulder?" Ned asked, going to the stove to get himself a cup of coffee.

"She's only telling you what she did," Al said.

Danny glanced at Uncle Al. Uncle Al had come out of the hospital thin, but now he looked very well.

"Ned, hurry up and get ready and come to church with me," Al said.

"You've been to church, haven't you?"

"I'm going to go to ten o'clock mass at Crucifixion church also."

"The true church isn't in any building. It's in the heart, in the love and beauty of life that God has created."

"But if you don't go to mass on Sundays and Holy Days of Obligation, it's a mortal sin."

"Who said so?" Ned asked Danny.

Liberty stuck her snout up against Ned's thigh. He gave her a piece of sugar.

"The Church."

"Can you show me where Jesus said that you commit mortal sin if you don't go to mass?"

"It's a commandment of the Church. And the Third Commandment is remember to keep holy the Sabbath."

"I can keep holy the Sabbath in my own home as well as in church. Suppose I stay home and read the words of Jesus instead of going to mass, do you mean to tell me that's a sin?" Ned asked.

"Yes, it is," Danny said, sincere and confident.

"I haven't anything against people going to church. It's a good thing. Only don't try and tell me that I'm sinning if I stay home and commune with God by myself."

"Yes, you are," Danny answered, screwing up his face, puzzled because he couldn't understand why Uncle Ned couldn't get it into his head that missing mass was a mortal sin.

Al noticed the clock.

"I have to hurry or I'll be late for mass. Ned, do me a favor and go to church," Al said.

"Maybe I will."

Al left the kitchen.

"Going to two masses, as if one wasn't enough. You'd think he was a murderer and had to do it."

"But, Uncle Ned, you don't go to mass because you sin."

"Well, why do you then?"

"Because you have to, and because you get grace if you do."

"Grace is within you."

"You don't think the Church is wrong, do you?"

"Of course not. I'm a Catholic."

"Well, what you say is against the Church."

"How?"

"What you say about mass. And you don't believe there is a Hell or a Purgatory. The Church teaches us there is."

"Rats. That's what old-fashioned Irish priests say to scare people."

"No it isn't."

"Do you mean to say that I'll burn in Hell if I don't go to mass?"

"Yes, if you don't go to confession and get absolution before you die."

Al came out to the kitchen wearing a derby and a black overcoat with a velvet collar.

"Hurry up, Ned, or you'll be late for mass."

"Don't worry about me."

"Mother, slip us a kiss before we go," Al said.

He hugged and kissed her.

"That's the girl."

"We'll be here when you come back, Al."

He left.

"Danny, you want to forget this hell-fire and damnation," Ned said.

Danny frowned. Yes, Uncle Ned just couldn't understand, that was all.

"Well, Mud, we're all going to be happy this Christmas," Ned said.

"Ah, me son Al is a fine boy," Mrs. O'Flaherty remarked as she watched Al go out the back gate.

V

"Merry Christmas, Boy. I was expecting you," Jim said, opening the door.

"Merry Christmas, Papa," Danny said, handing Jim a box of candy. He'd used some of his Christmas-present money to buy this for his mother and father.

"What's this?"

"I . . . I brought it to you and Mama as a present."

"You're a fine boy. Thanks."

Danny beamed.

"Take your coat off and come in the parlor, Dan."

Danny pulled off his sheepskin and followed his father into the front room. The parlor was cleaned up, all spick and span.

"Papa, this is for you from Uncle Al, and this is for you and Mama from Uncle Al, and this, for you and Mama from Uncle Ned, and this, for you and Mama from Aunt Peg," Danny said, handing his father cigars and envelopes containing money.

"Say, that was nice of them. But they didn't have to bother about it. You thank them for your mother and me," Jim said, rather embarrassed.

"Oh, my son! My son, my prodigal son," Lizz cried out, rushing into the room and hugging and kissing Danny.

"Merry Christmas, Mama."

"Lizz, we just got these presents from your people," Jim said, handing her the envelopes.

"I knew my people wouldn't forget me on Christmas," Lizz said, tearing open the envelopes and looking at the money in them.

"And look, Lizz, Danny brought this to you and me," Jim said, handing her the box of candy.

"Kiss your baby sister Merry Christmas," Lizz said as Catherine entered the room.

Danny shyly kissed his sister. She was a pretty little thing and a nice kid, and she never talked much to him, Danny thought. He wished that she and Little Margaret were as well-dressed as Roslyn and her sister.

"Want to see what I got for Christmas?" Catherine asked.

He nodded. She ran out of the room and returned with a large doll. It was pink-cheeked and clothed in a white dress with a blue sash.

"My Papa gave this doll to his best girl," Catherine said.

"Merry Christmas," Bob and Dennis chorused, joining them.

"Merry Christmas," Danny replied.

"Papa, why do people say there's a Santa Claus when there isn't one?" Bob asked.

"They tell it to kids."

"But why do they when it isn't true?"

"Say, how do you know there isn't a Santa Claus?" Lizz asked.

"I never saw him. Yesterday we were at two different stores, and there were two different men, and both of them were dressed up like Santa Claus, and there were more of them on the street for the Salvation Army. And Denny told me there isn't any Santa Claus."

"Why get me into this?" Dennis complained.

"I guess they always just tell it to boys and girls of your age and Catherine's. I guess it's just a Christmas custom and part of the Christmas spirit," Jim said.

"But if there isn't a Santa Claus, why does everybody pretend there is one?"

"Bob, I guess it's like I just told you it was. That's all there is to it," Jim said, and Bob seemed disappointed because he hadn't received a more satisfactory answer.

"Son, look at our Christmas tree," Lizz said, pointing to the small Christmas tree on the floor by the center window. It reached a little above the window sill and was decorated with ornaments from the five-and-ten-cent store.

"It's nice," Danny said; he had caught himself in time before he had blurted out that the tree at home was much bigger and was decorated with colored electric bulbs.

"Say, Lizz, I almost forgot something," Jim said, rushing out of the room.

He returned almost immediately with an envelope.

"Here. Don't think your father and mother forgot any of their children on Christmas Day," Jim said, handing the envelope to Danny.

Master Daniel O'Neill

His name was written on it.

"Open it, Son," Lizz said to him, smiling joyfully.

Inside, Danny found a brand-new one-dollar bill with a little card.

Merry Christmas to Danny
From Papa and Mama
Christmas 1918

Bob and Dennis looked wide-eyed at the crisp green bill in Danny's hand.

"Gee, thank you, Mama, and thank you, Papa," Danny said to his happy parents.

Jim patted Danny's curly head.

"Your father and I received Holy Communion at eight o'clock mass. We came home and fixed the turkey up, and we're going to start the bird cooking in a little while," Lizz said.

"Pa, why didn't you get chicken instead of turkey for today?" Bob asked.

"Because turkey's better, Bobbie."

"Is it really?"

"Wait and see."

"Well, if it is, it must be good, because chicken's good and I like it," Bob said.

"Sure it is. Don't you know that much, you?" Dennis said to Bob.

"I never ate turkey," said Bob.

"Yes you did, but you don't remember it," Jim said.

"Where?"

"In the cottage. And, boy, you're going to have turkey every Christmas from now on."

"Danny, see my pretty new bow," Catherine said, coming up to him and pointing to her blue hair ribbon; he hadn't even noticed it before.

"I swear, Doll Lily, you're going to be a flirt," Lizz said.

"I just want him to see my new bow." She pointed to her ribbon.

"You look pretty in it, Dolly," Danny said.

"My brother Bill gave it to me," she said.

"Is your sister coming over this morning?" Jim asked.

"Yes. Little Margaret went to a late mass. And Mother said I should ask you all to come over and see her this afternoon. She has something for Dennis and Bob and Catherine and Bill and for you, Papa, and for Mama, too, but she wants to give it to all of you herself."

"Yes, we'll be over this afternoon," Jim said.

Jim casually glanced out the window.

"Well, I'll be goddamned!" he exclaimed.

Everyone in the room turned to the window. They saw Bill smoking a cigarette as he walked along on the other side of the street with two fellows.

"Jesus Mary and Joseph!" Lizz exclaimed. She turned to Jim. "Jim, you're not going to beat him for this, are you?"

"Hit him? Know what I'm going to do? I'm going to give him a cigar."

Danny was relieved. He'd feared for a moment that Papa would get sore and sock Bill when Bill came home.

"Well, I'll be damned," Jim said, laughing heartily.

"Jim, you must get busy on the bird now," Lizz said.

"Yes, I better get busy on it," Jim said.

"I got to go now, Pa," Danny said.

"Will you be home when we come over?"

"I might. But I'm going to a movie this afternoon," Danny said.

"Well, be good."

Danny went to the hall and put on his coat.

"Here, Son," Lizz said, furtively sticking a crumpled dollar bill in his hand. She kissed him goodbye.

9

I

Danny sprawled out on the parlor floor. Liberty watched him with that look he loved. She had her ears cocked, and her tail was wagging away almost like a machine. He played with her, rolled her around, scratched her skull between the eyes just at the point she seemed to like. She was a dandy dog, and it was swell to have a dog. She was thin now after having puppies, and they'd gotten rid of the little dogs, too. He got to his feet, and the dog looked after him, downcast.

He could not remember one day in the whole of 1918 that had been as lousy as today, the last one of the year. Well, it would soon end now. In a little while the whistles would be blowing, and Kid 1919 would knock out 1918. That meant a fresh start. He was going to take a tip from Uncle Ned. For 1919 he was going to wish stronger than he'd ever wished before.

He got an old copy of *The Saturday Evening Post* and sat down opposite Uncle Al at the reading table in the back parlor. Al was breathing asthmatically and kept his eyes glued on a book. Danny had wanted to go to the midnight show at the Prairie Theater, but Uncle Al had put his foot down and said no, he had to stay home for New Year's Eve. Danny had crabbed, and Uncle Al had almost hit him and had said to him that he was not the only one who made sacrifices. Right this minute, all of the gang was at Roslyn's New Year's Eve party. Even Fat Malloy had been invited. On Halloween, in seventh grade, they'd had a surprise party on Billie Morris, and before they'd gone to it they'd had to ditch Fat because Fat wasn't wanted. Now even Fat was wanted. But Danny O'Neill wasn't. He tried to read. Uncle Al looked at him but said nothing. Uncle Al knew he was sore about being kept in tonight.

Twelve o'clock ought to come any minute now. He lay down the magazine and just waited for midnight. Let it hurry up and come.

Suddenly they heard whistles outside. From the street below people were blowing horns.

"Happy New Year, Dan," Uncle Al said, laying down his book.

"Happy New Year, Uncle Al," Danny answered, forgetting his grievance against his uncle and smiling happily.

Mrs. O'Flaherty, Ned, and Little Margaret rushed into the room to join in the good wishes. Everyone kissed Mrs. O'Flaherty.

"Let's all kneel down and say a little prayer," Al said.

They knelt, blessed themselves, and silently prayed. Danny fervently asked God for a good New Year for all of them, and for his father, mother, brothers and sisters. Everyone made the sign of the cross and got up.

"God willing, this is going to be our best year. And, Sport, if it is, I'll be able to send you to some swell high school, one like University High School on the Midway, where you can make the right contacts with the right kind of fellows," Uncle Al said.

He hadn't said a word to them yet about how he was thinking about the call.

"Come on out in the kitchen. I'll make some coffee and we'll have a midnight snack," Uncle Ned said, and they all trooped out to the kitchen.

II

After putting on his pajamas to go to bed, Danny went to the desk in the corner of his bedroom. Uncle Ned had brought it back from Madison when he'd come home to live with them, and this was the only place for it. So he had his own desk. He took out a diary he'd bought. He was sure in his own mind that 1919 was going to be his year, and he wanted to keep a diary of it. He opened the book to the blank page for January 1st.

He could put down in this diary what he really felt and hide it so nobody could see it and read it. But suppose it was found? Suppose Little Margaret found it and knew his feelings? She was nosey. He couldn't let such a thing happen.

He dipped his pen in ink, and sat, moody and reflective. He wanted to describe how he felt about not being invited to Roslyn's party. Was the party over now? Were they going home? They'd all probably had a good time, and they'd played kissing games, and Roslyn had kissed everyone there. Maybe not one of them even mentioned his name all evening.

Or if any of them did, it was probably only to laugh at him.

Well, they could all put this in their pipe and smoke it. Danny O'Neill's day was coming. They'd had their fun tonight. His fun would come. He was glad he hadn't been invited. Things like this must be looked at as obstacles. The more obstacles, the better, because he would get over every obstacle, and then victory would be sweet for him. Like *Carrying the Message to Garcia* that he'd read. Well, he was carrying his message—carrying his message to fate. And it was an ultimatum.

He wanted to write as the first line in his diary:

This is the year of my destiny.

And he didn't care if anyone found it and read it.

He wrote:

This is the

He halted. Yes? No?

first day of 1919. I hope it is a good year. I stayed home tonight, and at twelve o'clock we knelt down and prayed to start the New Year off right. I made resolutions to study hard and win a scholarship to one of the Catholic high schools in June. And I also made resolutions to make the nine first Fridays, and not to eat candy or go to shows during Lent this year. Tonight I beat Uncle Ned four games out of six in checkers.

Danny yawned. He hadn't written his real feelings in the diary. But he would keep it every day, and as soon as he was sure that he had a really safe place to hide it, he would put down what he felt about Roslyn and about everything.

He hid the diary in a corner of the closet. He turned out the light, knelt by the bed to say his evening prayers, and then opened the window and climbed into bed.

III

"Daniel O'Neill," Sister suddenly said, closing her history book.

It was almost the end of the class day. Danny stood up by his seat.

"Where did you go last Sunday?" she asked.

He was taken aback for a moment by the question. The way she had asked it led him to feel that she had something on somebody.

"I went to a movie at Fifty-eighth and Prairie, the Prairie Theater."

"Whom did you go with?"

"I went by myself."

"Did you see anybody there?"

"Nobody . . . Oh, yes, Sister, I saw some kids I know from the public school."

"William Morris," she called.

Danny sat down, confused by her questions. Billie Morris stood up. Whenever Billie was called on to recite, he always clamped his heels together and pointed one foot straight ahead and the other out to the side, because that was the way they'd been taught to stand in their elocution lessons. Danny thought Billie looked goofy standing that way.

"Where were you last Sunday, William?"

"The Michigan Theater."

"Whom did you see there?"

"Dick Buckford, Ralph, Glenn, Thomas O'Connor, Walter Regan, Roslyn Hayes, Natalie O'Reedy, Andrew Houlihan, Mary Conroy, and, oh, a couple of other kids from school."

"What did you do after the show?" she asked.

"We had an ice cream soda, and then we walked home."

They hadn't asked him to go with them. Last Saturday he'd even asked Billie and Dick what about going to a show on Sunday afternoon, and they'd said they couldn't do it. Well, he was glad Sister had heard about what they did.

"Have you boys been going to the show regularly with the girls from this school, William?"

"We have for three or four weeks on Sunday, ever since New Year's Day."

So they had been doing this ever since New Year's Day, and they hadn't even said a word about it to him?

"I have been hearing stories about my boys associating too freely with Sister Bernadette's girls. Have you just been going to the show together, William?"

"Yes, Sister, that's all. Except going skating sometimes, or playing around Glenn's house, we sometimes see the girls because Roslyn Hayes is his cousin and is around there a lot."

"Do you play any games?"

"Maybe once in a while we play tag or we talk to them."

They could feel sure that Danny O'Neill wouldn't forget that they didn't want him around. Well, soon he could be playing baseball every day in Washington Park and then he wouldn't even give them half a thought.

"Walter Regan," Sister called.

Regan, a lanky kid, stood up. Billie sat down, blushing. Danny looked at Regan's back, hating him. In sixth grade he'd licked Regan with boxing gloves and twice he'd challenged him to fights, but Regan wouldn't fight him.

"Do you think that anything you boys do is wrong when you see the girls? Do you do anything you would be ashamed of?"

"Not that I know of, Sister. We talk a little about school, and skating, games, and other kids, that's all," Walter Regan added.

They talked about other kids. Fat Malloy had told him about how Dick Buckford had imitated him at Roslyn's New Year's Eve party, and they'd all laughed behind his back. They talked about other kids, did they? That meant him.

Billie Morris raised his hand. Sister recognized him with a nod.

"Sister, there isn't anything wrong in our seeing the girls like we did, is there?" Billie asked.

She glanced around the room scrutinizingly. Most of the pupils were listening, eager and curious.

"Of course there's nothing wrong in boys talking with girls. But some of you shouldn't be giving girls too much of your time and attention. You still have examinations to pass if you want to graduate, and if you don't toe the mark and study your lessons, you might be sorry when it's too late. And next week I am going to begin working with a select list of boys to prepare them for the scholarship examinations which the Catholic high schools hold in June. Of course, I can't work with boys whose minds are too much on girls instead of on their studies."

Sister showed that she didn't like the kids seeing the girls by the tone of her voice. She was different now from the way she usually was. But she didn't have anything on him. It was the others she was sore at. Maybe she would pick him as one of the group she'd help prepare for the scholarship exams, and maybe he'd win one, and then on graduation night, when he received his diploma, Father Gilhooley would announce this good news before the whole parish. That would be his victory and his revenge on them all.

IV

"Danny, I was pleased to learn that you're not one of the boys in the group that is tagging after girls," Sister said, alone with Danny in the classroom.

Danny didn't know what to say to her.

"Someone told Sister Bernadette that you were running after a girl in eighth grade all of the time."

"Who said it?" Danny asked, his sudden anger half-simulated.

Natalie O'Reedy's name came to his mind right away. He didn't have any real reason for feeling sure that she had done it, but still he felt that she was the one. She was a good friend of Roslyn and, yes, he was certain she was the one.

"I can't tell you who it was, Daniel."

"I don't know why anyone says things like that about me. I don't have much to do with girls."

"Well, stories like that have been carried behind your back. I called on you to ask questions about girls today because I knew that it would be a chance for you to show that they aren't true."

"They're not true, Sister."

It wasn't a lie exactly. He didn't chase after her. Of course, he often went to school by way of Sixty-first Street, hoping to see her. But no one could prove that he chased after Roslyn.

"Sister, who said that about me?"

"I can't tell you that. All I can do as your friend is to warn you that you have enemies in this school," she answered, her grave dark eyes meeting his.

This meant that he had no chance with Roslyn, ever. Because one of her friends must have told this story to the nuns. It must be Natalie. Natalie and Roslyn must talk about him and laugh at him behind his back. In sixth grade Roslyn had once called him a pie-face. They probably called him many other names.

"I also asked you to remain after school for another reason." Sister paused a moment. "We nuns have been hearing stories that the eighth-grade boys and girls might be violating the Sixth Commandment."

He felt like sinking through the floor. Sister was mentioning this subject in a way that meant she knew he had an idea what it all meant. Her eyes were planted on him. He glanced aside.

"Danny, do you know if these stories are true or not?"

"No, Sister."

She put him in one hell of a hole, asking him a question like that. She wanted him to be a snitcher. He wouldn't be one. Well, he was certainly glad he didn't know anything here and didn't have to lie or to snitch, either.

"Did you go to Roslyn Hayes' New Year's Eve party?"

"No, Sister."

"You were at Glenn's party last fall, weren't you?"

"Yes, Sister."

"Were there any violations of the Sixth Commandment then?"

"No, Sister. Roslyn's parents and Glenn's mother and father were right there all the time, and there was nothing wrong happened at the party."

Kissing games weren't a sin.

"You haven't heard the boys mention anything that would suggest any such goings-on?"

"No, Sister, never."

"If you do, I want you to promise me as a friend that you'll tell me. Promise me that, Danny."

"Yes, Sister."

What else could he say to her in answer?

"I know that you will keep your promise. I know that your word is as good as gold."

He knew that he really wasn't any good, and here Sister had this high opinion of him. How could he ever live up to it?

"That's all I wanted to say to you, Danny, except this. I think you stand a very good chance to win a scholarship, and you're to be in the group I'll work with preparing for the examinations."

"I'm going to try hard to get one."

"I know you will, Danny." She rose. "And, Danny, you are not to say a word to any of the boys about this talk we have had."

He shook his head that he understood.

He walked downstairs with her. She left him at the back door of the convent.

He came out the side gate of the schoolyard. Down toward Sixtieth and Indiana, he could see some of the guys and girls, Roslyn, Natalie, Fritzie Lonigan, Billie, Tom O'Connor, Dick, Fat Malloy and Regan. He went home along Sixty-first Street to avoid them.

He was always being made fun of and treated like a goof. The public school kids he knew treated him the same way as the kids did here. No matter what he did or said, it seemed just goofy. What was the matter with him? Why did he seem different from other kids? He could fight, wrestle, play ball better than most kids. But many of them got respect for just being themselves. He had to fight kids to make them respect him or play ball better than they did. Well, he would.

Was it that he had the call?

He stopped by the elevated station. He should have gone down Indiana Avenue and bumped into them and taken a poke at the first one who made a crack. He imagined himself cleaning them up, one after the other, pounding them bloody and groggy.

Well, tomorrow and every other morning he was going to school with a chip on his shoulder.

V

He'd wanted to go home and think about his new resolutions and about what Sister had just told him, but Mama had spotted him from the window as he was going by and she'd called him in. He sat with Papa in the dining room. The tables were full of dishes. He watched his father closely, thinking that maybe if Papa had gone into the ring, he'd have been a great prize fighter, even a world's champion. Papa was a swell fighter. And would it have been something, to have your father a champ! But if that had happened, he wouldn't ever have lived with Mother and Uncle Al, because then Papa wouldn't have been so poor.

"Say, what is this snow-brigade business at school that I hear about?" Jim asked.

"I'm a marshal in the snow brigade," Danny answered proudly.

"Jim, the Sister likes him so much she made him a marshal in the snow brigade. That's what she thinks of our son."

"Do you get paid for it?"

"No, but this spring we're going to get off school opening day to see the White Sox for the work we've done in the snow brigade."

"What work do you do?"

"Whenever it snows, we go up to the school and shovel the snow off the sidewalk in front of the church property."

"That's what I call nerve," Jim said, looking at Lizz. He turned to Danny. "Your tuition money is paid, isn't it?"

"Yes."

"There are lots of poor devils out of work who could shovel snow. And what do they do? They have the boys from school do this work, kids who aren't formed and developed physically. Every Sunday I go to church, I hear Father Gilhooley complaining that the collections aren't big enough. Well, I want to know—is it the Church of God or the Church of Gold when it acts that way?"

"Jim, it's a sin to speak against the Church."

"Papa, the last time I shoveled snow Father Gilhooley came out and praised us and gave each of us a nickel."

"You hear that?" Jim cried out, turning to Lizz.

"Well, wasn't that fine of him?" Lizz replied.

"How many were you?" Jim asked, turning again to face Danny.

"Five."

"Is that the hull snow brigade, five of you?"

"No, a lot of kids didn't show up."

"They were smart," Jim said.

Papa didn't understand it.

"Five of them, a nickel a piece. Twenty-five cents to get more than the hull block shoveled."

He had to stand up for the Church, even against Papa. He had to say something.

"But, Papa, it's an honor. Sister doesn't let every kid be in the snow brigade."

"Well, you tell her to find other kids instead of you."

"Don't you do it, Son," Lizz said.

"I can't do that, Papa. Why, Sister Magdalen is my friend. I couldn't say that to her."

"And what would my mother say?" asked Lizz.

"I'm his father, and let your old mother put that in her corncob pipe and smoke it."

"It doesn't do him any harm, Jim."

"I got to go home and take the dog out," Danny said, his voice timid and tentative.

"Come again and see us, Dan, and don't forget what I told you," Jim said.

As soon as he got outside, he forgot about what Papa had said. If Papa told him to quit the snow brigade again, he'd think up some excuse. He wouldn't quit it. He hurried home. After taking the dog out, Danny wandered into the parlor, thinking about fighting. He hadn't been licked in a fight since Ralph Borax beat him in fifth grade. Since then, he'd boxed Ralph even. But he shouldn't let himself get over-confident and he shouldn't neglect his fighting. Most kids never gave it a thought and then, when they got in a fight, they just rushed and slugged. He always tried to fight scientifically. He studied other kids' style of fighting and worked out campaigns to use against them in case he ever had to scrap with them. He had to be smarter than other kids in fighting, wrestling, and baseball, and so he had to keep studying these sports. The reason he licked Hugh Nolan last year was because he'd been smart. Hugh was heavier than he was, and all the kids thought Hugh would massacre him. But he knew Hugh's style. Hugh was slow and rushed in, swinging murderous right haymakers. He had used footwork and jabbed Hugh with his left, sometimes crossing with his right, until Hugh was all in and had a bloody nose. A couple of years ago when Studs Lonigan and the older guys used to take him around as a mascot and get him into fights, everybody used to think that he won them because he couldn't be hurt. That wasn't so. He won them because he fought scientifically.

He practiced left jabs before the low mirror. He had to make his left faster, sharper, and straight. If you punched straight, you could always beat hookers and roundhouse swingers to the punch. He tried out his favorite punch, a left to the guts and a right to the jaw. When he'd boxed Regan and licked him in a few seconds with that punch. And he had to get his footwork down better. With sluggers, he had to side-step. One of the reasons why he was almost the only kid in the neighborhood who'd licked Andy Le Gare was because he had side-stepped Andy's rushes, blocked, and uppercutted. He practiced this trick and then he worked patiently at a shift he wanted to perfect. You weren't supposed to lead with your right. But if he could perfect a sudden shift of feet to lead with a right jab and follow up with a left uppercut, it would be effective against some slow-thinking kid some day.

And he wanted to perfect weaving and bobbing. Jack Dempsey, the new heavyweight who'd probably be the next champ, weaved and bobbed. To fight this way he had to get his follow-up punches down pat. He was weak on that. He usually hit a kid a couple of times and then dropped into a defensive position and waited. Against light kids, a weaving-and-bobbing rushing fight ought to turn the trick for him. He lowered his head, swung his shoulders from side to side, and murdered the air with punches in imitation of Jack Dempsey.

He decided he'd practiced enough for today. But every day he would shadowbox for five or ten minutes. It would give him more confidence in himself. He was really afraid to fight, and when you were afraid you had to be good and conquer your fear. The best way to do it was to make yourself a perfect fighter and have a full repertoire of tricks. His idea of a fighter was Kid McCoy. Boy, if he could some day be a Kid McCoy!

10

I

Danny looked out from the shelter which stood near the Fifty-first Street end of the Washington Park baseball field. The wide stretch of grass and baseball diamonds was almost deserted. The sun had come out after the rain, and glistening raindrops clung to the grass. He'd come out hoping he could get in some game, but there were no games being played today. There weren't even any men hitting out flies. Halfway across the field some little kids were playing, but they were too small for him. He wore his spiked shoes, an old baseball shirt, a gray-and-green baseball cap, and his fielder's glove was slung over his left wrist.

So far this year he was having a good year. He was hitting pretty good, and his average for all the games he'd played so far was .320. He wanted to make this the best year he'd ever had in baseball, and he was going to play and practice as much as he possibly could. Now was the time for him to give everything he had if he wanted to be a big-league star when he grew up.

But what about the call? Sister had been talking to him about it a lot of late.

"Hello."

The speaker was a man about fifty years old, with a mustache and red hair. Danny had seen him around here pretty often, and the man knew all the fellows who played down near this end of the park. Danny was pleased that the man recognized him and talked. The man must have seen him playing.

"I see there's no baseball today," the man said, sitting down beside Danny.

"It rained."

"You like to play ball, don't you?"

"Yes."

"Don't you like the girls?"

Danny noticed the strange expression in the man's eyes. To avoid meeting his gaze, Danny glanced off across the park and acted as if he had not heard the man's question.

"How old are you?"

"Fifteen."

"Haven't you ever played hide the weenie with the girls out here at night? Lots of kids your age do."

Danny didn't like the man talking to him like this.

"You shouldn't blush. Don't you know it's nature?"

He wanted to get away. He didn't like the look in the man's eye.

"I got to go home."

"Don't be in such a hurry," the man said, laying a restraining hand on Danny's arm. "Where do you live?"

"Fifty-eighth Street."

"You needn't be ashamed when I talk to you. I know lots of kids around here and they all tell me about their girls."

He'd never had a man talk to him like this. Older guys had talked about girls and told him the trouble with him was that he pulled his pudding, but he didn't. Only he wondered what it was like to do that. Why did dirty things have to be? Why did there have to be dirty sins that sent so many souls to Hell to burn forever?

"What's your name?"

"Danny O'Neill."

"Danny, do you like girls?"

"No."

"That's funny. And you say you're fifteen. All boys at fifteen like girls."

"I never bother about girls," Danny said, still facing the man.

Nobody he knew was around.

"You're a funny boy."

"I have to get home," Danny said, getting up.

"Well, I'll walk part of the way home with you," the man said, walking at Danny's side.

He had never met a man who said things like this to him before.

II

Danny said nothing. He wanted to be home, away from this man. He was ashamed of himself.

"Yes, Danny, I can't understand you," the man said.

Danny smirked, confused.

"You don't do anything to yourself?"

"I don't know what you mean," Danny answered, but he did know what the man was talking about.

"You must. All boys do it. Haven't you ever heard talk about whipping the dummy?"

Danny felt that he must be red from ear to ear.

He looked ahead, seeing the driveway that turned eastward and went past the refectory. Maybe the man would leave him there.

"You don't mean to say that you don't know what I mean, Danny?" the man repeated, eyeing Danny closely.

"Don't know what?"

"What it means to whip the dummy? You do, you know that, now admit it."

"Yes."

"Well, don't you do it?"

Danny looked at the man, puzzled, afraid. He'd once tried to find out what it was like when he was too young and couldn't do anything. But he hadn't ever really done it.

The man suddenly grabbed Danny and felt his genital organs. Danny drew away. He blushed. He was afraid. He wanted to run and he was afraid. And what would this man say to the guys he played ball with? Gee, why had he ever come out to the park today to have this happen to him?

"You're pretty big. You feel like you whip it."

"I don't. I never did," Danny said, a note of protest and insistence coming into his high-pitched voice.

"That's funny. All kids do it."

"I go on across here," Danny said as they reached the driveway.

"I'll go with you."

He crossed the driveway, watching out for automobiles. He'd get out of the park and walk along by the tennis courts. There would be people around, and this awful man couldn't be grabbing at him again. They came out of the park and walked alongside of the fenced-in tennis courts. Danny felt safer now.

"Gee, you're a strange boy. Are you telling me the truth?"

"Yes," Danny said; he tried to be casual.

Shame because of his own body welled up within him. Why did people have to have the kind of bodies they did? Why hadn't God made people different?

"You ought to get wise to yourself."

And what did the man want? Why were there men like this who didn't mind their own business and asked a kid questions like this and grabbed at his john? And the man had such a funny expression on his face when he looked at him. This was all beyond him. Danny walked faster, but the man kept up with him.

"What grade you in?"

"Eighth."

"Don't the boys and girls in your school like to play with each other and see what they look like naked?"

"No, they ain't like that."

He once missed a show party when they lived over on Fifty-seventh and Indiana, but none of the girls were from Saint Patrick's. Girls in Catholic schools didn't want to do that; he knew they didn't.

They passed Fifty-seventh Street. Only one more block. Each step brought him one step nearer to getting away from this man. Left foot. One more step nearer to getting away. Right foot, one more step nearer to getting away.

"You can learn a lot out in the park."

"I always play ball out there."

He'd never let himself get alone with this man again. One step, another, another, less than half a block now.

"What do the girls talk about when you see them at your school?"

"I don't see them much."

"They must be human. I'm just talking to you about nature, that's all, Danny."

Nature was sin.

Closer now, and in a minute he'd be rid of this awful man.

"Yes, you want to get wisened up. You got tools now and you want to learn all the things you can do with your tools."

He wasn't sure he knew what the man was driving at. All he knew was that the man made him ashamed of himself and ashamed of everybody, boys and girls and men and women and even priests and nuns and everybody, because of the way they were made.

"I go here."

"Well, I want to talk to you again. I'm always around the shelter in Washington Park, and don't forget what I told you," the man said with that funny expression.

Danny turned to cross the street.

"Goodbye, Danny."

"Goodbye," Danny muttered without looking back.

He ran across the street and was almost hit by an automobile. Because of his spiked shoes, he had to go up the back stairs. He could go through the building gangway to reach them, but he ran down Fifty-eighth Street instead. Without knowing exactly why, he didn't want that man to see where he lived. He turned in the alley. The stone dulled his spikes, but he'd always liked the sound spikes made on stone.

Life seemed so dirty to him. But if he became a priest he would escape from all the dirtiness of life. Priests didn't have dirty thoughts and they were chaste.

His dog began barking from the porch as soon as he entered the back yard.

III

Danny was terrified. He sat alone in his bedroom, thinking about what had happened. Perhaps this man was a temptation of the Devil, and God had sent this temptation as a way of telling him that he really had the call. God had often sent the Devil to saints to tempt them. But, of course, God had given the saints the strength and grace to resist temptation. But he wasn't a saint and he had never been strong enough to resist temptations.

Could he ever be a saint?

Anybody would laugh at him if they knew he even asked himself such a question.

He couldn't be too sure that this old man had been put in his path as a way of letting him know that he was really called. He had no right to think that God was going out of His way for anybody like Danny O'Neill, did he? Of course he didn't.

Danny wandered restlessly to the parlor. He began to wonder if baseball scouts went to Washington Park. If they did, maybe one of them might see him on one of his good days. They might see how promising he was. If they did, would they get in touch with him?

But he had to give up that idea. He had to recognize that this question of the call had been on his mind for months. If it stuck in his mind so much, now mustn't it mean that it was the sign? If it kept coming back to him at so many different times, when he had so many different things in his mind or he was doing so many different things, why, didn't that mean something?

Sometimes it was like a voice inside of him talking to him, and the voice would say to him:

You know you have the call! You know you have the call! You know you got the call!

Did he? Now, there was that voice again, right now, this minute.

You know it! You know you have the call!

Suppose he did. He could first be a baseball player, and never marry, and then, when his playing days were over, he could be ordained. But if he really had the call, he wouldn't always be fighting with himself this way. If he had the call, and God had poured grace into his soul, he would want to be a priest. He wouldn't love Roslyn. He wouldn't be dreaming of being a baseball player the way he always did. Yes, he was convinced. He didn't have the call.

He jumped to his feet, happy, feeling a sudden lightness of mood.

But how could he tell Sister?

As soon as one worry left your mind, another took its place. Here was one. But then, Sister couldn't say that he had to be a priest when he didn't have the call. A person who didn't have a vocation shouldn't be a priest. That stood to reason.

IV

Danny sat at his desk with his bedroom door closed. He was elated. Just after he had made up his mind that he didn't have the call, the idea had come to him like an inspiration. And now he had gotten the letter finished, written carefully and legibly so that it looked as if a man had written it. It ought to work, too. Connie Mack was known above all other managers as the man to pick promising players off the sand lots and develop them into stars. Well, after receiving this letter, why shouldn't Connie send a scout out to Washington Park to look him over? And maybe the scout would see him on a good day and sign him up for a tryout with the Athletics a couple of years from now when he was old enough. Players had been signed up at fifteen before. There was the case of that pitcher, Hoyt. Proud of himself, he read the letter he'd just composed.

Mr. Connie Mack
Shibe Park
The Philadelphia Athletics
Philadelphia, Pennsylvania.

Dear Mr. Mack:

I am writing you this letter to tip you off about a kid named O'Neill who is to be seen playing ball in Washington Park in Chicago all of the time. He isn't ripe just yet because he is only fifteen or sixteen

That was a smart idea, to make out that the man who was supposed to be writing this letter didn't know too much about him, so it was best not to give his exact age.

but he is coming along fast for his age, and he will be ripe soon enough and he looks like a real comer. If you look him over you can pick up a promising youngster now for nothing and he seems destined for the big show. I am a baseball fan and like to see kids get a chance, and take pride in picking them. I picked some before and was a good picker. Years ago when George Moriarity was playing on the sand lots of Chicago I picked him, and I think you must admit I picked a big leaguer then because Moriarity is a big leaguer. You can pick this kid up now for nothing and you will never regret it. He plays out in Washington Park all of the time, and you can send a scout out there to look at him and easily find out who he is.

I know you will not be sorry for this tip.

A baseball fan, a real one

T. J. Walker

He was pleased and satisfied with his letter. All year he'd really felt that 1919 was going to be an important year for him. Maybe this letter might begin to prove that it was. He was smart to have thought up this idea.

He decided to write Uncle Al a letter, too, because he owed him one and had the time. He could mail both letters together. He got fresh paper and wrote.

Dear Uncle Al,

I meant to write you a letter sooner than this, but I have been busy with school and I have been playing ball a lot. I think I am going to have a good year playing ball this year, and I am hitting over three hundred in the games I played in. Two weeks ago on Sunday morning, I played with the men I often play with in Washington Park, and I got a two base hit and caught two flies, and last Sunday I played center field instead of right field where I usually play with these men. I got a texas leaguer to center field and caught three flies. And we made up an eighth grade team in school and won indoor games from the seventh and sixth grade classes and I pitched good games, and made a triple in one game to help win it. My average on my report card last month was ninety four. Sister has some of us during most of the noon hour studying for the scholarship examinations and I hope that I will be able to win a scholarship. It would be swell if I could. Everybody at home is happy and Aunt Margaret is well. Little Margaret and I have tried to do things at home and Little Margaret is going to school every day and everybody at home is happy. Liberty is lots of fun and I take her out every day and she hasn't done anything in the house. But she has a new habit. She goes down in the basement and catches rats and kills them and brings them up to us on the porch and looks at us to pat her and tell her she is a good dog. And sometimes she hides the dead rats on the porch and under the stove in the kitchen. Mother gets mad when she does that and we have to watch her. School is going to be out early in June and next week the graduating class gets its ribbons. The eighth grade boys are acting a play about Ireland and I am going to act the part of an English Lord named Lord Heathcote and I have to learn my part. I am going to try my best to do it as good as I can. I saw the opening game of the White Sox and Lefty Williams pitched a good game and the White Sox won it. I think they are going to win the pennant. But I wish they had Stuffy McInnis playing first base and I think Stuffy would like to play with them too, don't you? I think he is the greatest first base man in the game except for Hal Chase but Hal is getting old now. Stuffy is better than Sisler in the field.

Mother is in the kitchen now cooking supper and she is singing an Irish song.

Aunt Margaret is at work tonight. Uncle Ned has not come home for supper yet. We expect him any minute. He says he thinks he is going away again next week. I am forwarding your mail. I was over to Mama's and everybody there is happy and well. There is no trouble at home and everything is smooth. I will write to you again very soon and I will watch your mail and forward it to you. Mother received the money order for ten dollars last Saturday and I endorsed it for her and cashed it for her. When will you be home? We will be glad to see you.

Your nephew

Danny

Happy and eager, he dashed out of the apartment to get stamps and mail both letters.

11

I

It was a warm and sunny May afternoon. When school let out, Danny and the gang met Roslyn, Natalie, and some of the other girls. Roslyn walked beside Natalie, and Danny observed her unobtrusively. Natalie was prettier, but he didn't care, he loved Roslyn. Natalie had long, brown curly hair and the best legs of any girl in school. Roslyn was thin and bony, and her face was pointed. But if you looked at her at certain times she was pretty. She wore a white dress and white stockings, and her gold and blue class ribbons were much cleaner than his own.

"When I was a little kid in second and third grade, I used to think that it would be such a long long time before I'd be big and graduating from school," Roslyn said.

"You're not so big even now, and it must be a mistake that you're graduating," Glenn said.

"I got another year to go before I'm out. But I'm sure I won't graduate. I'll quituate," Fat Malloy said.

Glenn gave Roslyn a shove.

"If you tear my ribbon, I'll kill you," she said.

Glenn made a face at her. Natalie moved alongside of Glenn. He stopped teasing his cousin. Danny stared at Roslyn, too overwhelmed to say anything.

Roslyn smiled at him.

Maybe Roslyn did care for him, but was proud, or perhaps as bashful as he was. At those parties at his house in sixth grade, it was Roslyn who had asked to be his partner. That was how he had gotten to know her. Before then he'd thought he was in love with red-haired Helen Scanlan. One summer day a long time ago, he had ridden on a grocery wagon with Helen. And he used to play tin-tin and other games with her and the Indiana kids when he lived on Indiana. Helen was walking ahead with Dick and Ralph. She was beginning to have breasts. Roslyn didn't. He'd take Roslyn to Helen every day in the week and twice on Sunday. Helen and sixth grade and all that was past. Many things were all over now, and grammar school was just about over, too. He was growing up and he didn't exactly feel as if he was even though his class ribbons told all the world he was graduating. The class prophecy predicted that he would be the lightweight champion of the world. What would he really be?

He looked at Roslyn.

"You didn't win a scholarship, did you?" Roslyn asked.

"No, I didn't," he said apologetically.

"I thought you would because you're pretty smart. You got higher averages than I did."

Even though he hadn't won a scholarship, she knew that he wasn't a dummy.

"What school you going to?" she asked.

He still wasn't sure what school he was going to because of his problem about the call.

"I guess I'll go to Saint Stanislaus," he answered, glad to be talking to her and for the conversation to be about him.

"That's a good school."

"I'm going to Saint Paul's."

That was the best girls' school on the South Side, and girls whose fathers had money usually went there.

"It's a good school," he said.

She pursed her lips as if she were thinking. He could see she was friendly. They were lagging behind the others, and no one was paying attention to them. He had waited since sixth grade for a moment like this. And here it was.

"I hope I'll like Saint Paul's."

"You ought to," he said, his voice a bit strained.

He wished they were both in seventh grade now and had another year because he was convinced that she really cared about him.

"Maybe I'll like it, and maybe I won't."

"I guess you ought to."

She faced him. He liked her blue eyes.

"I'll give you three guesses why I won't."

"I don't know," he said, screwing up his face.

"Can't you even guess?"

"Well, I can guess."

"Will you like going to high school?"

"I don't know anything about it."

"Will you miss anyone, for instance?"

"Well, of course I will."

"Maybe I might, too," she said.

Was she trying to tell him she'd miss him? Why couldn't he just tell her he would miss her? He couldn't say the words.

"I wonder what everybody'll be like when we're all graduating from high school?" she asked pensively.

Would she be his girl then?

How would they remember grammar school then? He would always remember walking beside her like this. He was sure that he'd remember it as long as he lived.

"I don't know," he said.

She looked at him quizzically. Had he said something he shouldn't have said?

"We're almost alone. Look how far the rest of them are ahead of us," she said.

"Yes, they're on the other side of Sixtieth."

He couldn't say any of the things he so much wanted to say.

She pouted at him and started walking faster. He kept up with her. She had suddenly changed and didn't seem to want to talk. He said nothing. If he had been sure what she was driving at, he might have said different things.

"Roslyn," he suddenly said, determined.

"We have to hurry up and catch up to the others," she answered coolly.

When they reached the other kids, the entire group strolled lazily along Indiana Avenue.

II

Danny waited for Sister to speak. He was alone with her on the stage of the basement auditorium beneath the church. She sat on a camp chair, facing him. After rehearsal for the play was over, he had tried to run out before she could catch him. He knew that he had to have a final talk with her about his decision, and he had been trying to put it off from day to day. Now it had come. He couldn't stall Sister because that would really be trying to fool God and his own conscience.

"You've made up your mind, haven't you, Danny?"

He didn't speak.

"I can tell. I know you have the call."

"Well, Sister, I have thought about it all year."

"And after all that, you still have the feeling that you might have it?"

"Yes, Sister."

"You couldn't want a better sign."

He looked down at his feet. Then he faced her.

"I guess you're right."

"Going to Quigley, Danny, doesn't commit you finally. It isn't taking a vow. And there is enough reason to believe that you have a vocation. Everything about you makes me believe that you are marked for the priesthood."

He should feel honored and happy to hear her tell him this. There must be something wrong with him when he didn't.

"Danny, you ought to register at Quigley Seminary. If you have any remaining doubts after a couple of years there, they will be cleared up. You will be taking no step that you can't retrace in time by doing this."

"Yes, Sister."

Under the circumstances, he couldn't do anything but agree with her. What reasons could he offer against it? Roslyn had spoken to him again this morning in front of school. Baseball? These reasons weighed nothing in the scales, and he knew they didn't. And Sister wasn't forcing him. She was only doing what was right and considering his soul and his duty. What was really forcing him was the voice of his conscience, a feeling within him that he had to go through with it or else he would be ruining his whole life and turning his back on God.

"There isn't something else you want to be, is there?"

"No, Sister."

"There isn't any girl?"

"No, Sister."

The lie had come out of his mouth before he'd thought, and now what could he do? But such lies were only venial sins.

"You're sure enough to take the first step?"

"Yes, Sister," Danny said, feeling as if he were someone in a dream and not himself.

He looked out at the chairs facing the stage, placed irregularly and out of order.

"I'm sure your grandmother will be the happiest woman in the world when she hears this news," Sister said.

He didn't answer.

"Danny, I can see a wonderful career ahead of you as a priest, a career in which you will do great good work."

He wanted to do good. And he was doing the right thing. Now he'd be able to confess about that bad confession, and then his soul wouldn't be black with sacrileges. His mind was made up, and he felt the same kind of relief that he felt after going to confession and receiving absolution. A weight was lifted from him.

"Well, Danny, I have many things to attend to over at the convent. But this news is of the kind to make me very happy and gratified."

"Yes, Sister."

"You know, Danny, I am proud of you."

He walked out of the auditorium with her.

After he left her, he walked slowly. He had to pray to fortify himself to go through with this. But it was his duty to do it. God gave a different duty to everyone, and everyone had to fulfill the duty God gave them. He thought about the parable of *The Master in the Vineyard.*

Just think, some day he might be celebrating his first mass and delivering his first sermon.

He drooped along.

III

"Mother, I want to tell you something," Danny said.

"Yes, Son."

"Mother, I'm going to be a priest."

"What did you say, Son?" she asked, after recovering somewhat from her surprise.

"Next year I want to register to go to Quigley Seminary."

"Well, the Lord bless us! It's a fine priest you'll be, Son."

"Can I, Mother?"

"Ask the Lord, don't ask me. And talk to Al about it tonight."

Danny went to his room and sat on the bed. He was going to do what God wanted him to do. And this was nothing compared with what the saints and the martyrs had sacrificed for God. They had died, happy because they were giving their very lives for God. He should be happy, very happy at this very minute. After all, what was it in the eyes of Almighty God to be Ty Cobb or Eddie Collins as compared with being a priest, saving mortal souls from the everlasting fires and the eternal pains of Hell? What was the matter with him?

It was dark and shadowy in his room because the window faced the building next door. He looked blankly at the wall.

IV

Danny faced both his uncles in the front bedroom. He didn't know what was coming, and all he wished was that he could get this interview over as quickly as possible. He suddenly hoped that Uncle Al would put his foot down and say he couldn't study for the priesthood. But Uncle Al would be flouting the will of God if he did such a thing. He couldn't ask to have his problems solved by wishing that Uncle Al do such a thing, risking eternal damnation.

"You're pretty young, aren't you, to be deciding things like this?" Uncle Ned asked.

"Sport, I don't want to dissuade you, but I do want you to think about it. It's a very important step you're taking," Uncle Al said.

"I know it is," Danny answered weakly.

"How long have you thought about this decision?" Uncle Al asked.

"All year."

"How is it you didn't say anything sooner to us?"

"I hadn't made up my mind before. I did today and told Sister."

"You talked with her but not with Uncle Al or me?" asked Ned.

"Well, she's my teacher, and she's my friend."

"And we're mud, I suppose?"

"Dan, you should have talked to me about it, too," Uncle Al said, disappointed.

"Gee, I didn't think."

"Well, Sport, we'll talk about it some other time," Al said. Danny looked down and awkwardly left the room.

V

"Rats! Such nonsense," Ned exclaimed, sitting with Al in the parlor.

"What's that, Ned?"

"Of course it's a fine thing that some young fellows become priests, but Danny—that's different. How does he know his own mind? Hell, he's just a little boy. And he ought to consider us, you and Mud and all that you've done for him. And there's his brothers and sisters. When he gets older, he has to help them out, doesn't he? When he comes back from the movie, I'm going to talk to him. I'll settle this business."

"No, don't do that, Ned."

"Why?"

"There's lots of time. We mustn't be precipitate."

Al puffed on his cigar, a faraway look in his eyes. He thought of how for all these years he had nursed such plans and dreams for Danny's future. He wanted to give him the best education he could, assist him in every possible way to become a successful lawyer and an educated man who would really count in the community. Of course, if Danny truly felt in his heart that he had to be a priest, what could he do? He would have to accept Danny's decision and get adjusted to it.

"You see, Ned, if he has a vocation—well, there is nothing for us to do. Then it's the will of God."

"Al, don't fall for that stuff. I can see the whole thing clear as a nutshell. This Sister just sold him all these notions, that's all there's to it. Didn't you hear him say that she was his friend? Sure, that's what happened."

"The thing we have to find out is if this is really what he has to be or if it isn't."

"You can't tell me Danny's made for it. Now, Al, I tell you, let me handle this and I'll take care of it."

"Well, let's wait. School is almost over, and he has the whole summer to play in, and let's see if it sticks in his mind. A proposition like this is a delicate one. We have to be careful in our tactics and be sure that what we do is right."

"Right? Sure we're right. There are plenty of kids his age who are pushed into the priesthood when they don't belong in it. And they are unhappy the rest of their life. It's too serious a thing for a boy his age to make up his mind about. And I'm going to talk to him."

"No, Ned, don't until I say so. We'll wait and let him alone and see what further decision he comes to," Al said.

VI

"Mother, I'm so happy," Lizz said, sitting in the O'Flaherty kitchen.

"It's the will of the Lord."

"I can't wait until I tell Jim. And, Mother, on the Sunday when my son says his first mass, you and I will drive to church in an automobile."

"I won't ride in an automobile. I'm swell. I want a fine horse and carriage."

"Mother, they're out of date. The swells nowadays go in automobiles."

"In the old country the finest people in the land, the gentlemen and their ladies, always rode in a carriage. And I'll have you know that I'll ride in a carriage myself."

"Mother, I'll bet this is Father's doing. Remember, Danny was always the apple of Pa's eye."

"May his soul rest in peace. But, Lizz, sit down, don't go. Have a cup of tea."

"Oh, no, Mother, I must go back to my chicks. Goodbye, Mother. And tell my son to come over and see us."

"Once I let me grandson over to see you when you lived on Forty-fifth Street and he almost got the diphtheria from you. Good night."

Lizz left by the back stairs. She walked over to the Fifty-eighth Street elevated station. She was going down to tell the news to the O'Reilleys, and would she lord it over them! She had known all along that her son, Daniel, was cut out for the priesthood. And she could see herself attending his first mass, sitting in the front pew, dressed in elegant clothes and letting the women of the parish eat themselves up with envy of her because she was the mother of Father O'Neill. What a day that would be!

She should have fixed herself up before going down to the O'Reilleys, but if she went home to bother about that, it would be too late when she got down there. She was poor, honorably poor. If they didn't like her because of the way she looked, let them tie a can to themselves. Would any of the O'Reilley children be a priest? No. Well, let them say anything to her because of her poverty when she had raised a son to be a priest.

Lizz took a seat in the elevated train. Noticing that other passengers looked at her, she frowned. Let rubbernecks look their eyes out. They didn't know the lady they were looking at.

Tomorrow she would go to church and give thanks to God on her knees.

The train had already stopped at Fifty-first Street.

"Conductor! Conductor! Hold it," she cried, and everyone in the train looked at her.

But it was too late. The conductor had closed the train gate and signaled for the train to go on. The train started. She lost her balance and almost fell in a man's lap.

"Can't you hear?" she yelled at the conductor as he stepped into the car from the vestibule.

"You called me too late. You mustn't have been watching for your station, lady."

"I told you to hold it. I'm a poor mother with sore feet and I can't run. Since when is it a rule of the company that a poor woman has to run to get off at her station?" she shouted, while the passengers listened and looked on with amusement.

"Sorry, lady. It was a mistake. You can take a train right back to your station and it won't be so inconvenient."

"Say, who asked you to give me your two cents' worth of lip?"

He looked at her perplexed. She quickly grabbed hold of a strap in order to preserve her balance. She glared at him.

"I'm going to turn you in. If you knew who I was you'd tremble for your job. I'm going to see my cousin, he's the closest friend of the District Attorney. You won't have that badge and stand in trains insulting ladies any more, oh, no, you won't, not when I get through with you," she yelled at him, the rumble of the train half drowning her words.

"I told you I was sorry, lady, but it wasn't my fault," the conductor said.

"If my man was with me, he'd smash your face in," she yelled, swinging her arms and almost falling.

"All right, lady, but you'll have to get off this train if you're going to talk that way."

"Get off, with pleasure," she said, smiling ironically and bowing to him. "With pleasure I'll get off." Her face hardened. "Why did you hold me on?"

"I told you, lady, that it was your own fault."

The train drew into the Forty-seventh Street station.

"Forty-seventh Street! Forty-seventh Street! The next stop is Forty-third," the conductor yelled.

He turned his back on Lizz and went to call the same information into the car behind. He pulled the gates open. Lizz hurried off and faced him as he stood between the cars.

"You dirty dog, insulting a woman," she yelled, brandishing her fist, paying no heed to the small audience she had drawn.

The conductor closed the gates and gave the signal for the train to start. When it started to move, Lizz shook her fist after the conductor. She hurried downstairs. She hoped Joe O'Reilley would be home so she could tell Joe about how she had been insulted. Maybe she could sue the elevated company. She walked along Forty-seventh Street and began rehearsing in her mind how she would announce the news about Danny to the O'Reilley sisters.

VII

"Oh, Jim, it tickles me pink," Lizz said while Jim sat drinking his second cup of coffee after having eaten ham and eggs; it was about two o'clock in the afternoon.

"I don't know what I think about it."

"Well, you wouldn't set yourself against the will of God?"

"How do I know it's the will of God? And it seems to me that since I'm his father, the least he could have done was to talk it over with me before making up his mind."

"Jim, a family that gives a boy to the holy priesthood will always be lucky."

"He's too young a boy to be making up his mind like this."

"The priest with his fingers can change the bread and wine into the body and blood of Christ. And he can work miracles, too."

"Maybe so. And the boy who works and brings in money to put bread in the stomachs of his younger brothers and sisters and helps give them a chance in the world is doing something, too. The way I see it, it's just as fine a thing as anything the priest does. You don't have to be a priest in order to do good."

Jim looked idly out the window. Spring sunshine flooded the empty prairie.

"Jim, wait until I tell you what I told the O'Reilleys last night. My, my, did I rub it into them!"

Jim glanced at her, bored. He had long ago developed the habit of not hearing what she said when she gossiped this way. As she began, he sat patiently facing her and hearing not a word she said.

VIII

Danny stood in a corner of the little room to the left of the stage in the basement auditorium. It was crowded with his classmates and their parents. He clasped his graduating diploma, a diploma in Irish history, and a Palmer Method certificate for writing. He wore a double-breasted blue suit made of coarse material. The trousers were hooked below the knee, and they bulged so much that his legs looked very skinny. His face was shiny, his hair was combed, and he wore a stiff collar which irritated his neck and made him feel uncomfortable. He had been ashamed about the suit. All the other kids had single-breasted belted suits. And this suit came from Mother's sister. It was one of the suits given to her for the boys in her orphan asylum in Brooklyn. Sister had written to Mother when she sent the suit, saying she hoped her grandnephew would one day celebrate his golden jubilee as a priest, as she would soon do as a nun.

He walked over to Sister Magdalen.

"Goodbye, Daniel," she said.

"Goodbye, Sister," he replied, his voice catching.

"Danny, we shan't be leaving the convent here for another week. You come around and see me. I want to talk to you about the summer."

"Yes, Sister, I will."

She shook hands with him. He turned away. He was almost crying. He shouldn't be like this. He didn't know why he was. But he was. He was leaving. Father Gilhooley's talk at the graduation exercises tonight made him feel so sad. He went out alone. Out in front there were only a few people around. The crowd was gone. He looked for Mother, but he couldn't find her.

"What kept you, Dan?" Jim asked, coming up to him.

"I had to say goodbye to Sister."

"Well, let me tell you that your father's proud of you," Jim said in a sudden wave of feeling.

Danny didn't know what to answer.

"I stayed off work to see you graduate," Jim said, glancing at Danny's diplomas.

Danny caught his glance. He couldn't give them to Papa. If he didn't bring them home to Mother, she'd raise all holy Cain, and he'd never hear the end of it.

"I'll go home with you. Your mother and your brothers and sisters have all gone over there already," Jim said.

Danny walked beside his father, clutching his diplomas. Papa was like some of the fathers of kids in school, with rough hands and rough skin on his face, but he was different from Glenn's father, and Roslyn's, and Billie's. They were all more like Uncle Al, business men and not like workingmen.

Neither Jim nor Danny spoke for a while as they walked slowly along the picket fence enclosing the schoolyard. Danny saw lights in the convent at the other end of the yard.

They crossed Indiana, and by the drugstore on the opposite corner he saw Roslyn with her family. They hadn't all come in their automobile, he guessed. She smiled to him, and he smiled back.

"Well, you're growing up to be a man now," Jim said.

Danny gulped.

"And your old man is damned proud of you."

Danny still didn't know what to say. Growing up to be a man meant many things, and one of them was the changes in his own body. He was very shy now with his father.

"Here's a graduation present for you," Jim said, handing Danny a dollar.

"Thank you, Papa."

Jim patted Danny on the back.

"So you're going to be a priest, you think?" Jim said after they had walked almost half a block in silence.

"Yes," Danny answered, and here was something else he didn't like to talk about.

"How'd you come to decide to do that?"

"I think I got the call."

"You know, Danny, you can be good and a fine fellow without being a priest."

"Uh huh," Danny muttered, apprehensive of what would come next.

"I want you to think this over some more. You still have time and you're young."

Danny walked on at his father's side.

"Will you promise me to do that?"

"Yes, Papa."

"You're a good boy. And you're an O'Neill. Never forget that."

They walked along. It seemed as if they had nothing more to say to each other.

IX

It was all over now, and Danny was alone in his bedroom. Papa and Mama and the kids and everybody had talked and had ice cream in the kitchen, and he had squirmed because they had kept talking about him. Mother told Papa again and again that she was going to hang the diplomas on the wall in a gold frame, and he had been fearful that Papa would get sore at the way Mother was rubbing it in, but Papa had kept his temper. He looked at his class colors and took them off. He laid them on his untidy dresser. He got his class picture out of a drawer. There he was in the back row. And there was Roslyn in the front row with the other girls, all wearing their white graduation dresses. Roslyn had looked awful pretty tonight. As long as he lived, he was going to keep this picture. No matter what happened to him in life, no matter what happened to Roslyn, he would have this picture as a memorial. Even if she would never love him, he'd loved her, and this picture would be the holy shrine of his love. But he was going to be a priest! Even so, he could keep this picture, couldn't he? He kissed the image of Roslyn and then carefully put away the photograph in the bottom drawer of his dresser.

He tried to keep his tears back. He couldn't. He lay on the bed and sobbed. Suddenly he got to his feet. He hadn't kept his diary all year as he'd intended to. He'd start in again tonight. He kind of thought that maybe he wouldn't be a priest. Perhaps Papa and Uncle Ned were right, and he was too young to make up his mind. But no matter if he did or didn't have the call, tonight was like an historic night in his life.

He got his diary out of the hiding place in the closet and went to his desk. He was suddenly certain that he didn't have the call. He stared at his diary. He wanted to write in it that he loved Roslyn, that she had said goodbye to him tonight with a smile, and that he would go on loving and seeing her. He wanted to write in his diary how sad he felt to be graduating from school.

He scratched out the date January 2nd and wrote the present date in its place. He dipped his pen in ink. With tears streaming down his face, he wrote:

I graduated from Saint Patrick's. It is a night of destiny. Now I will play ball all summer, practice, and I will go to high school in the fall and try to make the high-school baseball team. Tonight starts me on my career.

12

I

It was a pleasant August night. After supper Danny had gone out to play ball in Washington Park. When he came in, Uncle Ned called him.

"Danny, come here, I want to talk to you," Uncle Ned said, speaking very seriously.

What did Uncle Ned want?

Danny went to his uncle's bedroom. Uncle Ned closed the door.

"Now sit down on the bed."

Danny obeyed.

"Are you still thinking of being a priest?"

"What?"

"What makes you think you want to be a priest?"

He didn't answer quickly. He couldn't drag out of himself the thoughts he had—he couldn't tell anyone even if he wanted to.

"I don't know, I just thought so."

"That's not a good reason. Now, why don't you get it out of your head? You aren't made to be a priest. What school do you want to go to?"

"Gee, I don't know."

"What do you want to be when you grow up?"

He couldn't say he wanted to be a big-leaguer. He couldn't say that, either.

"Haven't you ever thought about it?"

"No, not much."

"Well, what would you like to be?"

"I think I'd like to be a shoe salesman, like you and Uncle Al"

"Well, that's not bad."

He didn't have the vocation and he didn't have to go to Quigley. He felt as if some terrible trouble and fear had been lifted suddenly from his mind.

"Well, you want to pick some other school, then, instead of the seminary, is that right?"

"Yes, I don't think I knew what I wanted to do and be when I said I wanted to be a priest."

"Well, come on in the parlor and talk to your Uncle Al about high school."

Danny followed Uncle Ned to the parlor. Uncle Al put down the book he was reading.

"He doesn't know what high school he wants to go to and is going to talk to you about it."

"Well, what do you say, Sport? Don't you want to go to the seminary? I won't stand in your way, you know," Al said, smiling.

"No, I just thought I wanted to."

"Where do you think you want to go?"

"Saint Stanislaus," Danny said.

"Well, you find out and let me know the tuition."

"I will."

"And here, will you run down and get us a quart of ice cream?"

Danny took a dollar bill from Uncle Al. He dashed out of the apartment and ran with sheer relief and joy. Just like that, he had made up his mind. He didn't have to be a priest. He now could be a ball player if he was good enough. He had his chance. And if he made good, then Roslyn would surely love him and respect him.

II

It was beginning. Now he could call himself a high-school student. But would he ever be smart enough to learn studies like Latin and algebra? How would he fare here at Saint Stanislaus with all these strange kids? He had a clean page to write for himself. If he watched his step, he wouldn't be treated like a goof. Would he get in fights and be licked?

Danny sat in the center of a large classroom, one of about fifty new students. The only two he knew were Ralph and Jack Connelly from Saint Patrick's, but he'd missed his chance to sit near them. They were over in the first row, toward the front. A number of the lads were talking, introducing themselves to one another and saying where they came from. He wanted to talk to someone, but he couldn't bring himself to do it. He had determined to talk with the fellow behind him, a lanky, freckle-faced kid in long pants, but he hadn't. His tongue seemed to desert him.

They waited for a priest. At Saint Patrick's when no one was in the room, they'd yelled and thrown erasers at one another, but here no one did that. He glanced around the room, trying to size up his new classmates, but he avoided meeting anyone's eyes. The kid behind him poked him. He pretended not to notice or feel it. The guy was bigger than he was and looked tough. He was poked again, this time harder.

"Cut it out!" Danny said, turning around.

"What?"

"Cut it out!" Danny repeated, breathing almost in gasps and turning pale.

"Suppose I don't?"

"Well, cut it out!"

He was in for it. Why didn't he just happen to have another seat or another kid in back of him?

"Are you tough?"

"No, but I don't like gettin' poked in the back."

"You don't, huh?"

"No!"

"I suppose you wanna scrap?"

"No, but I ain't afraid of you."

Just then, a tall, handsome, pink-cheeked priest strode into the room and sat down at the teacher's desk on a dais. Everyone stopped talking. The priest scowled and let his eyes drift around the room.

"I'm Father Powers. If you don't know me or never heard of me, you will!"

The priest had a deep, gruff voice, and Danny was scared, both because of his voice and his looks.

Father Powers scowled again. He stepped off the dais and walked to the blackboard on the left side of the room. He wrote a list of textbooks on the board and turned to the class.

"Copy this list of books and have them tomorrow morning. You can get them at the bookstore in the hall right outside the door of this room."

He returned to his desk. There was a small sheet of paper and a form on every desk. Danny took out a pencil and copied the list. The other students did likewise, those not having pencils borrowing them.

Fox and McMillan's Deharbe's *Full Catechism of the Catholic Religion.*

Bennett, *First Year Latin.*

Hawkes, Luby and Touton, *First Course in Algebra.*

Brooks, *English Composition, Book One.*

Betten, *Ancient World.*

Maury-Simonds, *Physical Geography.*

Curry, *Mind and Voice.*

Finishing, Danny looked up, hoping the priest would notice that he had copied the list quickly.

A small boy who looked Polish, in the row on Danny's left and in the third seat, finished copying and began watching the priest.

"You!" the priest exclaimed, pointing at this boy.

"Yes, Fadder," the boy answered.

"Yes, you!" the priest declared, still pointing.

"Me?" the boy asked in a timid voice, his face flushing.

"Well, I don't mean your grandmother."

"Me?" the boy asked while many laughed.

"Yes, you!"

"My name's Smilga."

"Are you tough, Smilga?"

"No, Fadder."

"I just wanted to know. I was wondering if anyone in the room thinks he's a tough guy. Because if he does, I'll take him on with one hand."

Some of the boys laughed.

"And don't laugh. You can all hear me. You are here for us priests to educate, God save the mark. I don't want you to think this room is a circus, either, even though you all look like monkeys." He paused. "Maybe it would be easier for me if you were monkeys. Monkeys would be easier to teach than you guys. Judging from your appearance, I'd say that there isn't a man in the crowd of you. We used to get real fellows here, but now, every year, the freshmen get smaller and smaller. Well, pretty soon we can open a kindergarten. I'll be ready for one after a class such as the likes of you."

He paused again. With a twinkle in his dark eyes, he glanced about. He yawned.

"Tomorrow morning I want you all here at ten minutes to nine, ten minutes to nine sharp, and no later. I'm going to bite my initials on the ear of any one of you who comes in late. And you there, cockeyes, don't laugh."

He pointed at Danny.

"Me, I ain't laughing," Danny said in an injured tone of voice.

"I know it. You were trying to, but all you could get out was a snicker."

Danny shook his head from side to side. He was being laughed at on the very first day of class.

"And don't talk back to me, either, or else we'll put on a demonstration up here to open the educational proceedings for the year. Do you want to fight me?"

Danny was silent.

"I asked you, do you want to fight me?"

"No . . . No . . . No, Father," Danny meekly answered.

"Well, then watch your step. Prudence is the better part of valor . . . for all shrimps."

The class laughed again.

"And the rest of you can quit snickering."

They stopped laughing.

"Now, my unpleasant task is to hammer some Physical Geography into your heads. I suppose you don't know what that is, but you will before I get through with you. When I'm done with you, if you don't know anything about it, well, you won't have any heads left. But anyway, it's a useless task. I know that much in advance. However, with the help of the Lord, I'll get a little knowledge into a head here and there. And there are several warnings I want to give you. Don't any one of you fellows ever dare to come in here with your lessons unprepared. That will be rash of you. More rash than getting tough, because when you get tough, I'll just lick you. But when you come without your homework, by the ghost of great Caesar's ghost I'll not only lick you, I'll bite my initials in your face." He looked around. "But I am sorry that none of you are big. If a couple of you were big bruisers, then, when I fought with you, it would be more interesting for the shrimps in the class to watch." He laughed gruffly. "And quit snickering. And no talking in class. I'll do all the talking unless I ask you a question. I can do all the necessary talking without any help. Remember that, unless you want the wrath to descend on you. And now, there is a form slip of paper on every desk. I want each of you to write your name on it, that is, if you know how to write, and leave the slip up here. Class is dismissed. I don't feel well and I'll postpone the torture of teaching you shrimps for one more day."

The students filled out their forms and brought them to the desk. The freckled-faced kid in the seat behind Danny stopped him at the door.

"What's your name?"

"Danny O'Neill."

"Mine's Tom Garrity. Shake hands, you're all right."

They shook hands. Downstairs Danny met Ralph and they walked home together.

13

I

"I'll finish the kids' shoes tomorrow," Jim said, standing up and leaving his tools and materials in the dining-room corner where he had been half-soling a pair of Dennis' shoes.

"Don't you feel well, Jim?"

"I'm all right. I just have a little headache. Now and then for the last couple of days I've had them. I need glasses. I think I'll go downtown tomorrow and see about getting fitted to a pair."

"Jim, maybe you better go and lie down. And if you don't feel well, I'll go out to the drugstore and call up to say you can't go to work tonight."

"I'm all right. But maybe I will take a little nap."

"Jim, you must get glasses."

"Lizz, for years I've been after you to have your teeth fixed. Now if I get glasses you got to go to the dentist."

"I will, Jim."

"You promised me that last spring. I'm going to take you, my lady."

"Danny started to high school today, Jim."

"He gave up his idea of being a priest?"

"He can still change his mind."

"Whatever he decides to do seems to be none of his father's business."

"Jim, you go lay down now and rest."

"I think I'll play some phonograph records first, and then take a nap."

"I have to go down to the basement and finish the washing. Is there anything you want me to do for you before I go?"

"No, that's all right."

Jim went to the parlor. He didn't feel at all himself today. He felt a bit dizzy;

he had been having little dizzy spells on and off for the last couple of weeks. He dropped into his Morris chair and looked out the window. It was a fine, sunny day. He saw children, too young for school, playing on the sidewalk. All his were in school.

His spirits seemed depressed. It must be because he felt so low. He had a sickish headache. Listless, he continued to stare out the window. Closing his eyes, he had a strange sense of his own body. He felt that his eyes were very large in his head, and his right arm scarcely seemed his own. It was almost asleep. If he'd been drinking, he could understand it. But Lizz had insisted on his taking the pledge, and this time he'd kept it for almost a year.

He opened his eyes. The spots were gone. No, he was all right. Some little indisposition, that was all there was to it. The strongest man felt a little sick, a little faint, now and then, and it meant nothing at all.

He stood up, but again he felt dizzy. He dropped back into his chair. What in the name of God was it? Let's see, what had he eaten? It must be his stomach. Black spots danced before his eyes so vividly that he had an impulse to clutch one of them. He must need glasses. That would explain the dizziness and the headaches. Hadn't he been telling himself these last weeks that he needed glasses and ought to attend to getting them? If he felt just a little better, he'd go and settle the matter today. Well, tomorrow would be soon enough.

He was weak. Could his eyes do that to him? He better knock off an hour or so of sleep. He'd wake up feeling better. The dizzy spell he'd had at work last night had passed and he had gone on working without any trouble. Come to think of it, for a week or so he hadn't been getting enough sleep. The best engine in the world could be run down. Just like an engine needed gas, so did a man need rest.

Jim stood up. His mind was engulfed in darkness. He fell to the floor and crumpled up into a semi-reclining position, his back resting against the Morris chair. His wide-open eyes were focused on nothing. His head slanted down, and his chin almost touched his chest. His cheeks were blown out, especially the right one. His right eyelid began to droop. A ray of sunlight cut through the dusty parlor window and spread across his flaccid right leg just where it was turned in at the ankle. His right arm was close to his body, bent at the elbow, and his slightly flexed fingers rested on the torn edge of the carpet.

Little children shouted outside the window and then ran away. An automobile backfired as it passed on the street. The room was silent. Jim did not stir. His glassy eyes gave him an almost inhuman appearance.

He began to drool.

Time passed in the quiet room.

SECTION TWO

1922

14

I

Tall, sallow, bespectacled, and clad in the brown robe of his order, Father Michael looked out the window by the second-floor landing. He hocked, pulled a handkerchief from his trouser pocket beneath his habit, and held it to his lips a moment. He touched his biretta as if to arrange it.

Danny O'Neill emerged from the lavatory. His sheepskin coat was unbuttoned, revealing a brown pullover sweater on which black S.S. letters were sewed across the front. He had one hand in the pocket of his long trousers. His gold-rimmed glasses were bent, and he adjusted the bows behind his ears to make them fit more comfortably.

"Good afternoon, Father."

Father Michael swung around from the window.

"Oh, it's you, O'Neill. I want to see you."

"Since it's retreat this week, you can't make me study any Latin."

"You never let well enough alone, do you, O'Neill?"

Danny fiddled with his gray cap, waiting and wondering what Father Michael wanted to see him about.

"O'Neill, your marks these last months could be better than they have been."

"Father, I study and do my homework. I try. Of course, I'm not too good in Latin, but I don't think you can blame me for that. After all, Father, I'm a live guy and Latin's a dead language. How can somebody alive learn something dead?"

"Never mind joking now. If you joked less and applied yourself more in my Latin class, you would do much better."

Danny grinned at the priest. He wasn't afraid because he knew he'd done nothing for which Father Michael could seriously take him to task.

"O'Neill, we priests are more concerned with educating you fellows than we are with turning you into athletes."

Danny recalled how, last fall, Father Michael had shown no interest in the football team and had even laughed at him in uniform.

"Father, I wouldn't be showing much school spirit, would I, if I didn't go out for the teams and play on them when I can make them?"

"I know all that. I just wanted to warn you not to make the mistake of giving all your attention to athletics. All sport and no study won't make you a bright boy, you know. It will hamper you from gaining the benefits of schooling for which you are here. You are capable of doing much better in your studies than you have been doing. In your first two years here, your general average ranged between 85 and 90: this year, it is ranging between 80 and 85. That would be very good for most pupils. But you have already proven that you can be a 90 student."

"I'll have to try harder, I guess."

"Yes, I think you ought to. I have no real complaint against you except that you are sometimes a little . . . boisterous." Father Michael smiled knowingly. "But I haven't been Prefect of Discipline here for years for nothing. I can handle boisterousness." Father Michael paused. "And there's another matter. Have you thought more about the priesthood? Last year you told us that you were interested in knowing more about how we train young men for the priesthood. Have you given this matter more serious thought and made up your mind about it?"

"Well, Father," Danny began, embarrassed. "Not exactly, Father. You know my dad had that stroke when I was in first year. Of course, he's working now, but I know that I'll be needed to help out at home when I leave school."

"I understand, O'Neill. I just want you to be sure that you are doing the right thing. If you definitely do not seem to have the call for the priesthood, then it would be a mistake to urge you on. Likewise, if you do have it, it would be a serious misfortune were you to ignore it. And this week the annual student retreat affords you a most favorable time to examine your own mind and heart carefully, so that you may know how you feel."

"I will, Father."

"And don't forget, a little more study will do you no harm. Even a little more interest in old Cicero won't do any damage."

"Father, I'd like Cicero better if he wrote in English."

"O'Neill, that's a bum joke."

"I know it is, Father. Don't you remember you sprang it on me in class last month?"

Father Michael frowned. Danny grinned at him.

"O'Neill, you needn't be so fresh."

Danny didn't answer. He quietly gloated because he had pulled a fast one on Father Michael. Wait until he told the guys about it.

"Goodness, it's time to ring the bell," Father Michael said.

Danny started running downstairs.

"Don't forget what I've said to you, O'Neill."

"Yes, Father."

Father Michael took a cowbell off the window ledge and marched downstairs to ring it.

II

"This afternoon, I shall speak to you about the Sixth Commandment," Father Robert Geraghty said.

The third-year class watched and listened in grim and awed silence. The heavy-set priest stuck his nicotine-stained hands inside his brown robe and surveyed the room. Danny, sitting in the second seat of the third aisle from the window, slanted his gaze in order to avoid meeting Father Robert's eyes. Father Robert had a bull-dog face. He was freckled, and his light brown hair receded from a prominent forehead. His sharp gray eyes pierced from behind gold-rimmed glasses.

"The Sixth Commandment of God tells us: *Thou shalt not commit adultery,*" Father Robert said, enunciating his words carefully and speaking with poise and a sense of authority. "This Commandment of God commands us to lead pure, wholesome, virtuous lives. It enjoins us to be chaste in mind and body. Our bodies are temples of the Holy Ghost; they are stamped with the image and likeness of God. This Commandment requires us to treat our bodies in a manner consistent with the dignity with which God has endowed them. It commands us to control our animal nature because we are Christians, men with immortal souls who receive the body and blood of Christ in Holy Communion, and because we are destined to be the future inhabitants of the Kingdom of Heaven."

Danny had been waiting all week for this talk, and now here he was listening to it. The Dominican retreat master had talked to them about the Sixth Commandment after mass this morning, but he hadn't really told them anything. Would Father Robert tell them something they didn't already know? Would Father Robert tell them what it was really like? What he really wanted to know was what did it feel like?

"God, by the Sixth Commandment, forbids all sins of impurity. This Commandment forbids all immodest and unchaste actions, either with another, or alone. It forbids impure desires, thoughts, and intentions. I think that this is explicit enough. You all know what I mean."

Father Robert was so sure of himself that Danny felt he had to be right. Every word he uttered carried conviction. Yes, he was a priest who knew what he was talking about, and there was reason, all right, why so many fellows thought that Father Robert was the brainiest priest on the faculty.

"This Commandment establishes the divine law controlling what is called Sex. Now, what is sex?"

Sex. He repeated the word to himself, *Sex. Sex!* That was what caused him so much trouble. Would Father Robert make it all clear, simple, understandable to him? He leaned forward, absorbed.

"God in His wisdom shares with man the power of reproduction, the power of creation. He permits a man and a woman to bring into the world a creature more astonishing than the stars, than all the heavenly bodies, the flowers, the plants, the mountains, the lakes, the rivers and oceans. God has given to men the power to bring into the world creatures who will outlive everything else that God has created. This is the power of fatherhood and motherhood. It is called sex.

"Sex is an instinct. God means this instinct to be noble, beautiful, dignified. And sex is noble, beautiful, dignified, when it is controlled by the dictates of natural law, restrained and used for its proper purposes.

"Let me tell you a little story. A young man and a young girl met. He was fine, clean, manly. He had fought nobly and with success to master the instinct of sex in him. She was a beautiful girl. She was sweet, pure, chaste. They fell in love. To them, the most important thing in the world was that they should vow to live together, never to part."

Danny thought of how he would like to shout out one of Father Robert's own jokes: the boy and girl preferred double wretchedness to single blessedness. But he knew better than to interrupt Father Robert with a wisecrack.

"The boy and the girl had many dreams. They built castles in Spain. They were married in the Church. Their union was blessed and strengthened by God. God approved of their marriage. And God shared with them His creative power. A boy was born to them."

Father Robert paused, waited a moment for effect.

"This is the story of your own mother and father."

It was hard for him to see it that way. But Papa and Mama must have been young, romantic, full of dreams, building castles in Spain—they must have been like this once.

"This is the story of decent men and women in all ages. And this should be your own story."

This was what he wanted. He wanted the story to be his and Roslyn's. He hadn't seen Roslyn in a year, but he still loved her. He wanted to vow that he would love Roslyn always and forever. He wanted her to be Mrs. Daniel O'Neill some day. Yes, it was worth while to struggle to preserve his purity for the day when he might be Roslyn's husband. The fellows called it keeping your cherry. And they laughed at any kid who had kept his cherry. But still, yes, yes, it was worth it, even though he had to wait for years yet until he would be in a position to get married.

Concentrating on his own thoughts, he did not hear what Father Robert was saying. A question was raised in his mind. He wanted sex the way Father Robert had described it. If he got it that way, it would not be a sin. It would be love. Suppose he thought of himself and Roslyn married. Then if he imagined them doing it, would that be a sin, a dirty thought? Doing it that way was beautiful, dignified, noble. Father Robert had just said so. He imagined himself and Roslyn on the night they got married. His fantasies titillated him. He twisted in his seat. Thinking of doing it as man and wife and without sin was as exciting as thinking about it in a sinful way. But there must be something wrong somewhere in his argument. There must be some sophistry. But still, he couldn't see where it was. It seemed sound reasoning to him, and if it did, then he had a right to think of sex as much as he liked, just as long as he thought of it with a girl he loved whom he truly wanted to be his wife.

"God has so created men and women that they enjoy a great and an intense pleasure when they engage in the act of reproduction."

But what was it like? Back in first year, he used to masturbate. He had given it up, disgusted with himself. That was not such an intense pleasure. Was the real thing so much more than that had been? It must be, he guessed, judging from the way people all wanted it. But how did Father Robert know about it? He was a priest, and he had taken a vow of chastity.

"There are two principal reasons why God made the sensations of sex so exquisitely pleasurable. One: The pleasure associated with this act serves as an inducement to man to further God's purpose of perpetuating the race. Two: Sex is man's testing. It offers the greatest trial of worthiness before God that man must face. If man can meet this test, then he has proven to God that he is worthy of entering the Kingdom of Heaven."

Father Robert strode over to the teacher's desk by the window.

"Any person who does not believe in God has a strange slant on life. He is out of step with most of the human race. Law, natural and divine, is meaningless and silly to him. He asks why he should restrain himself. For what? After all, if there is no God, there can be no Heaven and Hell. Man cannot be punished for his sins. If you abolish God, there is no sin."

If a man really believed that there is no God, then he could do anything he wanted to without being punished for his actions, because he would not consider it a sin. But how could a man really believe that there is no God? The fact that God exists is as plain as the nose on anybody's face. The fool cried out in his heart that there is no God. Only the fool could believe this.

"For the atheist, pleasure can be the only end of life. Live for today, because tomorrow you die. That is his creed. But we Catholics know that after death comes the Judgment. And I repeat, it is principally sins violating the Sixth Commandment which, more than any other sins, will condemn souls to Hell.

"There is a purpose to life, and we learned this purpose in our very first catechism lessons.

"Why did God make you?

"God made me to love Him and serve Him here on earth, and to be happy with Him forever in Heaven.

"The wisest words of the greatest of philosophers could not improve on this simple explanation of the purpose of life. The purpose of life is the love and service of God. And what is the end of life? Death is the end of life. We are put here on earth to save our souls in order that we may be inhabitants of the Kingdom of Heaven. God has presented us with the terrible alternatives of either a future life of joy and untold bliss in Heaven, or else one of endless torment in Hell. Man lives but to die. This very minute, every one of us is racing, rushing onward to death. Every one of us is nearer to death right now than he was when he entered this classroom after the lunch-hour period."

Father Robert paused in order that his words might have their proper effect.

"God knows the year, the month, the day, the hour, the minute, the precise second when each of us will die, because God knows everything."

God did. He could sit in class and fool the priest by pretending to listen when he wasn't listening. He could even wallow in dirty thoughts without being suspected. But he couldn't fool God. Danny was limp. He wished the talk were over. He wanted to forget the awfulness of life, the terrible possibilities of the future. He told himself that he was young, and that he had many years of life ahead of him. Death was far off. For a number of years yet, he had death licked.

But, he shouldn't be so confident. Death stole up upon one like a thief in the night. And even the longest life was short. He would be eighteen years old at the end of the month. Eighteen years of life gone, and they seemed so brief. He was already more than halfway through high school. Eighteen more years and he would be thirty-six, almost an old man.

"The meaning of death is the warning sign for us. It tells us we must constantly be on our guard. We must constantly struggle to keep our souls free of sin, especially sins of impurity. Sins of impurity are not only sins against God, they are also sins against life. They are hideous to man as well as to God. The hospitals of our city are full of the victims of these sins, those who have been ruined by lust and indulgence. But the hideousness of such diseased persons is as nothing if it is contrasted with the hideousness of the soul on which is marked the guilt of sins against the Sixth Commandment. Such being the case, we can readily perceive that it is folly, blind, stupid, unbelievable folly, for anyone to risk his immortal soul merely in order to experience a few brief moments of illicit sensual pleasure. Yes, when we understand what the stakes are in the drama of the human soul, we know that it is not so hard to avoid sin, not so hard as the world pretends it to be. If we keep in mind that Heaven is the reward for chastity, then it is not so difficult to preserve our chastity."

Every word Father Robert said was true. And yet, at times it was hard, almost impossible, to resist the temptation to indulge in dirty thoughts and to nurse immoral desires.

"Evil and worldly influences constantly seek to destroy your purity. You must fight these off. The only way you can successfully do this is to embark on a program of virtue. You must hold aloft the ideal of purity and you must take practical steps to realize that ideal concretely. The purpose of our annual student retreat is to furnish you with a program of virtue. Your retreat master tomorrow morning will deal with this question.

"Now, I think that I have told you all that you need to know concerning the Sixth Commandment. You will form ranks and go downstairs to church. This afternoon is the time set aside for the members of this class to make their confession."

III

Because of Father Robert's talk, he was determined. He was going to make a general confession. Then he would walk out of church a different person. He would feel free as air. After all these years in which he had carried the guilt of a bad confession on his soul, he would at last be absolved from his sin. Yes, he was determined to make the first truly good confession of his whole life.

But this resolution was so much easier to make than it was to carry out. He had to examine his conscience as carefully as possible and try to remember every sin he had ever committed, or, at least, every mortal sin. He had to confess to sins against the Sixth Commandment which he had already confessed in the past. He had to tell the priest everything of what he was. He had to go into one of the confessional boxes, kneel down, and admit that for years he had been a spiritual coward, and because he had been one, he had let himself sink into the deepest pits of sin. He had committed sacrileges year after year.

Danny knelt by himself toward the rear on the righthand side of the small church. It was located on the first floor of the school building. The windows were of stained glass, but plain, without any figures. Up front, there were statues much like those in Saint Patrick's. There were entrances on either side of the rear, and behind Danny and to his left was a small choir. His classmates were scattered about the church. Some knelt in pews, examining their consciences. Others formed lines before the confessional boxes along the righthand wall or up by the altar, where the Dominican retreat master was hearing confessions.

He had to stop thinking of how he would feel when he got it over with, and get on with the examination of his conscience. He was sorry for his sins. But was his sorrow pure? He ought to be sorry for his sins because they offended God. But he was also sorry for his sins because in a couple of minutes he had to acknowledge them to a priest, and some of his sins were intimate and painful. He had to attain purer contrition. Since this would be a general confession, he had to be in the right mood for it. He closed his eyes and carefully, slowly, almost painfully, enunciated the words of the *Act of Contrition.*

Now he would examine his conscience.

First Commandment: *I am the Lord thy God, and thou shalt not have strange gods before me.*

He had never denied that God exists, worshiped idols, nor in any way violated the First Commandment.

He glanced around the church. Big Garrity was finished. And Tim Doolan, too. Wistfully he watched them kneel down and say their penances. He turned his mind back to the examination of his conscience.

IV

Danny was alone with God. He felt his heart palpitating. His breath was jerky. He knelt in the confessional box. Howe was in the other side, and he could hear mumbling. Cramped and anxious, he asked God to give him the strength to go through with it. Even though he had to confess shameful sins, he would not shirk. Once and for all he was going to straighten out the problems of his conscience. He still heard the mumbling, but he couldn't make out any words. If you heard anyone else confessing, you were supposed to close your ears and not listen. He didn't want to hear. He only wanted Howe to finish, so that it would be his turn. He could not stand the strain much longer.

He heard Father Michael's mumbling voice. It was the granting of absolution. He breathed deeply. In a second now.

The slide opened, and through a wire grating he could perceive Father Michael seated sidewise in the center of the box. Father Michael did not look at him.

"Bless me, Father, for I have sinned," Danny whispered in a frightened voice. "Father, my last confession was two months, and four days ago, and, Father, I want to make a general confession."

Father Michael blessed Danny. He spoke so rapidly and in such a low whisper that his words were inaudible to Danny. They seemed like a hasty mumble of sounds.

"Father, I made a bad confession."

"Yes!"

"Father, when I made my first communion, I didn't tell all of my sins. My brother and I stole something, and I let him take the blame at home and get a whipping, and I didn't get any blame and told on him."

He waited, as if for a stroke of thunder.

"Go ahead!"

"Father, I want to make a general confession. Since I made my bad confession, I went to confession and Communion many times, committing sacrileges.

"Father, I took the name of the Lord in vain, many times, sometimes as much as ten times a day, sometimes maybe forty or fifty times. I sometimes made blasphemous jokes about the Lord's name, too, Father.

"I missed mass ten or fifteen times in my life, but not once on my own account since I was in fifth grade, about six years ago.

"Father, I was disobedient to my parents and my elders and in school, talked back to them, caused trouble in classrooms, and did things like that, many, many times, perhaps maybe on an average of ten to twenty times a week.

"Father, I had thoughts of other things than God many times in mass, and sometimes immoral thoughts even.

"Father, I had fights with other fellows, maybe twenty in my life, I started fights, got other fellows to fight, and lost my temper maybe as much as thirty times a week.

"Father, I broke the Sixth Commandment by thoughts, words, and deeds. I broke the Sixth Commandment by myself maybe a hundred times or more, but not since a year and three months ago. I had immoral thoughts for years, thirty or fifty a week, or even more. Even today, Father, when I was receiving moral instruction, I had immoral wishes and thoughts. I had immoral wishes and entertained them, from ten to thirty times a week or more, for years. I tried to look at girls naked ten times. I listened to immoral words maybe as much as ten or twenty times a week or more for years."

Danny paused.

"Go ahead!" Father Michael said, his voice even and without anger.

The priest's manner and tone of voice encouraged Danny. He felt more confident, less humiliated.

"Father, I lied hundreds of times. And I envied others when I shouldn't have done it, oh, hundreds of times, too. And I wanted to have things other fellows owned, hundreds of times. And I bore false witness against my older brother many times, and against others I know about three or four hundred times in my life. And I cheated in school three times on my homework since I have been in high school. And sometimes in grammar school I cheated in my homework. And, Father, I have stolen, maybe as much as between five and ten dollars in my life from stores and cheating rides on the railroad and elevated and sneaking into moving picture shows."

Danny halted.

"Did you do anything else?"

"Oh, yes, Father, I sometimes was disrespectful of priests and nuns."

"How?"

"I answered them back, and called them names. For instance, Father, the nun I had in seventh grade, we called her Battling Bertha."

"Is that all?"

"Yes, Father," Danny said, feeling weak, a trifle faint.

But he was happy. It was over. For once he had made a good confession. He waited, apprehensive of what the priest would say to him, but hoping he wouldn't be bawled out. But come what may, he had honestly confessed everything to God.

"Now you . . ."

"Oh, yes, Father, when I was in fourth grade, I went to communion after I had a piece of bread to eat in the morning because my mother said it would be all right for me to do it."

"Is that all now?"

"Yes, Father."

"Now, you must pray regularly and receive the Sacraments regularly in order to receive grace. That will help you to resist temptation. You must avoid the occasion of sin and, above all, you must avoid bad company. If you avoid bad company, you have won half of the battle in your fight against temptation. And before you go to confession always examine your conscience as carefully as you can. You must never be afraid to confess your sins to the priest. He is the representative of God in the confessional box. When you speak to him, you are, in essence, speaking to God. As God's representative, the priest is in the confessional box to help you and to absolve you of your sins. Now, for your penance, say fifteen *Hail Marys* and fifteen *Our Fathers* and make a good *Act of Contrition.*"

Father Michael hastily mumbled the words of absolution. With painful slowness and sincerity, Danny carefully whispered the words of the *Act of Contrition.*

Father Michael finished before Danny and waited.

"God bless you! Go and sin no more," Father Michael said, closing the slide.

V

Danny came out of the confessional box, feeling as if he had actually lost weight. Yes, it was over. His soul was in the state of grace. He wished that he could take wings and fly.

He knelt down in a pew close to the confessional box. Just think, he had been afraid for years to do what he had just done. And it was so easy. It was over with so quickly. He hadn't come out of the confessional box humiliated, either. He had come out feeling more free than he had ever felt before in his whole life. His conscience was now at ease. He could face God. If he were to die this very minute, he would be ready to meet his God. He had shed sin, the ugliest of sins, from his soul. Yes, to think he had not dared to do this for years. What a fool he had been.

He blessed himself and slowly said his penance. He forced his mind to concentrate on God as he prayed. But he anticipated how, just as soon as the penance was said, he would dwell with pleasure on his present state of grace.

Finishing his penance, Danny blessed himself and left the church. He bounded down the back stairs and out into the narrow, brick-paved schoolyard, which was bounded on one side by a five-foot brick wall. He dashed across the yard and on down a short distance to the corner where the students often gathered. It was a chilly but sunny February afternoon, and the snow on the street was thawing. Some of his classmates were hanging around, talking.

"Here's the sinner," Tim Doolan said.

Tim was a small, wiry, bowlegged lad with blond hair and boyish blue eyes.

"Did you get thrown out of confession?" Marty Mulligan asked, laughing; Marty was plump, broad-shouldered. He had a genial, ruddy face and a slow, easy-going way of moving. He and Tim, like Danny, wore school letters.

"What penance did you get?" Kelly asked.

"Fifteen *Our Fathers* and fifteen *Hail Marys.*"

"O'Neill, you must be worse than me. I only got ten and ten," Marty said.

"Who did you go to?" baby-faced, curly-haired Al Corkerry asked.

"Flaming Michael," Danny said.

"Is he easy?" asked Tim.

"Yes, he's soft in confession. But I wouldn't try Geraghty," Danny said.

"Me, neither. Say, I'd walk miles to go to another church to confession before I'd risk going to Geraghty."

"Galloping Geraghty comes out to my parish in Morgan Park on weekends to hear confessions and say mass. I know fellows who went to him. They say he's stiff," Gregory Hickmann said.

"Well, what'll we do?" asked Marty.

"Let's go and practice shooting baskets," Danny said.

"Sounds too much like work," Marty said.

"You lights can't cop anything this year. Why bother about it?" Tim said.

"Might as well do something. Come on, who's coming?"

No one answered. He looked at Corkerry who was on the lightweight basketball team. Corkerry shook his head.

"Well, I'm goin'. So long," Danny said.

He walked over to the Illinois Central Station to get a southbound train to Seventy-fifth Street.

15

I

Jim left his small office on the platform to have a look around. The moment he stepped outside onto the platform he was grateful for the stove by his desk. Cold blasts of wind swept in through the driveways. He could see his own breath. Hustling to keep warm, platform men were loading vehicles as fast as they could. But everything was behind schedule tonight. Lambert and Morgan had been slow in getting vehicles in for the freight. Pete Hecht complained that he didn't have enough help to get the wagons loaded more quickly. But behind schedule or not, things were humming.

Jim walked with a hitch in his gait, dragging his right foot with every step. He wore glasses, and his cheeks were sunken. He threaded his way in and out of the busy freight handlers. The noises of crashing boxes, the steady echo of shouting voices, the sputtering of motors being cranked all disturbed him. He heard the bells of a railroad engine. Since that stroke, he had not been able to accustom himself to noise as easily as he used to. It confused him, and sometimes he had to pause a moment on the platform to get his bearings. It was almost like pinching yourself to know that you were awake.

Pete Hecht, the platform foreman, came up to Jim.

"How many more you need?" Jim asked, shouting to be heard above the noise.

"Two more stake trucks, another gascar, and I have one extra trailer load."

"I'll call for 'em."

Pete hurried away. Jim passed a series of bins filled with miscellaneous freight. He suddenly paused, noticing a gray-haired man struggle to get a heavy box onto a platform truck. The man failed and let the box rest on the floor. He looked at it and rested a moment.

"Here, let me give you a hand," Jim said.

"I can handle it myself."

"Come on, Pop, we'll get it.

Jim and the gray-haired man grabbed at opposite ends of the box. They lifted, straining their muscles. Jim's end sagged. He couldn't quite make it. The gray-haired man got his end on the truck. Jim gritted his teeth and heaved. The old man helped him, and they managed to slide the box securely onto the truck.

"Thanks, mister."

"Don't mention it," Jim said, turning away.

A few years ago he could have picked up that box alone. And now, for a moment, he'd thought he was going to drop it. The old man had been able to lift better than he could.

He walked on, knowing that there was something gone out of him. He had lived all his life in a world where men made their bread with the strength of their backs. He knew what it meant to lose your strength. Well, he was lucky. Where would he be today, if Patsy McLaughlin hadn't promoted him to the supervision during the war boom? He looked at his wrists. They were a little bit thinner than they used to be. His left side was good, and his left arm was powerful. He could still lay many a man out with a left.

Well, you old sonofabitch, you ain't the man you used to be.

How many times hadn't he heard that remark passed in jest. Many a jest was more than a jest.

He traversed the length of the platform. Things were picking up now. He'd be cleaned up in good time tonight despite the delay in getting vehicles. He cut back to his office.

Inside, he picked up the telephone.

"Local 360."

He waited.

"Hello, Lambert? This is Jim O'Neill."

"Oh, hello, Jim. How you feeling?"

"Pretty good. How's yourself?"

So many fellows asked him how he felt. The question had a different meaning to him now from what it used to have. Now when somebody asked him how he felt, he sensed that they were being sorry for him.

"Say, Lambert, I need two more gascars, and would you tell them up there also to get us an extra stake truck and another empty trailer?"

"That's what we're here for, Jim. And take care of yourself."

Jim hung up. *Take care of yourself.* They all told him that. They needn't pity him. For all they knew, he might be working long after they were six feet under the ground. He sat for a moment. Suddenly he sat up rigid. The sudden noise of an automobile backfiring had frightened him. He laughed, realizing what it had been. He had to get better control over himself. He was used to all the noises at a terminal or depot. It was just that at some moments he would be caught off guard and then some of these noises would make him jump. It wasn't anything.

The work here, at Jefferson Street Depot, was a little harder than it had been in the Call Department. For almost ten months after he had had that stroke, he had worked on sheets as a Dispatcher up in the Call Department. That had been a snap. Then Wolfe had transferred him here. Well, he would handle his job here.

"Hi, Mr. O'Neill," a young driver said, entering.

"What can I do for you, Shaughnessy?"

"Put me to work."

"All right, back your truck in at the north end of the platform. There's a load of valuables for Atlantic I want to get right out of here."

Shaughnessy left. Jim checked off a notation he had made about the load of values for Atlantic, and wrote Shaughnessy's name down alongside the check mark.

II

The night was getting along. Jim had cleaned up all his transfer freight. There wasn't much for him to do for a little while now until wagons began coming in with freight that had to be unloaded and sorted for delivery in the morning. And there was a train due in a half hour that always had a lot of stuff on it.

Jim stood glancing out of the dirty window of his cooplike office. He began to brood. He remembered the day he had been stricken. He had gotten up from his chair, and then he had caved in, passing out as he fell. The memory of that moment almost suffocated him. It seemed even more horrible than the actual experience had been. Feeling suddenly weak, he sat down. He feared that another stroke was coming on him. He was convinced that his right hand had lost all its power. He started sweating. He was alone and trapped in this little coop.

He grabbed a pencil and wrote out his name. He read his signature. It was all right. He had only had a foolish fear. It had been nothing, just his imagination getting to work, that was all. A man could give himself all kinds of imaginary troubles if he didn't watch himself. What kind of a fellow was he getting to be? Who was Jim O'Neill, to be pitying himself? He had never gone in for pitying himself before and he wouldn't begin now. Life was a fight, and he would go on fighting. When he went down, it would be fighting. And that wasn't just yet. There was still something in Jim O'Neill. There were no complaints about the way he was running the place. He did his work every night as well as it could be done, and there could be no kickbacks about him.

He looked out and watched sweating platform men work. The gray-haired old man whom he had helped rolled a barrel by. A buck Negro passed singing and carrying long rods. A clock on the desk behind him ticked away the seconds.

Hell, he could go on for years. He wasn't a cripple yet, not by a damned sight. He hated these hours of the night with so little to do, with himself feeling cooped up in the place.

III

"What time does he get out of school?" Jim asked.

"Two-thirty," Lizz answered.

"Well, that gives us time."

"You must tell Danny to pin the pay envelope inside of his coat."

"Hell, he won't lose it. He's seventeen, isn't he?"

"He's going on sixteen."

"Wait a minute. He was born in 1904, and this is 1922. He's going on eighteen," Jim said.

"He's sixteen."

"Sixteen in a pig's eye."

"I think that I ought to know how old my son is."

"Of course you should. Why don't you?"

"Say, you, what's eating you today?"

"Nothing's eating me. Only listen to me! Ever since the war, I've been getting Dispatcher's pay. And what have we got to show for it? We've hardly a nickel in the bank, and here again payday comes around and we've only got a couple of nickels in the house."

"Don't look at me that way. It ain't my fault, we got all these little mouths to feed."

"More money comes into our house, with Bill's pay and mine, than comes into a hell of a lot of homes. Take Heinie Mueller. He only gets Dispatcher's pay and he gets along better than we do."

"His mother bought him a home of his own on the West Side."

"It's high time that we saved some money."

"As true as there is God in Heaven, I don't waste a cent."

"I don't say that you do. All I say is that with the money that's been coming into this house, we got damned little to show for it."

"Good God Almighty, what do you look at me for?"

"Lizz, now listen, we've got to save some money. We got to cut down on expenses. We got to, that's all. Suppose something happened to me? What would we do?"

"God forbid!"

"But suppose it did. I don't expect it to, but I say suppose it did, because I want to make you see why we got to watch our p's and q's, and save something."

"Jim, nothing is going to happen to you. Our Lord and His Blessed Mother watch over this household."

"God helps those that help themselves. Now, Lizz, from now on, every payday, we have to put a little money in the bank."

"It costs money to feed and clothe all our little ones and to keep them in school."

"I ain't complaining. I'm only saying that it's time we watched our step."

"Jim, I'm as careful as any woman could be. Don't I know that my son and my bread winner—"

"All right, Lizz," Jim interrupted. "Now we got to provide in case of a rainy day."

"As God is my judge, I don't waste money."

"I don't say you do or you don't. All I say is that we ought to look ahead."

"God will always provide for me and mine."

"Yes, and let me tell you again, God helps those that help themselves."

IV

Lizz searched for paper on which to write a letter. She found an old composition book of one of the children and tore a sheet of paper out of it. She sat down at the dining-room table and wrote in a scrawling and scarcely legible handwriting.

> *Dear Al*
> *Please send me ten dollars if you can spare it. My expenses are so heavy and Jim is under the doctor's care and with the children in school and tuition and food and clothings things are hard. I wouldn't write you if I didn't need it and God will bless you and I'll pray for you, and please send your sister this if you can. I said a whole station of the Cross for you yesterday in church. God bless you and Mary look down on you and St. Vincent protect you from accident and Saint Joseph protect you from harm.*
> *Your loving sister Elizabeth*
> *Mrs. James O'Neill*

Her family ought to help her more. They owed it to her to do it.

V

"I'm sorry I had to bother you and bring you home from school to go downtown with me, but I've got to get the money back home to your mother. Your brother, Bill, gets paid today, but he isn't comin' home to supper tonight because he has to go to school for that bookkeepin' course he's takin'," Jim said, walking to the Fifty-eighth Street elevated station with Danny.

"Oh, it's all right, Papa," Danny said, masking his disappointments; he had wanted to practice basketball today.

"What do you do with yourself after school?" Jim asked him.

"Well, most of the time, I play basketball."

"You like it?"

"Yes."

"Are you any good at it?"

"This is my second year as a regular on the lightweights."

"Maybe I'll try to come and see you play sometime."

"That would be swell," Danny said, but he didn't really mean it.

He didn't think Papa would like it. Papa looked like a workingman. Many of the fathers of fellows at school looked and dressed like business men. Whenever any one at school asked him what his father did, he always said his father was in charge of wagons and trucks at the express company, speaking of it in a way that made Papa's job sound much bigger than it was.

Danny watched his father limp without letting him know that he was observing it. He knew that Papa had been hampered at work ever since the stroke. He remembered how he had worked all summer between first and second year at the Wagon Call Department of the express company. For a while he had been on the ten-to-eight shift and he'd worked across the board from Papa. He'd had a chance to see Papa keep sheets. Papa had been slow and often he'd had difficulty hearing correctly over the phone. He hoped nothing would happen to Papa which would handicap him any more in his work.

Jim paid the elevated fare. They went upstairs to the station and boarded a downtown express train.

Danny stared idly out of the window. The train passed over the vacant lot on Calumet near Fifty-first where he used to play. He waited for Papa to talk to him. Jim said nothing.

Danny reflected that Papa had never bawled him out for having been fired from the express company last summer after working a month. He'd been glad the day that Omar James told him he was canned, because it had freed him to play ball every day in Washington Park. Papa and Mama had made a lot of fuss about his pay envelope, too. Two years ago he had opened his own pay envelope and had given Mama five dollars every two weeks. Mother had kept the rest for him, and he had spent it on things he needed and to pay his second year tuition of eighty dollars. But Papa and Mama believed the O'Flahertys had taken his money. They were specially angry because two years ago he had gotten over a hundred dollars back pay besides his salary, and they said the O'Flahertys had spent that money. So last summer he had to bring his pay envelope to Papa, and

Papa said he was banking most of it. There was fifty-five dollars in the bank now in a joint account in his name and Papa's. Anyway, Mama and Papa were still sore about the money he earned two years ago. He couldn't make them believe he had really spent it on himself.

The train stopped at Indiana Avenue. Danny stared at a girl in a raccoon coat who stood on the platform. She wore galoshes. He looked at her legs, seeing the part that was visible between the top of the galoshes and the edge of her coat. When you saw that much of a girl's leg, it was sometimes more exciting than to see a girl's whole leg bare when she was in a swimming suit. The train passed on. He wanted a girl, one as pretty as that girl. He wondered if Roslyn had grown up into a pretty girl. Would he ever have a girl? Think of it, to some day be married to a beautiful girl, so that you could see her naked and do it to her as much as you wanted to without sinning. But he had years to wait before he could be married like that. If he was married, his wife would see him naked. Would he feel funny, embarrassed, standing naked before a girl?

"What do you want to do a year from June, Dan, when you graduate from high school?"

"Uncle Al wants me to go to college."

"That's good. It seems to me you ought to be able to work your way through college."

Danny nodded. But he didn't want to do that. He wanted to go to college and be a football star. Since he had been star end on the school team last fall he had dreams of college in terms of football. And he was beginning to think that in college he wanted to belong to a fraternity and live a college life. Last fall Hugh McNeill had started a high-school fraternity and he'd been made a charter member of it, but he'd never taken it seriously or gone to meetings. He'd been suspended. He was thinking that he ought to go back into it and be a regular member. It would help him to know girls, and through being in a fraternity he might learn to dance. And that was the kind of a life he wanted when he went to college. If he had to work his way through college, what was the use of going?

"I might be able to fix it up for you to get something nights at the company while you're going to college. If not, then you could work days and go to school nights like your brother is doing now."

"I haven't made up my mind yet what I want to do."

Jim looked sharply at Danny. Danny realized immediately that he had said the wrong thing.

"Your mind isn't the only one that has to be made up. Before you go to college, you're going to discuss it with me."

Yes, he'd stuck his foot in it. Well, he was glad that his going to college was still over a year away.

"Is it too late for you to try and get your third and last year in one?"

"The priests at school wouldn't allow it."

The train was now moving slowly. Danny had not been paying attention to the stations and he realized that they had already passed Roosevelt Road.

"I'm not against your studying. I don't want you to think I am. But there's something I don't want you ever to forget. You don't come from rich people. You come from poor people. And you don't want to try and be a dude and ever start acting like you was rich. You haven't got any right to act that way unless you earn it, and you got to work to earn it."

Danny cautiously nodded his head in agreement with his father.

"You know, when you worked at the company, you made a damned fool out of me. I told them I needed to have you work, and then you went and said you lived with your grandmother when I had made them think you lived with me. And you showed off and told them about buying box-seat tickets for the ball games as if the bleachers wasn't good enough for you."

"I didn't know it or I wouldn't have done it," Danny said, remembering how sore his father had been at him when he had done these things.

"We'll forget that. But you're getting older now and you don't want to start pickin' up any high-falutin' notions."

The train stopped at Adams Street, and they rushed off.

VI

"Well! Well! Well!" Lambert exclaimed.

"Hello, Lambert," Jim said.

"Hello, Jim, how you feeling?"

"Oh, pretty good! Nothing to complain of."

"And how are you, young fellow?"

"Pretty good," Danny answered.

There was a line of five men at the payroll window in the room. Jim went over to it, and Danny stood with Lambert. Lambert was as thin and sallow-faced as ever.

"Are you getting yourself a lot of education these days, young fellow?" Lambert asked.

"All I can take in."

"What you going to do with it when you come out of school?"

"I suppose use it," Danny said.

"Well, that's something."

"How's everybody in the Call Department?" asked Danny.

"The same as ever. Your friend James isn't on days there any more, and Simon Murray's got his place."

Danny grinned. He had always liked Lambert and done better work for him than he'd done for the day force.

"Young fellow, I was sorry you got fired last summer. I think it was Mr. Wolfe."

"I was wrestling in the office, but my time was up. I wasn't wrestling on company time."

Jim rejoined them.

"Well, Jim, be taking care of yourself."

"I always do that."

"And take care of yourself, young fellow," Lambert said.

"We'll make a scholar of him yet, Lambert, and he'll be teaching us things soon," Jim said, laughing.

"Lambert's a nice fellow, and I always got along good with him," Danny said as Jim and he left.

In the hall Jim stopped and tore open his pay envelope. He counted the money in it and took out a dollar and a half. He pinned the rest in the torn envelope and handed it to Danny.

"Tell your mother there's a hundred and ten dollars in there. Say I took a dollar and a half and that the other dollar missing was subtracted for my company sick-benefit payment."

Danny nodded.

"Don't lose it! And now let's find a drugstore, and I'll buy you a soda before I leave you."

They left the building.

"You're a good lad, Dan," Jim said, walking toward a drugstore with Danny.

VII

Jim stopped playing the phonograph and sat back in his Morris chair. On and off since yesterday afternoon when he'd ridden downtown with Danny, he had been thinking about the lad. Danny was at the age where he had to be watched. And Danny was the only one of his kids he was worried about. He could watch over the other boys because he had them right under his eye.

The doorbell rang. He let Lizz answer it.

"Jim!" Lizz called excitedly.

Jim hurried to the door. A policeman stepped in with Bob. Sniffling, Bob was very frightened.

"Is this your son?" the policeman asked.

"Officer, he's a good boy," Lizz exclaimed.

"Officer, come into the front here," Jim said.

They all entered the parlor.

"Has this boy ever stolen anything before?" the policeman asked.

"Why, Officer, he never did. And, Officer, do you know my cousin, Sergeant O'Leary?" Lizz asked.

"Is he your cousin, Mrs. O'Neill?"

"He's my mother's first cousin. You just tell him you met Cousin Mary's daughter."

"What kind of a boy are you to be doing this and you the cousin of Sergeant O'Leary?" the officer asked, fixing a stern gaze on Bob.

"I didn't mean it. The kids dared me to do it and said I was afraid."

"What did he do, Officer?"

"He was stealing candy in a store."

"How much did you take?" Jim asked, looking sternly at Bob.

"Just some Hershey bars," Bob answered.

"I'll pay for them, Officer, and I promise you he'll get something that'll teach him never to do a thing like this again," Jim said.

"Well, you know I ought to bring him in."

"Oh, Officer, please don't. We're poor people, and the boy's father there works nights, and he is only getting over a stroke," Lizz said; Jim tried to signal her to shut up.

"What made you do it? Don't you know you can't break the law?" the policeman said harshly, turning to Bob.

"I didn't think," Bob said.

"You ought to be ashamed of yourself. Wait till I fix you. Trying to disgrace a decent and hard-working father and mother," Lizz said.

"You hear what your mother is saying to you? You a boy from the Sisters' school and with the name of O'Neill?"

Bob was too frightened to speak.

"Are you a dummy? Can't you at least answer the policeman?" Lizz yelled at Bob.

"If I let you go, how do I know you're not going to do this again?"

"Officer, he won't," Lizz said.

"He won't, I'll tell you that!" Jim said.

"Well, I'm not going to do anything this time. I got him running out before he'd eaten any of the candy, but the next time he tries any stunts like this it'll go hard on him."

"Oh, thank you, Officer. And when I see my cousin, Tim O'Leary, I'm going to say a good word for you. Officer, what is your name?" Lizz asked.

"Harrington."

"Are you any relation to the Harringtons who used to live at Twenty-fourth and Wabash about fifteen years ago?"

"No, mam, I don't think I am."

"Officer, can I make you a cup of tea?" Lizz asked.

"No, thanks, mam. And good day to you and Mr. O'Neill, and I hope you tell that little fellow he can't break the law. We'll forget it this time."

"Well, thank you, Officer," Jim said.

Jim accompanied the policeman to the front door.

"We sure soft-soaped that flatfoot," Lizz said when Jim came back to the parlor.

"Go get me the razor strap!" Jim commanded Bob, ignoring Lizz.

"Papa, please don't hit me," Bob pleaded.

"I told you to get me the razor strap!"

"Jim, please don't hit him this time. He won't do it again," Lizz said.

"You keep out of this, Lizz. You let the kids walk all over you."

Bob slowly walked out of the room. He returned with the strap. He was crying. Jim snatched the strap. He took Bob by the scruff of the neck, dragged him into the bedroom, and closed the door.

"Take your pants down and lay on that bed!"

"Please, Papa."

"Do what you're told!"

Bob obeyed.

Jim grasped the strap in both hands. He swung left-handed, bringing the strap down hard on the boy's bare buttocks.

"We have enough trouble without you getting in trouble with the police," Jim said while the boy moaned.

Jim brought down the strap again, reddening the boy's buttocks. Bob moaned.

"Crying won't help you. Take your punishment like a man," Jim said, striking again.

He hit Bob three times more.

"You knew you shouldn't steal, didn't you?"

"Yes, Papa," Bob sobbed.

"Why did you do it?"

"I'm sorry. I wanted the candy."

"Are you ever going to do it again?"

"Honest, I won't, Papa!"

"Well, see that you don't!"

Jim left the room, went to the bathroom, and hitched the razor strap back on a hook.

"I hope you didn't hurt him," Lizz said when Jim came out to the back of the house.

"You got to hurt them when they do things like that. A policeman bringing a boy of mine home for stealing! What the hell are we coming to?"

"The dirty little stinker disgracing us," Lizz said.

"Lizz, fix my lunch. I have to go to work now," Jim said.

Christ, a man was always having worries and troubles bringing up his kids.

16

I

Danny stood near the victrola, leaning on the oil mop. Every Saturday it was the same story. He had to do his chores, run the oil mop over the floors, and dust the furniture. And he would mope and take more time getting himself to do this work than actually it took to do them. He went to the window and looked out. Washington Park was covered with snow. He could see skaters moving on the lagoon. He turned from the window and just stood there, clasping the mop. He had been reading in the papers about flaming youth, modern youth, jazz-age youth, and he was beginning to think that he was missing something. He wanted to be a flaming youth himself. That was why yesterday at the basketball game he'd told Hugh McNeill that he wanted to get reinstated in the fraternity. He could learn to wear classy clothes and be as doggy as young fellows like Phil Rolfe and Young Rocky who hung around the Greek poolroom at Fifty-eighth Street. He perfunctorily ran the mop over the patch of floor near the windows. He leaned on the mop again, a faroff look in his eyes.

Suddenly he heard Aunt Margaret yelling for Uncle Ned to get out of the bathroom and let her in.

II

Margaret rushed out to the kitchen.

"Mother, do you remember even one morning when I ever could get into the bathroom since that bum came home from Madison?"

"Ah, sure don't be getting excited, Peg," Mrs. O'Flaherty said, filling her corncob pipe as she talked.

"Mother, I ask you, what am I going to do?"

Mrs. O'Flaherty lit her pipe and puffed on it meditatively. She took it out of her mouth and held it in her hand.

"Peg, don't let him get your goat."

"Mother, I'm sick and tired of him! Mother, he won't work, and all he does is sit in the bathroom. I never in my life heard of a man who will live and die in the bathroom the way he does," Margaret yelled.

Margaret went back to the bathroom and pounded the door.

III

Ned sank relaxed in the warm water of the bathtub. Enjoyably he inhaled his first cigarette of the day. He was always able to think better in the bathtub than anywhere else, and now he had a real whirlwind idea, something entirely new in advertising women's shoes. He had never seen this one embodied in an ad. The idea was that a woman's personality could be told by the shoes she wore. Tell me what shoes you garb your slender foot in, and I'll tell you what kind of a doll you are. That expressed the content of the slogan, but he had to put it in snappy, classy, catchy language. The word doll had to go out. *I'll tell you what kind of a lady you are.* Lady was the best word here. He inhaled again, closed his eyes, and sought the precise words for his slogan. He had the words almost on the tip of his tongue. He had a sense of what they were but he couldn't just hit upon them. He snapped his fingers as if that would help him formulate the slogan.

He sat up, shocked, a pained expression on his face. Margaret was wildly banging on the door.

"For Christ sake! I want to get in there, you dirty, stinking, lazy bum!"

"I'm coming right out, Peg," he replied in a conciliatory tone.

Hell, she wouldn't give a man half a chance. She wouldn't even give him time to close his pores with cold water. He pulled up the stopper and carefully climbed out of the tub. He hastily tried to rub himself dry. Didn't she have any decency? What kind of a woman was she? Didn't she even know that there was such a thing as delicacy? With all her yelling and banging and cursing, she was announcing that she had to go to the toilet. It was disgusting.

Half dry, he put on his pajamas and robe and fled down the hall to his bedroom.

IV

Danny carelessly ran a dust cloth over the parlor rocking chair. The whole neighborhood could hear her yell. He guessed that she was probably right, and that

Uncle Ned ought to work and not take all morning in the bathroom. Uncle Al didn't. But even so, she didn't have to scream. There she did it again.

"Jesus Christ!" Aunt Margaret yelled from the rear of the apartment.

Out of habit, Danny bowed his head at hearing the Lord's name.

He hoped she wouldn't go off the wagon. She hadn't gotten drunk in over a year now. But she'd stayed sober for more than a year before and then gone out and gotten drunk. Would they have to go through the whole darned business all over again? He hoped that she would cool off, go to work, and forget it. But anyway, she no longer tried to commit suicide the way she used to when she got drunk at Fifty-first and Prairie.

He put away the dust rag and got out his composition book. He had to write his weekly composition to hand in to Father Robert on Monday. If he could get it done now, then he'd be free from study until Monday. He had done the rest of his homework. He had an idea of a story to write, too. But with her yelling like that, the circumstances and conditions at home weren't conducive to such work. Anyway, he would sit down and try to get it done.

Danny looked up from the table in the back parlor. His right hand was smeared with ink, and he chewed on the end of his pen. He had a swell idea for a story, and he was sure that Father Robert would read it out loud in class, give him a good mark, and even print it in the *Aureole*. He leaned over to write. He sat up, tense and still. How could he write in a house like this?

Aunt Margaret was right outside the room, banging at the closed door to the front bedroom and screaming at Uncle Ned again at the top of her voice.

"You goddamn mollycoddle, letting your sister support you!" she screamed.

Danny winced. Uncle Ned didn't answer her.

"When are you going to get a job and go to work like a man? Putting all of the burden on my poor shoulders and on your poor brother!"

Still Ned didn't answer her.

Danny set down the pen and stuck his fingers in his ears. She always said this house would drive her mad. Well, if she kept doing this for many more Saturday mornings, she'd drive him nuts.

"Ned O'Flaherty! I say before the world that you're worse than a whoremaster. You killed your sick wife. You're a goddamn bum. Yes, I ain't ashamed to tell the world. You're a goddamn dirty no-good bum!"

He felt like yelling himself, giving her a piece of his mind. He got up, strode past her in the hall, and went out to the back. His sister, Little Margaret, stood in the dining room in bare feet and a thin nightgown. She was a tall, skinny girl, but her breasts were still immature. Unable to resist temptation, he looked at her. Fearful that Little Margaret had spotted his curious gaze, he glanced away.

"She's at it again," Danny said, bored.

"I'm on her side."

"I just wish she wouldn't yell so loud."

"She's got a right to yell. I'd yell, too. He's a bum."

Aunt Margaret rushed through the dining room, her kimono open, her hair falling down her back.

"Mother, I'm through! I give up. Never again does a penny of mine go to support that whoremaster son of yours."

"You're on his side," Little Margaret suddenly said, melodramatically imitating her aunt.

Danny didn't answer. He left the room, determined to try again to get on with his story.

"Hey, you, Ned O'Flaherty!" Margaret shouted from the kitchen. "You get a job and get the hell out of my home, do you hear me? I'm goddamned sick and tired of supporting you."

Danny bent over his composition book. Again she was rapping at the front bedroom door.

"The gentleman of leisure! He's primping himself. What the hell you primping yourself for? Why in the name of Jesus Christ don't you go out and get a woman and get married? Let some other woman support you, let her take care of you in the goddamned style you're accustomed to! Why must I support you? Why do you rob the bread of life from us, from your old mother, and the little children? Yes, I'm talking to you, you, Ned O'Flaherty!"

"That's right, tell it to the neighborhood," Ned called back to her from behind the closed door.

"You're goddamned right, I will! I want the neighborhood to know! I want the world to know what I put up with, supporting a no-good brother, keeping him while he lives like a gentleman!"

Danny put down his pen, stared glumly at the wall, and waited for her to shut up.

V

Margaret sat disconsolate on the hall tree, clutching the telephone. She glanced around at the closed door of the front bedroom. Ned had just heard her telephoning two hotels to try and find Lorry Robinson. Ned was around here, spying on her broken heart, snooping on the tragic loss of her life. Her face set in determination. She'd fix him. She'd shame him as he had never been shamed before.

She telephoned Dora, using a slug instead of a nickel.

"Dora, I'm losing my mind," Margaret said, sobbing for Dora to hear.

"Peg, are you all right? Can I do anything for you? Are you sober?"

There was a click in the ear piece. Margaret knew what it was. It was a party line. Someone was listening. Well, let them listen. Let them know of her sad life.

"Dora, I got to leave home," Margaret sobbed, her body shaking as she spoke.

"Tell me what's the trouble, Peggy?" Dora said sympathetically.

Yes, it was probably that nosey old bitch, Stallings, downstairs on the phone. Let her hear!

"Dora, the dirty bum of a brother of mine is around here all morning. He won't work. I got to get to work, and he won't even let me in the bathroom."

"Now, Peggy, don't take it so serious. You mustn't let things affect you so hard."

"Oh, Dora, you don't understand! You don't have a mollycoddle around the house all the time, lounging about in a filthy bathrobe. He'll have my poor brother Al and me in the poorhouse supporting him."

"Peg, control your nerves. You come over and see me and I'll cheer you up."

"I have to go to work. I'm not a person of leisure like he is. Someone has to bring money in to keep the home here going. We can't afford to have more than one person of leisure on our backs, and we have that gentleman."

"We're having a party tonight. Come when you finish work," Dora said.

"I'll be so tired. I'll be a nervous wreck. Dora, I can't stand it any longer. I can't! I give up. Every day that bum is around here. You'd think that if he wanted to live off the fat of the land he'd get some rich woman to marry him and live off her instead of us. And with all the trouble we've had, does he care? Burying a sick father, a sick sister, and what has he ever done? He just lays around the house like a gentleman, a gentleman bum. Oh, Dora, I can't stand it any longer. I'm getting old. My nerves are going. My head is throbbing as I talk to you. I can't stand it. Dora, if anything happens to me, you'll know the reason why."

Margaret hung up.

She had to hurry or she'd be late for work. She went to the bathroom and soaked her face in water and then went to the bedroom, dressed, and tried to powder up her face to hide the signs of her tears. She looked neat and attractive in a blue tailored suit.

"Mother, it's a crime. He drives me to work every day in such a state! How can I work? And I'm going to be late because of him," she said in the kitchen.

"Peg, I know. But you be a good girl."

Margaret left, sobbing as she went out the back door.

VI

At two-fifteen Ned came out to the kitchen with his coat on his arm. He was dressed, shaved, and combed; his shoes were shined, his suit pressed and brushed, and his derby rested on his head at the proper rakish angle.

"Mud, can you spare a dollar? I expect to have some money next week and I'll pay it back to you," he asked.

Mrs. O'Flaherty gave him a dollar.

"Thanks, Mud. I'll be home for supper."

He went to the parlor, gave his appearance a final check-up, and went out the front door.

VII

It was quiet in the house now. Danny put down his pen. His fingers were cramped and his right arm ached. But he had finished the story and he knew that it was good. It was one of the best compositions he'd ever written for Father Robert, and he was sure that it would be printed in the *Aureole*. Gratified, he read his story, half aloud.

The Fruits of Sacrifice

Early in the reign of Queen Elizabeth, John Anthony, a young Englishman, returned without his parents' consent or knowledge, to God's true religion; and he secretly cherished an ambition to be a priest. John's father, a wealthy English officer, was a bitter anti-Catholic. When John finally made known his conversion and his plans, there was a bitter scene between father and son, but John, in spite of his father's opposition, clung to his determination to study for the priesthood.

Two days later, leaving everything that was near and dear to him, the noble Englishman set out for Rome where he intended to prepare himself for his priestly duties. Owing to his lack of funds, John was forced to journey on foot, and at that time, as travel was arduous, he reached the center of Catholicity, only after enduring severe hardships and privations. The aspiring Briton had a keen, retentive brain, and it was not long before he became the leader of his class.

Finally, the goal for which he had striven so long and so earnestly was attained; John Anthony was ordained a priest; he became a representative of Christ on earth. He celebrated Holy Mass for the first time in a little church on the outskirts of Rome, and words cannot describe his joy, as he, for the first time, renewed the Sacrifice of Mount Calvary. A week after his ordination, Father Anthony volunteered to labor in Ireland.

At that time, Ireland was undergoing bitter persecutions. All the malice and hatred of bigoted and unscrupulous English statesmen, abetted by the great Queen Elizabeth, was directed against the Catholic Church. A priest was a hunted animal, considered a more dangerous member of society than the worst criminal, and a price was placed on his head.

After many adventures and narrow escapes, John, cleverly disguised, reached the Emerald Isle and presented himself to his Bishop, who was also in disguise and in hiding. Then he began his labors to keep bright the Flame of Faith in Ireland. For three years, Father Anthony zealously and devotedly served his God by administering the rites of the Church to the poor Irish peasants. Usually his home was a cave in the barren waste, while a cold, hard rock served him as a pillow; and a price of twenty pounds was on his head. Despite the fact that he was a hunted man whom the British greatly desired to capture, he consistently eluded the priest-hunters; although frequently the homes of Irish peasants suspected of harboring him were burned to the ground.

Finally a traitor, desirous of securing the reward for Father Anthony's capture, revealed to the British authorities the fact that the priest was to celebrate Mass Easter Sunday on a near-by hill.

Easter Sunday dawned; it was one of those cold, gloomy days, which are quite frequent in Ireland. Nevertheless, the sturdy peasants came from the entire countryside, and there on a barren hill they gathered to participate in the renewal of the Sacrifice of the Cross. A large rock, sheltered by a small dilapidated shed, served as an alter, while all around the faithful knelt in the mud, their weary bodies chilled by the wind and the bitter cold; and their bared heads whipped and cut by the driving sleet. Despite the hardships which they endured, the shabby peasants were happy, their eyes shining with a radiance which only comes from a supernatural happiness. Before the altar Father Anthony, gaunt and hollow-eyed, celebrated Mass. Suddenly the appalling cry, "the British, the British," rang out. Terrified, the little band scattered in all directions, as the savage blood-thirsty redcoats of "good Queen Bess" appeared out of the mist. The barren hill, which had so recently served as a tabernacle of God, was dyed a deep crimson; and the rock, which served as an altar, was bathed in the blood of a new martyr, Father Anthony.

Bending over the figure of the dead priest, the leader of the British forces looked down into the face of his son!

The scene shifts to the magnificent court of Queen Elizabeth. That tyrant, whose slightest whim was law, ostentatiously dressed in queenly robes, was haughtily sitting upon the imperial throne, when the father of John Anthony was brought in, in chains and closely guarded. Brought to his senses by his son's heroic sacrifice and death, the senior Anthony had resigned his commission in the Queen's Army, and openly proclaimed his return to the true Faith. The Queen, of whom the soldier had been a favorite, first by liberal and tempting promises and then by threats, endeavored to shake Anthony's resolution. Anthony remained firm, however, and was condemned to death for treason, and two weeks later, after receiving the last rites of the Church, he went to meet his son, to whose sacrifices and prayers he undoubtedly owed the grace of his conversion and happy death.

Danny sat back in his chair. Yes, despite all the yelling that had gone on at home this morning, he had gotten this story written.

17

I

Riding home in a half-crowded elevated car, Margaret kept asking herself why shouldn't she go to Dora's party. She needed a little fun, a little company. If she went home, what had she to look forward to? Talking to her mother or perhaps to her sister, Lizz? And that man would probably be home.

What kind of a life was she leading? She worked herself to the breaking point. She had a responsible job as cashier at the hotel and as if that wasn't enough, she had to cook and do housework at home. She gave up her salary to support her mother, not to mention a whole kit and kaboodle of O'Neills, and the laziest and most criminal brother that any decent girl ever had. What did she get out of life? Nothing. She was thirty-five years old already, and she'd be thirty-six before she knew it. She was getting to be an old woman, and she had to wear glasses all the time. She had hardly a stitch of clothes worth owning. Most of the girls she used to know were married. Why, even her old friend, Myrtle Peck, had remarried. They were their own bosses. And look at where she was, after all the chances that she had had in life? She had been a fool for her family.

Here she was, a grown, self-supporting woman, and yet she was worrying about whether or not she should go out to a little party and have some harmless fun with friends. And she was in such a state of worry when it was a Saturday night, and tomorrow she was off. My God, look at what she'd become! Why, was there any other girl her age, with her appearance and brains, who would even snap her fingers about such a matter? No!

This morning, when she had left home, she had been so upset, so nervous, that she had trembled and her hands had been shaking. She didn't know how she had gotten through her day's work, handling the large sums she'd had to without making mistakes.

She noticed that the train had stopped at Forty-seventh Street. Several couples entered the car. Young girls going out on dates with their fellows. One beautiful blonde girl, such a doll, so sweet, so young, so innocent, sat opposite her. She had been like that once. She had hoped for joy and happiness, for love once. Well, she wished this girl more luck than Margaret O'Flaherty had ever had. And she hoped that this young girl would not be the fool that Margaret O'Flaherty had been. Just think, she had been young once and she had had men at her feet, begging her to marry them.

She was still an attractive woman, even though she did wear glasses. She was distinguished-looking. Many people had told her so. Yes, to this day it was a puzzle to friends of hers why she had never married.

Fifty-first Street! Oh, how she hated this very station. The most unhappy time of her whole life had been spent in the days when she used to get off at this station to go home, to go to a bleak home that had nothing for her but misery and sorrow. She had been younger then. And she had been seeing Lorry. And the station made her think of her poor dear father, and her dear sister Louise, both of them dead for over ten years. The train was passing the yard and the greenhouses in back of the building they'd lived in on Prairie Avenue. Now she was past the yard. Good riddance. She could never pass Fifty-first Street without remembering, remembering so many things that she wanted to forget.

Margaret got off the train at Fifty-eighth Street. She decided to go to Dora's party. She waited a few moments on the crowded platform and boarded an Englewood train. Sitting alone, she thought of Lorry Robinson. If she had only seen him one more time and made him realize that she loved him and that she was the best woman in the world for him. Just think, if that had happened, Lorry might have divorced his wife, and today she might be Mrs. Lorry Robinson, the happiest woman in the world.

Life had played a filthy trick on her.

She was on the verge of tears. She looked at her hand. It was shaking. Her poor nerves. She shouldn't be suffering this way. And she wouldn't, either, if it hadn't been for Ned. To think that such a man was her own brother!

She wished that she were already at Dora's. Who'd be there? She'd bet that most of the men would be pikers. There wouldn't be any man there to interest her, a woman of her character and ability.

It had been months and months since she'd had anything to do with a man. The last time, she'd needed some money, and she'd borrowed it from Tom, who had charge of the waiters, and she'd had a little affair with him. He was a nice man, but who was he for a woman like herself? It was just before he was married. Tom was decent to her, and she still owed him a hundred and fifty dollars. Sometimes she was bothered by it, but not much. God, if men knew how women could do without them when they didn't love them! If men knew the opinions she had of most of them!

She wondered what Lorry was doing this minute. It was years now since she'd seen him. Over five years. He had gone on living and so had she, every minute of the years, and they had loved each other, yes, they had, and now their ways were parted, and she hadn't seen him for years. Oh, the cheap, dirty little tricks life played on people. Love, what did it all amount to? What did anything amount to?

There couldn't be a God. There wasn't. She didn't believe in God. She didn't believe in anything. What kind of a God was God to let her live the unhappy, terrible life she had lived, and to leave her at thirty-five, a good-looking woman, facing an empty future? Who could answer her that question? No one could.

There was no God! There was no God!

II

"How about a little drink, girls?" Bill Hilton asked, coming into the parlor in his shirt sleeves; he was a husky, deep-voiced, impressively masculine man with heavy brows and dark eyes.

"I wouldn't touch it. Not if you paid me a million dollars, but thanks just the same," Margaret said, smiling wanly.

"Bill is proud of that fire-water he brought home," Dora said; she was a large-boned, well-built, dull blonde woman in her thirties; her face was long, her features were even, and she had blue eyes.

"Why shouldn't I be proud of it? It comes from Canada and it cost me six and a half bucks," Bill boasted.

"What about my drink, Bill?" asked Dora.

"Straight or with something to flavor it, Dor?"

"Straight."

"See, Peg, my Dora there, she's a real hard-drinking gal."

"I'm not going to get drunk tonight. I'll just have one now before the people come."

"Good, you ought to have some fun taking care of me for a change," Bill said.

"I've done that plenty," Dora said.

"Not as much as I've taken care of you," Bill said.

"You better hurry up, and then put a tie and collar and your coat on before everybody comes."

"I'll write your ticket for you, Dor. Peg, sure you won't change your mind?"

"No, Bill. As God is my judge, I wouldn't take a drink if you paid me. Bill, I have great will power. When I say no, nothing can change my mind."

"All right as far as I'm concerned, girlie. After all, Bill Hilton was never a man to push a girl into the forbidden ways. Of course, if she likes them, well, you know me. But that's another matter. I always do right by everybody. Take Dora. Well, after I met her and came home with her, the next morning, I pushed back the bed covers and said, well, we might as well consummate this peccadillo with the ring and the jingle bells," Bill said, grinning. He left the room.

"Dora, I wish my brothers were like Bill. Al is straightlaced, and I vowed walking here that I wouldn't talk about Ned. If I do, I'll break a blood vessel."

"Now, Peggy dear, you're going to forget everything and be happy tonight and have a good time," Dora said, squeezing Margaret's hand.

"Yes, I'm going to be happy and I'm going to have a good time," Margaret replied, staring straight before her as if she were in a trance.

"Peg, you don't want to be a damned fool."

"Dora, if you knew what I've gone through in my life. If you only knew. But no one knows. No one knows," Margaret said, still acting as if she were in a trance.

"Forget it. Peg, tonight's tonight. Forget it."

"Oh, if I only could forget. If I only could forget."

"I wish my sister Cynthia was here. She can recite the loveliest poems about forgetting and about everything."

"How is dear Cynthia?"

"The last time I saw her, she was cockeyed. But then, she doesn't have to worry about anything. She gets three hundred dollars a month alimony and she lives like a queen."

"Cynthia is a good girl. I don't envy her her luck. Dora, I don't envy any woman what she has."

"Peg, why don't you be sensible? You can find some guy to marry you. Marry him. Divorce him and live off the alimony. If Cynthia can do it, you can."

"That mob at home wouldn't let me."

"Peg, you've done enough for your family. Tell them to hop in the bowl."

"Oh, Dora, you don't know what I've gone through."

"It's not too late to tie a can to them. You're still young."

"I'm an old woman. An old woman," Margaret said, sighing.

"Peggy darling, I know what's the matter with you. You're melancholy. You're melancholy. And nothing in the world is as good for melancholy as a nice good drink. Come on, Peg."

"No, I said I wouldn't drink. Dora, you know me. You know what will power I got. No!"

Bill came back, wearing a collar and tie and his blue suit coat. He carried two jiggers of whiskey and two chasers on a tray. Dora took one drink.

"Spittin' in your eye, Babe," Bill said, tipping glasses with Dora.

They drank.

"Hits the spot. Damned good stuff," Bill said, patting his paunch.

Margaret grinned at them feebly, a weak grin of assumed understanding.

"Bill, Peg is melancholy. Tell her to have a drink."

"Liquor won't cure what's the matter with me."

"Nothing's happened to you. You ain't in trouble, are you?" Bill asked.

"Bill, you know better than that."

"It's her family, Bill."

"I'm a good sport, but the ache in my heart is hard to forget, hard to forget," Margaret said, crying.

"Peggy, I'm going to make you forget. The gang that's coming is a swell gang," Dora said.

"Don't mind me. I'm all right now. But without you and Bill tonight I don't know what I would have done. I might have even made an end to myself. You're such good friends to me."

"Sure we are, Peg. You just forget. Now, let me get you a drink."

"No, Bill, I said I wouldn't drink it and I won't."

"You know best."

All three of them were suddenly silent. They waited for the guests. Margaret gazed at her image in the long mirror. She reflected that she was a good-looking woman. She was more attractive than Dora and had a more intelligent face.

Bill offered them cigarettes, and they lit up.

III

The parlor was crowded and the gang was noisy. Bill had put two bottles of gin, a pitcher of water, ice, and ginger ale on a table in a corner, and the guests kept pushing over to it for drinks. Margaret sat on a couch, smoking a cigarette and looking on while others had a good time. She guessed that these people were all right, but they were crude. With most of them drinking while she was cold sober, how could she have a good time? And how could these people do anything that would ease the ache in her heart? What could they do to help cure the sickness of sorrow in her soul?

Dora towed a good-looking, well-set-up man over to Margaret.

"Peg, meet Tom Cameron. He's a swell fellow."

"How do you do?" Margaret said, polite, but formal.

"Can I get you a drink?"

"No, thank you."

"You don't imbibe?"

"Sure she does. Tom, this girl friend of mine, if she wants to, she could drink a horse under the table," Dora said.

"Why, Dora, how can you say such a thing?" Margaret said.

"Peg and I, we been so drunk together, Tom, and we gave Bill plenty of trouble trying to take care of us. But Tom, Bill's a swell fellow. Swell fellow. Takes care of me when I take a fall for this stuff," she said, studying her glass.

"Maybe Miss O'Flaherty would change her mind and let me fix her a drink."

"No thank you. I'm not drinking."

"Aw come on, Peg, be a sport."

"No, Dora."

"Still treading the paths of virtue, huh, Peg?" Bill asked, joining them.

Margaret smiled at Bill.

"I was just asking Miss O'Flaherty, Bill, if I could fix her up a light potation," Tom said.

"Light potation, hell; if she wants a drink, give her the bottle."

"Why, Bill, you and Dora are giving me a dreadful reputation."

"Hell, we are. We're all drinking. And, Peg, let me tell you something, You're a swell girl. Swell girl. I want my friend, Tom Cameron, to know that I think you're a jewel of a girlie, because you are," Bill said.

"Peg, be a sport. Have a drink."

"Honest, Dora, I don't want to drink."

"Well, I do!" Dora shouted.

She finished her glass, spilling some on her dress. She wiped her chin with the back of her hand. She lurched to the table in the corner for another drink. Bill followed her.

Margaret glanced around. All these people were having a good time. She was bored. All these people were happy and carefree. She wasn't. She watched that blonde girl, Mrs. Marshall, ogle a man. She recognized the man's face, but couldn't remember his name. The man was running his hand up and down Marshall's thigh, and Marshall didn't seem to mind it. Well, what if the man wanted Marshall, and Marshall wanted it, what did she care?

"May I sit down, Miss O'Flaherty?" Tom Cameron asked.

"Why, yes, of course."

"I suppose you are thinking badly of us all here in our frivolity."

"Why should you think that?"

"Well, you seem so sober and serious, and you seem to have such an intelligent expression writ upon your countenance."

A moment ago, when Dora introduced her to him, she hadn't been interested in him, but she might as well be pleasant, even though she did feel he was trying to give her a lot of soft soap.

"I like people to have a good time," she said, watching a man and woman shimmy.

"Would you like to dance, Miss O'Flaherty?" Tom asked.

Margaret stood up. He put his arm around her, and they tried to dance in the small and crowded room. They got bumped, their bodies touching. He clasped her firmly and held her close to him. Well, let him. She didn't mind it at all. She needed fun, release. They danced, almost hugging one another and scarcely moving their feet. The floor got so crowded, there was no use trying to dance. When the victrola stopped they moved off to a corner of the room.

"That's the girl, Peg. Have a good time. Don't have the blues," Dora drunkenly shouted in Margaret's face.

Dora staggered off.

"Dora has a real sense of life," Tom said.

"Yes, she has."

Margaret tried to size him up. He seemed more refined than the other men here, and his grammar was good. She liked a man to use good grammar.

"Are you sure you wouldn't like to change your mind and have a drink?"

Why not? Everyone else was having a good time. Why shouldn't she? Why go on forever being blue? A couple of drinks would make her feel like a different person. And she didn't have to get drunk. Look at the will power she had already shown in having gone for so long a time without a drink. Yes, she could now control herself, have a few drinks and a good time, without really getting drunk.

"Yes, would you mind getting it for me?"

"With pleasure," he answered, grinning.

She waited for him.

"You're sober, Peg," a man named Al Hansen said, staggering before her.

"So are you, Al."

"Oh, I don't think you know the half of it."

"Half of what?"

"Half of how sober I ain't," he said, bursting into laughter.

"Daddy, dance with me," Martha Hansen said, grabbing him.

Tom returned with two glasses.

"Thank you."

"May I drink to you, an intelligent woman?" Tom said, raising his glass.

She smiled and tipped glasses with him.

A couple of drinks was what she needed. There wasn't anything wrong with it. She drank. It was good stuff.

Mort Rankin, a pudgy, gray-haired man, joined them.

"Say, this is a swell party, swell party. Certainly is a swell gang."

"You still handing out flowers, Mort," a big blonde woman named Katy Kendall said.

"Katy, I was just saying to my friends here that this is a swell party, a swell bunch, a swell gang," Mort said.

"It's awfully crowded here, and rather smoky. Let's go out on the porch a moment for some air, if you don't mind," Tom suggested.

Margaret and Tom Cameron left the room.

Everybody was talking, dancing, and drinking. The victrola filled the room with jazz music.

IV

"I just want to forget," Margaret said on the porch.

"Yes, I can understand that."

"I just want to forget," she repeated, her voice throbbing with self-pity.

She and Tom drank.

"The stars are out tonight. Oh, if the stars only knew. Maybe they do," Margaret said with an affected sigh.

"You're too smart a woman, Margaret, to be unhappy," Tom said, putting his arm around her.

She began to cry. He kissed her salty tears.

Why shouldn't she have some consolation? Why shouldn't she have some fun? He was a nice man. This wasn't wrong.

She responded to his kisses. He led her by the arm, back into the kitchen. A couple was hugging by the pantry, oblivious of Tom and Margaret. They heard the steady noises of raucous talk and music from the front of the apartment. They went to a darkened bedroom off the dining room. Tom switched on the light. It was empty. Coats were piled on the bed. He pushed them off onto the floor. He closed the door and, noticing a key in the lock, locked the door.

"Turn the light off," Margaret said.

He obeyed her wish.

He grasped her in the dark, and she was willing in his arms. She would be happy and forget for a minute, for a few minutes. She could make herself pretend that Tom was Lorry. Oh, if it only were Lorry.

V

Margaret returned to the parlor and slipped into a chair in a corner. Tom followed her.

"Tom, will you get me a drink."

Tom went over to the table to get her a drink.

After being with Tom in the bedroom, there was still an ache in her heart. Everything she did, what did it mean? She felt cheated. Life was always cheating her. And look at these people, all of them yelling, drinking, having such a good time. She was so different from these people.

Suddenly Dora looked down at Margaret, bleary-eyed. She couldn't stand up straight, and her hair was disheveled.

"Peggy, where you been?"

"Dora, you're drunk and you don't remember. I just had a drink with you ten minutes ago. I've been right here all along."

"Huh?"

"Of course I've been here."

"Oh, Peg!" Dora said; she squealed with laughter.

Margaret watched her, annoyed.

"But I'm your friend. I won't tell."

"Dora, you're drunk."

"I'm drunk as a lord."

Tom got back through the crowd with drinks and handed a glass to Margaret.

"Tom, where you been?"

"Dora, where were you?"

Margaret thought that Tom was a gentleman.

"He just danced with you, Dora," Margaret said.

"No, he didn't."

"Dora, you're drunk," Margaret said, catching a wink from Tom; she winked back and took a drink.

VI

Margaret jammed her way to the liquor table and made herself a drink. They were a swell bunch, and she was having a swell time, and she wasn't drunk, only happy.

"That's the sport, Peg," Bill said, blowing spittle and an alcoholic breath in her face.

"Bill, this is a swell party."

"Where's Dora?"

"Ain't she passed out yet?" Margaret asked.

"She can't."

"Anybody can. But not me. I'm not drunk."

"Dora can't, because it's my turn to pass out and have her put me to bed."

"Bill, I used to be unhappy. I'm not unhappy now."

"Give me a kiss on that, girlie."

Margaret kissed him.

"Whoa, what's my husband doing?" Dora shouted, floundering up to them.

"Kissing your girl chum because she's happy."

"Then kiss me."

Bill embraced her.

"Kiss me," Dora said, turning to Margaret.

Margaret kissed her.

"Everybody's drunk and happy. Whoops, I want a drink," Dora yelled.

Margaret wandered over to Al Hansen.

"Everybody's happy!" she said.

"Everybody's happy," he repeated.

"Oh, here you are! You happy?" Margaret said to Tom, who joined them.

"Know what I always say?" Tom said with drunken dignity.

"What?"

"Take the bird on the wing because tomorrow you may be dead."

"What's that?" Al Hansen asked.

"I want to tell you something," Margaret said, leading Tom out to the hall.

Margaret embraced Tom. He responded coldly to her kisses. She clung to him, hugged and kissed him until she rekindled his desires. Taking his hand, she pulled him out to the bedroom off the dining room.

"Jesus Christ!" a woman yelled from the bed, caught with a man.

Margaret and Tom retreated hastily and went to the bathroom. Margaret locked the door and put her arms around him.

"I want to forget everything," she said, panting.

VII

"Bill," Margaret sobbed, putting her head on his shoulder.

"Jesus, a cryin' jag."

"Bill, let's commit suicide."

"What the hell for, girlie?"

"Just for fun."

"Let's have a drink instead."

They touched glasses and drank.

"Drink enough of this and you won't want to be playin' hokum kari, as the Chinkees say," Bill said.

Someone dragged Bill away. Margaret glanced around the room. The room seemed vague. It seemed as if there was dust in the air that prevented her from seeing clearly. Everyone was yelling, drinking, pawing, and staggering around. She saw faces through the dust. Her head began to swim. Her legs seemed rubbery, a little warm in the thigh muscles.

"Listen to me," she said, pulling a man into a corner.

"What for?"

"I said listen to me."

"All right, I will."

"Friends, Romans, drunkards, lend me your ears," she yelled.

"How much interest will you pay me on 'em?"

"Lend me your ears."

"What's your name?"

"Oh, you don't know me, do you?"

"No, can't say that I do."

"Well, I don't know you."

"That makes it one up. Mitt me, my name is Andy Hough."

"I heard that name before. Where did I hear that name before?"

"Guess."

"Know who I am?"

"Who?"

"I'm Margaret O'Flaherty."

"You are? Who's that?"

"Me."

"Oh, you."

"Yes, goddamn it, me! I want to say something."

"Well, babe, you ain't got padlocks on your tongue."

"All right, listen."

"I am."

"Look at me!"

"I am."

"Know what you're looking at?"

"You."

"Just a minute," she said, snatching the drink out of his hand.

"Is that what you wanted?"

She gulped down his drink.

"Know what I could have been?" she asked.

"What?"

"Anything I wanted to."

"Well, why didn't you?"

"Because I'm a tragic woman."

"What the hell's that?"

"Dora!" Margaret yelled, spotting Dora near her. She grabbed Dora's arm and pulled her over. "Dora, tell this man who I am."

"I'll be damned, it's Andy Hough," Dora said.

"How you doing?" Andy asked.

"Dora, tell this man about me," Margaret said.

"Andy, this is my bes' friend. Peg O'Flaherty."

"Dora, am I or am I not the most intelligent woman you ever met?" Margaret asked; she pushed back wisps of hair and looked foolishly at Dora.

"You are," Dora said.

"Dora, couldn't I have been a great woman?"

"You could. Yes, she could. Andy, you should know how smart my bes' friend is. She's so smart. She's smarter than . . . well, goddamn it, she's smart."

"Well, what have I got to do about it?" Andy asked.

"I want you to know."

"Dora, am I a capable business woman?"

"Yes, you are."

"Am I an honorable friend?"

"You are."

"Say, what the hell is this gag?" Andy asked.

"Just a minute. Lend me those ears, Roman, and shut up," Margaret yelled.

"Say, who the hell you think you're talking to?"

"You, you good-for-nothing little fart," Margaret shouted at Andy.

"What did you call me?"

"A good-for-nothing little fart."

"Say that again, and I'll sock you!" Andy Hough said.

"You're a good-for-nothing little fart!"

"Get away from me, you drunken bitch," Andy sneered, shoving Margaret in the face.

"Don't mistreat my girl friend," Dora yelled, clutching at Andy.

"Get away from me, you, too," Andy said, giving Dora a push.

Bill rushed at Andy.

"Now, you filthy . . ." Andy started to say to Margaret.

Bill clipped Andy on the jaw. Andy went down. He tried to get up, but Bill was over him, pumping his fists into Andy's face.

"No man's touching my wife," Bill yelled as several fellows dragged him away.

Dora screamed.

"Come on out in the alley and finish this, you," Andy yelled at Bill; his face was marked, and his tie was askew.

Margaret staggered up to Andy. She snapped her fingers under his nose and turned her back on him. Andy made a move to sock Margaret, but Bill, breaking loose, rushed him. Bill split Andy's lip. The other men separated Bill and Andy a second time, and Al Hansen gave Andy the bum's rush out the front door.

"You dirty drunkards, don't you hit my man!" Mrs. Hough yelled; she was a dowdy, overdressed blonde.

Mrs. Hough went for Margaret. They clinched and grappled. Margaret pushed Mrs. Hough into a corner. She sank her teeth into Mrs. Hough's right arm. Mrs. Hough screamed in pain.

Out in the hallway, Andy tried to shove his way back into the apartment, but Al Hansen knocked him silly with a punch in the jaw.

Three men pried Margaret loose from Mrs. Hough.

"I'll kill the whore," Margaret screamed, trying to break loose and claw Mrs. Hough; she was restrained.

Mrs. Hough was thrown out of the house. Katy Kendall flung her wraps and Andy's hat and coat after them. Mort slammed the door, leaving them in the hallway, nursing their bruises.

"What was the matter?" Bill asked Margaret.

"He insulted me and Dora, the little two-bit cigar. Where's his whore? Let me get my hands on his whore!"

"Come on, everybody, and have a drink. We're all friends," Mort yelled.

"Gimme a drink," Margaret yelled.

Dora stumbled up to Margaret, put her arms around her, sank her head on Margaret's shoulder, and sobbed.

VIII

Cynthia Gray, Dora's sister, arrived with her friend, Joe Jerome. Cynthia had a well-preserved appearance: she had lustrous black hair, black eyes, and a fine figure. She wore a stylish black evening gown with a low cut bosom. Joe looked sleek and greasy. He had an angular face and wore a thin mustache.

"Oh, my dear friend Cynthia," Margaret said as the two women embraced.

"Peg, you're ahead of me on drinks," Cynthia said.

"Come on, have a drink," Margaret said.

"Joe, get us ladies drinks," Cynthia commanded Joe.

"I brought this," Joe said, pulling out a bottle of whiskey and handing it to Bill.

"Cynthia dear, I'm so glad to see you."

"Where have you been, Peg?"

"Cynthia, I'm so miserable."

"You don't look it."

"Cynthia, looks are deceiving."

Tom joined them, and started making eyes at Cynthia.

"Cynthia, this is Tom, Tom . . . well, he's a gentleman."

"Tom Cameron is my name. How do you do. I'm delighted to meet you," Tom said.

"Well, that's nice of you," Cynthia said.

"It's a pleasure to me."

"Peg, your friend has a line."

"Oh, you misinterpret me," Tom said.

"Did you rehearse your speech?" Cynthia asked him.

Joe brought drinks to Margaret and Cynthia.

"Peg, to you, my dear friend," Cynthia said.

"And to my dearest friend, Cynthia."

They drank.

"Hello, Joe! How the hell are you?" Margaret shouted at Joe Jerome.

"Him, he ain't. Are you, Joe?" Cynthia said, emptying her glass.

"Cynthia, tell Tom here. Am I the most intelligent woman in the room or am I not?" Margaret said.

"Of course you are, Peg, next to me," Cynthia answered. She turned to Joe and handed him her glass. "Get me a drink!"

"Cynthia, let me cry on your shoulder."

"You'll spoil my dress, Peg."

"Hey! Hey! Hey!" Al Hansen exclaimed enthusiastically as he joined them. "Come on out in the dining room. They got a game of strip poker going. Come on out and see the sights."

Margaret grabbed Cynthia and pulled her out to the dining room. The others followed. Three men and three women sat around the oval dining-room table, playing cards in varying states of undress. One of the men had his shirt off, and another was without his collar and tie. Katy Kendall sat in her corset and underwear.

"Boy, what breastworks," Cynthia exclaimed, pointing at Katy's big and sloppy bosom.

"Hey, wanna get in the game," one of the men yelled, grinning lasciviously at Cynthia.

"I don't want your pants," Cynthia answered, laughing lewdly.

The game continued.

IX

"I should have played this game," Cynthia said drunkenly; she laughed and pointed at Katy and another naked woman who sat at the table, calm and composed.

"It ain't too late," Katy said.

"I should have played this game because I got a more beautiful body than anyone in the house."

"Cynthia, we better go home," Joe Jerome said, taking her arm.

"Joe, you tell them. Who has the most beautiful body in this room?"

"You have. But, dear, let's go. It's pretty late."

"There! Did all of you hear that?" Cynthia shouted.

The strip poker game was almost over. A man sat with cards in his hand, pitting his BVD's against a woman's chemise.

"I got a beautiful body, too," Margaret said, wavering in front of Cynthia.

"Like hell you have," Al Hansen said.

"What did you say? Are you talking to me?" Margaret asked.

"I'm talkin' to both of you dames," Al Hansen answered.

"Cynthia, we have to go," Joe Jerome said, clinging to Cynthia's arm.

"If you think you got something special, show it to us," Katy Kendall yelled at Cynthia.

Cynthia broke away from Joe. Dora wandered around the room, mumbling to herself in a stupor. She sat down on a couch on one side of the room and cried.

"For the last time, Cynthia, we have to go," Joe said.

"Have a drink, Joe, and let me alone."

"You're afraid to prove what you said about your chassis there," Al Hansen said.

"Who's afraid?" Cynthia asked.

"You are," Katy said.

"Prove what?" Cynthia asked.

"What you said."

"What did I say?" Cynthia asked.

"You're welshing," Al said.

"I'll dare you to disrobe," Tom said, snickering and leering at Cynthia's side.

"I got a beautiful body," Margaret said, stumbling up to Tom.

"You dames can brag about your bodies, but there ain't one of you that's got ankles like me," Tim Carr said; he was a wizened, gray-haired old man.

"Who cares?" asked Cynthia.

"Damn it, I do," Tim answered.

"Well, care then," Cynthia said.

Tim took off his pants. He stood with his black silk socks gaitered over his long woolen underwear. He took off his socks and rolled up his underwear. He walked around, taking mincing steps.

"Say, what the hell is this, a whorehouse," Bill asked.

"No, it's a beauty contest," said Katy Kendall.

Tim put his left foot on the table. His ankle was thin and bony, with small gray hairs growing over the jutting bone.

"I say, there's slender ankles for you."

"You ain't got nothing," Cynthia told Tim.

Tim pointed to his ankle.

"I got a lovely body," she yelled.

"Who the hell believes it?" Tim replied.

"Doesn't anybody believe it?"

There was a chorus of noes.

"Well, I'm going to show you goddamn doubting Thomases. I'll be damned if I don't," Cynthia yelled, and the men clapped.

"I got a beautiful body," Margaret mumbled.

Cynthia unhooked her dress, let it fall to the floor, and stepped out of it. The men clapped boisterously while she slipped off her petticoat. She took off her corset and quickly removed her underwear. Wearing only her black pumps and silk stockings, she walked confidently around the room.

"Now, who's right?" she asked.

Joe Jerome left the house in disgust.

"I got better than you," Margaret mumbled to Cynthia.

Cynthia didn't answer. She stood rigid at one end of the room.

Margaret quickly stripped. Bleary-eyed and without her glasses, she stood alongside of Cynthia. Both women had well-formed and mature figures, with well-proportioned upright breasts. Cynthia's hips were broader than Margaret's.

Tom brought them each a drink.

"To our bodies," Cynthia flaunted, tipping glasses with Margaret.

"Uh huh!" Margaret responded.

They drank. Margaret spilled liquor on her chin.

"Now, goddamn it, look, all of you. Look at what you can't get," Cynthia said.

Dora stumbled up to them.

"I got something too," she said.

She made fumbling efforts to get her clothes off.

"You cut it out," Bill said, dragging her away.

"Well, any of you busting any buttons?" Cynthia yelled, taking another drink.

Margaret began to sway from side to side. Her eyes were puffed and swollen. Her face was dirty, and its expression one of stupefaction. Suddenly, she crumbled.

"She passed out," Al Hansen said.

Bill carried Margaret to the cot at the side of the room and dumped her on it. He got a rag and wiped her face. Then he put a pillow under her head and covered her up and let her lie there.

The party lost its spirit. Everyone started getting ready to leave.

18

I

Margaret awoke from a feverish, drunken sleep with a splitting headache. The sunlight pouring through the window made her blink and pained her eyes. For a moment she did not know where she was. The windows were closed, and the air in the room was stale. Her clothes lay in a heap near the dining-room table. The floor was littered with ashes and cigarette butts. She remembered now. She was at Dora's, and she had slept in the dining room on the cot.

She had been drunk, and she was in bed without a stitch of clothes on. It was Sunday morning. The apartment was quiet. She was alone in this room, and Bill and Dora were probably asleep in the bedroom right behind her.

Why had she done it?

And what had she done?

She was overcome with shame. She couldn't remember going to bed. Who had put her to bed? Now she could remember. There was something being said about beautiful bodies, and she and Cynthia were standing before them all, naked. How could she have done such a thing? And then she had passed out, and from that moment to this she couldn't remember anything except a kind of blind excitement and a feeling, even in her sleep, that she was sick and suffering.

A streak of pain knifed through her head. She was tired, very tired, and she felt all the old symptoms of a hangover. She knew what she had to face today. Nervousness. Shame. Disgust with herself. The blues. The fact that her life was sad and empty. Yesterday her soul ached, and today there was even more ache in her soul. Oh, what a poor creature she was.

On her way here last night she had denied to herself that there was a God. There was a God. She beseeched Him. She, a miserable, pitiful, and unhappy creature whose life was ruined, she begged Him to forgive her, to take pity upon her, to have mercy on her.

If she could sleep. But she was awake, and she couldn't sleep.

II

Margaret heard Bill and Dora mumbling behind the closed door of their bedroom. She wanted to call in to them, but she didn't. She waited, nervous and depressed. Still naked, she felt her body as something ugly and dirty, a disgusting heavy mass that weighed down her spirit as if with lead. Why couldn't they come out? Didn't it even occur to them that she might need some care and attention? She wanted them to come out because she hated being alone with herself, alone with this body of hers.

At last, the door opened.

"Oh, good morning, Bill," she said guiltily.

"Morning, Peg. How you feeling?"

"I'm so sorry about last night. What happened to me?"

"Oh, you were raring to go. You were hell on wheels last night. But tell me, feel all right?"

"I feel terrible. I'm so sorry, Bill."

"Forget it, Peg. If you got a hangover, do what I'm gonna do, take a hot bath and sweat it all out. I got a head that's splitting open. Boy, that was a party!"

"How's Dora?"

"Sick as a dog. She puked all over the bedroom last night." Bill was a nice fellow but he was crude, blunt, vulgar.

"Tell me what happened?"

"Don't you remember?"

"As true as I'm lying here, Bill, I don't. If I did anything, I'm not responsible. I didn't know what I was doing."

She was glad that Dora'd been drunk, too. That took a little of the curse off her.

"You and Cynthia gave a private beauty show. Boy, the two of you kept saying you had beautiful bodies, and the first thing I knew, there you two were, naked, and then the next thing you passed out cold. All I could do with you was put you to bed like you are. Dora was too far gone to help me."

"I suppose Joe Jerome took Cynthia home."

"Nope, he didn't. He got sore at her and blew. Tom took Cynthia home."

"Him!" Margaret said with contempt.

"I thought you went for him."

"I certainly did not. That fifteen-cent piker."

"Well, we all have our likes and dislikes. How about some coffee?"

"Can't I get up and make it?" Margaret answered, hoping that he'd say no.

"Stay where you are. I'll make it. But, say, the gang sure wrecked the house," Bill said, going out to the kitchen.

III

"Peg, I'm a wreck," Dora said, sitting up in bed with toast and coffee on a tray before her.

Bill and Margaret sat by the bed with their breakfast on a card table. Margaret wore a nightgown and dressing robe of Dora's. Her eyelids were swollen. Suddenly her lips quivered. She took a sip of coffee.

"Why do I do such things?" Margaret asked, her voice oozing self-pity.

"I don't even remember what you did. I was that blind," Dora said.

"You wanted to pull the same stunt she and your sister pulled, but I stopped you in time," Bill told Dora.

He would stop Dora but not her, Margaret reflected bitterly.

"It must have been a scream," Dora said, laughing.

"Why did I ever do such a thing?" Margaret asked tragically.

"Forget it, Peg. A good bat doesn't do anybody any harm. I like a good bat now and then. You blow off steam that way," Bill said.

Dora belched.

"Still feeling it, huh, Dor?" Bill asked sympathetically.

"It must be what I drank. It was no good."

"Sure it was, but you drank too much of it," Bill answered.

Margaret looked at them, glum.

"Anybody want more coffee?" Bill asked.

"Not me. Jesus, no, not with my guts," Dora said.

Margaret shoved her cup over to Bill. He picked it up along with his own.

"Bill, you're such a dear friend," Margaret said.

"Save the rain checks, Peg girlie," Bill said, leaving the room with the coffee cups.

"Dora, I'm so sorry for what I did," Margaret said.

"Peg, everybody was stinko," Dora said.

"I didn't mean to drink."

"It did you good."

"Yesterday, I was in such a terrible state of the blues."

Bill returned with two cups of black coffee. Margaret drank the coffee quickly, hoping it would make her feel better.

IV

"What the hell business is it of my family if I don't come home? Getting that snot-nose nephew of mine, Danny, to call up here and ask for me. I'm a grown woman and I can stay with a friend for the night if I want to. The goddamn no-good buttinski O'Flahertys," Margaret said vindictively.

"Leave 'em, Peg," Dora said lifelessly.

Unwashed, and filling the bedroom with their body odors, Margaret and Dora lay side by side, their eyes fixed vacantly on the ceiling.

"Dora, what'd you do with a family like mine?"

Not answering, Dora turned to the wall and dozed off. Margaret started to cry. She could still hear Bill working away cleaning up the apartment. She wanted to get up and she didn't have it in her. She felt dirty. Her body seemed to her like something filthy, violated, something that had been dragged in mud. She wanted to take a bath and get cleaned up, and she knew that if she did, she would feel better. She lay in bed, crying.

She watched Dora sleep with her mouth open and felt a sudden revulsion for her friend. There was Dora sleeping like a cow, unworried, with nothing on her soul. She and Dora were so different, and she suffered as it was impossible for Dora to suffer. Dora had no conscience. She turned away from Dora and watched the curtain flap. Outside, the world seemed so far away.

She felt the sweat between her legs, under her armpits, and between her toes. Why did she lie here and not take a bath and clean up? She had gotten up three times to do it, but each time she had felt so weak that she'd come back to bed. The minute she stood up, her head got light.

She realized she had done such awful things last night. She was so sorry. If she could only drive her feeling of guilt out of her mind. Cynthia had called up, and she'd talked to Cynthia, and Cynthia thought it was all funny and laughed about it. Why was she different from other girls? But she was. She had a soul. They didn't. It was because she had a soul they didn't have that she felt different and suffered more.

Oh, God.

She put her hand over her eyes. She saw bright colors in her mind's eye. She pressed her eyelids. They pained. She still saw those beautiful colors before her eyes.

Opening her eyes upon the dimmed and darkened room, she watched the curtain flaps, saw the sun-shot day cut little knives of light through the sides between the curtain and the sill and paneling.

Dora snored. Margaret looked at her, disgusted. She heard Bill working away, cleaning the house.

V

Because of sheer weariness and exhaustion, Margaret sat with Dora. The day was almost shot now. She heard Bill snoring in the bedroom, while Dora was sitting here, drinking, gradually getting drunk all over again.

Dora started crying.

"Peg, I want a baby."

Margaret pitied Dora. But what would Dora do with a baby? Dora could never learn to take care of one.

She remembered the idiot child of Lorry's she'd had—years ago. She felt too sad to cry. No, she had better drive memories like that out of her mind. It never did you any good to remember. The curse of a woman's life was memory.

"Peg, I hate myself. It's my fault. That time before I met Bill and got caught, I should have gone through with it, even if the baby would have been a bastard. I almost killed myself getting rid of it, and now I can never have a child. Peg, never have an abortion."

Margaret didn't answer. Dora's tears irritated her.

"Bill would have married me, even if I did have an illegitimate baby. Bill's broadminded. And Bill would like a kid himself and he'd be a swell father. Just think, Peg, I meet some fellow, and what I do, after all, it's natural. It's crap that a woman doesn't want it as much as a man because we do. I do. I love it, Peg. So I sleep with a guy, and that's not wrong, and then what happens to me? I'm knocked up. Knocked up, and I got to go to some damned butcher, and pay him a couple of hundred bucks, and look at me, look at the price I got to pay."

"The woman always pays," Margaret said bitterly.

"Cynthia hates kids. But think she'd get caught and have it happen to her? Not by a damned sight. She's too lucky. Me, I'm unlucky."

"You're not as unlucky as me," Margaret said.

"Have a drink, Peg," Dora urged.

"No, I won't," Margaret said.

"Oh, have a drink."

"You have one."

"Damned right I will," Dora said.

Dora poured herself a drink.

"Peg, why does God do things to us and not to others?"

"There is no God!"

"Isn't there?" Dora asked, looking at Margaret, startled.

"There can't be!"

"Are you sure?"

"If there is a God, why has He let a girl like me receive the treatment I have gotten from life?"

"Peg, you sure?"

"Yes! There is no God!" Margaret said, focusing her blood-shot eyes on nothing.

"Peg, you're not an atheist, are you?"

"I don't believe in anything."

Dora took a drink. Margaret looked at her with disgust.

"When I get old, I'm gonna be a Catholic. I wouldn't be one now because I'd damn my soul . . ."

Why didn't Dora shut up? The drunken slob!

"I'd damn my soul because I couldn't stay virtuous. I like it too much to stay virtuous. But after I get my change of life, then I can be a Catholic and save my soul. I'd love being a Catholic if I could only keep myself from sinning. But look at me! Know what I am? I'm a sinner. Oh, Peg, I'm a terrible sinner."

Margaret lit a cigarette.

"Peg, you ain't a terrible sinner like me, are you?"

"Dora, don't be ridiculous."

"Peg, tell me, there is a God, ain't there?"

"I don't know."

"Yes, you do. You know so much. Gee, I'm so dumb and you're so smart. Bill says he loves me but that I'm a dumb Dora. So I say, 'Sure I am.' Peg, have a drink."

Margaret still heard Bill snoring. She got up, determined.

"Peg, what you gonna do?"

"I have to go home."

"Aw, Peg, please don't."

"Dora dear, I have to. And thank you and Bill, you've been such darlings. I'll never forget how sweet you were to me."

"Please stay. And here, have a drink."

"No, I have to go."

Dora cried like a baby.

VI

"Peg, is that you?" Mrs. O'Flaherty called when the front door opened.

Margaret didn't answer.

"Where were you?" Mrs. O'Flaherty asked, meeting Margaret in the hallway.

Margaret walked past her mother, went to her bedroom, and slammed the door. Mrs. O'Flaherty blessed herself. She hurried in to Ned in the front.

"Mud, is she drunk?"

Mrs. O'Flaherty shook her head affirmatively.

"The goddamn slut!"

"Ned, what'll we do?"

"Let her sleep it off. She ought to be arrested."

Ned and Mrs. O'Flaherty sat in the darkened parlor, silent, waiting to see if Margaret would do anything. Margaret lay on her bed, her legs wide apart, her mouth open. She snored.

19

I

"Where did you get the idea that Poland has suffered more than Ireland?" Cyril Lynch shouted at Smilga.

Lynch and Smilga, both frail and slight, stood in the center of a group of students who were hanging around the corner near the schoolyard, waiting for the afternoon bell to ring.

"Hey, Smilga, which makes the best puttin'? A Polish broad or an Irish housemaid?" Danny O'Neill yelled, leering.

"Poland is de defender of civilization," Smilga passionately proclaimed.

"When Poland was a forest full of barbarians, Ireland was the isle of saints and scholars and the cradle of civilization," Cyril orated.

"When de Turks were at de gates of Vienna, John Sobieski saved Christendom," Smilga said, speaking rapidly and nervously.

"Smilga, better not let Father Robert hear you murder those th's," bow-legged Tim Doolan said, holding a lighted cigarette.

"The Poles can't even learn to speak the English language," Cyril said contemptuously, and Smilga flushed.

"Pilsudski saved Europe and de Church from Trotsky and de Reds," Smilga said.

"Who the hell did you say that guy, Suds, was, Smilga?" Danny O'Neill asked.

"Hey, Lynch, why don't you and Smilga join the League of Nations and shut up," said Hugh McNeill, the school cake-eater.

"Because it's no good," Lynch answered.

"How do you get that way?" asked Danny.

"The League of Nations never did anything for Ireland," Lynch said.

"You're nuts," Danny said.

"Hey, O'Neill, do you want a soapbox, too?" plump Marty Mulligan asked, puffing on a butt.

"Poland has always fought de tyrants," Smilga said.

"So has Ireland," Lynch yelled.

Smilga cast a withering look of contempt on Lynch.

"Jiggers, here comes Michael," Red Keene yelled.

Marty Mulligan and Tim Doolan quickly threw away their cigarettes.

"Father Hock! Hock!" Danny said, hearing Father Michael hocking and spitting around the corner.

Holding his handkerchief to his mouth, Father Michael appeared. He put away his handkerchief and smiled, but his eyes traveled suspiciously from one student to another.

"What's going on here?" he asked.

"Cyril is fighting the King of England again, Father," Norton said.

"Fadder, I was explaining about de fight of my people for liberty," Smilga said.

"I was telling him that Ireland has fought more for freedom than Poland," Cyril Lynch said.

"I'm sure none of you fellows threw that there," the priest said, pointing to a cigarette butt on the sidewalk.

"Not us, Father," Marty said, looking down at the butt.

"Mulligan, don't let me catch you smoking," Father Michael said.

Marty stared seriously at the priest, but said nothing.

"I'm glad that all the shouting was only about Poland and Ireland. You were making enough noise to raise the dead," Father Michael said; he turned to go back around the corner.

"Father," Ike Dugan called.

"Yes?" Father Michael asked, turning around.

"Did you hear about the latest thing in shoes?"

"What is it?" asked Father Michael.

"Feet."

Father Michael walked over to Ike and patted him on the back.

"Dugan, pick up the marbles. Your jokes are even worse than O'Neill's," Father Michael said; he walked away.

"Smilga, Poland never suffered from Black and Tans the way Ireland did," Lynch said.

II

"O'Neill," Father Dennis called.

Father Dennis was a fleshy young priest of about thirty, with glasses, a nasal voice, and a shock of wavy black hair.

"What do you want, Father?" Danny asked, standing up.

"Some day I want to take you to a gymnasium with me and swing you around for exercise. I won't have to pay a fee for the use of dumbbells then."

The class laughed. Father Dennis joined them in enjoying his own joke, and when he laughed he revealed several gold crowns.

"Now, would you mind telling me what a past participle used with *avoir* agrees with?" Father Dennis asked when the laughter had subsided.

"With the preceding direct object."

"So far, so good. Can you give me an example."

Danny cleared his throat.

"Ah . . . *Qui* . . . *Qui* . . .

"Is this an example? *Qui a écrit les lettres que vous avez reçues ce matin?*"

Danny looked at the priest with a blank face.

"Sit down, O'Neill!"

Danny sat down.

"*Pauvre bête! Pauvre bête!*" the priest exclaimed.

Father Dennis glanced around the room with a glint in his eye.

"Now, where is the Mulligan stew?"

"Yes, Father," Marty Mulligan said, arising.

"Did you hear the example I just gave your fellow omadhaun, O'Neill?"

Marty shook his head.

"What was it?"

"I don't remember."

"But you heard it?"

"Yes, I heard it."

"Mulligan, if your ears are washed, listen. *Qui a écrit les lettres que vous avez reçues ce matin?* Is that sentence an example of the grammatical rule concerning *avoir* which O'Neill just mentioned?"

"No, Father."

"How do you know it isn't?"

"Because if it was, you wouldn't have recited it. You wanted to catch me."

"Mulligan, sit down and go back to sleep," Father Dennis said. He clenched his fists and raised his arms. "Ah, *diable! Diable! Diable!*"

Father Dennis waited for the class to stop laughing.

"Baby-face Corkerry, a past participle used as an adjective agrees with what?"

"Why, it agrees with itself, Father."

"Corkerry, I am afraid that because of you there is going to be a mishap in this classroom."

"Miss Who, Father?" Corkerry asked.

"Corkerry, for your private information, a past participle agrees with the noun or pronoun to which it relates. Now, sit down before I brain you."

"Father, how can you brain a guy who hasn't any brains?" Tim Doolan said.

"Doolan, quit sitting on your own brains. Stand up." Father Dennis again waited for the class to stop laughing. "Now, Doolan, listen closely to the following sentence and tell me if it illustrates one of the rules just mentioned concerning the past participle. Listen! *La dame qui j'ai entendue chanter est une de vos amies.*"

"Yes, Father, it is."

"What does it illustrate?"

"One of the rules about the past participle."

"What might the sentence mean, Doolan?"

"It's about a dame who sings."

"I knew you'd understand the word *dame.* Sit down, you're abusing my patience."

Danny, bored with class, turned around to Smilga, who sat directly behind him.

"Frank McDonald," Father Dennis called.

"Father, you called on me yesterday."

"And I am calling on you today."

"Father, won't these other pupils here object? They pay their tuition, and if you call on me too much, they might think they're getting cheated out of their money's worth."

The class roared.

"Do you fellows think I am cheating you out of any education by calling on McDonald to recite French two days in succession?"

"No, Father!" many of the students roared out.

"All right, McDonald. In the following sentence I want you to tell me whether or not the participle is variable or invariable."

"I don't know in advance, Father."

"Listen, Smilga, you can't goof me. I know you're a cake-eater and that you take girls out every night," Danny said.

Danny imagined himself as a cake-eater who was always having dates with girls.

"Hey, Smilga, you'll get a dose if you don't cut it out," Pat Carrigan whispered; he sat opposite Danny and lived around Fifty-eighth Street.

Smilga fixed his eyes on his French textbook.

"Smilga, don't you even know it's a sin?" Carrigan whispered.

Smilga jumped out of his seat and leaped through the air, landing on Carrigan and knocking him to the floor. Smilga sat on Pat and tried to claw him. The class was stunned by the suddenness of what had happened. Father Dennis sped down the aisle and dragged Smilga off Carrigan.

"What's the matter? What happened to you, Smilga?" asked Father Dennis.

“Fadder, I have my honor.”

“Well, what’s that got to do with flying through the air like a hyena? Who insulted your honor?”

Smilga pointed at Carrigan.

“I didn’t say nothin’ to him. He just went off his nut,” Carrigan said.

“Carrigan, if I fly at you, there won’t even be a grease spot left on the floor where you once were,” Father Dennis said.

“Fadder, it’s an individual matter. I had to defend my honor,” Smilga said, with intense seriousness.

“Well, would you mind defending your honor more quietly the next time?” Father Dennis asked.

“Yes, Fadder.”

“Thank you, Smilga.”

“You’re welcome, Fadder,” Smilga said, still utterly serious.

Father Dennis motioned to Smilga to sit down.

“Borax, stand up and justify your existence.”

Danny didn’t pay attention while Father Dennis asked Borax questions. A note from Smilga landed on his desk. He opened it and read.

> *I will meet you to defend my honor with bare fists in gladiatorial combat after school this afternoon.*
>
> *Anthony Smilga*

Bewildered, Danny turned around. Smilga met him with an unflinching gaze.

“O’Neill, go outside and kneel down in the hall,” Father Dennis said.

Danny got up and sauntered out of the room. He stood by the door. Father Dennis came out.

“I told you to kneel down, O’Neill.”

Danny knelt down.

III

“Are you ready?” Smilga asked, approaching Danny by the large handball board in the schoolyard.

“What is this, a game?” Danny asked.

“You know what I’m talking about. Are you ready to fight me?”

Danny looked to a few of his classmates who were gathered around. He addressed himself to Pat Carrigan.

“Pat, can’t you convince him?”

“He says he’s satisfied his honor with me and now it’s your turn.”

“I don’t want to fight you, Smilga,” Danny said.

"I tried to tell him, but it's no use. He demands a fight with you, O'Neill," Corkerry said.

Danny shrugged his shoulders.

"I insist that you allow me to avenge my honor," Smilga said.

"Don't be a sap, Smilga," Danny said.

Smilga dropped his books and rushed Danny. Enraged, he acted like a child having tantrums. Outweighed and clumsy, he tried to rain girlish punches on Danny, but Danny blocked with his arms and elbows. Smilga rushed a second time, and Danny held his hands before him to fend off Smilga's punches. Smilga accidentally ran into Danny's left elbow.

"Isn't that enough?" Danny asked, sorry about the accident, but perceiving that Smilga was not seriously hurt.

"All right," Smilga said, putting a handkerchief to his watery and reddened eye.

"Don't you want to shake hands, Tony?" Danny asked.

Smilga shook hands with Danny. He faced the others.

"I have lost all but honor."

He picked up his books and walked off.

"So long, Smilga," Danny called after him.

Danny left the schoolyard to go to practice basketball.

IV

Since Saint Stanislaus had no gymnasium, the school rented a meeting hall on Seventy-fifth Street in which to play its home games. The hall was relatively small for a basketball court. One basket hung over a stage and the other beneath a gallery.

Danny was alone in the hall. He wore a sweater over his basketball suit. Father Theo, the Athletic Director, had bought him a mask to enable him to wear his glasses during the games, and he now wore the mask also. It was constructed like a baseball catcher's mask and covered his eyes and a portion of his face below them, as well as the lower forehead. He patiently practiced.

The basketball season was more than half over, and the lightweights were in second division in the Catholic League. They couldn't hope for much this year. But Danny was playing a dandy game at guard and had become one of the best players in school. He couldn't rest on any laurels. There was still plenty to know about basketball, plenty of shots and tricks to perfect. The good player had to learn to shoot fast and from all positions and angles. Diligently, Danny tried angle shots, one-handed spinning and twisting flips, and one-handed overhead tosses. It was boring. But he kept at it in the chilly hall.

He had developed so far as a basketball player by practicing and playing as much as he could ever since he had entered high school. Last fall he had gone out for football just to have something to do, and he'd ended the season as a star end. Practice had helped toward making perfect in both football and basketball. He continued practicing and experimenting. He switched to long shots, and then to free throws, and then to dribbling. He had to get everything down pat. Next year was going to be his senior year. He was preparing for next year. Other fellows didn't go out of their way like this to develop themselves as he did. Well, he would collect his dividends for it. He was tempted to quit and go home, but he determined to keep at it a while longer, boring as it was.

V

"So you're joining Mike's frat?" Glenn said, sitting alone with Danny in Mike Flood's parlor on Cornell Avenue, near Sixty-ninth Street.

"I'm not joining. I'm being reinstated."

Glenn seemed totally uninterested in Danny's correction. Danny hadn't seen him in over a year. Glenn had not grown very much. His hair was darker than it had been back in eighth grade at Saint Patrick's and he combed it pompadour. Glenn wore a classy gray suit with wide trousers. He sat there, cool, aloof, treating Danny practically as a stranger. They heard murmurs from the fraternity meeting in progress in the dining room. Danny, growing nervous, crossed his legs and twisted about in his chair, letting his eyes wander about the room. The Floods must have money. Their furniture looked expensive and they had a baby grand piano.

"How you like it at Park High?" Danny asked.

"It's a swell school."

Glenn languidly held out a package of cigarettes for Danny to take one.

"No thanks, I don't smoke," Danny said.

Glenn gave Danny a condescending expression and lit a cigarette.

"You're on the teams at Saint Stanislaus, aren't you?"

Danny nodded. He wanted to ask Glenn about Roslyn, but he hesitated. Particularly because of the way Glenn was acting, he had better not be the one to bring up Roslyn's name. But he did hope that Glenn would tell Roslyn he'd seen Danny O'Neill and that Danny O'Neill was in a fraternity with fellows like Mike Flood. But he wasn't in yet. They were voting on him tonight.

Glenn belonged to the world of dances, dates, parties, fraternities, and sororities, which were all a mystery to Danny. In the presence of this world, Danny felt inferior and out of place. He wished he hadn't asked to be reinstated. He felt that he was right originally in not having paid any attention to this fraternity after it had been formed last fall. McNeill had made him a charter member because he turned out to be a good football player, but he had never even attended one meeting.

It was taking them a long time to decide on him. And if they didn't vote to reinstate him, Mike would tell Glenn, and Glenn might tell Roslyn. Would he go on forever feeling that he didn't belong as other fellows seemed to belong?

"I'm in Sigma at Park. I came over tonight for the card game after the meeting."

That was a high-school fraternity, but he didn't know anything about it.

Glenn was high-hatting him. And who was Glenn? And what was he? He ought to laugh at Glenn and tell him to go screw himself. But instead of doing that he felt ill at ease.

Marty Mulligan motioned to Danny from the parlor entrance. Danny jumped to his feet and crossed the parlor, relieved that the waiting with Glenn was over.

"We just voted to reinstate you, Dan. Congratulations. I'm glad," Marty said, shaking hands with Danny. Marty was a husky, slouching, genial lad of Danny's own age.

Danny followed Marty into the dining room. Hugh McNeill sat at the head of the long, narrow table, and Mike Flood, Tim Doolan, Tommy Collins, Ike Dugan, Jimmie Halloran, Red Keene, and Joe Carberry, from Loyola, were grouped on either side of Hugh. A cloud of cigarette smoke hung over the room.

Hugh shook hands with Danny. Nineteen years old, he looked much more mature than the other fraternity brothers. He had a good build. His black hair was greased and parted in the center. He wore long sideburns and, though clean shaven, his face was blackish because of his heavy beard. He was wearing a blue herringbone suit with twenty-inch bell-bottom trousers.

"Danny, as president of Beta Lambda, I want to welcome you back and to tell you we're all glad that you're with us as a fraternity brother. When I founded our fraternity I explained its aims, and I don't think I have to go into it now. Let me just say now that our aim is to be brothers to each other, and not in name only. We want to help one another, have good times together, and work and plan and build together to make ours a national fraternity."

Danny sat down, glad that Hugh didn't go on any more. He glanced around the table self-consciously.

"Now, what is the next order of business on the agenda?" Hugh asked.

VI

She came up to his shoulder and she wasn't at all bad to look at. He liked her dark, bobbed hair, and he kept wanting to put his hand on her big breasts which shook as she walked beside him in Jackson Park. Corkerry trailed along behind him, trying to get some place with her stumpy, bow-legged friend.

After all the talk he had heard around school and from the Fifty-eighth Street fellows about making broads and hunting gash, here was his first pickup. He glanced at her out of the corner of his eye. Not at all bad to look at. She did have a wart on her chin, but then, you couldn't expect to get Mae Murray or Gloria Swanson the first time you went over to Jackson Park determined to pick up a girl.

The two couples strolled along a path in the park. It was a warm and sunny early April afternoon. Danny and Corkerry were off from school because the physics laboratory could accommodate only half of the third-year class at a time; they had been in the group doing experiments last week so they were free this week.

Danny led his pickup into the Japanese house, and stood in a corner with her. He embraced her.

"Don't."

"Why?" he asked, his voice a trifle husky.

"We'll be seen."

He roughly pulled her to him and kissed her. It was his first kiss since he had been in eighth grade. The contact emboldened him, drove him on, excited him with desire. He fumbled for her breasts. He was surprised at how tender, how soft they felt under her dress. She struggled with him, but he kissed her again. Tugging and wrestling, he tried to put his hand under her dress. She wore no pants, and he felt her bare thighs. The muscles were firm and hard. He wanted more. He didn't care where he was. He thought of nothing but contact with this girl. He tried to push her into a corner, but she eluded him and skipped outside.

"Let's go back," he said, walking beside her on the path away from the Japanese house.

"No."

"Why?"

She didn't answer. He linked his arm in hers and they strolled on. She sat down on an empty bench. Corkerry and the bow-legged one sat down at the other end of the bench, and Danny noticed that Corkerry was pawing at his pickup.

"What's your name?" he asked.

"Sarah."

"Sarah what?"

"Just call me Sarah."

"Give me a kiss."

"Not in public."

"There's no one around."

"It's not nice. I don't even know your name."

"Sam. Just call me Sam."

"I don't believe it's Sam."

He grabbed her and tried to kiss her.

"You're rough," she said, laughing and freeing herself from him.

"Let's go in the bushes," he said.

She giggled.

"Come on," he said, grabbing again.

She pushed him away.

"Your name's Sarah?"

"Uh huh!"

"Sarah, we got to go," the bow-legged girl said.

Both girls got up and walked off, saying goodbye.

"We could have laid them if it was dark," Danny said casually.

"Uh huh. I ain't never had a lay either," Corkerry said.

Danny said nothing. Let Corkerry think he was experienced.

"Well, Danny, this was better than monkeying around with magnets and all that stuff," Corkerry said.

Danny shook his head.

"I got to hurry up now and get dressed and out for baseball practice," Danny said, increasing his pace.

VII

Wearing his baseball suit, Danny crossed Stony Island at Sixty-fourth Street and walked toward school. His state of dejection showed in his slow and aimless gait. He scraped his spiked shoes on the sidewalk and twirled his fielder's glove.

Back on the Jackson Park baseball field, S.S. was losing to Saint Marks. And it was his doing. Although he usually hit southpaws, he had faced a lefthander three times this afternoon with the bases full. Now instead of talking about Casey at the bat, they could talk about Danny O'Neill up there. He was supposed to be a slugger, too, and he had struck out three times with the bags loaded. He remembered the taunts from the crowd.

"You swing like a rusty gate."

"Four-eyes couldn't hit the blind side of a barn!"

"Try hitting it with your head!"

And then, that ball that had come to him in left field. Why had he run in on it? There he had been in left field, waiting, confident that he would catch anything he got his hands on. The sacks were filled. A line drive was hit. With the crack of the bat, he'd come forward instead of running back. The ball had gone over his head for a home run.

Well, the baseball season was over at S.S. The team had had a disastrous season. He was ashamed to have played on it. They'd lost one game twenty-six to nothing, and another eighteen to two. And he hadn't been a star himself. Yes, he had made two long doubles against Augustine, one of them with the bases full. And yes, he had smacked out a triple in another game. But he had gone hitless in some games, and then today, look what he'd done. He remembered the last strike he'd missed. He'd swung so hard that he'd lost his balance and fallen down. Boy, if he had ever connected! But the simple fact was that he hadn't connected.

Some of the fellows had said that it was a dark day and that O'Neill had bad eyes and couldn't see the ball. Well, he did have bad eyes. But that was no excuse. If he wanted to be a big-league star, he had to make the grade with what eyesight he had. And he just wasn't developing as a ball player.

For three years he had daydreamed of how he would be a scintillating high-school baseball star and how he would hit a home run with the bases full. And look at the way he had folded up in a pinch. Yes, after kidding himself about his destiny, and having the nerve to think that he would be a star like Ty Cobb or Eddie Collins, he was a miserable failure. Whenever he was in a tight situation, he was a bust, a flat tire. He didn't have what it takes. He was eighteen years old, and he was no good. He lacked something—nerve, confidence. In a pinch, it was always the same. He lost his confidence. When he didn't have time, a few seconds in which to think, it was different. That was why he was better in football and basketball than he was in baseball. In baseball when you batted, there were those few seconds and fractions of a second between pitches, when your mind undid you. In football and basketball, you didn't have the time to think as you did in baseball. That made the difference. And it was in just that period of a few important seconds that he was no good. Yes, even though he was considered one of the best athletes in school, he was never really going to be any good.

Well, he had another year. Next year was going to be his big year in all sports. But there he was again, filling himself full of crap.

He walked through the schoolyard and downstairs. He stood alone under a shower, berating himself, telling himself that he was never going to be any good.

VIII

Danny dressed in a hurry and left the school building before the other players returned from the game. He couldn't face them.

Riding home on the elevated train, he looked through the final issue of the year of the *Aureole*. Father Robert had told Shanley, the editor, to use his story, *The Fruits of Sacrifice*. He looked at his name in print and proudly read his story.

Then he turned to the Sports Department and read what he had written as Assistant Athletic Editor.

FOOTBALL

Next fall, Saint Stanislaus is determined to win the undisputed football championship of the Catholic League. Will we get it? We will, if every student at Saint Stanislaus will do his part. If not, victory will not perch on the banner of the red and black.

On the first day of practice next September, we want a record turnout. It is the duty of every student to try for the team regardless of weight or experience. Remember that weight is not absolutely essential. A light, speedy player is, by far, more valuable to a team than a slow, heavy, lumbering fellow. You have a whole summer to get yourself in shape for football. Remember, too, that football will better you physically and mentally. Next fall, if Coach McBride is greeted by an enthusiastic, determined, and conditioned squad, he will work wonders, and if it is humanly possible, the Stanislaus squad will make its mark in the league.

Let us start now to make next year the banner year in Saint Stanislaus athletics. And don't let us forget our fine school cheer:

Red and black,
Smack, smack, smack.

D. O'N.

20

I

"Mother told me that Danny is taking out that Anna Sheehan to a party tonight. She's up in the air and she says she ought to blister that one's behind," Lizz said, sitting down with Jim while he ate supper.

"It seems to me that he ought to have other things to do besides chasing girls. Now that he's out of school for the summer, he ought to be thinking of getting a job instead of taking girls out."

"That's just what I said to my mother. I told her that before my son goes running after skirts he ought to work and bring in some money to his mother and father."

"Yesterday, I asked about getting him back to work at the express company, but I can't do anything. They don't want him in the Call Department."

"I told my mother, Danny works this summer and his pay comes to me."

"I'm glad you did. Mark my words, Lizz, that boy isn't going to run around like a bum this summer."

"And to think of it, taking out Anna Sheehan. Why, she's nothing. What have the Sheehans got, Jim? Nothing. That one isn't good enough for my son."

"It's better he's going out with a poor girl than a rich one."

"Jim, those Sheehan twins are flirts. Flirts! They have fellows coming up to their house every night in the week."

"The more I think of it, the more I'm convinced that we never should have let him live with your people."

"Jim, if those Sheehan girls don't let my son alone, I'm going to make a public spectacle of them. I'll stop them in front of church before the whole parish and I'll make a holy show of them."

"Well, Lizz, if it's just an innocent party, why, there's nothing wrong in it. But he'll have time enough later on to be taking girls out on dates."

II

"Son, be sure that you have a clean handkerchief when you take the girl out," Mrs. O'Flaherty said at supper.

Danny didn't answer. There was every other subject under the sun to talk about beside his date, and they talked about this. Wasn't it his private business?

"Peg, won't he be a hot sketch, taking a girl out?" Ned said.

"Think of it, Little Brother is going to have a girl," Margaret said, with a doting smile at him.

"She's not my girl. It's just a party, and every guy has to bring a girl, so I got to."

"Son, is that Sheehan one the best you could do?" asked Mrs. O'Flaherty.

"She's a very nice girl. All of Mrs. Sheehan's daughters are lovely girls," Ned said.

"They're not good enough for my grandson."

Danny felt like squirming. Couldn't they talk about something else?

"Who the hell do you think your grandson is? They're too damned good for him if you ask me," Ned said.

"Indeed they're not."

"Mother, nobody is too good for our Little Brother," Margaret said.

"Calling a big guy like him Little Brother," Ned said.

"Hello, Little Brother," Little Margaret said, watching Danny in a manner calculated to make him feel uncomfortable.

"You keep still!" Danny told his sister.

"Little Brother. It makes me laugh," Little Margaret said.

"Little Brother!" Ned said.

"It seems to me some people could mind their own business," Danny said.

"Now, nobody tease Little Brother," said Margaret, smiling affectionately at her nephew.

"Are you going to dance?" Little Margaret asked.

"I can't dance," Danny answered curtly.

"Don't dance with her, Son. Dancing is the sport of the Devil," Mrs. O'Flaherty said.

Danny glared at his grandmother.

III

It was a quarter after eight. He was supposed to call for her at nine. He nervously paced back and forth across his bedroom, wishing the time would pass more quickly. He felt trapped, a prisoner. If he went in other rooms of the house, they'd come and start talking to him about his date, asking him questions. Whenever he had a date from now on, he wasn't going to tell them unless he had to. Of course, he couldn't keep a date with Anna Sheehan a secret because she lived in the same building with them.

Should he be on time when he called for her? Some fellows said that a girl wouldn't go for you or respect you unless you came late when you called to take her out. Was this so? If he called late, how late should he be? And if he was late, would she be sore at him? She was a nice girl. He didn't want her for his girl, and he was taking her only because he couldn't think of any other girl to take. He had wracked his brain for a long time, trying to make up his mind what girl to ask to the frat party, and then finally he had met Anna Sheehan one day in the hall and he had blurted out the question, and she'd said she'd like to go with him. But even though he was only taking her as a stopgap, he didn't want her to be sore at him.

And there were other questions that bothered him. What about dancing? If he didn't even make a stab at it, that would look bad. And if he did, he'd make a fool of himself and be laughed at. And then, what did you say to a girl when you took her out? On a date you were supposed to have a line. He didn't have a line. What would he talk about? Anna Sheehan was a decent girl, and, of course, he wouldn't have to try anything with her. From what he heard other guys say, it seemed that if you took out a girl who wasn't decent, and didn't try to fool around with her, she'd think you were a hick and a pretty awful lug, and that if you took out a decent girl and tried to fool around with her, she'd get sore and never go out with you again. And then, a lot of fellows who had monkeyed around with girls said they'd bet that no matter how decent a girl was, she could be put if the right guy came along and tried the right technique on her. All sorts of things about girls and dating girls puzzled him. Suppose a decent girl had to go to the bathroom when she was out on a date with a fellow? Didn't she blush or feel funny or ashamed while he waited for her? And wouldn't a fellow feel the same way if he had to leave her to go and take a leak? Yes, all sorts of questions like these bothered him.

He wished that he hadn't let himself in for this. If he hadn't gone back into the frat, he wouldn't be facing this ordeal now. But he wanted to be in the frat. He looked down on fellows who didn't belong to a fraternity.

"Dan," Uncle Ned said from the bedroom door.

"Yes," Danny replied, on the defensive for fear Uncle Ned would start talking about his date.

"Here, take this in case you need it, and have a good time," Uncle Ned said, handing him a dollar.

"Oh, thanks, Uncle Ned."

"So long. And have a good time," Uncle Ned said, leaving him.

Uncle Ned was all right.

He now had six bucks. He counted his money, enjoying the feel of the green dollar bills. Except for the times he had been working last summer and the summer before, he hadn't often had six dollars to spend as he did now. He had enough to take a taxicab each way.

IV

Danny viewed himself in the bathroom mirror. He'd shaved today without cutting himself. He shaved once a week, but even then, he had only a few dark hairs on his chin and upper lip. He wished he would quickly reach the day when he would have a real beard to shave. The first time he'd shaved, he'd cut his face and some of the fellows at school had razzed him. He stepped back a pace and smoothed his vaselined hair which was combed pompadour. He wanted to let it grow longer and wear sideburns, but he was leary of doing it. It would look as if he were trying to play the sheik. He felt guilty about saying or doing or wearing what was fashionable, because he really didn't have the feeling that he belonged in the kind of a world he was trying to crash.

He smoothed his cravat, a tie with green, black, and brown stripes which clashed with his yellow shirt. His suit was a dark brownish gray, with a stylish belted back. Uncle Al had bought him this suit, and he liked it except that the trousers weren't wide enough. Not that he wanted wide bell bottoms, but he would like trousers a little wider than these were. He guessed that he looked all right, in fact, pretty nifty.

He left the bathroom. It was still too early to call for Anna. He took a peppermint out of his pocket, sucked it because he wanted to have a good breath.

"Brother," Aunt Margaret called.

"Yeh, what do you want?" he answered, surly.

"Come here," she said.

He made a face, and met her in the dining room.

"Here, Brother, I wanted to give you this for tonight."

"Thanks."

"Now, you have a good time. Let me see how you look," she said, turning on the dining-room light to see him better.

She made him feel miserable, but he said nothing.

"Why, Brother, you look so nice. You look sweet." She raised her voice. "Mother, come and look at Little Brother."

"Ah, the devil take him. Come and read me the rest of the death notices," Mrs. O'Flaherty answered from the bedroom.

He wandered restlessly into the parlor and put *Dapper Dan* on the victrola. Hearing the chorus, he dreamed of how he wanted to be a slick Dapper Dan himself.

V

"Son! Son!" Mrs. O'Flaherty called to him from the door.

"What do you want? I'm all right," he answered.

He waited and she came skirting down the hall to him.

"Son, here, you be a good boy, and now, you mind your p's and q's and have a good time," she said, and she handed him a dollar.

"Thanks, Mother."

"Goodbye, Son!"

"Goodbye, Little Brother, have a good time," Aunt Margaret called from the rear.

"Goodbye," he responded and closed the door.

He stood in the hallway, outside his door. He breathed rapidly, and his heart pounded. He must now go upstairs and ring the Sheehan bell.

They might all know how he felt. Somehow he felt that he was not made for this kind of a life, and that they would know that he wasn't. That was one of the reasons why he felt the way he did, he guessed.

He took a few steps and then stood against the railing.

He had to go through with it.

He would try to act as if he were really accustomed to calling on a girl and taking her out on a date.

He walked slowly up the steps. He stood outside the Sheehan door, nervous.

VI

He rang the bell. Mrs. Sheehan opened the door. She was a large and well-padded woman, with a jolly, robust, red-cheeked face, gray hair, and a very ample bosom.

"Oh, hello, Danny. Come right in. Anna is fixing herself up and she'll be ready in a jiffy."

"Good evening," Danny said shyly.

She took his hat, an expensive but old gray hand-me-down from Uncle Al. After hanging it on the hall tree, she led him into the parlor and turned on the light. They had an old piano, old furniture, lots of knickknacks, and the wall and top of the piano were crowded with photographs. In one corner there was a picture of Christ as a youth.

"Well, we're glad to see you. You've never come up, and lots of fellows are always here."

"I usually had studies or something," Danny said.

"Yes, your grandmother tells me how hard you study."

Danny heard Anna moving about and talking to her twin sister, Amelia.

"Anna will be ready soon. She and her sister did the supper dishes for me before she started to get dressed. That's why she isn't ready."

"Oh, that's all right."

He wished he could think of something else to say.

"How is your grandmother?"

"She's fine, thank you," Danny said stiffly.

"She's a fine woman."

Danny looked around. The Sheehans didn't have a lot of money, but they were nice people. It must be hard on the girls knowing that so many other girls had more money and nicer dresses than they had. That was something that must bother girls more than it did fellows. But it bothered fellows, too.

He wished Anna were ready. He wondered what Mrs. Sheehan was thinking about.

"You're out of school now, Danny?"

"Yes, we're finished for the year."

"The girls have a week or two more, and so have the youngsters at Saint Patrick's."

"We get out a little early."

"Mother," Anna called.

"Excuse me, the girl wants me," Mrs. Sheehan said.

Danny sat, nervous. He started sucking another pepperment. If he only hadn't let himself in for this.

"Hello, Dan. I'm sorry I kept you waiting," Anna Sheehan said, breezing into the parlor.

"Oh, that's all right," Danny said, rising.

She was a slender, blonde-haired girl with blue eyes and a thin face. She was rather pretty, Danny reflected. But she could be prettier. And she had put too much powder on. Anyway, she wasn't homely. She wore a black dress which fell just below the knees. It didn't look too new, but then, she looked all right.

He asked himself why hadn't he asked her twin sister, Amelia? Amelia was as nice a girl as Anna, and prettier, a moon-faced, black-haired girl with wonderful dark eyes. He had been dumb in not having thought of it. Well, it was too late, and he had to make the best of Anna now.

"Have a good time, and don't be out too late," Mrs. Sheehan called to Anna as they left.

VII

She wasn't a gold digger. When he'd suggested taking a cab, she'd said for him not to be silly, taking a cab so far when they could go by street car. They strolled along South Park Avenue. He became confused as they came to Fifty-ninth

Street. Should he or shouldn't he take her arm crossing a street? He couldn't get himself to take her arm. They crossed Fifty-ninth Street.

It was twilight. People strolled lazily along; there was a steady stream of automobiles passing in either direction. He thought that it could be a romantic scene in a moving picture. Himself taking a girl out, both of them happy and as much in love with each other as a fellow and a girl in a movie. But if he was a fellow in a picture or a story, he wouldn't be a damned mummy. If he went on all night scarcely talking, she might think he was as bad as a hayseed. She might tell others. It might get around Fifty-eighth Street that he was a dope and a goof for fair.

"Are you out of school yet?" he asked, merely to make talk.

"I just wish I was."

She was in first year at Englewood High, a public school. Most of the girls at the party tonight would be Saint Paul girls. He wished he were taking out an S.P. girl.

"Why do you wish you were out of school?" he asked, grinning and trying to banter.

"I'd like to work. I worked last summer at the Fair, and my older sister, Mary, she's going to get me a job there again this summer."

"You like to work?"

"I like it much better than I do school."

Sixtieth Street. Again he couldn't get himself to take her arm crossing the street.

This was such a familiar street. How many times had he walked this same block, thinking of Roslyn? And that had been only a few short years ago. And now, here he was on his first date, and it wasn't with Roslyn. There were lots of girls who'd rate more than she. The last time he'd seen her, she had been thin, not so pretty, kind of bony.

In the old days he'd never dreamed that he'd be walking to Sixty-first Street with Anna Sheehan on the night of his first date. He'd never even known her then. She'd been living in Springfield, Illinois.

Speechless, but with sudden courage, he took her arm and guided her across Sixty-first Street. They waited for a street car.

VIII

The party was being held in the clubhouse of a small golf club located on the Southeast side of Chicago. The building was squat and red-bricked. The ballroom was medium-sized, with a stage at one end, and mirrors flanking the other three sides. Through opened doors, a full moon and a clear sky was visible, and the steady song of grasshoppers could be heard.

Five couples were present when Danny and Anna arrived, and others were coming. Danny stood waiting with his hands in his pockets. Anna had said that she'd had to powder her nose and gone to the ladies' room. She hadn't shown any embarrassment either when she'd told him this.

"Where's your woman?" Mike Flood asked him.

Mike was smaller than Danny. He had big ears and an angular face. He was sleeked out in a new gray tweed suit.

Danny pointed toward the ladies' room in answer to Mike's question.

"Oh!" Mike exclaimed.

The three-piece orchestra struck up a fox trot. Danny watched the dancing, trying to appear casual. Marty Mulligan and Ella McGrail danced gracefully by him, Marty smiling cordially. The mere sight of Ella McGrail made Danny feel sorry for Anna Sheehan. Alongside of Ella, Anna seemed common. Danny's eyes followed Ella. She was slender and had lovely curled brown bobbed hair. She wore an organdy dress, and she and Marty formed a fine picture when they danced. She was Marty's steady Friday-night date. He watched Marty dance, hoping to get an idea, but it was useless. He had to dance in a couple of seconds now, and he didn't know how.

Maggie Joyce joined Mike. She had red hair, and was pretty, prettier than Anna. Mike didn't even introduce her to Danny. He danced her off.

Mike was a snob, high-hat. If Mike knew that Anna's father was only a motorman, he'd be even more tony. Then Mike would always say to him: How's the motorman's daughter?

Anna joined him, a thin smile on her face.

Now he had to dance. He was sure that she must sense his discomfort. Yes, he was certain it must be written legibly on his face.

"Want to dance?" he asked hoarsely, speaking as if the words had to be forced out of him.

She put her left arm on his shoulder and held out her right hand for him to take. He encircled her with his right arm, and grasped her right hand. Her hair brushed his cheeks. His confusion seemed to empty his mind of will. Like an automaton, he took a step with his left foot, his movement stiff. He stepped on her toe. He walked, almost as if he were a stilt-walker. There was no bend, no grace, no resilience in his body. Tense, unrelaxed, he took one step after another, paying no heed to the music. He didn't like the smell of her perfume; it was getting stale. He could feel her left breast against his chest. He liked the feel of it, but it made him uncomfortable. He had to pretend that he didn't even know her breast was touching him. He kept stepping on her toes, and she tried her best to dodge his awkward feet.

Couples danced by and around them. Danny noticed Dopey Carberry standing on the side, grinning at him. He and Anna collided head on with Marty and Ella McGrail.

"Sorry," Marty said, and he was off, dancing in rapidly graceful movements, taking long and easy strides and expertly whirling Ella around and around.

Danny's throat was dry. He didn't know what to say. He felt foolish. He tried to keep off her toes and not to bump her into others, and he was grateful when the orchestra stopped playing.

They stood silent, uncomfortable, while the orchestra prepared to play a new tune. He glanced around. He gulped. He had to talk. He couldn't be a goddamned dummy all night.

"Nice place," he said in a strained voice.

"Yes, isn't it?"

Was she silently laughing at him? Disappointed in him?

"I like this," Anna said when the orchestra started playing *The Sheik.*

"So do I," he said.

He tried again to dance.

"I'm sorry," he said, after stepping on her foot.

"Oh, it was my fault."

She danced with her upper torso bent forward and her buttocks protruding, in order to avoid abdominal contact with him. Her left breast brushed against his chest. He danced her into Carberry, and because of the collision his thigh touched hers. Didn't this kind of contact make a girl want to blush?

"Did you see *The Sheik?*" she asked.

"No, I didn't."

"I adored it."

"I'm sorry I missed it," he said, and again he stepped on her toes.

She smiled.

Both of them were relieved when the orchestra stopped. They slowly walked off the floor to sit down near the mirrors on the right.

IX

"Would you like to dance?" Danny asked, sitting beside Anna.

"No, thanks, I'm tired."

Some couples were dancing, and others, including Mike Flood and Marty, were standing a few feet away in a gay and laughing group. None of them turned to ask Anna and him to join them. All night, most of his fraternity brothers had scarcely paid the slightest attention to him. Mike had not bothered with him at all. The others had been friendly if he talked to them, but hadn't made any effort to talk to him.

Danny wished the party were over. All he could do was sit with her, try vainly to find something to say, and pretend that both he and she enjoyed this pretense. She wasn't acting as if she were sore, but she couldn't be having a good time. And it was his fault. He had let her in for this. He felt lousy.

Mike Flood flashed by with Ella McGrail, his nose stuck conceitedly in the air. Danny saw Maggie Joyce walk over to some Saint Paul girls sitting in a corner with Tommy Collins and Ike Dugan. Marty approached Danny and Anna.

"Would you like to dance, Miss Sheehan?"

"Do you mind?" Anna asked, looking at Danny.

"No, of course not."

She had, it was true, just said she was too tired to dance with him, but then he didn't blame her. Why should he complain? He was glad that Marty had come over. And after the dance, when Marty walked off the floor with Anna, this would give him a chance to join in with the bunch. That would be better than sitting alone all night with Anna.

Dopey Carberry sauntered over to Danny. His girl was in the washroom. Dopey was a thin, languid, curly-haired fellow with thick, sensuous lips. He moved and sat in a limp way, as if he were always determined to expend a minimum of energy.

"Well, high-stepper, how goes it?" Dopey asked.

"All right."

"This is a dumb party."

"What's the matter?"

"Nothing to drink, no excitement, not enough people here. Hell!"

Danny didn't answer.

Hugh McNeill grinned at them as he danced by with his girl, Patricia Carmon.

"One thing about Mac, he always gets nice women," Dopey said.

Danny nodded. He watched Marty talking to Anna as they danced. He was grateful to Marty.

He wondered would he ever learn to dance, so as not to be the spectacle he had made of himself tonight? He was the same at this party as he used to be at parties in grammar school. He didn't feel at home at a party. He not only didn't know what to say, but he didn't know how to act.

Well, perhaps the girls here would think him a goof. Let them. On the gridiron, the basketball court, the baseball field next year, he wouldn't be. If they saw him there, they would see a different Danny O'Neill. He didn't have to step down to any fellow in this room when it came to athletics, not even to Tim Doolan.

X

Danny and Anna sat on opposite sides of the Yellow Cab. He thought that perhaps he really ought to try and kiss her. He wanted to. Even if she didn't rate as did the girls the other fellows had taken to the party, he still wanted to take her in his arms and kiss her. But he didn't dare take the chance.

"That Marty Mulligan is a nice fellow. I liked him," Anna said.

"He's a swell guy. My best friend."

"He's a very good dancer, and jolly," Anna said.

The others had gone some place to eat, but there hadn't been room for him and Anna in any of the automobiles. Even in the frat he was treated like a kind of poor relation. But anyway, Anna had said that she better go home.

The taxicab sped along Cottage Grove Avenue, past the lighted Sixty-third Street amusement area. He saw a number of people on the street. The cab turned into Washington Park. In a couple of minutes they'd both be home. It would be all over, an evening of agony for him. If this was what taking out girls was like, it wasn't any fun. But it wasn't the same for other fellows. There was something wrong with him, that was the trouble.

The cab stopped in front of the gray stone building on South Park. They both got out, and Danny paid the bill. He followed her up the stone steps and into the hallway.

"I don't have a key," she said, ringing her bell.

Danny inserted his key in the lock of the lower hall doorway, and at the same moment the buzzer sounded.

He trudged upstairs after her. They faced each other outside his door at the second floor landing.

"Thank you, Danny, for a very lovely evening. And good night," she said cheerfully.

He grinned foolishly.

She ran upstairs, and he heard Mrs. Sheehan talking as she let Anna in. He opened his own door. Everyone was asleep. He went to his room on tiptoe. He undressed, glum and doleful. He got into bed and lay there, thinking that he had made a holy show of himself. He was a goof. He had no right taking girls out. He was a clown.

But damn it, he'd change. He'd learn how to dance. He'd have as beautiful a girl as any of the fellows. Someday at parties he'd be the center of attention.

But wasn't he kidding himself? What a goof he'd really been tonight? Everyone seeing him try to dance must have laughed. Anna mustn't like him. She couldn't have had a good time. The girls had cut her, and the fellows hadn't paid much attention to her.

And he lay here now saying he'd some day be somebody. And that they'd sing a different tune about him some day. And that they'd some day remember they knew him and be proud of it. It was all going to change. He was serving notice on them, the girls who paid no attention to him, the fellows who laughed at him; he was serving notice on them all that some day they'd hear about a different Danny O'Neill. They would!

21

I

Jim kept moving about the house, restless, not knowing quite what to do with himself.

"Jim, why don't you take a nap," Lizz said.

"I don't feel like taking one."

He went to his room and got an old straw hat.

"Lizz, I'm going to run down the street and get an afternoon paper."

He left the house. It was a pleasant, sunny August afternoon. Jim limped along Calumet Avenue. The weather was a good augur for his vacation. If he had ten straight days like today he would offer no complaints. Time was when he didn't get any vacation. Well, now he did, and he needed it this year especially, because he felt more tired than usual. He was going to get himself good and rested. He'd sit in the sun, take in some ball games, and he and Lizz would go see some movies together. And for ten straight nights he could eat supper with his family and stay home with them. He felt free.

Passing the drugstore at Fifty-eighth and Calumet, Jim saw Danny leaning on the counter and talking to the soda fountain girl. Here it was already August, and Danny hadn't been able to find work. A shame to be losing so much time, and for what? To be hanging around a drugstore gassing with some girl. He limped on toward the elevated station. None of the bums were in front of the poolroom today. He guessed that they must be cooling their lazy asses in the shade some place. Coming back, he entered the drugstore.

"Oh, hello, Pa."

"Hello, Dan. Want a drink?"

"No, thanks, Pa, I just had one."

"Can you fix me up a Coca-Cola?" Jim asked the girl.

Danny waited beside his father while Jim drank his Coca-Cola.

"Come on, walk home with me."

Danny couldn't refuse. Jim laid a nickel on the marble counter and he and Danny left the store.

"I just came from downtown. I got a job," Danny said, as they walked along the shady side of Calumet Avenue.

"Good. What doin'?"

"It's only Saturdays. Wrapping shoes. I get three dollars every Saturday for doing it. I start next Saturday."

"Oh!" Jim exclaimed, disappointed.

"Uncle Al got it for me. It'll give me a little spending money."

It never occurred to Danny that he ought to give his mother a dollar of his pay just for the principle of the thing. Jim decided that there was no use mentioning the matter to Danny, since the amount was so small.

"I guess such work is better than nothing," Jim said.

"I don't mind it."

Jim looked sharply at Danny. They walked on a stretch without speaking.

"What have you been doing with yourself these days?"

"I've been going swimming a lot. That is, in the afternoons. Most mornings I went downtown to see if I could get work," Danny answered, thinking that, after all, Papa didn't know this was a lie and couldn't prove that he hadn't tried to get a job.

"I'm on my vacation. I want you to come over to supper some night this week. Can you come tonight?"

"I can't tonight. I promised a fellow I'd go swimming with him."

"How about tomorrow night?"

"Yes, I can come tomorrow night."

"You won't have to take it up with your social secretary, will you?"

"What? I ain't got no social secretary," Danny said before he realized his father was being sarcastic.

"Come in a while and we'll talk," Jim said, and, apprehensive, Danny followed Jim into the apartment building.

II

"Danny, you're too good to wrap shoes," Lizz said.

"No honest work is beneath you. Remember that," Jim told Danny.

Danny sat between his father and mother, uncomfortable.

"Jim, what would the O'Reilleys say if they knew that after all Danny's education and bringing-up, they were to find out that he was wrapping shoes in a store?" Lizz said.

"I don't give a good goddamn what the O'Reilleys or anybody else says," Jim replied.

"Mama, it ain't their business," Danny said.

"That's right, boy," Jim said.

"Jim, you got him work where the money came rolling in, and we let them have it," Lizz said.

"Mama, they didn't take the money I made at the express company. I bought a suit, and paid my tuition in second year, and got new glasses, and last summer you and Papa put it in the bank for me," Danny said.

"This innocent boy, Jim, don't know what they did."

"What's past is past," Jim said.

Danny wished they'd talk about something else.

"When you work now, pay attention to your p's and q's. Let your experience at the express company be a lesson to you, boy."

"I will, Papa."

"Lizz, it seems to me that if your brothers were half as important as they seem to think they are, and half as smart as they pretend to be, they could have done better by him."

"It wasn't their fault, Papa."

"Don't tell me. You don't need to stick up for them against me in my own house," Jim said.

"I didn't mean to be doing that," Danny said, thinking that Papa just didn't understand.

"Will I give the O'Flahertys a piece of my mind!" Lizz said.

"You'll do nothing of the kind. The less you have to do with your relations, the better," Jim said.

Danny wanted to go, but he couldn't think up a good excuse. He sat there, timid.

III

After Danny left, Jim took a nap. When he woke up he discovered that Lizz was out.

He knew where she was. She'd gone to church again. Every time she had a chance she went to church. Couldn't she stay home once in a while?

Jim scrutinized the dining room. Lizz hadn't removed the luncheon dishes from the table, and the big glass cake jar was full of crumbs. He kicked an old rag in a corner. Dust. Dust everywhere. Papers on the table and papers on the floor.

He went to the kitchen. The bread had not been put away. Dirty dishes were in the sink! Flies all over the place. He went to the parlor. More papers on the floor. Rags in a corner. Yes, the house was filthy. And she had to be off to church again. Now that he was on his vacation, she was probably planning to eat and sleep in church.

Jesus Christ!

She'd already said enough prayers in her lifetime to save the souls of the entire human race five times over. What did God want of her? How many prayers? How many Stations of the Cross? How many holy candles? How many masses?

Goddamn it!

As far back as he could remember, their house had always been the same and she had been leaving it to go to church. Wasn't it high time that she got wise to herself? God didn't demand all this devotion from her, not when she was a wife and a mother. What in the name of God was the matter with her? Why in the name of God couldn't she at least wash the dishes before she was off to church?

He was fed up!

He felt like going up to church and dragging her home.

He fumed back and forth across the parlor.

IV

Wearing a soiled black dress, Lizz knelt in the aisle of Saint Patrick's Church and lifted her eyes to the picture. Lost in the shadows, it represented one of the Stations of the Cross. She palmed her hands together and closed her eyes like one entranced. She prayed to Christ for herself, her husband, her children, her mother, her brothers and sister, her dead relations, for all who needed prayers.

In her mind, she saw Christ carrying the heavy wooden cross.

Christ was a tall man wearing loose but fine garments. He wore His crown of thorns, and His sacred blood flowed down His cheeks. She saw the agonizing Christ stop on the road. And she imagined Veronica wiping His face. The imprint of Christ's face was stamped on that cloth. Oh, that she had lived in Jerusalem then! She would have followed the Saviour to Calvary. She would have wiped His face as had Veronica.

Lizz rose and slowly moved on to the next Station. In her mind, she plodded after Christ along His terrible road to Calvary.

V

Jim saw Lizz from the parlor window. God, what a sight. He noticed that one of her shoe laces was untied. And her hat looked as if it had been dragged through the prairie. My God, she looked like a beggar's wife. What would people think of him when they saw his wife going around like this? Suppose some men from the express company saw her now? And didn't she have any consideration for the kids? Didn't she ever stop to think what the children in the neighborhood might say to the kids about their mother? And she was still wearing that dirty rag under her chin. Why? She wasn't complaining of neuralgia now.

Lizz saw him in the window and waved.

He turned away and waited for her, his anger mounting. He heard her fumbling at the front door lock.

"Hello, Jim."

He didn't answer.

"I'm so tired," she said, entering the parlor. "I ran up to church to say the Stations of the Cross." She suddenly noticed that his face was livid. "But what's the matter, Jim?"

"Don't you take any interest in your home?"

"What? You begrudge me a half hour with my God?"

"You could apply your time better by cleaning your home and taking care of yourself."

"Say, what's eating you?"

"Go look at yourself in the mirror."

"That's a fine thing to say to me after I come from the House of God."

"Judging from the sight of you, God Himself wouldn't be pleased with you going to church looking like you do."

"I'm acceptable in the sight of God."

"Well, you look like a filthy beggar woman to me."

"Don't you insult me or I'll get the carving knife to you!"

"Oh shut up! The house is filthy. The dishes aren't washed. The table isn't cleared off from lunch. Rags, papers, every damn thing under the sun is thrun all over the house."

She took off her hat and laid it on a chair. The dirty rag around her face and neck became untied, and she pulled it off and held it.

"And you're still wearing that goddamn rag under your chin," Jim said cuttingly.

"Say, you, if I hadn't worn a rag under my chin as much as I have, my neck wouldn't be without a wrinkle today."

"Lizz, are you a complete fool?"

"Jim O'Neill, the Blessed Mother of God protects me. If you say a word against my character, you'll answer not to me but to the Mother of God."

"Shut up. You give me a pain in the ass," Jim said.

"I won't shut up! Hit me, kill me, but I won't shut up!"

"Why in the name of God don't you wash your face?"

"Insult me, go ahead! You're worse than an infidel. You talk like a Saracen," she yelled.

"And you rave like a crazy woman. You should have seen the sight you were coming down the street."

"The Son of God had no place to lay His head."

"Well, you have. And the Saints never looked like you. If they did, they'd have been thrun out of Heaven."

"It's not enough to insult me. You have to blaspheme."

"Lizz, I'm sick and tired of this. Now, from now on, you are going to change your ways. You hear me!"

"I owe more to my God than to you, Jim O'Neill."

"God doesn't ask you to pay him back in rags."

"I am not ashamed of my poverty. My poverty will win me a crown in Heaven," she loudly proclaimed.

"Crap!" Jim yelled, turning his back on her.

She left the room indignantly.

Jim slumped in his chair. He saw her old hat on the chair. He got up in a rage and ripped off the brim of the hat. He tore off the crushed, dusty flowers. He walked deliberately into the dining room, flung the destroyed hat at her feet, and then left the room.

VI

"God won't let you off lightly, Jim O'Neill," Lizz said at the parlor entrance.

Jim turned his back on her. He went to the window. This all had to happen on his vacation, too.

"What will your son Arty think of you, looking down from Heaven on what you did to me."

"I have no ears. I can't hear a word of what you say."

"Many a time you came home to me like a drunken stew bum, with your face all cut up from fights, and you in such a condition that you didn't know if you were coming or going. And I took care of you. I put you to bed when the stink of alcohol would almost have killed anyone else. I took care of you. I put you to bed in your drunken, stinking vomit. And this is what I get."

"Lizz, you're talking to yourself. And people who talk to themselves are often considered crazy."

"I was crazy to marry a long-legged beggar like you."

"And you certainly get yourself up to look the part of a beggar's wife."

"You didn't say that to me when you married me."

"And it's a pity I didn't."

"I was good enough for you then."

"I've heard all this time and time again. Put on a new record, Lizz, the old one's scratched."

"I was an innocent little girl. A virgin. And fool that I was, I fell for a dirty drunken bum of a brute like you."

"Will you shut up?" he asked, turning and facing her, his face tight.

"No, I'll never shut up. I'll go to the archbishop and tell him what you did to me."

"You'd do much better if you cleaned up your house."

"You go to hell, Jim O'Neill."

"It'll be much pleasanter there than in this goddamn dump."

"Well, it's your home. If you can do any better providing than this, then look to yourself. Go and see yourself in a mirror."

"I can look myself in a mirror without breaking it."

"Oh, God, take me into Your bosom. Take me up with my father and my little angel son, Arty," she sighed, spreading out her arms.

He brushed past her and went into the bathroom.

"I'll tell Father Gilhooley," Lizz yelled at him through the bathroom door.

Jim didn't answer.

"Little Arty in Heaven saw what you did to his mother. Your conscience will never let you forget the insult you paid to your dead angel. You put your dirty boots on him. You kicked his memory. You blasphemed your pure angel son who lives cold and dead in the graveyard. That's what you did, you dirty stew bum!"

Jim flung the bathroom door open, rushed at Lizz, and drove her into the wall with a punch in the jaw.

"You goddamn hypocrite!" he yelled.

"Help! Murder!" she screamed, sitting on the floor.

Jim left the apartment, slamming the door.

VII

Jim limped slowly down to Sixtieth Street. He was sorry for what he had done. But a man's patience did not last forever. He went over to Washington Park and found an empty bench under a shady tree. Opposite him the sun filtered through leafy green shrubbery. Jim bit off a chew of tobacco from his plug. An old man hobbled by on a cane. Would he come to that some day?

He would rather be dead than helpless. Well, thank God, he wasn't helpless. Even if he was impaired, he was still doing a full-time man's job, and doing it well.

He spat tobacco juice. The old man passed out of sight.

It was very quiet and very restful. He watched sparrows hopping about, sticking their little heads down as they searched for food. A fat pigeon flew in their midst, and the sparrows were off, chattering.

He heard automobiles from South Park Avenue behind him. There was a tennis game, and he could hear voices.

"Forty love."

Tennis seemed to him to be a hell of a game; not a man's game, not by a damned sight.

Why hadn't he just walked out of the house on Lizz? He wished that he'd paid no attention to her, let her go on saying anything she wished. He hadn't meant to lose his temper. He didn't want to hit her. But finally, when she started on about Arty, he'd seen red and he hadn't known what he was doing.

He watched the sun filtering through the green shrubbery.

VIII

"My goodness, Jim, what did you get?" Lizz asked when Jim came home laden with boxes.

"Never mind," Jim answered, while the younger children crowded around him.

Jim opened one box and brought out a black dress.

"Oh, Jim, you shouldn't have done that. We're too poor."

"Mama's new dress," Catherine said.

"Nothing is too nice for you, Lizz."

Jim held the dress against her.

"You got my size, too, Jim. But you shouldn't have bothered."

Jim opened another box and pulled out a soft dark blue dress with ruffles around the collar.

"This is for your mother, too," Jim said, facing the kids.

"My goodness, Jim, we can't afford it."

"Never mind that talk. You got to get dressed up. Tonight you're going to put on one of these new dresses, and I'm going to take you out stepping. Little Margaret can come over and watch the kids."

Jim opened two more boxes. One of them contained a dress for Lizz and the other a dress for Catherine.

"I had a cab-driver's holiday today, Lizz. I went in and chatted with McGinty and the other men on days at the Wagon Department, and I had lunch with Bill," Jim said.

Jim kissed Lizz. He still regretted having hit her yesterday afternoon.

"Jim, I want to run up to church and say a prayer," Lizz said.

"All right, Liz, but don't be long. Promise me that. I want to take you out tonight."

"I'll only be gone a jiffy."

"Wear one of your new dresses."

"Jim, I'd spoil it kneeling down."

"Fix yourself up before you go to church."

Lizz went to fix up; Jim played *Dardanella* on the victrola.

After Lizz left for church, Jim looked in her bedroom closet. It was packed with old clothes, dresses which Lizz had had for years. Some of them were dirty, torn, and falling apart. He pulled out all the old dresses and dropped them on the floor in a heap. He carted the pile downstairs and threw the dresses in with the ashes in a large garbage can.

She was going to be dressed up from now on. And if she was, she was a damned handsome woman. He didn't give a damn what she'd say about his having thrown away her old clothes. She was going to change her ways.

IX

Lizz seemed like a different woman. She looked clean, healthy, even distinguished. Her lustrous black hair was neatly parted in the center and knotted at the nape of her neck. Her skin was almost shiny, and her complexion was very clear. Her cheeks were tinged with red. She wore the new blue dress with the ruffles around the collar and she had put on an old corset to hold in her figure. Her bosom seemed matronly. Jim was dressed up in his black suit, a white shirt, a large stiff collar, and a black knit tie, the last a present from Al O'Flaherty.

"We used to go out a lot when we were young, didn't we?" Jim said, guiding Lizz along Calumet Avenue.

It was a mild summer evening at twilight. The street was very peaceful. People sat in front of a few buildings. Windows were opened, and from one there came the sound of a victrola.

Jim remembered how he used to call for Lizz before they were married. Her dead sister, Louise, was then a kid. Al and Ned were young fellows, and Al was working in a shoe store and always talking about shoes and crabbing about how you could ruin your feet if you didn't get the right fit. And Peg worked in a candy store.

They walked over Fifty-eighth Street.

And the old lady would tell him that any man with the name of O'Neill would never have bad luck, and the old fellow would be there, and many a night the old fellow would rush the can, and he and the old fellow and Mary would drink it. He could see old Tom O'Flaherty still, sitting in the crowded little room on Blue Island Avenue, taking the can from Mary, drinking, wiping his chin with the back of his hand. And then Lizz would be ready, and he and she would leave.

They passed a crowd of young fellows in front of the Greek poolroom. Jim wanted to recapture the feelings of those days when he courted Lizz. They seemed so far away. He took her arm and guided her along, pulling his right leg along with each step.

X

"I don't care so much about moving pictures, Jim," Lizz said, sitting with him in the ice cream parlor, having a soda.

"Well, it's nice to see one once in a while."

Jim thought of how it was so pleasant to have nights off in the summer, to walk around, to go to a show, to see the people strolling and taking it easy. He felt strange doing this in the evening. He was so used to working at nights that he felt funny now, not working. He had this same feeling every vacation.

He finished his soda and pushed the glass away.

"Jim, we didn't have nickel shows like this to go to when we were young, did we?"

"No. But we had other things. I like the things we used to have. Remember the trolley parties? They used to be fun," Jim said.

"Didn't they? And the dances. Jim, I don't think I'd know how to dance now. But you were the dancer. Oh, but I was proud of my Jim when we danced," Lizz said, smiling, showing her decayed teeth.

"I guess I couldn't dance now with this leg of mine."

"Of course you could, Jim."

"Well, we better start home. We don't want to keep Little Margaret up too late, watching the kids."

He got up, paid the check, and they left the store. The sky was a deep blue, and the summer air was almost enervating. The streets were quiet, except for the automobiles passing on Garfield Boulevard, and the irregular echoes from elevated trains a few blocks off. They walked along Indiana Avenue. The Methodist Church at Fifty-sixth was pure white, and strange, almost fantastic, against the night. People were sitting on front porches and on the steps of the apartment buildings.

Jim slipped his arm around Lizz.

"My Jim!" she exclaimed with feeling.

22

I

Jim pulled down the shade of the narrow bedroom window to keep out the light. He took off his dirty clothes, got into bed, and pulled a sheet over his fatigued body. He was all in. He had a pain in his back, and his arms, shoulders, and legs were tired. His insteps were sore. His eyelids seemed heavy. His throat and nostrils were dried, irritated from dust.

Well, he was satisfied. The house was clean, spick and span. Lizz and the kids had helped, but he had done most of the work himself. He had swept the whole house, beat the rugs, washed the windows, dusted and polished, and thrown out paper, rags, all sorts of junk. There was all the difference in the world between a clean home and a dirty one, all the difference in the world on a man's thoughts. A clean home gave you the feeling that there was tidiness, order, security, regularity to your life. And he had lived in a house all messed up for so long, it was a real treat now to lie down and know that the house had been put in apple-pie order. But it had to stay clean. It really took much less time and much less trouble to be orderly than it did to be disorderly.

He turned over on his side. Why should he be so tired? Many a day he'd done more work than he had today without becoming as tired as he was now. Well, he wasn't so used to it as he was once.

His mind was lulled into a state of half-sleeping and half-waking. With his eyes closed, his body inert, and all his muscles relaxed, he had a dimmed sense of the bedroom. It seemed contracted in size. The whole world which he sensed, the apartment, the building, Calumet Avenue out front, the alley in the rear, the vacant lot below the window, all seemed to have become lessened in their proportions. In his mind's eye the sky seemed closer to the earth than it actually appeared to the ordinary vision. And this contracted world seemed vague, nebulous. Images filtered through it, willy-nilly. He thought of Lizz downstairs, washing over a tub, and then he thought of his dead father-in-law, Tom O'Flaherty. Tom O'Flaherty drifted out of his mind, and he remembered himself leaving the stables one Saturday night, going to a near-by saloon and drinking a jigger of whiskey.

He turned over and lay on his back with his mouth hanging open. He was awake, but the world was vague to him. He heard kids in the vacant lot, and one kid was yelling to others that they couldn't catch him, and then they were all shouting.

And he thought of Little Arty, and suddenly a profound sadness pervaded his drifting thoughts. He told himself that if they had only gotten Dr. Geraghty on time, and he recalled the first night he came home when Arty was sick and they'd thought it was a cold, and he imagined himself going out for a doctor, and imagined the doctor coming back. He imagined Arty well after being taken down with diphtheria, and everything the same at the cottage as it was before Arty had died. He tried to imagine Arty now alive, and in school, and himself helping Arty to learn his ABC's and telling the boy why he had to learn them.

He thought of the express company, and of himself returning to work when his vacation was over, and being asked how had he enjoyed the vacation. And he remembered when he had worked in the Call Department and used to come down on summer nights, Danny would be across from him, keeping record sheets and answering telephone calls. He recalled Danny when it was time to go, getting up and going out to the can, and then coming back and leaving, saying so long to everybody. His mind blurred. He lay inert, breathing easily, and he suddenly was asleep.

II

Come, Jim, it's time to go, Lizz said to him.

Lizz, we can't go with you looking like that, he said, seeing her old clothes and the rag tied under her chin.

Jim, when they're hanging my son, what does it matter what I wear.

He put on his hat, and they left the house. There was a great sadness in him. He and Lizz began walking down an endless street in which every block seemed to look like the block on Calumet Avenue between Fifty-ninth and Sixtieth. They kept walking down this endless street, and they passed the vacant lot next to the apartment building in which they lived, and then they walked on and they passed a vacant lot that looked just like the one they had already passed, and Jim saw the same kind of rusty tin can standing on a mound of sand as he had a moment ago, and they walked on, and still they were walking along an endless street that never looked any different from the block on Calumet Avenue between Fifty-ninth and Sixtieth.

People were on the street. Suddenly women began opening windows and looking at them.

There goes the father and mother whose boy is going to die on the gallows, a woman cried out.

There goes the father and mother whose boy is going to die on the gallows, another woman repeated.

And other women kept opening windows and saying the same thing.

Let's get off this street, Jim. We can't face this disgrace, Lizz said.

Jim knew they could not leave this street because at the end of it stood the hangman's house. And they had to hurry to get to the hangman's house on time, because the hangman had told them that he would not delay hanging their son one minute after nine o'clock in the morning, and if they wanted to see Danny hanged, they had to be there on time.

Jim and Lizz walked straight down the long street that never seemed to end and never seemed to change but was always the same, and the women kept opening their windows and looking at him and Lizz, and all the women looked alike, but while he knew that he knew the women, he didn't know just who they were, and he couldn't place their names in his mind, and the women kept yelling from window to window:

There goes the father and mother whose boy is going to die on the gallows.

They came to a building that looked like the entrance to the main office building of the express company in the Loop, where Jim went to collect his pay. He walked to the elevator, and there was one of the men who used to be the elevator man at the main office.

Hurry up if you want to see them hang your son, the elevator man said.

Jim and Lizz stepped into the elevator, and it went up and up, and it seemed as if they never would get to the top of the building in time to see Danny hanged on the gallows, and the elevator kept going up and up.

III

Fither, Arty exclaimed, smiling. Jim was working days now, and he enjoyed it much better, and every day this summer when he came home the sun was still shining, and now when he got home, there was Arty, standing alone in the parlor, waiting for him.

Jim was very happy and relieved because he had been worried about Arty all of the way home, and he didn't know precisely why he was worried about him, but he had been worried, and he had thought there was something seriously and disturbingly wrong about Arty, and he didn't just know what it was. And here was Arty, healthy and happy and smiling at him.

Where's your mother?

Mither gone to church.

Where's your brothers and sisters?

Gone to church.

Why didn't you go to church?

Fither!

He sat down, and Arty sat down on the floor, looking up at him with those big eyes of his, and Arty did not move, and Jim sat there and watched him with an exquisite joy in his heart because Arty was alive.

IV

Jim swept the parlor floor with a brand-new broom. The dust was in a heap and he looked around. It was dirty again. But he had just swept it. And it was dirty again. He didn't know what was wrong. He swept the floor again. And he looked around, and it was dirty again.

Lizz came into the parlor.

I swept the floor, and it's dirty again, Jim told her, leaning on the broom.

I sweep it every day.

And why does it get so dirty?

Because it isn't clean.

But if you sweep it, it should be clean.

But it isn't.

Now watch me, Jim said, sweeping the floor again.

Lizz watched him, standing motionless like a statue.

Did you see me sweep the floor?

You swept it.

He looked around the room pleased. But it was dirty again.

What the hell is it? he asked.

I sweep the floor every day, she said.

And what happens?

It gets dirty again.

Jim stood in the midst of dirt and dust, puzzled. He looked all around. In a corner he saw the heap of dirt and dust that he had already swept up.

Lizz, I'm not going to stop until I get this floor swept, he said, but Lizz was gone.

No dirty floor was going to stop him. He swept and swept, but the floor was still dirty.

V

Jim was lying in a bed in a darkened room. There was a small candle on the dresser near by. Lizz was suddenly beside him.

What's the matter, Lizz? he asked.

Jim, you're going to die.

He knew that. Lizz had come into the room where he lay to tell him that he was going to die.

How soon?

In two minutes. Doctor Mike was just here and he told me to tell you you're going to die, she said.

Why didn't he examine me?

He examined me instead of you, and he said for me to tell my husband that he'd die in two minutes.

The room was very cramped and very dark. The candle was dim on the dresser. When it burned down, he would die. He and Lizz watched the candle burning with a yellow flame, and the candle was burning down. He was watching himself die because he knew that just as soon as that candle burned down, he would be dead.

Lizz, what'll the kids do?

Starve.

And what'll you do?

Starve.

Jim tried to get up, because if he could get up and squash the candle out, he'd live. He tried to get up and he couldn't move. He was weak, and powerless.

Jim, your time has come.

Yes, his time had come, and it didn't have to come, because if he could get up and squash out that candle before it burned down, he'd live, but since he couldn't, his time had come.

He looked at the candle. It was slowly but steadily burning down. He had very little time to live. The room was getting darker, because as the candle burned down it gave off less light. Jim thought how all his life he had realized that some day he was going to die, and now his time had come.

The priest is coming, Jim, Lizz said.

But he won't get here before I die.

He has to, Lizz said.

But look at the candle.

The priest has to get here or you'll go to Hell.

But the priest couldn't reach him in time, and the room was getting darker, and the candle flame was growing feebler. Jim felt his strength ebbing. What could he do? He told himself that he'd get up and squash out the candle flame. He exerted all his will, but he was too weak to move.

Lizz knelt beside the bed, praying silently.

Again he exerted all his will power, and he bounded out of bed. He felt a sudden surge of hopefulness. He was on his feet. He had saved his life.

It won't do any good, Jim. Your time has come.

He leaned over the candle. He blew. The weak flame persisted.

The time was when he could have blown out a candle. He was reduced to the point where he could not even blow out a candle flame to save his life.

It won't do any good. Jim, your time has come. The priest will be here.

Jim blew again. The candle still burned.

He blew again.

The candle burned down slowly.

He staggered back to bed. The room was darker, and he could barely see Lizz praying at the bedside, and the flame was growing weaker and weaker. He was facing death. His children were somewhere else, and he couldn't even see them before he died. After all these years, he was a dying man, and now he was looking on as Death smothered the room in darkness. Nothing could save his life. He tried again to get up and blow out the candle. He was powerless to move. It was so dark in the room now that he couldn't even see Lizz beside the bed. The candle barely flickered.

In sadness and terror, he waited for death.

VI

Sweating, Jim opened his eyes. He didn't know where he was. He was surprised to learn that he was alive. Looking around, he realized he was in his own bed. He had just been dreaming that he was dying.

"Don't talk so loud or you'll wake Papa," he heard Catherine saying to one of the boys.

He was stiff and tired. There were pains in his shoulders, and his eyes seemed weighted at the lids. He moved his arms and legs to assure himself that nothing had happened to him.

"You stinkers keep quiet. Your father is asleep," he heard Lizz yell at the kids in the back of the apartment.

He was all right. But the fear from his dream remained. Now, knowing that he was all right, he lay suddenly rigid. Had that dream come to him as an omen? Nonsense. Everybody dreamed of all kinds of things. Lizz believed in dreams. But a man would go crazy if he believed in dreams. Nonsense. But it might have meant something.

There are more things in this world, Horatio, he recited to himself.

He yawned. He told himself that he was on his vacation and that he didn't have to do anything he didn't want to. He could rest all night, and all day tomorrow, too, if he wanted to. He was all right.

He still felt stiff and tired. But he'd done a lot of work, and often after an afternoon nap he woke up this way.

He sat up.

Again he went rigid.

That had been a terrible goddamn dream.

He got up, dressed himself, and went to the bathroom. He washed and felt better after dipping his face in a bowl of cold water. He went out to the dining room. The kids were sitting on the floor, and Lizz was in the kitchen fixing supper. He looked gently at his three youngest children. Catherine ran to him. He picked her up and kissed her.

"What were you doing?"

"We were playing jacks," she said.

"Can I play with you," he said.

"Of course."

Jim sat on the floor and played jacks with Catherine, Dennis, and Bob.

VII

After supper, Jim sat down in the parlor to read the newspaper Bill had brought home.

"G'wan, you sonofabitch!"

He got to his feet and went to the open parlor window.

"Bob!" Jim called.

"What do you want?" Bob yelled from the sidewalk.

"Come in or I'll come out and get you!"

"Gee, I didn't do anything!"

"I told you to come in!"

Bob lowered his head, kicked the grass, and walked to the entranceway to the building. Jim met Bob at the doorway and dragged him into the parlor by the scruff of his neck.

"I didn't do anything, Pa," he whined.

"What's the matter? What's the matter?" Lizz asked, rushing in.

"He was cursing out on the street!"

"Were you, you little brat?" Lizz asked.

"No, I didn't curse. Honest to God, I didn't, Mama."

"You stand there and lie to my face after I heard you?" Jim asked Bob.

"It was Joey Morrell who was swearin'! He always curses."

"Jim, that Joey Morrell is a dirty little tramp. He's a tramp. His father's no good," Lizz said.

"Did you curse out there now, calling somebody a bad name, or didn't you?" Jim asked Bob, looking the boy directly in the eye.

"No, Papa, I didn't."

"Jim, my Bob wouldn't tell a lie. It was that stinker, Joey Morrell," Lizz interrupted.

"He called some kid a sonofabitch," Jim said to Lizz.

"Papa, I didn't say it. Honest, I didn't."

"You'll stand there and lie to me when I just heard you?"

"Promise me you won't say that dirty word again?" Lizz asked Bob.

"I never said it, Mama, so I don't have to promise you."

Seeing how frightened Bob was, Jim had an impulse to let the boy off. But no, he had to do his duty. It wasn't only the cursing, which was bad enough coming from a boy his age, but also the lying on top of it. If Bob could get away with this, he'd try to get away with more.

"I'm giving you your last chance. Will you tell me the truth now?" Jim said sternly.

"Yes, Papa!"

"Did you or didn't you swear right before the window just a little while ago?"

"I didn't, Papa."

Jim slapped Bob in the face.

"Don't hit me, Papa," he pleaded, whimpering.

"Did you lie to me just now?"

"I didn't. I hope to die if I did."

Jim dragged Bob to the bathroom. He got his razor strap. He pulled Bob to the bedroom.

"I'll teach my kids to tell the truth. If it's the last thing I do, I'll teach them to be honest and to use decent language. No son of mine is going to grow up a liar."

Jim hit Bob with the strap.

VIII

"ALLIALLIOUTSINFREE!"

It was Susie Prout yelling. The kids were playing hide-and-go-seek. And here he was. Papa wouldn't let him out. And Papa had hurt him like hell with the razor strap. Gee, if he only had thought soon enough, he wouldn't have called Joey Morrell a sonofabitch. But Joey Morrell had tried to trip him. Gee, why did Papa have to be where he could hear through the window?

He could hear the kids playing. He wanted to ask to be let out, but he could see that Papa would only get sore again, and maybe give him another licking if he asked. And Mama couldn't fix it with Papa this time, because Papa was so sore.

Papa was sore. It wasn't right of Papa. Papa said sonofabitch, and so did Mama, and Uncle Al, and Uncle Ned, and he even heard Bill say it, and Mama sometimes lied to Papa, and they all didn't get a licking like he had.

Why did he have to get treated differently from other people? If the word was so bad, why did Papa and Mama ever use it?

Whenever he got into trouble like this, he always felt he wasn't wanted. Did other kids feel that their mothers and fathers didn't want them?

He sat at the table, feeling that they didn't want him here.

23

I

Danny sat in the midst of a group of fellows and girls on the sand at Fifty-first Street beach. He watched Antonina Sidney come out of the water and approach their group. As she came closer, he kept his eyes on her almost as if he were transfixed. Her wet, tight-fitting, gray one-piece bathing suit clung to her lovely slender body. Her coat of tan enhanced her attractiveness. Watching her, Danny tried to imagine her naked and at the same time, he thought of her as an almost bodiless spirit, as lovely as a cloud, a creature who belonged with air and sun rather than with human beings. Unaware of his gaze, she sat down beside Sarah Windlemann. Sarah was a dark-haired Jewish girl who was attractive despite her large bones and prominent nose.

"Danny, you and Rocky here are coming to my beach party tomorrow night, aren't you?" Sarah asked.

"Try and keep us away," Young Rocky answered, stretched out near Danny on the sand.

Danny had been palling around with Young Rocky all summer. He was a tall, well-built, tan-skinned lad of eighteen.

"I hate to see this week go," Young Rocky said.

"Why?" asked Sarah.

"I only got another week of my vacation, and I had such swell weather."

"Be like me, and don't work," Danny said.

"You told me you was starting to work tomorrow in a shoe store," Young Rocky said.

"That's only for one day a week."

"You're lucky."

"I'd rather work than go to school," Sarah said.

“Sarah, you and Antonina do me a favor. Cover me with sand,” Young Rocky said.

Danny joined the two girls in piling sand over Young Rocky.

“Nice to have slaves,” Young Rocky said.

“You want to be covered, Danny?” Antonina asked when they had covered Young Rocky and put a handkerchief over his eyes.

“Sure,” Danny said, grateful that Antonina had shown this much interest in him.

Danny lay beside Young Rocky and the two girls piled sand over him. Gradually he could feel the sand covering his arms and legs and body until he was encased in a mound.

“This is swell,” Danny said.

“I’ll put this over your eyes now,” Sarah said, laying a ribbon over his eyes.

Danny lay there. He had a sense suddenly of being far, far away from the world. He felt as if he were half asleep. He heard noises, but he wasn’t at all sure how far or how near the noises were. The steady sounds of the waves beating against the sand was soft, soothing, rhythmic, almost like music. He sensed people walking near him. He heard voices. He seemed to see little in his mind, little other than a kind of red and sunny color. Then, he turned his head slightly and, still keeping his eyes closed, he saw in his mind’s eye the lake far out upon the horizon. He was absorbed in the sight of the lake in his mind’s eye, and the sounds of life all about him seemed muffled, farther away than they had seemed only a moment ago. He was warm and cosy, and he felt as if he were living in a comfortable dream removed from the world, all by himself.

“This is the nuts,” Young Rocky said.

Danny was too absorbed in himself to answer.

“O’Neill, this is the nuts. Do you feel as good as I do?” Young Rocky asked.

Danny still didn’t answer. He let his tongue play around his mouth, touching cavities which seemed pretty big. He oughtn’t to think about cavities now. Again he thought of the lake, far out. The whole beach diminished for him into a distant faraway life and then vanished. He was alone in a warm dream, free of his body, seeing water and blue sky and white clouds. And he thought of Antonina and of her tan body as part of this world. He yearned to be alone with Antonina, bodiless and riding clouds out upon the far horizon where water and sky seemed to meet.

II

Danny stood by himself in front of the poolroom, wondering what to do. Studs Lonigan and a few of the older fellows were grouped together a few paces away from him.

"Hey, O'Neill, you better let it alone. You don't want to go to the booby hatch, do you?" Studs Lonigan yelled at him.

"Yeh, O'Neill, you ain't got them pimples on your face for nothing," big Slug Mason said.

Danny walked by them without saying a word, hearing them laugh. The big bastards! Studs Lonigan used to like him when he was a punk. Now Studs hardly ever spoke to him, except to make some wisecrack at his expense.

He wandered over to the park. There was nothing to do. Young Rocky had a date for tonight. The other younger fellows around the poolroom had gone off somewhere before he'd come around. Andy Le Gate had wanted him to take in a movie, but he didn't want to go with Andy.

He and Andy used to be close friends when they were kids living on Indiana Avenue. Andy hadn't changed much since then, except that he was older and heavier. Andy would still suddenly burst out laughing when there was nothing to laugh at, just as he used to five or six years ago. In those days Andy used to bang his head against a stone wall to make everyone laugh. He liked Andy, but Andy was always wanting to talk about the Democratic Party, the Ku Klux Klan, or the White Sox, and nobody cared what Andy had to say about any of these subjects. Andy had worse luck with the girls than he did.

It was a cool, clear night, and there was a steady wind humming in the trees. The shadows of the trees were clearly etched against the background of darkness. There was no moon out tonight. It was the kind of summer night that made him feel lonesome. Would he find anyone over in the boathouse?

The summer was more than half gone, and he had just goofed it away. He hadn't played any baseball and, in fact, he hardly even read the box scores any more. He would still like to be a ball player, but he didn't have the energy and interest any more to go out and play. This summer he had hoped to learn how to dance, but so far he hadn't. He still had no girl, and he hadn't had a date since the one with Anna Sheehan. Every time he ran into Anna he felt guilty, but she was friendly, and she hadn't told anyone about the awful way he danced or what a lousy time she'd had on a date with him.

The boathouse was almost deserted. In one corner he saw some Negro lads of his own age. He frowned. The shines shouldn't be allowed in the park. It was a white man's park. He strolled back and forth along the path passing the boathouse.

He wished it was already tomorrow night. Antonina would be at the beach party. At the beach this afternoon the whole gang had gone in the water and they had been ducking, and he and Antonina had ducked together, and under water she had had her lips pursed for him to kiss her, and he knew she'd wanted to be kissed, but he just hadn't acted. Antonina had seemed friendly up to that moment, and from then on she hadn't paid any attention to him. Coming home from the beach this afternoon, Young Rocky and some of the other fellows had talked about how Antonina had let them throw her around in the water and grab her any place they wanted to, and they had all just about felt everything she had. Young Rocky offered to bet a half a buck he could lay her and there hadn't been anyone who'd take the bet. That proved what a sap he had been to think of her the way he had when he had been lying on the beach covered up with sand. And she must think he was a pretty slow dope who didn't know what it was all about. Well, did he really know what it was all about?

He remembered the day last spring when he and Corkerry had picked up those janes in Jackson Park. That was the most he had ever had to do with a girl.

He didn't know what to do with himself tonight.

III

"O'Neill, don't tell me that a nice clean boy like you was over in the park hunting for gash," Edmond Lanson said.

Danny sat next to Edmond Lanson and Willie Kiernan on a park bench. He was friendly with Lanson but didn't know him too well. Lanson was taller than Danny, dark-skinned, with hazel brown eyes, curly hair, and a rich, deep voice. Danny knew that Edmond was a knockout with the girls and that he was also quite a fighter. Kiernan was a blond young lad who had recently come from Iowa. He spoke in a twangy voice. Danny liked him.

"Have a drink, O'Neill?" Willie said, pulling out a bottle.

"No, thanks."

"Hey, Kiernan, O'Neill is a decent kid. What do you want to put him off on the primrose path for?" Lanson said.

"Here, quit talking flowery, pal, and drink," Willie said, handing Lanson the bottle.

Danny was tempted to drink. He wanted to be a regular fellow like these two. Most of the fellows his age who hung around the poolroom drank. And so did his fraternity brothers, Marty, Hugh, Tim, even Ike Dugan, who was only going into his sophomore year this fall. He ought to drink. But he was afraid to take whiskey. The smell alone almost made him sick.

Edmond drank and passed the bottle back to Willie. Willie took a good drink from the bottle.

"O'Neill, know what I did tonight?" Edmond said.

"What?"

"I left home. I had a fight with my mother. I was dancing with her last night at a party we had, and I thought I'd have some fun, so I did a little rubbing it in. She slapped me in the can to cut it out, and her hand hit a gat I had in my back pocket. I had a row, and the old man got sore, and so I left home."

"O'Neill, Ed and I here are pals. Know what our motto is: Through thick and thin, we share everything but gash," Willie said.

"O'Neill, don't you become like me," Edmond said.

"Why, you're all right, ain't you?"

"I'm no goddamn good. I'm never going to amount to a screwy row of toothpicks." He looked toward Kiernan. "Am I, buddy?"

Grinning and curious, Danny watched them drink. He always hung around drunks to see what they did and hear what they said. And he kept wondering should he drink or shouldn't he? These days, fellows all bragged about how much they drank. But he knew what drink did to people. Look at all the trouble Aunt Margaret had caused for years now by drinking.

"How much money have you got?" Lanson asked Kiernan after they had finished their bottle.

"A ten spot, pal. And what's mine is yours."

"That's enough to do what I want to do."

"What's that?" Danny asked, his manner supercilious.

"Well, what I'm going to do is go to a can house and make a gift of my lily pure body."

"Say, I could use a piece of tail myself."

"Let's go," Edmond said. He stood up. "Forward march."

"Got any dough, O'Neill?" Willie asked.

"Hell, no, not a sou."

"Well, that don't make any difference. I'll stand you to it."

"I can't tonight. I don't feel like it."

"Now what the hell, you know a man never wants to turn down tail," Willie said, putting his arm around Danny's shoulders and blowing a moonshine breath in his face. "Come along as a pal of me and my buddy."

He would see a naked woman. He would then be able to say he had lost his cherry.

"I got to get home. I got lots of things to do," Danny said, weakly.

They went off, noisy and gay. Danny walked in the opposite direction. He ought to be proud of himself for having resisted temptation. He had refused to sin. But he knew that it had not been any virtue in himself that had kept him from going. He had been afraid to go, that was what it was. He had wanted to go. He wished now that he had gone. And he knew that he had just been too afraid to go and do it. Instead, he would walk home now, regretting his decision and thinking of naked girls and what it would be like to be with one of them.

IV

Wading out of the cool, calm, shallow water with Young Rocky, Danny thought that it was just the right kind of a night for a beach party. The moon and the stars were out, and the water wasn't too cold. They stood for a moment by the edge of the beach. Small waves broke at their feet. They were on the beach at Jackson Park, just north of the regular fenced-in beach. Several fires were lit along the stretch of sand, and from somewhere in the distance they could hear singing and a banjo.

Danny and Young Rocky dashed across the sand to a fire where a mixed group were gathered. Sarah Windlemann, in a swimming suit, was bent over the fire, roasting marshmallows. She handed some up to Danny and Young Rocky.

"Sarah, you win the cat's meow and his asbestos whiskers," Young Rocky said.

Danny and Young Rocky sat down. Danny scanned the faces around the fire, searching for Antonina. She had gone off over a half hour ago with some fellow, and he hadn't seen her since. He remembered the bet Young Rocky had offered to make coming home from the beach the other day.

"You look dopey tonight. What's itching you?" Young Rocky asked.

"Nothing."

"Then wake up and hear the birdies sing."

"Having a good time, Vinc?" Danny asked, noticing Vinc Curley sitting opposite him: Vinc was a big, awkward young man with an overlarge head and an obtuse face.

"Say, Curley, you want to be careful," Young Rocky said.

"Why?"

"Somebody's liable to take that head of yours and sell it for kindling wood," Young Rocky said, and they both laughed.

"Have you seen Mary the Wop?" Young Rocky asked.

"Who's she?"

"Don't you know Mary the Wop, a friend of Sarah's? She's hot necking," Young Rocky said.

"Where is she?"

"That's what I want to know. Sarah just told me she's been necking the boys one after the other while we were in swimming."

Just then a baby-faced girl, wearing an old white dress, approached the fire.

"There she is," Young Rocky said.

Danny had sensed that it was Mary the Wop. He was on his feet before Young Rocky had identified her. Without thinking, Danny grabbed her hand and dragged her away, halting about five yards from the fire. He clumsily leaned forward to kiss her. She put her arms around his neck, clung to him, and returned his kiss. Pressing herself tightly against him, she began to French-kiss. He'd never been French-kissed before.

She muttered a protest because in his excitement he had grasped her so tightly that he'd hurt her.

"Break it up! Break it up!" Young Rocky yelled, imitating a policeman.

Danny released her. Young Rocky grabbed her by the hand and pulled her away.

"The bastard!" Danny said, disappointed.

He returned to the fire.

"Hello, Danny."

Danny looked at Natalie O'Reedy, surprised.

"Hello," he replied, still not recovered from his surprise at meeting her here.

"Danny O'Neill, this is Eddie Feeley," she said, introducing him to a pimply-faced fellow who stood beside her.

Danny looked down at both of them. Natalie was very small, but even prettier than she'd been in grammar school. She now wore her hair bobbed. He wondered what she could see in a runt like Feeley, who hardly came up to his shoulder and wasn't very much taller than Natalie.

"I've hardly seen you in a couple of years," Natalie said.

Danny was struck by the cordiality in her voice. He remembered how Sister Magdalen had once told him that he had an enemy in school, and for some reason he had thought it was Natalie. If that were so, she wasn't acting like it now.

She and Feeley sat down near the fire, and she motioned for him to join them. He saw her face momentarily brightened by the flames. Yes, she was pretty.

V

Danny and Young Rocky walked back to the group, wet and invigorated from a swim.

"Natalie is a swell girl, isn't she?" Young Rocky said.

"Yes, she is."

"She's too decent for guys like us."

"Uh huh."

"Look!" Young Rocky said, pointing at Vinc Curley, who was kissing Mary the Wop.

"Hey, Vinc, jiggers the cop!" Danny yelled.

Vinc ran away. Young Rocky grabbed Mary the Wop and ran off with her. Danny walked back to the fire.

"Want a sandwich?" Sarah asked.

"Oh, thanks," he said, accepting a sandwich from her.

While Danny was eating his sandwich, a snotty-faced, stocky drunk approached them.

"Well, what the hell is this, a sewing circle?"

Danny knew the fellow by name only, Stan Skillen.

"Oh, Stan, you're never funny when you drink," Antonina said.

"Huh, kid?" he asked.

Danny and Young Rocky looked at each other. Skillen staggered away.

"That guy is asking to have one laid against his chin," Young Rocky said.

"He's awful fresh," Natalie said.

Danny didn't say anything. He felt that he should shut the guy up if he tried cursing again in front of Natalie. He should have done it then. It was a chance to impress Natalie. He would just as soon as not—because suppose the guy could fight. But what the hell, was he yellow?

"Well, he's gone, and good riddance to him," Feeley said.

VI

Young Rocky and Sarah were toasting marshmallows and handing them out. A few feet away, another group was singing to a guitar.

"Goddamn it, what in the name of Christ is this?" Skillen shouted, returning.

"Watch the language," Danny said.

"I said goddamn it what the hell kind of a goddamn screwy party is this?"

Danny jumped to his feet.

"What the hell do you want?" the other demanded.

"There's decent girls present. Cut your swearing out!" Danny said.

"Who the hell for?"

"Me!"

"What the hell is this, a game?"

Danny gave him a shove. He tumbled into the sand.

"Don't fight, boys!" Antonina yelled, while Danny stood over Skillen with clenched fists.

"You gonna cut it out?" Danny asked.

"I didn't mean anything," Skillen said, getting up.

"Then you better apologize to the girls."

Skillen looked down at the girls.

"I'm sorry. Please accept my apologies."

Natalie smiled sweetly.

"Forget it, Stan, and don't be a nuisance," Antonina said.

"You better blow now," Danny said, feeling himself the master of the situation and proud of the role he played,

Danny and Young Rocky watched Skillen stagger away.

"He ain't as drunk as he acts. Somebody hit him with a bartender's towel," Young Rocky said.

"I didn't mean to make any trouble, but we had to call him, the way he was talking," Danny said.

"He was a nuisance," Natalie said, smiling at Danny.

Danny was certain that he'd won Natalie's respect by his conduct.

"Let's sing," Young Rocky said.

Danny listened to the songs, not singing because of his foghorn voice. He kept his eyes on Natalie. The moon played on her face. She was beautiful. It was like being in a movie almost, sitting this way, singing, looking at her. All these years, here was the girl he wanted to fall in love with, and he hadn't even realized it.

24

I

Jim waited for Lizz to get ready to go to confession with him.

A week of his vacation had already gone by, and he had to be back on the job next Friday. He hadn't done half the things he'd intended to on this vacation. Well, he still had a few more days, and he did feel rested up. That was most important.

Lizz had wanted him to take off an extra week without pay. Some of the Dispatchers did that, but he couldn't afford it. The last couple of days he'd been doing a lot of thinking about money. They had hardly a penny in the bank. After all the time since 1918, four years, that he'd been in the supervision, they had nothing to show for it except a few dollars in the bank. How many times hadn't he already had it out with Lizz about money, but what good had it done? She didn't seem to know just how the money went, and neither did he. What did they have, with the money he and Bill earned? He made two twenty-five a month and Bill knocked down a hundred and thirty-five, over three hundred dollars a month. Now if that wasn't enough to keep them going, he'd eat his shirt. Neither he nor Lizz spent much on themselves. She still hadn't gone and gotten her teeth fixed. Still, the money went.

Of course the kids cost money for schooling. But that was only three dollars a month tuition, with books and the other expenses added, such as collections. When you sent your kids to a parochial school, you always had to keep chipping in for mission collections, and God knows what.

And there was gas, electricity, food, insurance, lots of expenses, but still, they ought to be saving something.

Yes, where did the money go to?

"I'll be ready in a minute, Jim," Lizz called from the bedroom.

"That's all right, Lizz. Take your time."

Jim wondered what the future had in store for him. He guessed that he would just go along and do the same thing he had been doing, raising and providing for his family. But he wasn't complaining. If his health were a little better, and they were saving a little money, he'd be sitting on top of the world. Well, he should be able to go on for years in the condition he was in.

But it did seem to him that they ought to have tried to buy a little house. They could pay down something on it every payday. If they'd done that right after his promotion, by now they'd probably have a neat little place of their own completely paid for. Some of the men at the company who made no more money than he did had done this, and now they owned their own homes. He'd wanted to find a place on the West Side that they could buy that way, but Lizz had been all for living near her mother, and she'd found this place. And they'd just signed a lease on the apartment for another year. Lizz said she didn't want to move and they couldn't do much better than this for fifty dollars a month, and he'd said all right and signed up. But they should have tried to get a place of their own. Owning your own home made all the difference in the world for a man.

He felt suddenly gloomy. He told himself that he shouldn't let himself be the victim of so many moody fits of depression. But they sometimes came on him, and he couldn't shake them off. He kept thinking this way, worrying about money, wondering about the future, thinking of what condition his family might be in if something did happen to him.

Look at all the men in the world who went on for years, drinking like a fish, doing any damned thing they wanted to, ignoring their responsibilities, and yet they had their health and not a worry in the world! Look at some of these rich bastards, born to the purple, who had all they wanted and didn't have to lift a finger, and screwed around as much as they damned well pleased, and sucked the blood out of poor workingmen! What happened to them? Some of them lived to a ripe old age.

There wasn't a great deal of justice in this world. He had lived long enough and gone through enough to know that much. And to know it well. He tried to impress on his kids that they had to do right, and if they did right everything would come out good for them. Of course he wanted them to do right, and if they didn't they would have to answer plenty to him. But would doing right get them anywhere? Look at him! Well, he'd fought his way up from nothing, and he'd gotten somewhere. He was supporting his family, living a decent life and dependent on nobody. He could have pride, too, that he'd done right. But still, there wasn't a lot of justice in the world. For every decent man who got anywhere, two sonofabitches lifted themselves up over the backs of others.

What were his kids going to do? What were they going to be? You couldn't tell much about them. He hoped he would live many years, and that he would be able to see them all grown and amount to something.

He saw himself dead in a coffin, Lizz mourning, all the little kids around it. It couldn't happen. It wouldn't. His time wouldn't come that way, too soon, with a family not raised to leave behind him. God wouldn't have things that way. Why should he die? Here he was, trying to do right, bring his family up decent, and if he died, they would be thrown on the world, and his kids wouldn't have a chance. No, it wouldn't be. And the world was getting different. Many workingmen weren't as poor as they used to be. Take at the express company. The men on the wagons got much better pay than he used to get and they lived a better life. Some of them were buying automobiles, and their kids were getting a better chance than most kids got when he was young. Yes, the world was getting better and different from what it used to be. He could see that right from his own experience.

"All right, Jim," Lizz called.

II

"Jim, it's such a nice night," Lizz said.

"Isn't it," he said, taking her arm and guiding her across Sixtieth Street.

"Jim, wouldn't it be grand to have an automobile? My Bill could learn to drive it and he would take us to mass every Sunday morning."

"Let's not be having pipe dreams. We can't afford an automobile."

"I wasn't saying we could. But there's no harm in talking about how it would be if we could. Some day my Bill and my Danny boy will buy their mother an automobile."

"Lizz, we can't count too much on our children. Many a father and mother have rued the day they did. Kids grow up, and go off and get married, and forget the old man and the old lady."

"Mine never will."

"I like to think that. Only a man and woman don't really know their kids and what they are going to be like later on."

"I know mine. Oh, wait until they grow up and see how they take care of their father and mother."

"Lizz, I'd hate to see the day when you and I had to depend on anyone but myself."

III

Jim knelt in the quiet, dim, and almost empty church and finished saying his penance of seven Our Fathers and seven Hail Marys. He sat back in his pew. He had to wait a while for Lizz. She prayed before the altar of the Blessed Virgin. Lizz had gone into the confessional box ahead of him, and while he'd waited his turn he'd heard her murmuring voice going on and on. Someone would think that she'd been guilty of something like murder from the time she'd taken. And what sins could she commit?

He let his eyes wander around the church. The ceiling was low and calcimined, and the interior of the church as a whole was barnlike. Father Gilhooley came out of his confessional box near the Blessed Virgin's altar and paced back and forth along the side aisle. Behind Jim a door of Father Doneggan's box closed.

Jim yawned. A few moments ago he'd confessed that he used things so that he and Lizz wouldn't have any more kids. Father Doneggan had warned him against doing this. Now that didn't seem right, not for a man his age and a woman Lizz's age, after all the kids they'd had and all they'd been through. No, he didn't think it was a sin. The priest had to say certain things to people to keep them in line, just like a father had to to do the same kind of thing with his kids. That was the reason for some of the rules of the Church, he guessed. Rules like the one about not preventing kids being born weren't made for a man in his circumstances. It wasn't a sin on his soul.

Jim kind of wished that Lizz would get finished. But it wasn't so bad sitting here in church. In fact, it was sort of pleasant. Although he sometimes did crab about priests and money, he was proud to be a Catholic. Like he had often heard said, if you had the chance to cross the ocean in a steamship or a rowboat, which would you choose? Well, the Church was a steamship, and other religions were just leaky rowboats by comparison. He was proud to think that ever since the days of Christ the Church had gone on teaching the same truths. Yes, even if he did like to gripe about Father Gilhooley, he was proud to be a Catholic. Sitting there, a sense of mystery stirred in him. He thought of Christ dying on the Cross. And people still went on doing all sorts of lousy things even after Christ had died for them. He liked to think that Christ was born in a poor man's home, and never in His life was He rich. That was one of the lessons in Christ. It was a lesson for all men who wanted to get rich by stepping on other people's backs. Christ was the poor man's God, too. A lot of people ought never to forget that.

He watched Lizz light some candles, genuflect, and then walk away from the altar. He met her in the aisle and led her out of the church.

"I hope you're not going to be sore because you waited for me," she said in a defensively belligerent tone.

"It was nice in church. I didn't mind at all," Jim answered.

IV

"Jim and me just went to confession," Lizz said proudly to her mother and Ned in the O'Flaherty parlor.

"Fine, fine, glad to hear it," Ned said.

"Where's Dan?" Jim asked.

"He's gone to a beach party," Mrs. O'Flaherty said.

"Did he work today?" Jim asked.

"Yes, he did. But that's no work for my grandson to be doing."

"It won't hurt him. In fact, I think that it'll be good if he keeps at it during school. If he has to work every Saturday, he won't be playing football," Ned said.

"Football won't hurt Danny, will it?" Lizz asked.

"It won't do him any good," Jim said.

"Cripes, he'll be coming home here a wreck one of these days from football. And then what's he going to do?" Ned said.

"Sure, and I saw them playing football in the park last year, and the way they lep on one another, and fall on each other, sure I don't know how they weren't all killed. And I was talking to Mrs. Sheehan. Her oldest boy does play football, too, and it has the heart torn out of the poor woman. I don't like football. It's a left-handed game. They won't let the fellows run with the ball but they knock them down every time," Mrs. O'Flaherty said.

"Hell, it's a game where they kill one another. There ought to be a law against it," Ned said.

"Well, let him work on Saturdays instead of playin'. He might learn the value of money if he earns his own spending money," Jim said.

"That's what I think," Ned said.

"How's the shoe business?" Jim asked.

"Slow, Jim! Slow. Al goes out on the road again in a couple of weeks, and I'm seeing a man I'm expecting to tie up with. I hope I'll be going out on the road, too, in September."

"And, Mother, that Swede in my building, Hanson's her name. She's only got herself and her man, and you'd think she'd have a woman do her washing. But them Swedes are penny-pinching. Every time I go down to do the washing for Jim and the kids, there she is. Mother, you can thank your stars you don't have Swedes in your building," Lizz said.

They went on talking.

V

Everyone was in bed, but he wasn't tired, and he was glad he'd gone to church and then walked over to see the O'Flahertys with Lizz. Ned wasn't a bad fellow. Jim went to the bedroom and got out an old one-volume edition of Shakespeare's plays. The cover was torn and the pages were dusty. He hadn't read Shakespeare in years and he used to like to. He opened the volume to *Julius Caesar* and began reading it, thinking of Brutus. He liked Brutus best of all the characters in the play.

Jim sat alone in the parlor reading *Julius Caesar.*

VI

"Papa, don't you wanna bat 'em out?" Dennis yelled.

Jim shook his head. He stood behind the boys who were catching balls batted out by Al McGlynn, a kid who went around with Dennis. They were near the Fifty-fifth Street end of the Washington Park ball field. Jim pounded the catcher's mitt he was using, and waited. He bobbled a grounder, picked up the ball, and flung it in to Al McGlynn. These days he didn't function right playing around with a ball. Even so, this was good for him, toned up his muscles. And the sun today would do him good.

Al McGlynn waved for all in the field to come in. He and Dennis chose sides.

"Mr. O'Neill, won't you umpire for us?" Al McGlynn asked.

"No, I had enough. I'll sit under the tree and watch you kids play."

He found himself a shady spot and looked on while the kids played a game, easy pitching. Dennis came up to bat. Jim liked the way Dennis swung. The boy might be good when he grew up. Dennis hit the ball past third and made two bases, but the next kid up struck out. They changed sides. Bob came in and batted. He turned his cap around backward, grinned, and fooled around with the bat.

"Cut it out and play ball," Dennis yelled at him.

"Come on, O'Neill, bat and quit breaking up the game," yelled Morty Miller, a kid in Dennis's gang.

Bob rubbed his hands in the dirt. He motioned the kids in the field to go way out. He spat on his hands and rubbed them on his pants.

"We can't spend all day on you," Dennis yelled.

Bob batted. The bat was too heavy for him and he topped a little roller to Dennis.

"Bob! Come here!" Jim called.

"What do you want?"

"I said come here! Hurry up!"

Bob reluctantly went over to his father.

"Quit acting like a clown and dynamiting the game," Jim said.

"I was only getting their goat," he said.

"Don't give me any lip! I told you to play with them kids and quit fooling around as if you thought you were a Keystone comedy."

"I wasn't doing anything."

"That's enough. Go on back, and don't let me see any more monkeyshines out of you or I'll bat your ears for you. Get me?"

Bob shook his head. He walked back to the game.

Jim didn't see why Bob had to be playing the clown when he wasn't at all funny. He couldn't understand Bob. Bob was different from Denny. Jim bit off a chew of tobacco and watched the kids play.

VII

Jim gave Dennis and Bob each a nickel for a soda and left them. He just thought he'd listen in on what the Bug Club had to say. The Bug Club met in a hilly spot near some trees on the other side of the park and not far from Fifty-sixth and Cottage Grove. There was a large crowd present. A major circle of listeners surrounded a speaker. Other speakers were addressing smaller groups, and still other people were listening to, or participating in, noisy, free-for-all arguments.

Jim approached a small group which was listening while four or five fellows in the center jawed at one another. He reflected that the Bug Club couldn't have a better name than the one it had.

"There is action, and then there is reaction," said a tall thin fellow with shaggy eyebrows.

Jim wondered what the fellow was selling.

"Vat do you mean, action and reaction?" said a stout fellow.

"Just what I said, action and reaction," the tall young lad repeated.

"Vell, the action is the work of the workers, and the reaction is the work of the bosses."

"Action and reaction in everything are the laws of the world and everything in it."

Jim wandered off to another group.

"Unless you are born again, you'll not be saved," a mealy-mouthed, pudgy-faced man in a blue suit was saying.

"What's that you're after saying, man?" a gray-haired man asked with a brogue.

"Brother, unless you are washed in the blood of the lamb—"

"Won't that be a dirty little job for Jesus," the Irishman interrupted, and most of the spectators laughed.

Jim thought it was funny, an Irishman blaspheming that way.

He went over to the big circle and sat down on the edge of the crowd. He recognized the speaker, a blind man named Edelson.

"And the Republican candidate was elected on a campaign of going back to normalcy. My friends, get that—back to normalcy," Edelson said in a slightly high-pitched, but firm and clear, voice.

Jim looked around. All kinds of people came out here, long-haired men and short-haired women, old codgers, nuts, businessmen, Polacks, atheistic Irishmen, all kinds of people.

"So we went back to normalcy! Tell that to a man out of work! Tell that to a young soldier who was shot and maimed for life in the war that was supposed to save the world for democracy! Tell that to the poor! Tell that to the workingman who gets subsistence wages! My friends, tell that to most of the American people who are prevented from receiving the fruits of their toil! Tell them that we are going back to normalcy with Warren Gamaliel Harding!"

The speaker paused.

Jim thought that this fellow, Edelson, was smart and brainy. And what he said was the truth. Times always were better for the workingman when the Democrats were in. It was when Wilson was president that conditions improved at the express company. The business was put under government regulation, and look at the raises that had been granted.

"We fought a war that we had no business fighting!"

"You said enough there, you Bolshevik," some fellow yelled from the audience.

"Quiet, let the man speak!" someone else shouted.

Jim glanced around to see who was doing the interrupting. He spotted the fellow. Just as he'd thought, some young punk.

"My friend, if you want to refute me, come up here and try it. Your heckling won't get you any place."

"Don't talk against the government."

"Hey, silence. You ain't got the floor," someone yelled.

"I'm an American," the heckler interrupted.

"My friend, there are other Americans here, and they want to hear me speak, not you. When I am finished you can have the floor," Edelson said.

He paused.

"I said we fought a war we had no business fighting. That war brought a peace that can be no peace. The lives of American boys were sacrificed in vain, in vain, on the battlefields and in the mud of France—all in vain."

Jim felt that we didn't have any business fighting in the war. What scrap of ours was it?

"My friends, the story of how we went to war and why this country sent its manhood across an ocean to fight in a war of steel and gold, has not been told. Some day that story will be told. And when it is, the reputations of many statesmen will crumble into the dust of historic obloquy."

Jim sat listening, chewing grass, interested.

VIII

After Edelson finished, Jim moved over to a small group.

"There's only one rule, and that's the Golden Rule."

It was Ned O'Flaherty arguing in a small group. Ned wore white flannel trousers and a silk shirt and had on a straw sailor hat.

"Stranger, do you believe in justice?" a man asked Ned.

"Karl Marx said that religion is the opium of the people," a small Jewish fellow interrupted in a Yiddish accent.

"Who the hell was he?" Ned asked.

"Karl Marx? He was Karl Marx."

"Hell, I suppose he was another guy with long whiskers," Ned said, getting a laugh.

"What has Karl Marx's whiskers got to do with exploitation?" the Jewish fellow yelled.

"His whiskers were probably as long as some of the words you fellows use," Ned said, and some in the group laughed.

"Stranger, what do you believe in?" another man asked Ned.

Jim looked at his watch. It was after five. He limped away. He'd never thought that Ned O'Flaherty was a Bug. Why, Ned had been arguing just like the other Bugs. He guessed Ned went to the Bug Club because Ned enjoyed the sound of his own voice so much. His brother, Al, was the same way.

The sun was still strong, and the park was full of people, some strolling about, others sitting on the grass. Jim passed a fellow and a girl who were wandering aimlessly with their hands clasped, their eyes continually turned on one another. The girl was just beginning to bloom. Just the time when a girl was loveliest to men. Jim stole a glance at her and turned his eyes away, resigned. Yes, she was beautiful, something lovely that he would never have again. He glanced out on the lagoon. Lots of rowboats out. He skirted a family group which sat eating a picnic lunch, and one of the brood of kids almost ran into him. He suddenly realized that there was no reason why he shouldn't take his family over to the park on Sundays for a picnic. He limped around the edge of the lagoon and turned onto the path which ran by the boathouse and around to Fifty-eighth Street. Young cake-eaters stood in front of the boathouse, giving the once-over to some passing girls.

The park was a spectacle, a spectacle of so much life. And suddenly Jim felt like a stranger. Often since he had had that stroke, he had had this same feeling. Without warning, a mood would come over him, and he would feel himself to be half a stranger to life. He would remember the awful moment of his stroke, the awful moments after he had come to again, the time he had been in bed recovering, regaining some use of his limbs, and he would think that perhaps he was not too long for this world.

Jim limped on, noticing the young men with their girls, the children, the fat women, the elderly couples, the changing panorama of the Sunday park.

IX

Jim let himself in by the front door. Dennis, Bob, and Catherine lapsed into sudden silence when Jim entered the parlor.

"Where's your mother?" he asked.

"Mama left a half hour ago. She said to tell you that Anna McCormack is dead, and she went down, and for you to make us supper and get Little Margaret to come over and stay with us so you can go to the wake," Dennis said.

"How did she find out about it?" Jim asked.

"Danny came over from Mother's and said they had called up there to tell Mama," Dennis answered.

Jim was silent for a few moments, and the kids sat watching him. He noticed that the parlor was again disordered.

"She could have waited to cook supper at least," he said with sudden bitterness.

"Papa, I'm hungry," Catherine said.

"I'll fix your supper in a few minutes. And look, you kids pick the papers off the floor and put them together in a pile on the table."

The children obeyed him, and Jim walked out of the parlor. Bill came in.

"Hello, Bill, how was the ball game?" Jim asked.

"The Sox got skunked again."

"Anna McCormack is dead, and your mother has gone down there. I'm going to cook supper," Jim said.

"Want me to help you?" Bill asked.

"No, that's all right. I'll fix supper up. Are you hungry?"

"No, I'm not, Pa. I had some red hots at the ball game."

Jim went out to the dining room.

"Jesus Christ!" he exclaimed.

He saw the dinner dishes still on the table. And she was out traipsing to a wake. He was going to give her a piece of his mind the like of which he had never given her.

He sat down in a chair. He had given her a piece of his mind more than once. He had tried to persuade her. He had argued and fought with her. He had cursed her. He had even socked her. He was sorry he had ever hit her. But some things would try the patience of Job. And now what could he say? She flew, leaving everything a mess the minute she heard someone was dead. What was there in wakes that got her that way? And why did she have to neglect family, husband, everything, to sit all night with a corpse? It was ghoulish!

Jim shrugged his shoulders.

He began taking the dishes out and dumping them into the sink, and he noticed that she hadn't even put the food away. The kitchen was full of flies.

He rolled up his sleeves and got busy.

X

All the dishes were in the dishpan, and it was full of lukewarm, soapy water. As he slowly washed each dish, Jim kept thinking that this was unfair. Why couldn't Lizz see that it was? Of course, a woman had to bear things that a man didn't have to. But it wasn't asking her too much to take care of the house. That was a woman's place and a woman's duty. If the man was a good provider up to the best of his ability, why shouldn't he ask the woman to take care of the house?

After washing the dishes, he rinsed and dried them. Then he cleaned up the kitchen and started to make a salad that he and the kids liked. Lizz was never any good for salads. He set the table, put the cold meat from dinner and the salad on the table, made tea, and then called the kids to supper.

"What's the matter with my kids? I'm not going to bite you. Why don't you say something?" Jim said, noticing how silent the children were.

"Papa, why do people have to die?" Bob asked.

"Bob, you give me a grand and glorious feeling," Bill said.

"If you asked fewer questions and read your catechism, you'd know. It tells why people die," Dennis said.

Jim's face clouded.

"Well, I know they die because God made them the way they are, but I never could figure out why God made them that way," Bob said.

"Bob, you sure are a lulu. You even ask why God does things," Bill said.

"Papa, why do you think God has people die?" Bob asked.

"Shut up!" Jim said in sudden anger.

The table was jolted into silence. Bob looked around, bewildered.

They finished the meat and lettuce and had tea and Ward's Cake. Setting down his cup after a sip, Jim spilled tea. It disturbed him. Was his right hand getting worse? Nonsense! Anybody could spill tea. He picked up the cup again and drank without spilling. His nerves were getting jerky these days. He should control them.

They finished supper.

25

I

The enormous corpse of Anna McCormack was laid out in an expensive casket and surrounded by wreaths and flowers in the parlor of the frame house which the McCormacks owned on Laflin near Thirty-fifth Street. Her once ruddy face was powdered and waxen. Her gray hair was simply arranged. A pair of rosary beads rested in the folded, chubby hands. In the dimly lit room, Lizz sat between Katie, the daughter, and Martha, the daughter-in-law of the deceased.

"You could have knocked me over with a feather, Katie dear, when you telephoned me and said Mother was dead," Martha said in a low-pitched, tremulous voice.

"As soon as I heard the sad news, I hurried right down here. My Jim was out in the park with the boys. I didn't even wait for him to come home," Lizz said.

"It was so good of you, Lizz, to come," Katie said.

"It was the least I could do," Lizz said.

"Poor Mother! Only a week ago she seemed so healthy. Who would have ever expected that by today she would be gone? I went to ten o'clock mass with her a week ago today. She came home and she cooked dinner. And now she's gone," Katie said.

"God calls us all," Lizz said.

Katie began to sob. Lizz and Martha patted and caressed her.

"Now, come, dear, I know how you feel. When my poor father died, I couldn't sleep. I couldn't eat. I know how you feel. Dear, let me make you a cup of tea," Lizz said.

"What'll we ever do without our mother? What will poor Father do? What will the boys do? What'll I do?" Katie said, continuing to sob.

"Your angel mother is in Heaven. Don't cry, Katie. The will of God is beyond and above us, and we must bow to it," Lizz said.

"Mother is gone," Katie said, speaking like one in a trance.

She dried her eyes.

"That's the brave girl," Lizz said as Katie dried her eyes.

"Last night Mother didn't feel well and she went to bed after supper. She hardly pecked at her food. It was her heart. With her weight, her poor heart couldn't do the work it had to. You know, I remember now how she puffed when we walked up the steps of the church to go to mass last Sunday. But she had such a peaceful death. So peaceful. Mother just went to sleep," Katie said.

Katie and Martha began sobbing hysterically. Lizz, with tears in her own eyes, turned from one to the other, wondering which she should comfort first.

II

"Oh, Marty, I feel so heartbroken," Lizz said sadly, meeting Martin McCormack in the kitchen.

"Yes, I understand. Mother was a wonderful woman," Martin said; he was an awkward and bulky, but gentle, man with bushy brows.

"Poor Anna, she was one of my Jim's favorite cousins," Lizz said.

Old Mike McCormack limped into the kitchen, using his blackthorn stick. He was a short and chunky man, with gray hair, ruddy cheeks, and a weatherbeaten face.

"Oh, Mike, I'm so sorry," Lizz said.

"Ah, I know! I know. Does my cousin, Jim, know?" Mike asked.

"Jim will be down tonight."

"Marty boy, get your father a jigger of whiskey. There's some in the pantry."

"Yes, Dad."

"Have a jigger yourself."

"No, thanks, Dad."

Martin got a bottle of whiskey from the kitchen and handed his father a shot. Old Mike drank it down. He leaned on his blackthorn, a silent and severe figure.

"Well, I'll be soon following my Anna. We are all called. Her time has come, and soon Old Mike will be going to meet her in the beyond," Mike said, breaking the silence.

"Dad, you're the picture of health," Martin said.

"Martin, your mother and I, we have been man and wife nigh onto forty years." Old Mike paused. "That was before you were born, Martin, my lad."

"Anna was such a lovely woman," Lizz said.

"No man ever had a wife to hold a candle to her. Martin, when you are married, you'll be the lucky man if you get a girl who's worth the little finger of your mother."

"I know it, Dad."

"Forty years! But what is man? A straw in the wind. What is the life of man? The flame of a candle that goes out in a flash. And then we go to the great beyond to meet our Master. Well, no woman ever went before her Master with a purer heart and a finer soul than my Anna did at six o'clock this morning. Martin, my boy, get your father another jigger of whiskey," Mike said.

He leaned on his blackthorn, and his stern face was rigid.

Martin handed him another glass of whiskey.

"Thank you, my lad."

He drank it down. He looked at the green-bordered wallpaper.

Katie came out in the kitchen like one in a trance. She was a tall and stately girl with flaxen hair and blue eyes. Her eyes were red and rimmed from tears. She began to sob.

Martin went to her and awkwardly stroked her head.

"Come now, Sis. We must brace up."

"Let her cry. If it does you good, girl, cry," Old Mike said.

"Yes, dear, you just have a good cry if you find it does you good," Lizz said, hovering over Katie.

III

"Hello, Mother," Lizz said, speaking into the telephone from a drugstore booth.

"Hello! Hello, yourself!"

"Mother, this is your daughter, Elizabeth."

"Ah, Lizz, how is she laid out?"

"Oh, Mother, you should see her. She's laid out beautiful."

"What did you say, Lizz?"

"Mother, I said she was laid out beautiful. They must have spent a fortune on the casket."

"What did she die of, Lizz?"

"She was perfectly all right yesterday, walking around. And then last night she felt a little indisposed."

"What did you say, Lizz?"

"She was indisposed. She couldn't eat much, and she went to bed not feeling well, but nobody thought that it was serious. But she got worse. It was the heart, Mother. The heart. That was the reason. She was too heavy. Her heart just stopped. But, Mother, it was the most beautiful death. She just went to sleep."

"You don't say. How did they take it?" Mrs. O'Flaherty yelled into the telephone.

"Oh, Mother, I don't know what they would have done if I didn't come to console them."

"What's that you say, Lizz?"

"Mother, can you come to the wake tonight?"

"Peg's working. I'll come with Peg tomorrow night. When are they burying her?"

"Tuesday morning at a high mass. And then they go by automobile to Mount Carmel."

"Couldn't they afford to bury her in Calvary?"

"I don't know. They have a burial ground in Mount Carmel."

"You don't say?"

"Mother, I can't talk any more. They need me here. Old Mike is taking it hard."

"He is?"

"Yes, he is. Everyone asked for you. They asked me, 'How is your mother?'"

"They did! How old was she, Lizz?"

"Sixty-five. She was sixty-five last March, Mother."

"Pity, pity it is. Such a young woman, and so fat. Why, she must have weighed three hundred pounds," Mrs. O'Flaherty said.

"Mother, all of Jim's people will turn out for the funeral. Can you come, too? I want the O'Flahertys to be represented. I don't want them to say that me and Jim didn't turn out with our family."

"How old did you say she was, Lizz?"

"Sixty-five. She was sixty-five last March. Last Sunday, when her daughter, Katie, went to mass with her, Katie said she noticed that Anna puffed when she walked up the steps of the church, and she was puffing and out of breath. That was last Sunday. And now, Mother, she lies dead. But, Mother, I got to hang up. They need me. I'm at a drugstore at Thirty-fifth and Laflin."

"You don't say."

"I got to get back."

"I'll pray for her."

"Goodbye, Mother."

Mrs. O'Flaherty hung up.

Perspiring, Lizz left the booth. She walked out of the drugstore, but suddenly she stopped in front of it. She had telephoned the O'Flahertys to ask them to send someone over to tell Jim to be sure and come to the wake tonight. And she had forgotten to tell that to her mother. She went back into the drugstore to telephone again.

IV

The parlor was crowded with women who sat on camp chairs or stood in corners, their talk muffled. Lizz sat near Katie and Martha, and on the right of Annie O'Reilley. People kept coming steadily. They approached the casket, prayed, looked at the corpse, and paid their condolences to Katie and Martha. Then the women found places in the room, and the men went downstairs.

"As soon as I heard about poor Anna, I rushed right down here," Lizz boasted to Annie O'Reilley.

"Lizz, you're so good. I'm sure they need you," Annie said with a smile; she was a faded woman in her early forties.

"You know, I feel the same about Jim's people as I do about my own. Why, Annie, if the same thing happened to you—and God forbid that it would—I'd leave everything and come down, and I'd stay up all night watching you, too, as if you were my own," Lizz replied, returning Annie O'Reilley's smile with a most beneficent one of her own.

Annie sat silent, and Lizz watched her from the corner of her eye.

"But God forbid that any more of Jim's people pass away soon. You know, Annie, it seems as if my people have a longer life than Jim's. My mother is already over seventy, and she hasn't a gray hair in her head, and my poor father lived to a good ripe old age. Jim's father and mother, and yours, were called at an earlier age, weren't they, Annie?" Lizz said, a twinkle in her eyes.

"Of course, I'm not related to Jim by blood, but by marriage," Annie said.

"Sure, and didn't I see the good woman only Tuesday, going to the store," Mrs. Muldoon, a neighbor, said, interrupting Lizz.

"Oh, Annie, you must meet Mrs. Muldoon. Mrs. Muldoon, this is Mrs. O'Reilley. Her man is a cousin of Mr. McCormack," Lizz said.

"How do you do? Are yez closely related to Mr. McCormack?" Mrs. Muldoon asked.

"Her man is a second cousin. He's a plumber," Lizz said.

"Oh!" Mrs. Muldoon exclaimed.

Lizz watched two women come forward, bend low, and then move away.

"Do yez live near here, Mrs. O'Reilley?" Mrs. Muldoon asked.

"No, she used to live back of the yards, Mrs. Muldoon, until she was married. Now she lives over in a swell neighborhood on Forty-first Street, don't you, Annie?" Lizz said, smiling at Mrs. Muldoon.

"You don't say!" Mrs. Muldoon exclaimed.

Annie O'Reilley looked at Liz, annoyed.

"Did yez say that your man is a plumber?" Mrs. Muldoon asked. "My son wants to be one, and I sez to him, sez I, 'Mickey, that's no job for a lad of your stripe to go after.' Sez I to me Mickey, 'Sure, now, why don't you get yourself a nice job where yez can wear a collar and tie to work?' But I hear tell there's good money in plumbing, Mrs. O'Reilley."

Lizz's eyes lit up. She saw Jim enter the parlor.

V

Jim met old Mike near the kitchen doorway as he was starting to go down the stairs to the basement room.

"Ah, Jim, come here," Old Mike said, pulling Jim into the kitchen. "Jim, I'll never be the same man again."

"I know it's hard, Mike. But we all are called," Jim remarked.

"Ah, Jim, life is short. It seems like it was only yesterday that Anna was my blushing bride. And now Anna lies dead, and my life is over, and I'm an old man with a cane, just sitting out my days."

"Yes, Mike, I know how it is."

Mike limped to the pantry and came out with a bottle of whiskey.

"Have one with me, Jim?"

"No, Mike, I can't drink any more," Jim answered.

"Ah, Jim, for my sake. A good shot of whiskey never did man nor devil any harm," Mike said.

"All right. One," Jim said.

He poured two small glasses of whiskey. Jim knew that he shouldn't drink. Well, one wouldn't hurt.

"Jim, we often drank on happy occasions, but tonight we're not," Mike said, handing Jim a drink.

Jim raised the glass. They drank.

"Sit down, Jim, and talk to me," Mike said.

They sat down alone in the kitchen.

"Man is born to die, Jim. Vanity, vanity, all is vanity, Jim, lad," Old Mike said, fixing his gaze on the stove.

"Yes," Jim said quietly.

Old Mike leaned on his cane.

"Jim, I'm glad you came. I wanted to see you. How are you feeling yourself, Jim lad?"

"Pretty good, Mike. I'm on my vacation, and I got some good rest."

"You're thinner, Jim."

"Yes, Mike, I lost a little weight."

Jim thought of the corpse in the front, the waxiness of a face that was once so ruddy with life. He waited for Old Mike to speak. Aware of how deeply he sympathized with Old Mike, he couldn't think of anything worth saying that would express his feelings. When you most wanted to tell another man something, you were least able to do so. Jim felt a sudden and profound loneliness. He felt himself all alone in a world of men. He felt himself forced always to be alone with himself. The words he could say to another man, they did not get him closer to that man. Even with Liz, he was still alone with himself, alone in the world. He thought of death as a figure, dark and mysterious, a figure which wrote every man's name down and prepared to visit him. Some day he would be dead, and people would be gathered at his wake as they were now gathered at poor Anna's—God have mercy on her soul.

"Jim, I say to myself, 'Mike, you're dreaming.' And then I look around me and I know I'm not. Well, the Master wanted her and the Master took her to Himself.

Jim could see how hard the old man was taking it. If he could do something for him, he would. He remembered himself crying when he buried his Little Arty.

"Dust, and to dust we must return. Ah, Jim, what is a man's life but the snap of one's fingers," Old Mike said.

Old Mike stood up.

"Jim, you better go down and see the boys. They're downstairs. I'll be coming down later."

"Yes, Mike. I'll see you later," Jim said.

VI

The basement room was large, well lit, and thick with cigar and cigarette smoke. There was a constant hum of masculine talk. Jim sat with Patsy McLaughlin in a corner, while Joe O'Reilley and Dennis Gorman, the lawyer, were on Patsy's right. Chewing on a cigar, Patsy carefully but unobtrusively looked at Jim. Patsy was a bluff, rough-and-ready-looking man with gray hair, sharp eyes, and a long, straight nose.

"Well, Jim, I'm glad to hear that you've been enjoying your vacation," Patsy said.

"Yes, I'm getting good and rested."

"Good. Jim, you want to take care of yourself. When you go back to work now, don't kill yourself. I don't expect more from any man than he's able to give, and I don't want anyone to kill himself workin' for me."

"I go along. You know me, Patsy."

"How's the family?" Patsy asked, glancing down and looking at Jim's thin right wrist.

"Fine, fine, everything's jake with me, Patsy."

"McGinty was in to see me yesterday morning about your older boy. He wants to put him on the tractor board, says he'll be a big help. So I told Wade Norris to go ahead and okay the change. Your lad will get a single wagon driver's pay. I think that's a little more than he's getting now," Patsy said.

Jim beamed with pride. Just then Martin McCormack appeared over them with a box of cigars. They both shook their heads in the negative.

"A lot of people came for mother. There's quite a crowd of men in the room now," Martin said.

"You know, Marty, a man never knows how much he needs and depends on a mother or a wife until she's gone," Patsy said.

Martin nodded agreement. Jim thought that yes, this was so true, and he regretted all the quarrels and squabbles and fights that he had ever had with Lizz. She had faced a lot with him. He thanked God that she was still with him. And she didn't get out too much, and if she did come to a wake and stay a long time at it, now that was no real cause for him to complain.

"Say, Jim, haven't you lost a little weight?" Martin asked.

"Not of late. I used to be heavier before I had my stroke, of course," Jim said.

"Going to play football again this year?" Patsy asked Martin.

"I'll have to come out and see you play. But me, Marty, I'm an old-timer. I don't know much about football," Jim said.

"Well, it's a great game, Jim. I love it. Of course, it's only a job to me. I make extra dough, and pretty good dough, too, and it helps me out, too, in other ways. My chief seems pleased. He always talks of it. He smiles and says now all those other guys in the professional league had to go to college to become football players, but McCormack there, an ordinary dick, he didn't, and he's right up with them. There's good money in it, and professional football is going to come up stronger all the time," Martin said.

"You don't think it will take the place of baseball?" Patsy asked, his voice rather anxious.

"Nope, Patsy, I don't think that."

"My kid, Danny, plays. He seems crazy about it. The folks are all worried that he'll get hurt," Jim said.

"Jim, if a kid wants to play football, the best thing to do is to let him. Come to think of it, one of my team mates, Joe McBride, coaches him."

"There's money in it, you say, Marty?"

"Yes, there is, Jim. But, say, will you excuse me? I have to be getting around and see about everybody," Martin said.

"Joe, you think there's any chance to get this fellow Thompson out of the Hall next year?" Patsy asked, turning to Joe O'Reilley; Joe was a handsome gray-haired man.

"Well, it'll be a tough fight. I'm swinging with this fellow, Judge Dever."

"He's a reformer, isn't he?"

"The best man to lick Mayor Thompson is a reformer."

"The trouble with these reformers is that they don't know that you can't change human nature," Patsy said.

Joe O'Reilley puffed comfortably on his cigar.

Jim didn't feel at ease in this room. In it there were cousins of his and men like Gorman whom he'd known for a long time. A number of these men were more successful than he. Patsy was his own boss. Joe and Dinny Gorman were successful lawyers with their fingers in politics, and they were still going up the ladder. Most of the men in the room looked in good health. And here he was, not in really decent shape and with nothing to fall back on. He glanced at Joe and Patsy and then across the room at Alderman Paddy Slattery, his mother-in-law's cousin. They all had a look and a manner of confidence. When they talked about politics, they spoke as insiders sharing a common knowledge that nobody else had. He noticed, too, how poor relations looked up to these men, even ass-holed before them. Well, he didn't and wouldn't. But he felt that he must look different from them. He remembered how, as a young man, he used to drink with Patsy. Patsy was only driving then. But Patsy had lifted himself up by his bootstraps, and he deserved it. It wasn't that he envied them or anything like that. He didn't. He felt a difference. He felt it in what they said, what they talked about, their manner, the look in their eyes. Even were he in the best of health, he knew that he'd feel different from these men.

While they went on talking, Jim was silent, moody. He now regretted the mistakes, the carefreeness and carelessness of his youth. He might have done what Joe had done. He hadn't. Now he could see where he was wrong. But he couldn't do anything about his mistakes, except try to make his children profit by them. He continued to glance around the room, seeing familiar and unfamiliar faces in a cloud of tobacco smoke. There was Old Mike leaning on his stick in a corner. He thought of the dead woman upstairs, and the chill fear of death curdled in him. Every man in this room would some day die. Who would be the next? Would he? Would Joe and Patsy and others here sit at his wake? He heard some fellow near him saying that well, after all is said and done, we're here today and we're gone tomorrow.

"Jim, it must be a great comfort to a man to have kids. Where would old Mike be if he didn't have any?" Patsy said.

"Yes, it is; if you bring 'em up right they're a comfort," Jim said.

"Well, Jim, there's no use crying over spilled milk. Mary and I haven't any, and it's too late," Patsy said wistfully.

Jim didn't say anything. Patsy had his regrets, too. He wondered about Joe. Joe was a bachelor. He thought that life was strange. He recalled a night many years ago when he and Joe and Patsy had sat in a saloon drinking beer. Joe had talked about the future, full of plans for his career. He had quietly been scornful of Joe. And now here they were, the same three men with the years in between then and now. He had gone the roughest road of the three. But what was the use of stewing about such things?

He listened to them talk.

VII

"Himself has gone home?" Mrs. Muldoon asked.

"Oh, yes. He needs his rest."

They were alone in the parlor. The house was very quiet. The sweet odors of the flowers permeated the room. They sat in the dim light, side by side, close to the coffin.

"Ah, sad it is to see someone go, to see their loved ones crying, and sad, sad it is, Mrs. O'Neill. I always do be saying to himself, sez I to himself, 'The day will come, Paddy, when you and I will be dust'."

"There's no gainsaying that, Mrs. Muldoon."

"Mrs. O'Neill, do yez think that she might be rising up and talking to us?"

"What did you say, Mrs. Muldoon?"

"I was after asking you if we might be seeing her ghost?"

"I don't know. It isn't everyone that has the privilege and the power to see souls from the other world."

Mrs. Muldoon yawned.

"Late it is. Are they all in bed?" she asked.

"I put the girls in bed. I told them they needed rest and that I'd be here and sit up with their mother," Lizz said.

They sat side by side in silence.

"Let's pray for her departed soul," Lizz suddenly suggested.

Both knelt down before the casket. While they prayed half audibly, Lizz glanced sidewise at Mrs. Muldoon. She would remain on her knees in prayer longer than this biddy. She quickly lowered her head to escape Mrs. Muldoon's darting eyes. Lizz prayed with all the mannerisms of intense piety. Mrs. Muldoon breathed asthmatically as her lips murmured in continuing prayer. Lizz stole another glimpse of Mrs. Muldoon and, confident, she prayed on. Sighing and wheezing, Mrs. Muldoon lifted her bulky body, looked at the corpse, and went to her chair. She sat with her hands crossed in her lap. Lizz remained praying for about five minutes and then took her chair beside Mrs. Muldoon without saying a word.

Mrs. Muldoon yawned. They sat in solemn silence. A sense of the presence of the dead woman seemed to pervade the room.

VIII

The gray dawn crept through the parlor blinds. The odor of fast-fading flowers mingled with the stale air. Perspiring, Mrs. Muldoon slept sitting up, her ample chin sunken against her chest. Lizz wiped her face with a handkerchief. A snore from Mrs. Muldoon attracted her attention. Proud of her own superior endurance, she watched her neighbor sleep on.

Suddenly Mrs. Muldoon woke up.

"What time is it?" she asked, sleepily rubbing her eyes.

"It's almost morning."

"I just passed off to sleep."

"She came to me and talked to me while you were asleep."

"What's that you're saying?"

"She sat right up in the coffin," Lizz said.

"Why didn't you wake me up?"

"You were so tired, I let you sleep."

"You say she sat up and talked to you?"

"Oh, yes. For about fifteen minutes."

"You must have been dreaming. Sure, why would the dead be rising to talk to you, and me, her neighbor for twenty years sitting here. Sure, if she came back, she would have woke me up to talk to me."

"She said that you were her friend and she would pray for you."

Mrs. Muldoon looked at Lizz, speechless. Her face revealed her painful perplexity.

"Anna told me things she didn't want anyone else to know," Lizz said.

"What?"

"I couldn't betray a secret confidence with the dead. No, I'd never do that. But she did say that she would think of you in the other world."

"Thank you, Mrs. O'Neill," Mrs. Muldoon snapped curtly.

Lizz did not answer. Mrs. Muldoon sat up straight and unrelaxed. Subtly watching Lizz from the corner of her eye, she began to sniff as if Lizz were a disturbing odor. Lizz beamed contentment and satisfaction.

"Did you ever hear tell of them that is possessed?" Mrs. Muldoon asked.

"Oh, yes, I know all about the possessed. Why, I drive the Devil before me wherever I go. No devils will dare to steal in and try to grab the soul of the dear departed with me around."

"There was a woman down the block, Mrs. Cafferty. The poor thing was always seeing the dead, and lo and behold, she was possessed, and they had to take her away. Did you ever know Mrs. Cafferty?"

"Did I know her? Say, I knew her mother. There was a bad streak in that family. Her mother's name was Muldoon before she married a Cafferty."

"That wasn't the same one."

"Oh, yes, it was. I knew the Caffertys."

"If it was, tell me the name of Mary Cafferty's husband, Tim?" Mrs. Muldoon asked, speaking low and making a stern effort to control her rising anger.

"Why, Tim Cafferty. My mother knew him."

"Well, she was possessed. Sure, she was always seeing the dead at wakes, and it was the hand of the Devil behind it. Did you say you saw Anna McCormack? Are you sure that it wasn't the work of the old one?"

"Oh, yes. The Devil is afraid to come in the room I'm in. Anna talked about you, too."

"What did she say?"

"Nothing will happen to you. She'll watch over you. Thanks to her, none of yours will be drunkards."

Mrs. Muldoon rose and faced Lizz defiantly.

"I'll not be standing here having you blaspheme my dead friend, bringing the Devil himself to the very room in which she lies waking," she said.

"Please be careful and don't be talking loud in this house of sadness," Lizz said.

Mrs. Muldoon put her hands on her hips.

"I can see the Devil in your eyes."

"No one ever has had a minute's luck who said an unkind word to me. That dead woman is protecting me this very minute. Don't you think you are getting away with anything."

"Well, you'll never have a minute's good luck from this day forth, defaming that poor dead woman."

"Say, you, you better get the hell out of here before the McCormacks wake up. You can't talk to me that way."

"I wouldn't insult myself by talking to the likes of you," Mrs. Muldoon said.

Mrs. Muldoon sat down opposite Lizz. They faced one another stonily, and the pale dawn continued to seep through the drawn blinds.

Old Mike hobbled into the room and, leaning on his blackthorn, he looked at his departed wife.

"Thank you, thank you," he said, turning from Lizz to Mrs. Muldoon.

He hobbled out. They glared at one another.

26

I

"And, Bill, if you're not transferred in with McGinty today, I wouldn't let on that I heard anything about it. You just forget that I told you what Patsy told me," Jim said, eating breakfast with Bill.

"Of course I will."

"This promotion, Bill, it won't mean that you're not going to go on with your bookkeepin' course this fall?"

"No, no, Pa. I'm going to go through with my course."

"Good. And I was talkin' to Marty McCormack about football last night."

"He's a pro football star."

"Do you think your brother might become a good football player?"

"Gee, I don't know, Pa. I never saw him play."

"Of course, a young fellow's bones are soft, and he's different from a man. Young fellows shouldn't be playing football until they are developed. I was wondering about Danny. After all, if he has a chance in that line, there isn't any use of my putting my foot down and telling him that he can't play football at school this year."

"I agree with that, Pa."

"I'm worried about your brother. I'm afraid that thanks to your mother's people, he's not an O'Neill."

"Dan is all right. I say that, and I always say it. He's going to come out all right."

"Do you think so, Bill?"

"Pa, I know so. I have all the confidence in the world in that kid."

"If Marty can become a football player and make good at it, why can't Danny?" Jim asked reflectively.

Bill got up to go to work.

II

Jim checked his anger. After all, Danny had only come over with the message Lizz had given him on the phone about her staying on down at the McCormacks'. There wasn't any reason for him to be taking it out on Danny.

Danny stood before Jim, hands in pocket. He wore an old pair of cuffless, gray-checked trousers and a white shirt with the collar turned in and the sleeves rolled up. His hair was greased and parted in the center. He had medium-length sideburns. Jim studied Danny. The lad didn't look tough, and he wasn't so heavy, except that he had pretty wide shoulders and long arms. Jim guessed that Danny got his shoulders and arms from him.

"Football starts when you go to school next month?" Jim asked.

"It'll start right away, as soon as school begins, so we can get into condition."

"Aren't you afraid you'll get hurt playing?"

"I played all last year and didn't get hurt. I'm heavier this year."

"You're not very heavy."

"I don't get hurt easy. And I got pretty good shoulders. If you know how to play football, how to tackle right and to fall when you're tackled, you're not as likely to get hurt as if you don't."

"Well, I was against your playing and I wanted to talk to you about it."

Danny turned pale.

"But I guess it'll be all right," Jim said.

Danny sighed with relief and smiled.

"As long as you keep in condition and train. You don't smoke, do you?"

"No, Pa, I don't."

"Good. That'll help your wind. By the way, how did it go workin' in the shoe store last Saturday?"

"Oh, all right. It took me an hour or two to get the hang of it, but then it was all right."

"Don't lay down on the job. Always remember this, no matter what you got to do, do it well. Dan, and you know, in baseball or football, there has to be team play. Well, the same holds true in life. Always hold up your end of the stick."

Danny nodded agreement. He left, and Jim sat for a moment. Danny would turn out all right. He seemed to be an innocent kid.

Jim got up and started tidying up the house a bit.

III

"Papa, when will Mama be home?" Bob asked at the supper table.

"Oh, gee, Mama won't come back until the funeral. She never does when any cousins die. Isn't that right, Pa?" Dennis interrupted.

"How do you know?"

"Well, isn't that what happened when Mr. Ganley died?" Dennis asked.

"Papa, I like you to cook supper better than I do Mama," Catherine said.

"You do?" Jim remarked.

"Yes, I do. I like the salad you make us. Mama doesn't like to make salads," Catherine said.

"Well, forget it," Jim said.

"Papa, will you take us to the wake tonight?" asked Bob.

"No, you kids stay home. Little Margaret is coming over again."

The three younger children showed disappointment.

"Bill, I wouldn't be going if your mother wasn't camping out there. Tonight, by God, I'm going to bring her home!" Jim said.

They went on eating.

IV

"That's not fair," Catherine said to Bob, who lay on the couch and made faces.

"Why?" asked Bob.

"Because we're playing wake, and you're the dead person, and a person that's dead can't make faces and laugh and talk. A person that's dead is dead and doesn't move, just like my brother, Little Arty, didn't move when he was dead. If you're going to play wake with us, you got to lay still," Catherine said.

"If you don't cut it out, I'll sock you one," Dennis yelled at Bob.

"Oh, all right," Bob said.

He lay still.

"Dennis, you're Pa. I'm Mama, and Catherine is Annie O'Reilley. Now you walk in," Little Margaret said.

Dennis went to the parlor entrance and walked in.

"Oh, no, that's not right," Catherine said. "Dennis, if you are playing Papa, you got to limp like Papa does."

"All right," Dennis said.

Dennis walked forward, limping, pulling along his right foot in a good imitation of his father.

"Oh, here's my Jim, Annie," Little Margaret said.

"I'm waiting for my Tom to come," Catherine said.

Bob sat up and screwed up his face. He was listening to something.

"Bob, I hate you. You're dead and supposed to be still," Catherine cried.

"Damn you!" Dennis yelled, rushing at Bob.

"Please, Dennis, stop, I heard something," Bob cried out as Dennis was grappling with him trying to punch him.

"Dennis, don't hit him. Let me fix him," Little Margaret said.

Dennis relaxed his hold.

"Little Margaret, listen. Listen, everybody!" Bob said, urgent.

They were silent.

"It's nothing," Dennis said.

Bob put up his hand. There was a scratching noise coming from the dining room, and it seemed to be the window.

They were motionless with fright.

"Burglars and kidnapers," Catherine said, starting to cry.

"I'll see," Bob said.

"No, you'll get shot," Little Margaret said.

"I'll get Bill's gun," Dennis said.

"It's rusty, and there's no bullets, and it don't shoot," Bob said.

"You would say that. How would the burglars know?" Dennis asked.

"Listen," Little Margaret said.

The four children were quiet. The only sounds to be heard in the apartment were scratching noises from the dining room.

"We got to do something," Bob said.

Dennis ran into the front bedroom. Bob jumped off the couch and followed him. Little Margaret and Catherine timidly tiptoed after Bob. Bob peeked around the corner of the hall and saw a man outside the window, trying to jimmy it.

"It's a robber. Make all the noise you can, right away quick. Catherine, get Denny," Bob whispered.

"Papa, get your gun, there's robbers," Bob shouted at the top of his voice.

"Mama, call the police, there's robbers," Little Margaret yelled.

"Throw things," Bob whispered.

He took off his shoe and threw it hard against the wall below the window ledge.

Dennis ran to them with a worn-out, useless old revolver. He pointed the gun around the corner of the hallway wall.

"Hands up!" he screamed, trying to imitate Papa's voice.

Little Margaret and Bob yelled and threw things on the floor that Catherine kept bringing from the parlor.

"Hands up or I'll shoot!" Dennis repeated, again trying vainly to imitate his father's voice.

He peeked. The man was gone.

"We scared him," Dennis said.

He ran to the window. In the moonlight he saw a man legging it across the prairie and disappearing in the alley.

Little Margaret turned on the light in the dining room.

"I would have shot him, if there was bullets," Dennis said.

"Kids, we got to turn on all the lights so he doesn't come back," Little Margaret said.

They turned on every light in the house.

"Let's look at all the windows," Bob said.

He climbed onto the dining-room window sills and examined them.

"Gee, I just had to lock the kitchen window. It wasn't locked. If he tried it instead of the dining room, he'd a gotten in," Dennis said.

"Lock it, you funny monkey," Little Margaret said.

"I did," Dennis said, waving the revolver.

V

They sat around the dining-room table. Little Margaret held the carving knife. Dennis fingered the revolver. Bob brandished the saw-edged butcher knife. Catherine clutched a broom.

"Did you hear anything at the parlor window?" Catherine asked.

"Nobody could come in the front. They'd be seen," Dennis said.

"I thought I heard something," Catherine said.

"You're imagining," Dennis said.

"Gee, how soon will they come home?" Little Margaret asked.

"I want my Papa," Catherine cried.

"Come on, Catherine, they didn't get in, and with all the lights on, they'll think that everybody is here and be afraid," said Little Margaret.

"Boy, I wish there was bullets in this gun," Dennis said.

"Let me hold the gun a while, Denny," Bob said.

"Gee, when will they come?" said Little Margaret.

"I want my Papa," Catherine said, still crying.

"Listen!" Dennis said.

They sat stiff and silent, their faces taut with terror. They heard a crack on the floor. No one moved.

The house was quiet.

"I want my Papa," Catherine sobbed.

27

I

Carrying his lunch wrapped up in a newspaper, Jim left for work. Catherine was waiting for him in front of the building.

"How is Papa's Doll?" Jim asked.

"Papa, I like it better when you are on vacations than when you aren't."

"Why, Dollie?" Jim asked, taking her hand.

"I just do."

Jim looked down at her. Their eyes met. She smiled.

"I was playing jacks, and it was my turn, but I knew it was time for you to be going to work so I gave up my turn. I told the kids I had to walk to work with my Papa," she said.

"What did they say?"

"They said their Papas worked days, and not nights."

"What did you say to that?"

"I said it was better to have a Papa who worked nights."

"Why did you say that?"

"Because you're my Papa and you work nights."

"Well, Dollie, some day we might all be rich, and then your father will be home with you more," Jim said, but he didn't believe that he would ever be a rich man, and not have to work, and he couldn't even imagine what he'd do with himself if he were in such circumstances.

"And then I can have all the dresses I want," she said.

Jim led her cater-corner across Fifty-eighth Street, and they walked on the half block to the elevated station. In front of the station he picked her up with his left arm and kissed her.

"Papa's Doll Lily is getting to be such a big girl that she's heavy," he said, setting her down and giving her a nickel. “Now you be a good girl and Papa will see you tomorrow.”

“’Bye, Papa,” she said.

II

Jefferson Street Depot was the same familiar sight with the line-up of vehicles to be unloaded, and the hustling freight handlers. But the noise confused him for a moment. There seemed to be a ringing in his head. He heard engines ringing and chugging. Men were shouting and yelling. Motors were being started and stopped. All the usual noises of the depot now seemed strange, almost paralyzing. On his vacation, he’d completely forgotten how noisy it was at work.

Standing on the platform by the small stairway, he was suddenly dizzy. He felt his head growing light and he quickly supported himself against a side wall. The spell passed. He limped along the bustling platform to the coop.

“Ah, the stranger home from the wars,” Phil Heston, the daytime Wagon Dispatcher, remarked as Jim entered the coop. “How was the vacation?”

“Pretty good, pretty good. I got a good rest and I feel fine after it,” Jim said, hanging up his hat and coat on a hook.

“Well, the joint is still here, Jim.”

“I see,” Jim said.

“I go on my vacation next Monday. Me and the old lady, we’ll get in a Ford and roust about for a week or so,” Phil said.

Phil put on his hat and coat.

“See you in heaven,” he said, leaving.

“Don’t take any wooden nickels,” Jim called after him.

Jim sharpened a pencil, got out his sheets, and got ready for the night’s work.

III

“Well, Jim, it’s nice to have you back. Sure you won’t have a cup of java?” Pete Hecht said, sitting in the coop with Jim, while the noises from outside were steady and persistent.

“No, thanks, Pete,” Jim said, writing out a wagon departure on his depot record sheet.

“Yes, Jim, I’m glad you’re back. You and me, we been here together how long now? Over two years. Every night over two years, except Sundays and vacations, and when one of us is off sick,” Pete said.

“Yeh, it doesn’t seem that long either, does it?”

“Time sure flies, Jim.”

A driver came in, a man of about fifty, with graying temples.

"If I am not deceived by my failing eyesight, Jim, I'd say that I can smell Kirkland," Pete said.

"Yes, and my ears tell me Pete Hecht is here. Say, Pete, don't you ever wear your ass out," Kirkland said.

"Kirkland, my boy, I've given this ass of mine years of practice in sitting down. There ain't an ass in this whole city that has the training in sitting that this here practiced ass of mine has."

"Well, I guess you said a mouthful then," Kirkland said.

"Yes, sir, when I was young my boy, I decided that the best part of me was my ass. So I started right in then and there to train it. And that's the secret of my success. That's why Pete Hecht has got the best sittingest ass in the whole damned express company," Pete said.

"Pete, you're a card," Kirkland said as he and Jim laughed.

"Well, Kirkland, what can I do for you?" Jim asked.

"Put your John Hancock here for me. I'm leaving now, Jim, with that stiff for 5500 North."

"Why don't you change places with the stiff? Nobody won't know the difference," Pete said.

"Because a corpse reminds me too much of you," Kirkland said while Jim signed his ticket.

"Say, Jim, know what I heard about this bastard, Kirkland?"

"What, Pete?"

"Well, someone was telling me that he killed his wife and collected the insurance."

Kirkland left, grinning.

"Kirkland's got a sense of humor," Pete said.

Jim telephoned the Wagon Department to give Lambert Kirkland's departure time. Pete sipped coffee from a tin cup.

IV

"Hello, Clancy, what can I do for you?" Jim asked, returning to the coop from the lavatory and finding a wagon man waiting for him.

"I'm empty."

"Well, I ain't got nothin' for you. Call up Wagon."

Jim looked at the sheets on his desk while Clancy phoned.

"Sign me out. I got to go up to the Wagon Department," Clancy said.

Jim signed the ticket. Clancy left. Jim bent over his desk. Suddenly he looked up and saw Mr. Wolfe, the night Assistant Superintendent, watching him from outside the coop window. Mr. Wolfe was a tall, straight man, well-built and bronzed. When he watched anyone, he shoved his head forward and seemed to be smelling as much as he was observing. Jim went on working, paying no attention to Wolfe.

"Everything going all right tonight, O'Neill?" Mr. Wolfe asked, entering the coop.

"Yes, it is, Mr. Wolfe. Not a stick of outgoing freight is left, and I got that corpse on the way now. Kirkland is deliverin' it."

"Good," Mr. Wolfe said, sitting down on a stool.

The phone rang, and Jim answered it.

"Hello, Jim. I'm at mother's and I just thought I'd call you up."

"Yes, well, listen, I'm busy. He is? I'm glad. No, that's all right."

"Jim, what's the matter with you?"

"Nothing. I'm glad you called to tell me. You better go home now, Lizz."

"Jim, are you all right?"

"Yes, Lizz, I'm glad you called. I got to hang up now, and you better go back."

Jim hung up.

"That was my wife. One of the kids had a cold. She called me up to tell me he was better," Jim said, not wanting Wolfe to think he was tying up the depot line with outside personal calls. Jim waited for what Mr. Wolfe had to say.

"O'Neill, tell me, have you noticed anything about this here fellow Clancy?"

"No, I haven't. He seems like a nice kid."

"I just saw him smoking a cigarette on the job as he drove out of here."

"I didn't see him. He was in here and I signed him out. He always goes along and does his work and doesn't have any lip to him."

"I wish you'd watch and see if any more of them smoke going out of here."

"All right, I will, when I get a chance. I don't get much time to be hopping off the platform, though, and watching them drive away."

"Another matter. In some of the depots, the wagon men have been going to the toilets and staying there a long time, stalling. I want to check up on them. The company is losing a lot of the time it's paying them for while they stall in the toilets."

Jim remembered his own days as a wagon man, and how a fellow felt and liked to knock off five or ten minutes in the midst of his work. It didn't do any harm. The freight got moved just the same.

"I haven't noticed any of them pulling any stunts here. I make them tend to their business."

"Well, keep your eyes open and, oh, yes, have you noticed anything about Schmeling on a gascar?"

"He was in here with a load last night, but I didn't notice anything particular."

"Well, if you smell any liquor on his breath, let me know."

"I never have."

"I have some bad reports on him."

Jim waited for further questions and remarks.

"That's all, O'Neill," Mr. Wolfe said, getting up and leaving.

Jim told himself that his work was to take care of wagons and get the freight moved out of the place, not to be a stool pigeon or a gum-shoe.

He could see why they called him Hiram the Wolfe. He liked working for a man like Patsy rather than Wolfe. Well, Patsy was the real boss, and if anything came up between him and Wolfe, he'd go to Patsy. But then he never gave Wolfe cause for a complaint against him.

V

Jim heard the receding echo of engine bells. He stretched and looked at the clock. Two-thirty. The clock was ticking away, each tick beating out another second of his life. Jim was tired. It was just the same as ever, and he was used to being back in the harness. In fact, it seemed as if he hadn't been away at all on a vacation.

He heard the sudden and unexpected crash of a box outside. He looked out and saw a crowd of platform men collecting near the tail gate of a truck which was backed against the platform. Someone was hurt. He hastened out of the coop, and as he approached the scene of the accident he heard a man moaning. He pushed through a small crowd and saw a thin, tall fellow with graying hair, who was moaning; a large box had crushed his leg. Three huskies were lifting off the box. The man continued to moan. His foot was mangled and blood was mixed with his crushed shoe and smashed bones. Jim turned aside a moment. The sight almost made him retch.

"Bring him into the coop right away," Jim said.

Several huskies lifted the man. His injured leg dangled as one held it by the thigh. He continued to moan. A crowd of platform men followed, and Pete Hecht turned to them and said:

"You fellows better get on with the work."

The injured man was set on the floor of the coop, and Pete went to the telephone.

"Have any of you fellows got a bottle on you?" Jim asked.

The huskies all shook their head no.

"My foot, my foot!" the fellow moaned.

Jim bent down and looked at the foot. It was mangled a little above the ankle; blood still oozed from it.

"Better not touch it, Jim. Let the docs do it. We might make it worse," Pete said, turning from the telephone.

Jim could see that it was best not to try to take the shoe off such a foot. The man let out such a harrowing moan, it made Jim tense with fright.

"Pete, can't you find anyone here who has a bottle?"

"I'll see, Jim."

He hustled out of the coop. Jim took off his coat and set it under the injured man's head to serve as a pillow.

"There now. A doctor will be here in a jiffy, and you'll be all right," Jim said.

"Oh, Christ! Oh, good Jesus Christ!"

Jim knew how the fellow must feel. He knelt there beside the suffering man, feeling utterly helpless. The man continued to moan.

Pete came back with a platform man who had a bottle of liquor. It was unlabeled moonshine. Pete bent down with the bottle.

"Here now, man, take a good swig," he said consolingly.

The man drank.

"Here, take another. It'll pull you together."

The man drank again.

The platform men who had carried him in stood there, looking helplessly from one to the other.

"How did it happen?" Jim asked.

"I didn't see," a bushy-browed, chunky fellow answered.

"He slipped when we was pulling it, and I don't know what happened. The box fell on him. That's all I know."

The man was quiet.

"Now, you'll be all right. Here, have another drink," Pete said.

Jim gazed down at the man. He knew how the fellow felt, how he would feel and worry about his family if something similar happened to him. He vaguely remembered the pain, too, when he'd been young and worked in a factory and lost a finger. Nobody had been able to do anything for him then while they'd waited around him for a doctor to come. Nobody had been able to say anything to help him. There was nothing to say. This fellow would probably lose his leg, from below the knee, too.

An interne, dressed in white, entered with a bag and bent down over the injured man who again began to moan.

VI

Riding home on the elevated, Jim couldn't get that man out of his mind. His name was Swing. He'd been working on the platform for nine months, and everyone said he was a nice fellow. Jim hadn't known him except by sight and to say hello. He looked out the window at the dark hulks of the buildings and then over them at the blue sky. The sky seemed to move as the train rumbled on. What made it worse was that Swing had kids. Nothing could be done to save that leg. Jim remembered Swing lying on the floor of the coop, remembered the bloody crushed pulp of leg, blood, bone, flesh, sock, overall, and shoe leather all mashed together like some jelly. Something like that could happen to any man. And when it did, where was he? What would he and his family do? The incident made him fearful about himself. He looked out the window again, moody and brooding. The moon was still out, clear, full, silvery. It was beginning to lighten. There was a gray mist hanging from the sky. He shuddered, remembering Swing again, his moans, the beaten, fearful, harassed expression on his face, and the way the man had kept asking the young doctor if he would lose his leg. Jesus!

He got off at Fifty-eighth Street. He had a pain in his back and he wanted to get home. He wanted to sleep and blot out of his mind the memory of that man, lying on the floor of the coop with that bleeding, useless leg. He wanted to forget what that meant to this man and his family in terms of the vital necessities of which they were robbed.

He limped down Calumet Avenue in the gray mist. Saturday morning. Tonight, work again, and tomorrow was Sunday, and he was off. Back to the regular routine now after his vacation. He had forgotten about how quiet the street was at this time when he walked home. It was damp and cool, and there was a freshness in the very air of the new and young day. He heard a bird chirping.

28

I

Danny walked into the Feinberg & O'Shaughnessy chain shoestore on State Street at ten o'clock on the dot. The store was pretty dead. The salesmen hung around waiting for the rush that would come later in the day. A tall Jewish salesman sat on his little stool, carefully fitting a fat woman.

"Good morning, Mr. Dorian," Danny said to the manager; he was a medium-sized gray-haired man and he was wearing a gray summer suit.

"Good morning. How's the uncle?" Mr. Dorian said; his eye traveled to the clock in the rear of the store.

"He's all right."

Danny walked to the cashier's cage in the rear of the store. He punched the time clock, hung up his hat and coat, rolled up his sleeves, and stood behind a caged-in counter next to the cashier's cage, ready for work. Miss Fiedelson was wearing a black dress. The moment he got behind his counter on Saturdays, he was aware of her right near him. He thought of her as watching his actions. All day as he wrapped shoes, he would have a sense of her in his mind, and she would act as a sort of audience. She was about eighteen or nineteen and awfully pretty, just the type he liked. She came up just about to his shoulder and was a little bit plump. She seemed to be ready to smile at almost any minute, and when she smiled she had a dimple in her chin. She had dark eyes, curly bobbed hair, and a nice figure. When he looked at her, he wanted to take her in his arms and hold her, pet her, run his fingers through her hair and kiss her. He didn't think of her for any more than that because he was sure she was a decent girl. She looked so sweet and innocent.

She looked up from some figuring she'd been doing and smiled a good-morning greeting to him, and he returned the smile. If it weren't for her, the prospect of the day ahead would be completely dull. He had to stand behind this counter all day and wrap shoes. He'd always been pretty clumsy with his hands, and he'd started in on this job without any confidence in his ability to do it well. He'd learned quickly enough, but he couldn't guarantee always to wrap a neat package and to be fast. It wasn't hard, but in about twenty or thirty minutes, the rush would start, and from then on he'd be busy all day and there'd be few breathing spells.

Miss Fiedelson pushed a pair of low-heeled woman's shoes over to him. He put the shoes together, made a neat package of them, and tied the bundle. He made a face. Trying to break the string, he'd run it over his finger, and it hurt. He never quit here on Saturday without having three or four cuts on his fingers. He stuck the bill under the string and set the package before the cage for the salesman to get it. He was learning, and today he ought to do better than he had on other Saturdays. This was his third one here.

Miss Fiedelson glanced at him. When their eyes met, she smiled cordially.

"I wish the day was over," he said.

"Why? It's only begun," she said.

"I'm going swimming tonight," he said, wanting her to think he was a guy who went places.

Another pair of shoes to wrap. He wrapped them and put the package in front of the cage.

She hummed a tune. After he learned to dance, he'd like to date her up, say for a dance on a date with Marty and his frat brothers. He'd introduce her to all of them. He could just imagine Marty Mulligan saying she was a sweet girl. And he saw himself taking her home in a cab, putting his arms around her, and kissing her.

Two more packages, one man's and the other, woman's shoes. He wrapped them speedily.

Through the cage he saw a blonde girl sitting on a bench, her leg out while a salesman tried on a shoe. A hot mama, all right. Shoe salesmen could get a few eyefuls now and then and they could touch girls' legs. They had a swell chance to get to know girls and date them up. He kind of envied shoe salesmen.

"Another PM. for me. I'm going places today," the dapper, redheaded salesman said, pushing a pair of high-heeled suede shoes through the cage to Miss Fiedelson.

She marked off the premium, made change, and slid the shoes over to Danny.

"Hi, boy!" the redheaded salesman said to him.

"Hello," he answered, wrapping the shoes.

He leaned over the counter and waited for more work. It was a long time to go until seven o'clock. He watched Miss Fiedelson out of the corner of his eye.

II

The redhead stood by the cage and talked to her. Danny wished he'd go away.

"Well, baby, how's tricks?" he asked.

"What tricks?" she replied.

Danny listened. He had to learn to get a line and he might learn a little from the redhead, even if he didn't like him.

"Tricks! Tricks!" the red-haired salesman said.

"I donno," she said.

"You got circles under your eyes. I'd hate to think what you were doing last night."

"Nothing," she said.

"Want me to believe that?"

"It's true."

"That makes it worse, then."

"Why?" she asked, flirtatiously.

"All that time's gone to waste. Last night was a nice night, moonlight, and that sort of thing, going to waste. And I wasn't doing anything either," the red-haired salesman said.

"Mr. Dorian is watching you," Miss Fiedelson said.

He walked off. She hummed a tune.

III

He sweated, and his shirt was wet. Pairs of shoes were piled up at his left, and he wrapped them as fast as he could. He had to start over again on a group of three pairs of men's brogues, and that gummed up the works.

Miss Fiedelson stepped over to him, and helped him. He struggled with the three pairs, and finally made an unwieldy bundle and pushed it out. Mr. Dorian was watching him, too. Another pair. This one he got more neatly. Another. The salesman kept dashing down with shoes and money. She was hopping now, too, and didn't get much chance to help him. He wished he didn't have to do this goddamned work. Why didn't he belong to a family that had lots of dough?

IV

He had three cuts on his first finger. Although he favored it, he kept forgetting and using his finger to break the string, hurting the raw spots more. Couldn't he ever learn to avoid this? Yes, he never could do things with his hands.

Well, soon it would be school, and then he'd play football on Saturdays and wouldn't have to work. But before that happened, he had to get to know Miss Fiedelson better and get her telephone number. He wished he could call her Louise and that she would call him Danny.

"Two P.M.'s, number seven," the tall, dark, Jewish salesman shouted, leaving the shoes and even change.

He dashed off.

The store was jammed.

"Five-fifty even," the red-haired salesman yelled, leaving a pair of shoes and shooting away.

Danny worked as speedily as he could, but he couldn't keep up now. The shoes to be wrapped were stacked at his side, and as fast as he wrapped one pair, another pair was pushed over to him.

Miss Fiedelson couldn't help him much either, because she had to make change, keep a record of the P.M.'s sold, and watch her cash because she was responsible for shortages. The salesmen kept telling him to snap it up, and the customers were waiting. Out front, he could see the people sitting in the rows of chairs, the salesmen measuring feet, rushing off and returning with boxes, trying on successive pairs.

"Try to pep it up, O'Neill," Mr. Dorian said, coming behind the cage.

"Yes, sir."

"He's very good, Mr. Dorian. We're just rushed to death today, we got so much business," Miss Fiedelson said.

Danny was grateful. His fingers hurt. He'd cut them again.

Mr. Dorian picked out a pair of shoes, wrapped a very neat bundle, broke the string with his fingers without hurting them, set them in front of the cage, and picked up two other pairs that went together in the same order and wrapped them efficiently.

"Watch the paper there. You use a lot of paper and string," Mr. Dorian said, working to help Danny catch up.

"Yes, sir," Danny said, going right ahead, folding over the paper, lapping down the ends, holding it, and running the string around the package.

"And try to make them neater. Your packages aren't always too neat," Mr. Dorian said.

"Yes, sir."

The rush was cleared up with Mr. Dorian's assistance. The boss walked away.

"He's a little cranky today," Miss Fiedelson said.

Another rush started. Danny sweated away, wrapping one package after another. But anyway, the busier it was, the sooner the day passed, and the quicker he would be finished.

V

One more hour to go. Now the rush petered out, and the last hour would go slower and slower. He looked at the clock again. Going on one minute after six. Sometimes the last two summers at the express company, he'd watched the clock that way. When you watched the clock and work was slow, time seemed almost to stand still.

"Well, I'll be glad when it's nine o'clock. You're lucky. You go home at seven. I stay until nine," Miss Fiedelson said.

"I'll be glad when it's seven," he said.

"And won't I be when it's nine," she said.

"All right, here you are, bright eyes, another P.M.," the red-haired salesman said.

"Oh, it's you again," she said.

"Quit flirting with the wrapping boy and take care of me, sister," he said.

Danny flushed. He wrapped up the shoes and gave them to the redhead.

"I'm ready to swoon," she said.

"Well, I'm going to like it swimming tonight," he said.

"I'll bet you're a devil with the girls," she said.

"Not at all," he said, trying to pass it off.

"I bet you are," she said.

He looked at the clock. Twenty after. Forty minutes to go.

VI

"Well, five minutes and I'm through," he said.

He wrapped a pair of low-heeled sport shoes. It was a neat bundle this time and maybe the last one for the day.

Three minutes to go.

"Yes, I'm not sorry the day's over and I can go," he said.

"Have a good time," she said.

"Don't worry, I will," he bragged.

He was getting so he could talk with her.

"Don't get drowned," she said.

"No danger," he said.

"And don't do anything I wouldn't do."

"What's that?" he asked, looking at her, smiling.

"You'd like to know," she said, winking at him.

"I couldn't even guess."

"I'll bet you might be able to."

And he liked her very much now, seeing her with that sweet smile, her perfect white teeth, her eyes so dark, the dimple in her chin so attractive when she smiled.

It was seven o'clock. He would like to stay on a little, now that he was talking to her this way.

"Well, you can go. You're released. But think of me, still two hours to go," she said.

"I'll pray for you," he kidded.

"Oh, don't do that. Maybe it'd be blasphemy."

"It couldn't be, not for you."

"You'll never know."

She hummed the tune of *It's Three O'Clock in the Morning*. He liked that.

He slowly rolled down his sleeves, put on his hat and coat, and punched his time card. She handed him an envelope containing three dollars.

"Good night, and have a good time."

"So long."

He wanted to add Louise. He didn't. He left the store, thinking that he could fall in love with her just as easy as he could with Natalie O'Reedy.

He walked to the Van Buren Street elevated station, thinking that all day he had wished for this moment, and now that it had come he wished he was back in the store, talking with Miss Fiedelson. He was going swimming with Young Rocky, but they probably wouldn't meet any girls tonight.

SECTION THREE

1922–1923

29

I

Hatless, with his hair vaselined, Danny stood chatting with the fellows on the corner near school. He wore his brownish gray suit with the belted coat.

"I don't know why Mike Flood's old man sent him to Middlehurst Military Academy," thin-faced, pale Ike Dugan said.

"Boy, I wouldn't want to be sent to that jail, no, sir," Marty Mulligan said.

"What'll his women do?" Red Keene asked; he was a rangy, callow sophomore.

"I'll take care of that," Ike said.

"You!" Danny exclaimed.

"Our All-American end," Red said.

Danny thought that this year he wanted to become All-Catholic end.

A newcomer in short trousers stopped and looked at the group.

"Cake-eaters!" he exclaimed.

He walked on. The fellows acted as if they hadn't heard him.

Danny wandered around the corner to the schoolyard. It was the same as ever, with the fence, the building, the handball court, the baskets for basketball. A regular opening-day sight. The yard crowded, and timid newcomers all over, most of them in short trousers. He remembered his own first day at S.S. He had been leary when he entered this yard. Then he was fifteen. Now he was eighteen years old, a senior, one of the leading athletes in school. And this was his year. Danny strutted around the yard and then back out to the corner.

"Hello, Dope," Tim Doolan said.

"The bow-legged cavalry sergeant is back," Danny said.

"Well, boys, in a couple of minutes we'll all go back to jail," Tommy Collins said.

"You barely missed jail in Ireland this summer, didn't you, Tommy?" Ike said.

"Yes, sir. They had a revolution there. They called it the troubles. It wasn't any fun."

"It must be fun traveling," Danny said, wistfully wondering if he would ever travel, would ever cross the ocean as Tommy had done.

"Did you get seasick and puke up Doolan all over the boat?" Marty Mulligan asked, laughing.

"No, he crapped up Mulligan," Tim said.

"Well, my hearties, we ain't got many more minutes of freedom left," Tommy Collins said.

They heard the bell and straggled along to the schoolyard.

II

Joe McBride faced a formation of thirty-five Saint Stanislaus students on the Jackson Park baseball field. Joe was a broad and burly man, built like a barrel. The students waited for orders. Danny, Tim, Marty, and other veterans of last year wore brand-new football suits. Others wore the suits left over from last season, and a few wore makeshift suits or else old clothes of their own.

"All right, you fellows! Duck walk! Duck walk!" Joe yelled, megaphoning through his hands.

They squatted, and walked with bent knees in a squatting position. Some of them kept losing their balance and toppling. Earnestly, they duck-walked in circles. It seemed as if they had done it for a long period. Joe watched them, his face impassive.

"A little more ginger in your behinds there," he yelled.

He kept them at it for about eight minutes.

"All right, stand up!"

Relieved, they stood up.

The calisthenics continued.

III

"Well, how do you like being back in the harness, Dan?"

"I never did like this part of it, this damned duck-walking, calisthenics, and the rest of it."

Danny and Joe were going back to school, and Joe, beside Danny, walked in a rolling, almost waddling, manner.

"You got to get in condition," Joe said.

"But still, you don't have to like it. It's dull."

"I suppose you go around and complain to all the fellows that you don't like it."

"What do you mean, Joe?" Danny asked, surprised.

"Don't you see that an attitude like that hurts the morale of the team? I don't want one of my veterans to go around complaining."

"I wasn't complaining, I was just saying that, hell, I don't like the dull stuff we got to do."

"You got to like it on my team," Joe said, sore.

Danny didn't see why Joe should get sore. Hell, you had to be a damned dope to like these preliminary workouts. Ten laps around the field, squatting, getting up, squatting, getting up, running with your knees in the air, and all the rest of it.

"Joe, I'd rather play fullback this year than end," Danny said.

"I'm running this team."

"But I thought I might be better at full than at end."

"I'll do all the thinking that's necessary on this team."

"But I was thinking, particularly on defense, I might be more useful."

"I'll decide who's useful and where on this team. All you got to do is to go out and learn how to play football."

Danny didn't say anything. He walked beside Joe to the showers.

IV

"O'Neill."

Danny turned and saw Father Jim motioning to him in the third-floor corridor. He didn't like Father Jim. He was a small and nervous priest with glasses, dark hair, and a large mouth.

"I notice that your tuition isn't paid for this quarter or for the final quarter of last year."

"My uncle just forgot. I'll tell him, Father."

"All right, O'Neill, I just wanted to remind you. I was checking through my books last night and I noticed it."

Danny walked off, ashamed. Father Jim might mention it to the other priests. Uncle Al wasn't doing so well and he'd said that the tuition would have to wait until later.

V

Danny got off the elevated train at Fifty-eighth Street. He began walking down the stairs slowly, carefully. He was so damned stiff that he could hardly move. He felt the muscles in his legs. A charley horse in both legs. His whole body was tired. It was just like last year after the first few days of practice. Slowly, he descended the stairs, limping, holding on to the banister. He walked stiffly and slowly out of the station. Some fellows were in front of the poolroom. They'd see him this way and know he was a football player.

"What's the matter with you, O'Neill? You walk like you had your pants full of crap," dapper Phil Rolfe said.

"I got charley horses from football," Danny casually answered.

"Who the hell do you play football with?" asked Rolfe.

"Saint Stanislaus," Danny answered modestly.

"Expect us to believe that crap?"

Danny thought that he would like to tackle Phil Rolfe just once, that was all. He walked away stiffly, his thigh muscles paining him as he moved.

"There goes the All-American drawback," Phil Rolfe said.

VI

"Al, he couldn't even walk up the stairs," Mrs. O'Flaherty said at supper.

"Oh, I just got charley horses. They'll go 'way. Everybody gets charley horses when you start training."

"What do you play on the team, fall guy?" Ned asked.

"I'm end."

"What the hell good is it going to do you to play football and get half killed?" Ned asked.

"I'm not half killed."

"Last night you went to bed at seven-thirty, dead to the world."

"That's because of the training we're doing. We got to get into condition, don't we?"

"Did you hear that, Al? Getting into condition! Cripes, I never heard tell of that one before. He can't hardly walk home, and he crawls into bed, and he calls that getting into condition."

Danny sulked.

"If you get a broken leg, will the school pay your doctor bill and for the hospital?"

"No, they can't afford it," Danny said.

"Al, did you ever hear the beat of that?"

They just didn't understand how he felt.

"Al, don't let him play," Mrs. O'Flaherty said.

"What the hell do you want to play football for?"

"I'm doing it for my school."

Uncle Ned looked at him in bewilderment and then laughed.

Danny finished supper and hobbled to his room. He wanted to go to bed. He didn't dare to, lest they see how tired he was. His eyelids seemed heavy. He was stiff all over. He determined that he was going to play football whether or not they gave him permission. He didn't care what they said. If they didn't let him play football, he wouldn't go to school. He'd run away from school, go on the bum, hop freight trains, and fix them. He didn't care what they said, he'd play football.

He telephoned Marty Mulligan and arranged to go to Marty's.

"Where you going?" Uncle Al asked.

"To Marty Mulligan's.

"Haven't you any lessons?"

"I'm going to do them with Marty."

"Well, see that you get home early."

He left by the front door, slowly and painfully walking down the steps. He didn't have any money. He'd meant to ask, but after what was said at supper, he didn't dare to. He thought he'd go over to Mama's. Mama might give him something. Maybe he and Marty would go to a movie, if he could only stay awake.

VII

"Got a date yet for the party?" Ike Dugan asked Danny, sitting with him at the Greek's Ice Cream parlor during the lunch period.

"No, I haven't bothered yet," Danny replied casually.

"Well, I dated up Ella McGrail. She's a wonderful kid."

"Yes, she is," Danny said.

The party was a couple of weeks off. But here it was, time for another frat party, and he still couldn't dance. The whole summer had passed without his having had a date or learned to dance. What was he going to do about it now? If things went on this way, he'd never be able to dance.

He let his tongue play around his decayed teeth. The cavities on both sides of his mouth were getting bigger. He ought to get them fixed. Gee, as it was, things were bad enough at home, and Uncle Al still hadn't paid his tuition. How could he get Uncle Al to pay a dentist's bill?

"Boy, hasn't the frat grown? We got two chapters now, and it's only a year old. And Mac says we ought to have a Pullman chapter, too, and get some more guys from school who live out there."

"Yes, it has. It was a good idea to have one chapter of the fellows in school and the other of those who work," Danny said.

VIII

Danny walked along North Clark Street, past stores, cheap hotels and cabarets, looking for the dancing school he'd picked from the classified telephone directory. He reasoned with himself that no one would know that he'd learned how to dance this way. Still, he felt almost as badly as if he were going to a dentist. Well, he was determined to go through with it. He would be able to dance for the party. But whom would he take? Natalie? He was a little leary about asking her for fear she'd say no.

Right at this minute, the squad was out practicing. All last year he had skipped practice only once, and that was after the Saint Luke game, when he was so shot that he had to go home at noon and go to bed. If Joe McBride only knew that his star end had cut practice to take dancing lessons!

He found his address in the 400 north block. He climbed a stairway to the second floor and stood before a girl at a desk who was asking him his name.

"Daniel Smith," he answered, not knowing why he hadn't given his real name.

"All right, Mr. Smith, that will cost you one dollar," she said, writing and ringing a bell.

A drab and slightly stout girl appeared.

"Miss Cox, this is Mr. Smith. Will you take him?"

"How do you do, Mr. Smith."

"How do you do," he answered shyly.

He followed Miss Cox into a small, bare room. The floor was waxed, and there was a scratched victrola in one corner.

"Have you ever danced, Mr. Smith?" she asked him, closing the door.

Why hadn't he gotten a prettier girl to teach him to dance instead of this one? Well, she didn't know him from Adam, and he was here for a purpose, and that was all there was to it. Still, he wished that he hadn't come.

"No, I never did."

"Well, I think we ought to start with the waltz. That's the simplest dance to learn," she said.

He faced her, his stance awkward.

"Mr. Smith, the waltz steps are very easy. You start with your left foot like this," she illustrated standing beside him. "You take a short step like this with your left foot." She took a step. "And then you draw your right foot to meet the left, and then you take a short step with your left foot, and then with your right, and bring your left to meet the right, and you keep doing it that way, left foot, right, short left step, right. Do you understand that?"

"Yes," he said shaking his head, but confused.

"Before I put on the music, try it with me," she said.

He clasped her in a dance embrace.

"Now left, right, left," she said.

He got all mixed up and stepped on her toe.

"Watch me, Mr. Smith."

She seemed annoyed as she illustrated again. He wondered, was she quietly laughing at him and thinking that he was just a chump, maybe some hick just in from the country.

"All right, try it again," she said.

Again he clasped her in a dance embrace.

"Left, right, left, right, left, right," she repeated, stepping with him.

She freed herself and stepped back.

"That's better. Now let me see you do it by yourself."

If anybody he knew saw him now, they'd get a good laugh. Well, he didn't care. He had to learn this, and he would.

"Go ahead now."

He tried, seriously and with determination. His legs were stiff, and he moved without rhythm. He swung his left foot out from him, and then slid his right foot over to meet it. He slid his left foot forward a few inches. He slid his right foot forward and at an angle in a longer stride, and brought his left foot together with the right foot.

"Good. Now we'll try it to music," she said after he had repeated these steps for the length of the room.

She wound the victrola and put on a record.

"That's a nice record," he said, hearing the first bars of *It's Three O'Clock in the Morning.*

He tried the steps with her to the music. She seemed to be so limber, so lithe, so easy on her feet. He felt himself to be so clumsy. His feet seemed to be much bigger than they really were.

"You were doing good and you missed. Now start again," she said.

He tried again. Stiff as he was, he was getting one step down. If he learned this step, he could pick up the others later. In time he'd dance as gracefully as Marty Mulligan.

"All right, now try it again, Mr. Smith."

He tried, seeing his feet in his mind, his big gunboats. He was ashamed of the size of his feet. He was without grace, just a damned oaf. Well, if others could learn, he could.

"All right now, Mr. Smith, one two, one, one two, one, one two, one," she singsonged while Danny tried diligently.

IX

Danny got off the elevated train at Fifty-eighth and went over to Prairie Avenue. He was determined to do it this minute. Before he did anything else, he would get a date. All the way home from his dancing lesson he'd rehearsed what he'd say. Now it was do or die.

Eleanor Feinberg was behind the counter in the Walgreen Drugstore. She was sweet and he liked her.

"Hello," he said.

He was able to talk to her, and that was more than he was able to do with some girls. If he didn't get the date, he might ask her. When she smiled, her dimpled chin was awfully pretty. "I haven't seen you so much of late," she said.

"I've been busy. We got football practice every day, and I'm pretty tired after it," he said.

"Where do you play?"

"Saint Stanislaus," he said.

"On the school team?"

"Yes," he said casually.

"Isn't that wonderful! I'm just crazy about football."

"I'll take you to a game sometime," he said casually.

"I'd love to go, but I have to work every Saturday afternoon."

"Can't you get off one Saturday?"

"No, I couldn't. Are you going to play with Rocky and the fellows on Sunday afternoons, too?"

"That team?" he said with contempt.

"Aren't they any good?"

"They aren't trained and coached. Can I have two nickels?" He pushed a dime through the cage, and she gave him two nickels.

"I know what you're going to do," she said, smiling knowingly.

"Nope, I'm just going to call a fellow up."

He strutted off and down to the phone booths in a corner. He bent over the book, to look up her number. He got it. He lost his breath. He could do it tomorrow and he'd have time to think up what to say. He stood before the booth, feeling helpless, hopeless, like a goof. He couldn't risk being turned down.

He plunged into the telephone booth, dropped his nickel in the slot, and waited, breathless, telling himself that he would cross the Rubicon.

X

"Hello, Natalie?"

"Yes."

He liked the sweet, gentle voice coming through the phone.

"This is Danny O'Neill."

"Oh, hello. I haven't seen you since that beach party."

"I know it. How are you?"

"I'm fine, thanks. How are you?"

Now what? He'd often heard that it was best to talk a while before you sprung the question for the date.

"Natalie, my frat is giving a party. It's a surprise party for one of the fellows, Tommy Collins, and . . . would you like to go with me?"

"When is it?"

"Two weeks from Friday?"

"Why, yes, I'd love to go."

And as simple as that.

"I'll call for you about nine o'clock, is that all right?"

"You say it's two weeks from Friday, just a minute."

"Yes," he said, suddenly plunged into gloom.

"Oh, two weeks from Friday, now let's see, yes," she said.

While he waited he tried to think up something insulting to say in case she changed her mind now after giving him the date.

"You remember Roslyn Hayes?"

"Yes, of course."

"Her father and mother are going to be away that weekend, and she's going to stay with me. Do you think you could get a fellow for her?"

He relaxed.

"I don't know. I'll try. One of the fellows in our frat knows Glenn, but he's away at school, Mike Flood."

"Oh, he's nice."

"Yes, he's a swell fellow. I'll try to get one of the fellows and I'll call you and let you know. And anyway, I'll call for you two weeks from Friday at nine o'clock."

"Yes, Danny."

There was a pause.

"Well, goodbye."

"Goodbye, and thank you, Danny."

He came out of the booth, all smiles. He tried to hum *My Wild Irish Rose.* The song was like Natalie, and Natalie was like the song, and he wished it was the night of the party already. He'd fall in love with her, and she would be his girl.

XI

"O'Neill, since you've missed practice two days this week, you can do ten laps around the field," Joe said very sharply. Some of the squad laughed. "And the rest of you fellows wipe the grins off your face. If you don't take this team seriously, you can turn in your uniform. I don't care how good you think you are."

Danny started jogging slowly around the Jackson Park field. Ten laps was a pretty long jolt to give him. He ran at a slow trot. If he thought of Natalie, it would be easier, because he wouldn't notice anything else, and it wouldn't be boring.

He trotted down to the baseball backstop at the south end of the field, and alongside the backstop, and then around the farther edge of the grass bordering the field. The squad was practicing fundamentals on the patch of grass beyond the skin baseball field, and near the fenced-in playground. Danny trotted to that end of the field. Joe suddenly appeared behind him, snapping at his legs with a switch.

"I said run, not crawl. Pep it up," Joe yelled. While the squad laughed, Joe pursued Danny for about a hundred yards. Danny ran to escape the switch, and then when Joe left off, he fell back to a jog trot and slowly pounded around the field, wondering if his wind would hold out, and thinking of Natalie.

XII

Danny joined the squad. Despite his ten laps, he felt fresh and peppy. All his swimming last summer had done him good. He'd always had good wind, though. He stood with hands on hips in a circle, while Joe threw the ball toward one or another player who fell on it. Joe rolled it toward him. He went for it, twisted his body sidewise, left his feet, encircled the ball with his arms, slid on the ground, and curled up around the ball. He knew he'd done it correctly. He got up casually and tossed the ball to Joe.

"Now form a double line, facing one another," Joe ordered.

Danny stood facing Ike. He knew what was coming and was glad he happened to get Ike. Since they didn't have a tackling machine, they had to be each other's dummies for tackling practice.

Joe walked along between the two rows of players. He stopped before Danny and Ike.

"Dugan, you come out of there."

Ike stepped forward. Danny grinned. Joe was going to make it harder for him. Joe walked on with Ike at his side and halted before Fireman Fagin, a third-year fellow who was the heaviest man on the squad. Fagin came down to face Danny. Joe took a position at one end of the double line.

"Now, you fellows take turns tackling. When I blow a whistle, first one side and then the other side tackles by turn. You take one step forward, leave your feet, and when you tackle, you drive your shoulder into the other fellow's midriff."

He blew his whistle. Fireman took a step. Danny relaxed to be better prepared for the shock. Fireman Fagin smacked Danny down with his one hundred and eighty pounds. Danny was shaken up. He remembered this same practice last year, the way he would get knocked down, get up, get knocked down, have a shoulder driven into his guts, and how he would gasp and ache and wish for it to end.

He liked the other half of it, though. There was no thrill in sport to match leaving your feet, flying through the air, and hitting a man clean and hard. The idea in tackling was to tackle your man every time so that you knocked him out.

The whistle.

Danny took a step and flew at Fagin. He crashed into him and set him sprawling. He got up, his face grim. He turned and walked back into position.

It went on. Fagin and Danny both hit hard, and by turn they rammed into one another. Danny's head was aching. His guts were sore. His charley horses bothered him again. He ached and was sore all over. He would get set, and then he would be knocked into the hard ground with all the force of Fagin's bone and muscles.

And Fagin's heavier weight counted, too.

He didn't blame the Fireman for hitting hard. He had to. Joe was walking back and forth bawling out anyone who didn't hit hard enough.

The tackling practice went on, cruel and relentless. First one side smashed into the other, and then the reverse. Many members of the squad would pick up their bruised and tired bodies slowly. There was no rest. The whistle was the cruel signal. One side, and then the other. Danny gritted his teeth and waited each time for the Fireman to plunge, driving his broad shoulders into Danny's guts. Bang, he went down, his entire organism rocked by the shock of the collision. He would wearily pick himself up and wait for the whistle for his turn, and then he would drive into the Fireman. The Fireman's weight told on Danny, but because of his broad shoulders, Danny was more powerful than his actual weight indicated. He would drive these shoulders into Fagin's solar plexus each time he tackled, and Fagin would slowly get up and shake himself from the shock.

Joe went back and forth, his face stern, his manner clipped, barking out words, bawling out the sloppy tacklers.

"That's enough. Sit down and rest a few minutes, and then we'll have signals."

The weary squad of youths gratefully dropped onto the grass.

30

I

Jim moved about the house. He had never been nervous in his life, but now he was a nervous man. He was losing weight. He could see how skinny his arms were getting. He looked at his wrists. These weren't the same wrists he used to have. He was losing his appetite. At work, he had dizzy spells. Yes, he was just a worn-out machine. Ah, he could remember now with such pain the confident days of his youth when he didn't give two good goddamns for tomorrow. Sometimes when he passed the young fellows in front of the poolroom, he thought of this, and he figured that these young fellows had the same devil-don't-care attitude that he'd had. He knew a few of them, like that Doyle lad, and others only by name, like that kid Studs Lonigan. They made him angry, but still he felt sorry for them. One of the consolations he had was that Bill wasn't that way.

He didn't know what to do with himself, and he moved restlessly about the parlor.

The last time he'd seen Dr. Mike Geraghty, Mike had said his condition was about the same. He didn't trust that man, didn't have confidence in him. The reason he had Mike was because Lizz called him that time he'd had the stroke.

Jim sat down and looked out the window at the sunny September day. He was a prisoner. He felt himself chained up within his own body and his own mind. He was a lonely prisoner in life. Yes, he was the prisoner and the captive of death. And when would it come to him? Why couldn't he shake off these moods? Why did they have to come to him so often? Why, when he would be thinking of something else, going along, working, talking with Lizz or the kids, doing something, why, then, would this mood come back? Why would he suddenly tell himself that he was through? Why would he think of death? Why would he feel the passing of time as he did? Other men his age didn't. Pete didn't seem to keep thinking of how time was passing, and of how the passing of time meant the passing of your own life, the ebbing away of your strength. At work, every time he laughed at a joke or a wisecrack he felt that he wasn't really laughing. He felt that his grin was empty, hollow, and that everyone could see that it was. Once when he'd been a young buck, he'd had a tooth in the front of his mouth knocked out in a saloon fight. He remembered how, while that tooth was out, he'd felt that there was a great big hole in the center of his mouth. He'd felt self-conscious about laughing. He'd felt then that when he laughed, he looked like hell with that wide space in his mouth. He had found it hard to laugh. The reasons now were different, but he had the same kind of a feeling about his laughing. He would suddenly find himself in a daze. He would snap out of it and wonder what he had been thinking about. And he couldn't even remember what had been in his mind the minute before. He would come out of such a daze feeling the same kind of sadness he so often felt after a nap, as if the troubles of a dream remained when he woke up.

It used to be that when he got to feeling low, he'd go out on a drunk. After he had stowed away enough booze, had a good fight or raised some hell, he'd be all right. He was tempted many times these days to get drunk, forget it all, and paint up the town with scarlet. But now he didn't. Now it was too serious for him to drink. He couldn't gamble with his health and his blood pressure now, because there was too much dependent on him, his kids, his wife. If he collapsed, they would be sunk in poverty and have no one. No, he had to fight this out with himself, and he couldn't go off on a bat.

And Jesus God, what was he going to do?

He was acting like a coward. He wasn't a coward. He wasn't afraid for himself. He didn't give a damn for himself. There wasn't a man alive who could say that Jim O'Neill was a coward. He remembered that fight he'd had once when he was having some drinks in a saloon on the West Side. Some guy had pulled a knife on him. He'd gone at that fellow, grabbed his wrist, twisted it until he dropped the knife, and kicked the hell out of him, and turned to his friends and everyone in the saloon and asked them if anyone else wanted to mix with him. And then, with his head high, he had slowly walked out of the saloon. He wasn't a coward.

To be, or not to be, that is the question;

My God, that was a wonderful speech of Hamlet's.

Sicklied o'er with the pale cast of thought . . .

That was him. Every time he looked at his kids, he almost wanted to cry. A lump would rise in his throat. They didn't know. They'd never know, except perhaps Bill. Bill would understand. Maybe they all would when they got to be grown men and women and came into the autumn of life. What sometimes riled him so about Danny was that Danny, thanks to the O'Flahertys, could never understand any of this. How could he know? With all the dude notions that filled his conceited little head! How could a son of his be that way, swagger and strut and walk about like the cock of the walk? Good Jesus Christ, you'd think that that conceited puppy was the son of John D. Rockefeller. The boy thought that his old man didn't notice, didn't catch on, didn't know the tricks of this world. He came over with his hair full of grease, and now he had sideburns. He showed himself up with his walk. And with his going around without a hat the way the college guys did according to the pictures of them in the papers. What the hell was schooling coming to? He had always thought that schooling was to give you an education, develop your brains, help you to be something and somebody other than a conceited snob.

He stared idly out the window. An old lady passed, leaning on a cane as she walked. He felt sorry for her. He didn't have to be having such thoughts. It was all unnecessary. He was just worrying himself. Why, he would go on for years yet. Despite all the hard luck he had had, all the worries, misfortunes, troubles, he was destined to pull through. He went out to see Lizz in the dining room.

"Lizz, can you fix my lunch, and I'll take it with me."

"But, Jim, it's so early."

"I just thought I'd see a movie."

"Will you have time for that, Jim? It's around three o'clock."

"Well, I can see part of a show."

"All right, I'll fix it quicker than you can say Jack Robinson."

"Lizz, don't put any meat in it," he said.

"Why, Jim, I have some nice hamburger left over from supper last night."

"No, I don't want any meat. You know, Mike Geraghty says that I oughtn't to eat it."

"Say, who cares what that horse doctor thinks? A little hamburger won't do you any harm."

"No, Lizz, you better not. I don't feel like eating any meat. Make me lettuce and tomato sandwiches."

"I haven't any in the house," she said.

"I'll go across the street and get some."

"All right. But, Jim, are you well, are you all right?"

"Sure, I'm fit as a fiddle. I've felt well as all hell since I had my vacation and got a nice rest."

"A little hamburger won't do you any harm."

"No, Liz, I don't feel like eating any tonight. I'll have lettuce and tomato sandwiches. I like them, you know."

"Whatever you say goes, only I saved this hamburger from last night for your lunch."

"The kids can eat it. I'll be right back."

He put on his coat and went out for lettuce and tomatoes.

II

Catherine would be disappointed because she wouldn't be able to walk to the station with him tonight. Well, he better see Doctor Mike and find out if there was anything wrong with him. And he didn't want to tell Lizz where he was going, because there wasn't any use in worrying her. And it was such a nice day, he might as well walk over. He had the time.

Jim wore an old gray suit and a khaki shirt without any tie. He had his old teamster's cap set evenly on his head. He walked along, slow and lazy, conscious of his limp. He hated to go to the doctor. Every time he went, he was worried that the doctor would find out something and tell him he was worse. But suppose he was? Would not knowing it help him any? Suppose he was? Suppose his days were numbered? They still didn't have a penny saved up.

Why in the name of God couldn't Lizz save some money?

A nursemaid passed him, wheeling a baby buggy. He remembered the first time he'd pushed one. It was a Sunday. He'd had on his Sunday best and put Bill in a buggy. He'd felt like a rummy. He'd felt that a grown man shouldn't wheel a baby buggy. He'd thought that the men on the corners and in front of the saloons were laughing at him, and he recalled how he'd set himself to step up to the first fellow who laughed at him and poke him square in the nose. And nobody had paid any attention to him particularly. Fellows he knew had nodded or said hello. He had wheeled the buggy with Lizz at his side. Bill had been a cute little bugger, too, and he had been gurgling away. But before they'd gotten home, Bill had wet himself and was bawling and yelling at the top of his lungs.

And Bill was a grown man now.

At Fifty-seventh, Jim turned toward Prairie Avenue. He could smell autumn in the air. It was as if the feeling of autumn crept into a man's bones, into a man's very soul. A cop strolled along in front of him. Several kids passed, yelling and cursing at one another. He looked around and saw that they were imitating his limp.

"Go on, you little alley cats or I'll break your faces in," he called at them.

"Limpey! Limpey! Limpey!" a dirty-faced kid yelled at him.

"I told you to beat it before I crack your pusses in," he shouted at them.

"You got to catch us first," the dirty-faced kid yelled at him.

He started after them, and they ran. Seeing that he couldn't catch them, he gave it up.

"Go hop in the bowl and pull the chain, Limpey!" the dirty-faced kid yelled.

Jim was flushed with anger. He turned and walked on, slowly, to hide his limp.

31

I

Danny came out of Walgreen's drugstore after having telephoned Natalie. He started toward home. He had said he couldn't do anything about getting Roslyn a date for the party on Friday night. Well, the worm had turned for once. He hadn't even tried to do anything about it. That was payment to her for hardly ever speaking to him when they were in grammar school. What in the devil had he seen in Roslyn when Natalie was in the same school? Why, alongside of Natalie, what was Eleanor Feinberg or Miss Fiedelson either?

"Hello, Dan."

Danny turned and saw his father near the entrance to the Fifty-eighth Street elevated station. Jim was unshaven and wearing his work clothes. He had his lunch wrapped up under his arm. Danny was ashamed of his father's appearance. He wouldn't want Natalie or his fraternity brothers to see his father going to work dressed this way.

"You haven't been over to see us of late," Jim said.

"Until this week I was busy every day after school with football practice. But now Uncle Al said I got to give it up and can't play on the team," Danny answered; as he spoke, he noticed that his father's eyes were a little sunken and that he looked pretty thin.

"Well, I've been thinking about it. It won't hurt you not to. You might get some broken bones. And besides, you can work Saturday in the shoestore if you don't play."

Danny didn't answer. No use trying to talk back to Papa. It was even easier to argue with Uncle Al than with Papa.

"Well, I have to be getting along to work. But come over and see me. So long, Dan."

"Goodbye, Pa," Danny said, watching Jim limp over to the entrance doors of the station.

Jim couldn't push the heavy swinging doors with his hands. He turned slightly and shoved through them with his left shoulder.

Danny walked off. His father wasn't well or strong any more. He was stronger than Pa and could push through the elevated station doors more easily.

He had never stopped to think that some day Pa would get old, or sick, or become weak. He felt that perhaps his father wouldn't live very long. Papa was weak. He had never realized this until a few minutes ago when he'd watched his father.

The image of his father struggling against those doors persisted in his mind and made him sad. He felt sorry for Papa. He remembered how when he worked at the express company and Papa was up there, he was slow in keeping sheets, and sometimes Pa wouldn't hear well. But he had never thought much about it until now. Now he could see that it might be serious. If anything happened to Papa, it would be terrible. He'd have to quit school and go to work, and even then it would be awful hard because he couldn't make enough money to take Pa's place, and neither could Bill.

He climbed the back stairs, still thinking of his father.

"Were you playing that pagan football again?" Mrs. O'Flaherty asked when he entered the kitchen.

"No, I wasn't," he answered crossly.

"When you talk to me, you can keep a civil tongue in your head."

II

Danny came out of the delicatessen on Sixty-third Street where he'd just eaten lunch. He met Marty Mulligan, and they strolled idly back to school.

"I copped some of my old man's wine for the party tonight," Marty said proudly.

"Swell. Don't forget me."

"Hell, I go for the idea, seeing you maggoty."

Danny grinned.

They met Hugh McNeill. He had long sideburns and bell bottoms.

"Say, Danny, what the hell is this business about you not playing tomorrow against Saint Luke's?" Hugh asked.

"My uncle and my old man both said I can't play this year."

"Can't you play anyway?"

"How?"

"He has to work in the shoestore tomorrow. Hell, with the party and having to get up early, he'll be a wreck."

"Listen, you can stay at my house tonight. Don't go to work tomorrow. The team needs you. And the frat meeting is at your house Monday. I'll fix it up with your folks. They like me. You got to do this. You got to for the honor of the school. You got to do it, Dan, for our frat. We got to have as many of our frat brothers on the team as we can. And since Tim Doolan is hurt, you and Marty got to go out there tomorrow and hold up for us," Hugh said, talking like a cheer leader.

Danny looked from one to the other. There were things more important than obeying Uncle Al and Pa. Suppose he played and they found out? Well, even if they raised hell, wouldn't it be worth it? He was eighteen, old enough to have some independence.

"I'll play."

"That's the stuff. Shake, and it's for our frat," Hugh said, and they shook, using the complicated fraternity grip.

Marty patted him on the back.

III

Danny had waited until the squad was dressed and out on the practice field before he put on his football togs. Alone in the damp locker and shower room, he saw himself as resembling a character in a book. His life was now beginning to unfold almost like a story in a book. A party tonight, and he was taking as sweet a girl as anyone described in a story. And now he'd play in the opening game. The captain, Tim Doolan, was hurt. He was the star end. Everything looked dark. And he shows up to play. Maybe tomorrow he would play the game of his career and win it for S.S. singlehanded.

He left the school building and began trotting over to Jackson Park, his cleats scraping on the sidewalk. When he got near the park, he halted to get his wind. He walked slowly, his gait drooping, his expression noncommittal. He wanted them to notice his casual and nonchalant appearance at practice after having quit the squad. He wanted to be nonchalant in athletics as in everything else. The team was running signals on the Jackson Park ball field, and no one noticed Danny until he joined the subs following behind the regular eleven.

"Joe, I'm going to play tomorrow," Danny said.

Joe turned and looked at him for a moment, surprised.

"All right, follow along with the others, O'Neill."

"Father Theo out today?" he asked Ike Dugan.

"No, I saw him go off some place."

"I wanted to tell him I was going to play tomorrow," Danny said.

"Boy, you got guts," Tim Doolan said, joining him. "You just walked up and say you're going to play, after being away from practice for a week. You'd think you was running the team."

Tim was not in uniform. He had wrenched his shoulder playing Sunday football out in Pullman. He held his shoulder in close to his body, and every so often he winced.

"Well, I'm playing tomorrow."

"That's the stuff, O'Neill," Tim said, patting Danny's back.

"O'Neill, take over right end," Joe ordered.

Danny took his place in the lineup.

IV

Red Keene and Ike Dugan had promised to call for him in Red's old Ford at a quarter to nine, and here it was, nine-thirty already, and they hadn't shown up. Where were they? What would Natalie think, being kept waiting so long?

He looked out the parlor window, anxiously watching the stream of passing automobiles. Suppose they had had an accident and couldn't get here, and he didn't hear, and he kept waiting and he never did get to call for Natalie? But then maybe it was just as well, and you ought to keep a girl waiting a while. If you did, then maybe she'd like you better.

He paced back and forth across the darkened parlor. He turned on the light. He counted his money, five dollars. Mother had given him some money, Mama had given him a dollar, and so had Uncle Al. He could take a cab home, if necessary. What time would they come? He went back to the window.

Twenty minutes to ten. He rushed to telephone Natalie.

"Hello, Natalie, this is Danny O'Neill. I called to tell you I'm going to be a little bit late. The fellows who were supposed to call for me haven't come, but they ought to be here any minute."

"Why, that's all right. I'll be here, and thank you for calling to let me know."

He hung up. He sat by the phone, wondering if he had done the wrong thing in telephoning her.

The phone rang. He grabbed it eagerly.

"Hello."

"O'Neill, this is Red. I'm going to be late. I'm just starting after you now," Red said.

"Well, hurry up."

"All right, I couldn't help it, keep your shirt on."

Red hung up. Well, anyway, they were on the way.

He practiced waltz steps in the parlor. He'd taken a few lessons, but he wasn't sure of himself about dancing. Well, he had to trust to luck. Maybe he wouldn't be as bad as he expected. If you didn't trust to luck sometimes, you never got anywhere in this world.

V

The party was being held in a large basement room at Tommy Collins' home because it offered the best dancing space. Danny stood facing some of the girls who sat together primly on a couch. Most of the fellows had left the basement and gone upstairs to the kitchen to drink wine and try to feel up Emma Munn, the tramp Marty had brought to the party.

"Where's everybody?" Josephine Flanagan asked.

"Around," Danny answered.

Josephine was at the party as Tommy Collins' date. She was supposed to be the keenest girl at Saint Paul's. Bobbed-haired, pretty, insouciant, she was wearing a red dress which made her doubly attractive. Natalie, wearing a black velvet dress, sat beside Josephine. Danny decided he wouldn't trade Natalie for Josephine. Two other Saint Paul girls were also with them, Madelaine Tracy and Pauline Sweeney.

Danny glanced from one to the other. He struggled with himself to think up something clever to say. His eyes met those of Pauline Sweeney. He shifted his gaze quickly. He was afraid of her. She was supposed to be snooty and sharp-tongued. She was bovine and sat at the edge of the couch utterly at ease and contented with herself.

"Some of us got to play football tomorrow," Danny said, hoping Natalie would say she wanted to see the game.

Natalie smiled formally, but neither she nor the others spoke.

"And, boy, if our coach knew what we were doing tonight . . . well, he wouldn't like it nohow."

Again Natalie smiled but said nothing.

Feeling that he had to do something with his hands, Danny stuck them in his pockets. He wished he could get away. He couldn't stand in front of these girls and act like a mummy. And he couldn't think of what to say to excuse himself.

"This bunch will get better marks for parties than they will for their studies in class," he said.

"One can get good marks and still go to parties," Natalie said.

"I guess so. But who cares what marks he gets so long as he gets by?" Danny said.

"I do," Natalie answered.

"You do?"

"Of course. Only I don't get good marks in math. I wish I did, but I don't. Ever since I was at Saint Patrick's, I was never good at anything connected with math."

"I used to do pretty good in math back in the days when I studied," Danny said casually.

"What do you mean? Don't you ever study?" Natalie asked.

"I never crack a book," Danny said, imagining himself a real nonchalant.

The three girls sat. They disconcerted him. He wanted to impress them.

"But I ride a swell pony in Latin," he said, laughing.

Tommy Collins and Ike came over. Tommy held out his hand and pulled up Josephine Flanagan, and they danced.

"O'Neill, do you mind if I dance with Natalie?" Ike asked.

"Why, no," he said.

"May I?" he asked Natalie.

"Do you mind?" she asked, looking at Danny.

"Of course not, Natalie."

He saw Ike dance off with her. He walked across the basement feeling like a clown. He'd been as big a bust dancing tonight as he'd been with Anna Sheehan. He went upstairs to join the gang in the kitchen.

"Who's this?" Emma asked in a loud voice; she was a skinny blonde, not particularly good-looking.

"Don't you know Danny O'Neill?" Marty asked.

"No, I don't," she said.

"Well, there he is. Now you do," Marty said.

"I know you," she said, pointing at Red Keene and ignoring Danny.

"It's all right knowing that big dumb redhead, but don't forget, baby, I took you here," Marty said.

"You ain't dumb, are you, Red?" she asked.

He grinned.

"Sure he's dumb," Danny said.

"You ain't been asked to be heard from," Emma snapped at Danny.

He sulked. What the hell was she? She was no good. Marty said she even put out to her punk fifteen-year-old brother. Think of her, and then think of a girl like Natalie.

Marty handed Danny a glass of wine. Although he didn't like the taste, Danny took a sip. He made a face.

He saw Emma leading Red into the pantry.

VI

Two, three, four blocks, with neither of them talking. He wished that he had her home. She couldn't have had a good time at the party.

Another block in silence. The cab turned into Jackson Park. What a wonderful place to kiss her, with the park, the trees. The cab shot around a bend, and he was jolted toward her. He liked the transient and accidental feel of Natalie against him.

"Pardon me," he muttered, moving away.

She didn't answer.

"Well, it's not so awful late," he said.

"No."

"I'm awful sorry that I was so late calling for you, but it wasn't my fault."

"Oh, that was all right."

The park was quiet. Even the wind seemed romantic. Here he was, doing what he had hoped and dreamed of doing, going to parties, taking a girl home in a cab, and tomorrow getting his chance to be a football hero. And still it wasn't like he had hoped it would be.

"Tommy Collins was to Ireland this summer," he said.

"Yes, I heard he was. It must be fun to travel."

If he could only say to her, wouldn't it be fun if he and she were married and could travel to Ireland and all around the world on a honeymoon, and make love in the moonlight on a ship in the middle of the ocean?

"Yes. Some day I'm going to travel," he said.

And he was. Some day he was going to do many things, and be many things. Maybe he'd made a chump out of himself, but some day he would be something, and then she wouldn't be sorry she had gone out with Danny O'Neill.

"Yes, it would be fun to travel," he said while the cab sped along the midway.

"It would be wonderful."

"Well, Tommy's lucky. He's traveled already."

"Yes."

"He's a nice fellow."

"Yes."

They passed the buildings of the University of Chicago. In a few minutes he would leave her. He wished that the ride was over. He wished that it wasn't and he could make an impression on her. All night she had hardly ever talked to him unless he first said something to her.

"Well, it wasn't such a long ride at that," he said as the cab entered Washington Park.

"No, it wasn't."

He gave up trying to talk. He felt that even his voice changed when he tried to say anything, that it sounded false. The cab headed west on Sixtieth Street. When he left her, should he try to kiss her good night? Fellows said after you took a girl out and spent money on her, the least she could do was kiss you good night.

The cab pulled up in front of the building where she lived.

"Just a minute," he said to the driver.

He got out of the cab awkwardly and walked beside her up to the outer door.

She turned and smiled at him, and he so loved that round pretty face of hers, those dark eyes, the white teeth, the curly bobbed hair peaking out of her hat.

"Well, good night, Danny, and thank you very much. I had a very good time."

"Oh, that's nothing. Say, Natalie, would you like to go out tomorrow night, to a show?" he asked in a faltering voice.

"I'm terribly sorry, but I can't."

He grinned, feeling that the grin on his face was silly beyond words and that it made him look like a goof.

"Well, good night. I had a lovely time."

She opened the door and went in. He watched her ring the bell and walk upstairs.

VII

Outside, it was raining drearily, and Danny waited in Mac's hallway. He thought of the party. He must have looked like an ox trying to dance. He was damned glad that he hadn't fixed it up for Roslyn to have a date; she would have been there and seen what a chump he'd made out of himself. Well, maybe he'd made a chump out of himself, but tomorrow he wouldn't.

But if he wanted to play a decent game, he had to get to bed and rest. Standing on his feet here wouldn't help him, either. He sat down on the mat.

Where the hell were they?

If only Natalie would be at the game tomorrow, she would see him in a different role. But he hadn't the guts to ask her and when he'd hinted, she hadn't said anything.

He imagined himself in a muddy uniform, coming off the field after he had just made a spectacular one-handed catch of a forward pass and scored the winning touchdown. He would stop by her in the stands. And she would say to him: Danny, you were wonderful. I was so thrilled.

And she'd wait for him and ride home with him, and when he left her at her doorway he would put his arms around her and kiss her.

Bored with sitting down, he got to his feet. He stood in the damp and chilly hallway. Suddenly a car stopped. It wasn't Mac's. Two men got out. He was frightened. What could he do? He closed his fists and waited. As they approached the doorway, he could tell that they were dicks. He unclenched his fists. They entered the hallway.

"What are you doing here," one of them asked.

"I'm waiting for a friend who lives here, and I don't want to wake his family up."

"What's his name?"

"McNeill. You can see it on the bell."

"What's your name?" the other dick asked.

"Daniel O'Neill. I've been to a party with my friend, Hugh McNeill. His family owns this building. He and I are fraternity brothers. I'm supposed to stay with him all night."

"Where is he?"

"He had to take his girl home. He didn't have room in his car, and I took mine home in a cab."

"What do you do?"

"I live at Fifty-eighth and South Park, and I go to Saint Stanislaus high school, and my cousin, Martin McCormack, is on the force, maybe you know him."

"You say you're waiting to stay here all night with this fellow?" the other dick asked.

"Yes, sir."

"And you go to high school?"

"Yes, sir."

The two dicks looked at one another. Danny waited, hoping that they wouldn't do anything. But he wasn't too afraid, because he hadn't done anything and he could get out easily if they took him in.

"How soon is this fellow coming home?"

"He ought to be here any minute."

"How do you know he ain't home already?"

"Because I asked at the garage where he keeps his car. It ain't in yet."

"Well, listen, kid, don't make any noise. We got a call that there was a prowler around here. Don't make any noise waiting."

Danny watched them leave the hallway, get into the squad car, and drive off. He looked out at the dark and foggy night. He sat down. Now he had something to tell Mac and Tim when they got here.

He waited. It was chilly and lonely and very quiet.

VIII

Danny walked away from Father Theo. Father Theo had just said that he'd called up Uncle Al this morning. Father Theo had gotten Uncle Al to agree to let Danny play football this year. He was pleased about this. Playing today wasn't going to get him in dutch at home.

He joined the team, grouped around Joe McBride in the dressing room.

"Now, listen to me, you fellows," Joe said, facing the squad in the dressing room. "I want you fellows to go out there and fight. These fellows you're playing are heavier than you are. You have to play a fast, hard game. Lots of football games are won in the first minutes of play. Try to sweep them off their feet before they get started. Every time you tackle a man, hit him as hard as you can, as if you were going to knock him down so that he won't get up. Don't be afraid of hurting anyone. Football isn't mahjong. Football is football. To play this game, you got to play hard."

Joe paused. He glanced around the dressing room.

"Your captain isn't going to be with you. Thanks to his school spirit and his loyalty to the team, he played prairie football last Sunday and got his shoulder wrenched."

"I'm sorry, Joe. I won't do it again," Tim Doolan said.

"I'm doing all the talking now, Doolan."

His eyes fell on Danny, and a number of the players looked from Danny to Mulligan. Danny grinned foolishly.

"I don't know what some of you were doing last night, O'Neill and Mulligan, but I'm going to be watching what you're doing this afternoon. Now the starting lineup is Kennealy at quarterback, Kavanaugh and McDonald halfbacks, and Nolan fullback. Ends, Morrisey and Sachs; tackles, Fagin and Mulligan; guards, Hanighen and Delehanty; center, Tom Moss. Now go out and let me see what stuff you got."

The team ran out of the dressing room. Danny tagged after them. Wearing an old sweater, Danny sat on the bench between Tim and Ike.

"You'll be in there soon," Tim said.

Danny watched the team run through signal practice. When he did get in, he'd show Joe. Party or no party last night, he'd show him.

IX

"O'Neill, take your sweater off and warm up," Joe ordered.

Danny pulled off his sweater, grabbed a head guard, and ran up and down by the bench. He heard words of encouragement from some of the S.S. rooters in the stand.

"All right, O'Neill, take Sachs' end. Tell Kennealy to play out further on his end. Now let's see what you got."

Danny ran out and reported to the referee. He took his position at right end. Saint Luke had the ball on their own forty-yard line. He stood, hands on hips, waiting, poised, confident, sure of himself.

X

ST. STANISLAUS "LIGHTS" HOLD POWERFUL ST. LUKE HEAVIES TO TWO TOUCHDOWNS

St. Stanislaus upset all the "dope" in the opening of the Catholic League schedule against St. Luke at St. Basil's field.

Outweighed thirty pounds or more to the man, St. Stanislaus nevertheless played St. Luke's off their feet in the first half, and were finally defeated only because of the sheer weight of their opponents. Had Doolan, Jablownski, and Borowik been able to play, it is certain that the result of the game would have been far different. That a light green team should make such a showing against St. Luke's is a mighty tribute to the gameness and spirit of our team.

Marty Mulligan, his knee wrenched so badly that he was not able to straighten his leg, was the star of the line. McGee performed exceptionally well on the defense, breaking up the Luke formations repeatedly. Moss, opposed by Shellenback, Luke's 200 pound center, gave a magnificent exhibition of courage. Kavanaugh at end proved himself a worthy newcomer to our game eleven. O'Neill, at the other end, played his usual spectacular game.

In the third quarter Luke's weight told, and the Black and Red goal was crossed twice. The rest of the game's laurels go to our "Lights." The close found everyone in the stands enthusiastically cheering our plucky team. Our "Lights" had covered themselves with glory even in defeat, and it was the unanimous opinion of the Luke rooters and of their team that St. Luke had met a "game" foe.

32

I

Drivers were crowded into the coop.

"Here, Mr. O'Neill, sign me out, please," one of them said, handing him a ticket.

"Just a minute! Just a minute!" Jim said, feeling weak and dizzy.

The telephone rang.

"Hello, Jefferson Depot, Jim O'Neill speaking."

"Jim, this is Lambert. I haven't gotten any of my gascar moves yet from your place. Anything wrong over there?"

"No, I got 'em all here. I ain't had the time. I'll call you back on them just as soon as I get the time."

"All right, Jim."

"Now, one at a time, you fellows," Jim said.

He took a ticket to sign it. The telephone rang again. The drivers crowded around him. From outside came a steady noise from the platform. The telephone continued ringing. Jim picked up a pencil. His right hand was numb, and he couldn't feel anything.

"Goddamn it," he exclaimed as the pencil fell to the floor.

He grabbed the phone.

"Hello, Jim O'Neill speaking. . . . No, wrong place, buddy."

Jim hung up.

"Where the hell is that pencil?" Jim said.

He was sweating. His stomach seemed to be upset. He was very weak and dizzy. The noise from the platform seemed faraway. He felt that his right side was swollen. He bent down to find the pencil on the floor. He wanted just to sit down and never get up. That's all he wanted. Strange faraway noises. Had to get these wagonmen signed out of here. He got down on his hands and knees to find the pencil.

He crumbled on the floor of the coop, unconscious.

II

He was all right now. He could have finished the night at work, but Mr. Wolfe had come in to see him and had said he better go home. He'd insisted anyway that he could go home alone.

Suddenly he felt weak and dizzy again. He stood on the elevated platform, dressed in his work clothes, his khaki shirt, his old teamster's cap, and an old overcoat which hung loose and open. He felt his face. Needed a shave. He would go home and he would go to bed.

A well-dressed woman watched him. His inflamed eyes were ringed with red, bloodshot, and the pupils were enlarged. He looked like a crazy man. When his eyes met hers, she glanced aside. He wavered a bit like a drunken man. Jim felt that the woman was looking at him in a very strange way and acting as if she were frightened by him. What was he, a bogey man? What did she think he was, a bum, a drunken bum?

Lady, I'm not a bum! Lady, I'm a sick man!

The woman's face was suddenly a little blurred. He saw her as if she had welled up out of a vague gray background in a dream. She stood as if transfixed, her eyes fastened on him. He still felt so weak and a little dizzy. He had to pull himself together. Why did she look at him the way she did?

"Lady," he said hoarsely, in a troubled voice.

He staggered to her, limping pitifully.

She drew back a step.

"Please, lady."

She faced him, fearful.

"Lady, I'm not drunk. I'm just a sick man. I had to leave work because of an attack. That's all, lady. Don't look at me like I was a drunkard," he said, speaking more slowly than usual and pronouncing with difficulty.

A train pulled into the station.

"What train do you want?" she asked, grabbing his arm as he wavered.

"Jackson Park or Englewood."

She guided him into the car and set him in a seat by himself. She moved off to another seat. He looked almost glassy-eyed at those near him. The right side of his face seemed heavy, and the right side of his lip seemed pulled slightly out of position.

A young fellow started to sit down opposite Jim, but, noticing him, he found another seat. The motion of the car shook him up. He told himself that he was all right. He sat slouched, looking out of the window. People looked at him so funny. He saw them as if they were not human. He shook his head. Suddenly it cleared. But he was very weak. Must be his stomach. He broke out into a sweat and he felt faint. He felt as if he were withering away inside of himself. His head seemed to go round. There seemed to be grooves inside of his head, and his consciousness seemed to whirl on grooves, to whirl and whirl, and suddenly his head cleared. He was proud, as if his own will power and determination had saved him from losing consciousness again. The elevated train raced on along the express track.

III

Jim staggered off the train at Fifty-eighth Street. He was weak on his feet, but it was only a little way to home. He walked unevenly, dragging his foot to the stairs. He held on to the banister and slowly began to descend. Landing on a step with his right foot, he almost fell. God, had it come? He couldn't let it. He clung to the banister with all the power in his left hand and landed on each succeeding step with his left foot, then pulling down his right foot.

He reached the bottom of the steps and staggered over to the exit doors. A stranger behind him pushed the doors open for him.

"Thank you. I ain't drunk. I'm sick and going home because I had to leave work. I ain't drunk, Mister."

"Do you want me to help you home?"

"No, I only have a block and a half. I'm all right."

"Are you sure?"

"Yes, thank you."

Jim turned slowly, unevenly, pulling his right leg after him with each step and, determined, he limped toward home.

IV

"Son, your father had a stroke," Mrs. O'Flaherty said when Danny came home after having gone to a movie with Hugh and Marty.

"When?"

"Now, just a minute, Mud. Your father came home from work not feeling well. Dr. Geraghty said he might be all right and he ought to rest a week or so. It mightn't be serious," Uncle Ned said.

"Can I go over to see him?"

"It's too late now."

“Will I have to quit school and go to work?” Danny asked.

“Now, listen, don’t be crossing bridges until you come to them,” Ned said.

Al came out to the kitchen in his shirtsleeves.

“I went home with Mike and conversed with him for a little while. He thinks it mightn’t be serious. He says that with a little rest Jim will be all right.”

“Oh, God, why does everything have to befall us?” Margaret sighed.

“Cheer up now, Peg, cheer up,” Al said.

“Yes, cheer up when this befalls us.”

“For God’s sake, Peg,” Ned said.

Margaret looked at him, suddenly angry.

“If you were any kind of a man, you’d be making money,” she said to Ned.

“Now, what called for that?” Ned asked.

Danny sat there, pained, worried.

“If he dies, we can’t let him be buried in my plot in Calvary. That’s for me, for these poor old bones of mine,” Mrs. O’Flaherty said.

“Mother, what the hell kind of talk is that?” Ned asked sharply.

“You let Mother alone and go out and get a job, you dirty bum,” Margaret screamed at Ned.

“Now, what the hell caused this? What did I say? What did I do?” Ned asked.

Danny went to his bedroom.

“Al, I can’t stand it any more. With Jim sick, I can’t bear the burden,” Margaret said loudly.

“Please, Peg, now you go to bed and get some rest. You’re nervous,” Danny heard his Uncle Al say.

He started undressing.

“Cripes, I’m going to bed. Let damned fools be damned fools,” Ned said angrily, and walked to his bedroom and closed the door.

V

Danny had been neglecting to say his good-night prayers. He knelt down and prayed. He promised God that he wouldn’t neglect them again, and asked God to protect his father.

He climbed into bed and lay there. He heard Aunt Margaret yelling and screaming and Uncle Al mumbling, quietly trying to persuade her. He turned to the wall. Why did such things have to happen in his house and in his family? Why did his father have to be sick?

If anything happened to Pa, he’d have to quit school, give up football, and go to work. He would have to give up his chances in life. Everything would change if Papa was sick. He remembered the last time he'd seen Papa, meeting him on Fifty-eighth Street, noticing how hard it was for Papa to open the doors at the elevated station.

There was always trouble in his family. The same troubles weren't always happening in the homes of his fraternity brothers. Nobody seemed to get drunk in their homes and be a disgrace. There weren't the same worries over money. The other fellows had fathers who could pay their tuition for them and not have to give excuses like he'd had to to Father Jim. They were all going to be able to go to college without having to work their way.

Aunt Margaret was still yelling.

What kind of a person was he, thinking about these things when his father was so sick? Thinking of what it would mean to him!

God forgive him.

VI

It was a sharp, clear, crisp morning. Wearing a sheepskin coat and carrying his strapped books, Danny left home early in order to see his father before he went to school. He'd hardly slept and he felt dopey. He didn't know how he'd ever get through football this afternoon.

He ran up the steps at the Calumet apartment. His mother let him in and kissed him.

"Is Pa awake?"

"Yes, he's in bed."

Mama led him into the bedroom. There was that familiar musty smell, and the small dim room was in disorder. Jim lay propped up with pillows at his back. He looked thin and haggard and needed a shave. His right arm rested outside the covers, the hand turned inward.

"Hello, Dan," he said softly.

"How are you, Papa?"

"Oh, Dan, I'm all right. I just had a bad spell. I'll be up in a few days and back to work in a week or so. I'm not in a bad way."

"Gee, I'm glad," Danny said, feeling that anything he would say would be embarrassing.

"Are you on your way to school now?"

Danny shook his head affirmatively.

"Danny, you want to study hard and get all you can out of school. You know, I always regret that I never had an education. I was foolish and wouldn't try to get myself one. I don't want my children to make the same mistake," Jim said in a very wearied voice.

Danny noticed how very tired his father looked. His hair was getting gray, and he had a peculiar stare in his eyes. Danny didn't know what to say.

"I have to go now to get to school. But I'll come over tonight."

"Yes, goodbye," Jim said, his voice still weary.

VII

Danny trudged upstairs to see if he could find someone who'd let him copy the Latin homework. He hadn't done any Latin homework for three nights. He hated Latin, and Vergil was way over his head.

"I see that you are doing us a favor and getting here on time this morning," Father Michael said ironically, standing at the second-floor landing.

Danny grinned feebly.

"You have been late several mornings. You'll have to stop that."

"Well, sometimes, Father, the bell rings before I get here," Danny said.

"O'Neill, I'm not fooling. Even though you're a senior now, you're still a pupil."

"Father, you know, a couple of years ago, my father had a stroke. Well, last night, he had to come home from work, and I wanted to ask you if you would pray for his recovery."

"Did he have another stroke?" Father Michael asked, his whole manner changing.

"No, I don't think so. The doctor thinks he'll be all right, but he's in bed, and naturally, Father, we're worried, and maybe it would help if you and the priests here prayed for him."

"Of course we will, Dan. I'll offer up my mass tomorrow morning for him."

"Thank you, Father," Danny said.

Father Michael patted Danny on the shoulder.

VIII

Samuel Howard was in the classroom. He was a gawky, callow boy, about Danny's size, but with narrower shoulders. He looked like a rube. He had long hair and gray eyes. He was awkward in all his movements. Samuel always paid attention in class, didn't date girls, and read books, and he was just too smart for words. Danny thought that the straw was sticking out of his ears.

"Howard, do me a favor?"

"No. If you're too damned lazy to do your own homework, you can take the consequences."

"Oh, come on, be a sport, Howard. I'll do you a favor sometime."

"What? Offer to let me copy your mistakes in Latin if you ever get the ambition to do that much?"

"It's not going to hurt you if you let me copy your Latin. I didn't have time to get it done. My father came home seriously sick last night."

"I don't believe in cheating."

"This isn't cheating, what the hell? Who cares about Latin anyway?"

"You don't." Howard looked scornfully at Danny. "I had to spend time doing my work, and you want to cheat and get the same mark as I do without doing any work."

"Oh, Howard, you're just the guy I'm lookin' for. Listen, let me copy the Latin homework in Vergil, will you? Hell, I couldn't get the damned stuff done," Marty Mulligan said, entering the room.

"No!"

"What the hell? Why?"

"If I can do it, you can."

"Hell, you're smart. You know everything."

"I never learned anything by copying."

"You got it done?" Marty asked Danny.

"Me?" Danny responded.

"Come on, Howard. I'll do you a good turn sometime," Marty said.

Samuel Howard picked up his Latin composition book and walked out of the room without saying a word.

"Now, that's what I call a first-class heel," Marty said.

"Hey, Smilga, let me copy your Latin, will you?" Danny yelled as Smilga entered the classroom.

Smilga handed Danny his Latin composition book, smiling as if Danny were doing him a favor. Danny and Marty sat down to copy Smilga's homework. Just then the bell rang, to start classes for the day.

IX

Clouds of steam rose to the ceiling of the damp, warm, and dimly lit shower and dressing room. It smelled of soap, water, sweat, and urine. It was a reconverted storeroom on the basement floor of the school building. The showers were fixed up in wooden booths on one side, and next to them were toilets and a urinal. On the opposite side of the room there were wooden booths and benches for dressing. The football players were in various stages of dress and undress, and everyone was yelling and shouting.

Danny stood under a warm shower with Tim, Marty, and Red Keene. Dreamy, he wanted the warm water to needle and flow endlessly over his body and over his wrenched shoulder. He didn't pay any attention to his teammates under the shower with him, and because of his shoulder they were careful not to shove him while they shoved one another.

Tom Moss, the center, stood before their shower, naked. He was a handsome lad with attractive curly hair.

"Do you fellows pay rent on the shower? How long do you want to take?" he yelled.

"Come on in and shut up," Marty yelled back at him.

"There isn't room. Come on out and give someone else a chance."

Marty thumbed his nose at Tom.

Danny suddenly winced. He had moved his shoulder the wrong way. He stood in the rear of the booth, letting the warm water hit his shoulder. The heat seemed to take some of the soreness out of it.

"Mulligan, did anyone ever tell you you were a pain?" Moss yelled.

Marty rushed out of the shower and faced Moss.

"Don't get snotty with me. I don't like you."

"Take your shower and give someone else a chance. You don't own the school," Moss said, speaking in the contemptuous tone he seemed incapable of avoiding.

Marty drove him across the room with a punch in the jaw. Before Marty could follow up, some of the others got between them. Holding his jaw, Moss said nothing. Marty went back under the shower. Tim turned on the cold water and they splashed a moment and got out of the shower. Moss quietly took his shower.

"Marty, dry my back?" Danny asked.

"Who was your servant last year?"

"I can't use my right shoulder."

"Oh, I forgot," Marty said; he took the towel from Danny and carefully dried his back for him.

Danny suddenly winced.

"I'm sorry, Dan. I'll be more careful."

"That's all right."

Danny started dressing slowly. Some fellows were singing under the shower.

"Hey, sing faraway, you bastards," Tim yelled.

They went on singing.

"Listen, Morrisey, you're a damned fool playing football with your rib like it is," Marty said, sitting beside Morrisey on a bench,

Morrisey, a slender sophomore with a thin neck and a goofy look, said nothing.

"Last year I got a broken rib. I know what it is," Marty said.

Tim Doolan tied Danny's tie and helped him on with his sweater.

"Jesus, with these damned charley horses, I got to walk like I crapped in my pants," Danny yelled.

Just then Father Theo entered. He was a rangy, sandy-haired young priest who looked like an athlete.

Embarrassed and afraid, Danny looked away from the priest. Father Theo approached him.

"How you feeling, O'Neill?"

"All right, except for my shoulder."

"Take care of yourself, boy. We need you Saturday against Saint Basil."

"Father, after losing three games, our team looks like the wreck of the Hesperus with injuries," Tim yelled.

"Your shoulder better?"

Tim nodded.

"How's your rib, Morrisey?"

"Father, I'll be able to play Saturday, but Mulligan here was saying I shouldn't and I shouldn't come out to practice any more."

"What do you mean?" Father Theo asked, turning angrily to Marty.

"Why, nothing, Theo. I was only telling him I had a broken rib last year and he oughtn't to play with his rib in bad shape."

"Are you a doctor?"

"No, Father, but I had a broken rib."

"Who asked you to give Morrisey advice?"

"Nobody, but I know what it means to have a broken—"

Father Theo hauled off on Marty and punched him square in the jaw.

"That'll teach you to mind your own business."

Holding his jaw, Marty sulked silently. The fellows became very quiet and hurriedly finished dressing and left.

X

Danny ascended the steps at the Dorchester elevated station. With each step he mounted, he was stabbed in the thigh muscles by a sharp pain. He paused halfway up and gazed wistfully at the remaining stairs he had to climb. If he only had reached them. And when he got off the train, he had to go downstairs at Fifty-eighth, and then he had to climb two flights more to get home. He carefully went up one step after another, limping, holding his injured right shoulder close to his body and carrying his books in his left hand.

Danny sat alone in the elevated train. It had been exciting in the shower room tonight, Marty socking Moss and then Theo poking Marty. Marty and Theo had both done wrong in swinging with such little provocation.

It was just his luck to go and get a wrenched shoulder. This week everything seemed to be looking jake for him. And then he had to wrench his shoulder. He was proud, though, of the way he'd been injured. In scrimmage on Monday, Joe McBride had been showing Rory McGann how to plunge and he'd been playing defensive fullback. Joe had come ploughing through the line, over two hundred pounds of bone and muscle. He had tackled Joe head on and shaken him up. But he'd wrenched his shoulder making the tackle. And his shoulder had just been healing after the game against Joliet a week ago Saturday, when he'd hurt it making a diving tackle over the interference to nail the Joliet quarterback in his tracks on a punt. He'd been thinking that now, for the fourth game of the season, he'd be in condition and able to play up to form. And he was needed against Basil, the South Side rivals of S.S. Basil had a much better and heavier team. If he was out, S.S. would be further weakened. He had to be ready to play. Tonight he would soak his shoulder in hot water as long as he possibly could.

Yes, this week everything had started to look good for him. Pa was better and going back to work tonight. Dr. Geraghty said he thought Pa would be all right now. Last Saturday there'd been a little party at Hugh's, and he'd danced with Hugh's sister and done all right. He was learning how to dance. And then, bang, this damned injury.

He hadn't telephoned Natalie since the party almost three weeks ago. He'd thought of her every day and he had even gone so far as to get in a telephone booth and give the operator her number. But then he'd hung up. He wanted a date with her. He wanted her to see him play football. He wanted her to know that he was better than he had seemed when he had taken her to the party at Tommy Collins'. What kind of a guy was he? He wasn't afraid to tackle Joe McBride head on when Joe outweighed him by almost a hundred pounds. But he was afraid to call up Natalie and ask her for a date.

Before he went home he'd go to the drugstore and telephone her. He would be damned if he was going to lose out by having a faint heart.

XI

"Hello, Natalie? This is Danny O'Neill."

"Oh, hello."

"Natalie, are you doing anything Friday night?"

"I'm sorry, I have a date."

"Saturday?"

"Gee, I have one Saturday, too."

"How about Sunday night?"

"I'm so sorry, Danny, but I have one then, too."

"How about Monday night?" Danny asked; he'd skip the frat meeting.

"I can't go out on weekday nights."

"How about a week from Saturday?"

"I'm so sorry, Danny, but I have a date then, too. But call me some other time."

"All right. But don't forget, I put in a reservation," he said, thinking it was a clever crack.

"And thank you very much for calling me, Danny."

He heard the click of the receiver and came out of the telephone booth. He wished he hadn't called. You never wanted to stick your chin out to a girl. And he'd done that. Suppose she told other girls at Saint Paul's that he couldn't dance, was a dull date, always pestered girls? That would give him a hell of a rep. He started walking home, haltingly.

XII

"What's the matter?" Al asked, seeing Ned's drawn, worried face when Ned returned to the supper table from the telephone.

"That was the express company. Jim collapsed at work and they're bringing him home," Ned said.

"Good Jesus Christ!" Al exclaimed.

Everyone at the table was struck with terror and gazed impotently at one another.

"Ned, is it serious?"

"Mud, I told you all that I know. He's had another stroke and they're bringing him home," Ned said.

"Al, that poor man will never work another day. Mark my words," Mrs. O'Flaherty said.

Little Margaret began to cry. Danny's face was white. He said nothing.

"Mud, don't talk like that. Wait until you know more," Ned said.

"I'm going to call Mike to get him over to the O'Neills for Jim right away," Al said, rising and going to the telephone in the hall.

"Al, call Peg up at work and tell her," Mrs. O'Flaherty said.

"What the hell do you want to bother Peg for? She can't do any good at work. It'll only upset her. Cripes, last week when Jim had to come home with an attack, she kept us up all night yelling. You would think she was the one who was sick," Ned said.

They sat finishing their coffee and dessert without saying anything. They heard Al talking over the telephone with Mike Geraghty.

"Dan, you hustle over and tell your mother Mike will be right over," Al said, returning to the dining room.

"And, here, give this to your mother in case she has to get anything for your father," Al said, following Danny into the bedroom and handing him a five-dollar bill.

Danny was dangling with his coat.

"What the hell's the matter with you? Here, hurry up," Al said, taking the coat, and in doing so handling Danny a little roughly, so that his shoulder pained and he grimaced.

"Be careful," Danny said.

"Are you hurt?"

"Nothing, just a little stiffness in my shoulder. But it's all right," Danny said, still wincing from pain.

"Gee, I'm sorry. Maybe you had better have Mike look at it."

"My coach did. It's nothing. A little twist or something, only those things hurt for a day or two."

"Go ahead, Dan," Al said.

Walking stiffly on his aching legs, Danny went out.

XIII

"Hello, Dan. How's the football player?" Bill said.

He heard the younger kids talking and playing.

"Bill, Papa . . ." Danny said.

"Mama! Mama! Mama!" Bill called excitedly, his face turning white.

"Papa is coming home. The express company called up and said he had a stroke at work and they are bringing him home."

Bill was pale. He said nothing. He turned his face away. Danny knew why.

"Ah, my prize package came over to see me," Lizz said, rushing into the parlor as Danny was carefully getting his right arm out of his coat sleeve.

"Mama, Papa had a stroke and they are bringing him home. Uncle Al called Doctor Mike; he's on the way here now, too."

"Saint Joseph guard me!" Lizz exclaimed.

She ran to her bedroom, turned on the light, blessed herself from the holy water fount by the doorway, and knelt down before a picture of the Blessed Virgin which hung on the wall.

"Danny, will you take me to see you play football Saturday?" Bob asked, entering the parlor. Dennis and Catherine followed him.

"Wait to see how Papa is. If he's all right, I'll take you."

Bob saw how solemn and serious Bill and Danny were.

"What's the matter?" he asked.

"Get the hell out of here, all you kids but Dollie," Bill said.

"Well, what's the matter?"

"Get out of here before I sock you," Bill said, jumping off the chair, and Bob fled.

Bill sat down.

"Bill, what's the matter?" Catherine said.

"Pa is coming home sick, Dollie."

She began to cry.

"I just walked to the station with him a little while ago for him to go to work. He kissed me goodbye, but he said I was too big a girl for him to take me in his arms any more," she said.

She sat in a corner and wiped her eyes.

Danny wished he could think of something to say to Bill. He was worried himself. He didn't want Papa sick. Maybe Pa was dying, and he ought to get the priest. They couldn't let Papa die without the priest.

And what would they all do? Maybe he would have to go to work. He would hate to have to give up football. And he didn't want Papa not well.

"They didn't say how sick Pa was?" Bill asked.

"Uncle Ned talked to them. He said just what I told you."

"Dan, kneel down and say a prayer for Pa with me," Bill said.

They both knelt, blessed themselves, and prayed fervently. Bill sat down again, and Danny made faces as he got off his knees, because of the stiffness of his muscles.

"Let's hope for the best. I told Pa last night that today was much too soon for him to go back to work, but he thought he was all right," Bill said.

"Maybe it won't be serious," Danny said.

Bill and Danny heard Lizz telling Bob and Dennis that their father was coming home. Then Lizz came into the parlor.

Bill got up and went to his room, almost in tears.

"Mama, last week after his attack, I asked the priests at school to pray that Pa would be all right," Danny said.

"The power of prayer can cure anything, Son," Lizz said.

"Mama, I don't want anything to happen to my Papa," Catherine said.

Bob and Dennis came into the parlor.

Lizz suddenly got to her feet.

"Goodness, I got to fix things up. The bed isn't made, and I got to get out the holy candle. Dennis, you go and get the priest and have him come down here for your father," Lizz said.

"Can I go with him?" asked Bob.

"Me, too?" asked Catherine.

"Yes, go ahead. And don't be dallying on the way," Lizz said.

Lizz went to fix the room for Jim.

XIV

"How you coming out in football?" Bill asked.

"Our team is light, and there are a lot of injuries. I got charley horses and a wrenched shoulder," Danny said.

"Won any games yet?"

"No, but we are going to try our darnedest to win Saturday." Danny felt guilty talking with Bill. With Pa sick, he would be playing football while Bill was working.

"I'd like to have a crack at your team in basketball. I'd like to see what stuff you got," Bill said.

"You play any more?" Danny asked, remembering that Bill used to play and was a good center and a crack shot.

"This year I was thinking of playing with my council in the Order of Columbus," Bill said.

"Gee, maybe you can."

"Dan, remember when we were kids. We used to have fun, didn't we?" Bill said moodily.

"Uh huh," Danny said wistfully, but thinking, fun as it was, it wasn't as much fun as he was having these days.

He and Bill were different now, too, what with girls, dancing, the fraternity. He didn't know if Bill had a girl, and didn't think that Bill knew how to dance. They were much different.

"Remember Ed Walsh's no-hit game, Dan?"

"Uh huh."

Bill was silent again. Lizz was busy fixing up the bedroom for Jim. Danny and Bill sat, waiting for their father to be carried home, paralyzed.

33

I

It was a sunny afternoon, almost too warm for football. A crowd of between five and six hundred was out to see the game between Saint Stanislaus and Saint Basil. Most of those present were students of one or the other school and they stood along the side lines. Others were seated in the stands behind the north goal post. Amid cheers, the teams lined up for the opening kickoff, the black and red S.S. team to kick and the brown St. Basil team to receive.

A loud cheer went up. The whistle blew. Tim Doolan signaled ready, ran forward, booted the ball. It soared and arched through the sunny air, and the crowd watched the moving pattern of colored jerseys, silent until Glynn, the Basil quarterback, caught the kickoff. Then it let out a cheer. Glynn cut toward the right side lines and then tried to reverse his field.

Danny, playing without a helmet to show off as he had done all season, tore down the side line as fast as he could with his stiff legs. Acting as if by instinct, he side-stepped Basil linesmen who hurtled themselves at him, striving to cut him down. By quick dodging he avoided being clipped. When Glynn caught the ball, he cut in. He guessed what Glynn was going to do and checked himself and waited. Glynn reversed his field, preceded by a three-man interference. Danny cut behind the interference, left his feet, and nailed Glynn from the side, a clean, neat flying tackle. Glynn and Danny got up slowly. Glynn was shaken up. Danny's shoulder pained him.

He heard S.S. students giving seven rahs for O'Neill.

"That's the All-American end stuff, kid," Fireman Fagin said enthusiastically, patting Danny on the back.

Danny's face was impassive.

He determined that, shoulder or no shoulder, he'd go on. He'd made that tackle, hadn't he, and diagnosed what was going to happen perfectly? He put his hands to his shoulder. No, forget worrying about his injuries. He had an image in his mind of O'Neill, the curly-headed right end without a helmet, playing like a sensation, electrifying the side lines, even the bastards from Saint Basil.

Basil lined up in a balanced line formation. Danny stood poised, with hands on hips, a few yards from Marty Mulligan at right tackle.

Glynn barked out signals. The shift to the left, the pass, and the Basil backfield tore around end at Danny. Keeping his feet, Danny drove the ball carrier inside, and his classmate, Jablownski, made the tackle.

From the side lines the S.S. rooters cheered loudly and lustily. Their light and despised team had held the vaunted Basil crew without a gain on the first play.

II

Failing to gain, Glynn punted. Tim Doolan returned the punt and was downed on the S.S. twenty-yard line. S.S. hepped into an unbalanced line formation. Danny crouched beside Marty Mulligan and looked up at Hurley, the husky Basil left tackle. With the pass from center, Danny leaped forward. He locked his left arm around Hurley's thigh. Holding Hurley, he kicked the tackle's underpinnings with his left foot. Hurley went down with Danny on top of him. Nolan made five yards through the hole Danny had made.

"Hey, watch your holdin'," Hurley yelled at Danny, sore.

Impassive, Danny turned aside and didn't look at Hurley.

What the referee didn't see didn't hurt.

S.S. lined up and hepped to the left, Danny crouched a yard behind the line, waiting. With the pass, he broke into the open field, hurtled himself at a defensive halfback, and was slapped into the dirt. He got up slowly, wincing. He'd landed on his shoulder. Jablownski had lost three yards on the play.

Tim called signals. The shift to the right. The pass. Hurley mashed Danny into Mulligan, using his fist instead of his open hand. Danny kicked out his foot and tripped Hurley. Nolan, carrying the ball, fell over Hurley, losing a yard.

With fourth down and nine yards to go, Tim called for a punt. Danny dodged past Hurley and ran straight down the field, fighting off blockers who tried to cut him down. Hearing the sound of the punt, he glanced over his shoulder in order to gauge the direction of the ball. It was a long, high punt, traveling down field in the center. Danny raced on. Just as Glynn caught the ball, Danny got a grip on his heel. Glynn tried to drag Danny along, but Danny nailed him without a gain.

Danny got to his feet, nonchalant.

"Get that sonofabitch without the helmet," he heard a Basil player yell.

Danny stood off by himself. He had forgotten about the crowd and the cheering on the sidelines. Now he heard the yelling, heard his name being shouted.

The minute you got in the game, you forgot the crowd. But in moments like this, you heard it again. It was wonderful to hear his name cheered.

III

Bob O'Neill stood on the side lines. He wished that they would all know that it was his brother. He was proud of Danny. He'd just seen him make a tackle. He watched the teams line up. The Basil quarterback broke through for about twenty yards. Gee, Danny's team had to do better. He watched the teams line up. Then a forward pass, and Saint Basil gained another first down.

"Come on, Danny!" he yelled pleadingly.

But Saint Basil went on down to the ten-yard line. Bob ran down the side lines and squeezed in in front of some guys behind the goal line.

There was wild yelling from all sides. Basil lined up and smashed forward. There was a brutal clash of bodies. Second down, and another brutal clash of bodies. Time was called out, and Bob watched Danny's coach go out on the field, followed by a kid carrying a bucket of water. He saw a player with a black-and-red jersey stretched out on the ground. But it wasn't Danny. He was glad.

Rah! Rah! Rah! Rah! Rah! Rah! Rah! Fagin! Yea!

The injured player got up. He walked slowly around and then put on his head guard.

Bob watched Danny. He sat alone on the ground. When the time-out period ended, he got up slowly and took his position, now playing close in to his tackle. The play came, a surging drive forward, and there was a massing of bodies near the goal line. The referee disentangled the players, and the crowd waited breathless to see if the man had gone over.

The S.S. rooters yelled with hysterical glee. S.S. had held. The S.S. rooters pleaded, beseeched their team to hold now on this last down.

Bob's face was tense with interest. He watched Danny in the lineup. There was the play. Again Bob watched the piling up and the referee disentangling the bodies.

The S.S. rooters yelled wildly.

Their team had held right on the goal line.

IV

When Tim kicked from behind his own goal line, Danny lunged down the field to cover the punt. A brown-clad Basil back hit him head on, and Danny landed on his right shoulder with a thud. He rose to his feet, slowly, wearied.

"Want me to call time out?" Tim asked anxiously, running up to him.

"No, I'm all right, just a bump."

"We got to hold 'em now," Tim said, turning and running back to take up his position as defensive quarterback.

Danny didn't care about his shoulder. He'd go on.

He took his position as defensive end, about five yards out from Marty at tackle. He stood, anxious and tense. His poise was gone. The pain in his shoulder was almost like the pain of a toothache.

Glynn called signals and came flying around Danny's end.

Determined, Danny wove in between the interference. Against his will, he half-heartedly tried to make a one-arm tackle but he couldn't hold his man. Glynn raced on for a fifteen-yard gain.

Danny got up. He told himself that he'd tackle hard the next time, regardless of his shoulder. Now both his shoulders pained him. He'd wrenched something in the left shoulder on that play. He wished the game were over. He wished he were on the side lines. It was hot. He was dry and parched. He ought to have time called and get himself taken out. No, lots of players had played spectacularly through a whole game with injuries worse than his. He wouldn't.

But on that last play, he'd favored himself. He was scared. He got in line and waited.

The play went around the other end, and Danny was grateful. Basil made a first down on the S.S. thirty-five-yard line. They had to hold now, here. Danny got set, waited, tense, unrelaxed, nervous. The play would come at him this time. He'd not favor his shoulder. He'd tackle hard.

The ball was snapped. A massed formation drove at Danny. He tried to beat off the interference with his left arm. A blocker crashed him squarely in the thighs. He dropped. He picked himself up after the play, the thigh muscles sore from the blow. He'd been hit just where he'd been bothered by charley horses.

Danny gritted his teeth. If he could only forget his shoulders. The hell with them. He waited for the next play, his hands out before him, ready for use in beating down interference. The ball was snapped. They were coming at him again. Thought they had a weak spot. Three brown-jerseyed backfield men coming at him low. Forget those shoulders. He side-stepped one blocker, but the other two boxed him in. He lunged and reached out with his left hand and caught the ball carrier's flying left ankle. The ball carrier lost his balance and Marty Mulligan knocked him down.

Danny got up. He'd broken up the play after they'd boxed him. But it was just luck. He had to go on, forget his shoulder. He wished it was the half. He wished he'd be taken out.

I can't be yellow, he told himself.

But he felt that he was being yellow today. He waited in position, and when the ball was snapped, he sensed that it would be a forward pass. He dropped back, and the pass came in his direction. He leaped up, snatched the ball, and ran. Three Basil tacklers converged on him and hit simultaneously. He landed on his head. A thudding pain shot through his head and neck, and another streaked a path of agony down his shoulder. He lay on the ground not wanting to get up, shaken from head to heels. He picked himself up. Mulligan and Tim patted him on the back.

Tim called signals. The line shifted to the left. Danny crouched a yard behind the line. Moss passed. Nolan came forward on a left tackle drive. Danny waited. Nolan slipped the ball to Danny. Head down, Danny cross-bucked. As he plunged he turned sidewise to hit with his left shoulder. He drove and stumbled forward for four yards, when three Basil men pushed him to the ground.

Just then the period ended with the score nothing to nothing.

V

Danny sat on the bench, watching Basil plough through the weakened and battered S.S. line. Basil led 13 to 0 and there was about five minutes to go. Basil made first down on the Stanislaus ten-yard line. Danny wanted them to hold. It wouldn't be so bad losing to Basil by only two touchdowns. In the second half they'd even threatened Basil. He'd caught a pass for a first down, and then Tim had gone fifty yards to the ten-yard line on a quarterback sneak. If only another pass had been thrown to him. But on the next play Nolan had fumbled, and then Basil had swept down the field for its first touchdown.

He watched the Basil backfield go into the Stanislaus line for four bone-crushing drives. They were stopped about two yards short on the last down, and the S.S. rooting section was cheering like hell. It was a moral victory to hold Basil three times within the ten-yard line as S.S. had today. Danny was thrilled. But he wished he'd been in there for this last stand.

Tim got set to punt behind his own goal line, and Danny imagined himself going down the field on the kick and making a spectacular tackle. He was disconsolate, and his interest drifted from the game. He thought of the way he had played until he'd been taken out at the end of the third quarter. From the second quarter on, he'd tried getting his man from the side with a slicing one-armed tackle. He had gone down the field on punts, full of determination, but, despite the best intentions in the world, he couldn't hit hard and head-on. This was something that had never happened to him before. There was something in him stronger than his will. It was a pain. It had seemed as if his shoulder would laugh at his mind. Every time his mind had said yes, go ahead, his shoulder had said no. At the last instant, when he had to hit, his shoulder just wouldn't hit for him.

How did others forget that they were hurt? He had always dreamed of doing this, and now, when he had a chance to, he'd favored his injuries. What was there in him that made him do that?

The game was over. Danny got up.

"You played a swell game," Bob said, joining him.

"How you feel, Dan?" Joe McBride asked.

"All right."

"You played a good game. How does your shoulder feel?"

"I tried to play with it, Joe, but it wasn't any good. It's hard to tackle with a wrenched shoulder."

"I'm satisfied with your game, Danny. I took you out because I saw you were hurt."

He was yellow, he bitterly told himself.

A group of Basil students jeered at Danny at the exit gate. One of them lip-farted at him.

"How you heels like getting stepped on?" a second asked.

"Look at the guy. He got his shoulder hurt. Too bad you didn't get your face stepped on, you bastard," another yelled.

Danny said nothing. He walked stiffly, with his right arm limp.

"Maybe you'll win next Saturday," Bob said.

He was tired. He ached all over. He only wanted to stand under a shower and let hot water fall soothingly on his bruised and battered body.

34

I

Jim couldn't get used to what had happened to him. It was still difficult for him to believe it. He was a paralytic. He was a cripple. It was going to take time before he'd be able to accustom himself to his new condition and his new circumstances.

He sat in his armchair, thinking. It was a gray and sunless day. The kids were in school, and Lizz was washing in the cellar. He had only been sitting up now a couple of days. Doctor Mike Geraghty had told him he might get better, but he knew that it had been said only to encourage him. He knew that he would never get better. And what he couldn't get used to was the realization that from this day forth until his death, he was helpless. Why, he couldn't even hold a pencil. He couldn't even write an X for his own signature.

Since he had been carried home from work, he was a different man. He felt that others didn't understand life and that he did. *Vanity, all is vanity.* Yes, he understood everything so differently now. Lying alone in bed, as he began coming back to himself, lying there so much alone, he had felt half in this world and half not in it, watching it. Yes, men tried and fought and raised hell and wanted all kinds of things, and yes, yes, *vanity, all is vanity.*

He looked out the window at some small children across the street as they ran and scuffled. There was something sad about seeing those little boys and girls playing on this gray day in autumn. There was something sad, not in him but in them. They didn't know. They were so innocent.

He was lethargic. His graying hair was unkempt and uncombed. He had a three-day growth of beard. His right foot, encased in an old carpet slipper, was turned inward; it seemed heavier to him than his left foot. His lifeless right arm drooped on his lap, and he sensed that it and his right foot were both swollen, larger than normal. He wore a dirty old blue shirt, no tie, a spotted gray vest, and a pair of old pants with frayed cuffs.

He watched a man with a brief case walk briskly by. That man was active. He could get up in the morning and shave himself. That man could cook himself a supper if he had to. And above all, that man could go out and earn his own living.

His son Bill had gone out on the wagons and was a helper on a truck now. He had had to give up his bookkeeping course, at least for the present. There was more money to be earned on the wagons, and there were mouths to be fed in this home, not only of the children and of Lizz, but of himself. That was what it was hard to understand. That was what it was taking time for him to get used to.

How many times had he not asked himself, why did this happen to him? Was it punishment for his sins? When he was young, after all, he had been a hell raiser. Was God taking this out on him for the sins of his youth? Hadn't he atoned for them by settling down and taking care of his family to the best of his abilities? Why did it have to happen to him?

The day was passing slowly. He would sit here now many days and they would just pass slowly. Each second of time was the same. Each tick of the clock marked off a second, no longer and no shorter than the next second, or the second before it. But take a day like this and consider how much longer it was than a day at work. It seemed five times as long as a day at work.

A woman pushed a baby buggy beneath the window. Sitting by the window these last few days, he had begun to see the street differently. Little things were repeated every day. The same cur dogs kept running by. There was one old bitch of a bulldog that was usually around, and three male dogs were generally sniffing after her. A big black cat was always passing in front of the window. There was an old man with a hefty cane who walked by in the morning and in the afternoon. He was beginning to recognize people. Some of them passed at about the same time every day, others at odd moments. He saw the same trucks and automobiles go by. He was beginning to see how all these little things were part of the street, and to recognize them.

He heard an elevated train from half a block away, and then it was quiet again. In a little while the kids would be out of school. His own kids would come home for lunch. Others would stream past the window. That was one of the big events of the day on this street. The street came to life then. You could hear the kids talking and laughing, and you could see them running and mauling and racing with so much health, so much life in them. The sight gave you the feeling that it was all so sad because they, too, were going to lose that innocence of theirs. They were going to have to learn the hard lessons of life and they were one day going to lose their health.

Since he had been allowed to get up a few hours a day, he had had a sleepy feeling, a feeling as if he were on the verge of falling asleep, and he felt as if there were foggy spaces in his mind. He would start to think of one thing, and suddenly he would be thinking of something else, and things would come into his mind the way they did when he was lying in bed three-quarters asleep. He looked out the window again. A little girl was running home crying while her playmates watched her. He could always notice little happenings like that when he watched the children play.

"How are you feeling, Jim?"

Jim turned. He hadn't heard Lizz come upstairs.

"Oh, all right, Lizz. A little better," he said.

"The children will be coming home soon. I came upstairs to fix their lunch."

"I'll help you," Jim said, getting up.

"No, you just sit there and take it easy. You need rest."

"Well, I'll come out and sit with you."

II

Jim pushed hard with his fork to crush the lettuce on his plate. Lizz went to him. She took a knife and fork and cut his lettuce and tomatoes.

"You didn't have to do that, Lizz. I could have done it all right. You sit down and eat your lunch," he said.

"Papa, I knew my catechism lesson this morning, and Sister said I was good," Catherine said while Lizz went back to her place.

"Good! Good!" Jim said.

"You eat now, Jim," Lizz said.

"I am," Jim said, spearing some lettuce.

He was clumsy. Little details of living required him to make new adjustments now.

He chewed the lettuce and turned to Bob.

"How did you do in school?"

"I was all right, Papa."

"You better be. I'm going to keep my eye on all of you kids."

"Papa, I went to the board in arithmetic and was the first one to get the problems done," Dennis said.

"I'm proud to hear that, Dennis."

"Papa, when will you go back to work?" Catherine asked.

"Oh, in a little while. It won't be long now. And then when I do, what are you going to do?"

"I'm going to walk to the elevated station with you every night, like I did before you got sick," she said.

"That's the girl," Jim said.

"Go ahead, Jim, and eat."

"I am, Lizz."

III

"How you feeling, Pa?" Danny asked, coming into the parlor.

Everybody asked him how he was feeling. He didn't like the sympathy they put into their voices when they asked him. When a man was well, he never realized all kinds of little things about not being well. Funny, the number of things that a man never thought about unless something happened to him. But he hadn't even answered Danny.

"Oh, I'm all right, Dan. Sit down. Bob told me you hurt your shoulder."

"It's all right now, Pa."

"Is your team winning any games?"

"We haven't yet."

"You haven't got much of a team, have you?"

"Well, we got a light team. It fights hard."

Danny sat watching Jim. Pa looked bad. Mother and Aunt Peg were surprised that he had even pulled through after this stroke.

"Where's Bill?"

"He's gone to a movie. Bill goes out on the wagons now," Jim said.

Danny didn't say anything. Bill was on the wagons working hard, and here he was in school. And playing football. He was worried about Bill. Bill didn't look healthy. He was skinny, and his face looked pasty. Out on the wagons he might get sick or get pneumonia or something. And the work was hard, too.

"Well, when you get out of school in June, we'll get you back in the company, and it's going to be O'Neill's Express Company."

He wouldn't be able to go to college and make a name for himself as a college football star. He wouldn't be able to be in a fraternity and live the life of a college man.

They sat for a few silent moments.

"Papa, I can quit now and go to work," Danny said, but he hated to have to do this.

"You finish it out this year. I'll be back at work sooner than it looks, too. I'm feeling better already. I'll get a week or two more of rest, and then I'll start taking walks. I'll be in shape in no time."

Papa seemed so sad when he talked like that. Did Papa really believe it?

"You do your lessons every night, Dan?"

"Yes," Danny said, knowing how much he was lying and how he studied only enough to get by.

"Maybe when I get back to work and you're earning money, we can get a bigger place to live in, and then I'll have you and your sister come back to live here where you both belong."

Danny didn't answer to that. He didn't want to contradict Pa. But it worried him. He didn't want to live with Papa and Mama.

"Yes, I've got lots of plans. I've been working them out in my mind while I've been home here with nothing else to do."

Danny nodded.

"Get the checker board," Jim said after another silence.

They played five games of checkers, and Danny let his father win four of them.

"I got to go now, Pa," Danny said, getting up.

"What's the hurry?"

"I got to go home and do my homework."

"Well, come over again tomorrow."

When Danny got outside, he decided that he'd go down to the poolroom and see who was there. He could get by without having his homework tomorrow. Instead of walking, he did a fox trot along Calumet Avenue.

35

I

It was a balmy November evening. Coming home from confession, Danny limped stiff-leggedly and made very slow progress. His right knee was uncomfortably taped and bandaged and it pained him. He tried to move a little faster than he had been, but he felt the strain and had to slow down immediately.

Disappointed, he thought that if he had been able to play the full game today against Christian, he might have earned himself a berth on one of the All-Catholic teams that would be picked in about two weeks. Even though Christian had trimmed S.S. thirty to six, Danny felt that he had covered himself with glory. Today for the first time this season, he'd felt right, in good condition. His charley horses and wrenched shoulders were gone. He had reaped the full fruits of two years of football today by playing a game that made the crowd stand up and notice him more than once.

He carefully hopped off the curb at Prairie Avenue and drearily struggled across to the opposite curb. He carefully stepped onto it. He thought of how, time and again, the big Christian backs had come tearing and charging around his end, and he had busted up their plays, spilled the interference, and nailed the ball carrier. He recalled the time he'd leaped in the air between two Christian backs and snared a forward pass from Tim Doolan, one-handed. But the play he was most proud of was his run back of that kickoff. He recalled catching the ball on the five-yard line and cutting in toward the center of the field. Then, when the Christian team was swooping down on him and had him trapped, he'd reversed his field and raced down the side lines, pumping his knees high for a run of about fifty or sixty yards. And wasn't it just his luck that when he had dodged by the safety man and was free to go on for a touchdown, he should slip in the one muddy spot on the whole field? Only for a few damned yards of mud, he would have run a kickoff back for a touchdown against the champions of the league. Such a tough break! If only he hadn't slipped.

And his tackling today had been sharp and clean. He got a bigger thrill out of tackling than he did out of anything else in football, and today he had covered punt after punt of Tim Doolan's and nailed his man in his tracks. Yes, after his in-and-out season, he'd been hot today. He'd done everything on the field right. And then, early in the second quarter, he had to get hurt. Schillinger, the Christian left half, had started a swing around the other end, and he had dumped him from behind. Fireman Fagin had piled on after the tackle, only instead of landing on Schillinger, Fagin had fallen on his knee. His knee had suddenly started feeling peculiar. It seemed as if there were cords in his joint tightening up on him. He'd looked at it, and it was swollen up like a sponge. Joe came on the field to look at it and had told him to come out. He'd refused to move. Joe sent Kavanaugh in to take his place, and the referee chased him off the field. He could remember himself limping off the field, while rooters from both sides had given him a big hand. That was glory. It might be the last time he'd ever walk off a gridiron for S.S., because it didn't seem as if his knee would be in shape for the final game of the year against Athanasius next Saturday. What a lousy break. Maybe if he'd been able to play the entire game, he'd have been even more sensational, and on the strength of his play he might have earned himself a ride to some college. With Pa laid up, that was the only way he'd ever be able to go to college. Yes, today he'd been the nuts, and then, just at his peak, he had to get hurt.

Well, even though today might be the end of him, he'd gotten something. He'd won a memory. If you loved football, any sacrifice for it was justified. And he loved it. He hobbled along South Park Avenue, painfully slow, walking like one for whom each step was agony. Yes, he loved football and he would always remember the game, and now, today, he had justified his career. All year he had played to the grandstand, even pretending to be kicked in the nuts when he hadn't been, in order to get a few cheers. Well, today he had made up for all that grandstanding. Today he'd played football as it should be played.

He felt his bandaged leg. He had three blocks to go, and then two flights of stairs to climb. The pain in his leg was sharp and steady. His leg was tired. His wrenched and swollen knee was very sore. Still, he was proud of it, as if it were a medal. He wanted people to see him limping. He wanted them to know how he'd earned his injury.

II

The swelling in Danny's knee was going down. It was getting dark. Walking with a slight limp, Danny left Jackson Park with Joe after the practice session. Danny had caught a few passes, and for the rest of the time he had kidded and goofed around. He wouldn't have come out at all to practice except that it was the last week of the season. Athanasius was their own weight, and they were hoping to win their first game of the season. If they won, they were going to claim the lightweight championship of the Catholic League.

"Danny, I'm disappointed in you," Joe said.

"What?"

"I don't like your attitude. You haven't come out to practice regularly this year as you did last, and you demoralize the team."

"How?"

"You don't always try. Of course, I don't expect you to do much now with your knee hurt, but you kid around, and last week you were laying down in practice."

"Well, what the hell, Joe, I don't like to kill myself in practice. What's the use?"

Joe looked at him, startled.

"Danny, the trouble with you is that you're good, and you know it."

"I can do some things on a football field. So why the hell should I break my neck in practice?" Danny said, limping beside the burly coach.

"Suppose you weren't good? I know you are, and that's why I put you in the game. With the attitude you've shown, I wouldn't have if I didn't need you. But suppose you weren't good?"

"I'd quit the team. I wouldn't be a sucker like some of the guys and come out and get battered all over in practice just to sit on the bench with a suit on and watch others play. That's good in story books, but I wouldn't do it in real life. If I couldn't be a regular on a team, I wouldn't be any heroic unknown soldier on a football squad."

"Do you say things like this to the other fellows?"

"No, but you just asked me questions, so I'm saying them to you. I'm not going to stop suckers from being suckers."

"Danny, if I didn't like you, I'd talk differently to you. I don't think you're going to get anywhere, not only in sports but in life, with that attitude."

Danny grinned at Joe rather foolishly.

"You go out and play a game like you did Saturday and then you talk to me like this. Why do you play football?"

"I like it. It's fun."

"It's more than fun. It's training for life. You got to fight in life the way you fight on the gridiron. That's what I want you kids to learn, that's the lesson I want you to get. To be sportsmen, hard fighters, and to learn to be loyal," Joe said.

"Football's a dirty game."

Joe looked at Danny, perplexed.

"Well, it is. We all play dirty sometimes. I hold and trip every time I think I can get away with it, and I'm not the only one. Everyone does."

"That's no way to play the game. It's no way to play the game of life."

Danny smirked. He was surprised at the thoughts that came into his head. Did he really believe them? Yes, in the main, he did.

Joe and Danny walked on in the fading twilight.

III

The football banquet was being held in the refectory room on the second floor of the school building where the priests ate. Father Robert Geraghty, the master of ceremonies, rose at the speakers' table after Tim Doolan was applauded for his speech.

"Now I'm going to call on our star end, Danny O'Neill."

Danny's teammates clapped for him as he slowly arose. Nervous, he painfully remembered how at last year's banquet he had risen, said he had nothing to say, and sat down again. This year he had to say something.

"We heard a lot of speeches about how good we are. Well, we weren't as good as we've been told, and we oughtn't to kid ourselves."

He paused. He didn't know why he had started speaking this way. He sensed Father Robert's eyes on him, stern and sharp. He hemmed and hawed a moment. A voice inside of him said for him to go on, and to tell the truth.

"Fellows, we got skinned in every game this year but the one against Athanasius. Tonight I've been thinking about the season. I can't think it was just tough luck we lost so many games. We weren't so hot. We weren't loyal enough. We didn't play hard enough. We didn't give everything we got. We weren't any good. We don't deserve all these encomiums and laudations we got. Those of us that are getting letters shouldn't feel too puffed up because we're getting our double S. We had a lousy team. We didn't really go down fighting. I'm talking about myself, too, here. I say this because maybe next year the squad will profit by what I say and will try to make next year's eleven what we dreamed of making this year's team and didn't . . . uh . . . uh . . . that's all I got to say."

Danny sat down, tense and apprehensive. He was perfunctorily applauded by his shocked teammates. He felt that he hadn't made a good impression. His first public speech, and what a frost it was.

Father Robert stood up, his face flushed.

"I want you all to forget what your *star* end has just said. His speech was unworthy of his team, unworthy of his own feats under our school colors. You have been a football team that has brought honor to your school."

But Father Robert had seen only one game.

"You gave the best you had. You had good training. But you were a young and green team, and you performed remarkably well against all odds."

Father Robert fixed his eyes on Danny. Danny felt like shriveling up inside. But still, he'd told the truth. What he had said had made up to himself for his own grandstanding and posing, and for the things he'd done which he shouldn't have done. It was true. They had been just a half-ass team.

"O'Neill, you have spoken against your own teammates, your own comrades who fought side by side with you in the mud and went through the fire with you. What you have said here tonight reflects on them. I don't think that you really meant what you said. I think that all of your teammates will take a charitable attitude toward what you said here tonight, and that it will be forgotten. We don't want those to whom we award our letter to have such thoughts as yours."

Father Robert paused. There was loud and enthusiastic applause. Blushing, Danny clapped. But he had told the truth.

IV

"I nominate Rory McGann for captain," Danny said.

"I second it," Marty said.

"Who else is nominated?" Father Robert asked, looking around the room.

No one spoke up. Rory sat across the table from Danny. He was only a freshman, but he had been one of the best players on the team, and he promised to develop into a real star. He was a dopey, freckle-faced kid, and Danny suddenly recalled hearing all kinds of stories about how dumb he was in the classroom and how he was always getting in trouble with Father Robert. He had nominated Rory because he thought that Rory was the best prospect on the whole team and ought to be captain because, dumb or not otherwise, he was not dumb on the field, and everybody liked him.

"No more nominations?" Father Robert asked.

The fellows glanced from one to another. Danny guessed they just couldn't think of anyone and that they probably wanted Rory the same as he did.

"We have to have more than one nomination," Father Robert said.

"Father, then I'll nominate Moss," Pat Nolan said.

"I'll second it," McDonald said.

"Father, I want to nominate . . ."

"That's enough, Sachs. Nominations are closed," Father Robert said.

You couldn't go against Father Robert. That's where he'd put his foot in it.

"Doolan, you count the votes, and, Jablownski, you and Mulligan collect them. There is a little card before each plate for you to vote on," Father Robert said.

He sat down, and there was chatting while the votes were cast, collected, and counted.

"McGann, nineteen, Moss, eleven," Tim Doolan announced. They cheered.

"Just a minute!" Father Robert called out sharply. "You have to vote again. McGann is only a freshman and we have to have a captain such as Moss, who is a better student than McGann."

V

"What was eating you to make that speech?" Marty asked Danny as they were walking away from school in a group after the banquet.

"I don't know. I just got up and I started talking."

"You sure talked a mouthful," Ike said.

"Say, what's Galloping Geraghty got against Rory? He wouldn't let him be captain," Tim asked, lighting a cigarette.

"He elected that pk, Moss, captain," Marty said.

"Geraghty always gets his pets. Look at Shanley," Danny said.

"Boy, Shanley even had to be taking up a collection at the banquet," Marty said.

"The school ought to give Shanley a rebate on the dough he collects for mission, and God knows what else," Tim said.

"Come to think of it, guys, there is always a collection for something comin' up. It was for the Foreign Mission Society tonight, wasn't it?" Ike said.

"Yes, and, Ike, you ought to ask for something out of that Foreign Mission collection. You're a foreigner," Red Keene said.

"Wise guy," Ike said to Red.

"Anyway, I don't see why he has the right to nullify our election the way he did," Marty said.

"Well, when he first came and we were first year, the guys in third year fought with him, remember? And he screwed them up and down, and they hardly got a medal, and nobody from their class was even put on the *Aureole* staff," Danny said.

"I tell you, if you ain't in good with him, you're s.o.l.," Ike said.

"And I'm in Dutch with him," Danny said.

"It's your own damned fault. You spilled your own beans by shootin' off your trap."

Danny guessed they were right. Why had he done it? He'd been a fool. But, damn it, he had told the truth.

"You didn't have to say that the crap they gave us is all crap," Tim said.

"What the hell. It's all right at a banquet," Marty said.

They walked on down Stony Island.

"Say, guys, I got a date with Sheila Cullen for the Alumni Hop," Danny said; he'd meant to tell them this news sooner and it had slipped his mind.

"Congratulations. She rates," Marty said.

36

I

I just saw his nibs," Jim said, heatedly, coming in from a short walk.

"Who?" Lizz asked.

"His nibs, your son." Jim paused a moment. "My eyes nearly popped out of my head. I didn't say a word, and he didn't see me. He just walks along as swell as you please—wearing a goddamned pair of spats."

"Maybe the young fellows are all wearing spats these days."

"The damned dude! I should have walked up to him and given him a slap in the puss to let him know who he is."

"Jim, you're taking it too serious. There's nothing wrong in the boy wearing spats. Maybe they're an old pair of Ned's."

"Don't you stick up for him. That bucko has a swelled head. Did you ever watch that prancing, dancing walk he has sometimes? Goddamn it, he walks like he thought he was the Prince of Wales. Well, if he goes on the way he's started, he'll turn out to be the Pimp of Wales. A pauper's son wearing—spats."

"Well, Jim, it's not my doing."

"I suppose that the next thing we know, Daniel O'Neill Esquire will be coming over to see us with a cane. And do you see all the grease he puts on his hair? He can't part his hair on the side like a man. He's got to part it in the middle like those damned pups who hang around that poolroom."

"Jim, now you know you're not supposed to let yourself get excited."

"Oh, what does it matter? The world will be better off with me out of it."

"Jim, you better lay down and take a nap."

"I was over at your mother's the night he had his fraternity meeting there, and I was sittin' in the parlor, listenin' to them talk. Lizz, those boys come from richer homes than his and they'll make a bum out of him. He didn't think I knew what they were talking about with their dances and shenanigans, sayin' we'll pay at the door and I'm taking this girl and you're takin' that, and he'll go with spats and play the gentleman. Lizz, aren't you proud of the son we left with your relations to raise?"

"Oh, Jim, Danny isn't bad, if only those O'Flahertys don't influence him."

"If I'm ever able to go back to work, that lad comes home where he belongs."

Jim looked out the window at the fading day. If he ever went back to work!

He dragged himself off to the bedroom and dropped on the bed. His anger had worn him out. A lethargy seemed to permeate his whole body. Here he was, lying alone, alone in all the world, a sick and a dying man.

He drowsed off to sleep.

II

As soon as Danny came home from downtown wearing his new pair of spats, he put on his blue trousers and looked at himself in the mirror. The trousers fell neatly over them, and he ought to look classy for his Friday night date. Of course, he was self-conscious about wearing spats. But then, Phil Rolfe around the poolroom wore spats. And so did Tommy Collins. If they could, why couldn't he?

He went to his bedroom and took off the spats and trousers and put his school pants back on. He looked at the cloth-top shoes he'd worn downtown. Pa had given them to him, and they fit him snugly. But they had the ugliest damned gray and brown checked tops. No one wore shoes like that. If he dared to wear them, he could just imagine Ike, and Red, or someone asking him what the hell did he think he was, a museum. But these were the only decent pair of shoes he had to wear to the dance, and he had been stumped with what to do about shoes until he'd hit upon the idea of spats. And then he'd had luck last night at the frat meeting and won three bucks in blackjack. So now he was set for his date to take Sheila Cullen to the Alumni Dance. It was his first dance at a hotel. Just think, less than a year ago he had despaired of ever learning how to dance, and now, well, while he couldn't dance as good as Hugh or Marty, he could dance better than Tim and a lot of other fellows. He still had the problem of money. He'd been saving out of his lunch money for two weeks, and he could get by if he didn't have to take a cab. He had to phone Hugh tonight to see if he couldn't go in the new Reo Hugh's old man had just bought. Perc Dineen, whom he'd known at Crucifixion, had a Marmon to go around in. He could see himself, driving a Marmon or a Lincoln.

He was getting places. But this problem that he'd just solved about the shoes was only one instance of how it wasn't as easy for him to be a high-school fraternity man as it was for the other fellows. He had to wear hand-me-down clothes, an overcoat out of style with a velvet collar that Uncle Al had given him, Pa's cloth-tops, pleated shirts from Uncle Ned. Yes, Fate treated him different than it did his friends. Well, so much the more to overcome. He picked up his English textbook and studied the lesson for tomorrow. Since his talk at the football banquet, Galloping Geraghty had been making him recite every day. He couldn't fall down on his lesson with the Galloper now.

III

"You say you haven't any school today?" Jim asked, idly glancing out of the window.

"No," Danny said.

"That's right. Neither have the kids. It's too bad that you haven't a job to do so you could earn a little money when you have free time. What happened about that shoe-store job?" Jim asked.

"Mr. Dorian, he's the manager of the store, said he didn't need me any more."

While Jim had his eyes turned toward the window, Danny observed him closely. Pa had changed so much. His hair was almost entirely gray. The right side of his face was twisted a bit, particularly at the mouth. And there was a strange stare about his eyes. Pa didn't look at all like what he once did. Danny tried to remember his father from the days in the cottage. Pa had been heavier then, and he'd been strong and could do all kinds of things. But it was difficult to recall to mind just what Pa had looked like. Now he was so different. He tried, but still he could not form a clear image of what his father had looked like before his first stroke.

"I want to get a drink of water. I'll be right back," Danny said.

Jim didn't answer. His lips were quivering.

"Son, what's your father doing in the front?" Lizz asked while washing dishes.

"He's just sitting there, Mama."

"He's not been feeling so well today."

Danny didn't say much. He knew that Pa wasn't going to live long. He didn't like to think about Pa dying.

Danny got a drink of water and went back to the parlor. Jim was lying crumpled on the floor and foaming out of the mouth, his eyes open but seemingly sightless.

"Mama! Mama!" Danny shouted.

Lizz came rushing into the room.

"Something's happened to Pa," Danny said, terrified at the sight of his father.

"Oh, merciful God!" Lizz exclaimed.

She bent down to Jim.

"Jim! Jim! Jim!" she said frantically.

"Can I do anything, Mama?" Danny asked, convinced that his father was dying.

"Here, help me get him in the chair," she said.

Danny and Lizz bent down and tried to lift Jim's limp body from the floor. He was difficult to lift, but they got him propped in a chair. The only sign of life Jim showed was his gasping. His mouth hung open.

"Mama, I better get the priest," Danny said.

"Yes, Son, and telephone Docter Mike. Get a nickel out of my pocketbook," she said.

"I got a nickel."

He grabbed his coat and flew out of the house.

IV

After speaking with Doctor Mike, Danny hurried out of the drugstore at Sixty-first and Calumet. The time had come. Pa was dying. Danny ran along Sixty-first Street and as he neared Prairie Avenue he got a stitch in his side. He had to walk.

His father was dying. And on the very day that he had a date to go to the dance. He couldn't go to a dance with his father dying. Perhaps Pa would even be dead by the time he was due to call for Sheila. Perhaps the Sacrament of Extreme Unction would save Pa's life. God might not call Papa. A man wasn't dead until he was dead, and God might save him.

If God had made up His mind, how could you persuade God to change His mind by prayers? That was a question he often thought about and never could settle. He ought to ask about it sometime in his Christian Doctrine class at school.

He dashed in front of a rumbling truck at Prairie Avenue and was almost run over.

He couldn't run because that pain in his side came back. Sixty-first Street was so familiar to him. The stores and the people. Women with baby buggies and little kids. Passing street cars. And yet it wasn't familiar. It was strange. Here he was walking along it now under such different circumstances. Not going to church or to school or anything like that, but going for the priest while his father was dying. Pa might be dead when he got back.

Pain in the side or not, he had to get the priest. He couldn't be responsible for Pa dying without the last rites of the church because of a pain in the side. He ran, holding his side, grim and resolute.

V

"Hello, Dan," Father Doneggan said as he entered the reception room of the priest's house; Father Doneggan was a small, nervous priest.

Danny liked him. He was glad he was seeing Father Doneggan.

"Father, I think my father is dying. Can you come to him right away?" Danny said, out of breath.

"Sure. What's the matter, Danny?"

"I think he's had another stroke. I think he's dying. I went out to the kitchen to get a drink of water and when I came back to him he was on the floor. He was unconscious. He looked like he was dying," Danny said.

"Wait for me. I'll go right with you," Father Doneggan said, starting to unbutton his cassock as he walked out of the room.

VI

He was walking along Sixty-first Street with Father Doneggan, and Father Doneggan was carrying the sacred Host. What should you say to a priest who was carrying God with him on the street?

"How are you doing these days, Dan?" Father Doneggan asked.

"I'm all right," Danny said, surprised that Father Doneggan would ask such a question when he was carrying with him God and the holy oil for the anointing.

"Playing on any of the school teams?"

"I was on the football team and I'm captain of the heavyweight basketball team. My picture ought to be in the *Chronicle* next week."

"I'll watch for it."

They walked a stretch in silence and turned down Calumet Avenue. He hoped they'd arrive in time.

"How's your mother?"

"She's all right, Father."

"She's a fine woman. Say, your two brothers sometimes serve mass for me. Good boys."

"One of them is in eighth grade now."

"Yes, isn't his name Dennis?"

"Yes, Father."

"The other one is a bright boy, too, the southpaw. That's Bob."

"Here we are," Danny said.

VII

Danny sat alone in the dining room, looking idly out at some young kids playing in the vacant lot. He couldn't see his brothers out there. He didn't like being present on occasions like this. He could hear voices, Mama, Father Doneggan, Doctor Mike. Would Pa live or would he die? He wasn't in with them because Mama had said for him to wait outside.

"I think your father is going to be all right, Son," Lizz said, entering the room.

"Yes?" he answered, going limp in sudden relief.

"Son, you go and leave this at the drugstore on Fifty-eighth Street," she said, handing him a prescription.

Danny put on his coat and hurried out. He could go to the dance and Papa wouldn't die.

VIII

When he came back from the drugstore, Doctor Mike was gone. Pa was propped up in the bedroom, and Father Doneggan was in the hallway, just ready to leave.

"Father, please take this for a mass for my dead father," Lizz said, trying to give the priest a dollar bill.

"Mrs. O'Neill, you keep it. I'll say the mass anyway. You need it for yourself and for your family."

"Father, here's my angel. Father, he's in fourth-year high school now and he's going to graduate in June," Lizz said.

"Dan's an old friend of mine," Father Doneggan said, giving Danny a friendly poke in the ribs.

"Father, do you know my mother thinks the world of you?"

Father Doneggan edged toward the door.

"Why, she thinks that the sun never sets on you."

"A fine woman, your mother."

"And how is your father?"

"He's all right. I didn't know you knew him."

"I know who he is."

Father Doneggan edged closer to the door.

"Oh, Father," Lizz began.

"I have to go, Mrs. O'Neill, and I'll come back. I think your husband will be all right," Father Doneggan said.

"You were so good, Father. I know it was your coming that saved him."

"I wouldn't say that. But goodbye, Mrs. O'Neill."

The priest turned to Danny. "Keep your chin up, Dan."
Lizz pursued him to the sidewalk.

IX

Suppressing his excitement and acting calmly, as if such dates were usual occurrences to him, Danny helped Sheila Cullen out of the Reo. They entered the Warwick Hotel on Fifty-third Street, near Lake Park Avenue. Followed by Tim and Mary Boylan, and Hugh and Marty with their girls, they strolled casually across the ornate hotel lobby. Sheila was a moon-faced, bovine girl, with lovely shiny black hair which she arranged simply. She wore a pale green dress underneath her muskrat coat.

"Excuse me while I powder my nose," she said after Danny had helped her off with her coat.

She and the girls went to the ladies' room. Danny checked his and Sheila's coats in the checkroom. After brushing up in the lavatory, Danny and the fellows waited for the girls by the entrance to the Glass Room, hearing strains of music from within. Couples drifted idly by them to go in and dance. Danny stuck his hands in his pockets and tried to imitate Hugh's blasé manner. He glanced down at his spats. None of the fellows had kidded him about them. He hadn't said much to Sheila, but he'd find his tongue when they danced.

X

Sheila was in his arms, dancing, following him so perfectly that he felt almost as if he were dancing with himself. It seemed to him like a scene in a moving picture. Everything was just right, wonderful.

The polished half-filled dance floor was surrounded by gilt-framed mirrors. A large crystal chandelier hung from the center of the high ceiling. The orchestra played overhead in a balcony.

Looking over her shoulder, Danny watched his image in the mirrors. He was beginning to get some glide and rhythm into his dancing. With a little more practice he'd be as good as Marty or any of his frat brothers. But he ought to say something to Sheila.

"This is good music," he said.

"Yes, isn't it," she answered as Danny bent down and held his face close to hers to hear.

He glided her into a corner, turned and took long easy steps down one side of the floor.

"Yes, it is good music," he said.

"Yes, it is."

He whirled her in another corner.

"What's the name of this piece?" she asked.

"Gee, now, what is it?"

He seemed visibly to be racking his memory to recall the name of the dance tune.

"I heard it before, but I just can't place the name," he said.

Just then the orchestra stopped. Danny joined the other dancers in clapping politely.

"Say, now that's funny. I've heard that piece, and still the name just won't come to me," he said.

Girls like Sheila seemed to wait for a fellow to talk to them. They didn't offer much themselves. But then, why should they? They could get all the fellows they wanted.

"Well, it's turning out to be a pretty good dance."

"Yes," she said.

The orchestra started playing again.

XI

Danny felt the bulge in his pocket. Sheila had asked him to keep her purse for her. He was discovering that little things like that added to the charm and pleasure of taking a girl out. Holding her purse for her made you realize that you were her escort.

Walking off the floor with Sheila, he courageously took her arm. The sounds of conversation about them were hushed, low; the laughter was restrained. Everyone at the dance was polite and well-mannered. The expression on Danny's face was serious, as was that on the faces of other fellows. It was as if they were all performing an accepted ritual which demanded seriousness of demeanor and restraint of voice. And Danny was thrilled with the idea of it all. He was actually at a dance with a nice girl, and he was showing that he knew how to behave. He kept watching Hugh and others out of the corner of his eye and trying to imitate them.

Danny and Sheila joined the others by a lounge in the lobby. Sheila sat down with the girls. Just as Father Henry, the head of the alumni, passed, Tim and Marty lit cigarettes. Father Henry waved a greeting to them and walked on.

"He didn't bat an eye with you fellows smoking," Danny said.

"We're not under his authority now. We can smoke here," Tim said.

"Say, that's good music," Marty said.

Somehow when Marty said this, it didn't seem forced; when he said it, he feared his voice was artificial and strained and that the girls would know this.

"Yes, swell band," Tommy Collins said with a professional air.

Danny took a good look at Hugh's date. She was a husky blonde, but damned pretty and well built. She never seemed to stop smiling. She looked nice, but, no, he wouldn't trade her for Sheila.

"Our frat has the nicest girls at the dance," Hugh bragged, smiling at the girls.

Danny stood facing Sheila, hands in pockets, alertly following the conversation. He was thinking that he ought to ask some of the fellows to exchange dances, but he didn't know which ones to ask. He didn't know which girls it would be easiest to talk to and which ones would want to dance with him.

Red Keene, who'd come as a stag, strolled over to Danny.

"Ah, here's the torch head," Danny said.

"Don't you ever get tired of the same gags?" Ike asked Danny.

Danny couldn't think of a comeback to put Ike in his place.

Just then they heard music for the next dance.

"Shall we dance?"

"All right, but let's let some others get on the floor first. I don't like to be the first on the floor," Sheila answered.

He should have waited a moment. He guessed it was a *faux pas* to be the first one on the dance floor.

Hugh and his girl moved on, and the others following. Sheila rose. Danny walked at her side. He saw Natalie enter the Glass Room with Eddie Feeley. Natalie would see he had a good date and that he could dance now.

Just as Danny and Sheila began to dance, the lights went out. Spotlights from the balcony played over the dancers. The band groaned out the *Roses of Picardy* in slow measures. Danny was touched and moved. This was romance. If he could only find words to say, having this girl in his arms now, dancing smoothly with her, smelling her perfume, smelling her hair, feeling now and then a brush of her hair against his cheeks. Did she feel what he did?

A red spot momentarily played on Danny and Sheila. He tried almost frantically to think of something to say, to have the whole floor see him in what appeared to be intimate talk with Sheila. He wanted it to look to everyone as if he were in love. He wanted Natalie to see that he was in love, and that she meant nothing at all in the world to him. But his mind was blank, and his throat was dry. Words seem to choke on him. A yellow spotlight was turned on another couple. Saying not a word, he danced with Sheila.

XII

"That was keen," Danny said, clapping.

Sheila grinned.

Noticing that Natalie and Feeley were near by, he led Sheila to them.

"Hello, Danny," Natalie said.

"Natalie O'Reedy, this is Sheila Cullen. And this is Mr. Feeley," Danny said, and they all acknowledged the introductions.

"Keen music," Danny said.

"Yes, it isn't at all bad," Feeley said with reserve.

The four of them stood there, waiting for the orchestra to resume, looking at one another without saying a word.

XIII

"You've taken French, haven't you?" he asked, gliding Sheila to a corner.

"Of course, but I'm not very good at it."

"Neither am I. But I got one thing out of French."

"What's that?"

"Oh, a motto. A good one."

"What is it?"

"Toujours de l'audace."

"Did you make it up yourself?"

"Uh huh," he muttered, hoping that she hadn't read *The Drums of Jeopardy* in *The Saturday Evening Post*, because that's where he'd learned the motto.

"That's nice," she said.

They danced silently. She would think he was a dope if he didn't keep on talking. He'd learned how to dance. Now if he wanted to be somebody in the eyes of girls, he had to learn how to talk.

"Say, that was a keen idea the orchestra had, jazzing up *Adeste Fidelis* in the last dance, wasn't it?" he said.

"Yes."

"The fellow who thought that one up was clever. It was a keen idea."

Sheila didn't answer.

XIV

Danny helped Sheila out of the automobile and walked with her to her hallway.

"Thank you, and I had a very nice time," she said inside the hallway.

He shoved his face forward with his lips pursed.

"Don't," she said.

"Aren't you gonna kiss me good night?" he asked huskily, grabbing her.

She turned her face aside. He kissed her ear. She freed herself and stuck the key into the lock of the outer door. He stood helpless, like a fool.

"Good night."

"Good night."

He watched her go.

He walked slowly back to the Reo. He saw Tim and Mary Boylan necking in the back seat. He felt like a chump. He hadn't known what to do and how to go about it. He sank into the front seat with Ike alongside of him, and as Hugh drove on he kept thinking of Sheila.

XV

Riding home from school on the elevated train, Danny saw a picture of himself on the sporting page of *The Daily Chronicle*. In the photograph, he stood with feet spread apart and with skinny arms outstretched, guarding Bart Daly, who held a basketball ready to pass it. Bart was one of the smartest fellows in fourth year. But hell, if his name wasn't under the picture, nobody would know it was him. He looked almost like a Chinaman.

He read the article accompanying the picture.

SAINT STANISLAUS PLAYERS SHOW GOOD SPIRIT

by Albert Michaelson

Distance lends enchantment to the basketball aspirations of the Saint Stanislaus boys, who every afternoon make the jaunt from their school near Jackson Park to a hall at Grand Crossing for practice. With such determination in overcoming what would be a handicap for a less spirited team, it is not to be wondered at that in the Catholic League contests these black-and-red-jerseyed lads should put up a battle for the league scalp lock.

Several Veterans Back

Ably coached by Father Theodore and captained by their classmate, O'Neill, the heavies are displaying a fighting spirit which should place them higher on the list than last year's position of fourth. Most of the old team are back, with two new prospects among the early turnout, Nolan and Moss, who centered for the school eleven.

Of the veterans, Danny O'Neill and Mulligan take senior precedence with Borowik, who comes from last year's lightweights. Mulligan and O'Neill will fill the respective positions of guard and forward, while two third-year men, Harrington and Fagin, will complete the floor partnership. Harrington, who has a keen eye for free throws, will be employed for most of the tallies.

He got off at Fifty-eighth Street and stopped into the poolroom. It was smoky and crowded, and he saw Studs Lonigan shooting straight pool. Studs didn't say anything. He'd like Studs to say he saw the article in the paper and the picture. Studs went on shooting pool.

"Hey, why you holding out on us?" Wils Gillen asked Danny.

"Huh?"

"I seen your picture in the paper and read what was said about you," Wils said.

"Oh, that," Danny said modestly.

"I never knew you was good. Hey, guys!" Wils yelled.

Phil Rolfe and some of the fellows turned toward Wils.

"Hey, did you see O'Neill's picture in the paper tonight?" Wils yelled.

"What for? Was he arrested to be put in the loony house?" Studs Lonigan asked.

"He's a basketball star," Wils yelled.

"That's all spelled C R A P, punk," Studs said, chalking his cue.

"I never knew you was good, shake on it," Wils said. Danny smiled self-consciously. He was arriving. These guys never had their pictures in the paper or had write-ups.

"Let's play a game of slop pool," Wils said.

"All right," Danny said.

XVI

Danny walked home, thinking how all kinds of people in Chicago would read *The Chronicle* tonight. They'd read about him and see his picture in the paper. That was something to be proud of.

He only hoped that Sheila and Natalie would see it. And, yes, that Roslyn Hayes would see it, too, and that it would make her sorry she'd once thrown away a chance to get him.

He turned in the alley to go up the back stairs and again he thought of how all kinds of men in the city would turn to that sports page and there see the picture of Danny O'Neill. That made him more famous than the guys around the poolroom. Let the older guys kid him. Studs Lonigan never had his picture in the paper. He was on the road now, on the road to being somebody.

He sang.

I could just go right on dancing, forever, dear, with you . . .

37

I

Danny studied himself in the mirror which ran along the wall above the line of wash bowls in the Bourbon Palace lavatory. He looked all right. The pimples he'd had on his forehead a couple of days ago were gone. He was proud of his loud-striped tie and he hoped that it would help him to cop off dances with some good-looking girls.

Others were also giving themselves a final once-over. A cake-eater carefully recombed his hair. A man with a pancake haircut straightened his tie. A pimply young lad washed his hands and turned to the drying machine. He stepped on the treadle and held his hands in the current of hot air that roared out of the machine.

Leaving, Danny almost collided with Wils Gillen at the doorway.

"I see you come up to compete with Valentino tonight," Wils said.

Danny waited for Wils to take a leak and give himself the once-over. They left the lavatory together and ascended the carpeted steps. There was an ornate mirror at the landing halfway up.

"Plenty of babes to jig with tonight," Wils said, and Danny nodded.

Upstairs, the large and overdecorated foyer to the dance floor was already jammed, although it was only nine o'clock.

"I'll see you by this table here. I'm going to get me a jig," Wils said as the orchestra played a jazz tune.

II

Danny had been moving around, trying to get up the courage to ask some girl to dance with him. He pushed through the crowd toward the dance floor. It was the largest dance floor in Chicago and was as smooth as glass. Oval in shape, it was surrounded by marble pillars. A promenade, with Louis Quatorze chairs, circled it on two sides. Danny edged along the promenade and stopped at a pillar. He stood there watching the dancers. He noticed a girl near him. She was a little too plump and had straight bobbed hair and bangs over her forehead. Her velvet dress looked cheap. Not good-looking enough to bother about, he decided.

He saw Wils whirl past with a hot blonde mama dressed in white. They quickly disappeared in the whirling crowd.

The dance floor was becoming more crowded every minute. He wanted keenly to be out there dancing, but he stood watching as if he were casually surveying the crowd. Suppose the girl in velvet was a Polack and nothing to write home about, he could ask her to dance, couldn't he? She was better than nothing.

A bell-bottomed young fellow in a greenish suit with a striped tie approached the girl in velvet.

"Are you dancing?" Danny heard him ask her.

"No," she replied tartly.

"Well, babe, there's roller skatin' on the sixth floor," the fellow said sarcastically, and then he walked on.

Her face expressionless, she watched the dancers.

"Would you like to dance?" Danny asked, approaching her.

"No!"

"Well, you must have come here under the misapprehension that it's an ice-skating palace," he said, but she walked away from him before he finished his insult.

Well, that was a Polack for you!

III

He found Gillen in the crowded foyer. All about them there was a steady hum of conversation.

"Get a jig?" asked Wils.

"I'll grab off the next hop."

"I had a babe. Boy, all she did was talk about Valentino, but was she luscious! And know what I did? I got her in a corner and socked it in, and I said, 'Umm, sister, Valentino can't give you anything better.' And she just laid it right back to me and said, well, if she couldn't have Ruddy, I'd do. So I got another hop with her. If she's got a girl friend, maybe we can take them home and lay 'em."

The orchestra started up again. Wils pushed off, and Danny was caught in a jam of couples who were shoving toward the dance floor.

IV

Four straight refusals. But he was determined to dance, no matter what he danced with. He approached a bony girl in a pink dress who stood by a pillar at the end of the floor near the foyer.

"Are you dancing?"

She stepped onto the floor and waited for him. He danced with her. Someone from behind bumped him.

"I beg your pardon," Danny said, stepping on the girl's toes.

"Oh, that's all right."

He would just as soon not be dancing as with this one. Not pretty. She smelled of cheap perfume gone stale. Or of something. He didn't like her odor. He pressed himself close to her. She shimmied with him. He gave her a meaningful, knowing look as he held her body tightly to his. Their feet scarcely moved in a jammed up crowd.

"It sure is crowded. I never seen it so crowded," she said.

"Yes, it is. Well, Valentino can pack them in."

"He's grand," she said.

He maneuvered her until they could slide sidewise and shimmy.

"Do you come here often?" she asked him.

"No."

"I never seen a crowd like this."

"Yes, it's a mob."

"I never seen a crowd like this."

Maybe she didn't have much of a face, but she sure had her features, Danny thought, liking what she was giving him. Continuing to shimmy, she threw her head back and sang to the music.

You gotta see your mama every night,
Or you can't see mama at all.

V

Tired and sweating, Danny pushed back and forth along the promenade. The place was teaming with girls, and he couldn't find a partner. The crowd was so big that you could hardly dance on the large floor. It was just one huge pack. From the balcony upstairs, the dancers looked like a mob. He continued back toward the end of the floor, near the stairs and large foyer, keeping his eyes peeled for girls. Many fellows and men were doing likewise. Finally, he took a chair between two pillars and sat watching the couples endlessly move by. He saw a husky bouncer in a tuxedo, sidling through the crowd and tapping a couple on the shoulders. The next time he danced he'd have to watch out for the bouncers. But it was pretty hard for them to stop people from shaking it in a crowd this size.

He spotted the mama in white with whom Wils had danced. She was in the arms of a greasy fellow with long sideburns. She was keen to look at. He wondered how such a pretty girl could like to dance with the greasy fellow she had as a partner. Why, all you had to do was to look at such a guy and know that he was a pk.

The lights dimmed and spotlights played over the dancers, red, and then blue and then violet, and the orchestra played *Peggy O'Neill.* Danny remembered how he had danced with Sheila to this song. But how different she was from girls who came here. How different she was from girls like that blonde with the greasy cake. Girls like Natalie and Sheila who rated didn't come here or to other public dance halls. Of course, all the girls who went to public dance halls weren't bums and tramps, but a lot of them were, and Saint Paul girls who were keen and rated, they never went to such places. He thought of how he would like to be dancing with Sheila to this music, with spotlights playing over the darkened dance hall. He got up and strolled on, moody, wanting a girl to dance with him.

He spotted one who wasn't too bad to look at, though she was a bit thin. She was leaning against a post and had on a blue dress. He leaned against an opposite pillar and looked at her. Was she aware of him?

The orchestra halted, and the lights went on. There was loud applause, and the couples on the floor waited for the next piece.

"Would you like to dance?"

"No, thank you."

Danny slunk off. Turning around, he saw that some guy had asked the same girl and she was stepping onto the dance floor with him.

What was there about him? Was there something in the way he looked? In the way he spoke? In the tone of his voice? What? What was there about him that had made so many girls refuse him a dance as they'd done tonight?

VI

"Well, Wils, when you get as famous as Valentino, you'll be able to pack them in this way," Danny said; he was sitting with Wils, and they were sipping ginger ale in the jammed refreshment parlor in the balcony.

"Hell, Dan, he's workin' for us. He brings them here, and then we do the rest."

Wils could say that. He'd gotten practically every dance tonight, and with some of the neatest tricks in the place, too.

"Say, you were telling me about the swell frat you belong to. How about me getting pledged to it?"

Immediately, it seemed a good idea. If he did this for Wils, that would show he had stock. Wils rated with girls, and it would be easier to get dates and that sort of thing if he palled with Wils.

"Say, I'd like to do that. I'll bring you to a meeting next Monday night. Noel Merton from our neighborhood is being brought that night. Can you call for me at eight-thirty Monday?" Wils nodded affirmatively.

Danny took a sip of ginger ale. He felt a real sense of power, being able to get Wils pledged. Wouldn't he have been a chump not to have gone back into the frat?

VII

Although she was dumpy, you could look at her without getting sore eyes.

"Isn't it simply beautiful here?" she said, getting close to him.

There was something almost electric in the feel of a girl's body against him this way.

"Gee, I hope the Sheik is as wonderful as Julio. I don't go to places like this. My mother doesn't like me to. But I came tonight because I wanted to see him. Did you see him in *The Four Horsemen?*"

"Yes."

"Julio," she sighed.

Danny felt like a nobody. What could she think of him when she had Valentino on her mind? And it wasn't only girls who came to a public dance hall, either, who went into ecstasies over the Sheik. The girls at the Alumni dance in their bunch had talked a lot of Valentino. Even Little Margaret did.

"You think he'll be good?" she asked.

"I guess so," he answered, shrugging his shoulders and guiding her against the stage where Valentino would soon be appearing.

Progress was slow because the crowd crushed in around them, and they could hardly move and were pressed there against each other.

"You don't hang out here?" he asked, his voice rather hoarse.

"I should say not. I don't *hang out* any place."

The hell she didn't. She was the kind. He could tell from the way she danced. Well, she could dance that way with him all she wanted.

The orchestra stopped. They stood there near the stage.

"You know, I'm not like the girls here. I go only so far, you know, and then no farther. All right to toddle a little, but—"

"I never thought you were. That's why I asked you to dance with me."

"You see, my subconscious mind stops me from doing anything more," she said.

The orchestra started up again.

"Hot music," he said, pressing her tightly, feeling her crushed against him, both of them taking very short sidesteps, constantly halted because of the crowd that hemmed them in.

"Like I was saying, my subconscious mind stops me if a fellow wants to do more than a little toddling."

"Your sub-which? What's that?" he asked.

He'd heard Uncle Ned speak of the subconscious mind, but he thought he'd play dumb and maybe get off some cracks to make an impression.

"Say, you know what it is. Why, you look and talk like one of these college boys."

"Me? The only school I ever went to was reform school," he said.

"Well, your subconscious mind is—it's that thing that tells you when you're doin' wrong," she said.

They were clear of the stage. He glided her backward. She danced like a clinging vine. He was flattered to think that he could find a girl who'd dance that way with him.

"Well, maybe we all ought to give our subconscious minds some chloroform," he said.

Just then the orchestra stopped. There was a spirited burst of clapping.

"That was good. They ought to play us another jig," he said.

The orchestra moved off its dais.

"Maybe we can have the next hop together," he said, leaving the dance floor with her.

"I'll meet you at this post for the third one from now."

"Don't forget what to do with that subconscious thing you got there," he said, smiling.

He bowed and walked off to meet Wils in the foyer.

VIII

Danny and Wils stood together in the center of the dance floor. Conversation buzzed all around them. They eyed the stage. There was a sudden burst of applause when the curtain was thrown back. They waited. They were pressed forward from behind.

"Well, we'll see what the bastard's got now," Wils said.

An orchestra dressed in Arabian costume seated itself on the stage, and there was more clapping. They twanged away at the strings of the banjos, playing *The Sheik.* They sang while the crowd continued to shove forward.

I'm the sheik of Araby,
Your love belongs to me;
At night when you're asleep,
Into your tent I'll creep.
The stars that shine above,
Will light our way to love.
You'll rule this land with me,
The Sheik of Araby.

Hysterical cries arose.

"The Sheik!"

"The Sheik!"

"There he is!"

"Air! Air! A woman's fainted."

All around him Danny heard cries and shouts, handclapping, girls and women yelling and shrieking and screaming, men cheering and whistling. And there upon the stage stood Rudolph Valentino, with his wife at his side.

Danny felt so unimportant. What was he in this mob? Who was he? Women were throwing things up toward the stage, jewels, rings, handkerchiefs. Girls were jumping up on their toes, waving their hands, waving handkerchiefs, blowing him kisses.

Rudolph Valentino was tall, dark, with a vapid, pretty face. He wore a wide-brimmed black sombrero, a white silk shirt, a woven and varicolored sash, black velvet trousers, and black boots. He bowed as the crowd continued to cheer and scream; the cheering and screaming continued.

"God, the dames is passin' out all over the place and tossin' rings and diamonds at him. Some dame has just thrown a diamond up at him," a husky fellow in back of Danny and Wils said.

"Say, Tony, you can't tell me all this ain't a publicity stunt for the spic," another fellow said.

"Handsome brute, but I go for his babe," Wils said.

His wife was a slender woman, and her skin seemed pale beside Valentino's. She was dressed in black and red, and wore a large, beautiful black shawl draped over her shoulder.

"The Sheik!"

"The Sheik!"

The cry went up again and again.

Danny and Wils tried to press closer, but couldn't. The people were now packed and jammed tightly against each other.

IX

While Valentino and his wife tangoed, a spotlight followed them. The crowd watched in silence. Danny stood on tiptoe, uncomfortable, wishing he were in Valentino's place. Valentino danced, lithe and supple, graceful. He led his partner in four gliding steps, the two of them walking side by side, and then he twirled her, and they swished and turned and curved and suddenly fell into a series of short quick steps and then into long and graceful ones. His hair glistened under the spotlight. The hall was hushed.

The balls of Danny's feet were tired, but he watched, keeping his eyes more on the woman than on the man on the stage and observing the dancing as closely as he could, to see if he could learn any steps. But the dance now was too intricate for him to imprint the steps clearly on his mind. The tango music ran in his head. He admired the simple grace of Valentino, who was again whirling his partner and then leading her at his side in those long and measured steps, facing her, each of them bending on one knee, rising, and without missing a beat swinging into fast whirls again. Hell, he could never dance like that.

X

After his encore dance, Rudolph Valentino stepped to the front of the stage. He waited while the applause rose persistently and girls and women shrieked and screamed. Danny saw a blonde snatch off a necklace and wildly fling it toward the stage.

"Ruddy!" she yelled.

"The spic's got something that you and I ain't got, Dan," Wils said.

And Rudolph Valentino stood before this throng, hearing the cries of admiration, his pretty face blank and expressionless, his sensuous lips turned in a slight smile, his famed hair glistening.

Danny watched him. He wouldn't like to look like that, dark, and almost not masculine. But he would like to be famous. Boy, to have all the babes go nuts for you that way. They were still yelling.

"The Sheik!"

"The Sheik!"

The crowd quieted down.

"Ladies and gentlemen!" Rudolph Valentino began, speaking with a foreign accent.

He continued, halting now and then to hunt for words. Danny listened. The old salve. He has never in his life received such a reception. He appreciates their kindness.

"And, ladies and gentlemen, I tell you, there is no city in the world for me like—like your own Chicago."

A burst of applause interrupted him. He waited.

"Kin yuh beat dat? All dese dames floppin' for a guy dat can't even speak English," said a bull-necked fellow with cropped hair who was on Danny's right.

"Yeh, Mick, he ought to take the spaghetti out of his voice."

Danny craned his neck. Valentino was telling them that he was fighting to give the American public good clean pictures, and that he was fighting the moving picture people who controlled pictures, and that he was grateful for the support the public was giving him.

Danny never knew that Valentino was fighting the movie moguls. But he didn't care about speeches.

His speech finished, Rudolph Valentino made a graceful bow and left the stage. The applause was deafening.

"Another dame's just caved in over there," Wils said, pointing.

Danny saw people milling and heard someone yelling to make way. He saw two men carrying a girl. Her dress was askew, and he got a brief glimpse of her white thighs.

The orchestra played *The Sheik*.

"I got this hop with a hot number," Wils said, starting to smash his way through the crowd.

Danny edged his way off the floor, dodging and weaving in between dancing couples.

His eye caught a slender, pretty girl.

"How about this dance?" he asked.

She stuck her nose in the air and moved away without answering him.

He reached the promenade and joined the parade of males seeking dancing partners.

38

I

"I hope there's no hard feelings, Dan," Dwight Lawrence said. Dwight was a lean, callow fellow who lived on South Park Avenue near Danny.

"What the hell, it's all in a lifetime," Danny answered, hanging up his cue.

Swinging his arms at his side, Danny briskly walked out of the poolroom.

"What were you doing in there?" Jim Doyle asked, stopping him right outside on the sidewalk.

"Oh, I was shooting a few games of pool," Danny said; he grinned foolishly and waited for what was to come. He liked Jim Doyle better than any of the older fellows, but Jim was always lecturing him. Jim liked to make speeches.

"I'll bet you're not doing as well in high school as my cousin, Joe," Jim said.

Danny knew he wasn't.

"It's because you hang around here. Take my advice, because I'm telling you this for your own good. Quit hanging around the poolroom and study more, so that some day you can amount to something."

Danny smirked. Jim Doyle should know that he'd just lost four dollars of his Christmas money playing rotation pool for two bits a game. Then would he get a speech from Jim.

"Well, I got to run along. I only wanted to tell you something for your own good," Jim Doyle said, passing on.

Danny laughed at the idea of Jim Doyle giving him advice like that. He was doing pretty well. Suddenly his cavalier attitude was punctured. Dwight Lawrence was a better pool player than he was, and he had played game after game as a gesture. He had determined that he would show that, what the hell, he could win or lose dough without batting an eye. But despite the way he'd posed, he'd really felt very different inside. He had been tense and nervous and so worried that he'd scratched shots again and again when he'd had high balls set up for him.

He had been making hollow gestures, trying to pose as a romantic nonchalant like Ed Lanson or a carefree fellow like Wils Gillen. And when he did this, all he was really doing was playing himself for a chump.

He turned in the alley to go home, disgusted with himself, wondering why he'd tossed the money down the bowl so foolishly.

II

Shaved, combed, and wearing a clean white shirt, Jim sat at the table, with eyes of adoration watching Bill eat breakfast. There sat the best of his kids.

"Now, you getting enough to eat, Bill?" Jim asked, wanting to be solicitous and saying this to show his solicitude.

"Sure. Sure, Pa."

"Well, it's good the Christmas rush is over. You won't have it so hard now."

"I didn't mind it. It brought in good money. It was fun driving my own gascar. But now, of course, my extra truck will be knocked off and I'll go back helpin'."

"Maybe if I talked to Pasey I could get you fixed up drivin' a truck regular. Of course, it would be easier to do nights, but I don't want you working nights. I don't care if I have to go to the poorhouse, Bill, I won't have you driving all night. You're young, and I don't want you getting buried on a night shift."

"Pa, it's just a matter of time and I'll have the seniority and I can get a truck on a regular route."

"Maybe you could get one of those tractors from McGinty."

"The tractors are a lazy man's job. You don't have to be an expressman to drive a tractor," Bill said.

Jim grinned. The express company must be getting in the boy's bones, he thought. Well, it was an honest way of making a living.

"Bill, I was wondering, maybe I could get your brother on nights, working after school. He's getting to be a husky kid and he can work as well as you. You sacrificed finishing your bookkeepin' course."

"Since he's gone this far in school, we ought to let him finish and graduate. By June I ought to have a regular truck of my own, getting a hundred and fifty-six a month. And you're getting a little money from the company benefit plan. We'll get by, Pa, until Dan graduates, and then he can get a job. And, why, you might even be back at work by June."

"Yes, you know, Bill, your old man's made of pretty tough stuff. It takes more than I had already to lay me out. I'm getting stronger. Yes, by next Christmas, Bill, the old man will be holding up his end of the stick."

Bill almost gulped. He bent down and looked at his coffee and took a quick drink.

"You know, I like Christmas to have snow, don't you, Pa?" he said.

"Yes, Christmas doesn't seem the same without snow on the ground."

"Snow makes Christmas seem entirely different."

"Yes," Jim nodded reflectively.

III

Danny moodily stared out of the window. There was no sun this morning. The park was bare, and the wind shook the leafless trees. He could see the figures of a few skaters on the lagoon. He turned from the window and plopped into a chair.

Christmas, like his birthday, always brought memories of old times. He remembered Roslyn. He didn't remember Hortense Audrey or Virginia Powers from Crucifixion, but he remembered Roslyn. Why should he? He only wished to see Roslyn now under circumstances where he could show off in front of her and let her know that she didn't really interest him. And yet last night, when he'd gone to confession, he'd had the same feeling of expectation that he used to have in grammar school when he'd go to confession and hope he'd see her at church. He liked the memory of what he used to feel about her much more than he liked her. But there was a sadness in thinking of that memory, in thinking of old times. Yes, he was full of nostalgia. He wished he were back in the old times, and here he was, almost nineteen. Time was flying. If he was destined to live to be sixty, why he had already lived a third of his life.

He wondered where he would be and what he would be ten years from now? That would be 1932. Who would be alive and who would be dead in the family? What would they all be doing? Would Mother be alive? At last she was beginning to get gray hairs. Would this be her last Christmas? Would it be Pa's last Christmas? Where would Sheila Cullen be in ten years? He wanted to be in love with her, and she wouldn't give him another date. There were so many questions about the future that he could ponder and wonder over.

In a few days it would be 1923. What was 1923 going to bring to him? Would he advance in life in the coming year? Would he get to college? Would it lead him on the road to where he would be fixed so that he could be somebody? He wanted to travel all over the world and see many cities, New York, Cleveland, Detroit, Paris, Berlin, Dublin, Jerusalem, San Francisco, Washington. Would he ever travel? And would his name ever mean anything in Chicago, in cities all around the country? And would he ever get a girl who would be lovely and who would marry him?

He went to his room. He wanted to write all his thoughts down, all that he felt and thought, his dreams of what he wanted to become in life. He'd never continued that diary he'd started way back on New Year's Eve in eighth grade. He got it out of a bottom drawer of his dresser and sat before it, holding a pen.

He couldn't write a line of his feelings, and finally he put the diary away and decided that it was time to go over and see his father.

IV

Jim wore the carpet slippers Bill had given him. When Bill had handed them to him last night, he'd almost cried. He looked at the table to the opened box with the tie that Danny had just brought him.

"It was nice of you to remember your father," he said.

"Gee, Pa, it wasn't very much."

"It's the spirit that counts, not the gift. Well, your poor father couldn't give anybody any presents this year. Your brother works too hard for me to spend his money on presents."

Jim lapsed into a spell of brooding. Danny thought how more and more when he came to see Papa this happened. They would talk for a while and then Papa would sit and say nothing. He would brood and be moody. He didn't know what to say. Papa seemed like such a sad man. Pa still had that brooding look on his face. Was he going to get sore? Sometimes that happened, and Pa criticized him and bawled him out. And sometimes Pa didn't, and then, after sitting like that, he would say something.

"Did you receive Communion this morning?" Jim asked.

"Yes, at five o'clock mass."

"You don't miss mass on Sundays, do you?"

"No, Pa, I never miss mass."

"A fellow your age should go to confession at least once a month."

Danny was sure that Pa said this having girls and the Sixth Commandment in mind. Pa had been young and wild once, and he must have a good idea of what kind of thoughts a young fellow had.

"I'm not talking away like an old duck. I know a few things, get me! I know what I'm talking about when I tell you that you must go to confession at least once a month."

"I do, Pa. And of course we have mass at school every Thursday morning, and after mass, there is a sermon."

"It won't do you any harm."

Danny glanced off at the small Christmas tree on a stand by the mirror.

"Bill trimmed the little tree. Do you have one this year?"

"Yes, but not as big as the ones we used to have."

V

Catherine came in with a doll.

"I called my new doll Priscilla," she said.

"Why did you call it that, Dollie?" Jim asked.

"Oh, I don't know. I just did. Maggie Cafferty across the street, she calls her doll Rose. I don't like that name, and I wanted to give my new doll a better name, and so I just called her Priscilla. I asked Little Margaret to give me a better name than Rose, so she gave me that, and I gave it to my new dollie."

Danny smiled patronizingly at his sister.

"I have something for you for Christmas," Danny said.

She came to him, and he handed her a brand-new quarter.

"Gee, thank you."

"You can go to the show with that," Jim said.

"And I have something for Bob and Denny," Danny said.

"I'll give it to them. They're having coffee in the dining room," she said.

Danny handed her brand-new quarters for them. She ran out of the room.

"Where did you get the money for that?" Jim asked.

"Mother gave me some money this morning, and so did Uncle Al and Uncle Ned and Aunt Peg, for Christmas."

"Well, by next Christmas you'll be working and have your own money to give. Dan, a man should always work for a living and be self-dependent."

Danny didn't answer. He guessed that Pa was right. But he would just as soon have Pa or Uncle Al or Uncle Ned rich, and be self-dependent that way and have dough. There were lots of things in the world to do besides work your balls off. He knew that much.

Danny glanced idly out the window.

He saw two ladies with a Christmas basket getting out of an automobile. He sensed immediately that the women were coming here. A feeling of shame came over him. Charity! His father was being given charity. Such a disgrace. Suppose that it became known. He couldn't hold his head up then. Charity!

Jim saw the women coming into the building.

The bell rang. They heard Mama go to the door and talk to the women. The two women came into the parlor. It was a bit upset, and that was more disgrace.

One of the women was thin, with bad skin and a sharp nose. The other was bony and heavy, but not fat, and she had a long, ugly face.

"Mr. O'Neill?" the one with the bad skin asked.

"Yes," Jim said quietly.

"Your case was reported to us, and we came with this basket. We're from the Women's Committee for Charity. You're the father here?" she asked.

"Yes, I am."

"And you're injured and unable to work."

"Oh, Miss, when Mr. O'Neill worked he was a wonderful provider. He came home with his arms full all of the time, and we had frog legs and chickens and all kinds of things. He just had a little setback, a stroke, but Mr. O'Neill was a wonderful provider," Lizz said.

Jim winced but said nothing.

"That's a shame. Mr. O'Neill, we're awfully sorry. And our committee was organized for just such unfortunate cases as yours. We believe that Christmas day calls upon us all to remember one another in the name of Jesus whom we commemorate. Today we remember the true spirit of Christmas and think of one another and think of those that are less fortunate. That's why our committee was organized. We want to bring cheer and warmth and a feeling of Christmas into every possible home that needs it, regardless of race, religion, or creed. You're Catholic?"

"Yes," Jim said quietly.

"I'm Baptist, and Mrs. Sanders here is Presbyterian. But we're all under the one God. Is this your oldest son?" she asked, pointing to Danny.

Danny felt like sinking through the floor.

"He lives with his grandmother and is a student in high school. My oldest isn't here, and here are my others, all except a girl who lives with my mother. This is Robert, and this is Dennis, and this is my baby, Catherine," Lizz said, pointing to the younger children, who were standing in the doorway.

"Such sweet little ones. Merry Christmas, children," said Mrs. Sanders.

"How long have you been . . . in this condition, Mr. O'Neill?" asked the other woman.

"Since the fall. I'm going to be back at work soon," Jim said.

"Of course you are. What we must all have is faith in the goodness of God and our fellow men. We must not lose hope," she said.

"Oh, no, we haven't lost any hope," Lizz said.

"Well, I do so hope that your little family will have a lovely and a Merry Christmas. We must run on now, you know, we have so much to do. We'll come back and see you sometime and try to bring you some more little cheer. And a very Merry Christmas to you, Mr. O'Neill, and to you, Mrs. O'Neill, and to all the lovely little ones."

"Oh, thank you, and the same to you," Lizz said.

Jim's lips moved as if he were speaking, but Danny, who sat very close to his father, didn't hear a word. Jim didn't even mutter. He just moved his lips. Lizz was seeing them to the door.

"I have sunk so low, haven't I?" Jim said, his words throbbing, his voice on the verge of breaking, while he and Danny saw the women get into their automobile and drive off.

“Well, God bless us. Now, who gave our names in?” Lizz asked.

“Let whoever did be damned. Lizz, throw that goddamned junk out,” Jim said, pointing to the basket with his left hand.

“Oh, no, Jim, not since it’s here. Why, there’s a turkey; I’ll use it. But did you ever hear such jabber? Protestants, too, Baptists, and Presbyterians, well, may they burn those ugly faces of theirs in the fires of hell. Such jabber,” Lizz said.

“I don’t know why I don’t go to the poorhouse and die there where I belong,” Jim said bitterly, sitting slumped in his chair.

Danny sat, shamed. He didn’t know what to say.

“Who asked those two bitches to come around? Who gave them our names? Whoever did, they can mind their own goddamned business.”

“That’s what I say, Jim. But since the stuff is here, why, we’ll use it. Did you hear me soft-soap them?” Lizz said.

Jim was pale, livid. He looked out the window at the gray Christmas day. A young fellow and a girl walked by, arm in arm. Lizz went back to cook dinner, and the kids ran out to play again in the dining room.

Danny sat alone with his brooding father. Neither of them spoke.

39

I

Danny opened Mike Flood's letter and saw that it was typed. He wished he owned a typewriter. He read the letter.

Middlesex Mil. Acad.
Feb. 8, 1923.

Dear Brother Dan
Received your letter and was very glad that I didn't introduce you to my sweet woman, "Kate." You know you are a dangerous fellow around women. I received a letter from Hugh today and he told me the fellows all had a wonderful time at some formal, but said that you weren't there. What's the matter? But I say pretty swell for my fraternity brothers to begin going to these full-dress affairs. Don't worry, old Mike gets to hear all about the parties you attend. I received a letter from Ella McGrail telling me that good-looking John McTeague took her to the formal. Trying to take her away from a poor fellow down at prison or something like Sing Sin. Well, I will get back at you bunch of Bums, when I get home you all better look out. I will be pretty busy next week on my exams. I am not fearing in the least. Middlesex is giving an informal dance next Saturday. I sent the adored Kate an invitation so here's hoping she can come. You know I was laid up in bed for a week with the Flu. I am now out and strong.

I received a letter from one of my various girl friends telling me that S.S. hasn't won a game yet. Well I wrote back and told them it was because they let big bums like Danny O'Neill play on their team. What say, Eh!

Have you a girl for the Frat party? If you haven't, call up good-looking Maggie Joyce. You and her would make a good team of truck horses. Ella McGrail told me she had a date with Ike Dugan. Tell him why don't he take Sally Cozzens to the party and give one of the other fellows a chance with Ella. What do you say, Ike, am I right.

Well, I am glad that none of you fellows know Kate Dillon for I think I would be out of luck when I get back to old Chicago. Just think, only four more months. Tears. Well Dan I think I will close now hoping to hear from you and the bunch in the near future.

With lots of Love and Kisses, Pardon me I thought I was sending a letter to one of my women.

The old boy
Mike Flood

P.S. Some typest.
Tell Hugh McNeill I had my steno type this letter.

Danny used to dislike Mike, but he didn't any more. Mike was all right, once you got to know him, but Mike wouldn't introduce any of the fellows to his new girl. Her name was Kate Dillon, and her old man was an influential politician and a rich contractor. She rated.

When was he going to get a girl like that? Sheila had turned him down for the party this week. Well, he had a date.

It was dull and gloomy at this time of the day when it was almost dark and just before supper. He decided to answer Mike's letter now in order to have something to do. He got out pen and ink and sat down to write. He liked to write letters, only he wasn't sure that he could write them as snappily as Mike.

II

"Well, Tim, while you're parlor dating we'll be going on a bender," Danny bragged, his mouth full of food.

"Fellows, he's being funny today," Tim said.

The fellows were sitting around the dining-room table at Tim Doolan's, having coffee and sandwiches after a Sunday afternoon blackjack game. Danny reached out and grabbed another sandwich. He bit into it, taking half the sandwich at one bite. He'd really been kidding Tim because he wanted to lead the conversation around to Sheila Cullen. Tim and Hugh had a parlor date tonight at Mary Boylan's and Sheila would be there. Hugh had a girl and he was just going along because he didn't have anything better to do. Why couldn't it be Tim and himself? They would each be with their girl, and talk, and dance a little, and kiss them, and have hot chocolate and sandwiches. And then, after leaving the house, he and Tim would go and sit in a restaurant and have coffee and waffles and talk about their date. But Sheila wouldn't give him another date.

"Since O'Neill took us into camp for eight bucks in blackjack, I think he ought to buy a bottle for our bender," Ike said.

"Yes, that's a good idea, Danny," handsome John McTeague said.

"I'll buy a bottle. We ought to celebrate because the heavies won their first league game Friday against Athanasius."

"Well, boys, I sure wish I could go with you, but I'm going out stepping tonight, too," Wils Gillen, one of the newest pledges, said.

"We ought to make Worm Gillen give up his date," Danny said.

"I ask the rest of you fellows, is it fair to make a worm, even if it's me, give up a piece and obey one of the brothers?" asked Wils.

"Hell, no. Worm Gillen, I order you to keep your date. My order is ahead of any O'Neill can now give, so you got to keep that date. And, listen, give her all the jazzing she can take," Tim said.

"That's my menu," Wils said, grinning.

Tim suddenly turned pale.

"What's the matter with me? If my mother or sister heard that, boy!" Tim said.

"Well, Tim, when you are having your effete parlor date tonight, just think of us," Danny said.

"Yes, I will, if that gives you any satisfaction," Tim said, and they went on eating.

III

Danny, with his fraternity brothers, Ike Dugan, Harry Allerdyce, John McTeague, Red Keene, and Otto Krauss, all emerged from a saloon on One hundred and sixteenth Street. A few doors down the dim block, they entered another saloon. It was dingy and dirty, with sawdust on the floor, moldy walls, and a generally dirty and musty appearance. Men were lined up along the bar. At one end a drunk in an old army coat floundered about, singing. They couldn't make out all the words of his song, but he seemed to conclude each stanza by naming some city and singing that if someone would buy him a drink he would go on to the next stanza and sing of another city.

"Ike, you better not get anything," Danny said, finding a place at the bar.

"Say, how come?"

"You don't want to be violating laws," Danny said.

"Crap," Ike said.

"Say, fellows, let's see how many damned laws we can break in one night," Danny said.

"Sounds good to me, fellows," Ike said.

"Too bad somebody hasn't got a car. We could break one law there by speeding and another by going on the wrong side of the street," Red said.

"Otto, can't you get your car tonight?" Danny asked.

"No, I can't," Otto answered.

"Well, what do you fellows want?" the bartender asked curtly.

"Give us all a shot of moon," Danny said.

"Chasers?"

"None for me," Danny said bravely while the others nodded that they'd take chasers.

Danny took the drink. He looked off from the others and gritted his teeth. The stuff he'd had in the last saloon had been lousy, and he'd had a tough time getting it down. Well, he'd get this stuff down.

He gulped down the moonshine. He sneezed and coughed. There was a burned taste in his mouth. He gagged. Worse than drinking varnish. But he held the liquor down.

"That's got a kick," Ike said.

"Could be more potent," Danny said casually.

He still had that taste in his mouth. He began to sweat. But he was still sober. He guessed he was going to show the world that he was the kind of a guy who could take his liquor and hold it like a man.

"Hey, Allerdyce, ain't there more saloons on this street?" Danny asked.

"There's sixteen of them in this one block and every one of them's wide open," Allerdyce said; he was a tall, thin lad of sixteen, with a very prominent Adam's apple.

"Well, come on, boys, tonight we're going to take in six barrooms in a night instead of six nights in a barroom," Danny said.

They paid fifteen cents each for their drinks and left to go to the saloon next door.

IV

"That makes seven saloons," Danny said, staggering out of another establishment.

They grouped together on the narrow sidewalk.

"Say, a buck and a half for a bottle, that ain't so expensive," Danny said, holding up an unlabelled bottle of moonshine.

"Quit makin' speeches and give me a drink," Ike said.

"Here, but leave some for the rest of us," Danny said, handing Ike the bottle.

Ike drank and quickly handed the bottle to Allerdyce. Allerdyce scarcely wet his lips with the liquor. Danny grabbed the bottle and took a good gulp, fighting to keep it down.

"O'Neill, you must have cast iron in your guts," Red said.

Danny grinned at him with drunken pride. His legs felt a little rubbery. There seemed to be a lump on his stomach, some place around the solar plexus. He suddenly recalled how there had been so much in the papers about people dying and going blind from moonshine whiskey and rotgut gin.

Oh, phrigg it!

He was going to show the world. He was going to get so goddamned drunk, and he was going to raise so goddamned much hell, that they would all know who he was and what he was.

"Hey, let's get a train for Sixty-third and Stony and get Marty. Then we're gonna get drunk. I mean we're gonna get drunk," Danny said.

They staggered uphill past more saloons.

"Hey, let's sing," Danny said.

"What'll we sing?" Ike asked.

Danny started the song he had learned from Tim and his gang out here in Pullman. They all joined in singing.

Oh, the game was played on Sunday
In old Saint Peter's yard,
With Jesus playing half back
And Noah, he played guard.
Oh, the angels on the side lines
My God, how they did yell
When Jesus made a touchdown
Against the team from Hell.

Go with Christ!
Go with Christ!
Go with Christ.
Moses on the five-yard line,
He can tackle goddamn fine.
Go with Christ.

They killed the bottle and staggered a few blocks to the Illinois Central station for their train.

V

Marty came out beyond the ticket-taker at Louisa Nolan's Dancing School. They could hear the orchestra playing jazz.

"Jesus, what a damned fine bunch of drunken hoods you guys are," Marty said, smiling.

"Marty, see all these guys?" Danny said. "All of them, but John here, they're Father Flaming Michael's higher Christian education."

"O'Neill, you're drunk," Marty said, laughing.

"Mulligan, we want a bottle at Whalen's," Danny said.

"Now you're talking business. Wait till I get my coat," Marty said.

They waited while Marty ran upstairs to the checkroom.

"Danny, you don't want to drink any more. Let's go have some coffee," John McTeague said.

Marty came down wearing his coat and smiling genially. They went downstairs and out onto Sixty-third, turned the corner, and staggered south along Stony Island Avenue.

"O'Neill, you're getting maggoty," Marty said.

Danny grinned.

In his whiskey-fogged brain he had an image of himself bravely and impressively drunk, raising hell, raising hell the way other fellows did when they got drunk, and he thought of how, after this bender, he would talk and brag to the guys about how drunk he had been, and of the brave and crazy and drunkenly humorous things that he'd done. And this time, he wouldn't be talking B.S. the way he had the time after the party at Tommy Collins' when he'd waited in Mac's hallway.

"Marty, we been making six barrooms in a night. Sixteen barrooms in a night out in Pullman. We've been in every goddamned kind of a saloon on earth," Danny said.

"You're all maggoty," Marty said.

"Marty, I got an idea. We go see Sheila Cullen," Danny said.

"You want to see her in the condition you're in?" said Marty.

"Why the hell not?" he said.

He wanted to go to Mary Boylan's and show off before Sheila Cullen. He wanted to let her see that he didn't give two good hoots. Because that was just how he felt. There wasn't one goddamned thing in this whole world that he gave a good goddamn for. And he was going to show tonight that he didn't. Not one goddamned thing.

"Know what I'm gonna do tonight, Marty? I'm gonna tell the whole phriggin' world to go screw itself. And know what I'm gonna do if it doesn't want to? I'm gonna screw it."

Danny bumped into a stranger.

"Hey, Bud, watch where you're going."

"Huh! Watch where I'm going? You watch where you're going. Get the hell out of my way when I come along."

"Come on, O'Neill, you drunken maggoty bastard," Marty said, smiling.

"Listen, I don't take sass, see!" the stranger said.

"You don't take sass. Well, let's see about that. You don't take sass. Well, I'm gonna give some sass," Danny said.

"Just a minute," Marty said, stepping in front of Danny.

Marty looked at the fellow.

"Listen, you, this fellow's my friend. He's drunk, see! I'm not. Now you blow while you're all together," Marty said.

The fellow looked at Marty. The others came up yelling. "It's last time I say it! Blow!" Marty said.

The fellow turned and walked off.

"Why didn't you let me fight him?" Danny said.

"Come on, you drunken bastard," Marty said.

He and Marty walked on, arm in arm, and the others followed.

VI

Whalen's was a cramped, smoky, and crowded joint. The fellows had a drink and stood around frowning, trying to look tough and romantic while Marty held a mysterious and whispered conversation with the bartender. The bartender then slipped Marty a pint bottle. Marty handed him a dollar for it and he walked furtively out of the place. They all followed him. They went across the street to Jackson Park and gathered by a bench just inside the park. Everybody chipped in to make up the dollar the liquor had cost.

"Gimme the bottle," Danny said, lurching forward to grab it.

Marty warded off Danny's arm. He uncorked the bottle and held it up.

"Well, boys, here goes."

He took a good-sized drink.

The bottle was passed around. Danny got it from Ike. He was so drunk that he no longer gagged when he drank.

"You don't want Sheila Cullen to see you in the state you're in," Marty said, taking the bottle from Danny.

"I'm goin' down there now," Danny answered.

"Me, too," Ike said.

"All right by me. Just a minute, though. You guys are way ahead on me. I want another drink," Marty said.

He took a good swig. The bottle was passed around again. Danny put the bottle to his lips, but he couldn't drink. He coughed it right up and sneezed.

"You had enough. You'll pass out, you bastard," Marty said, snatching the bottle from him.

They killed the bottle and left the park, Danny trailing after them and scarcely able to walk. They boarded a Sixty-third Street car and they edged up to the front of it.

Danny swayed. He knew where he was going. He was going to see Sheila Cullen. She was at Mary Boylan's with Tim and Hugh. That's where he was going. His eyes were bloodshot and swollen. There was spittle on his lips. His hat was askew. His face was dirty. He saw faces, and these faces didn't seem to him real.

They were funny faces. Marty stood beside him, but Marty didn't hold his face in one place.

"How you coming, O'Neill?" Ike asked, clinging tightly to a strap.

"Huh?" Danny asked in a heavy, drunken voice.

"How you coming?"

Danny grunted.

The car shook him up. He had a headache now. He was sweating and he felt dizzy. The faces before him seemed funnier than ever. He laughed. The faces were so funny that he had to laugh. He hiccoughed and almost retched. He tasted bile. He wavered, hanging onto his strap.

Gonna screw the world! Gonna show everybody. Gonna show Sheila Cullen. Didn't want a date with him. Show Sheila Cullen. He withdrew his hand from the strap. He stood on wobbly legs and looked glassy-eyed at Marty. Suddenly he collapsed.

Marty grabbed him under the shoulders before he fell. When the street car reached Cottage Grove, Marty and Red dragged Danny off.

VII

"I love Sheila Cullen. I wanna see Sheila Cullen," Danny drooled; he had his arms around the shoulders of Red and Allerdyce. His shoes and spats were messed with vomit. His hat was on askew. His glasses were bent. His eyes were swollen.

"Shut up. She's in the window up there and you're making a fool of yourself in front of her," Marty said.

The group was gathered by a lamppost in front of an old apartment building in the Fifty-five hundred block on Ingleside Avenue. Hugh, Tim, Mary Boylan, and Sheila looked down on them from a second-floor window.

Ike Dugan tried to climb the lamppost. Then he clumsily imitated an ice skater, going back and forth along the sidewalk.

"Hey, what are you guys doing?" Hugh yelled down from the opened window.

"We're on a bender," Red yelled.

"I wanna see Sheila Cullen," Danny shouted loudly.

"Look up, she's in the window."

"Sheila, I wanna come up and see you," he yelled.

"Oh, you can't. I'm going home in a few minutes," she called down.

"Huh?"

"She said you can't. You're too drunk," Marty said to him.

Danny broke loose from Red and Allerdyce. He lurched and stumbled toward the building entrance. He tried to go forward but he was powerless to control his movement. He was bent over with his shoulders hunched, when Marty and Red reached him in time to check him from falling.

"You won't see me?" he yelled up.

"Come on, O'Neill, we're going," Marty said.

"Won't you see me?" he yelled up.

"I can't," Sheila called down.

"Hey, Marty, he's cockeyed, take him away and sober him up," Hugh called down.

"Danny, come on, she won't see you," Marty said.

Tim came out from the building entrance, shivering without his overcoat.

"Hey, listen, guys, blow, will you? You're all pissy-assed," Tim said.

"Sheila Cullen, you're a dirty bitch," Danny yelled.

"You guys got to do something with him! He's blind. He doesn't know what the hell he's saying," Tim said urgently.

Marty dragged Danny about five yards off.

"Huh?"

"We're leaving," Marty said.

"I wanna talk to Sheila," Danny said; he broke away from Marty.

"Jesus, get him out of here," Tim said.

Danny stood under the window, trying to curse Sheila, but all that he could do was mumble.

"The girls are sore as hell," Tim said.

"I gotta do something with him. I'll knock him out, and that'll help him. He's disgracing himself with her," Marty said.

Marty grabbed Danny's arm, but Danny pulled free. Two others grabbed him, and he struggled free and again tried to curse Sheila.

"I gotta put him out, that's all," Marty said.

He measured Danny off and caught him flush on the jaw with a hard right. Danny sagged and dropped to the sidewalk. Struggling to get up, he got to his hands and knees. He fell back on his side and lay there on the cold stone, gasping.

"Let him lay there a minute," Marty said, bending over him.

"I gotta go back. I'm cold," Tim said.

The girls closed the window and pulled down the shade. Tim went back upstairs.

"What'll we do with him?" John McTeague asked.

"Here, I'll put my coat over him. Let him lay there a minute and then he'll come to," Marty said.

Marty spread his overcoat over Danny.

"Is he all right?" Ike asked, worried, shocked into sobriety.

"He just passed out. He'll come to in a minute and we'll give him raw tomatoes and black coffee in a restaurant, and he'll be all right," Marty said, shivering.

Danny lay there, unconscious, gasping, the coat thrown over his head.

VIII

Danny woke up and looked around the room, bewildered. Where was he? How did he get here? What time was it? Outside, it was a gray day.

A nurse entered the room.

"Good morning. How are you feeling?"

"I'm all right. Where am I?"

"You were brought in here last night."

"What happened to me? I feel all right."

"You must have drunk too much."

"When can I get out of here?"

"You'll go home today. I'll be right back with your breakfast," she said.

He watched her go out of the room. How did it all happen? What would he tell them at home? He couldn't let them know he was in a hospital. If he had only been drunk, why hadn't they sobered him up? Why did they have to bring him here? What kind of friends were they?

Well, he could tell Mother that he had stayed all night with Hugh, or Marty, or one of the fellows. This was Washington's birthday, and there wasn't any school. But the heavies were playing a practice game tonight in Whiting, Indiana. He had to get to it and play. But how was the bill going to be paid? It was a private room, too.

IX

The breakfast dishes were beside him. He talked into the telephone.

"But, Marty, how did I get here?"

"We had to take you. We thought you were gonna die. We took you to a restaurant and tried to feed you tomatoes and black coffee and it didn't do any good. You were vomiting and even coughing up blood. Christ, I was scared, Dan. I didn't know what to do, so I took you there. They pumped your stomach out. How are you feeling?"

"I'm raring to go."

"That's what you just said to my mother. She knows all about it. She was sore as hell with me."

"How does she know?"

"Your grandmother called her, woke her up at about three o'clock this morning."

"My grandmother?"

"We had to call your folks. When I got you to the hospital, we didn't have enough dough. And we were afraid you'd die. They let you lay there until your uncle came over in a cab and paid them for pumping your stomach," Marty said.

"I'm ruined."

"No, your uncle wasn't sore. He was worried. And, say, the rest of the guys were pie-eyed. I never want to go through what I did last night. It was all up to me. I had to make the decision and, Christ, I didn't know what to do."

"What did I do?"

"Say, you were so blind—wait until I see you, and I'll tell you what you did and what you told Sheila Cullen."

"When did I see her?"

"Don't you remember?"

"The last I remember is getting on the street car."

"That the last you remember? Boy, you don't know half of it. Don't you remember me socking you?"

"No."

"I had to knock you out because you wouldn't stop cursing at Sheila. We washed your face in snow to bring you to and did everything we could think of. And all the time Ike was bellyaching. He thought you were going to die and that there would be a scandal. Your folks talked to his mother, too, and even to Otto Krauss's. I talked to Otto this morning. He's afraid his old man is going to make him quit the frat." Marty laughed. "On account of his bad companions, meaning you. Next to you, I'm getting the rap."

"Gee, I'm sorry, Marty."

"It could have happened to any of us. But I tell you, I've seen fellows drunk but not like you was. Talk about being maggoty."

"What did Sheila say?"

"She was sore as hell. And she ought to be."

"Mr. O'Neill, our car is ready to take you home now," the nurse said.

"Well, Marty, they're taking me home. I'll call you later."

X

Danny lay in bed. Thank God, Uncle Al had had to go away. Uncle Ned wasn't home, either. He looked around his bedroom. The day was dreary, and the room was almost dark.

"There you are!" Mrs. O'Flaherty said, coming into the room. "Blessed Mother of God, at three o'clock in the morning, me poor son had to go out in the snow and pay ten dollars to the hospital for you. Blessed Mother of God. And you out with the tinkers."

"Mother, I tell you I'm sorry. I won't do it again."

"If your poor father knew this, what would he say, that poor cripple!"

"Does he know?"

"Thank the Lord he doesn't. I told your mother, but she swore that she wouldn't tell him. Ah, he'd fix you. And if he got his hands on the tinkers you were out with! You can thank your stars your crippled father doesn't know of your shenanigans."

"Mother, please forgive me."

"Don't talk to me, you devil," she said, leaving his bedroom.

He turned his face to the wall. He tried to distract himself by playing a basketball game in his mind. But he couldn't rid himself of his regrets, his shame, his disgust with himself.

XI

As soon as Al was in his room in the hotel in Indianapolis, he sat down and wrote Danny a letter. All the way down on the train he had thought and worried about last night.

Feb. 22, 1923
Indianapolis, Ind.

Dear Dan:

I am sorry that I had to leave before you came home today from the hospital. I wanted to talk to you but I couldn't miss my train. Sport, we are going to have no recriminations. Bygones are bygones. Everyone makes mistakes, and we must all try to learn by mistakes. I know that you are going to learn and that there are going to be no repetitions of what happened. We were all given a serious fright last night when I received the telephone call from your friend, Marty Mulligan. But nothing happened that cannot be repaired. You made a mistake, and I know that it will teach you not to repeat it in the future. We have had so much trouble in our home because of drink that I am sure you will be able to weigh the dangers of it. Sport, it's no fun. You must promise me that you'll never take another drop. I am not going to ask any more than that of you and when I return home, we are going to go on as if this never happened. We are not going to drag it up or speak about it. No nagging, no reminders. It was a moment of weakness, and if you were older and had more experience I know that it never would have happened. So, Sport, keep a stiff upper lip and write to me. Be good to your grandmother and aunt study and lots of luck, all the luck in the world. I know that you are going to forget this unfortunate experience and profit by it. Be good, and watch my mail.

Yours,

A.O.F.

40

I

The weather was pleasant, with a promise of spring in the air. On his way over to the O'Flahertys, Jim walked along, throwing his left side forward and dragging his right leg after him. His anger against Danny mounted. His son a drunken bum, having to have his stomach pumped. For more than a year, in fact for years, he'd been worried about how Danny would turn out. How many times hadn't he told Lizz that Danny would come to no good. But he hadn't really believed what he was saying. He had only been expressing his worries. For once and for all, he was going to have it out with Danny. And if the O'Flahertys dipped their oar in, he would give them more than a piece of his mind. They had been given a full chance to raise Danny, and look what had happened.

At Fifty-ninth and Calumet Jim halted at the curbstone. He swung his body around to look toward South Park with his left eye. It was better than the right one. No automobiles were coming. He stepped off the curb, planting his left foot on the asphalt. Dragging his right limb along, he had that same impression that he'd been having so often of late. There was a good right leg, swinging from his hip, alongside of his bad leg, and he had a good right arm, a little shorter and thinner than his bad arm. With each step this good right arm swung in rhythm with his good right leg. He had feeling around the fingernails of his good right hand and he could feel his toes and move them in the good right foot, but he couldn't feel anything around the heels. He crossed the street slowly, seeing his three legs and three arms move in his mind as he took each step.

He stepped up onto the opposite curb and continued on his way. He thought of how he was going to tell Danny that from now on he had to get his father's permission to do anything. He formed the words he would use in his mind, and he imagined himself talking with his son. And he still had an impression of that good right leg hitched to his hip and that good right arm, and they were moving in his mind, mixed up with the image of Danny. He had a third leg that was his leg and that wasn't his leg, and it walked in his mind as he kept thinking of Danny. This might be a good omen. It might mean that he was going to get better. All his life he had never paid any attention to dreams and omens, but had that been right? If you were sick and going to get better, did your improvement start in your mind? It might, mightn't it? Why, this picture of his arm and leg as he walked along might well be a kind of omen telling him that he was on his way to recovery.

Well, recovery or no recovery, his son Danny was now going to be set on the right path once and for all, with no fooling and no shilly-shallying.

II

"Jim, make him toe the mark," Mrs. O'Flaherty said.

Danny thought that Mama must have told Pa about his drunk even though she had given her word not to do this.

"Mary, he's turning over a new leaf. I'm going to see to that," Jim said, speaking very slowly and encountering difficulty with his pronunciation.

Danny watched his father. Pa looked so old, with his gray hair and sunken cheeks. When he moved, he seemed to jerk his whole right side stiffly. The sight of Pa made him feel afraid and sorry at the same time. He wanted to turn his head away and not look at Pa at all.

Danny didn't know what to say, particularly because he wasn't sure how much Pa knew. If Pa didn't know about his drunk, he'd be a fool to make everything worse, and so he had to watch his step.

"Well, what the hell are you standing there for?" Jim asked.

"I'm ready, Pa."

"Jim, he's your son. You tell him what's what," Mrs. O'Flaherty said.

Ever since his drunk, Mother had been this way. She would hardly speak to him and she was always making insinuations and innuendoes.

"I'll get my hat and coat," Danny said, going to his bedroom.

He and his father went out the front door. Danny paused in the hallway, uncertain whether or not to let his father go down the stairs first.

"Go ahead," Jim said, giving Danny a push.

Danny started down the stairs. He could hear his father coming after him.

III

It was early March, and the days were beginning to lengthen. There was melting snow along the sidewalks. Jim and Danny walked slowly. Danny was on the outside, not daring to look at his father, but he was aware that his father's eye was on him.

"I suppose you're proud of yourself."

"No, I'm not. Pa, what's the matter?"

Danny watched a fellow and a girl go by in a shiny gray Stutz.

"That's what you'd like to be, isn't it, Prince Charming?" Jim said.

He hadn't thought his father had caught him watching the roadster. It had turned eastward at Sixtieth Street and was now out of sight.

"I saw you watching that fellow with the girl in the automobile."

"I hardly noticed it, honest, Pa. I was just thinking."

"What were you thinking about? Your own grandeur?"

"I was just thinking."

"If you thought, you'd have a brainstorm."

Pa had never been as sore at him as he was now. Pa must know. He wished that this ordeal were over. But it hadn't even begun.

"Why don't you say something to me?"

"I was just wishing that school was out and I was working, that's all."

"You're going to work tomorrow afternoon."

Danny walked slowly at his father's side, waiting for more information. Perhaps it was better, hard as it would be, for him to give up basketball and quit school. He'd have to forget all about college, a college frat, and the college life. But all that he wanted was simply what so many fellows had.

"After school, you go down to Terminal Q and report to Charley Josephs, the terminal agent. He'll put you to work. You're strong enough to hustle a few boxes and you'll make fifty-five cents an hour. You come to me with what you make, and I'll give you what you need."

"Yes, Pa, I will."

"You're damned right, you will."

Pa walked so slowly that it was taking them a long time to go over to the building on Calumet Avenue. He wanted to get it all over with. He decided that it was best to say as little as possible to his father.

"From now on, you don't go out at night unless I give you permission to."

Danny didn't answer. Pa was treating him as if he were fourteen years old.

"No more dances and parties. You've had enough of that stuff."

Yes, Pa must know. Was Pa going to talk about it? What could he say then? Say he was sorry? He was sorry. Yet at school he had bragged and boasted about his drunken experience. He had looked at his classmates many times and thought that none of them was the wild fellow he was.

"Every day you come over to see me. And no excuses will do. If you miss seeing me just one day, God pity you, that's all I say."

They turned the corner at Fifty-ninth and South Park. It had taken this long to walk a little less than a block.

Danny stuck his hands in his coat pockets. But he was self-conscious of them. He took them out. He was self-conscious even about the way he walked. Pa might not like that. And he couldn't blame Pa. He knew how Pa felt. Only Pa didn't understand him. That was the trouble.

"You—you're no son of mine!"

Danny grinned. He felt foolish. There was nothing to do but wait until Pa got it all out of his system.

"Look at me!"

Danny turned his eyes up at his father. Pa looked very sad. His face was drawn, and his lips were closed tightly. He swung his left arm outward in a gesture.

"You're nothing but the dribblings of a Chinese jerk off against a lamppost. That's all you are!"

He shouldn't take this from anyone, not even from his own father. But Pa was sick. He couldn't argue with him. And he was afraid of Pa. He felt that his father was going to punch him. He looked at his father blankly.

"I'm ashamed of you!" Jim said with unusual slowness, his voice choked with emotion.

Danny matched his pace to that of his father, and they continued slowly.

IV

The weather had changed. It was raw and cold, and a sharp wind whipped through the runways and across the unheated terminal platform. Even though he wore gloves, Danny's hands were cold. He had worked now for an hour and a half hustling freight and he had two and a half more hours to go. Along with five men, he helped unload a single wagon that had brought in a load of five-pound packages. The men worked fast and methodically, none of them talking. Danny stepped over the tail gate after a chunky Negro, picked up a package, emerged with it, and set it on a platform truck. The other men took out three and four packages at a time, but he kept on taking them one at a time. He wouldn't hurry. The packages could be around here after he went home, for all he cared. The work was hard enough as it was without having to be made harder by breaking your neck to hustle. As fast as you did one job, there was another waiting for you. And he had to be careful of the way he'd bend down. He'd hurt his side helping to unload some barrels, and if he moved or stooped in a certain way, he had a sharp pain. Otherwise the pain was dull and steady. He guessed that he had strained a muscle.

He saw Hiram Wolfe watching him. Mr. Wolfe wore an overcoat with a velvet collar, and his face was not tanned as it usually was in the summer time. He had the same tight look, and he seemed to be sniffing as if he could smell breaches of discipline. Mr. Wolfe did not speak to Danny. He walked away. Danny thought that Mr. Wolfe might have asked about Pa. Well, at all events, he wasn't working in Wolfe's department.

"Come on, Bud, this ain't no rest cure," a husky said to him.

Danny went for another package. He stooped and grimaced, feeling a sharp pain in his side. Danny worked on, bored.

"O'Neill, push that truck over to that there bin in the corner and start unloading it," Charley Josephs said.

Danny pushed the hand truck. One by one, he began removing the packages. Two platform men joined him and started throwing the packages off speedily.

"Come on, Four-Eyes. Quit dreamin'," one of them said.

Danny tried to work faster but his arms seemed leaden. The pain in his side persisted. If he said anything, they'd probably think he was stalling. Then Charley Josephs might tell Pa. And his ears were numb with cold. He wished he had brought ear laps.

"You college kids don't like work, do you?" one of the platform men said.

Danny gritted his teeth.

"All right, shake a leg and then go on and give them a hand with that there gascar down there," Josephs yelled at them.

Danny looked at the motor truck at which Josephs was pointing. It was jammed tight with huge crates that must weigh from one to two hundred pounds each. It was a quarter after seven. One hour and forty-five minutes to go.

V

"What's the matter? Oughtn't you be going to work?"

"I couldn't work today, Pa. I hurt my side," Danny said.

"What happened?"

"The first night I worked I wrenched a muscle in my side unloading barrels. I didn't know how I was going to get through to nine o'clock."

"Where is it?"

Danny pointed to his right side, just above the hip.

"Well, I guess the work is too heavy for you. Maybe I shouldn't have made you do it. I talked to your brother Bill last night, and that's what he thinks. When school lets out, you can get a regular job. We can manage until then. But it's hard on your brother, and we're going to need your help by June."

"I'll be able to go back to work in a day or so. But I just couldn't today. I had to come home after lunch and put hot towels on my side."

"No, I don't think you better, Dan. After all, I got a rupture lifting heavy boxes when I was too young."

"Pa, I wanted to ask you if I could go out tomorrow night."

"Where to?"

"I want to have supper with my friend, Marty Mulligan. We're going to do our homework together after school, and then we want to see a movie in the evening."

"Yes. It's all right, so long as you ask me and tell me the truth. Sure."

"I won't be able to come and see you."

"But what about the pay you got coming for working last night?"

"Oh, gee, I forgot about that."

"Well, you can go down and get it Saturday morning."

Jim began to drowse off.

VI

Danny left his father's feeling happy. He could go to the dance tomorrow night. He was stagging it, but he could bum a couple of dances. If Pa knew he'd lied. But how would Pa find out? He was young, and he'd only be young once. He wanted to go to dances. Pa had when he was young. And, yes sir, Pa had drunk his share of the world's whiskey.

He made a face, and his hand went to his side. He was afraid that he wouldn't be able to play in tomorrow's league basketball game. The team needed him badly. The season was going terribly, and he was having a rotten year himself. He had been trying to play a one-man game. He had to play the remaining games on the schedule, not only for the sake of the team, but also to redeem himself and prove that in his final year he was capable of some real playing. Uncle Al and Pa had both forbidden him to play, but he was going to play under the name of one of the subs so that when the score was printed in the papers they wouldn't see it. He hurried home to put more hot towels on his side. That was his only hope of fixing himself up to be in shape to play. If he was, he wouldn't grandstand. He'd play the way he was really capable of playing.

VII

"O'Neill," Father Theo called as Danny marched out of school with his class.

Danny got out of line.

"I won't be able to come out to practice today, but I want you to see that the heavies go through a good workout. Practice signals and shooting, and see to it that everybody's tail is dragging before you call off practice. You fellows looked terrible Friday losing to Christian thirty-six to five. You yourself were playing a one-man game. Now you've got to get together on some team work. We got two more league games and if we win them we can still finish third in the South Side heavyweight division."

"All right, Father," Danny said, disappointed that Father Theo had caught him; he'd intended to skip practice, but he couldn't very well do that now.

He left the school building to go to practice.

VIII

"Come on, you guys, quit fooling," Danny yelled at his team; he put his half baseball mask over his glasses and walked to the center of the floor.

"What you want now?" Nolan yelled.

"We got to practice. Gimme the ball," Danny yelled at Nolan.

"Come and get it."

Danny rushed at Tim. Tim tossed the ball to Marty Mulligan. Danny ran from one to the other as they tossed the basketball around. Suddenly he realized that here he was, captain, and look at the spectacle he was making of himself. Making him shag around in a circle to get the ball and laughing at him.

"Are we going to practice or not?" he asked them, sore.

"What say, kid?" Moss answered.

"Captain Jinks of the Horse Marines," Fagin yelled.

"No, of the Horse Turds," Nolan said.

Danny walked aside, and they goofed. They wouldn't do a damned thing he said.

"Marty," Danny called.

Marty walked over to him, grinning, his pudgy body white and clean in his suit.

"Marty, why don't you help me get discipline on the team?"

"They think you're a goof. And you act like one. If you can't make them respect you, what can I do? You're to blame yourself, O'Neill."

Danny looked at Marty, hurt.

"I'm telling you this because I like you and you're my friend and fraternity brother. I wouldn't otherwise. They laugh at you. So how can you expect them to obey you as captain?" Marty said.

Danny felt that Marty was telling him the truth. He said nothing. He sat on a chair. His players clowned with one another and did no serious practicing.

IX

Danny rode home by himself. He wanted to be alone. He had so often felt that he was considered a goof by the fellows. He couldn't be one of them. They didn't take him seriously. Girls didn't take him seriously. His own classmates didn't take him seriously. He tried to make wisecracks and he didn't get the laughs that other fellows got. He wanted to be popular and he couldn't. He wanted to be somebody, and no matter what his feats were in athletics, still he wasn't treated like somebody. All his efforts to be and to do spectacular things didn't avail him much. Again and again in his life, the same thing always happened. He got to know fellows, and they got to know him, and then they didn't treat him with respect, and he didn't have the feeling that he belonged. He wanted to be one of the guys but he could never feel completely confident that he was one of them. He had always been razzed more than other guys were in every group he'd ever been in.

What was the matter with him?

He got off the car at Sixty-first and Cottage Grove and waited to transfer to a west-bound Sixty-first Street car. He was still brooding. Even in the frat things did not go as he wanted them to. Marty was his best friend. But Marty and Tommy Collins were going out often on dates and seeing a lot of each other and not asking him. They talked in front of him as if they had something private to talk about. He was always catching little innuendoes which made him feel out of the swim.

He flipped his car before it stopped, handed his transfer to the conductor, and found a seat. He was glum. After almost four years in high school, he was still just a goof, as much of a goof as he had been at Crucifixion or Saint Patrick's. His best friend had told him as much today. His own team had laughed at him, their captain.

He had achieved his high-school dream. He had become an athletic hero of the school. He'd been injured for the school on the gridiron and he'd been voted captain of the heavyweight basketball team. Still, his athletic career had not panned out right. The end of his last basketball season was drawing to a close. He had helped ruin the team himself by individual playing. He hadn't developed as he should have. Last year, he had been developing both as a football and a basketball player. He had felt it himself. He had seen how he was coming along. And this year what had he done with his chances, his developing skill? He'd pissed them away.

He suddenly remembered his dog, Liberty. They had sent her to the country, because she was too much trouble and the neighbors complained about her. And she was dead now. He missed poor Liberty.

He got off the car at South Park Avenue. It was getting dark now. Again he was walking past the familiar buildings, each one of which was so imprinted on his memory. This was a street of memories, of ghosts. How many times had he walked down this street, full of his own dreams? Dreams of sports, of athletic heroism, of Roslyn, of love, of success, of being somebody, of fulfilling a destiny.

Oh wad some power the giftie gie us
To see oursels as others see us!

All his life he had been posing, acting, striving, trying to build up pictures of himself in other people's minds. He felt that his life had been a failure. He condemned himself. He was ashamed of the very name of Danny O'Neill, the name that he had wanted to be so shining and so famous.

41

I

"Watch me now," Jim said.

Danny saw his father fit a pencil between his right thumb and his third finger with the index finger resting over the pencil. It was painful to watch his father. There was something hideous, not human, in Pa's jerking paralytic movements. His right hand and arm were like an automatic machine that functioned badly. There was no flexibility in his father's movements, no naturalness. He watched, trying to keep the expression on his face interested and unrevealing. His father scrawled. Suddenly the pencil dropped out of his father's hand. Jim took the sheet of paper on which he had been trying to write and handed it to Danny. Danny studied the scrawling with assumed interest, his face hiding his contradictory feelings. Pa's scrawling bore only the most faint resemblance to letters.

"Of course, it takes time for me to regain the use of my right hand, but it's coming. I've been practicing writing my name, and of course that's not very good, but it's an improvement."

Danny nodded. It was worse than what a two-year-old child could do.

"I'm getting better. You watch and see if from now on I don't pick up. I'll be writing my own name again soon. And that's only the first step. I'm going to be able to go back to work."

Danny hoped that what Pa said would come true. He knew that it would never be. There his father sat in the fading light of day with shadows playing over his unshaven face. In a few months his hair had turned completely gray. He was almost pop-eyed and did not blink his right eye as he did his left. Pa seemed like something else beside his father. Pa sitting there seemed like the personification of Death.

"Well, Dan, we'll soon be having another spring," Jim said after a brooding period of silence.

"Yes, the weather is changing, and the snow is melting," Danny said.

"I'm going to walk a lot as soon as the weather changes. I was out the other day and it was slippery, and I fell down and strained my back. But it's all right now."

Danny had heard Mama tell Mother about how Pa lay on the sidewalk and couldn't get up, how he got on his knees and tried to raise himself on the left side and fell back, and how some stranger had come along and helped Pa get up and had taken him home by the arm.

"Yes, but my back is all right now. Anybody could slip on the icy sidewalks."

"About a month ago, I did, and I thought I hurt my back," Danny said.

"Sure, anybody can slip. But now spring is coming. What I need is to exercise my muscles. If I do some walking on my game leg, it's going to improve. You know, we got to use our limbs if we want to keep them in condition. And with the winter and the bad weather we had recently, I couldn't use mine much. Well, that is all past."

"If Winter comes, can Spring be far behind?" Danny quoted.

"What's that?"

"Shelley. A poem. I read it in my English book."

"Say it again."

"If Winter comes, can Spring be far behind?"

Jim got to his feet and limped to the bedroom, motioning Danny to follow. He pointed to a shelf in the smelly, disordered closet.

"There's a big book of poems up there. Get them down, Dan."

Danny dragged down a heavy book from under some old pillows. The binding was broken and the pages were frayed and torn. He carried it to the parlor. He held the dusty book in his lap and got dust in his nostrils.

"I bought that two years after we was married, your mother and me. I read it sometimes."

Danny thumbed through the book. Burns, Shelley, Keats, Swinburne, Browning. He had read fragments of their poetry in his English textbook, or at home. Uncle Al had a lot of little blue books about all kinds of subjects, all kinds of classics, and some of them were books of poems, and he'd read in them. He recognized some of the poems here.

"You like to read?" Jim asked.

"Yes, Pa, I do."

"Can you recite some Shakespeare for me, Dan?"

"At school, we had to memorize a lot of Shakespeare. Last year we studied *Julius Caesar*, *Hamlet*, and *Macbeth*. And I read some other plays of Shakespeare. I learned a lot of speeches of Shakespeare, Pa."

"Recite me Polonius' speech. That's something, boy, that you should learn and take to heart. I'm your father, and I couldn't give you any better advice. Polonius was speaking to his son, wasn't he?"

"Yes, to Laertes."

"That's it. Let's hear it."

Danny set down the heavy book of poetry selections. He coughed. He felt funny, reciting, although he often recited things to himself.

"Go ahead."

And these few precepts in thy memory keep.
See thou character. Give thy thoughts no tongue,
Nor any unproportion'd thought his act.
Be thou familiar, but by no means vulgar;
Those friends thou hast, and their adoption tried,
Grapple them to thy soul with hoops of steel,
But do not dull thy palm with entertainment
Of each new-hatched unfledg'd comrade. Beware
Of entrance to a quarrel; but being in,
Bear't that the opposed may beware of thee.
Give every man thy ear, but few thy voice;
Take each man's censure, but reserve thy judgement;
Costly thy habit as thy purse can buy,
But not express'd in fancy; rich, not gaudy;
For the apparel oft proclaims the man,
And they in France of the best rank and station
Are most select and generous in that.
Neither a borrower nor a lender be;
For loan oft loses both itself and friend,
And borrowing dulls the edge of husbandry.
This above all: to thine own self be true,
And it must follow, as the night the day,
Thou canst not then be false to any man.

"Good. There is sound advice there to remember," Jim said.

"Yes, Pa, it expresses a wonderful philosophy."

"Remember what it says," Jim said, wagging his left index finger at Danny.

II

After Danny's visit, Jim sat brooding. He hoped that the lad would take that speech from Shakespeare to heart. He thought of how he had now lost three of his children to the O'Flahertys. Because of his condition, Catherine was living there now, too.

But today, Danny's visit had been a nice one. In only a couple of months now, the boy would be out of school and ought to be able to find himself a job. They needed the money he'd earn. His being out of work was being felt more and more at home, and in many ways. He could see it in the food Lizz put on the table now.

He dragged himself to the dining room where Lizz was ironing.

"I talked with Dan," he said, taking a chair. "I should have taken him under my wing sooner. I can see a difference in him since I put my foot down after he got drunk this winter."

Lizz went on ironing.

"Where are the kids?"

"They're out playing."

"They ought to be getting in soon."

"Jim, they are going to have to work hard enough sooner than they think. Let them run in the prairie and play while they get the chance. But say, there is still a couple of dollars in that bank account of the money you banked for Danny when he worked two summers ago. We can get that."

"But I can't even write my name to draw it out."

"Danny can go downtown tomorrow. As soon as Dennis comes in, I'll send him over to my mother's to tell Danny."

"I have to go too. When I put that money in the bank, I fixed the account so he couldn't get it out alone."

"It's good you were shaved yesterday. You'll look all right to go downtown tomorrow."

"I don't care how I look. What am I? A pauper. Lizz, why doesn't my family send me to the Old People's Home? Why don't you just pack me off to River Forest? I don't belong here. I'm no good. I'm a weight on you and my children. Get rid of me. I'm no good alive," Jim said, speaking almost like a pouting child.

"Say, Jim, when you were able, no children had a better father. No wife had a better husband and provider. Jim, you're our Daddy Long Legs."

"What I was!" Jim said, abstracted. "Look at what I am."

III

Danny thought how he had often seen paralyzed men on the street and he had felt sorry for them. He had not even wanted to look at them. He was sure that most people wanted to turn their heads away when they saw anybody on the street who was as paralyzed as Pa was. Did Pa know this? Did Pa walk down the street and notice people looking away when they saw him? It was no disgrace for a man to be paralyzed. Woodrow Wilson, the greatest man alive, was in Washington now in the same condition as Pa. But you just hated to see it, the queer jerks, the lack of power in someone's arms and legs, the twisted face, the ugliness of it. It was terrible to see, and it made you think of how you were one day going to die. Here he was, young and healthy, and his future, whatever it might be, was ahead of him. You went on thinking you had life before you, and when such a thing happened in your family as what had happened to Pa here at his side, why, then you thought of many things the Church had always said. You came from dust and you returned to dust. You got old. Girls who were beautiful got old and wrinkled. Men who were strong got weak and old, and even helpless like Pa.

"You're pretty quiet today," Jim said.

"Oh, I was just thinking."

"Maybe you don't even like to talk to your father."

"Why no, Pa."

"Well, don't worry. I won't be here long. Soon I'll be under the earth and then you won't have to be ashamed of me any longer."

"Pa, I never feel that way."

Danny stood with Jim to cross at Fifty-eighth and Calumet. There were no automobiles coming, and he walked slowly at his father's side. Pa's right eye wasn't good, and he had to be watched crossing the street. They went on to the elevated station.

IV

At the bank, Danny for the first time looked at the book. His father and mother had drawn out all but five dollars of his money and they had not said a word to him about it. He didn't begrudge them the money. Only he was hurt, disappointed. They should have said something to him. The fact that you were a son of someone didn't mean that they should treat you as if you didn't have a word of your own to say. He was glad that they had used the money, but he noticed that it had been withdrawn before Pa's stroke last fall. He was glad they could use what was left of it now. He was contributing something. He was glad of that, because he was ashamed to be still going to school while Bill worked. But still, they could have at least told him. He didn't see why he was treated as if he was still ten years old.

"Come on, hurry up. After all your schooling, don't you even know enough to fill out a bank withdrawal slip?" Jim said.

Danny filled out the slip and signed his name. He could almost have cried to have to watch his father struggle to put an X down for his name. He took the slip and the book to a window, but he was sent to one of the officers, and the man asked him questions about Pa and filled out a new slip. Danny signed it, and Pa limped over and put his X on the new slip, and they got the money. Danny handed it to Jim.

V

Riding home, Danny felt betrayed. He didn't care that they had used the money. He was glad of that. It was the principle of it, the way they had treated him as if he was not to be considered in anything. If Pa wasn't sick, and he wasn't needed to work as soon as he graduated, he would run away and make his own life some place else, travel, see things, be his own boss. They could treat him different. Well, he was just past nineteen. Soon he would be working. Soon he would be twenty-one. He would give money home, but he wouldn't be told what to do. Priests at school, uncles at home, aunt, grandmother, father, mother, all telling him what to do, making him lie if he wanted to go out. He was fed up with the whole damned business. What did they think he was?

"Shakespeare said that a man's best friend is his pocketbook," Jim said to Danny in the elevated train.

Danny didn't answer.

"Don't forget that. You're going to be working soon. Don't forget that. Save what you can when you go to work."

"Uh huh."

"Do you like school?" Jim asked Danny after they had ridden a couple of stations without speaking.

"Yes, but I want to get a job and work."

"I hope I can get you back in the company. If not, you'll have to shift for yourself."

"I'm going to start looking soon for a job. Our class gets out ahead of the rest of the school because we're graduating. I'll be able to go to work before the end of May. That's only a little more than two months from now."

"Well, until you get out, study all you can. Study never hurt any man unless it gave him a swelled head."

He didn't care a damn about study. The hell with study. The hell with Latin. The hell with Vergil. The hell with chemistry. The hell with trigonometry. The hell with English. Well, yes. He couldn't ever write the way he liked to fancy he could. What experience did he have worth writing about? None. He had no romances, no real exciting experiences, no adventures, no exceptional happenings in his life. The hell with writing.

42

I

Danny waited with the rest of his classmates for the last hour of class to come to an end. Outside it was sunny and pleasant. Spring promised to come early this year. And now, again it was Friday. One more day, one more week over. As he drew toward the end of his school career, the days seemed longer. Time seemed slower. Today was heralding more than the end of the week. This afternoon he was going to play his last game of basketball for his school, and if they won over Athanasius, they'd finish the season in third place. The basketball season was a bigger one than the football season had been. Today was his last chance to redeem himself.

Danny twisted about in his seat and gazed at Father Powers. The pink-cheeked priest glanced about the room, frowning. Danny thought that Father Powers' bark was worse than his bite, but that he could be tough. Father Powers didn't like him.

"Well, I've been teaching you fellows one thing or another for almost four years," Father Powers said. He paused a moment. "Haven't I, O'Neill?"

"Yes, Father."

"Think that it has done you much good?"

"Yes, Father."

"You're an optimist, aren't you, O'Neill?"

"Yes, Father."

"Yes, I guess you are. I know that I haven't put much into the massive dome of your skull. The hemispheres of your brain seem to me to be full of bubbles and vast spaces, a vast bush like Australia, now just as they were when you came to us here, a little shrimp."

Danny grinned foolishly.

"Mulligan, are you awake today?" Father Powers asked.

"Yes, Father."

"Well, I'm glad to hear that. Mulligan, you didn't give any more promise than O'Neill, but thanks to your association with me, serving mass for me for two years, you've turned out better. Of course, I have had to compete with those friends of yours around the corner of Sixty-third and Stony Island, but even so, I have hammered a little through your skull."

"Yes, Father."

"Don't be so sure of yourself, however."

"Yes, Father."

"Shanley, have you learned much?"

"Father, I think that I have profited greatly by my education here," Shanley said.

"Well, you have."

Father Powers looked around the room.

"I still have a few more classes in which to try and teach you something. It's harder on me than on your other teachers. I only get you once a week on Friday afternoons for Christian Doctrine, and they get you all week. Well, I'll do the best I can. Everybody awake now?"

"Yes, Father," the class chorused.

"Good. I thank you, gentlemen."

There was a twinkle in his eye.

"Mulligan, do you remember those far-off days when I taught you physiology in the first year?"

"Yes, Father. I learned a lot."

"Do you remember what I said when I talked about alcohol?"

"Well, Father, you said that alcohol had bad effects on the human system, and . . ."

"On the liver," Danny called out.

"O'Neill, you don't have to show off. You haven't got a lot to show off with."

"Yes, Father, on the liver and the heart," Marty said.

"Well, Mulligan, despite all I said, I'm sure that you are going to have a red nose. Redder than mine."

The class roared.

"My red nose comes from other causes than Mulligan's will come from."

Again the students laughed.

"Smilga, how are you doing?"

"Me, Fadder?"

"Yes, you. Of course, you're still hard to see. You never did grow up, did you, Smilga?"

"Fadder, I don't smoke."

"No, I'm sure smoking hasn't stunted your growth. But I'm not so sure about Doolan back there."

"Father, I wouldn't touch a coffin nail."

"I guess you mean if you had to pay for it, is that it, Doolan?"

The class again laughed.

"That's enough of this horse play. Now, again, everybody wake up. We have important matters to discuss this afternoon," Father Powers said, his voice changing. He glanced around, serious and interested.

II

"You fellows are soon going to go out in the world. Here in school you are with your own kind. You have before you the example of priests. At home you have the example of your mothers and fathers. But soon you will leave us, and then everything is going to be different. You have been given a good education, even though it would be difficult to prove it by some of you. At all events, we have done the best we could with you. Now you are not going to be treated as others will be. You are going to be watched. You are going to be looked upon as Catholics, educated by us priests. You are going to go forth from here in June carrying the responsibility of being a Catholic."

Danny felt that he was a fine one to be carrying any responsibility.

"You cannot carry this responsibility lightly, either. A Catholic is always under scrutiny in this world. He has to act at all times so that he will be a credit to his Church and so that he will not bring unwarranted and bigoted criticism upon his Church.

"A Catholic young man who graduates from a Catholic institution of learning must be a guide. Goodness of conduct is not sufficient for such a person. He must also *know*. He must know how to answer criticism. He must be armed with the doctrines of the Church so that he can defend the faith.

"Now, infidelity, atheism, materialism, paganism are all gaining ground in the modern world. The enemies of the Church are active. You all know this from the activities of the Ku Klux Klan in recent years."

"Riding around trying to bully people by dressing up in nightshirts," Danny called out.

"Yes, that is so. The Klan wears nightgowns and does not dare come out in the light of day without masks."

Father Powers paused.

"For the rest of the year in our lessons, I am going to summarize all of the important doctrines of the Church. I am going to give you the arguments and the answers on important questions of faith and dogma which you may be called upon to explain when you go out into the world. First of all, I am going to discuss the question, is there a God?"

He yawned and then continued.

"Truly, it is a silly question to ask—Is there a God? All of us know that it is silly, fatuous. The fool cries out in his folly that there is no God, cries out that God does not exist when the entire harmony of the world tells us that there is a Creator.

"Now, suppose a pagan asks one of you to prove that there is a God. How are you going to answer him?"

The priest looked around the room.

"O'Neill, how are you going to answer him?"

"Well, Father, I'm going to say that a world so perfect as this one couldn't exist if somebody didn't make it. I would point to the sky, and if it was a nice night, with the stars and the moon out, I would tell him to look at them, look at the stars and the moon, and I would say to him, did he think that such beauties in the world made themselves. And he wouldn't be able to answer that. Of course, he might be bigoted and say something bigoted, but he couldn't answer my question."

"In other words, you would advance the argument that the proof of God is to be found in His works. Now, that is one of the important proofs that God exists. One of the great achievements of the Fathers of the Church and the great thinkers and theologians of the middle ages was to advance the same kind of a proof as O'Neill here. Of course, they perfected such arguments. But it is a good approach. Saint Paul, in his *Epistle to the Romans,* Chapter one, twentieth verse, says: *For the invisible things of Him, from the creation of the world, are clearly seen, being understood by the things that are made, even His eternal power and divinity.*" This text is the one that the Fathers and the theologians of the middle ages based their thoughts on when they perfected the argument that God is proven by His works. *Invisibilia Dei per ea quae facta sunt, intellecta conspiciuntur.* O'Neill, what does that mean?"

"I don't know, Father."

"You studied Latin under me in second year, didn't you?"

"Yes, Father."

"Do me a favor. Don't ever admit it. At all events, that is the beginning of the chapter of Paul I just quoted to you in English."

"I see," Danny said.

"Do you see, too, Doolan?"

"Of course, Father."

"Shanley, can you offer me another proof of the existence of God?"

"Yes, Father," Shanley said, standing up, a tall, slender boy, with a sensitive face, reddish hair, and awkward movements and gestures.

"Well, I give you the floor."

"The argument of the watch on the desert island."

"Yes, go ahead."

"Well, Father, suppose that you were alone on a desert island. There were no footmarks, no signs or traces to show that anyone had ever been there before. You were the first human being ever to have come to that island. And you found a watch. It worked perfectly and kept time perfectly."

Danny raised his hand.

"Yes, O'Neill?"

"Father, how could it keep time perfectly, and how could you know it kept time perfectly if you didn't have another watch? I was just thinking, suppose I was there, the person on that island, how would I know it kept the right time?"

"O'Neill, that question does not disturb the argument. Let Shanley go on."

He had just thought of that question, and he felt that he had asked it to show off, and so he got nicely told to shut up.

"Well, anyway, I would find this watch, Father, and I would see its perfection of mechanism. Everything about it is perfect. Now I would ask myself, how did the watch get here? The watch could not get there by itself. I would know that, because I know that every cause has to have an effect. So I would say that the watch had to have a maker. Well, Father, the watch, the watch that works the most perfectly, is simple, a simple mechanism if you contrast it with the universe. The universe is like a watch, only it is much more complicated, and yet it works in complete harmony. Now, if we agree that a watch has had to have a maker and that it could not have made itself, we have to argue that even more so is this true of the miraculously perfect universe in which we live. Therefore, there must have been a Maker of the world."

"Yes, good. Shanley, you know how to think."

He would never be as smart as a fellow like Shanley. He ought never even to dream that he might be. Shanley was the best writer in the class, too. He wished he could write like Shanley. Father Robert and all of the class thought that Shanley would someday be a famous journalist or a writer.

"Saint Thomas Aquinas perfected an argument of this kind. I shall try to state it simply for you fellows, and you try to remember it. Our senses tell us that there is movement in the world. Is that clear?"

Some of the students nodded their heads. Others looked blank.

"Mulligan, you seem stumped."

"Well, Father, I was just thinking that I didn't see what you were driving at."

"The earth revolves on its axis. Is that correct, Mulligan?"

"Sure, of course."

"Everything in the world moves."

"But what about rocks, Father?"

"Mulligan, aren't rocks part of the earth, which revolves on its axis?"

"I get you now, Father."

"I'm glad to know that. Now, if something moves, it must be capable of moving, isn't that so? Yes. It must have the potency of moving. Now, if it moves, it is in the act of moving. Now, something cannot be both in potency and in the act of moving."

He saw the many blank faces.

"What I am telling you here is that nothing can move by itself. It cannot be in potency and in the act of movement at the same time. If it can't be both at the same time, how does it move? It must have a mover. In other words, it is not logical to say, like the atheist and the materialist, that the world is made up of a series of movements, a series of causes and effects, connected with each other but lacking a first cause. If the world moves, it must have a mover. The earth could not crank itself up and revolve on its axis any more than an automobile could. Even when you have a self-starting automobile and don't have to crank it, you have to have someone to start the automobile. In other words, if there is all this movement in the world, the earth, the stars, the planets, there has to be a first mover. So when O'Neill makes the argument that the stars prove God exists, he can add another argument right with his. Not only the beauty of the stars cry out aloud with proof that someone made them. Also, the motion of the stars cry aloud to offer another proof that God exists. Is that clear to you fellows?"

There were noddings of heads, and many said "Yes, Father."

"So we say there is a First Mover in the world."

A sort of beginning of moving-day, the first of May, Danny thought. But the class today was too serious for him to call out and make that crack. He'd surely get socked if he did.

"We Catholics argue in terms of cause and effect that there is a God. But there are causes of different orders. If I take O'Neill and pick him up and let him drop out the window on his head so that he will break up the stones in the schoolyard, there are various causes for what happens. I have dropped him. And another cause is the law of gravity. There are orders of causes. Now, there must be an efficient cause behind everything. A man cranks an automobile and it moves. But the man who cranks the automobile did not make that automobile. Other men made it. In other words, we trace back through causes and effects. And when we do that, we come to the Efficient Cause. That Efficient Cause is God. The Efficient Cause of the universe must have generated all things in it. He must be the Cause which causes all the other causes. But when we say that there has to be a First Mover, we do not prove completely what we Catholics believe concerning our God and our Creator.

"Smilga, do you know why we haven't proved enough as yet?"

"Well, Fadder, let's see." Smilga scratched his head. His face suddenly lit up. "A Protestant, Fadder, could say the same thing."

"No, that's not quite right. I gave you a hint. But I'll go on. In the case of the watch on the desert island, the watch was there, and we argue backward that it must have had a maker. But the maker of the watch had the materials he needed in order to make a watch that is an exquisite instrument of perfection. Now, when we say that God is the First Mover, did He have the things already given to Him to move? If He did, you see, He did not create the world. He only cranked the machine. The machine was there. So He must have not only moved the world, He must also have made everything that He moves in the world. The argument of Efficient Cause must mean something more—it must be Creative Cause. God is not only the Efficient Cause of the universe: He is also the Creative Cause."

Father Powers smiled and cleared his throat.

"Here I have only touched on the great thought of great Catholic thinkers of the past, the saints who were not the martyrs but the thinkers of our religion. For the Church lays claim to its thinkers, too, and with justifiable pride. From what I have explained, you ought to realize the great beauty and the impeccable logic of the great thinkers of the Church. You see that they did not rest with an argument such as Shanley gave us about the watch on the desert island. Not that that is wrong. But they have explored every possibility. But let us get on. We have now gone so far as to see that there is an Efficient Cause—God. And that God is not only the First Mover; He is also the Creator of everything that He moves. We all have read and heard many stories about how the artist creates a fine work of art because he loves it. Now, God loves the world. God is the Supreme Artist. He has created the universe out of love. And His love moves the world. There were great thinkers before the Christian era who grasped something of the truth of God. But that is one point where they did not go far enough. They did not see how God loves the world He creates. Why does He love the world? Well, why do your father and your mother love you? Why does the artist love his work? The same is true on an infinitely vast scale of God. He created the world and loves His creation.

"Any questions?"

"Father, does God love earthquakes and such things?" Danny asked.

When some of them laughed at him, Danny was sorry he'd asked the question. But then they might think he'd asked it to be funny.

"That's not a good question. We are not able to conceive either the full character of God's love or the extent and nature of His purpose.

"Besides the proofs from logic, there is revelation. We know that God has created the world, not only by the use of our logical faculties. We know that God has created the world and every living thing in it, every inanimate object, every grain of sand on the beach, because God has told us so. God is the author of the

Bible, and the Bible is a book of revelation. Similarly, God sent us His son, who is co-equal with God the Father and the Holy Ghost, to redeem mankind. And we know from the Gospels of Jesus that the Church is the true Church, founded by Christ, our Lord, on the rock of Peter. Now, you fellows know all this. You have studied it for years in grammar school and four years in high school. This knowledge is as natural to you now as the air you breathe. I am not going to discuss it at length as I have other matters of faith. At all events, it is now time for school to let out, and we will continue next week."

43

I

It was spring. The weather had turned, and the days were just too wonderful to have to be cooped up in school. Danny didn't know just what to do with himself. He was counting the days. It was now mid April. He had always felt that he would be sad when the time came for him to be leaving S.S. Now it was coming, and coming along soon, and he wasn't sad. He couldn't wait for the time to come when he would be done with school, once and for all.

He stopped mooning and read the advertisement he was going to answer. He read through notes from his notebook which Father Robert had dictated on how to write letters, to be sure that he used the right form. He read through the draft of his letter which he had written in a notebook, and now he was all set to copy it out. He copied slowly, trying to form each letter with care because he had such a terrible scrawl unless he took the utmost pains with his handwriting.

April 16, 1923
5816½ South Park Ave.
Chicago, Ill.

Mr. A. R. Dorfman
The Clarion Publishing Co.
Beloit, Wis.

Dear Sir:
I desire to place my application in answer to your advertisement contained in today's issue of The Chicago Clarion.

This coming June, I shall be graduated from the Saint Stanislaus High School, which is located on the South Side of Chicago, Illinois.

I have had three years' experience conducting the athletic column of Saint Stan-

islaus' Aureole, *which during a state-wide contest was declared to be the most interesting school publication in Illinois.*

I have also competed in amateur wrestling tournaments and have received letters from my future alma mater for participating in the baseball, basketball and football activities of my school. This year, my senior year, I have been captain of the heavyweight basketball team at my school, which finished third in the South Side division of the Catholic League. These experiences should enable me to understand the player's version of sports.

As a salary I will expect one hundred and fifty dollars per month with a gradual increase, after I have proven my ability.

Hoping that you see fit to accept my application, I remain,

Yours truly

Daniel O'Neill

That might get him the job and open up a real career for him.

He copied out the next letter he was writing. He wasn't as interested in getting this job, but then, he had to get something to do.

April 16, 1923
5816½ South Park Ave.
Chicago, Ill.

L. Long
49 East Madison St.
Chicago, Ill.

Dear Sir:

I desire to place my application for the position of shipping clerk, which was advertised in today's issue of The Chicago Clarion.

This June, I shall be a graduate of Saint Stanislaus High School on the South Side of Chicago.

While I have never had any experience as a shipping clerk, I have been employed as a clerk in the Call Department of The Continental Express Company for two summer vacations. I think that my experience in that occupation affects the above-mentioned lack of mine. I have a general knowledge of the express business and its methods including that of routing the pickup and delivery service; and this will enable me to route automobiles and discharge the duties of a shipping clerk, in a capable manner.

Hoping that you see fit to accept my application, I remain,

Yours truly

Daniel O'Neill

Danny went out to mail his letters and pay his daily visit to his father.

II

"Dan, I've been thinking, Dan, that your cousin, Marty McCormack, might be able to get you a job playing on his football team. He makes good money at it."

Jim seemed pathetic to Danny when he said this. Danny could see that his father was worried about money, and about him. And Pa was trying to be friendly, to get near to him. Every time he was with Pa, there seemed to be something sad about their being together. He couldn't put his finger on just what it was that caused this, or on just why he and Pa never seemed able to understand each other better. And today Pa appeared to him to be even more sad than usual.

"Dan, I was sittin' here thinkin' that since you like football, and since they tell me you're pretty good at it, why not turn it to something? You can get a job weekdays, and then play Sundays with your cousin's team and make some extra money."

"I'm not good enough for that."

"Why?" Jim said, eyeing Danny closely.

"Well, I only played two years in high school, and I'm not heavy enough. Those fellows all played in college. Some of them were All-Americans."

"Your cousin never went to college."

"Well, look at how husky he is."

"We could put some beef on you."

Another one of those dreams of his. To be an All-American. To be Eddie Collins' successor. Gone! Danny Minus-Zero O'Neill.

"I don't know why you don't follow up my idea. Here you have been playing football, why not turn it to something? We need the money, and you got to make your way, and your cousin told me at his mother's wake last summer that there's good money in it."

"Pa, it would be swell, but I couldn't make it. I don't weigh enough and I haven't had the experience."

"Well, after all the to-do you made about it and all the time you gave it, that's a fine how-do-you-do."

Pa was accusing him. And he didn't want to argue with Pa. Pa just didn't understand.

"Well, Pa, maybe when I get a little heavier, I might try."

III

Danny waited apprehensively. They had finished discussing the coming initiations and now all the brothers sat in Marty Mulligan's parlor and prepared to start *critique*. Hugh McNeill, now grand president of the fraternity, had introduced the idea, and once a month they had *critique*.

"Well, who begins?" Hugh asked.

"Whoever wants to. The floor is open," Marty Mulligan, the new chapter president, said.

"Well, I'd like to say something," Ike Dugan said. "It's about O'Neill with girls. I been watchin' him. Danny, what I want to say is this. I don't think you're always serious when you're with certain kinds of girls. You say things that, well, they aren't funny, and the girls don't get a good impression of you."

"And sometimes if you can't date up a girl, you insult her," Tommy Collins said.

Yes, he did do that. But he did it when he was hurt and felt a girl would laugh at him. It was a reaction in self-defense.

"You called up Kate Flanagan, and after you asked her for a date and she said she was busy that night, you told her that she ought to hire a social secretary and that perhaps she could write a book on how it feels to be so popular," Red Keene said.

Well, it was a funny crack.

"Now, what is going to be thought of our frat, Dan, if you say things like that to decent girls?" Marty asked, looking at him intently.

"I guess you're right, fellows," he said, feeling that he must answer.

"I'm saying this, Dan, for your welfare as well as the good of the fraternity. It's not right, is it?" Marty said.

"No."

"And, oh yes, this," Marty said. "You ought to have more dignity than you do. For instance, when you were captain of the heavies in basketball, you couldn't make the fellows treat you like a captain. I think the reason is because you always like to goof around too much."

He had often felt things like this about himself, not wanting to believe them. Was this the reason why he had never been able really to fit in and be popular as other fellows were? Or what?

"Yes, O'Neill, you like to talk too much and your jabber wears people out," Ike Dugan said.

"Yes, O'Neill, Ike means you aren't as witty as you'd like to think you are. You're always making wisecracks that don't come off. You do it with us as well as with girls," Tim Doolan added.

"I'd like to say something here. You see, you got to have dignity sometimes when you are out on dates. Like that dance you were stagging a month or so ago."

"Yeh, Marty, that night Ella McGrail got sore as hell at him and thought he was goofy," Ike interrupted.

“Well, that’s an example,” Marty said.

He didn’t like to be reminded of all this. But he had to take it just as the others did when they had to face *critique*. The aim of *critique* was that the fraternity brothers should criticize one another and point out one another’s faults for everybody’s own good. But still, he didn’t like to sit here and be told these things. And all he could do was to sit and take it, and he knew he must be grinning weakly. He felt like a clown.

“Dan, I think that you ought to choose your ties with more care. Your ties are too loud, ties that Polacks and niggers wear. That’s not good form,” John McTeague said.

“I always thought that they were all right.”

“I don’t think girls like them that loud,” John said.

“I don’t agree with you there,” Hugh said.

Danny sat, waiting for more criticisms, feeling that he was being stripped bare and held up as a laughable spectacle.

IV

“I have here the answers and final results on the School Spirit contest, and those who submitted the winning definitions are going to get their one-dollar prizes today,” Father Robert said.

Danny wondered would he win any of the prizes. He was saving money for the Senior Prom, hoping that he’d be able to get a date for it.

“The first question was: ‘What is school spirit?’ The winning definition was submitted by Daniel O’Neill.”

Danny smiled with gratification. A victory for him.

“*School spirit is an ardent and enthusiastic participation in all school activities.*”

Father Robert came down toward Danny.

“You’re waiting for your prize, aren’t you?”

“Well, Father, since I won it.”

“We’re going to hold it. You haven’t paid your tuition yet, so we will deduct this dollar,” Father Robert said in a low voice. He faced the class. “Some of the other definitions which merit mention were the following: ‘*School spirit is the quality of defending your school even though the enemy is coming over the top and you are out of ammunition*,’ by Heyler, fourth year. Another, by Allen, class of ’24: ‘*School spirit is the seed which later develops into patriotism.*’

“The second question: ‘Why should every S.S. student have school spirit?’

“Shanley’s answer won that. I quote: ‘*Every Saint Stanislaus student should have school spirit for the same reason that every American should be ready to fight for his country.*’ Good. Very good.

"Third question: 'How may a student who lacks school spirit best be denounced in one sentence?'

"The best answer to this came from Francis Xavier Conlan, class of '25. I quote: *'An S.S. student who lacks school spirit is like an onion in a rosebed, an undesirable misfit.'*

"The class of '25, after learning of this definition, has started popularizing for next year the following slogan: 'Don't be an onion.'"

The priest walked down the aisle while the seniors laughed.

"Here is your prize dollar, Shanley."

He came to Danny, a broad grin on his face.

"On second thought, I have changed my mind, and so, Dan, here is your prize dollar," Father Robert said.

That was the way Father Robert always joked.

"Timothy Doolan won the prize for the last question. He says that the best way to punish a student lacking school spirit is as follows: I quote him: *'A student who lacks school spirit should be ostracized and ignored by the faculty and student body.'* Good. And one of the other answers was that of Howard. Howard's punishment for such unworthy students is less mild than Doolan's. Howard says: *'Duck him in the lagoon; expel him publicly; publish a slackers' list in the* Aureole; *call out his name and offense at a mass-meeting; ride him on a rail; drum him out of the school to the tune of the Rogues March.'*"

Howard smiled at Father Robert.

"Well, that's that. Here's your dollar, Doolan."

Tim walked up and took his dollar.

"Now, I have some more matters to bring up. This year, we are going to publish an annual. We are going to publish a brief biography and a picture of every one of you in the annual."

"Father, won't that be a Rogue's Gallery?" Danny asked.

"Those who live in glass houses should not throw bricks," Father Robert said.

The class laughed.

"Well, let me begin with the first rogue then, O'Neill. Shanley, you take down the information. First of all, O'Neill, you dropped out of the Debating Society this year. Debating Society and Literary Club, second and third year. Is that right?"

Danny nodded, and the priest went on getting the information.

V

"Father, I wanted to see you," Danny said, catching Father Michael in the third-floor corridor.

"Yes, Dan."

"Father, first I wanted to ask you if I could get out of school a little early so I could look for a job. I got to get one right away, you know, because of my father."

"Well, we're letting the senior class out at the end of May. That ought to give you a head start on most of the others who will be looking from other schools. And of course, if you want to take a day or so off to look for a job, that will be all right, only don't take too many off. I couldn't permit that."

"Thank you, Father."

"How is your father?'"

"He's the same. Father, I don't think he'll ever be able to work. He doesn't get any better."

"We'll keep on praying for him," Father Michael said, looking at Danny sympathetically.

"And, Father, I wanted to ask you something else. It's about my tuition." Danny halted a moment. "Well, Father, business has been bad for my uncle, and then on top of that there's my father, so, Father, I wanted to ask, could I graduate and pay you the tuition money I owe you after I'm working?"

"Certainly. How much is it?"

"Twenty dollars from last year and eighty for this year."

"Surely, I understand, Dan."

Danny was filled with gratitude and at the same time overwhelmed with shame. If this news got around? But it wouldn't. Father Michael wouldn't say anything.

"Don't worry about it."

"Thank you, Father."

Danny went off, thinking that Father Michael was all right, a swell priest. He was going to be sorry leaving—leaving a few priests like Father Michael, anyway.

VI

"I got a date for the Senior Prom," Danny said to Marty in front of big Emil Heiden.

Heiden had taunted him after the Alumni Spring Dance, saying he couldn't get a dance.

"Who?" asked Marty.

"Sis Hansen. She's keen," Danny said.

"If she's a mama with the stuff, she must have had a lapse or something, giving you a date," Heiden said.

"Heiden, this bastard always gets the keenest women. He never takes them out twice, but he always has a keen date," Marty said.

"They won't go out with him twice, huh?" Heiden jeered.

"It's because he treats them lousy, gets drunk on them, and is snotty. He's too snotty," Marty said.

They didn't know that if he was snotty, it was because he was hurt or afraid of being hurt by a girl. But now, for the Senior Prom, he had the most beautiful girl he'd ever taken out. He felt what difference did it make if twelve girls had refused him dates for the Spring Alumni Dance. His past experiences with girls had worked out right because they had meant that now he had found the right girl, Sis Hansen.

"Well, I'm from Missouri," Heiden said.

"You'll see her, Drink-of-Water," Danny said.

"Maybe," Heiden answered.

"You will," Danny said with aplomb.

He had a date to make them all sit up and take notice. And it was, let's see, thirty-four days to the dance. Thirty-four days, and then he would have a girl, the most beautiful girl any guy could ever have. She was only sixteen, but college guys took her out, and she was a knockout, a literal goddess, blonde and slim, and she was going to be his date, and, yes, his girl.

Heiden walked off.

"Say, the baseball team is playin' today. Let's go over and razz them," Danny said.

"All right. Say, Joe McBride was hurt that you didn't come out. He says you were influenced by our frat. He thinks our frat spoiled you. Boy, he should know the kind of a guy that would spoil the frat," Marty said, laughing.

"He wouldn't let me play first base," Danny said.

They paid their checks and, their arms around each other's shoulders, they strolled over to Jackson Park to watch S.S. play. Danny watched with a silly grin on his face. Most of the players were first- or second-year kids. He could have made the team and maybe he would have starred. He should have gone out for it.

"Hi, Joe," he called, catching the coach's eye.

Joe greeted him curtly. Danny watched, with that silly grin pasted on his face.

VII

Danny stood with his fraternity brothers in Tommy Collins' basement. The initiation was almost over, and it had been quite a card. The pledges, Noel

Merton and Wils Gillen, had been made to dress up in short pants with Buster Brown collars, and they'd had mustaches greased on their faces. They'd had to roller skate up and down Sixty-third Street. And then Merton had carried a box of toilet paper and Wils had walked at his side, taking out sheets and trying to give them away. On Danny's suggestion, the two worms had been ordered to go down to Sixty-third and Stony Island and Wils had had to make a speech trying to sell the toilet paper. It had been a scream, all right. Danny hadn't had as much fun or laughed as much in a hell of a long time. Talk about what it hadn't done to his funny bone!

And now, Wils and Noel were stripped to the waist and blindfolded. Tommy Collins hocked, and then Marty Mulligan fed them genuine oysters from a bucket, and they didn't know what they were eating. Everybody enjoyed it. Marty smeared Wils' chest with catsup, and Ike took the blindfolds off of Noel. He saw Wils smeared with catsup and it looked as if Wils were bleeding.

"You did that," Marty said in a challenging voice.

Noel looked at Marty, shocked.

"I did not."

"All the brothers are here to witness it," Marty said.

They all sat on chairs, now solemn-faced.

"I saw him. He cut him up with a knife," Danny yelled.

Ike Dugan hid his face in a handkerchief to hide how much he was laughing.

Noel caught on.

"Gee, I'm sorry. What can I do now to make up? I didn't mean to do it," Merton said, and that spoiled the fun.

"You're too smart. For that you get extra paddles," Marty said. He turned to Gillen. "Go over and wash the stuff off you, and then you worms get the paddles you were ordered to have here."

Gillen obeyed. They put on their shirts. They bent over in a corner, and the brothers lined up, Marty first. He took one of the paddles, a solid carved piece of wood about three feet long. He smacked Merton's buttocks three times and then he socked Gillen.

"Merton, I'm giving you one of the extra paddles, and the others will do the same."

One by one each brother took his turn. Merton and Gillen winced with the blows, and before the initiation was finished, they cried out and moaned. When Danny's turn came, he didn't have the heart to sock them. But he gritted his teeth. If the others did, he would. These fellows were worms, and the worms had to be made to appreciate the value of the fraternity before they were initiated. Otherwise they wouldn't be good brothers. He smacked them mightily. They winced in pain.

The paddling was finished. Wils and Noel sat down facing the brothers for the questioning period. This was the most interesting part of the initiation. The pledges would be asked whether or not they masturbated, and they would be questioned about what they said and did, and how they acted in sexual intercourse if they weren't virgins. After questioning, the solemn part of the initiation came. The pledges would take an oath, and Hugh McNeill, as grand president, would deliver a solemn lecture about the ideals of brotherhood and fraternity and what it meant to be a fraternity man. After that, Hugh and Wils would be brothers.

VIII

"Brothers, I can't wait until we have another initiation. Boy, what I won't do to some worm," Wils said, grinning.

"How many blisters you got on your can, Wils?" Danny asked.

"Plenty, but it was worth it," Wils said. "Sure was. To be a brother to you guys. You're a swell bunch of fellows anywhere."

Danny told himself that he would know them all his life and find them friends, tried and true. He was proud of his fraternity.

44

I

The sun was warm and pleasing, and Jim idled on the swing of the O'Flaherty back porch. He gazed off at the blue sky above the rear of the buildings on the opposite side of the alley.

He did not want to feel proud or happy because of the news he had just heard. No man's death was good news, and it did not change your condition. But it was, well, ironic. He had been sitting here, and the old lady had come out and told him that Mrs. Geraghty had just called up and said that Dr. Mike Geraghty had died today of heart failure. Here he was still alive, and his doctor was dead. Mike had been attending to him regularly since his stroke last fall. Think of it, himself a sick man, yes, a dying man, seeing the doctor who was healthy, and always it had been his condition that was the trouble and the cause of worry, not Mike's. Why, Doctor Mike had looked in the pink of condition, as if he had never known a day's sickness in his life. He had been to Mike's only Tuesday. Mike had seemed hale and healthy. He had examined him, had said that he was much the same but that there was some hope for him. He had walked away wondering if Mike was kidding him to make him feel good. And just think, then Mike's number was already up, and not another week was to pass before Mike would lay dead and he would be sitting here as he was on a sunny afternoon, thinking of how he was still alive and Mike was gone.

Jim got up and went in the kitchen.

"Mary, I'm going home. Lizz will want to hear the news. I'll be over again soon."

"Take care of yourself, Jim."

II

"Mother, I got to go over there," Lizz said excitedly in the O'Flaherty kitchen.

"They won't need you," Mrs. O'Flaherty answered.

"Mother, Nora Geraghty is a wonderful catch for our Al. She'll inherit a house, and I'm sure that Mike left an estate and insurance. Why, a lovely widow woman like that is a catch. And, Mother, if you want to know what I think, I think Al has always been sweet on her. I have to go over there and put in a good word for Al. Oh, Mother, I'm just the one to make a match like this."

"What in the name of God are you talking about? Go on home to that sick man. He needs you."

"Mother, if we don't get this for Al, some guy is going to come along and get her. And Al was Mike's best friend. Mike would want Al to take care of his widow."

"Don't say no more, Lizz. Don't say no more, or I'll not be responsible for what I do."

"But, Mother, look at that money, you don't want it to go to a stranger," Lizz said.

"The poor man is no sooner dead than you want to marry his wife. Sure, it's pagan," Mrs. O'Flaherty said.

III

Jim was alone in the house. When he had come back with the news of Mike, Lizz had rushed right over to the O'Flahertys, and the kids were out playing. It took some time for the realization that Doctor Mike had died to sink in his mind. Now he realized it. Being alone, with no one to talk to, no distractions from his thoughts, he was terrified. What was worst about it was the suddenness with which such a blow came, unexpected, without any previous hints and without any kind of warning. Now that Mike was dead, he no longer held anything against him for not having come to Arty, down in the cottage. He would harbor nothing against the dead. It was too bad. When a healthy man in his prime went off like that, it was always a tragedy. Yes, none of us knew when we'd be called.

And even more awful, too, was the fact that Mike Geraghty had gone off so suddenly that there had been no time for the priest. He was called off to meet his God without a warning. Now Mike Geraghty's soul faced God to be judged. Jim sat in his comfortable chair and thought of this, thought in awe and in terror. For that was the most terrible thing about Mike's death. He went before a priest could absolve him of his sins.

God spare me that fate, Jim prayed.

When we had our health, we rarely thought of death. When he had his health, he'd always acted as if he were going to live forever. Now he knew better. Now he often thought of death. Before this last stroke, he had feared death for what he would be leaving behind. Now he was ready to die, ready to face his God. His family would be better off without him. He was just a helpless old man taking bread from the mouths of his children, whose lives were ahead of them, while his was over with.

Yes, he was ready to go, and he would be better off dead, and still, still, no man wanted to die. Think of it. The world goes on after you. No matter how much you thought of what would happen after you were dead, you wouldn't know and be here to see it. You would see it from the other world, but how would you feel, and what would it be like in the other world? Suppose that after his death some of his kids, Danny, should go bad? How would he feel, watching it happen, watching the boy take the road to Hell, watching all that from the other world?

His eyes turned toward the window. He stared out at the street. Everything before him was so familiar that he scarcely saw anything now when he looked out the window. The scraggly lawn in front of the building, the street, the gray and tan brick of the apartment buildings across the street, the railing in front of the building facing him, all these seemed to melt away from him, and he saw them and did not see them. He seemed often these days to be thinking, and suddenly there was a cloudiness in his mind. What had been going on in his head a minute ago? Oh, yes, death. He was thinking of death.

It was the fear of that awful minute when you were dying that was the worst about the fear of death. His time was coming. What would he do when that awful minute came? What would he think? Could he go like a man? Would he whimper, be fearful, and lose his courage? The best way to go was like Mike Geraghty had, suddenly, except that if you went that way, you didn't have a chance to have the priest. When he had been younger, and in good health, he had taken his religion for granted. He had not known what it meant. So it was with men. Human folly. The folly of all men. They paid no attention to God when they were in their prime. Perhaps God punishes them for this, in this world or in the next.

Well, anyway, Mike Geraghty was dead. God have mercy on his soul. May he rest in peace.

It was so quiet in the house. He could almost hear himself breathing.

Why had Lizz left him alone? She must have been gone already over an hour. Suppose something should happen to him? He shouldn't be left alone. He limped back and forth through the house, complaining to himself because he had been left alone. He kept going to the window and looking out, but she wasn't coming. Suddenly he put his hat on and left, determined to get her and bring her home.

IV

Jim and Lizz walked slowly home from the O'Flahertys. Lizz was getting fatter all the time. She had not bothered to fix herself up, but had rushed over to her mother's just as she was, wearing a soiled apron and a splotched black dress. Jim wore old clothes, and a crushed and shapeless felt hat. The short distance between the O'Flahertys on South Park Avenue and the O'Neills on Calumet seemed interminable. They walked slowly, each one thinking his own thoughts, saying not a word.

"Jim, you ought to lay down. You walked over to my mother's twice," Lizz said when they got home.

"The second time I went to get you."

"But, Jim, I almost never get out of the house, what with all I have to do and the children."

Yes, that was so. She took care of him. She couldn't get away. He shouldn't begrudge her a few minutes with her mother.

"Lizz, I'm sorry. Come and give your fellow a kiss," Jim said.

"My Daddy Long Legs," she said affectionately, hugging him.

Jim grinned, and with his twisted mouth his grin looked grotesque, unreal.

"Lizz, I think I'll go up to confession."

"Jim, I don't like you crossing streets alone. You know you were almost hurt last week."

"I'm all right."

"Wait until the children come in, and one of them can go with you."

"I'm all right. Anything you need from the store?"

"Yes, Jim, will you get a cake in the bakery on Sixty-first Street for Bill's supper?"

Lizz went to her purse and handed him a five-dollar bill.

"That's every cent we got, you'll have to change it."

Jim put the money in his pocket and left for confession.

V

"Why, Jim, what's happened?"

Jim was breathing heavily. He was pale. He started to speak but said nothing, moving his lips soundlessly.

"Are you hurt? Tell me."

"I don't know how it happened. Lizz, I lost the money. I went back over the whole route, and I looked in church where I knelt. I don't know how I could have lost it."

Lizz sighed in relief. Jim was all right.

"I thought you were hurt, the way you looked."

"I don't know how I could have lost that money. Here, you search me and see if I missed finding it in my pocket."

"God, it was all we had, too. What'll we do?"

Lizz frantically searched his pockets, turned them inside out. The money was gone.

"Jim, I'll go with you, and we'll look for it," she said anxiously, putting on her hat.

"I don't know how it happened," Jim said, his voice utterly forlorn. He seemed to Lizz at that moment like a little boy, and he made her think of one of the children, Bob or Dennis.

They went out and vainly retraced the steps Jim had taken, looking for the lost money.

VI

"I don't know how I could have lost it."

"Now, Jim, don't you worry. We still have bread to eat," Lizz said, sitting opposite Jim, and writing out a note.

"What are you doing, Lizz?" Jim asked.

"I'm writing a note to put on the mailbox. In case anybody found it, they will return it to me."

Lizz put the note on her mailbox and came back. She saw Jim looking miserable and sitting motionless by the dining-room table. She turned away fearful that she might convey her fright and feelings to him. She knew now beyond doubt that Jim would never get better. She had felt all along that he wouldn't, but still, she had hoped. She had hoped against hope. Something would happen, some miracle. But now she knew better. Last week, he had gone out and he had walked into a sign, hitting his jaw against it. Today he had lost their last five dollars. Jim, her Jim, the father of her children, was not only sick, he was helpless.

Perhaps it would have been the mercy of God if Jim had been called today instead of Mike Geraghty.

"What's the matter, Lizz?"

"Nothing, Jim. I'm sure that the money will come back to us. Now, don't you worry."

She gathered dishes off the table and carted them out to the kitchen to wash them. Jim sat alone by the dining-room table. Lizz wiped her eyes. No, she couldn't give in. Jim was her man, and this was her brood. She had to guard them and take care of Jim. Helpless or not, she wanted Jim. Better for Jim to be home helpless than under the ground.

She washed the dishes, remembering Jim, remembering the tall, powerful, yes, handsome, man she had married. The Jim who had danced and waltzed her and once so thrilled her. The Jim who had loved her, given her children—there he was, a helpless old man. Like a child. She couldn't even let him go to the store any more. Yes, losing the money today, it was a sign. Jim would never be better. Soon, soon, her Jim was going to be cold and dead, just as Mike Geraghty was.

Oh, Blessed Virgin, stand by me in these trying hours.

She sniffed. She rubbed her chubby arm over her eyes and with determination set to washing the dishes.

Jim sat motionless, staring vacantly at nothing, his paralyzed right arm resting on the dining-room table.

45

I

Jim was up again and sitting idly in his parlor chair after reading his newspaper. The attack he had had, had not been so severe as it had seemed. He had had convulsions and had been comatose that Saturday night after he had gone to confession and lost the five-dollar bill. They had gotten Doctor O'Donnell, who had been the family doctor for the O'Flahertys before they'd had Mike Geraghty. Jim was almost back to what he had been before the attack, except that his hand was numb. His arm and hand always came back more slowly than his leg when he had these attacks. Time was flowing slowly through the sunny afternoon. It was funny how the past seemed to grow so far away, farther and farther away, more vague, more dim, more distant. The past seemed to become more and more like a fog. He would try to remember, and the pictures of himself, of the scenes in which he once moved, these all seemed a little clouded. And whenever he tried to remember more of past things, he would come on stumbling blocks. He could not drag things out of his mind, his memory, with the vividness he desired.

He remembered the spring day that he had come home to the cottage with the good news that he was to be a Wagon Dispatcher. It was still light out and he remembered the sun, over in the west, hanging above the railroad tracks on the far side of Fuller Park. And he remembered that the kids were home, and that he had walked in the kitchen and told Lizz, and that she had danced. He wanted to remember more, how he had sat down and planned and told Lizz what they were going to do now with their good fortune and their added income, and he couldn't drag these remembrances out of his mind. The effort tired him, and his thoughts wandered. With his lethargy there was that cloudiness in his mind, the sort of fogginess that seemed to cover every picture and image he formed.

He sat there, slumped in his chair.

II

"But, Jim, I just thought that if you went to the hospital for a little while, you could get better care than I can give you," Lizz said.

"And who is going to pay for it?"

"I was told there is a ward for expressmen at Saint Matthews Hospital. I was thinking of looking into it or I could see Joe O'Reilley or Patsy McLaughlin about trying to get you into Mercy."

Jim was silent.

"After this last attack, I was thinking, Jim, of how you need better care than I can give you. And Dr. O'Donnell told me that he thought you should go to a hospital for a little while."

"He did, did he?"

"But, Jim, he's a good doctor, and such a fine man. And he isn't charging us a cent."

"What the hell do I care what doctors say? What good did doctors ever do for me? For anybody? For Arty? Why, Mike Geraghty was such a good doctor that he didn't even know he had heart trouble. Doctors! And Mike didn't know what ailed himself even."

"But, Jim, I wouldn't say maybe a few weeks in the hospital is what you need if I didn't think it would be good for you and help you to get better. And oh my, then when you came home again, we would all be so happy to see our Daddy Long Legs."

Lizz stopped, uncertain whether or not she should say any more.

"I am going to stay home here to die where I belong, with my wife and children around me and not alone in some damned hospital where I'll be a charity patient."

Lizz didn't say a word. She sat a moment and then she got up and went to Jim and stroked his gray hair. She bent down and kissed him.

III

So this was what he had been reduced to? His own wife thinking he should go to the hospital, in a charity ward? Jim's humiliation was too deep for words. A powerful emotion swept through him, caused a lump in his throat, almost produced uncontrolled tears. He dropped into his old Morris chair, feeling weak. His head was light, and his breath came more rapidly than normal. His heart pounded. His pulse quickened. His face twitched. This was what he had been reduced to, a pauper.

His very existence was a weight upon them. His very presence was unnecessary. He was taking bread from the mouths of his children. He was forcing

Bill to work hard and give every cent home. He was probably going to be the cause of robbing Dennis of education, perhaps also the others. Of course, he had sacrificed himself for his family. He had never complained. They should not complain when they had to return to him something of what he had given them. But still, rob a man of his strength and his independence, and he might as well be dead.

He had to admit it to himself. He was better off dead. He had always known that this was a tough world. But he had never until now realized how really tough it was. If you were weak, it was no place for you. He could sit here from now until doomsday and see healthy people pass by the window, and he would bet that they would hardly even realize that there were men in the world in his condition. When he had been healthy, had he thought of men who were sick, paralyzed? Not much. The world was callous. It didn't even know. It didn't stop to take the time to know of the suffering in it. Such was the way of life.

Well, he could say that he had never dreamt that he would have to swallow pills as bitter as the ones he was swallowing. Go to a pauper's ward in a hospital, to be alone there, to be there on charity, passing his days with strangers, waiting that way for death. How could he do that? But maybe he ought to.

"Lizz," he called, but she was downstairs washing.

He would talk with her about it when she came up.

IV

"No, Pa, I don't want you to go to the hospital unless you got to," Bill said.

"Jim, you belong with us. You're our Daddy, our Pa. What would we do without you?" Lizz said.

"Pa, stay home here. You're going to get better. You're looking all right to me now."

"Am I, Bill?"

"Yes, Pa. I mean it."

"Oh, I don't belong here. Bill, ship me to the Old People's Home, ship me any place, what good am I?"

"Pa, don't talk like that."

"It's the truth."

"No, it isn't," Bill said.

They sat there, father, mother, eldest son, and the silence among them was strained, tense.

V

"Where did you get the money for that candy?" Jim asked.

"Father Doneggan gave it to me after I served mass this morning for him. Father Doneggan always gives us money. All the kids like to serve mass for him because he does," Bob answered.

"Are you telling me the truth?"

"Yes, Papa, honest, I am."

"Go get your brother," Jim ordered.

Bob went to the back and returned with Dennis.

"Dennis, what happens when Father Doneggan says mass and you serve?"

"He always gets through quicker than the other priests. I like to serve mass for him."

Jim looked at Bob, angry.

"Is that all?"

"What do you mean, Pa?"

"Anything else, any other reason why you like to serve mass for him?"

"Well, it's good to serve mass. And of course, he's better to us kids than the other priests. He gives us more money. I'm going to serve at a wedding mass next week. Gee, that's when you get something from him, serving wedding and funeral masses. He's swell to the kids then. He always gives us more than any of the other priests. Father Gilhooley hardly ever gives us anything, but Father Doneggan always does," Dennis said.

"What do you do when you get money that way?"

"I tell Mama. Don't you remember, Pa, the last time I served a funeral mass for Father Doneggan, I got a dollar and a half from him and I gave it to Mama, and she let me take Bob and Catherine to see a movie?"

"Did you tell me about it?"

"Sure I did, don't you remember?"

He believed Dennis, but he couldn't remember.

"Well, that's all right. Only both of you remember this, that you don't serve mass for money. You do it for God. You boys must always remember that. You must always remember that no matter what you do, God knows it. God watches you. God is your Father. You have to always act so that you aren't afraid that God will be displeased by what you do. That's one thing I want my kids never to forget—never forget your God and your church."

They looked at him, puzzled. Papa never used to talk like that before he got sick.

VI

"But, Mrs. Morrell, my man lost that five dollars your boy found," Lizz said to Mrs. Morrell in the front hallway.

"How can you prove that?" asked Mrs. Morrell; she was a stout, plain woman.

"I wouldn't lie. Didn't you see the note I had on my box?"

"How do you know it was the same money that my boy found?"

"Why, if my man lost it near the house and your boy picked it up, it must be."

"Why must it be? How do I know?"

"Mrs. Morrell, do you mean to say that you would keep the money lost by a poor crippled, helpless man with a big family?"

"How do I even know you lost it?"

"Do you mean to say I'm a liar?"

"I'm not saying nothing. All I'm saying is that my boy found that money and that it's ours, and you can't prove it isn't."

"Well, it will never bring you a day's luck. As long as you live, you'll never have a day's luck. Taking the bread out of the mouths of a cripple's family."

Mrs. Morrell glared at Lizz. She brushed by her.

"As long as you live, you'll never have luck," Lizz screamed after her as Mrs. Morrell hurried away. Lizz turned and went upstairs to her own apartment.

She wanted to tell Jim. But he was asleep, and she had better not wake him.

VII

"Where's Bob?" Jim asked, rubbing his eyes after his nap.

"I saw Mrs. Morrell in the hall and when I came back in the house, he was gone. But, Jim, I want to tell you about that one, and her son, the dirty little thief."

"Did Bob pass you in the hallway?"

"Why, no, he didn't."

"How did he get out then?"

"He must have gone out the window."

"I told him to stay in."

"I'll call him," Lizz said.

She went to the dining-room window and leaned out and screeched for Bob. But he wasn't around.

"I'm going to find him. I told him to stay in, and the minute my back is turned he's gone," Jim said, his lip quivering.

"But, Jim, you don't want to be tiring yourself."

Jim went to the front and put on his coat and an old cap.

"Jim, wait until I tell you. Mrs. Morrell's son found the five dollars that you lost and she won't give it back. Should I split her head open with the frying pan?"

Jim hastened by her, muttering to himself.

"Jim, don't go looking for Bob. He'll be home," Lizz yelled after him from the open parlor window.

Jim turned toward her and said something, but she did not hear him. She saw him limp on and cross the street to talk with some boys playing in front of the stores at the corner of Fifty-ninth and Calumet Avenue.

VIII

"Say, do any of you kids know my boy, Bobbie O'Neill?" Jim asked the children in front of the store.

"Sure, I know him."

"Did you see him, Bud?"

"He must be with his gang. I think they're in the alley somewhere between Cal and South Park."

"Thanks. If you see him, tell him his father wants him home."

Jim crossed back to the other side of Calumet, and the kids watched him. One of them laughed and imitated Jim's limp.

Jim started crossing the vacant lot outside his apartment.

"Jim, Jim," Lizz called from the side window.

He ignored her and dragged himself through the prairie, almost tripping in a hole and getting his foot caught in some old wire. He had to bend down and extricate his shoe from the wire. Then he went on and looked in the back yards along the alley.

Wait until he found that kid. Because the old man was sick, did Bob think he could do what he wanted? He had explicitly said to Bob to stay in. And the moment he lay down, Bob was out the window. Just wait, just wait until he found him! He limped along the alley, looking over every fence, seeing neat green yards. He came out of the alley on Sixtieth Street.

Where to now?

Maybe that kid had been wrong and meant the alley between Calumet and Prairie. He limped to it and entered the dusty alley. The elevated girders rose above him. When he walked, both the sole and heel of his right shoe dragged, and he scattered dust.

As long as he lived, his children were going to obey him. If they tried to take advantage of a sick father, what would they do when he was gone and they had to obey only their mother, soft and lenient as she was? There would be no holding them then. He crossed to a yard where some boys were playing ball.

"Hey," he called.

The boys went on playing.

He stepped into the yard. Seeing the unshaven paralytic in old clothes, the boys were frightened. He walked a few steps, and they drew back.

"Do you kids know my son, Bob O'Neill?" he asked.

"Mother! Mother!" one of the boys yelled.

A thin woman appeared on the first-floor back porch. Jim looked hurt, surprised.

"Go on and leave these children be," the woman yelled.

Jim was so shocked he did not know what to say. He approached her.

"I'll call the police," the woman yelled, grabbing a broom.

"Lady, I'm only looking for my son, and I wanted to ask these boys if they knew him and saw him."

A janitor came up from the basement.

"Get outta here, you!" the janitor yelled at Jim.

"I'm only looking for my boy," Jim said.

"Go on, get the hell outta here, quick, or I throw you out."

The man gave Jim a shove. Jim struggled to retain his balance. He doubled his fists.

"Come on out in the alley, and you'll pay for this, you!"

"Go on or I calla the police," the janitor said.

Jim dragged himself out of the yard and stood by the fence.

"Come on, you goddamned hunky, come on out here and fight me," he said, his voice throbbing with emotion.

The janitor laughed at him. Jim stood there in impotent anger. He turned and went on. His face was twitching and quivering. He could have cleaned up on that bastard, sick as he was.

Scattering dust, he limped down the alley, looking for Bob in every back yard.

IX

"Did you find him?"

"I looked all over but I couldn't find him. And, Lizz, just as certain as you see me before you, there's a goddamn wop or hunky janitor across the street that I'm going to clout," Jim said, wearied and dirty.

"What happened? What's the matter?"

"Oh, he acted as if I was a bum or something. I was in a yard looking for Bob, trying to ask some kids if they saw him, and he got snotty. I dared him to come out in the alley and fight me, and he wouldn't."

"Jim, you can't go fighting in your condition."

"Where is that boy? It's your fault, you spoiled him," Jim said melodramatically.

"My fault? Jim, I was outside talking to that rip, Mrs. Morrell, and you were with him."

"You let him walk all over you, so he thinks he can walk all over me."

"Why, Jim," Lizz began, but she stopped. She saw how Jim looked and didn't want to irritate him.

"You're protecting that boy, inciting him to disobey his own father, turning him against me."

"Why, I wasn't even here."

"Everybody is against me. Even my own wife, my own kids. To think that I should live to see such a day."

Lizz took his arm to lead him to the bedroom.

"Don't try to soft-soap me now. You know I tell you the truth," he said, jerking free of her.

Lizz had to struggle with herself to control her temper. But her Jim was a poor sick man, and the doctor said he mustn't be excited. She must treat him like a child. She mustn't quarrel or fight with him.

"Why do you take his side against me?"

"Oh, Jim, when I get my hands on him, I'll teach him not to disobey his father," she said.

Jim slumped in a chair. He sat there, frowning.

X

"Papa socked you," Dennis said.

"It didn't hurt," Bob said.

"You yelled."

"I wanted to make him think I was hurt so he would stop. It didn't hurt me."

"What did you run out for?"

"I told the kids I'd play ball with them. He had no right to make me stay in. I asked him why I had to stay in, and he said stay in. It wasn't fair."

"You better pray. Wait until Bill hears. Bill'll sock you, too."

"Well, I got my licking. But it didn't hurt."

XI

"Pa, let Bob go out," Bill said.

"I said no, and my word is final."

"But, Pa, it's so nice out. The kids will all have to work hard enough later on. Let them play when they have the chance."

"I told you what he did to me today," Jim said to Bill.

"But, Pa, you licked him."

"Don't you leave this house," Jim said, pointing his left hand at Bob to emphasize his command.

"Pa, I said let him go out."

Jim went to the bathroom and came back with the razor strap.

"You stay in," Jim said.

"Pa, he ain't done anything. It's no use keeping him in. I say let him go out and play."

Jim sat down. He seemed to crumple in his chair. He looked past Bill, his eyes focused vacantly on the dirty wallpaper.

"Go on out," Jim said lifelessly to Bob.

Bob looked at Bill.

"Go ahead."

Jim sat with Bill. The first time that Bill ever contradicted him. Well, Bill was supporting them now. Bill was the boss. He was no longer the master of his own home. He no longer had the authority of a father in his own household. He stared vacantly past Bill. Bill was uneasy, saddened by the sight of his father.

"I guess I was too hard on the kid," Jim said, his tone still lifeless.

"Pa, let me play the phonograph for you," Bill said.

Bill wound the phonograph and put on Jim's favorite piece.

> *Call me back through the years, pal of mine,*
> *Let me gaze in your eyes,*
> *Let me hear your sweet sighs . . .*

"Bill, no matter what happens, always remember that you only have one mother. Always take care of your mother," Jim said.

"Yes, Pa, I will."

"Bill, we learn things too late. Don't realize that you have a mother too late. Remember it always."

The record was finished. Bill played another of Jim's favorites, *Alexander's Ragtime Band.*

Jim listened wistfully, a faraway, moody expression in his eyes. Bill watched him. Never had his father seemed more sad. Bill bit his lip, moved. He had to control himself. There was this crippled man, gray-haired, tired-looking, helpless, and it was his father.

"Pa, I'll shave you now before I go to the show," Bill said, taking off the record.

"Don't bother. Do it some other time."

"No, come on, I'll do it now."

Jim obeyed Bill like a child. Bill picked up the razor strap, and Jim followed him into the bathroom. Bill sharpened the razor on the strap and lathered his father's face.

"I'm Tony, the barber, now," Bill said, forcing himself to be gay.

He shaved his father very carefully. He kept thinking that, yes, this man, this was Pa. Jim sat patiently while Bill went on shaving him, handling the razor almost tenderly.

46

I

Whenever she went over to see Papa, she would sit and watch Papa in his chair, and Papa would seem so sad. He would look at her, and just for him to look at her the way he did made her sad, because Papa was sad. Papa was sick. She had been sick with colds, and coughs, and bronchitis, and a sore throat, and chicken pox, and sick in the hospital with diphtheria when they lived in the cottage, but she had never been sick like Papa. Nobody was sick like Papa, and had to walk like he did, and had his arm like Papa's right arm. When kids saw anybody like Papa, they were afraid of him, like they were afraid of the man with St. Vitus dance who sold newspapers in front of church after mass on Sunday. But she wasn't ashamed of her Papa. She wasn't afraid of her Papa. Her Papa was very kind, and he was good to her, and he always spoke nice and almost never angry, like he sometimes spoke angry to Mama, or to Bob, or Dennis, or Danny. Papa never spoke angry to her or to her big brother, Bill.

Because Papa was sick she had to live over here with Mother, and sleep in bed with her big sister, Little Margaret, and her Aunt Margaret. It was nicer sleeping with them, because there was more room in the bed than there was sleeping with Mama and Papa, but she would rather be home and sleep with Mama and Papa.

Catherine sat alone in her grandmother's house, thinking of Papa. Mother, her grandmother, came into the parlor.

"Well, so this is what you're doing?"

"What, Mother?"

"Everybody can come in my son's house and take advantage of him. This is open house on my poor hard-working son, while he's away on the road, carrying those heavy grips."

Mother was always talking this way, always talking mean to her, saying she didn't like girls, and girls were no good. Papa never said anything like that. Mother would often be mean to her, and then Mother would change and give her nickels for candy. When she came home for lunch from school, Mother would give her good things to eat and tell her to sit down and eat while it was hot, and then sometimes Mother would no sooner say that than Mother would get mean and angry and tell her she didn't belong here. She didn't like it here, and didn't like Mother when Mother talked to her angry and mean.

"Don't stir yourself. It's all on my son's back. That father of yours will have all his children here on my poor son yet. Don't stir yourself. Sit where you are. Nobody worries where it comes from, the butter, and eggs and milk to feed you, nobody worries but me and me poor son," Mrs. O'Flaherty said and left the room.

Catherine looked after her, telling herself over and over again that she hated Mother.

II

Catherine had come over to play with the girls on Calumet Avenue, because she liked playing there better than she liked playing in the back yard, or on South Park Avenue or in Washington Park. They had just quit playing jacks, and they didn't know what they would do now.

"I seen your father, Katy O'Neill. He went that way," pigtailed Minnie Morrell said, pointing northward.

"He was taking a walk or something," Catherine said.

"He doesn't work, does he?" Anna Flynn asked.

"He used to work. He's sick."

"Minnie Morrell's father was drunk and walked worse than Katy O'Neill's father. Katy O'Neill's father walks like this," May Sweeney said. She imitated Jim's paralytic walk. Catherine's dark eyes flashed with hatred. "And Minnie Morrell's father walked like this," May Sweeney said, imitating a man trying to walk when dead drunk.

"May Sweeney, you lie," Minnie cried out.

"Minnie, you know it's true. You know we all saw your father walking that way. He fell down right on the sidewalk and he had the awfulest time to get up again, with lots of people all watching him like he was a holy show," May Sweeney answered.

"If I tell my father you talked about him, he'll fix your father," Minnie said.

"Let him try! Let him just try! Try, try, try, try!" May Sweeney shouted.

"You're it," Catherine said, touching May Sweeney's shoulder and running.

All the other girls ran, and May Sweeney chased them, and they had fun.

"I don't like tag," May called out, unable to catch anyone.

"Catch us," Catherine yelled.

"I ain't it. I won't play tag."

"May Sweeney's a spoil sport," Anna Flynn called.

"Spoil sport! Spoil sport! Spoil sport! Spoil sport!" the girls all chorused in singsong.

"I'm not a spoil sport," May yelled, but they singsonged more persistently than before that she was.

May Sweeney spied Lizz O'Neill across the street with a bundle in her arms. Lizz was in her house clothes, unkempt and dirty.

"I spy a witch! I spy a witch! I spy a witch!" May Sweeney cried out.

"That ain't a witch. That's Katy O'Neill's mother," Anna Flynn said.

"Well, can't Katy O'Neill's mother be a witch?" May Sweeney asked.

"I'd be afraid to meet her in the alley," Minnie said.

"Your mother is funny, look at her, Katy," May Sweeney said.

"She's not my mother."

"She lives in your house," Anna Flynn said.

"I know it. But she's just a poor old woman who had no father and mother and no home or any place to sleep and we keep her."

"She's your mother. My mother said so," Minnie said.

"She is not so. She's a poor old beggar lady that has no place to go and we keep her," Catherine said, boiling with shame because of the way Mama looked and the things the girls always said about Mama.

"Why, Katy O'Neill, you told a lie," Minnie said, pointing an accusing index finger at Catherine.

"I did not. She ain't my mother."

"Well, who is your mother?" May Sweeney asked.

"My mother's dead. She died of diphtheria when we lived on Forty-fifth Street, and we take care of that poor woman you seen."

They looked at her in awe, shocked because of her lie.

Catherine left to go back to her grandmother's. Catherine's face was dirty and she had torn her stocking when she fell playing stump-the-leader. Girls should not play stump-the-leader. It was a boy's game. She had to go home to Mother's for supper, and she wanted to go home to Papa's. She never knew when Mother would be mad. She liked the things she got to eat at Mother's, and she had lots of cake, too, and sometimes Aunt Margaret baked cake that tasted like no cake she ever got at Mama's. Mama bought cakes in the bakery and the delicatessen, and she liked them, but they tasted different from Aunt Margaret's cakes, and she would rather eat Aunt Margaret's cakes any day in the week. But she would rather be home with Papa and Mama, even if she couldn't have Aunt Margaret's cakes, and even if there was more things to eat and more goodies and nobody ever worried that there wasn't enough like they did at Mama's so much. And there was always so much to eat that there was never any question about the best things going to Bill, or Papa, and then the rest of them getting what was left, because she got as good things as her Uncle Al when he was home, or the rest of them. Except Mother was always giving her separate butter and saying she had to eat the servant's butter, but there was no servant except the nigger woman who came and did the wash on Tuesday. Mama had no nigger woman and did her own wash downstairs, and she was always fighting with Minnie Morrell's mother and other women about the laundry and who had the right to hang clothes in the back yard and the basement. There never seemed to be fights like that at Mother's, but Aunt Margaret was always fighting with Uncle Ned.

She walked slowly back to Mother's, wishing, wishing just as hard as she could possibly wish, that she didn't have to live there.

III

"So here you are, with your dirty face, coming in like a pauper's daughter. Go and wash yourself before you sit down to my son's victuals," Mrs. O'Flaherty said.

Mother was mad again. At noon Mother had given her a nickel and called her a darling and told her to buy herself some candy. And this afternoon, and again now, Mother was mad, mean to her. And she hadn't done anything. All kids got their hands a little dirty, and their faces, and how could you play and not get dirty? And she wasn't dirty, and she could clean her face and hands, and she would look pretty, too, if she could have dresses and coats of her own instead of having to wear old clothes that Little Margaret was too big to wear.

Sulky, she went to the bathroom and washed herself. She stood on tiptoes to look at herself in the bathroom mirror, but she was too small. When she came out, supper was on the table. She sat down timidly to eat.

IV

It still wasn't dark. She walked beside her big brother Danny, but Danny didn't say much to her. She liked Danny. He was good to her, and never mean, but her bigger brother, Bill, gave her more things and she guessed that in her family she liked Bill the best of all next to her Papa.

"Isn't there a Hayes kid in your class?" Danny asked.

"Yes, I like him. He has a sister named Roslyn that went to school with you. His family doesn't live in the parish, but he comes to school every day still. Sometimes his father brings him in an automobile," she said.

"Is he a nice kid?"

"Yes, he always dresses nice, and he's smart, and he doesn't act like a wild

Indian, like Bob does. Little Margaret had to see Mama again and tell her what Bob did in school, and Mama and Papa got mad at Bob. But Bob won a prize in arithmetic for last week."

"Does the Hayes kid win prizes?"

"He wins nearly all of them."

Danny glanced down at her. She was pretty. He wished for her to have pretty clothes, and to grow up to be as keen and as sweet as any girl. Maybe when he started working he could take care of her and even send her to Saint Paul's when she graduated from Saint Patrick's. Maybe he'd be able to. That was still sometime off. She was eleven going on twelve. Her face was pretty, and she was thin, with long legs, skinny, like nearly all girls were at her age. Gee, in a few years, she would be so different, bubbling, like girls he knew, and she would begin to have breasts, and that would only be part of it. How did girls feel when the monthlies start? They must have started for Little Margaret already.

And he wanted to say something to Catherine about the way Mother treated her. Mother had yelled at her again at supper, and there'd been a big row with Mother, with Uncle Ned and Aunt Margaret all yelling at each other. Catherine had cried.

"Mother didn't mean what she said. She's that way. She doesn't mean it," Danny said.

She looked up at him with a pathetic little smile on her face.

V

"Here you are, you hussy. Denying your mother," Lizz shouted, grabbing Catherine at the door and dragging her in the house.

"What's the matter, Mama?"

"Telling Minnie Morrell I wasn't your mother. Denying your mother. Oh, wait till I get my hands on you," Lizz said, slapping her. Catherine cried. "So I'm just a poor old beggar woman, am I?"

"Don't hit me, Mama. I didn't do nothing. Please don't, Mama."

VI

"I want you to hear this as well as Catherine there, Danny. You'll never have another mother. The most precious friend, the best friend any child on earth will ever have, is his or her mother."

Papa was awful sad tonight. And he kept saying the same things over and over about Mama, only Mama was not just like Papa said she was. She used to love Mama. Now she hated Mama. She hated Mama because Mama slapped her. And she hated Mama because the girls all teased her about the way Mama looked, and made her ashamed. And sometimes the girls all said, well, what could you expect, because after the way Katy O'Neill's mother dressed, you couldn't expect Katy O'Neill to have nice things.

"I have been with your mother here for a long, long time, years and years and years. After I'm gone, you children will thank me for what I say to you."

Papa spoke so slow, and how long was years and years and years? And after Papa was gone? Where was Papa going? She didn't want Papa to go away, go away to the Poorhouse or the Old People's Home like he was always saying he ought to, and she didn't want Papa to die and leave them.

"Your mother is your best friend. When everyone else in the world has deserted you, your mother will stand by you. When you have lost all friends, your mother will be at your side, firm as a rock. Never forget that. No matter what you do, no matter what any of you kids become, you must never forget your mother, and you must always remember that she's your best friend."

Papa was talking, talking. She could see that her big brother, Danny, wasn't paying much attention to Papa. She knew it because he was acting the way the boys in class sometimes acted when they weren't paying much attention to what Sister was saying.

"And now is the time to appreciate your mother. She will be gone soon enough. And then you'll miss her. Children should not wait until their mother is gone to appreciate how much she has done for them. I want all of you children to know that. I want you always to be proud of your mother. No children ever had a finer mother than you kids have. No children have ever had a mother who loved you more. Always be proud of your mother."

Papa was crying now as he talked. It made her so sad. She cried, too. And Papa went on still talking about Mama, saying the same things to them over and over again, and he was so awful sad.

VII

How could they all find out so quick what happened and what she said about Mama? But they did. When she and Danny came back here after being over at Papa's, Mother and Little Margaret said terrible things to her, and she couldn't stand it any more. Mother said she was a pauper's daughter.

Catherine lay in bed in the dark. Her aunt and big sister were asleep, and sometimes Aunt Margaret would snore, but she wouldn't make a lot of noise snoring. She had heard Uncle Al snore once, and he snored louder than Aunt Margaret. She was afraid in the dark, even if she was in bed with both of them. She hated this house. She wouldn't stand it any more.

Quietly, she crawled out of bed and took her clothes and sneaked into the dining room. Without making a sound, she dressed herself. She walked on tiptoe to the front door, reached up and unlatched the burglar's lock, opened it, slipped out, and gently closed the door. She tiptoed down the stairs and out into the darkness.

No one was on the street. It was dark. She was awful afraid and maybe she would be kidnaped before she got home. In the papers, she read about little girls being raped. She didn't know what it was except that it was something terrible, and even killed girls. Maybe somebody would rape her. Her tears flowed unchecked, and she quivered with fear. She ran as fast as she could, and she lost her breath. Her heart pounded in her flat chest. She wanted to go home to Papa because Papa would take care of her and protect her. She ran on fast. She fell, hurting her knees. She got up and went on.

A man was coming toward her on the other side of Fifty-ninth Street. He might rape her or kidnap her or hurt her. She got to the corner, turned it, and ran until she couldn't run any more, with her side hurting her. She looked back. The man wasn't in sight. He must have gone on down South Park Avenue. But the alley was ahead of her. Maybe somebody awful was hiding in the alley. She had to pass it, and she was sure there were awful men waiting for her there, and she cried and asked God not to let anything happen to her. No one came out of the alley at her, and she hurried on home.

"What's the matter, Dolly?" Bill asked letting her in.

"I want my Papa," she screamed.

Papa came out of the bedroom in a long nightgown. She ran to him.

"Papa, I hate that house. I won't stay there," she screamed.

Papa patted her head. He led her to the parlor, turned the light on, sat in his chair, and let her climb on his lap on his left side. He kissed her, and she sank her head against his breast, and she cried and cried.

"Papa, I won't live in that house," she said, looking up at him, and Papa was crying, too, and he kissed her.

"Papa's girl is going to live with Papa."

47

I

After Sunday morning mass, Danny and Wils had a coke in the drugstore at Fifty-eighth and Calumet Avenue. Coming out, they met Sis Hansen and Frances Lyman. Both girls wore King Tut dresses. Slender and well-formed, Sis had light blonde bobbed hair, a lovely and almost doll-like face, and a fine lithe figure. She walked with extraordinary dignity and innate grace. Wils and Frances were strolling ahead along Calumet Avenue. Danny kept side-glancing at Sis. Yes, it was hard to believe that he had really dated such a marvelous creature for the Senior Prom. And he didn't feel ill at ease with her. He was sure that he and Sis must be the right persons for each other. Walking beside her on such a sunny spring morning, Danny felt that this was living. Sis made him feel the spring morning so much, much more than he would have otherwise. She seemed a part of it, as if she were part of the air, the street, the sky, the sunshine.

"That's a keen dress you're wearing," he said.

"You like it?"

"Sure. It's keen. You look grand."

"Do you mean it? I wasn't sure if it was becoming. I liked King Tut dresses. But now every place you go, you see King Tut dresses."

"Well, other girls don't look like you do in them."

"How do I look?"

"Like the essence of perfection," he said, trying to turn his phrase with the proper casualness.

They turned the corner of Fifty-ninth Street. Washington Park ahead was green.

Sis lived on South Park, and she and Frances were going to her house. But it was just the morning for a walk with her in the park. They could stroll, and stand and look at the lagoon with the sun dancing on it, and meander over to the wooded island, walking under trees in the shade. He could take her arm to get her across a hole or across the stepping stones, maybe go rowing with her, and he'd drink in how lovely she was, no matter what they did.

"Let's take a walk in the park."

"Oh, I'd love to, but I have to go home. My mother is fitting a new dress she's making for me, and Frances is coming to look at it."

Frances and Wils, hand in hand, crossed in the middle of the street to the shady side.

"We won't cross in the middle of the street. Ladies don't do that," she said as Danny took her arm to follow them.

He should have realized this. The walk with her was ending, and he wanted it never to end. She walked so stately, like a queen. He looked sidewise at her. She was the most beautiful girl he'd ever dated. Her beauty was classic.

II

Father Robert had spent most of the class hour telling them about Boswell's *The Life of Samuel Johnson*. Danny had tried to listen, but somehow he kept falling asleep. He would keep waking up, frightened, fearful of being caught, but he just hadn't been able to keep his eyes open. He remembered hearing Father Robert tell what an eccentric person Johnson was, and how Johnson collected orange peelings. And he remembered Father Robert quoting Samuel Johnson saying something about the chains of habit being too weak to be felt until they are too strong to be broken, and he had been nodding his head and telling himself the chains of habit, the chains of habit, the chains of habit, and still again, he had gone off.

Father Robert was talking to Shanley. Danny waited in fright. Father Robert must have seen him sleeping and was going to punish him. And what a swell day, too, to be kept in the jug with a penance.

Shanley left, and Father Robert came down to Danny's desk.

"O'Neill, where's your English textbook?"

Danny rummaged in his desk. The book was missing.

"I don't know, Father. It was here."

"Did you take it home?"

"No, Father."

"Have you got one?"

"I had one, Father."

"Well, I'd like to see the proof. I looked in all the desks to check up and I found none in yours. How do I know that you have had one all year?"

"But I did. Honest, Father."

"Seeing is believing with me. I want to see your book. Every boy must show me his book as proof that he has had one before he graduates."

"Father, I had one. Maybe somebody stole it. I had one. But since we haven't been using our textbooks of late, I didn't pay any attention to it and thought it was here."

"If you want to graduate, I must see your book."

"But, Father, I tell you . . ." Danny began, looking at the priest, bewildered.

"Don't talk to me that way. I want to see that book, and if I don't you needn't figure on graduating. None of my students are going to put anything like this over on me, going through the year without even having the textbook."

"But I didn't."

"Show me, then. And I can tell if you bought a new one instead of the old one. That's all there is to it."

Father Robert left the room, Danny watching him still bewildered. This was worse than a penance. But he couldn't understand it. Where had his book gone to? He looked in some of the desks of other kids but couldn't find it. He left the room, wondering what he would do.

III

Danny sat in the elevated train at the Jackson Park station. It would start in a moment. He thought that he wouldn't be going from this station at this time of day much longer. Although the graduation exercises wouldn't be held until the middle of June, the seniors would be let out of school in two weeks. Two weeks from tonight the Senior Prom would be held. Showing up at the dance with a girl as beautiful as Sis, wouldn't that be an ending to his career at S.S.? Yes, sir, that would knock the boys for a row. But he still had to save all the dough he could so as to take her both ways in cabs and go out some place after the dance. Well, he'd save it. And tomorrow he was going downtown to Malloy and Horowitz's to charge a graduation suit to Uncle Al's account. He would be all dogged out for the dance. And he was all set about work. Even though he had gotten no response from the ads he'd answered, he had a job, starting in at the express company the day after the Prom.

The train started. He again reflected that he wouldn't be doing this much longer. But there'd be compensations. He would have a little spending money in his pockets without having to scrouge and mooch it. Once in a while he could have a date without having to pinch pennies and stint on his lunch money for a couple of weeks. Yes, even though he would have to get up early every morning and be tied down answering those damned telephones in the Wagon Call Department for eight hours a day, he was damned glad. He was tied down five hours a day, twisting and turning in his seat in a classroom, not interested in what went on, hating it, being treated like a kid by the priests.

He looked out the window. Below was Sixty-third Street. He passed above the roofs of the store buildings. He remembered how as a kid when he rode on the trains he used to look out the window and imagine himself seeing a sort of shadow of himself jumping from roof to roof. He would almost feel in himself as if he were jumping, feel his muscles as if he were running. He found himself doing that again. If Sis Hansen knew he had such childish notions in his mind, she'd laugh at him.

IV

"Father, I asked all the fellows, and I looked all over. I don't know what happened to my English textbook," Danny said to Father Robert.

"I told you, if you want to graduate, you have to show me that book."

"But, Father, I can't do that."

"Well, then, how do I know whether or not you ever had one?"

"How could I have studied, and done my lessons, and followed in class, if I didn't have it?"

"You could have borrowed some other fellow's book. I can't be sure unless I see the book. That's final, O'Neill, and you needn't try to change my mind. What kind of an example would I offer if other students knew they could get away with such a trick?"

"But I'm not pulling any tricks."

Father Robert didn't seem interested even in listening to him.

"But, Father, I'm telling you."

"That's enough," Father Robert interrupted.

Danny shrugged his shoulders. Only a week more in which to find that damned book, and he had tried everything, asked everybody in the class, and ransacked at home to be sure he hadn't left it there and forgotten about it.

"You better get that book, that's all," Father Robert said, leaving the room.

Danny stood blank and hopeless. After four years, not to get his diploma and graduate. Suppose he did get an offer for a ride to college somewhere, he couldn't go. Suppose he ever did have a chance to be sent to college by Uncle Al, he couldn't now because he wouldn't have his high-school diploma. And worse, just to be made to pay for something he hadn't done. When he was right, and knew it, and he couldn't prove it, it was a lousy break. This kind of thing always happened to him. In little things, and in bigger things, it was the same. There was a fate, a destiny over his head, and it was not a fortunate one. His destiny was a tragic one. He was going to die young, too. He always feared that he was.

Feeling glum, low, still hopeless, he drifted downstairs. He stood for a few minutes watching some of the fellows play handball and then he left the schoolyard. He wandered over to Sixty-third and Stony Island to see if any fellows were hanging around there. He knew the whole gang around the corner now, and they accepted him as one of them.

V

On an impulse he had gone to see her. Now he was standing before her in the same eighth-grade classroom, just as he used to. But the old days were so far away, so long ago, and so much had happened since he had used to talk to her here. He felt so different. He wasn't the same person. If she only knew that he had socked it in with girls at public dance halls and that he drank and had once almost died from bum moonshine. But Sister seemed the same. She didn't look older or different in any way.

"I had hoped that you would come and see me all these years, Danny," Sister Magdalen said, rather disappointed.

"I meant to, Sister," he answered, feeling guilty.

"You don't seem changed much. I have often asked Dennis about you. He told me how you were playing on all the teams at school, and I was proud of you. But are you graduating with a good scholastic record, Danny?"

"Pretty good, Sister. I have an average over eighty."

But he had dragged it down this year.

"I hoped you'd have even higher. Are you going to college?"

"Not right away. I'm going to work."

"Yes, I know about your poor father. I am worried about your brother, Dennis. He's been as good a pupil as you were. And just like you, he was very good for me in arithmetic. It must run in your family."

"Dennis is going to Saint Stanislaus next year."

"Danny, you never think about the priesthood any more?"

"Well, Sister, I came to the conclusion that I didn't have a vocation."

"I wonder. If I ever knew a boy who seemed cut out to be a priest, it was you," she said.

If what she said was true, look at what he had become. Look at what he was. But he wasn't as raucous a devil as he tried to make himself appear to be. Still, he had lain dead drunk in the gutter. That was dissipation.

"Well, one can never know. You still receive the Sacraments regularly?"

"Yes, Sister."

Until last year he'd gone at least once a month. Now he didn't go so often. But he had not missed mass all during his four years in high school.

It was strange to be with her now. He was sorry he had come, and was even embarrassed. What was there to talk about? Old times. Perfunctory questions.

Perfunctory answers. The old rapport with Sister Magdalen was broken forever. Suddenly, standing there, he wanted to be back in school with her and to have these last four years to live over, to have them ahead of him. Four years of life gone. He was still young, nineteen, but life was short, and now these four years were gone forever from his life and he had become that much older, with that many years less to live.

"I don't see much of the boys from your class. Do you?"

"No, except I see one of them once in a while at mass. Ralph, of course, is in Saint Stanislaus, and graduating."

Again, nothing to say.

"Well, I never had a better class than you boys."

The priests at school said the same, that the class of '23 was the best ever at S.S., and had won more medals, had many of its members on the teams, and participated in every form of school activity.

He wanted to get away. A false picture of himself was standing facing her, with nothing real to say to her.

"Well, Sister, I got to go."

"Good luck, Daniel. Come and see me again, and don't forget the lessons you have learned, now that you are going out into the world."

"Yes, Sister."

"And, Daniel, I want you to know I have always had faith in you. You will amount to something. You give your own virtues a chance, and that will win you the battle."

They shook hands, and she watched him leave the deserted classroom. He walked down the familiar back stairs again, and out of the yard to Indiana Avenue. She still had faith in him. Did many others? Did he have any faith in himself?

VI

Father Robert was speaking again today about literature. Danny half listened and looked at his red-covered, much-used copy of Brook's *English Composition.* He'd found the book back in his desk this morning. He didn't know who'd taken it, but anyway, there the book was. Everything was set, and he was graduating.

"One of Tennyson's greatest poems, and one of the finest poems in the English language, is *In Memoriam.*"

His mind wandered. Some day he would read *In Memoriam* and a lot more literature. He wanted to know all about literature. And in the meantime, it was so wonderful just to sit here and to daydream, build castles in Spain, and think that somehow, some way, the future was beckoning, and the future was going to be so much more . . . more beautiful than the present. Everything, somehow, some way, was coming to him in the future.

"Tennyson's friend died, and he was shaken with grief. The period was one much concerned about God because of Darwin's theory of evolution. Tennyson could not believe that man is descended from monkeys any more than any truly cultured man could or can."

Father Robert continued. Tennyson contemplated, brooded about death. *Death*. We all would die. He would grow old and one day die. But he wanted to live, yes, live, live, first, and he would, and die old and happy and great and successful, with wonderful memories to fill his life.

"Tennyson wasn't a Catholic. But he believed in God. He believed that there must be a hereafter. In one of his stanzas he writes:

> *My own dim life should teach me this,*
> *That life shall live for evermore,*
> *Else earth is darkness at the core,*
> *And dust and ashes all that is;*

No, life and the earth are not darkness. But damn it, he didn't want to do all this striving and fighting. He wanted to walk right along easy on the path to everything, and was he asking too much when that much was tossed into the lap of many others?

It was sunny out, a wonderful day. Clouds were floating in the sky. How many times hadn't he sat in this room this year, especially this spring, and just watched those clouds? It was almost two-thirty. Let's see, it was nine days and six and a half hours until he would call on Sis, and the date with her would not be an expectation but an actuality.

"And then take these lines:

> *O, yet we trust that somehow good*
> *Will be the final goal of ill,*

The bored class was relieved by the bell ending the day's classes. After class Danny handed Father Robert his English textbook.

"Father, the book was in my desk this morning."

Father Robert examined the book.

"Well, that settles that, and it's a good thing," Father Robert said, grinning genially.

But the priest's grin was such that maybe, Danny thought, he had been playing a practical joke. Sometimes he did play practical jokes like that. But if it had been that, then it was a pretty mean one, and if not, it was lousy of whoever did take his book.

"Now don't forget the moral of this, Dan," Father Robert said.

Danny shook his head affirmatively, but he wondered what the moral was.

VII

Danny lay on his belly, his chin resting in his hands. Classmates were sprawled near him on the grass in Jackson Park.

"Well, boys, it only seems like yesterday and we were punks, and now look at us," Marty said.

"Yes, look at us," Tim said.

"Shanley, what you going to do?" Bart Daly said.

"I'm going to study journalism at the University of Chicago, and Father Robert is getting me a job as reporter on *Catholic Life*," Shanley said.

Shanley would be a newspaper reporter, and that would be exciting. Could he ever be one? He didn't see how.

"I'm looking for a job next week, fellows," Marty said.

"I wonder what'll become of all of us, and what we'll all be twenty years from now?" Danny reflected aloud.

"What, O'Neill, you trying to be a philosopher?" Tim asked.

"Acting the philosopher ill becomes a guy who acts like an elephant trying to be a butterfly," Cecil Farley said.

"Well, I still wonder where we'll all be."

"O'Neill will be an athlete, or a drunkard," Marty said.

"And Marty's nose will be a sight for sore eyes from what he will drink," Danny said.

"Don't you guys realize that you're going out to fight the battle of life?" Tim kidded.

"Smilga here ought to be prime minister of Poland," Farley said.

"Boys, watch me light a cigarette. From now on, no one says to me can I or can't I smoke," Tim said.

"That's a significant accomplishment after four years of education," Howard said.

"Fellows, this is no time for fooling. You're making a retreat under Father Robert and you're allegedly going to become men," Tim said.

"Well, all kidding aside, it's been one swell time we all had," Marty exclaimed.

"You said it," Bart Daly said.

"Yes, everything considered, we ain't got no kicks coming. We got all the education we were capable of, and we've been treated fair, and we couldn't have gotten as much any place else," Marty said.

Danny looked off. They went on talking, and he was thinking. Destiny! What would all their destinies be? Where would the roads of all their lives lead to? Who would be the first to die? Who would be rich and poor? Who would be famous? He couldn't think of himself really being more famous than the smart fellows like Shanley, Daly, Farley. What would he become? And these memories, all of them would keep them forever, and they would come back to dances and alumni meetings and some day talk about these days now fading, even talk perhaps about this very day, with all of them lying here in the grass.

"Everybody is getting solemn. Look at O'Neill. You know, despite all his high jinks, I always thought he ought to have studied to be a priest," Tim said.

"Me?" Danny said, shocked, but still, there might be some truth in what Tim said. He had asked himself about this more than once since he had visited Sister Magdalen last week.

"What is this, a game?" Danny asked, trying to change the subject.

"O'Neill will do something. I know that," Smilga said.

They started back to school, singing songs as they drifted along.

48

I

"Hey, Dutch, here's grandma's boy," Casey yelled to Heinie Mueller when Danny walked into the Wagon Call Department at two minutes to ten.

"Well, well, well," gray-haired Simon Murray exclaimed, swinging around in his swivel chair.

The Wagon Call Department was just about the same in appearance as it had been when he'd worked under Omar James. There were some new clerks, but it was the same long room with the same long table. Keyboards were sunken into the table, and phones were attached to these keyboards. Every time there was a call on one of the keyboards, a small electric bulb flashed, and you knew it had to be answered. Simon Murray was the Chief Dispatcher now, and he sat at one end of the table, with Casey across from him, keeping his large record sheets. At the other end was Heinie Mueller, the Dispatcher in charge of special pickup service in the Loop. Before Heinie was the same rack with all the cubbyholes or bins into which were sorted the various calls taken for pickup service. The clerks sat before the boards answering phones. Gashouse McGinty, who had been Chief Dispatcher the first time Danny had worked in this office, was in a corner by the window. The tractor board before McGinty was new. It resembled a scoreboard with many ruled-off spaces. It contained peg holes and little buttons to be put into these peg holes. Each button represented a trailer, and the trailers were numbered, and whenever a tractor moved a trailer in transfer freight, the button for that trailer was moved accordingly. McGinty thus knew where all his tractors and trailers were at any minute. Beside Mac sat little Frankie Noonan, a Dispatcher who kept the sheets recording all the tractor and trailer moves for a permanent record.

"For Christ sake!" Heinie Mueller exclaimed, swinging around to see Danny.

Danny smiled self-consciously. He hung up his coat on one of the hooks by the iron strongbox to Murray's right.

"Ready for us, Bones?" Simon Murray asked.

He had been called Bones since he worked here before. It was Bill's nickname at the company, and they called him Bones and Young Bones.

"Yes, sir."

"See, Grandpa Murray, that's what he learned at school—how to say Sir at school," Casey said.

Danny glanced sharply at Casey. Casey was heavier than he'd been a couple of years ago. He had challenged Casey to fight more than once the first summer he worked. Maybe he'd have to settle with Casey. He didn't like him. Casey was a wise guy always razzing someone, shooting his mouth off too much. He knew Casey. And there was Francis McGillicuddy, curly-haired, soft and fleshy. McGillicuddy was always gassing with girls on the phones and stalling. The other clerks were new and they kept answering calls and shouting into their telephones.

"Hello, Mac," Danny said when McGinty turned around from his board.

"Oh, you here again? Jesus Christ!" Mac exclaimed; he was as big and fat and bull-necked as ever.

"Well, come on, come on, school's begun, sit down and knock off them lights," Mueller said, pointing to lighted bulbs in the keyboards.

"Come here, O'Neill," Murray said.

Danny went to Murray.

"What salary did Mr. Norris say you're to get?" he asked.

"Eighty-five a month."

"Hey, Dutch, come here, will you?" Murray called.

Heinie got out of his chair. Danny liked Heinie. He was a tall, thin man in his thirties. Heinie had hurt his left arm in the army, Danny recalled, and couldn't use it much. It was out of joint.

"Why should this kid get only eighty-five when the others are making a hundred and five? This kid's old man needs the money. Now, which of us ought to go to Norris and ask about this, you or me?"

"I don't care."

"Well, I will, but you back me up on it."

Mueller nodded. Murray went to the office next door to see Wade Norris, Patsy McLaughlin's chief clerk.

"How's your mother and the old man?"

"Pretty good, Heinie," Danny answered.

"Go on and see Mr. Norris, Bones," Murray said, coming back.

Danny went through the large front office to Norris' desk.

"Hello, O'Neill. You ready to go?"

"Yes, sir."

"Well, you'll get a hundred and five a month. You know what to do and you won't need to be broken in, so we can pay you what the other clerks get," Norris said.

"Yes, sir."

Norris turned back to his desk.

"Thank you, Mr. Norris."

He walked by Jew Becky, who didn't speak to him, and went back to the Call Department. Well, he had to start work now, answering telephone calls, answering them one after another until you were ready to go nuts. But a hundred and five a month was pretty good pay, more than most of the fellows in his class would get on their first jobs.

"Sit on the other side so I don't have to see your face, O'Neill. I'm too busy to have to laugh all the time," Mueller said.

The same old funny Dutchman with his sense of humor.

Murray gave him two soft lead pencils. He sharpened them and sat next to McGillicuddy, by the wall. He was going to answer incoming calls on the big keyboard.

McGillicuddy shook hands with Danny.

"All right, lights, lights," Mueller yelled.

"Yes, Bones, show us what you learned in high school," Casey called down to him.

He pulled a plug toward him, held the ear piece to his left ear, and spoke into the phone.

"Hello, Wagon Call Department."

"Who the hell is this?"

"Wagon Call Department."

"I know that. But who are you?"

"O'Neill, one of the clerks."

"I saw you this morning in my depot, Bones. Did they call you up?"

"No, this is his brother."

"Well, this is Collins, Dispatcher at the Atlantic. Give me Mueller."

"I got it, O'Neill, get another," Norris called; he must have been listening in on the call.

The keyboard was lighted up. He took another call.

"Hello, Wagon Call Department."

"Will you send the man for a package?"

"Yes, Mam, what's the address?"

"4909 Langley Avenue. Near Crucifixion Church."

"The name, please?"

"Keenan, and it's going to Muncie, Indiana."

"How much does it weigh?"

"Five pounds."

"All right, we'll get it this afternoon."

He had written the information on a call pad. He tore the slip off and threw across the call to the clerk beside Mueller, who sorted calls and put them in their cubbyholes in the rack. He pulled another plug.

"Hello, Wagon Department."

He couldn't hear this one.

"What is that? What? What?"

McGillicuddy came in on the same connection and took the call.

"You ain't learned nothing in school, have you, Bones?" Casey yelled.

"You got to get accustomed to the noise and the phones," Danny said.

"That's something you never did get to learn here, huh, kid?" Casey yelled.

Danny didn't answer.

He answered another call, nervous, straining to be sure to hear and not pull any bulls.

II

Danny's hours were ten to eight. He got off the elevated at Fifty-eighth Street at about a quarter to nine. It was almost totally dark now. He passed some fellows in front of the poolroom and went on home, hungry. Well, the first day had come and gone. It had been hard on him, because he had to get his ears accustomed to the phones and the noise. But he'd get along. From six to eight he had been with the men on the night shift, and he liked them. They all treated him better than the day men did. Lambert had been very friendly. Mr. Wolfe had come into the Department, looked at him, and said nothing and gone on to talk with Lambert. Then, coming back to go to his desk in the front office, Mr. Wolfe had asked him was he working regularly on this shift. He'd said yes, sir. Mr. Wolfe went out without saying any more. Wolfe didn't like him.

The Route Inspectors had all kidded him at noon when they came in to sort the calls for their pickup men. He knew them all from before, and they'd all asked him did he learn anything at high school, and big Mike Mulroney had asked him was this the best he could do after all his education. But he had tried hard, and this time he wasn't going to be taken for a goof like he had been before. Now it wasn't just summer work. It was work until he got some other job.

"Hello, Dan. I was waiting for you to come home," Jim said, meeting Danny at Calumet Avenue.

Pa needed a shave.

"How did it go?"

"All right, Pa."

"You did all right?"

"Yes, Pa. And oh, Pa, when I started, I was only supposed to get eighty-five, you know."

"Yes, what is it?" Jim asked anxiously.

"Heinie and Simon Murray fixed it up so I'll get a hundred and five. You said I should give half of my pay, and so I can bring Mama fifty-two fifty every payday instead of only forty-two and a half," Danny said.

Jim patted Danny on the back.

"Good boy, good boy, Dan. I want you kids all to stick together and take care of your mother, and we'll have a fine family. You understand me?"

Danny nodded that he did.

"If you kids all stick together, we're going to build a home yet. The O'Neills ain't through," Jim said, speaking with emotion.

Some of the older fellows from the poolroom, Tommy Doylan, Weber, and Studs Lonigan, approached.

"If they bump into me, watch me give them a belt," Jim said, clenching his fists.

They passed on.

"Here, take this. You'll be giving me many of them now, and take this, Dan," Jim said, handing Danny a dollar and patting him on the back.

"Thanks, Pa," Danny said.

He felt different with Pa already. Now he was working, doing his share, starting to give Pa money when Pa was sick. His feeling was different. He wasn't afraid of Pa. He felt sorry for Pa, and, yes, he was going to stick, and they were going to do something, the O'Neills were.

"Where are you going?"

"I'm going to have supper and then go out a while."

"How was the dance last night?"

"Good, Pa, good. Our class made money on it. The money goes to the fund for a new school building."

It had been just like most of his other dates. He'd spent seven dollars on Sis, and neither she nor he had had a good time. She wouldn't even kiss him good night. After leaving her, he'd felt like a chump.

"I'm glad to hear it. But come on, I'll walk home with you, Dan."

They walked toward South Park Avenue. With every step that he took, Jim scraped his right foot on the sidewalk.

"Dan, I only want you to do what's right. I don't care what you do as long as you do what's right. I want you to have a good time. You're young. But you got to do what's right, that's all," Jim said.

Danny didn't answer.

"You understand me, don't you?" Jim asked, looking down at his son.

"Yes, Pa."

Jim put his arm around Danny.

"I know you do. I know you'll turn out all right. I know all my kids will, and they'll take care of their mother, too. You know you'll never have another mother."

And Danny knew that he would never have another father, and that he wouldn't have his father long. Pa could only walk around a little. Bob had had to take him downtown this week to get new glasses because Pa couldn't go alone. Even with Bob to guide him, Pa had walked right into a sign. He could hardly see out of his right eye. He couldn't walk as well as he used to. Pa was a dying man, and Pa was sad.

"Don't you want to come up, Pa?" Danny asked in front of the building.

"No, I'm going on home. Come and see me whenever you get time."

"I'll be over tomorrow, Pa."

Danny watched Jim limp slowly away.

49

I

"They're gonna give you the sheepskin tonight, huh, Bones?" Casey called down to Danny.

"Yeah," Danny replied self-consciously.

He answered a call and shoved it over to Hogan, the clerk who sat next to Mueller and sorted the calls.

"What a waste of money it was sending you to school. Wasting your poor mother's money. What the hell good did it do you? Christ, you're as dumb now as you were when you first worked here," Heinie Mueller said.

"Never mind picking on the kid, Dutch, he's all right," Francis McGillicuddy said.

Danny answered another phone and took a call for a trunk to be picked up the next afternoon.

"Four years at high school and, Christ, he ain't even learned how to write," Heinie said.

Heinie passed one of Danny's calls under the rack to McGillicuddy. The handwriting was almost illegible. McGillicuddy passed it on down to Casey.

"The kid's all right, Heinie, only he's dumb, ain't that it?" Frankie Noonan said.

"You said it, Frankie," Heinie said.

Danny went on answering the telephone. The other clerks were busy taking calls, and the office was so noisy with everyone shouting into the telephones that Danny had difficulty hearing.

Murray looked at Danny's call which they had been passing around.

"Listen, O'Neill, you want to watch yourself. Take your time and take it easy," Murray said, taking the cigar out of his mouth.

"My kid ain't never been to school and he could do better than Chester Gump O'Neill over there," Heinie said.

Would he be ragged like this day after day? He could see that he'd have to get tough and call one of the clerks. That would win him respect, and then the men would treat him differently. He wondered should he call Casey or one of the others?

It was five o'clock. He was getting off at six this evening because of his graduation. When would he be off the ten-to-eight shift altogether? Casey and McGillicuddy were ready to leave.

"Bones, don't let them tell you nothing. Remember when you worked here before how you told us you won a Palmer Method diploma?" Casey yelled.

Danny jumped to his feet to call Casey, but Casey had left the office. Danny went out to the lavatory. It was old and rather dirty and smelly. He stood before a mirror and smoothed back his hair and straightened his tie. He studied himself in the mirror. Damn it, he wasn't so bad-looking. He hoped that after the exercises tonight he and his frat brothers could all get girls and go dancing some place. He'd tried to date Sis for tonight, but she'd turned him down. He'd missed his chance with her completely and he could scarcely figure out the reasons why.

McGinty came in the lavatory with the mouthpiece of his phone strapped around under his chin.

"Come on, Bones, better quit picking your nose and eatin' it, and get in there on the boards," he said.

They always used to say that to him when he worked here before. He stopped by the water bottle outside the lavatory for a drink and went back to the Department. He answered a couple of calls and then sat with a dreamy expression on his face. Schreiber, one of the clerks, was in Noonan's place over with McGinty, and Mac was kidding him. Danny stared at the unlighted keyboard. He was pretty good now on the calls. It was all coming back to him, and he was hearing better. If only he watched his handwriting.

He answered another call and passed it over to Hogan.

A young and pleasant-looking driver came in and went to Heinie.

"Hello, Smith," Heinie said.

The driver smiled. He pushed his uniform cap with the badge on it back on his head.

"Know it? It's young O'Neill," Heinie said, pointing at Danny.

"Bones' brother?"

"Yes, only there ain't nothin' else about them that's the same," Heinie said.

"He looks sweet to me," Smith said.

"Jesus Christ, look at him . . . Hey . . . Hey . . . Hey!"

"Are you talking to me?" Danny asked, roused from reverie and looking over at Smith and Heinie while they laughed.

Danny looked at them, his mouth agape, his expression one of puzzlement. He began chewing on his pencil. They laughed at him.

"Hey, goofy, take the pencil out of your mouth," Heinie said.

"Aw, go to hell," Danny said, sore.

"He better quit flagging the dummy," Smith said.

"Smith, he's graduating from high school tonight," Heinie said.

"They sure are getting dumber and dumber in the schools," Smith said.

"Take it in to the stables, Smith," Heinie said.

Danny watched Smith leave. Still more than a half hour of this. And then all day tomorrow from ten to eight, and all day every day but Sunday from ten to eight, yelling Hello Wagon, Hello Wagon, taking calls, giving them out to drivers, and listening to them treat him like a goof. Well, they should know what he was, a frat man and an athlete.

"Dutch, will it be all right to let the kid go now?" Murray called down.

"Christ yes, Simon. He ain't no use to me at this end of the board."

"All right, O'Neill, you can go now," Murray said.

It was five-thirty. Danny went out and cleaned up in the lavatory, came back, and put on his coat and hat.

"O'Neill, remember me to your father and mother, and good luck, kid," Heinie said.

"I will, Dutch," Danny said.

He went down to Murray and had Murray okay his time ticket, because he was getting off two and a half hours early, and if it weren't okayed by Murray, he'd be docked his pay for that much time.

"Don't get lost, O'Neill," Heinie yelled after Danny.

II

Danny sat in the second row on the stage of the large auditorium, looking out at row upon row of faces. Somewhere out in the audience were Mother and Pa. And there were friends of his, people he knew, and many girls. He wondered if any of the girls would have copies of the *Annual* and would read the eulogy to his athletic abilities it contained?

It was a sultry June evening and hot in the hall. Wearing his cap and gown, he perspired uncomfortably. Sam Howard read the class poem, but Danny didn't listen closely. He had marveled that Howard could write a poem, could think of what to say, and could put it in meter and rhyme. But Howard had done that. The poem spoke of calling the roll of the class, of her honor being strong, of scholarships and medals won, feats of its athletes, records written in the scroll of time, moral principles and the education everyone had gotten, and predicted how the class would go forth to life, their actions ever bold as their actions had been bold in school. Yes, it was an achievement for a person to write a poem.

Ages hence . . . the hour great . . . reflecting over the caravans of the ages . . . Danny wiped his face. He took off his glasses, cleaned them, and put them on again. . . . Honor bright shines on this my class. . . . Samuel Howard was finished, receiving a round of applause.

Tom Schreckenschmidt stepped forward to deliver the class oration. Father Robert had practically written it for Tom. With this oration Tom had won the senior oratorical contest. It told about the Order of Christopher and of the campaign to drive pro-British history textbooks out of American schools. Tom had a good speaking voice, deep and full, and he spoke naturally, with no oratorical flourishes. Hearing Tom, Danny felt like a mediocrity. Just as he couldn't have written the class poem as Samuel Howard had done, neither could he have given the class oration as Tom was doing. Speaking with great indignation, Tom was telling the audience how these pro-British textbooks called the American revolutionaries a band of rebels. The history of our great and glorious ancestors who fought for freedom at Lexington and Concord and Valley Forge and Yorktown, this had all been besmirched in American schools. A sleek cloak of British propaganda had been layed over it. Well, he was against anything so un-American. He agreed with Tom that it was a shame, a disgrace, and it was fortunate the Order of Christopher would not permit an outrage like this to continue.

Tom talked on, and Danny listened perfunctorily. He wanted the commencement exercises to end. He wished the time would come for him to walk forward and receive his diploma, and he wondered would he get loud applause. He wanted to receive loud applause as an honor at the end of his career. Well, he deserved it. He had fought for his school, and there was his athletic record listed for all to read in the *Annual.* If he didn't receive applause, it would be a slap in the face, too. He feared that just this would happen.

He glanced out at the audience, an indistinguishable sea of faces, and wondered did they like all the speeches. And there was Tom up forward on the stage in his gown and mortarboard, talking and gesturing, telling them that American history must, and would be, preserved, and that its glories and its lessons and its truths would not be lost because of lying pro-British propagandists. The great Catholic Order of Christopher was fighting this patriotic battle with relentless zeal.

Loud applause greeted the end of Tom's oration. Shanley stepped forward to deliver the valedictory. Danny mopped his brow. Tim Doolan grinned a few chairs down and ran a handkerchief over his face. The class sat, solemn and quiet. Angular and graceless, Shanley nervously repeated the title of his oration.

Success, the Open Door to the Future.

Danny was gloomy at the thought of the future. He didn't like to think of the future now as much as he used to.

> *Never before in the history of the world has there been the same possibility of success as exists today. The class of 1923 goes forth in the most promising time in history. From all corners there is to be heard the call for ambitious young men who will do persistent work, and who can, if they do, gain rich rewards.*

Maybe so, but Shanley wasn't talking about the express company. Look at his father. Look at Casey, still in the same job he was three years ago, and McGillicuddy, too. Or Bill, on a wagon.

For some, yes, there was a choice. For Shanley there must be. He envied Shanley. Of course, Shanley was in the limelight tonight and he wasn't. But Shanley had earned it by four years of study. Shanley would be a successful writer or a journalist, rich and famous. He used to look down on fellows like Shanley for studying so much, and for not drinking and dancing and futzing around the way he and Marty and Tim had. Well, Shanley was getting the first reward of his application tonight.

> *The voice of success resounds in our age. Men are wanted, wanted in all fields. The field of engineering calls for men. Literature cries out for new blood. And there is one field, the noblest, the most elevating, the most sacred of all, which asks for men.*
>
> *I speak of the holy priesthood, the life consecrated to God.*

Had he made the great mistake of his life in not studying for the priesthood? But if he had, with Pa sick, it was too late now.

Again Danny wiped the perspiration from his face. His shirt was wringing wet.

> *Business opportunities for the young man of today are unlimited. Almost every field of business endeavor is open to him. Business is waiting for youth. We of the class of '23 are walking out into the business world at the most opportune of times. If we on the stage here are failures, it will be the fault of none others than ourselves. Today there is no excuse for the failure of educated Christian young men.*
>
> *The reasons today for failure are laziness, sloth, lack of ambition, lack of the energy to develop one's brain, to work and study and prepare oneself for the future. We of the class of '23 do not feel that we are such young men, tainted by such lamentable weaknesses. We have received a sterling Catholic education. Some of us will go on to receive more Catholic education. But even those of us who will not do this, those of us who have decided to plunge into the world of business now, we know that we could not have been given better educational advantages than*

those which we did gain. Whatever we lack, it is our own fault. It was there for us, there to be given us by capable, conscientious, educated priests.

Maybe so. But somehow he felt unprepared. There seemed to be no connection between his education and the work he now did. Of course, he hadn't studied as he should have. And now it was too late.

Shanley still went on. What Shanley was saying made him apprehensive. What would his future be? What could it be? Yes, yes, he would be a success. He felt it in his bones. He had a deep faith, all right, but it seemed to be unfounded. Still, he had the faith that he would somehow be a success in life. No, his name was not going to be rubbed into insignificance.

My name is not writ on waters, he solemnly told himself.

Kidding himself. He knew he could not leave here tonight for the battle of life feeling as confident as could fellows like Shanley and Howard or Bart Daly. They all had more brains than he had, and brains counted. Youth owned the future. But it was youth like Shanley, not like himself—

We in America live in the richest country in the world. We are now the mightiest of nations, and our great nation is enshrined in the principles of liberty and justice and built upon the ideals of freedom and democracy.

Danny was suddenly sad, very sad. What Shanley was saying was all true. But he was no match for life. He didn't have the brains, and he didn't have the perseverance. He was just not able to make anything of the possibilities that life in America did offer to a young man graduating from high school. And out in that audience was Pa. This all meant nothing to Pa, a man who never really had a chance. Education was what enabled you to get along. Papa didn't have any education, due to his own fault, perhaps, but still, he didn't have any education. Maybe he himself also wasn't made to be educated.

Shanley was getting to his peroration now.

Danny glanced down at his classmates, all uncomfortable because of the sweltering heat. He wondered what was going on in their heads. How did they feel? What did they think of the future? Most of them were leaving school with better chances than he had.

We, the class of 1923, know that the future is ours. We go forth to conquer it, and to do our part in the furtherance of this great civilization of ours. We go forth to glorify our God and His Church, to abide by His will, and to mold ourselves to His purposes. We march into the ranks to serve our country, to earn our bread, and to build with our own hands and our brains, the little, perhaps the large, bricks that will be laid one on top of the other into the ever-rearing higher and higher tower of glory, of power, of prosperity, and of success that is our American democratic civilization.

The hall rocked with prolonged applause, the graduates on the stage all joining in it.

The exercises continued. The time had come for the distribution of diplomas. After that, the speech of the Cardinal-Archbishop would end the exercises. Still sweltering, Danny waited nervously on the edge of the camp chair. Would he get a good round of applause? If not, it would be like graduating in disgrace. Borax's name was called, and there was feeble applause. Would he? He waited, tense and apprehensive.

III

Danny walked home alone carrying his copy of the *Annual.* Well, he had gotten good applause, not as much as Shanley, of course, but it had been loud, and he hadn't been disgraced. At least he had graduated as someone in the class. But as he walked along Cottage Grove Avenue, there was a deep disappointment within him, and he could not clearly figure out what his disappointment was all about. He was bitter. Why should he be bitter? He had had his chances. He was still bitter, and he was envious.

He ought to forget it. He strolled on.

Mother had waited for him and taken his diploma. Pa had patted him on the back, but Pa hadn't said a word about the diploma. He didn't care who had it. What was it worth, and why should it mean so much to them? And he hadn't been able to get any date, although he'd tried to after the commencement exercises. Some of the fellows had, and had gone off to dance, and others had gone home. So there'd been nothing to do but walk on home himself.

Yes, he had reached a crossroad in his life. He was marching down some road. He didn't feel as he had when he had graduated from Saint Patrick's. He didn't feel now that he was walking down any road of his destiny, as he had felt that night. Again he thought of the applause he had received. It was empty. All this glory he had thought about in high school, that was all empty. He felt that there was something important in his high school career that was lacking. He didn't know what it was, but he felt some lack, something important that was missing. And those four years, they were all gone now. Time was fast. Four years gone and he had gotten so very little out of them. Perhaps it was his own fault. But he had expected so much more, dreamed of getting so much more, and all he had graduated with was a little false glory. He had really been a failure in school, a failure as a student, a failure as an athlete, too.

He walked on, past Saint Paul's school, a large, fenced-in building that was now dark.

He pitied himself. He was afraid of life. He was unprepared for it. He didn't see how he would fit into it any place, except as the goof of the Wagon Call Department. And he had only gotten that job because of Pa. Was he always going to go on in life being a goof and a failure?

He entered Washington Park. It was dark and shadowy, with the moon unevenly spilling over the grass and shrubbery. He felt more alone, more lonesome, than he had ever before felt in his life.

He stopped under a lamppost in the park. He opened the *Annual* and turned to the page containing his picture, without glasses, and his school record. He read what Shanley, the editor, had written about him.

Daniel O'Neill

Football, 2,3,4; *Basketball Lights,* 2,3; *Heavies, Captain,* 4; *Baseball,* 2,3; *Bronze Medal, Freethrow Tournament,* 3; *Second All-St. Stanislaus Basketball Team,* 3,4; *Athletic Editor,* Aureole, 2,3,4; *Vice-President, Athletic Association,* 4.

Danny is one of the best all-around athletes ever turned out at St. Stanislaus. He has taken a prominent part in every sport and in every phase of the school's athletic activity. During his course he has won nine major "S's," an unequalled record.

SECTION FOUR

1923

50

I

The day was just the same as any other in the office. Even though it was summer and business was supposed to be lighter than it would be in the fall, there were enough telephone calls to keep the clerks hopping at the phones. Danny looked up and saw Wade Norris talking to Simon Murray.

"Did the old man say why I'm being shifted?" Simon asked.

Danny let Hogan answer a call and sat listening.

"Simon, you know how it is in this game. When we receive orders, we have to carry them out. A man has to be a good soldier in this company and do his job," Wade Norris said.

Danny thought that now he was a soldier of industry. Working was much different from school. You had to work in a place like this in order to appreciate what a soft snap it was going to school.

Wade Norris went out. McGinty rushed over to Simon. Danny had to answer calls and couldn't hear what was being said. He looked up when the board was clean again and he had a breathing spell. Simon Murray was looking vacantly at the wall.

Hell, it was the same pay as this job, but Simon was certainly taking it hard that he should be sent to a depot. Pa had worked up here and then been sent to a depot, and lots of the men in the supervision were shifted around from time to time.

"Simon, remember the way I was yanked out of your chair for Omar James? Well, I was hittin' the ball and I was improvin' the service. But one day I get a letter informin' me I'm to go out and be a Route Inspector on West Madison Street. That's the way it is," McGinty said.

"I tried to hit the ball," Simon said, hurt.

Danny wondered what it would mean for him. Simon was easy on all the clerks, but was particularly decent to him. How would the new boss be?

Simon went out to the lavatory, and McGinty came over to Mueller.

"Dutch, why do you think they changed him?"

"I don't know. Maybe he was getting too many packages from the cake companies he picked up. It's bad business to be trying to get presents from shippers, and Simon didn't realize that," Heinie said.

Danny was learning all sorts of little things like this about the office and the company. Already he could see, too, that when you worked for a company like this, the company had more control over you than even the priests did at school. All the men had families just like Pa, and they had to keep their jobs and do what they were told and keep their eye on the ball when they worked, yes, for the sake of their families, if for no other reason. He remembered when he was a punk in short pants and he used to tell himself that when he was a man, he would be free. But here were men, and they were not free.

Simon came back from the lavatory, puffing on a cigar.

"Well, I tried to hit the ball the best I could," Simon said.

"Cheer up, Grandpaw Murray. Better times, friend," Casey said.

"Hey, Simon, can you take Chester Gump O'Neill along to the Atlantic with you?" Mueller called down.

Danny tried to think up a comeback but couldn't.

"I'll be glad to leave him," Simon answered.

"Hey, Dizzy," Heinie yelled at Danny.

Danny pretended not to hear.

"Stick a pin in it, Dutch, and see if it's awake," Noonan said.

"Wait till Barney Googles Collins sees him," McGinty said, and his huge fat frame trembled and quivered as he laughed heartily.

Danny answered a phone. No, he wasn't going to let them get his goat.

II

Danny was now working nine to six, and a new kid, a little cake-eater named Stratton, was on ten to eight. He'd changed with McGillicuddy on the eight-to-five shift for one day because he wanted to get home early tonight to go to a beach party. He got down at five to eight, and started rolling up his sleeves and sharpening his pencils for the day's work.

The door opened and a little man entered. He had bushy hair, and he wore a wide-brimmed straw hat. It seemed to float on his hair. He had a large face and very small bones. He wore a jazzbo tie, a belted gray suit, a blue broadcloth shirt, and narrow trousers that exposed white socks. Danny didn't like the looks of this man.

"I'm the new chief," he said.

"Hello, Barney," Frankie Noonan said.

McGinty looked at Willie Collins and laughed.

"Hey, Collins, where did you get that suit? It looks like you bought it on Maxwell Street and it got shrunk in the rain," McGinty said.

"Don't be too hard on the lad, Mac. He's still young," Noonan remarked dryly.

Collins ignored McGinty and shook hands with Morgan, the night Dispatcher. Danny sat down on Mueller's side of the board, next to Hogan's chair, and began answering phones.

"Heinie, your new office boy has come," McGinty said as Heinie Mueller came in, grinning.

Casey and Hogan dashed into the office. They shook hands with Collins and got to work.

Danny was too busy answering calls to pay attention to what was going on. At a quarter to nine, there was a sudden lull. He heard McGinty talking to one of the wagon dispatchers in the depots.

"Know who's here taking the place of Sam, the porter? Your old friend, Barney Googles. Yeh, Collins, the runt who lives out in Cicero with all the dagoes. Every time he gets in a crowd, he gets lost and someone steps on him by mistake. Sure, you need a pair of field glasses to see him. And, listen, I just noticed, he's starting to get bald."

"Come on, O'Neill, you're getting paid to work, not listen to what that balloon head McGinty says," Collins yelled at Danny, noticing that Danny was laughing and watching McGinty.

"And, listen, he has to go to the boy's department to get a suit of clothes that'll fit him," McGinty shouted into his phone.

"Look out, McGinty, before I kick your belly in," Collins yelled over at McGinty.

Danny broke his pencil and went down past Collins to sharpen it.

"How's the old man, O'Neill?" Collins asked.

"He seems to be feeling a little better this week than he has in the last few weeks," Danny said.

"I'm glad to hear it, my boy. If you're half the man your father is, you and I will never have any trouble," Collins said.

III

It was the busiest part of the afternoon. Bryan, who acted as Route Inspector on the street, supervising the special gascar service with the Chief Dispatcher in the Wagon Department, had been helping Collins through his first day. Patsy

McLaughlin called him away on important business, and Casey had to coach Collins and tell him what to do. Danny answered call after call, and then, suddenly, there was an unexpected lull and no lights on the board. He quickly went out to the lavatory.

He stood by the lavatory window, thinking how this was all a change from high school, from being Danny O'Neill, a prominent athlete, to Danny O'Neill, one of the punk clerks here. What was going to become of him? What was he going to be? Sometimes he liked to dream of going to college and being a football star and he would come out here and sit on the can and play football games in his mind, visioning himself as an All-American end. But daydreaming this way had a different meaning than it used to have for him three, four, and five years ago. Feeling that he'd stalled enough in the can and better go back, he returned to his place. It was ten after three. Still an hour and fifty minutes of work. He answered calls. There was another lull at three-thirty. He went down to Collins' place.

"Can I get another pencil?" he asked.

"Say, what the hell do you do with pencils? You got one this morning," Collins replied.

"I broke this one."

"He chews them, Collins. I guess he don't get enough to eat or something. He chews 'em," Casey said.

Collins went to Danny's place and picked up the chewed pencil which Danny had left there.

"Jesus Christ, is that all you learned at school?" Collins asked, examining the pencil stub again.

Danny felt foolish. He hadn't realized that he was chewing the pencil. He'd had this bad habit for years. He did it without knowing he did.

"All right, you can have one new pencil, but I don't give you another pencil this week," Collins said.

He handed Danny the key to the safe, and Danny took two pencils. He sharpened one, and sat down again to work.

At four-five, it got dull and slow, and there wasn't much to do. Danny twisted and squirmed in his chair. Every time he started to daydream about football, or girls, or tonight's beach party, a call would interrupt him. He took a pin out of a little bowl before him and stuck it in his mouth. Without realizing what he was doing, he chewed on the pin. He bent it in various ways, took it out of his mouth, put it back, bent it again. He wanted a girl. He wanted to be married to a wonderful girl, one who would be his *Wild Irish Rose* forever.

Danny suddenly stuck his finger in his throat. He coughed. He turned white.

"I swallowed it," Danny exclaimed, frightened.

"What?" Francis McGillicuddy asked.

"A pin. It was bent," Danny said.

McGillicuddy and Casey laughed.

"What the hell was that you said?" Mueller yelled.

"He swallowed a pin," McGillicuddy announced.

Neglecting business, everyone laughed at Danny.

"Collins, you better chain down the furniture or young O'Neill will eat it," Casey yelled, raising his voice because Collins was a little hard of hearing.

"What is this, a kindergarten?" Collins asked.

"Heinie, how about putting a requisition to the Supply Department for a couple of pounds of pins so Bones can eat 'em," Casey shouted.

"O'Neill, go to the can and try to vomit that up right away," Hogan said.

Danny went to the lavatory. He came back pale. He hadn't been able to vomit. Mr. Norris was standing over Mueller.

"This is a new one on me," Norris said, looking surprised at Danny.

"Listen, Wade, this is serious. The kid's liable to kill himself doing a thing like that, and his family needs his salary. You better send him over to the company doctor," Heinie said.

IV

"O'Neill, what did the sawbones say?" Hogan asked when Danny returned.

"He said there's nothing to do but hope for luck and take a physic," Danny answered.

"Well, let this be a lesson to you," Mueller said.

"I don't know how I did it," Danny said.

"I know a guy once who swallowed a needle, and it came out his right toe," McGillicuddy said.

"You better go home, O'Neill. It's a few minutes before your time, but go ahead. Hey, Collins, okay O'Neill's time ticket and let him go," Mueller said.

After his ticket was okayed, Danny left, knowing that they would talk about him and laugh at him behind his back. He was glad to get outside. The air was muggy. He bought a copy of *The Clarion* and went up on the elevated station at Dearborn. He got a seat in the train and started reading about a lurid sex crime, but he couldn't keep interested in the story.

He feared that he was going to die. He was afraid of death. And he was going to die for having done the goofiest thing in the world, swallowed a bent pin. Nothing could be done about it. He had to sit and wait, perhaps for death. Whether he lived or died now, it was in the hands of fate. He couldn't die this way. He couldn't. His destiny wouldn't be for him to die like this. But he might. And there were so many things in life he wanted to do. Why, he hadn't even had a girl yet. He had hardly done anything yet with his life. He had done nothing in his life to make him remembered after his death, and he wanted to be remembered. He didn't want to die.

It was only Tuesday. He had to wait until Saturday to go to confession. He couldn't very well go on the excuse that he had swallowed a pin and was afraid he might die. But he had to. Or else he would die in the state of mortal sin. He didn't think he had the nerve to go to the priest's house to have his confession heard.

He still wore the scapular, didn't he? All those who wore the scapular of Mary were promised that they would never die in the state of mortal sin. He might die any minute. He might die in the night, and in a state of mortal sin. He was doomed to Hell. He could see himself tortured by devils and burning in the red fires of Hell for all eternity. The greatest of the pains of Hell was that you knew you would never have any end of your suffering, and you knew that you would never see the sight of God except on that terrible last Day of Judgment when you were judged before all the world. He had read Dante this summer in one of Uncle Al's little blue five-cent books.

All hope abandon, ye who enter here.

He had felt hopeless many times in this world. But what would that feeling of hopelessness mean to the hopelessness of living, burning, suffering in Hell for all eternity? The purpose of Man was to die. He wanted his death to be years and years from now, when he was old and after he had lived a full life and was famous.

All hope abandon, ye who enter here.

But maybe he wouldn't die. Maybe it would just go out after he took a physic, and nothing would happen. Still, he couldn't shake off the feeling that he was living under a sentence of death. All men were, but men just didn't think about death very often. At least they didn't think of that sentence of execution when they were young as he was, only nineteen. And to think that he had put himself in such a state by having done such a damned fool thing. If he didn't die, would he ever live down what he'd done with the fellows at work? But that wasn't the question now. He would face that if God would allow him to live and save him from his own goofiness. All the things he wanted in life, all these might go, like smoke. And Pa was home, dying slowly. What would Pa say when he heard this? What would his family do if he died?

The train stopped at Forty-seventh Street. He watched a pretty girl walk by him on the platform. The train started up again. He had never ridden home under circumstances like this.

Yes, he might be looking into the very eyes of Death.

51

I

Danny yawned and looked around the office. He thought that it was a month ago that he'd swallowed the pin. Funny how he had forgotten all about it and how he'd stopped worrying over it. And the fellows in the office hadn't kidded him about it as much as he'd expected. He was bored with the work here. Every day, sitting here, answering one call after another, it got excruciatingly dull. And there was so little to look forward to. Pa was always talking about how he should go to night school and study, and he kept telling Pa that he would, but he didn't want to. He had really no idea of going to school. Going to school and getting knowledge was his only hope of advancement, but he didn't want to go to night school. Bill wasn't going back now, either, to finish his bookkeeping course.

"Well, the Chief is dead," Collins said philosophically.

"Your chief?" McGinty asked sarcastically.

"Mac, didn't you know that Barney here belongs to the Republican Club of Cicero?" Casey shouted.

Danny wanted to listen, but the damned keyboard lit up and he had to answer calls.

"Mac, Harding was planning to receive Collins at the White House when Collins goes on his vacation. They were both going to play ring-around-a-rosie with a delegation of boy scouts," Heinie Mueller said.

"Sure, Mac, Barney and Harding was close friends. They both belonged to the Elks," Frankie Noonan said.

"Bones, it don't mean nothin' to us whether a Democrat or a Republican gets elected. And it don't make no difference, either, no matter which one of them croaks. We punch the time clock at the same goddamn time every morning just the same, don't we, kid?"

"You said it, Casey."

"Who'll be president now, Bones? You ought to know that. You went to college and got an education," Casey said.

"Coolidge," Danny answered.

"See, Bones knows." He looked down and across the table at Danny. "Bones, you're my knowledge."

Danny answered more calls and then leaned back in his chair. He started chewing on a pencil and checked himself. He had to break that habit.

"It's a great loss to the American nation," Collins said.

McGinty looked over at Collins and sneered.

"A great loss to the American nation, I said," Collins yelled challengingly at McGinty. "It was Harding that put this country on its feet after the Democrats ran it broke. What the hell is the Democratic Party but a lot of shanty Irish like you, McGinty, and a lot of damned southern crackers and Ku Kluxers!"

"Yeah, Collins, and how about the niggers? They all vote Republican," McGinty retorted.

"And I suppose that Harding was a greater man than Wilson," Danny chirped in.

"You tell 'em, Bones! Knowledge, old boy," Casey said.

"Sure he was. He was a Republican. He was no Democrat," Collins said.

"Collins, the Republicans stand for big business," McGinty said.

Danny listened. He had thought that when he went to work the men would talk a lot about politics. He had to learn more about politics. He was a Democrat, and when he was old enough to vote, he was going to vote Democrat. What kind of an Irishman would he be if he didn't? He saw a light flash, but didn't take the call. Hogan answered it.

"You know, Heinie," McGinty said. "I think that bastard's job has gone to his peanut head. The job's got him. He's gotten egotistic about it. Christ, Dutch, if we ain't careful, that sonofabitch will begin to think he's Napoleon."

"Yes, lunkhead McGinty, it takes brains to vote the Republican ticket. Listen, you balloon head, I'm a Republican and proud of it, and all my kids will be Republicans too," Collins said.

"What brains does it take?" Danny asked Collins.

"Get them lights, O'Neill, and don't be so smart. You might have gone to high school, my boy, but still you got lots to learn. Answer them lights."

"Look out, Barney. Young O'Neill'll put you in place," McGinty said.

"That punk!" Collins said contemptuously.

Danny flushed, but said nothing. He wasn't afraid of Collins because of his job. He felt that he was pretty safe in his job and that he wouldn't lose it because of his father. But he had gotten to dislike Collins.

"Hello Wagon Department," Danny yelled into his phone.

Wade Norris came in and talked to Collins, Mac, and Heinie while Danny was busy. Danny caught snatches of what was said about a half holiday tomorrow because nearly all business houses were closing. When the lights were cleaned up, Danny leaned back in his chair.

"Well, brothers and sisters, I tell you we're getting a half day off tomorrow to celebrate Harding's funeral," Casey said when Norris left.

"Wahoo!" Hogan yelled.

"Mac, you can have O'Neill to keep your sheets," Collins said.

"I don't want that goofy punk," McGinty yelled.

"Aw, you go to hell, McGinty, I don't want you, either," Danny said.

"Say, you parrot punk!" McGinty said.

"O'Neill and Schreiber work the sheets on the tractor board," Collins said.

"I work the morning shift, O'Neill," Schreiber yelled; he was a husky, swarthy fellow.

"You do like hell," Danny shouted back.

"I do too. Hey, Mac! Hey, Collins, don't I get the morning shift?" Schreiber yelled.

"Why can't we toss for it, where we each get a fair and square break," Danny said.

"I asked first," Schreiber said.

"All right, Schreiber, you have the morning shift and O'Neill comes for the afternoon," Collins said.

"Hey, Mr. Collins, why can't Schreiber and I toss for the shifts? Ain't that fair?" Danny said.

"Hey, O'Neill, answer some of these calls," Schreiber said.

"What about you? You haven't a broken arm and you're not deaf," Danny said.

"I answer more calls than you do as it is," Schreiber said.

"B.S.," Danny said.

"You're a wise punk, O'Neill, ain't you?" Schreiber said.

"Yes I am," Danny answered.

"Listen, O'Neill, I can take care of running this department. I can settle who'll work afternoon and morning," Collins said.

"But why can't we toss for it?" asked Danny.

"I told you I'm handling that. Now answer them lights," Collins said.

Danny sulked and answered calls. Casey came over and stood by him.

"Schreiber is a wise guy. He pulled a fast one on you. You got to watch him, Bones," Casey said.

"He's a wise bastard," Danny said.

"Who?" Schreiber yelled.

"Not you. You couldn't be wise," Danny told Schreiber.

"O'Neill, what you think of Schreiber?" asked Casey.

"I'm his superior, mentally, morally, and physically. Why, he's conclusive proof of the Darwinian theory of evolution," Danny answered.

"What's that, Bones?" Casey asked.

"That man comes from a monkey."

"Hey, Heinie, hear what Bones just pulled on Schreiber? He used a lot of big words, but what he said was that Schreiber here came from a rat," Casey said.

"Listen, you punks, the next goddamn one of you who starts bellyaching and yelling goes into the front office," Collins roared.

They got down to work.

II

Time passed slowly. It was dull. Danny sat beside McGinty in front of the tractor board with large wagon record sheets arranged before him. They contained columns with the names of each tractor driver and the numbers of every trailer. Whenever a tractor moved, with or without a trailer, it was reported by phone to McGinty. Mac wrote it out on a slip of scratch paper, and Danny copied the information on his sheets. This was all that keeping sheets amounted to, although a great deal was made of it and it was supposed to be harder work and more important than answering calls from the public. Danny bent down and read from a small leather-covered book.

Think it no more;
For nature crescent does not grow alone
In thews and bulks, but, as this temple waxen,
The inward service of the mind and soul
Grows wide withal; perhaps he loves you now,

He quietly formed the words on his lips as he read, and struggled to understand them. He realized that there was nothing ahead of him at the express company, and he felt that if he wanted to get ahead he would have to become educated. He had been reading Uncle Al's series of little blue books. He had just finished reading the poems of Bobby Burns, and he'd liked *Tam O'Shanter* best of all, and now he was reading Shakespeare.

"Say, for Christ sake, what the hell are you doin'?" McGinty asked, looking at Danny.

Danny looked at McGinty, dreamily. He'd been concentrating so intensely on the book that he had forgotten the office. For a moment he seemed to exist mentally, half in the world of Shakespeare and half in the office.

"I'm reading Shakespeare," Danny said dopily.

"You're readin' Shakespeare? For Christ sake!" McGinty swung around to those over at the long table.

"Hey, did you fellows hear that? He's readin' Shakespeare. Holy Jumpin' Jesus! Readin' Shakespeare!"

Everyone laughed at Danny. Danny was silent.

"Hey, O'Neill, watch them sheets for the Gashouse. This ain't no place for readin'. You went to school. Never mind that stuff. You're here to work, my boy," Collins said with patronizing authority.

McGinty answered his phone and handed a note to Danny. Danny wrote on the sheets. He waited. He had only been working in this office a couple of months but he hated it. And he didn't see why he couldn't read if he did his work too, and he was keeping the sheets all right. Danny looked at the clock. Still two hours to go.

III

After supper, Danny read the newspaper accounts of the Harding funeral cortege. He felt sorry about President Harding. He went to the back parlor and got out the dictionary and a notebook. Inside the notebook were several sheets of paper with words on them. Every word he read or heard that he didn't understand he tried to remember, and then every night he looked up a few of them and used them in a sentence. If he wanted to be educated and a writer, he would have to know words. A large vocabulary was one of the beginnings of education and of writing. He had heard often of how Woodrow Wilson had such a wonderful vocabulary and that that was one reason why he had been such a fine master of English prose. Some day he would have to read Wilson's speeches.

He looked at the last sentence he had written.

> *Woodrow Wilson was great because he did not stoop to the ordinary tactics of* demagogy, *as do most politicians.*

He had used *was* because Wilson was a sick man. He must be dying of paralysis, as was Pa. Would Wilson live longer than Pa? Suppose they died on the same day? Wilson, the greatest man of the age, and Pa, just a man who never had a chance. Of course, Pa couldn't have been a great man like Wilson. Wilson hadn't been treated right or appreciated, either. But he had to get down to this work.

He read the next word on his list, *emanation*, and looked it up in the dictionary. He thought a moment and wrote:

> 51. *Success is but the* emanation *of perseverance.*

Success! Sometimes riding home in a crowded train, he wondered if people seeing him thought that they were looking at a young man who had a destiny. Success! Every day he answered telephones and people sometimes complained and said they didn't want to speak to a clerk, they wanted to speak to somebody, somebody in authority. *Somebody.* To be somebody.

Success is the emanation *of perseverance.*

Did he have perseverance?

He looked at the next word, looked it up, wrote another sentence.

52. *The helmeted warriors at Chateau Thierry were* doughty.

He went on.

53. *The* epitome *of man's thoughts should be summed up in God.*
54. *To be a* mendicant *for love of God, how noble; but to be because of laziness, how ignoble.*
55. *The* compendium *of my thoughts seems to be in these words, literary fame.*
56. *My dealings with my fellow workers have fallen one step short of making a* misanthrope *of me.*
57. *Heaven is* convivial *with smiles.*

He closed his book. He felt better for the little work he had done. A few words learned every day meant a large vocabulary in time, and that was indispensable for literary fame and for success in any other line.

He put on his straw hat and went over to the Greek poolroom.

52

I

"Mama, what's that we got for lunch?" Bob asked.

"You would ask questions like that. Now, you just wait until your father is served," Lizz said.

"But what is it?" Bob asked.

"Halibut steak," Lizz answered. She turned to Jim. "Since this is Friday, I thought I would get some nice fish for your lunch."

"And bran muffins. I like bran muffins," Catherine said.

"So do I," Bob said.

"You children hold your horses until your father is served," Lizz said, starting to serve Jim.

"It looks nice," Jim said.

"Jim, I went to Godoy's on Fifty-eighth Street, and do you know what that stinker said to me? He said 'Oh, hello, Mrs. O'Neill, I saw your sister in here this morning. She just left here.'"

"Well, what was wrong with that? Your people trade there, don't they?" Jim said.

"But he didn't mean Peg. He meant my mother. Thinking that my mother is my sister! Why, I'm never going to trade there again as long as I live," she said.

Jim toyed with the food before him.

"How was Mrs. Muldoon's wake last night?"

"Oh, my heart bled for the poor woman. There was hardly a person there, and not a soul but me to stay up with her. I didn't get home until this morning because my heart bled with pity for her. There was so few there, and not a one to sit up all night with her. So I stayed up and hustled home to make breakfast for my chicks and get my Bill off to work. She was Anna McCormack's neighbor, and as healthy as a horse, but she went out in the rain and caught pneumonia, poor thing."

Bob and Catherine reached for the last bran muffin at the same time.

"You can't have it. I reached first and you had three," Catherine said.

"So did you," Bob said.

"I didn't. I only had two," Catherine answered.

"Bob, don't you eat that!" Lizz screamed at him. "Put that muffin back on the plate or I'll sock you."

Bob reluctantly put the muffin on the plate.

"You don't care about anyone else. You don't care about anything but gorging yourselves. All of you. What if your father is sick? What if your brothers work and put the bread in your mouths, none of you care," Jim said, talking like a pouting child. He pointed an accusing finger at Lizz. "It's your doing."

He got up and left the room. He felt dizzy again, and he felt that pressure in his head. He felt that there was some mass in his head, and that it pressed down and down on him. He was fatigued. He was too tired even to be angry at what had happened. He lay in bed, staring emptily at the ceiling.

II

The Sisters had changed a rule of the school this year, and the sixth-grade boys and girls were in the same classroom, the girls sitting near the window, the boys by the door and blackboard. Bob stood by his desk in the second row.

"Robert O'Neill, if you didn't belong to the boy scouts and didn't spend so much time being a boy scout, you would have time to study your lesson," Sister Elizabeth said; she was a small and wizened nun.

"That ain't so," Bob said.

"What isn't so?"

"I did study my lesson," Bob said.

"If you did, tell me why you didn't know it when I asked you what was the Compromise of 1850 and what was Daniel Webster's stand on it? Why couldn't you answer those questions if you studied your lesson?"

"You asked me the wrong question. I could answer other ones," Bob said.

The class laughed. Bob looked around, puzzled. He didn't see what they were laughing at.

There was a knock on the door, and Sister Elizabeth answered it. The kids heard her talking to Father Doneggan. Suddenly she turned around and faced the class.

"Robert and Catherine O'Neill."

Bob walked forward. Catherine got out of her seat on the other side of the room. Bob was afraid. Maybe she had told Father Doneggan on him, and maybe Father Doneggan wouldn't let him serve mass any more. And he always got spending money for serving mass for Father Doneggan. And now that Dennis was at Saint Stanislaus, Father Doneggan was giving him more money this year and he was getting better breaks on funeral masses and weddings. He walked to the hall, afraid.

"Robert, I am very sorry I was just scolding you. There were things I didn't know," Sister Elizabeth said gently.

"Bobbie, your mother telephoned me. Both of you children hurry home. It's your father. And tell Mother I'll be down right away," Father Doneggan said.

Catherine whimpered. The nun led her aside and talked gently to her.

"Now, Bobbie, you're a man. You'll be brave."

"Is my father dead?" Bob asked, turning white.

"He's very sick. You children hurry home. You be good to your mother," Father Doneggan said.

"Yes, Father."

"Here," Father Doneggan said, handing him a quarter.

"Thank you, Father."

"Now, you and sister go right home," Father Doneggan said.

III

Mama let them in. They saw she was excited. She didn't say a word but went back to the parlor. There was Dr. O'Donnell and there was Papa in a chair. His eyes were rolling, and they had a spoon in his mouth, and he was trembling. Both children looked in awe at their father. Catherine bawled. Bob stared with curiosity.

"Now, we got to get your husband into bed, and I'm going to give him a hypodermic. He ought to be taken to the hospital," Dr. O'Donnell said.

Catherine looked at her father. Papa had been breathing almost like he was snoring, and now he wasn't making noises at all. His face was puffed out and his right cheek looked almost like it was swollen because of a toothache or something. She didn't want anything to happen to her Papa. Oh, she was so afraid.

And she felt so bad. Papa was trembling now, and she could see his pants wet. Papa wet his pants like a little baby. Oh, she wanted to do something. She wanted to die.

Dr. O'Donnell noticed her.

"You children go out in the back of the house," he said curtly.

Catherine cried. Bob took her by the hand and led her out of the parlor. The doorbell rang. Bob let in Father Doneggan. They went in the back and sat there, both of them quiet, staring at one another. They heard Papa being put to bed in the front and then they heard whispering from Mama, Father Doneggan, Dr. O'Donnell. They stared at each other.

Now they could hear Latin. Father Doneggan was praying.

"That's Extreme Unction," Bob said.

"I won't let my Papa die," Catherine said.

They heard the Latin and they heard Mama praying after Father Doneggan.

IV

"Oh, you poor little thing," Mrs. O'Flaherty said to Catherine.

Catherine didn't answer. They made her come over to stay at Mother's because Papa was sick and sleeping in the front bedroom, and there wasn't room for her. She was always pushed around. She had to wear Little Margaret's old dresses, and if there wasn't room for her because Papa was sick, she had to leave her Papa and come over here.

"Come, you little angel, and let your grandmother put something nice and warm in your stomach," Mrs. O'Flaherty said.

"I'm not hungry," Catherine said.

But her grandmother fixed her supper, and she ate everything Mother gave her. Mother had halibut steak, the same as Mama had for lunch today.

V

Mama was out calling up the hospital to get Papa taken in. Papa was what they called comatose. Papa couldn't talk, and didn't see anybody, and he rolled his eyes, and Papa wasn't like Papa.

And he and Catherine were alone and had to stay in the house. It was spooky. He wished Mama would come back. But they were the only ones who could stay here. Dennis worked on Saturday at the Flower Market for the express company, and Bill was working, and Danny was working, and Little Margaret had gone to confession for Papa. They had gone to confession, too, for Papa, and then Little Margaret had gone.

He had just this minute looked at Papa. Papa was the same. He had asked, Papa, how are you? But Papa couldn't talk.

"Let's play until Mama comes back," Bob said.

"What'll we play?"

"You say what, and I'll play," Bob said.

"We'll play beauty parlor. Now, you sit down, and I'll play I'm giving you a shampoo," Catherine said.

"You got to put a towel or something on me, don't you? You can't shampoo me without a towel," Bob said.

Bob waited in the dining room while Catherine went for a towel.

"Bob, go see Papa. He's making noises. I'm afraid. He's making funny noises in his throat," Catherine said.

"What are they like?" Bob asked.

"Go see," she insisted.

Bob didn't know why he did it, but he walked on tiptoe. He felt like he felt in church. He felt as if he shouldn't talk, and that he shouldn't have bad thoughts or anything. He heard the noises in Papa's throat, but they were not very loud. He tiptoed into the front bedroom. Now Papa wasn't making any noises in his throat. Papa was quiet. He was still, as still as little Arty had been in the cottage in Mama's arms. He ran out of the room.

"Papa's dead," he said.

Catherine ran into the bedroom. Bob followed her. He stood at the doorway. He still felt the same, like he shouldn't say a word or think about anything except God. Papa was dead. Papa was lying still on the bed, not making a movement. Papa, dead, made him feel like the room was holy.

Catherine went nearer to him and looked at him. She kissed Papa.

"Goodbye, Papa," she said.

She ran out of the bedroom. Just then Mama came home.

"Mama, go see Papa, he's dead," Bob said.

Lizz rushed to the bedroom. She screamed and rushed out of the house without even closing the door. They watched her from the parlor window, and she was going as fast as she could, and they knew Mama was going over to Mother's.

VI

"What else do you do to me in a beauty parlor?" Bob asked.

"I shampooed you. Now you got a shampoo. Your hair is drying. Let's see? I could curl your hair," Catherine said.

She went to the kitchen and found a rusty old curling iron. She used it on Bob's head.

"Ouch!" Bob yelled.

"I didn't hurt you," she said.

They heard Little Margaret yelling on the sidewalk.

"My Daddy's dead. My Daddy's dead!"

Catherine played with the curling iron, twisting Bob's close-cropped hair. Little Margaret came in. They hadn't closed the door after Mama. She found them in the dining room.

"What are you doing, you kids?" she asked; her eyes were red from tears.

"We're playing beauty parlor," Bob said.

"You ought to be ashamed of yourself. Playing, and Papa is dead. Have you kids any decency? Don't you respect Papa? Oh, what will I do? And you kids playing."

She slapped them. Catherine cried. Little Margaret's thin body quivered with sobs.

"Where is Papa?" she asked.

"In the front bedroom," Bob answered.

She ran in, yelling:

"Papa! Papa! Papa!"

"I know where Papa is," Bob said.

"Where?"

"Papa's in Heaven. Father Doneggan gave him Extreme Unction, and so Papa hasn't any sins on his soul."

"I don't want my Papa in Heaven. I want my Papa here."

53

I

"That's over with," Ed Lanson said, coming out of Saint Peter's church with Danny.

It was a clear, sharp autumn evening. Danny felt especially relieved after going to confession because yesterday his father had had another attack and was critically ill. Confession made up for the drinking he'd done of late.

"Yes, it's quite a change from what we did last Saturday night, Dan," Ed said, lighting a cigarette.

They strolled toward Van Buren Street to get an elevated train south. Yes, for the last three Saturday nights, he and Ed had gotten blind drunk at the Mongolia, a new chop-suey place at Fifty-third and Lake Park Avenue. Last Saturday night he had gone from booth to booth telling everyone that he was an All-Catholic end, and he'd charged the booths and the walls in order to show how you played the line. He'd damned near wrecked a booth and he had sprained his left hand taking a punch at a wall.

"Well, Ed, you'll be initiated in the frat now before Christmas."

"I won't mind it. Being a worm isn't half as bad as you'd think. Of course, you have to do crazy things, but, then, I like to do crazy things."

He had gotten Ed pledged, and he thought that Ed was the best pledge they'd gotten in the frat so far. In the last few weeks he and Ed had become the closest of friends.

The football season was almost over. S.S. had done much better this year than last, and he was going to see them next Thursday on Thanksgiving Day when they finished the season. In September, he had asked Father Theo, Father Michael, and Joe McBride if he couldn't come back to school and play. He could have worked nights at the express company and done this, but they'd said no soap. If only he had had this season. What with the team improved, his addition might have meant the championship, and he would have learned his lessons from last year and played the way he had played against Christian. Spilled milk. So much of life was spilled milk. Pa was home sick, and his whole life was spilled milk.

They climbed the elevated steps. Ed whistled gayly and Danny thought of his father.

II

"Go right over, Son, your father died," Mrs. O'Flaherty said when he came in the door.

The news was not a surprise to him. He didn't know exactly how to act, or what to say. A sudden thought came to him. He ought to know what he thought and felt. He might some day be a writer, and he ought to know and to remember how he felt at his own father's death. He hurried out to go over to Calumet Avenue.

It was a bit chilly. He saw himself walking along South Park Avenue, with buildings on one side and the park dark and black in shadow on the other, and a thin bit of the moon in the sky, and he was going over to a house of death that was the house of his own father. He had never really known his father, and his father had never really known him. Gee, what would Pa have felt and said if Pa knew how drunk he'd been last Saturday night? Just think, at this time a week ago, he was getting ready to go out on a date and dance and drink. He could remember the saxophone while he'd been dancing, the way it almost shivered up and down his back. The moaning saxophone had seemed to call something out of his heart and his soul, something in his body, and something in his mind, and something of his dreams. The nervous notes were a cry of his dreams for what he wanted in life. And was it wrong to want things? Was it wrong because Pa was sick? He had been doing everything asked of him since he graduated. Mama and Pa said that he should give half of what he made. And he gave Mother five dollars out of each pay for board. And he had to have lunch money, and buy clothes on time, and for the rest, he could manage one date a week. Last week he had felt that that one date a week was living, but now, with Pa dead, with the thoughts he had had, with his having gone to confession and his soul now being in a state of grace, he felt much different.

He rang the bell, and Lizz let him in and kissed him.

"My son! My son!" she cried.

"Where's Pa?"

"The undertaker just took your Daddy. Your brother is up there; go to McGann's on Sixty-first Street. You're my other man now, you and Bill," Lizz said.

Confused, Danny hastened up to McGann's undertaking parlor. He met Bill coming out. Bill had gone up just as he was from work, wearing his cap with the badge on it, an old coat, and a khaki shirt without any tie.

"I arranged everything. Pa will wake here and be buried Tuesday morning," Bill said.

Danny walked slowly back with Bill. His father was gone. It still took time to realize that Pa was dead, even though he had expected it. He'd last seen Pa for a few minutes on Tuesday night. Pa had seemed unchanged. They'd talked about the express company and Pa had again told him he ought to go to night school and study.

Bill began to cry. Danny wondered why Bill cried.

"I'll pay everything and take care of everything if it takes the last I got in me," Bill said. He wiped his eyes with the back of his hand. "Dan, the best friend we ever had is dead."

Death was supposed to be a dramatic moment, a moment of great sorrow and tragedy. But he felt empty more than he felt anything. Was there something wrong with him?

"What are you doing?" a policeman asked officiously, stopping them near Sixtieth and South Park.

Danny got sore. He opened his mouth to say something snotty, but Bill spoke ahead of him.

"What do you mean?"

"I told you. What are you doing?"

"We have just come from the undertaker's, where we took our dead father," Bill said, tears again coming to his eyes.

"I thought maybe you was prowlers. I'm sorry," the policeman said.

Danny sneered. What the hell business was it of a cop? Bill had working clothes on, and that was why the cop stopped them. He and Bill looked after the cop and walked on.

"I'll meet every obligation for Pa. Why did he have to die?" Bill said.

Danny said nothing. He felt more sorry for Bill than for his father. His father was dead. The dead did not feel. Bill was alive. Bill felt. What about himself?

To him there was something tragic about his father. He told himself that his father was a man who'd never had a chance. His father had been a strong man, and a proud man, and he had seen that pride broken, and it had been a very sad spectacle to witness.

When they got home, Uncle Al was there.

"Bill, I want to talk to you," Uncle Al began solemnly. He paused. "Now you are the man of the house."

He took out a cigar and handed it to Bill. Bill accepted it. "Do you need any money?"

"No thanks, Uncle Al. Mama spoke with Joe O'Reilley and borrowed it, and we'll pay it back out of the insurance."

"You're handling the funeral arrangements?"

"Yes."

"Bill, your father was a fine man. All you children must be worthy of him."

Bill said nothing. Uncle Al seemed embarrassed.

"I want to talk to your mother a minute," he said.

Danny flopped in a chair. Bill sat, his face blank. They heard their mother sobbing in the dining room.

The sense of Jim still seemed in the house, in the chair, in the victrola, in the glasses on the table. Something of Jim seemed to pervade everything in the house. Danny felt as if any moment his father would come into the parlor, dragging his leg the way he had since his last stroke. But no, Pa was dead. What exactly did it all mean?

III

Jim's corpse lay in a black coffin dressed in a black suit, black silk socks, patent-leather shoes, a white shirt, and a black knit tie. Jim's shaven and powdered face was set in repose. The signs of suffering seemed vanished from it. And his gray hair was long and wavy.

Danny looked at the corpse. Again that thought came back to him. His father had never had a chance in life. His father's death had made him understand something. Now that his father was dead, and it was all too late, he could understand the man better. Death was a kind of fact that closed a book. His father's book was closed, and all the might-have-beens now were inside that closed and locked book. He turned away.

There were small groups here and there in the undertaking parlor, friends of his or of the family, cousins, fellows from Fifty-eighth Street. Father Henry had come from Saint Stanislaus, talked a while, said the priests at school would pray for Pa's soul, and had gone. He was grateful that one of the priests had come. He had never liked Father Henry before, but now he did. People said they were sorry, and he knew how they felt saying it just as he would feel telling it to someone else who had lost a relative. Yes, his father's death was tragic, but still, it was the only thing that could have happened to Pa. Going on living, what would that have been like? Death was merciful to his father to take him. He felt that that was a fact to assuage the grief of everyone. Bill had taken it the hardest, but Bill was now talking a lot at the wake and even kidding a little here and there. Mama would cry, and then she would dry her eyes and talk too. He watched little Catherine. She went up and looked at her father. She tiptoed away and sat down by herself. Danny noticed the flowers. There were a few wreaths. One from some men at the express company, another from his father's council of the Order of Christopher, a third from his fraternity, and a fourth from some of the fellows around Fifty-eighth Street. There weren't many. Pa wasn't having a big wake. Few people really mourned him. Yes, Pa's going had not meant much in the world.

Danny looked around the funeral parlor, wondering whom to talk with. Camp chairs were arranged in rows. There were a few pictures on the walls. He could smell the odor of flowers. Bill motioned for him to come over.

"Jane, this is the kid brother. Dan, this is Jane. She might be your future sister-in-law," Bill said.

Danny saw his mother frown.

Jane was a tall girl, husky but well-proportioned. She smiled, embarrassed. Danny was glad to know Bill had a girl. He remembered how he would often see Bill during this last year. Bill would go out to a movie, talk to a friend, have a soda, come home, sleep, get up early for another day on the wagon. All last winter, in the freezing cold, Bill had worked hard and almost hopelessly. Bill said he liked working outside on the wagons and looked a bit healthier. Maybe it had been good for his health. But did Bill like it, and was Bill resigned to doing that all his life? It was hard work, and the wind ripped through you on those winter days. He wondered.

"The kid brother was supposed to be quite an athlete in high school, but I think I can still take him," Bill said.

Danny grinned. He remembered how he and Bill used to play games together as kids. Now they were worlds apart. Somehow, while he felt so proud of his world, his fraternity, dates at good hotels, and the rest of it, he felt ashamed of it all in the presence of Bill. He now had a frat pin and wore it on his vest so people would notice it. Suddenly he buttoned his coat. He stood there.

Mama dragged him off to meet Joe O'Reilley. He had heard of Joe O'Reilley all his life, and he'd even been proud to have a relative like Joe O'Reilley, a man in politics, and a lawyer of consequence. Joe O'Reilley was tall, gray-haired, and handsome. Danny shook hands with him. He wondered could he ever meet a man like this on terms of equality? He would like to impress Joe O'Reilley, but he didn't know how. He would be reserved and say nothing. Joe O'Reilley didn't say anything to him.

"Uncle Joe, who does my Danny take after?" Lizz asked.

This sort of thing always happened at wakes.

"He doesn't seem to take after Jim. He takes more after you," Joe said.

Lizz grinned. Danny saw Ed Lanson and Marty Mulligan come in.

"Excuse me," he said, going to them.

IV

Danny knelt in the pew with Bill and his mother. Mama was in mourning and she wore a new hat. She had gone to pieces when the coffin lid had been sealed down over Pa and she had cried all the way up to church. She sobbed now, and Bill helplessly nudged her. Danny was dazed and his mind wandered. Was his father in Heaven? He had tried to picture Heaven. He had listened to the singing and the organ music. The world seemed to him to be mystery and sadness, and the Church was the center and soul of that mystery. A mystery is something that cannot be understood by human reason. Death was a mystery. The soul, his father's soul, was a mystery. Heaven was a mystery. This mass, celebrated by Father Doneggan in purple vestments, was also a mystery. He sat back in the pew. Pa was not having a big funeral, but it was not so small as to be a disgrace. There would be eight or nine cars following the hearse. Joe O'Reilley hadn't been able to come, but his brother, Johnny, was one of the pallbearers. The other pallbearers were all expressmen.

Father Doneggan mounted the pulpit. He looked at the small, wiry priest and he was grateful that it wasn't any other priest who was saying his father's funeral mass. He waited, knowing that Father Doneggan would deliver a good sermon.

> *For we are sojourners before Thee, and strangers, as were all our fathers. Our days upon earth are as a shadow, and there is no stay.*
>
> *O Lord our God, all this store that we have prepared to build Thee a house for Thy holy name, is from Thy hand, and all things are Thine.*
>
> *Paralipomenon, Book I, chapter 29, verses 15 and 16.*

The priest paused and looked about the sparsely filled church.

> *We are all pilgrims journeying toward our Father's house. As we tread our path, knowing joy and sorrow, we build up stores along the way, stores for ourselves in our journey, and stores for those who will come after us. But these stores are not only of this world. These are of the spirit. We are all pilgrims. With this sentence, we can answer the question which has so troubled the human spirit in all ages: What is the meaning of life?*
>
> *For, my dear friends, it is occasions like that which brings us here in sorrow and in awe, occasions like this sad one that makes all, rich and poor, the man with the most acute brain and the humblest intellect alike, to ask himself: what is the meaning of life?*
>
> *And we know the answer. We are pilgrims, on the way to our Father's home. Today we gather in this little church and offer up the last services of the Church*

for one pilgrim who has returned to his Father's home. This man, a father himself, has gone to the loving Father of all. Just as he was a good father, a kind and loving father as I knew him, so has he gone to an even kinder and a more loving Father.

We are here now to say a last word in commemoration of a good and a humble man. He has gone from the bosom of his loved ones. His children, his devoted widow, his friends and relatives say the last prayers for him. The heartaches of those whom a dear departed has left behind him are heartaches which not we, but only God, can assuage. Just as I commend this good man's soul to God, so do I commend to God the sorrow and the grief of those who were nearest and dearest to him.

This man set up in this world a priceless store. It was a family. He gave to this world fine boys and girls, sons and daughters of the Church and citizens of the nation. He provided for them, and he watched over them. He set for them the example of a good father. He sent them to Catholic schools. On Sundays, they knew that not only they, but that he and their mother were also in this little church, paying worship to God. His life was not in vain. It was the life of one who toils in the vineyard and who reaps the fruit of the spirit.

He has been called. But the life he lived is in itself a consolation to the dear ones who now mourn him. The stores it set up were stores which count in the sight of God, stores more precious than the riches of this world. They were the stores of a fine Christian example, of a good and a generous Christian life. While we weep for him because he is no more with us, we know that he has gone on to a greater reward. From on high, he will watch over those who are below. He will see the noble example he has given by his life and his character. He will watch his children growing into fine, decent, Christian young men and women. And it will be his doing. He will want them to remember him. And they will. He will want them to carry on as good pilgrims along the paths of this world. And they will. He will want them to commemorate him by something that is finer than all the marble memorials of the world, by living lives as good as his. And they will.

I know this family. I grieve with them. For this man was my friend. I know their sorrow, and I know how irreparable is their loss. Their sorrow they will offer up to God. And the hallowed memory of this man will be in their lives. For, my friends, if one would want to know the answer to the meaning of life, they could look to the life of this man. It is to be as he was. To leave stores behind him such as he left. And then, when called, to approach the Master with a clear conscience. He is with God now. His bereaved family can take from his departure that high consolation. He built on this earth a house of which God is proud. He has now gone to the House of God.

For we are all sojourners before Thee, and sojourners as were all our fathers: our days on the earth are as a shadow.

In the name of the Father, and of the Son, and of the Holy Ghost, Amen.

The sad tones of the organ filled the church.

V

The long ride to the cemetery was over now and the casket was being put into the vault. Mama had cried all the way out, and he and Bill, and Mother, and Uncle Al in the same car hadn't been able to help her. They had all talked about the wonderful sermon. There had been tears in Bill's eyes after it. What Father Doneggan said about Pa was true. But now they were pushing the casket in the vault.

Lizz ran forward.

"Jim, Jim, come back to me," she cried.

Johnny O'Reilley took her by the shoulders and led her back.

The coffin was carried into the vault. It was a cold and windy day, gray, and without sun. Jim O'Neill's remains were sealed away. The last prayers had been said for him. The last farewells had been given to his corpse. The small group that had come miles to the cemetery turned and walked back to the waiting automobiles. About them was the cold earth, earth too hard to receive Jim O'Neill. The cars that had carried the little group to Mount Calvary passed back out of the cemetery in single file.

SECTION FIVE

1923

54

I

Danny walked in to work at nine o'clock sharp. It seemed as if he had been absent for more than four days. But everything looked the same. Everything was the same except himself. He felt that he had lived a much longer time than had actually elapsed since last Saturday at six P.M. and this morning at nine.

"Hello, Bones," McGinty said, very friendly.

Danny nodded.

"I was very sorry to hear about it," Hogan said.

Danny took off his coat and rolled up his sleeves. He sharpened a couple of pencils.

"Well, Bones, I knew your old man, and I'm afraid you'll never be the man he was," Collins said.

Danny sat down next to Hogan. He liked everyone in the office for the way they were trying to be friendly to him. He forgot all the reasons he had for hating the office, for disliking Casey and Collins and McGinty. He also remembered how they had all shown up at the wake and had chipped in to send flowers.

"Yes, it's a good man gone," Collins said mournfully.

"Hey, O'Neill, come here a minute," Heinie said.

Danny went a few steps to Heinie's chair while the other clerks answered calls.

"How's your mother? Has she taken it hard?" Heinie asked.

"She felt bad. But she's taking it pretty bravely."

"You kids got to be good to her now."

"Yes, we will," Danny said, trying suddenly to be and to appear very responsible.

"There will be a little time before she can collect the insurance money. Those things take time to be settled. If your mother needs a little money, you let me know and I can spare fifty or a hundred dollars," Heinie said, almost in a whisper so that the others couldn't hear him.

"I think that will be all right. She was able to borrow some money from my father's first cousin, Joe O'Reilley."

"Well, if she needs any money, let me know, and she can have it and pay it back when she gets her insurance money. And don't forget, you kids got to be good to her."

Danny nodded.

"And thanks, Heinie," Danny said, touched.

"And now, Stupid, see them lights," Heinie said.

Danny sat down again, determined. His father's helpless death stood in his mind as an example. He was not going to end up the same way. He was determined on that. He would show an interest in his work, and he would do it as well as he could, yes, he would try and do his work better than anyone else. Success, as he had so often read, was a matter of taking care of and tending to little details, and seeing that every little thing you did was done properly. As the papers, and books, and many people said, if you made yourself into a good man, they couldn't keep a good man down. He was seething with determination. He would do his job right, and some day he would be rewarded.

The board was suddenly dead. He would try and make as few mistakes as possible. He would answer calls, as many as he could. He would try to take more calls a day than anyone else, and he would try to take them right, and to write them legibly, and he would learn as much as he could of the express business. He would in every way possible make himself competent and reliable so that he would be the best clerk in the department. He would work his way up the ladder, starting with the given conditions.

He remembered a line from Kipling:

If you can fill the unforgiving minute with sixty seconds worth of distance run,

From now on that would be his motto.

There was a lighted bulb. He pulled the key eagerly.

"Hello . . . this is the Wagon Call Department, Continental Express Company. . . . Yes sir, we can take care of that this afternoon between two and five . . . and what is the name? . . . Yes sir, I have it, and the address, yes sir, and what are you shippin'? . . . And how much does it weigh? . . . And what is the destination of your shipment? Yes sir . . . the pickup man will call this afternoon . . . between two and five. . . . No, I'm very sorry, but I cannot stipulate a definite time . . . I shall mark your call for the man to pick your package up as close to two o'clock as possible. . . . Yes sir . . . all right . . . thank you sir."

"Hey, Bones, for Christ sake, try and get rid of them fools quicker and don't let them take up so much time on the calls," Hogan said.

Danny pulled another light and then looked at the clock. He marked down 9/24 in a corner of his pad. Another thing. He might as well put down the exact time of each call to the minute.

"Hello, Wagon Call Department . . ."

"Why in the name of Jesus Christ didn't you people come and get my package?"

"I'll have to investigate that, sir."

"Investigate, Christ! Investigate, hell! Listen, this is the fourth time I've called and asked you to get a package. What the hell do I have to do to get you people to come out and pick up a package?"

"Just call us up."

"Well, I called you eight times."

"There must have been some mistake on your call. I'll investigate it personally and see that the error is rectified."

"What the hell rectification can you do? I waited out here five whole afternoons for your wagon to come, and I'm still waitin'. Say, do you think you can get an expressman out here before the Day of Judgment?"

"Why, yes sir. If you'll give me your name and address, I'll see that he gets there this afternoon."

"Yeah, I heard that before. You been tellin' me that for a week. Say, what the hell do you guys do up there, sleep?"

"Why, no sir, we work."

"Well, I'd like to learn of it. Say, now why in the hell didn't you get my call?"

"I don't know. I'll have to check up, sir."

"The old bull. How do I know you'll check up?"

"Well, I'm assuring you."

"Do you want to know how valuable your assurance is? I think it's as valuable as toilet paper."

"Yes sir," Danny said. He suddenly realized that he had made a dumb remark. "Well sir, the best I can do is promise to investigate and see that the man calls this afternoon."

"You can go to hell. I'll ship my package parcel post. Crap on you."

"But sir, I can assure you that we'll have a man there without fail. I'll take the call and see to it personally that he will. I can assure you of the advantages of express service over parcel post."

"Yeah?" the guy said, wearied.

"The express service is quicker, faster, and it guarantees prompt delivery," Danny said.

"Well, for Christ sake, if that isn't nerve."

"There must have been some mistake. The clerk taking your call might have gotten the wrong address, or the driver taking it from us over the phone might have gotten the wrong address. Now, if you'll give me your name and address, I'll see that no such contingency happens again."

"You tell 'em, I stutter, O'Neill old boy," Casey yelled down.

"You got it."

"But I have to have it again so I can investigate."

"Well, it's 2143 Claybourne Avenue."

"Yes sir, 2143 Claybourne Avenue. And the name, sir?"

"Wright . . . W . . . R . . . I . . . G . . . H . . . T."

"Yes sir."

"You'll call today sure?"

"Yes sir."

"And what is your name?"

"Mr. O'Neill."

The fellow would think he was something more than a clerk.

"All right, Mr. O'Neill. Please take care of that, and thank you."

Danny hung up. He was proud. He had saved a piece of business for the company. To be a success, he would have to do things like that. He felt like going out and getting a drink of water now, but no, he was determined. He would sit here and work.

He answered calls steadily for fifteen minutes. Then there was another brief respite with the keyboard dead. He thought, too, that if he was cordial and efficient over the phone, and many people got to know him by name, that would be an asset and might lead to something. He still wanted to go get a drink and waste a few minutes in the can, but he resisted the temptation. He wished that they'd noticed him. But good work would be noticed sooner or later. If you did your job right, you'd be repaid for all the pains you took. He tried to make himself believe this.

He was tired of his work. It was so dull and so uninteresting. But many men had done dull and uninteresting work. The dull work had to be mastered. It was only by doing that, acquiring things, detail by detail, learning step by step, that you advanced. But there was a light. He pulled the plug. A wrong number. He dreamed of how his work and ambition would some day make him something big in the express business, way bigger than Patsy McLaughlin.

"Hey, Mr. O'Neill," Collins called sarcastically to him.

Danny glanced down to Collins.

"Get the coffee can and go out and get me a nickel's worth of coffee. And when you come back, get the broom and sweep up some of the paper here. Sam, the porter, was off sick last night."

Danny got out of his chair and went out to wash the coffee can in the lavatory.

JAMES T. FARRELL, author of a prodigious volume of work, dedicated his career to depicting the Irish-American, urban world in which he had grown up. Best known for his Studs Lonigan trilogy, Farrell also wrote four large fiction cycles, several volumes of critical writings, and approximately 250 short stories.

CHARLES FANNING is a professor of English and history and director of the Center for Irish Studies at Southern Illinois University in Carbondale. Fanning is the author or editor of several books and articles, including Farrell's *Chicago Stories*.

The text for this edition of *Father and Son* was taken from the 1940 first edition from the Vanguard Press.

The University of Illinois Press is a founding member of the Association of American University Presses.

Composed in 10/13 Janson Text
with Hoefler Titling display
by Jim Proefrock
at the University of Illinois Press
Designed by Dennis Roberts
Manufactured by Sheridan Books, Inc.

University of Illinois Press
1325 South Oak Street
Champaign, IL 61820-6903
www.press.uillinois.edu